STEEL DEMONS MC

BOOKS 4-6

USA TODAY BESTSELLING AUTHOR
CRYSTAL ASH

SDMC SERIES PLAYLIST

All American Nightmare - Hinder
Notorious - Adelitas Way
Hail to the King - Avenged Sevenfold
O Death - Ashley H
Joan of Arc - In This Moment
Radioactive - Imagine Dragons
Bad Company - Five Finger Death Punch
Love Me to Death - No Resolve
(Don't Fear) The Reaper - HIM
David - Noah Gunderson
Apocalyptic - Halestorm
Blue on Black - Five Finger Death Punch
Machine Gun Blues - Social Distortion
Wanted Dead or Alive - Chris Daughtry
I Get Off - Halestorm
You Shook Me All Night Long - AC/DC
Nobody Praying for Me - Seether
Loyal to No One - Dropkick Murpheys
Crazy in Love - Daniel De Bourg
Be Free - King Dude & Chelsea Wolfe
Raise Hell - Dorothy
Coming Home - Skylar Grey

Listen on Spotify at:
crystalashbooks.com/sdmc-playlist

CONTENT WARNINGS

This series is set in a dystopian world and contains graphically violent scenes throughout.

Please note the following content warnings for each book in this set:

Painless:
Death of a parent/spouse, gun violence,

Helpless:
Infection/injury, rough spanking, motorcycle accident

Heartless:
Assault and injury by a love interest (accident/unintentional)

PAINLESS

STEEL DEMONS MC BOOK FOUR

To the nurses and medical staff who risk their lives and mental health to save others.
You matter.
You're everything.

Prologue
SHADOW

SIX YEARS EARLIER

The woman flipped her skirt back down over her hips and stood from her kneeling position without a glance at me. She left my room, closing the door behind her, before I even discarded the condom.

Well, that was...fine. I guess.

I took my time cleaning myself off and re-fastened my pants. My fingers trembled slightly, either from needing a drink or nerves at what just happened, I wasn't sure.

The heat and numbness of alcohol called to me, more alluring than any woman. I didn't have any left in my room, so I'd have to go out to the dining area of this service center. Where more women walked around, serving food and drinks.

That wasn't so bad anymore, as long as they came and went quickly. But Jandro would be out there too. After how much he begged, goaded, and pleaded for me to do this, my biggest fear right then was his inability to keep his mouth shut.

I steeled myself with a breath in front of my door. With any luck, he'd be too drunk to remember, or preoccupied with his own woman for the night. I was fine with either option, as long as he didn't draw attention to me.

After a few more breaths, I left my room and squeezed down a staircase that was much too small for someone of my size. At least I remembered to duck under the beams this time.

"Yoooo, there he is!"

Fuck. No luck for me tonight.

I glowered all the way across the dining room, but it did nothing to deter Jandro's clapping and hollering. As I got closer, I noticed the six empty beer pitchers on his table, his flushed complexion, and how he was nearly sliding off the picnic bench seat.

"Are you done?" I grunted, grabbing his cut to pull him upright before he slid down to the floor.

"Bro, I'm jus' gettin' started." He leaned over the table, propped up on his forearms as he smiled woozily at me. "So how was it?"

"Can I get you anything, sir?"

The feminine voice sent my fists and jaw clenching. I stared hard at the table surface as I forced myself to breathe normally. My eyes lifted to Jandro's in a silent plea. His mouth tightened and he gave a small shake of his head.

Fuck. He was making me do this myself today.

"...Sir?"

"Whiskey," I ground out. "Your largest bottle. The whole thing."

She gathered up the empty beer pitchers and headed off without another word. I unclenched my hands while Jandro shot me a disappointed look.

"It won't kill you to say please," he lectured. "And to look at a server when they're talking to you."

"I forgot."

"Well, start remembering. I'm gettin' a little tired of reminding a grown-ass man to have manners."

The server flew by our table with another beer pitcher for Jandro and a handle of Jack Daniels for me.

"Thanks," I forced myself to mutter, but she was already several feet away tending to other tables.

"Doesn't count if they don't hear you." Jandro brought the beer to his lips with two hands.

"You know this doesn't come naturally to me," I told him, after taking a deep swallow from the bottle.

"It won't come at all if you don't practice. I'm not even asking you to say full sentences. But as my *tia* used to say, please and thank you is something every human being should know." He set the pitcher down and the giddy smile returned. "Now *please* tell me you were more successful at losing your virginity than speaking words."

I sighed before taking another deep drink. And I almost thought he'd be distracted enough to forget it. "It happened. So I guess it was successful."

"Did you come?"

"Yes."

"Did she?"

"I don't know."

"My man," Jandro shook his head, "You would know if she did. That's okay, though. Not everyone hits a home run their first time. Did you do what I told you?"

"No."

"No?" His jaw dropped, eyes narrowing at me. "Why the hell not?"

"I didn't really have the opportunity."

"You were alone with a naked woman in your room. Her *job* is to fuck. How is that not an opportunity? It's a two-way street, man, you gotta make it good for her, too. The clit is the center of a woman's pleasure, you can't just--"

"She made it pretty clear she didn't want me to touch her aside from...what was necessary."

"Did you at least kiss her some? Play with her nipples, maybe?"

"No and no."

"Shadow," Jandro groaned, lowering his forehead to the table. "You're killing me, dude."

"This was your idea," I reminded him. "The whole sex thing has never mattered to me."

"Because you don't know what you're missing!"

I shrugged with a grunt, then took another long drink to a memory I would be all too happy to erase. The small, hesitant knock at my door.

The curious glance at my face before jerking away with a soft gasp. Then the petite, red-haired woman climbed on all fours onto the bed, facing the wall. She pulled her underwear down, her dress up, and waited. Waited for me to take what she'd been paid for, and nothing else.

After Jandro and I left the prison, I started to figure out that most women weren't capable, nor had any motivation to treat me in the same manner as I'd been raised. Even so, women in general made me uncomfortable. Frightened women made me scared of myself.

I was capable of awful things. I killed men that rivaled my own size without breaking a sweat. But my brain was convinced the true enemies were half my size, coming at me with sharp blades, and taking joy in making my blood spill on the floor.

None of these women here wanted to hurt me, but my basic instincts seemed to keep missing the message. I'd never been able to fight back before. Now, every time someone came near me, I felt the need to defend myself.

What if I fucked up? What would happen if I was too rough with a woman much smaller than me? I used to fantasize about making my torturers suffer. Now I was afraid to find out what my strength was capable of.

I had seen the terror in women's eyes, the way they screamed and tried to flee as men began to violate them—before a Steel Demon put a bullet through their attackers' heads. The women out here avoided my eyes and made themselves smaller, as though hoping I wouldn't see them. It didn't take a genius to figure out that they expected me to hurt them in the exact same way other men did.

I should have just locked my door and jerked off.

"Bro, listen." Jandro flattened his palms on the table. "I hope this doesn't sound weird coming from me, but you're not a bad-lookin' dude."

"What?" I snarled at him, but it had little bite. The whiskey was finally making its way into my system, lulling me into delicious numbness. However, that didn't make his statement any less confusing.

"Every woman in this service center has checked you out at least once. But once they're in your line of sight, they scatter like mice."

"Because of my face," I told him. "Because of all this." I ran a hand up my forearm to indicate the extensive scarring under my sleeve.

"Nah, man. That ain't it." At least the loudmouth VP was talking quieter now. "It's because you look at everything as a threat. Like you've already fantasized about the most efficient way to kill something, and are just waiting for the chance to do it."

"That's not *always* true."

"I know, dude, because I know you. But that's the vibe you give off to people who *don't* know you. No one wants to get in your way because they want to keep their heads attached to their necks."

"Okay. So what do I do?"

"Well." Jandro rubbed the five o'clock shadow on his jaw, a side-effect from three straight days of riding. "You can carry on as you are and just not give a fuck. It might hurt you in the long-run, though. *Or* you can work to start changing how you come across to people. That would entail letting your guard down around women a bit. Pushing yourself out of your comfort zone, little by little, until you're comfortable with human interaction. Then, you never know. You might meet someone special."

I killed the bottle of Jack while listening to him, too embedded in my alcohol-soaked bubble to really consider his advice.

"I've never cared about, or needed, human interaction," I grumbled out with a shake of my head. "I just don't see the point."

"It probably didn't matter while you were some cunty bitches' endless blood sacrifice, but it does now," he insisted. "You're a person, dude. We're social animals. Not only that, you're part of an MC, the MC that brings true justice when the world has given up. I'm sorry, but you're gonna have to interact with people in ways that don't involve killing." He began gesticulating wildly with his hands. "And the longer you go without some kind of...affectionate human contact, the harder it'll be to connect with others."

Before I could retort, Daren stumbled out of the hallway into the dining room. His shirt was unbuttoned, and he was trying to get his pants zipped up as he walked.

"Hey guys, turn the radio on!" he yelled. "Something big is going down in DC. There's a journalist reporting it right now."

A half-dressed blonde woman followed Daren out from the hallway.

She jumped on his back, giggling and kissing his neck as she wrapped her legs around his waist. Yeah, women definitely didn't respond to me that way.

"What station, *burro*?" Jandro was already fiddling with knobs on the radio at our table.

"Don't matter. It's on all the stations."

"That can't be good," Jandro muttered as he settled on a frequency.

A quietness settled over the dining room as static from the speakers filled the air. Even the servers paused in their work to listen.

Only indistinguishable mumbling came through for the first minute, like people were having a conversation just out of range of the microphone. Then a voice charged with emotion addressed everyone listening, which, at this point, was probably the whole country.

"My fellow Americans, this is Emery Jones reporting with Freedom of Speech News," the reporter paused, their voice already cracking. "I've received multiple reports, and gotten eyewitness confirmation that...that..."

A long pause followed. Everyone in the dining room seemed to be holding their breath.

"Washington D.C. has fallen," the reporter finally continued in a harrowed tone. "All nine Supreme Court justices have been assassinated, gunned down right in...in the building. The Senate has been barricaded, with at least forty senators inside. They've set fire to the building and rescue teams are being blocked from getting in. A mob has...has stormed the White House and is vandalizing the building as we speak. We don't know if all these incidents were coordinated attacks. There's still been no word on the president, since he fled the country two weeks ago..."

The journalist continued reporting on the carnage all around them in a flat, emotionless voice, clearly in shock. Some of the servers began to cry. The rest of us just listened, in various stages of shock ourselves.

No one, however, looked surprised. I didn't care for politics, having been isolated most of my life, and even I knew this tension had been brewing for years.

"I don't know how we'll come back from this," the reporter went on, now sounding like they were trying not to cry. "The United States as we know it has... collapsed."

MARIPOSA

PRESENT DAY

"Your rodent is trying to kill me again."

"Freyja is not a rodent, *Rory!*" I scooped up the kitten who, in that moment, had just started vigorously grooming Reaper's stubble with her tongue. "She'll be hunting rodents soon, won't you, little girl?"

My black kitten squeaked out a meow followed by an enthusiastic purr. I laughed at my...companion? Familiar? There was no word to describe my bond with this animal.

"She's a rodent compared to Hades," Reaper chuckled, folding his hands behind his head. "And I don't understand why she curls up over my mouth and nose, if not to suffocate me."

"Probably because your breath is warm." I placed Freyja on the mattress and tickled her belly, earning needle-like teeth in my finger for my endeavors. "Or she likes how you smell, as much as I do."

Hades jumped up right then, placing his paws carefully on either side of the kitten as he bent down to sniff her. I realized Freyja's head wasn't much bigger than his nose as she batted at him with her tiny paws.

"You're goin' soft on me, Hades," Reaper groaned as the Doberman licked and nuzzled the kitten amidst her fierce assault on his nose.

Freyja zoomed across the mattress and down to the floor. Hades chased her while still taking care where he placed his paws and teeth. With them no longer smothering either of us, I scooted closer to lay my head on Reaper's chest. His arm slid around my back as he brushed a kiss across my forehead.

"Has she said anything to you yet?" he murmured, lips moving on my forehead.

"No, nothing." I drummed my fingers on his ribs in contemplation. "Maybe she's too young? When did Hades start talking to you?"

"About six months after I found him. I don't know if it has to do with age, or because that was the first time I had to kill someone after finding him."

Their lives are yours to take. Reap what has been sown.

Those words echoed like a drum in my head ever since the Steel Demons came to my and Gunner's rescue from skin traffickers, two weeks ago. Reaper had hinted about it before, but told me the full extent after we all made it back home.

Ever since he found Hades as a puppy, that voice told him who to kill or not kill. It could only come from the dog, who had bonded deeply with Reaper, and was clearly more intelligent than any normal animal. Reaper was certain that only he could hear the voice of Hades, until I confessed that he had spoken to me too.

He came to me in the rough, hazy form of a man and told me who he was. I wrote it off as a dream, until I saw that same vision while Hades the dog tore through the ankles of those holding Gunner and I captive.

Interestingly, Reaper never had any dreams or other interpretations of Hades, other than hearing his voice.

Gunner had a bond with his falcon, Horus, though theirs seemed entirely different. Gunner could see through Horus, as though he were in the falcon's body. But he never mentioned hearing voices or seeing him in another form either.

And now I had Freyja. Some kind of invisible pull brought me to the junk pile in Jandro's backyard where she had been stuck. Getting her out felt infinitely more important than just rescuing a kitten. I felt like I would lose a limb, part of myself, if I didn't rescue her. The only word that popped into my head was her name, and somehow I just knew she was meant to be with me.

As far as *what* she was or *why* I had to find her? That remained to be seen. But three of us in the SDMC now had these animals with strange, unique abilities. I had more questions than answers, and it made my head spin the more I thought about it. But I found comfort in knowing these creatures were here to help us, to guide us with their abilities and heightened intelligence. I just didn't know for what purpose.

Before finding myself with the Steel Demons, I would have driven myself insane looking for answers. As someone who owed their medical training to research and science, my little head would have exploded at the implication that something magical or paranormal was at play.

Strangely enough, it was using Reaper's approach that kept me from freaking out. He simply accepted that some things couldn't be explained. These animals had proved themselves to be trustworthy, protective of us in many cases. He wasn't going to pick apart theories and go hunting for answers when we lived in a time where survival was our number one priority. After Reaper and Gunner saved their animals, their own lives were saved in return. And that was all that mattered.

I could only wonder what the silly kitten flopping all over the floor would save me from one day.

Reaper and I watched them from bed like adoring parents for a few more minutes before I kissed his chest and reluctantly rolled away.

"I have to go to Tessa's," I said to his pouting expression.

"You just checked on her three days ago." He rolled toward me, pulling me back into his warmth.

"She's at least thirty-six weeks now. The baby's almost here." Briefly giving in to his hold, I peppered kisses underneath his jaw. "And she's stressed. She needs to be among friends. She and Big G are...kind of on the rocks, it seems."

"I know he's a dog," Reaper sighed into my hair. "She's a good woman. She deserves better."

I paused with my nose against his throat, the wheels turning in my head. Tessa seemed convinced that Reaper would never let her separate from Big G, that the club would see it as breaking up their family. But the Steel Demons president grew up in a matriarchal society, where women had multiple partners as a sign of devotion and trust from their men. Surely Reaper wouldn't force Tessa to stay in a situation where she was unhappy.

"What if Tessa and Big G had been part of your parents' community?" I asked him. "How would they handle a man's cheating?"

"Oh, he'd be kicked out within a week," Reaper grunted. "He's not the sharpest tool in the shed when it comes to social graces. They'd give him a few chances for making some remark, or being inappropriate with a taken woman, but he's too slow to adapt to such a different paradigm. He'd be gone long before he could actually stick his dick where it didn't belong."

"Hmm." I swirled a finger through the hair dusting his chest. If I brought it up *gently* to Tessa again and indicated Reaper did not approve of his behavior, she might be more receptive to moving out.

"That being said," Reaper continued. "The situation here is different."

"How so?"

"We're an MC, sugar, not a 'peace and love' hippie commune." He squeezed my waist. "I need men that can ride, fight, and follow orders. Unfortunately, that includes some men with unsavory habits when it comes to women."

"But that doesn't mean she has to stay *with* him, right?"

Reaper's eyes narrowed to slits. "What are you saying?"

"What if they both stayed in Sheol, but lived separately? He could be free to do whoever and she could find another man if she wanted."

"A divorce?" He propped his head up on his hand. "That's illegal," he said with a smirk that made it clear he was joking.

I dragged a finger down his abdomen, teasing at where the sheet covered him just below his waist. "Since when do you care about breaking the law?"

"Oh, I care *immensely*," he played along, breath hitching at my touch. "Do you know about the law of mandatory morning blowjobs?"

"Who came up with that bullshit?" I laughed.

"A very wise lawmaker." He pulled me back to him when I tried to roll away, tickling my sides until I was breathless.

"Really, though," I panted. "Did they get married before or after the Collapse?"

Divorce *was* made illegal in some jurisdictions before the Collapse. But afterward, because no recognized government bodies remained, marriages weren't legally binding. A couple couldn't get divorced if they weren't married in the first place.

"After," Reaper admitted. I knew he was following my logic. "I'll think about what you're saying, sugar, but I'm not sure separating them is the best option. You have to realize being with him protects her, too. No one here will hurt her, but if some of the guys see that she's free, they'll try what they can with her. It'll be harmless, but may be more trouble than she needs."

"That's true," I sighed. "Plus, there's no guarantee she'll actually want to leave him if it comes down to it."

He stroked a finger down my cheek before kissing me there. "If she or the boys were in danger, there would be no question of stepping in and getting them away from him. I mean that."

"I know you do." My palm cupped his handsome face. I never got tired of looking at him. "Thank you for telling me that."

A few more kisses and protests later, I finally rolled out of bed and started getting dressed. Freyja stopped playing with Hades and darted over to me to rub my ankles. Much like the other two animals with their humans, she followed me everywhere. Right after finding her, I tried locking her in the bedroom to no avail. Eventually I just gave up.

She was like a furry potato, with legs she could barely use, yet she still figured out how to turn doorknobs and squeeze through tiny gaps. No matter what, she wanted to be at my side. At first I could fit her in the pocket of my scrubs, but she was getting too big for them already. Balancing on my shoulders was a work in progress. She was daring and adventurous, but *damn* those little claws were sharp, and she was still getting the hang of balancing.

So, for the most part, she was happy to follow me down the street.

"What do you have going on today?" I asked Reaper as I pulled a brush through my hair.

"Besides admiring your ass from right here?" he grinned. "The scouting team is coming back today. I hope we get some good fuckin' news."

"Has Gunner seen anything about the drone?"

"No," he bit out, his jaw working with annoyance. "Even with Horus's eyes, he hasn't seen a damn thing."

While most of the club was at the traveling market, Shadow and a skeleton crew stayed back to guard Sheol. Their day was far less eventful than ours, except for Shadow shooting down a drone with a camera that flew dangerously close to the club.

The drone had to be controlled from a relatively close location, so Reaper sent teams out to comb the surrounding desert in search of whoever sent it out. Gunner also used his ability to see through Horus to scout high cliffs, mountains, and any other places motorcycles couldn't reach. The fact that he didn't find anything after two weeks didn't bode well.

I leaned over the bed to kiss Reaper again for reassurance. "Your guys are the best. They'll find something. And if they don't, it means there wasn't anything to find."

"God, I hope you're right, sugar," he sighed. "I hate feeling like I've got Tash's fucking eyeballs looming over my home."

"I know." I kissed his forehead. "I also know what kind of president you are. You'll find who's out there and make them regret ever playing with stupid toy planes."

He laughed and leaned his forehead against mine. "Damn, I fuckin' love you." His voice grew low and growly. His hands reached for me, and I stopped them with mine.

"I love you too, but I really have to go." Our lips collided for one final *final* time. "I'll come back here tonight so you can tell me how it went."

"Bring Jandro with you." He finally released me and delivered a walloping smack on my ass. Freyja arched and hissed at the loud noise. "Oh, you calm down, rodent," he scolded her. "Your human likes it. You'll see."

"Hm, some times more than others," I muttered, rubbing the sting on my right cheek. "Okay, I'll see you tonight."

"Ah, sugar."

"Yeah?" I spun around in the doorway to find Reaper sitting at the edge of the bed.

He looked thoughtful. Maybe even nervous, as his gaze slid to the walk-in closet.

"Uh, nothing." He shot me a sheepish grin. "I'll tell you later. I hope everything goes well with Tessa."

I hesitated. "You sure?"

"Yes, woman. Get out of here before I drag you back to bed and tear into you like my last meal."

Freyja was already pawing at the door, so I took my leave and wondered what that was about as we headed out for the day.

MARIPOSA

It wasn't Tessa, Big G, or even one of their boys, who greeted me at their front door, but Noelle.

"You came at the perfect time," she muttered, pulling me in and closing the door just as Freyja slipped through. "And also the worst time."

"What do you mean?"

The answer came in the form of a child's scream echoing through the house, like the call of a banshee. Toys and laundry littered the floor, creating quite the obstacle course as I followed Noelle through the house.

We passed by the kitchen where Tessa's youngest son squirmed in his high chair, his face red as a tomato. He was the source of the banshee cries and I quickly saw why. An upside down cereal bowl was on the floor, milk spreading out into a puddle, and soggy frosted flakes turning to mush.

The toddler's anguish was exacerbated by his older brother, who sat on the counter as he tore open the cereal box to rain the rest of the contents down like confetti. Big G emerged from the next room and rushed over to lift his youngest out of the high chair.

"Aw man, you're all wet," he groaned, holding the boy out away from him. Just then he noticed Noelle and I heading up the stairs. "What the hell am I supposed to do about all this?"

"I dunno, be a fucking parent to your kids," Noelle snapped back, stomping her feet louder.

"Hahaha, she said *fuck!*" the oldest boy cackled from the counter.

I wanted to simultaneously disappear and rush down to help clean up. But there was no steering Noelle, who led me back to the master bedroom. Tessa sat there, propped up against the headboard with piles of pillows. And she was crying.

"Oh my God, Tess!" I ran to her, throwing my arms around her shoulders. "What's wrong?"

"It's nothing," she sniffed, lifting her red eyes to me and forcing a smile. "Just pregnancy hormones. I'll be fine."

"That's not all it is," Noelle muttered, handing her a tissue box.

"Something to do with the war zone downstairs?" I ventured a guess.

"Please, you guys. I don't want to get into it." Tessa wiped her eyes and sniffed. "I just needed a break. Five fucking minutes to myself and he acts like the house is gonna fall in on him without me there to do everything."

"Yeah, God forbid he actually step up and act like a father," Noelle sneered. "My mom would have any one of my dads' balls if they didn't pull their weight."

"Nellie, please. I said not now."

I rubbed Tessa's arm. "You take as much time as you need. The three of them will live for the next few minutes."

Before she could reply, Tessa hissed in pain. Her hands flew to the lower side of her baby bump. "On top of everything else, I've been dealing with this little shit-kicker all day."

"He's been moving non-stop," Noelle added, with a tone of concern. "That's probably why you're so worn out lately."

"Moving is good," I said, pulling my stethoscope out of my case. "That means the baby's healthy. You ready for me, mama?"

Tessa nodded through winces of pain. "Do you think he'll come early if he's so active?"

"Not necessarily." I lifted her shirt and warmed the end of the stethoscope against my palm. "The other two were full-term, right?"

She nodded. "My oldest took almost 42 weeks, the little shit-head."

"It's normal for first births to be a bit late," I explained. "Now that your body is used to the process, your labor should be quicker, and this one's likely to come right on time."

"Big G's already begging me for another one," she groaned. "But I am fucking done."

"Fuck what that big man-child wants," Noelle growled.

"I'll get you on birth control right after this one arrives," I promised.

"He won't like that," Tessa frowned.

"Noelle's right, though." I moved the stethoscope over her belly in search of the little shit-kicker's heartbeat. "It's your body. He doesn't get a say."

"Thank you," Noelle huffed. "Finally someone is making sense."

I finally found the heartbeat, and frowned to myself. It seemed high.

"Is something wrong?" Tessa's eyes widened with worry.

"No, just..." I pulled the eartips out and let them hang around my neck. "He's in a weird position. I'm going to put some pressure on you, okay?"

The moment I pressed on her with my hands, I felt, and saw, the kicks and movements going on inside her.

"Oh fuck, here he goes again," Tessa moaned.

Noelle moved in to sit on her other side, rubbing her back. "Breathe, honey."

I gently pressed lower, down near Tessa's pubic bone, and felt the unmistakable shape of a foot. It was just as I feared.

"Tess." I tried not to sound grave. "The baby is in a breech position. His feet are down here and his head's up in your ribs."

"That's not good, is it?" She flinched at another kick.

"It's not ideal," I said carefully. "Breech deliveries are a bit riskier, but they can still be done. I think we should try to turn him around before you're due, to be safest."

"He's moving so much, though," she groaned, pressing a hand to her side.

"I know. It's possible he'll get into the right position on his own. Or if we are able to turn him, he'll flip right back around to a breech position."

"Stubborn ass." Noelle rubbed Tess's belly affectionately. "Why you gotta make it so hard for your mama, huh?"

"I say we give it another week." I placed the stethoscope eartips back in my ears and took out my blood pressure cuff. "If he doesn't flip back around, we'll start trying to turn him."

Tessa eyed me hard. "And if that doesn't work?"

"Then he's coming into the world feet first." I patted the hand on her side before wrapping my cuff around her bicep. "You've had a healthy pregnancy, so I'm not too concerned. I won't let anything happen to you, mama."

"Ugh, I want a fucking drink so bad," Tessa groaned. "Just a shot so this kid can mellow the fuck down."

Freyja jumped up right then and walked over the mattress toward Tessa. The black kitten sniffed at her swollen belly before rubbing her head against one of the feet pressing on her lower abdomen.

Tessa chuckled. "Well, aren't you a nice kitty."

"Aren't black cats supposed to be bad luck?" Noelle joked.

"I hope this one's not," I murmured, watching the blood pressure dial. "She's been my little shadow ever since I found her."

Tessa sighed, this time in relaxation as I finished taking her blood pressure and started putting my supplies away. Freyja purred up a storm as she rubbed her face and side against Tessa's belly.

"Well, your little kitty seems to have calmed the kid down finally," Tessa breathed. "Even my fucking cramps are hurting less. I'd call that a good luck charm."

"Good girl, Freyja." I scratched the kitten's ears and got a headbutt in return. "I wish I had a treat to give you."

The black cat stared at me, her green eyes holding an uncanny amount of wisdom. It almost felt humbling, and I knew I just got the first taste of what this animal was capable of.

"Did you train her to do that?" Noelle reached over to give some head scratches of her own.

"Nope." I stared at the little ball of fur, now grooming one of her front paws. "She did that all on her own."

MARIPOSA

T he deep, thumping bass of rap music floated down the street as I headed toward Jandro's shop. Having lunch together became our routine and was one of the highlights of my day. I touched the butterfly pendant at my throat, smiling when I saw him stretched out on a creeper, doing some kind of repair under a motorcycle.

His knees were bent, jeans worn down thin, beat-up work boots on the concrete floor. The white undershirt tank tops he wore while working looked so hot on him, even as they got covered in dirt and grease throughout the day.

As I got closer, I heard him rapping along to the song playing on the boombox. The music was loud enough that he didn't hear me walk up. He didn't even notice me there until I stepped one leg over his torso and sat down to straddle him.

"I really hope that's you, *Mariposita*, or someone's about to get a socket wrench up his ass."

"Damn. I really hope it's me too, then."

I lifted my feet so he could roll the creeper out from under the bike. If I wasn't already laughing, his smile would have done it for me. Seeing my sexy grease monkey always lifted my mood.

"Hi, *bonita*." He lifted up to plant a kiss on me, careful to avoid touching me with his hands.

"Hi, *guapito*. You hungry?"

"Always," he purred, kissing me again, deeper. His hips shifted underneath me, lighting heat in my core like a match.

I smiled against his lips before opening up to let our tongues meld together like they did so well. I had sat on him on a whim just to be silly, but quickly realized I might've gotten more than I bargained for.

He kissed my nose sweetly when our erotic tongue-fucking ended. "Let me up so I can wash my hands."

"Hmm." I ground into his lap instead, finding his bulge with the space between my legs. "I like you right here, actually."

"Mari," he groaned. "You can't complain about getting dirty when that mind of yours is so filthy."

"I think it'd be fun," I teased, tugging down the front of his tank top. "You can't get my scrubs all greasy, but I can touch you anywhere I want."

"Reaper!" Jandro yelled in mock despair, tossing his head back. "Help me, we've created a monster."

I kissed his throat, laughing as I finally stood up. "You love that I can't get enough of you both."

"My dick hasn't fallen off yet, so yes, that remains true." Grinning, he stood and headed off to the restroom to wash up.

I set up our lunch in the tiny kitchen, finding comfort in the small, domestic routine. Jandro kissed my cheek and thanked me for lunch when he returned, then flicked water droplets from his wet hands in my face. I aimed a punch at his bicep, but he batted my fist away and kissed me again. Ah, domestic bliss.

Freyja circled the small table as we ate. The humbling wisdom I'd seen in her eyes earlier was gone, replaced by eagerness to catch a piece of the steamed fish we had with our rice and beans today. In other words, she was just being a cat.

Gunner had recently set up a deal with a guy who stocked local ponds and lakes from a fish hatchery way up in the northern territories. It wasn't chicken or steak, but at least we had a regular source of protein and denser calories to eat.

"Reaper wants you over tonight," I told Jandro, once we stopped messing with each other. "Doesn't sound like he's expecting good news from the scouting team."

"He's always expecting the worst," Jandro said dismissively. "The way I see it, the first drone was destroyed and we haven't seen any more flying overhead. Tash, or whoever it was, tried something and it didn't work. That in itself is good for us."

"Makes sense. I just hope you can make Reaper see it that way."

"I try, but you know how he is." Jandro shrugged. "He sees it as his personal responsibility to expect the worst and prepare for it. After what happened to his mom's community, he's not even willing to risk cautious optimism. To him, it's the same as letting your guard down. And that's not something he's ever willing to do when it comes to protecting his people." He nudged my shoulder playfully. "Until you came along, he never let his guard down at all. Now he's only crotchety when it comes to running the club, and that's a huge improvement."

I smiled at him. "I do love seeing both of you happy. Like actually happy, and not just celebrating being alive for another day. It makes me hopeful for the future."

"I feel the same way, *Mariposita*." He leaned in for a kiss, but I pulled back, making a face at him because he'd just taken a big bite of fish.

We finished lunch with more lighthearted banter, then he made a big show of sticking a piece of gum in his mouth while I cleaned up the table.

"I'll see you tonight," I said, finally tilting my head up for a kiss. "Have a good da—"

"Oh no, *diablita*." Jandro grabbed my hips with a devilish grin and pulled me flush against him. "You don't get to sit on me and tease me like that without answering for it."

"I have patients waiting." But none of them were emergencies and I wasn't really concerned. My core ignited, like embers roaring to a flame from the perfect gust of wind. Only it was Jandro's hands on me that ignited the fire.

"Let them wait." He guided me backward until the freshly-cleaned table hit the back of my thighs. With an effortless lift, Jandro sat me on the table top and nudged his way between my legs. "You belong to both members of Steel Demons leadership. No one's gonna raise a stink if you're five minutes late."

"Five minutes? That's all you got in you?" I teased.

"Just warming you up for tonight," he groaned, taking a nibble at the edge of my jaw. "And the prospects are coming back from their lunch soon," he added apologetically. "So as much as I'd like to take my time with you on this table, I probably shouldn't."

"Hmm, I'll accept that." My teeth grazed his earlobe, earning another hot groan from him. "For now."

He stepped away, only to slide my pants and underwear down my legs. When he returned, his hand came between us, caressing me into an aching, hollow need for him.

"Fuck, I wish I could eat you for dessert," he moaned, slicking his fingers through my folds.

"Tonight," I reminded him, as I unclasped his jeans and freed his hot, heavy length from his boxers. I barely had time to stroke him before he nudged against my entrance.

"Why does tonight have to be like, *six* hours away?" he said in a choked whisper as he pressed in, his thumb still on my clit as his length slowly disappeared inside me.

"Because *you* decided you wanted me at lunch time." I locked my ankles behind his back, drawing him in, with my thighs glued to his hips.

"*You* snuck up on me and trapped me under that bike," he argued back, now fully sheathed inside me. "Caught me in a vulnerable position...coulda had your way with me and I wouldn't have been able to escape."

His breaths grew ragged as he rocked in and out of me, filling me up so deliciously, before leaving me empty and wanting more. He held me secure on the table with one strong hand on my waist, the other still working my clit into a rapid build up of sparks that lit up my whole body.

"Maybe I really will trap you under there one day," I panted, my fingers digging into the back of his broad shoulders. "When you least expect it."

"Baby, I'm going to be dreaming about it every day until it happens." His hips crashed against my thighs. "Trapped under a bike and in the best pussy I ever had. My two favorite places."

"Wouldn't that be a dream come true?" My laughter choked off as I felt him swell inside me, hitting spots that made me see stars.

"You know it," he grunted through gritted teeth, fighting to hold himself back.

"I'm right there," I whimpered, my body so tightly coiled on the edge of release. "Come with me, Jandro."

"Fuck, Mari..."

He held me so tightly as he climaxed, like I would break apart. I did, milking and draining all of him into me, but the love of this man kept me whole.

"Fuck...Damn." He shuddered as another convulsion of my orgasm squeezed around him. "You feel too good to be real." His forehead leaned against mine, eyes hooded and sated. "Sometimes I can't believe you're really mine. I love you, Mari."

"*Te amo, Alejandro,*" I murmured over the heavy thud of my pulse in my ears, running a finger over his gorgeous jaw.

My skin still buzzed with pleasure even as we separated and got dressed. I just got my pants back on as Larkan and Stephan's voices floated through the garage.

"You still eatin', boss?" Stephan poked his head into the kitchen.

"Nah." Jandro grinned as he hooked an arm around my waist and pulled me to him, pressing a slow, open kiss to the side of my face. "We're all done. For now."

REAPER

I almost did it. I was close. But I wasn't ready yet.

Quit kidding yourself, Rory. You chickened the fuck out.

The conversation in my head on the way to the clubhouse was an odd mix of tearing into myself for being a little bitch and psyching myself up for my next chance.

I almost gave Mari the ring this morning. Seeing Jandro's butterfly pendant around her neck reminded me of it every time. He was coming over tonight, so I couldn't do it then. I wanted the moment private, between just us.

I couldn't pinpoint why I was taking so fucking long to give it to her. I had the thing made at the market two weeks ago. Sure, scouting around for whoever was spying on us kept me busy, but that was just an excuse. I knew she'd probably like it, even love it. Not just the ring itself, but what it symbolized.

Years before the Collapse, men gave rings to their women as a sign of commitment. A symbol of his devotion to her, his willingness to stay by her side through thick and thin. An engagement, it was called. And it was not something taken lightly. Along with offering the ring, the man would ask for marriage—the same commitment from his woman in return. By the time a relationship reached that point, a 'yes' was usually expected. But there was always a chance she could say no.

Marriage didn't exist anymore, not in the legal sense. But people still held ceremonies and gave each other tokens of commitment. Mariposa was already mine in body, heart, and soul. The chances were low, maybe even non-existent, that she'd refuse my ring.

But that tiny, minuscule chance that she could, was enough to hold me back.

"President."

The mumbled greetings of my men drew me out of my own head, for the time being, and back to the matter at hand.

"By all means." I dropped into my chair at the head of the table, Hades sitting at my right side. "Don't leave me in suspense."

"Horus saw footprints and evidence of a campfire in a little valley in this mountain range." Gunner unfolded a map on the table and pointed at a spot roughly three miles away. "However, we can't scale that elevation on our current rides. The terrain is far too steep and wild, even for dirt bikes. We need Jeeps, ATVs, or some shit, to get up there. I'm willing to buy them if you think it's necessary, but those kinds of vehicles are costly."

"Anything else?" I looked up, Gunner and Horus both meeting my gaze. It didn't matter that Horus was a bird, those eyes with binocular vision were unsettling.

"No other signs of people in the area for twenty miles in every direction, boss."

I steepled my fingers in front of me, taking in this information.

"Everyone out." I swept my arm over the table. "Except Gunner."

He wasted no time in elaborating the moment the door closed. Most people assumed Gunner trained his falcon. They didn't all need to know he literally *saw* through Horus. I needed to hear him speak freely, without anyone getting weirded out at how he was able to know these things.

"The campfire was old, just a circle of rocks with barely any ash left," he explained. "It could have been set up and abandoned that same day Shadow shot down the drone."

"And there's literally nothing else?" I repeated, not wanting to believe it.

He shook his head. "The footprints disappeared halfway down the mountain. Too much time has passed with all the wind and sand around here. Honestly, I saw all there was to see. It's not worth getting off-road vehicles just for this, in my opinion."

"No tire tracks? No personal belongings left at the campsite?"

"Reaper," Gunner sighed. "You know I'm nothing, if not thorough. There was nothing there."

"So what the fuck am I supposed to do now?" I brought a fist down on the table. "We never should have gone to that stupid fucking market, least of all because of what happened to you and Mari."

"A little too late for that now, Pres." Gunner stood from his seat and leaned against the table. "I'm working on building up our arsenal. We're decently armed now, but I'm making sure we build up to where we were when we were supplying Tash. I'm also keeping double guards posted on the perimeter. If some asshole so much as throws a rock at us, we'll know."

"I'm tired of fucking sitting around and waiting for him to come to us." My fists closed, causing my fingernails to bite into my palms. "I want to hit him where it hurts. Sitting around and getting too comfortable was how he was able to infiltrate us in the first place."

"We need intel and allies for that," he reminded me. "I'm working on that aspect too." He reached up to stroke one of Horus's wings. "It's just hard to know who we can trust."

Hades stuck his nose in my lap and licked my arm. I unclenched one fist to pet him, the rage already simmering down to a manageable level—for now. I just hated feeling like I always had to look over my shoulder, and expect to see Tash's smug grin looking back. This whole drone thing was even making me lose sleep.

"Anything else?" I sighed, eager for my woman, a fat cigar, and three fingers of whiskey, in that order.

"Uh, yeah. Kinda." Gunner suddenly looked nervous. "Nothing to do with this, though."

I peered at him curiously. "What, then?"

"I was thinking of taking Mari out to the coast. Since you showed her where you're from and all, I just..." He trailed off, lifting one shoulder into a shrug. "I kinda wanted to do the same. Spend some time with her, get to know her a little better."

"You mean you're not fucking done testing the waters before diving in?" I demanded. "Fuck me with a rattlesnake, Gun. When are you gonna quit jerking her around and make up your mind?"

"I'm not jerking her around, I'm just going about it slow. Look, I take this shit seriously, alright?"

"What, like you think I don't?" I shot back. "Like Jandro doesn't? We knew what we wanted, so we went all in. You're the one acting like she's a side piece you can just drop and pick up when it suits you."

Now his fist came down on the table, and it made me glad to see. If he didn't care about her, he would have no reaction.

"That's not what she is to me," he hissed. "I *do* want her, just sharing her with you two kinda squicks me out, that's all."

"Then you don't want her. Not enough, anyway. Now tell her, so she can get the fuck over you."

"No, dude. Come on, I—" He brought a hand to his forehead with a sigh, then scrubbed his palm down his face. "I just want to be sure. I want to make absolutely sure this is the right choice, okay? None of us have known her for that long, if you think about it."

"The length of time doesn't matter," I argued. "We could die tomorrow, you know that. It's why Jandro and I love her so hard. If one of Tash's scouts picks you off with a sniper rifle tomorrow, are you going to feel good about *taking it slow?* Will you have lived without regrets? If you can look me in the eye and tell me *honestly* the answer is yes, then I'll never give you shit about this again."

He couldn't, as I expected.

"I just wanted your blessing to take her out for a day," he muttered, shoving his hands in his cut. "Guess the answer's no."

"My *blessing?* What am I, her father?" I scoffed. "She's my woman, but I'm not her keeper. You want to take her somewhere, you're asking the wrong person."

A tiny light bulb seemed to go off in his head as he shot me a skeptical glance. "Yeah?"

"Yeah, Gun. It's not all that complicated. If she tells you to fuck off, I trust you'll honor that answer."

He nodded to himself, the wheels turning in his blonde head. "Okay. Well, if that's all, president—"

"Look, if she says yes, the coast is romantic and all, but I need you here," I interrupted. "And we need to be pragmatic. Mari's getting her tattoo soon, but that's not always enough. She needs to learn how to defend herself."

He glanced at me, the question lighting up his eyes. "And you want me to...?"

"You're the best person for the job. I want her to learn weapons and hand-to-hand combat." I humored him with a smirk. "And if things don't develop between you two then, well, I got no hope for you."

MARIPOSA

"How'd it go?" I asked Reaper, as he and Hades came through the door.

"They found a whole lotta nothin'," he grumbled, shrugging off his cut to drape it on the back of a chair. "Just as I thought."

"Which isn't a bad thing," Jandro piped up from his spot on the couch beside me. "Like I told you, it means whoever wanted to fuck with us is miles away from here."

Reaper muttered something unintelligible as he rummaged through the kitchen. "You want wine, sugar?"

"Yes, please!"

I stretched my legs out on the couch, so my feet would have their place in his lap while Jandro's chest made a nice pillow for my head.

Hades stood in the center of the room, looking torn. Jandro and I took up the length of the couch, while Freyja's tiny black form was curled up in the center of his massive dog bed next to the fireplace.

"What a sucker," Jandro chuckled. "Just pick her up and move her, Hades."

"He got a nose full of claws last time he did that." Reaper returned from the kitchen and held my glass out to me. "The little rodent just walks all over him."

"Who does that remind you of?" Jandro poked me in the ribs as Reaper lifted my legs to take his spot on the couch.

"I do *not* walk all over you two!"

"Not in the bedroom, you don't." Reaper brought my feet into his lap, his hands sweeping over my ankles and calves in a way that turned me to jelly. "But we're yours, sugar. Utterly and completely. I hope you know that."

"I dunno," I joked, despite his words turning me to mush. "Rub my arches a little more and maybe you'll convince me."

He proceeded to lift my foot and close his teeth around my big toe, making me shriek and kick like a madwoman. The two of them found it totally hilarious. I barely noticed Jandro taking my wine so I wouldn't spill it.

By the time we settled down, Hades took up the love seat across from us. Reaper usually didn't want him on the furniture, but I noticed him growing more relaxed with his dog in recent weeks.

"Oh, Dallas said that Andrea finished the prospect's cut," Reaper said over me to Jandro, his hands now back to treating my feet properly. "We're all set for tomorrow."

"Good." I could hear the grin in the VP's voice. "I can't fucking wait to see what he thinks of his road name."

I tilted my head back on his chest to look up at him. "You didn't let him pick his own name?"

"All his ideas sucked." Jandro dropped a kiss on my forehead. "The one I picked for him is perfect."

"Can I have a hint?"

He caressed my jaw, grinning down at me. "Nope."

I pouted and he kissed my lower lip.

"He ain't sayin' shit. Not even I know what it is." Reaper's massage moved up to my calves and shins.

I slid down Jandro's torso, snuggling under his arm. "I'm just proud of Stephan, honestly." I refused to call him *prospect*. "After all you've put him through, he deserves some respect and recognition."

"He's a good kid," Reaper agreed. "Smart, and loyal down to his bones. He'll make a fine Demon."

Jandro's arm squeezed around my waist. "You're gonna be part of the ceremony, you know."

"Me? Why?"

"You're the president's old lady," Reaper grinned. "You're just gonna put the cut on him when I say to. Not much more to it than that."

"Then we're gonna fuckin' party!" Jandro raised a fist in the air. 'Cause fuck knows we all deserve one."

I rolled my eyes. "Like you guys ever need a reason to party."

Stephan's patching ceremony was held right after breakfast the next morning. Everyone gathered in front of the front gate where a crudely-assembled platform, similar to the one at Python's execution, was set up to provide a stage.

I stood off to the side where Stephan's cut draped over my arm. The Steel Demons skull grinned up at me from the back, freshly sewn on by Andrea, Dallas's wife. Jandro instructed me not to peek at the front, where Stephan's new road name was embroidered. I resisted, tempting as it was.

Reaper and Jandro stood on the rickety, wooden stage together, both trying to hide elated grins. They waited for everyone to gather and quiet down before Reaper addressed them.

"The Steel Demons recently lost a member," he began. "But we're about to gain one who is ten times the man Python was."

I stole a glance at Bones, who kept his eyes trained on the president with no change in expression. Reaper, and my guess, Hades, had determined Bones's innocence, and allowed him to stay in the club with no repercussions.

"Admittance into this club is *not* handed out lightly," Reaper continued. "We are demanding. We are harsh. We don't tolerate bullshit. And that's exactly why we've survived for this long, while other clubs have eaten dust."

A low murmur of agreements and nodding heads came back from the crowd.

"But once you've earned my trust and respect," he placed a hand over his heart, "Once you've proved your loyalty, the Demons will never turn their back on you. You become part of our family and we always take care of our own." His hand lowered again to his side. "Today we're making someone an official part of our family."

Reaper took a step back and allowed Jandro to step forward. "Stephan, come on up."

The young man, his face already pink from the warm morning sun, slid through the crowd to join his president and VP on the stage. Jandro directed him to face Reaper, who began asking him a series of questions.

"Stephan, do you swear to obey and uphold all laws of the Steel Demons MC, current and future?"

"I swear, president," the prospect answered solemnly.

"Will you obey orders from me, your VP, and any of your senior officers, to the fullest extent and without question?"

"I will, president."

The questions continued for another minute, before Reaper turned to me with a nod. I drew in a deep breath as I ascended the stage, my heart pounding with nerves and excitement for Stephan.

"Then with my full authority as president," Reaper said. "I declare you, from this day forward, a fully patched member of the SDMC." He nodded at me again, and I couldn't help but beam as I held out Stephan's cut.

The young man never looked so happy as he turned his back to me, arms extended behind him. I slid the leather over one arm and then the other before tugging it in place over his shoulders. He turned back to me as cheers and applause erupted from the club, his brothers, and I couldn't stop myself from planting a kiss on his cheek.

"Congratulations," I told him, a grin splitting my face.

"Thank you, Mari—ma'am." He turned beet red, much to the amusement of everyone watching.

I stepped back to stand at Reaper's side, while Jandro came up to throw an arm around Stephan's shoulders.

"Stephan the prospect is no more." Jandro slapped a hand on the young man's chest, right over his new name patch. "You're a Demon now, and your road name is Slick."

"Hm," Reaper mused quietly at my side.

"Before you all get any ideas," Jandro raised an index finger to the crowd, "like he's slick with the ladies or some shit, let me set the record straight. Here's how I came up with his name."

Stephan groaned and brought a palm to his face, but that just riled everyone up and earned an affectionate ruffling of his hair from Jandro.

"The first day this kid started working in my shop," Jandro declared. "I told him to hand me a tool that was in a box across the bay. This young fucker walks over there, gets it, but on his way back to me..." He could barely get the words out from trying so hard to contain his laughter. "This motherfucker...slips on an oil slick and eats shit!"

The laughter rippling through the crowd was contagious. Even Shadow appeared to crack a smile.

"Oh my God, that's awful." I covered my mouth to hold in my own giggles, but some escaped anyway.

"It's pretty fuckin' funny." Reaper chuckled, hooking an arm around my waist as he brushed a kiss along my forehead. "He's a good sport, though. And it fits him."

It was true. Stephan's joy was uncontrolled, like a kid on Christmas. Reaper and I stood watching him like proud parents, Jandro messing with him like a little brother. The happiness and feelings of celebration were intense now, but everyone seemed to understand it would be short-lived.

It dawned on me right then, why Reaper was so protective of his club, why the Steel Demons found every possible excuse to party and have a good time. This kind of life gave so few opportunities to laugh, smile, and feel good, so they took those moments and lived them to the fullest.

Especially with enemies still lurking.

SHADOW

F ive.
    Five tries was how many it took before I worked up the nerve to actually step into Mariposa's office. The first time, I made it to the end of my street before the anxiety overtook me. The third time, I got inside the clubhouse door.

I had to. There was no more getting out of this. I had talked myself out of going to her office every day for the past two weeks. But this morning, I woke up on the floor with my face covered in blood from a cut on my head. My mattress had been flipped up and leaned against the wall. My ribs were fucking sore and I was tired of this. I needed some help.

Now on my fifth and final attempt, she looked up from the counter with surprise. Those greenish-brown eyes and her smile wiped my memory of what I was doing here.

"Shadow! I didn't expect to see you here. How are you today?"

"Fine," I mumbled, my heart feeling like it was going to crash out of my chest. "And you?"

"Good, thanks." She turned on her wheeled stool to face me. Her smile accentuated the apples of her cheeks, flushing a delicate pink. "What can I do for you?"

"I, uh..."

...fucking forgot what I was going to say. Again.

I wanted to slam my fist into my forehead at how stupid I was. Why was this so fucking hard for me? I even practiced what to say, which I was certain nobody else did. Just having a mundane fucking conversation came so naturally to everyone, except me.

"Did the sleep aids work for you?" Mariposa's eyes fell to the plastic orange pill bottle I'd started crushing in my fist.

Fucking idiot.

"Um, yes. Sorry about that." I placed the now-dented plastic container on the counter. "You said to come see you if they worked."

"Yes, I'm glad to hear they were successful." She paid no mind to the ruined bottle. "So would you like to continue taking them?"

"Yes, if you would, um, advise that."

"If they're helping you, then certainly." She flashed me another smile before turning to open a set of cabinets. "So, no nightmares, then?"

"No." An aching breath escaped my chest. I felt a bit less like an idiot when she wasn't looking at me. "None during the nights I took them."

She nodded, still examining the various medications in the cabinet. "How's the quality of your sleep? Are you sleeping solidly through the night, or are you waking up frequently?"

"Pretty solid through the night." Much like last time I was here, the anxiety began to subside as we talked more and I got used to her presence. "The last three nights I, um..."

She looked over at me and the tightness in my chest nearly choked off my breath. "Yes?"

I forced the words out through the fear gripping me. "I didn't drink before bed. I didn't use alcohol to pass out at all. I just...fell asleep naturally."

Her expression morphed into one that had never once been aimed at me.

"Shadow, that's great!" She moved toward me with her hands extended, and now the fear running through me was of her touching me.

"It is?" I stepped back to put more space between us.

Do not *let her touch you. Reaper and Jandro will never forgive you.*

"Yes!" She stopped abruptly, dropping her hands to her sides with a sheepish smile. "Sorry, I just got excited for you. The drinking concerns me, honestly. I wanted to tackle that as a separate issue when you were ready. But it looks like you're curbing it on your own, which is fantastic to hear."

"It concerns you?" I stared at her, bewildered. "Why?"

"Because at the rate you were going, it could kill you, Shadow."

"You're...*concerned* about me dying?"

"Of course I am!" She said it like she never considered an alternative. "I'm the club medic. I'm responsible for keeping all of the Steel Demons alive and healthy. Besides, who would I say good morning to if you died?"

"You can say good morning to anyone," I pointed out.

She smiled and my chest tightened again, but it didn't feel like anxiety this time.

"I like saying it to you, though."

Why?

The statement was so utterly confusing to me. She knew how much I struggled with the most basic interactions. What possible enjoyment could she get out of talking to *me*, of all people?

Before I could ask the question rattling around in my head, a small black blur zipped through the office door. It slid across the smooth tiled floor and crashed head first into the lower cabinets.

"Freyja!" Mariposa bent to pick the thing up and placed it on the countertop. "You crazy kitten."

It was indeed a small cat, covered in dense black fur with green eyes. The kitten didn't appear to be hurt, as it immediately bounced across the counter to where Mariposa was sorting medications.

"No, I don't need your fur getting into everything." She picked up the animal around the midsection and turned it to face the opposite direction. "Go bug Shadow while I do this."

"Um—"

Before I could protest, the animal flopped over its own legs and crashed into my hand resting on the counter.

"She's about twelve weeks old, by my estimate," Mari laughed. "Still working on her coordination."

"Is she like Hades and Horus?" I asked, watching the tiny, furry thing play with my hand. I didn't move a muscle, but she jumped over my palm, chewed on my fingers, and kicked at my hand with her back legs.

"I think so," Mariposa said in a quieter voice. "Her name came to me as soon as I found her in the scrap pile behind Jandro's shop. Before I even heard her meowing, I felt this pull to look and find her. Reaper knew exactly what it was." She looked up at me with a small smile, her face pinker than usual. "Sounds weird as hell, right?"

Nothing is as weird as me.

"Considering we have three of these animals now, I suppose it's not all that weird."

"Maybe not," she mused, watching the kitten continue to attack my hand. "You can pet her if you want."

Again, such a simple thing didn't occur to me. I curled a finger and allowed it to scratch over the kitten's head. Freyja's skull felt so fragile under the weight of my hand, I worried about hurting her.

But when I lifted my finger away, the kitten pressed up and head-butted it. She began rubbing her head against my knuckles so hard, she nearly fell over. A tiny rumbling sound came from her, like the smallest motorcycle engine. Confused, I looked up at Mariposa.

"What's that noise? Did I hurt her?"

"She's purring," the grinning medic answered. "It means she's happy."

"Why is she rubbing her head on me?"

"She likes you. She's marking you with her scent to claim you as hers." Mariposa laughed as the kitten flopped over on the counter, wrapping her tiny front paws around my finger as she continued to purr and rub her cheeks against my hand. "Scratch that. She's utterly in love with you."

"Huh." I extended a finger to run over the kitten's belly. "You're a funny little animal with strange taste in humans."

"So, for your sleep meds," Mari turned back to her array of pills after another minute of watching the kitten and me. "I'd like to put you on a two-week dose this time. Take one at night before bed, just like before.

These do have a risk of dependency so if they stop becoming effective, or new symptoms come up, let me know, okay?"

"Okay. That sounds good." The kitten was distracting me so much, it was like I forgot to feel anxious. Was this what people meant by baby animals being "cute"?

I jerked my gaze back up to Mariposa, hoping I didn't offend her with my distracted response. "Thank you."

"You're welcome, Shadow." She tucked a strand of hair behind her ear, eyes darting around, looking everywhere but at me.

Fuck. She really was scared of me, no matter how much she tried not to treat me any differently. I pulled my hand away from the kitten, and turned to leave.

"I'll leave you to your work. Thank you again—"

"We should do this tattoo soon, right?" she asked the words in a jumbled rush. "The Steel Demons tattoo."

"Um, yes." I paused in the doorway, which Freyja took as an opportunity to scramble off of the counter and rub herself against my ankles. "If you are comfortable with me doing it. Reaper wanted you to have it done as soon as possible."

She nodded with a swallow, her nervous gaze continuing to bounce around the room. An ache squeezed my throat, all the way down to my stomach. It was probably for the best, but I felt some kind of internal discomfort with the confirmation that she didn't want me to touch her. At all.

I may not have known how to act around women, but I knew how to be a professional tattoo artist. When Jandro told me to just imagine her bare skin as a blank canvas, it helped. I did good work, and after some time to think about it, I felt confident I could work with her.

Plus, I wouldn't mind just seeing her and talking to her again. After a few minutes of conversation, she had a warm, calming effect on me that not even booze could replicate. She eased my nerves without numbing me. I could still feel, and while I wasn't used to feeling this way—whatever *this* was—she made me want to feel it often.

But the fear in her eyes hurt me, in a way I didn't even know was possible to experience pain.

"It doesn't have to be from me," I told her, ignoring the odd pain sensation. "I can recommend an artist in the next town over. He's probably booked out for months, though."

"No, Shadow." Her eyes refocused on me. "I want you to be the one doing it."

"Are you...sure?" I was so confused.

"Yeah, I'm just nervous," she laughed lightly. "It's my first tattoo. And it needs to be pretty big, from what I understand."

"Oh, right. The pain." I hadn't felt physical pain in so long, I had forgotten it was part of the tattooing process.

"Yeah." Her smile was nervous, but her gaze remained on me. "Just go easy on me in case I'm a total wuss, okay?"

"We can do it over multiple sessions if it becomes too much." I reached down to pick up Freyja, worried about trampling her. The kitten squirmed, her whole body fitting into the palm of my hand as I placed her back on the counter. She just ran back down to weave her little body between my boots again.

"Thanks, that makes me feel better." Mariposa laughed, watching the kitten's antics.

"You've taken good care of me in your field of expertise. I'll make sure to do the same."

Shit. Was that too much or okay to say? Fuck, how do I know? She's smiling, but looking away. What does that mean?

"That's sweet, Shadow. Thank you." Her voice grew soft, almost taking on the same breathy quality as when she was riding me.

Fuck! No, don't think about that. I was doing so well...

"I'll let you know what my schedule's like one of these days when I'm over with Jandro."

"Okay. Sure, yes. That sounds good."

"Hey, before you go." She pressed a cap down on a bottle of pills and held it out to me. "Don't forget these."

"Oh, right." Careful to step over Freyja and not on top of her, I crossed the room to take my medication from Mariposa. I forgot all about being careful not to touch her however, and her fingers brushed mine with a gentle heat. "Thank you."

"You're welcome, Shadow." She smiled with a small head tilt toward her shoulder. It made my chest squeeze with that odd, non-painful sensation again. "Are you coming to Stephan—I mean Slick's, patching-in party tonight?"

"Yes, I'll be tattooing him during the event."

"Great. I'll get to see you in action then."

Something about the words she used heated my body up a few degrees. "Yes," I agreed. "You'll see it's actually not a bad experience."

Truthfully, that depended on where Slick chose to have his tattoo done, but I wasn't about to spook her with those details.

"Sounds good." She gave a small wave, her eyes never wavering from me. "I'll see you there."

I suddenly didn't want to leave, but forced myself to turn toward the office door.

"See you then, Mariposa."

GUNNER

I broke the surface of the water, taking a deep breath as I slicked my hair back. The calm silence of being underwater shifted to the din of the party in full swing. Some EDM music from the mid-2000s played on an ancient set of speakers as people drank, laughed, and jumped into the pool.

In the background, I heard the buzz of Shadow's tattoo gun as he permanently sealed the Demon into Slick's body forever. It had been a good day, and I was never one to drag down a party, so I couldn't place why I preferred the quiet solitude of being underwater over celebrating with everyone else.

Maybe I just wasn't drunk enough yet.

Hoisting my upper body onto the pool deck, I fished a beer out of a nearby ice bucket, then slid back into the water as I opened it with my teeth.

I hadn't heard a peep from my uncle yet and that worried me. It had been weeks, nearly a month, since I hightailed it out of Colorado. Or Jerriton, rather. General Tash was not one to sit around idly. If he was gonna make a move to fuck over Uncle Jerry, he would've done it by now.

Could the shifty general have actually given my uncle a part of his territory? Anything was possible, of course, but I could not wrap my head around that logic. Why steamroll entire towns all over the Southwest? Why snatch up territories so ruthlessly, only to give them up to your competitors? I couldn't see Tash doing it, not for any reason that would benefit him. For all the lies he told us, I knew for certain that he'd protect his own interests at all costs.

I took a long pull of my beer and set it down on the pool deck, releasing it to dunk my head back underwater. Too much noise, too much thinking. It was so much more peaceful under the surface.

I swam to the far edge and kicked off, cutting through the water with long strokes. Just before I hit the opposite wall, a pair of feet dipped into the water. Slender, feminine feet.

When I broke the surface to take a breath, Mari smiled at me from her perch on the pool's edge. Her navy-blue bikini hugged her beautiful form in ways I only wish I could.

You don't have to just wish, a small voice reminded me. It sounded like the devil whispering into my ear, urging me to give in to temptations, to partake of what would, surely, feel so good. The other voice, the one keeping me on the righteous path, had been oddly silent as of late.

"Hey, baby girl." I slicked my hair back and cleared the water from my nose. "Coming in?"

"That depends." She kicked her legs, making small splashes. "You gonna make sure I don't drown?"

"You don't need me for that," I laughed. "But is your cat gonna defy the rules of the animal kingdom and follow you in?"

A few feet away, Freyja leaned as far as she could over the edge without falling in. Green eyes dilated, her tiny black nose flexed as she sniffed the water. Then she gingerly extended one paw to bat at the wet, blue stuff.

"I have faith in her," Mari declared. "I don't think those two will let her drown anyway."

Hades reclined nearby at Reaper's side. The dog was relaxed, gnawing on a bone, but his eyes remained on his new furry sidekick. Horus was also close by, perched on the wrought-iron fence surrounding the pool. I didn't have to slip my consciousness into him to know he took note of every single one of the kitten's movements. Those talons would be ready to push off, wings ready to dive, if she ended up in the pool.

Immediately after Mari found her, the animals went into protective mode. They guarded and took to her like she was one of their own. Maybe their animal forms were all different species, but the three of us knew they were cut from the same cloth. We just didn't know what that cloth was made of.

I raised a hand from the water and hovered it over Freyja. The water droplets falling onto her may as well have been acid with how she hissed and ran back to Hades.

"You're so mean!" Mari cried, but she was laughing.

"Nah, *this* is mean."

I wrapped my arms around her bare waist in a hug, and dragged her into the water with me.

"Gunner!" she shrieked, but didn't fight me. "I wasn't ready!"

"Keep psyching yourself up and you'll never be ready," I grinned, loosening my hold on her. "At least I didn't jump in with you this time."

"Yeah, *so* considerate," she groaned. Her fingertips lingered on my abs and she made no move to pull them away.

"Aw, come on, your feet touch the bottom here. You're no damsel in distress." I pulled away from her to grab my beer. Her touch on me felt good. Too good.

A quietness settled between us. I took sips of my drink while she gradually lowered more of herself into the water, until only her face was uncovered.

"There you go," I encouraged her. "See, it's not all that scary."

"I think I'm more scared of getting my tattoo now than water," she admitted with a nervous laugh.

"Oh, no way. Drowning's a lot scarier. You can't die from a tattoo, not even a bad one."

"Unless the needle has Hepatitis," she retorted. "Or HIV. Or I get a bad bacterial infection—"

"I get Shadow disposable needles," I assured her. "And he is meticulous about keeping his area clean."

She lifted an eyebrow. "Really?" she said, and looked over her shoulder.

Slick was stretched out a table, Shadow bent over him and oblivious to his surroundings as he inked the Demon onto Slick's torso. A few people gathered around to watch and pour alcohol into Slick's mouth when he requested it.

"No one's got food around him," I pointed out. "And look, Shadow's wearing gloves, see?"

Mari's eyes narrowed but she didn't argue. "Does it have to be so...public?"

"I mean, if you want to throw a party in honor of *you* becoming official, no one's gonna say no. But if you want yours done privately, no one's gonna tell the president's old lady otherwise."

Her eyes lit up at the title and she gave a small smile. My heart squeezed in my chest. She really did love being his. Hell, she was a natural at the patching-in ceremony this morning. And I had to admit, Reaper and her looked good together. All three of them seemed to have an easy, natural dynamic. I was beginning to see it the more I looked. But trying to see where I fit in felt like sticking a square peg in a round hole. I adored Mari, and would've made her mine in a heartbeat if there had been no one else. But what could I possibly give her that she didn't already have from those two?

"Can I be honest with you about something?" She had drifted closer to me and asked the question in a hushed voice.

"Always, baby girl." Fuck, her eyes looked so pretty with the pool water reflecting in them.

"I don't want Reaper and Jandro there while I'm getting tattooed."

"Really?" I almost choked on my beer. "Why not?"

"You know how they are," she murmured. "If my finger even twitches like I'm in pain, Reaper will go all crazy over-protective. Jandro will keep trying to make me laugh to distract me, and that could mess up the tattoo."

"True enough," I agreed. "Want me to be there with you?"

The look on her face proved that was exactly what she hoped I would say.

"Could you, Gun? If you're not too busy? I feel like I can handle Shadow on my own, I'm just not sure how well *he'll* handle it."

"Consider it done," I grinned. "I'll make sure the whole thing is so painless, you'll end up taking a nap."

"Somehow I doubt that," she mused skeptically, but returned my grin. "Thank you, Gun. I—" Her lips slammed shut, a deep, rosy flush filling her skin.

"You what?" I prompted. "Tell me, or we're both going under." I snaked my non-beer hand around her waist in a tight hold. She knew I was kidding, though.

"When something scares me, I just—" her heart brushed against my chest, betraying its rapid beating. "I feel safer, calmer, whenever you're around." She tilted her face up to look at me, almost resting her head on my shoulder. "That's all."

She said it like it was a silly, childish confession, but it meant everything to me. Here it was, the place where I could fit. The calm in her storm, her anchor and her safety. As she leaned on me, looking so damn kissable and perfect and mine, I started to think that this really could work.

"I miss you," I confessed like a lovesick teenager. "It's been a hell of a couple of weeks since our time in that cave, but I swear I haven't been ignoring you, Mari."

"I know," she assured me, sliding an arm around my waist under the water. "Finding out who sent the drone took priority. I get it."

"You haven't been starved for attention, I'm sure." It was meant to be a joke, but the words slipped out coated in my insecurities and doubts. "Sorry. Fuck, I'm sorry."

All the smiles disappeared from her face. "I've missed you too, Gun. *You*, specifically. Yes, Reaper and Jandro are always there for me, and it feels nice. But that's what I'm trying to tell you with this tattoo thing— you're not all interchangeable to me. You're all people I care about, but the three of you drive me fucking crazy for different reasons too."

"You're totally right and that was a dick thing to say. I'm sorry, it's just—" I sucked in a tight breath. "Old habits, I guess. Which is no excuse, really. But it's like I'm trying to unlearn everything I was taught my whole life, you know?"

Her expression softened. "Yeah, I get it. Me too. Although I guess it's different for me, since I'm the one at the center of this whole thing. Sometimes it still hits me hard and I panic."

"About what?"

"About being fair to all of you. I have to keep two, potentially three, men happy while you all just have me. Once I start to relax, I get hit with this worry that someone might feel neglected or ignored. I don't want to hurt anyone like that, not ever."

"I never thought about it like that," I said, cocking my head. "It is a pretty big responsibility to put on you, huh?"

"One I don't take lightly," she replied solemnly. Only after she said that did a light, blissful smile spread on her face. "But it's so worth it to me. I feel so loved, so cherished. Seeing how Reaper looks at me, how Jandro holds me—I feel like I'm made of sunlight and I just want to give that kind of love back to them, so they can feel it too."

I want that.

Those three words hovered on the tip of my tongue, but never left my mouth. I didn't just want that feeling she talked about, I wanted it from her, and her alone. I wanted to be a reason she smiled so big and glowed like a little ball of sunlight. Did it really matter that I wasn't the only one who made her feel like that? Was it really so bad that she had the capacity to love more than one man at a time?

I wanted to tell myself no, it didn't matter. But doing so felt like stepping off the edge of a cliff. It felt like putting my heart in a box without knowing if it would be thrown in a blender or looked after with care.

What the fuck did I even know what love was?

"I'm glad," was all I could tell her. "That they make you feel that way. You deserve nothing less, baby girl."

Mari's eyes seemed to search me, like she was trying to figure out what I really meant to say. "I wasn't trying to rub it in your face—"

"You weren't." I dropped a kiss to the top of her head, sliding an arm around her shoulders to hug her close. "I just kept turning it over in my head, trying to see it from all angles like I do with everything. You've cleared up a lot for me, really."

"I have?"

"Yeah." I held her close enough to feel her heart beat again. "Just seeing that look on your face, knowing for sure that they're good to you and make you feel like that... It's a big weight off my mind."

Warm fingertips slid up my back, making water trail down my skin.

"It doesn't mean I don't miss you, Gunner."

MARIPOSA

"I cannot believe this!" Jandro whined dramatically. "I'm getting kicked out of my own house."

"You were going to the shop anyway," I reminded him, watching Shadow wipe down a chair with bleach out of the corner of my eye.

"I was going to ditch and make the prospects do the work so I could watch you!"

"Prospect, singular," I reminded him. "Larkan is the only one now."

"Slick is still my little bitch," he grinned viciously, leaning into me.

"Stop." I tried in vain to dodge his attempts to tickle and kiss me. "This is why I didn't want you here! You'll make Shadow's work look like chicken scratch."

"You were one of my squirmiest clients," Shadow added. The large, quiet man seemed at ease as he set up his tattooing area. Every passing day in my company seemed to make him more and more comfortable with me. That moment in my office with Freyja seemed to break another one of the many barriers between us. He looked like he'd never pet a kitten before, and it was oddly wholesome to watch.

The kitten in question was curled up in Gunner's lap, who reclined on the couch with his feet on the coffee table. His long fingers dragged luxurious scratches over Freyja's head, if her halfway closed eyes were a sign of anything. On Gunner's shoulder, Horus kept staring at the cat, either protectively or like he wanted to eat her.

"That's 'cause it was my ribs, dude!" Jandro protested. "That shit hurts."

"You picked the placement. My job is the same no matter what spot you choose. So maybe think ahead next time."

My eyes bounced back and forth between the two of them. Watching them talk and banter like two normal friends was utterly surreal. Usually it was Shadow being silent while Jandro spoke close to his ear. Judging by Gunner craning his neck to look, he didn't see this often either.

"Fine, I'm a bad example. I can take a hint." Grabbing hold of my arms, Jandro gave me a deep, toe-tingling kiss. "But I wanna see it right after."

"We'll see you and Reap by the pool when we're done," I told him, almost wishing he wouldn't let go. My heart started to pound. It was almost time.

He cocked an eyebrow. "We?"

"Gunner's coming too."

Jandro clicked his tongue in surprise, his gaze sliding over to the blonde man on the couch. "All right then. See you both there."

He stole another kiss and went out the door. The moment it shut behind him, I turned nervously to face Shadow. For the first time since I walked in, he looked just as stricken with nerves as I felt.

"Have you, ahem," he cleared his throat, "decided where you would like the tattoo?"

I nodded just as Gunner came up behind me, placing a kiss on the back of my head as he rubbed warmth into my arms. A small bit of tension immediately released from my shoulders.

"I would like it on my upper back, please."

Gunner hissed in a breath, then I felt his smile on my cheek and an affectionate squeeze around my shoulders. "We're gonna match, baby girl."

"Yeah," I grinned back at him. "It just seemed like the best place to be able to see it."

"Okay," Shadow said. His jaw clenched as his dark eye settled on Gunner's face above my head. Was he blushing too? "I'll need to, um—"

"Don't worry, Shadow." I couldn't resist shooting him a teasing smile. "I *did* think this through."

Both guys seemed to hold their breaths as I peeled off my scrub top. Underneath I wore a halter camisole over a strapless bra. Taking the rubber band around my wrist, I piled my hair on top of my head in a messy bun.

"Will this work?" I turned my back to Shadow. With the exception of the halter strap across the back of my neck, my upper back was completely bare.

"Yes," he grunted out. I didn't catch his expression, and when I turned back around, he was rummaging through the supplies on his desk. "Let me get you a towel. Your arms will be resting on the back of the chair for a while."

He took off quickly into the house, and Gunner looked moments away from laughing his ass off.

"A towel, huh? I think your little strip tease made him jizz his pants."

"Don't be a dick." I swatted at him, only to be dodged and have my wrist grabbed.

"This reminds me," he smirked, playfully pinning my wrists to my sides. "Reaper wants me to teach you self-defense stuff. Weapons and hand-to-hand combat. You down for that, baby girl?"

"Sure." I tried to ignore the heat in my body that erupted, seemingly out of nowhere. It could only be from his gentle, playful restraint. "It'll probably be useful."

"Let's hope you won't ever have to use it 'cause you'll have one of us there." He released my wrists, trailing his fingertips up my forearms. "But it's better to know than not. In case that tattoo doesn't deter someone."

Someone like Corinne, only more evil and deranged. He didn't have to say it, but we both knew what he meant. She was going to make him a sex slave anyway, tattoo or not.

At the sound of Shadow's heavy footsteps returning, I turned to see him place a folded towel over the back of the chair. "There. That should be more comfortable for you."

I smiled at him. "Thank you, Shadow."

He nodded and turned back to his desk, pulling on a pair of gloves as he sat on a wheeled stool, a bigger version of the one I had in my office.

"If you don't mind," he muttered with a glance at me. "I'd like to draw the design directly on you first, to make sure I have the proportions correct and it fits the whole area."

"I'm fine with that. Just sit with my back to you?"

"Yes."

"Here, baby girl." Gunner pulled another chair over, placing it directly behind mine. "Just hop on, straddle that thing, and look into my eyes."

I chuckled at his innuendo as I took my seat, resting my forearms on the towel Shadow placed and stared into his gorgeous blue eyes.

"I'm, uh," Shadow stammered behind me. "I'm going to clean your skin with some rubbing alcohol, okay?"

"Okay."

"Relax, man," Gunner said over me to him. "It's nothing you've never done before."

Shadow muttered something under his breath in reply. I felt nothing for a few long moments, maybe almost a full minute. But then a damp, cotton pad gently wiped across my upper back, from my shoulders to my bra line. When my skin dried, the tip of a pen pressed gently as it moved across my flesh. I could tell Shadow was trying not to press too hard, but still felt the edge of his gloved hand, warm and heavy on my back.

"What was getting your tattoo like?" I asked Gunner, resting my chin on my hands as Shadow drew on my back.

"Same as you, pretty much." He leaned back in his chair, raking his hair back to put it in a bun like mine. "Shadow likes to draw on the body first to make sure the tattoo fits and flows well. I didn't get no towel for my armrest, though!" He glared at Shadow over my shoulder, who only grunted in response.

I got the sense that Shadow didn't like to be bothered while he worked. The lightest breeze of air from his breaths hit my skin as he drew, and I wondered if he noticed my goosebumps.

Shadow rides in the rear because he's the last line of defense, Jandro had told me. *Nothing gets past him.*

The large man at my back felt like nothing short of a shield. Even though he was drawing so carefully on my skin, I felt completely protected. The house could collapse in on us and I wouldn't get a scratch on me, because of Shadow.

"There were some parts," Gunner continued his tattoo story, "that had me white-knuckle gripping my chair. And I'm no puss, but fuck."

"Oh no." I felt the blood drain away from my face. "Did I end up picking the most painful spot?"

"No, the spinal column will be the worst part," Shadow said. "Because of the bones and nerves in there. But we can stop at any time, like I told you before." He seemed to lean in closer and said in a low voice, hovering just over my skin, "And Gunner *was* being a puss."

"I heard that!"

A giggle burst out of me, and I tried not to let my shoulders shake too much. Shadow made a throaty sound that could have been a chuckle. I smiled behind my hand, feeling like we just shared a private joke.

"Okay," he said, the pressure of his hand moving away from my skin. "The sketch is done. Take a look in the mirror."

I stood from the chair and walked to the hallway mirror, turning around to look over my shoulder.

"Wow!"

My jaw dropped. Sketched in rough purple lines, the Steel Demons skull grinned at me from between my shoulder blades. Its horns swept up along the back of my shoulders toward the base of my neck. The words *Steel Demons* flowed in an elegant banner just beneath the skull. He made it look more feminine somehow, fitting the contours of my body while still representing the club where I had found my home.

"Oh my god, Shadow." I kept turning and twisting in the mirror to see it from different angles. All the fear melted away at the sight of it, and now I couldn't wait to make this symbol a permanent part of me.

"Do you like it?" He sounded apprehensive.

"I *love* it!" I shot a face-splitting grin at his shocked expression as I returned to my seat, propping my arms up on the back of the chair. "Can't wait to get started now."

"I'm glad you like it," Shadow mumbled from behind me. I heard him rip a plastic package open, which I assumed to be the needle.

"Aww, look at you." Gunner scooted forward, his grin matching mine as he rested his fingertips on my knees that were splayed out on either side of the chair. "Baby girl's all excited about her first ink now. What do you need me for?"

"Don't go." I clasped one of his hands on my leg. "I'm excited now, but I'll probably start chickening out halfway through."

"I'm not going anywhere." His breath fanned over my face, gorgeous blue eyes falling to my lips as his forehead barely brushed mine. "I wouldn't miss this for the world."

A buzzing sound from behind me startled me out of the moment. Holy shit, this was really about to happen. I was tying myself to this club forever.

"Are you ready, Mariposa?" Shadow asked.

I sucked in a deep breath, my vision consumed with Gunner's face. His eyes lit up as he gave a comforting squeeze to my hand, and brushed a soft kiss along my forehead.

"Yes, I'm ready."

"Here we go. Tell me to stop any time you need it."

The buzzing filled my ears again and my heart felt ready to jump out of my chest. The warmth of Shadow's hand returned to my back, followed by a sharp, scratching sensation on my left shoulder blade.

"Oh." I released a breath. "That's not bad at all."

"You won't feel much of anything in a few minutes," Gunner assured me. "The adrenaline takes over and you'll be numbed to most of it."

He was right. Once I got over the initial shock, it felt like little more than scratching or even tickling in some areas. I rested my cheek on my hands, gazing at Gunner while Shadow worked.

"Tell me about you," I murmured to the beautiful man in front of me. "It feels like I know so little about you."

He huffed out a dark laugh through a lopsided smile. "There's not much to know, baby girl. I try to separate myself from my past as much as I can."

"Why?"

"Because my family's a bunch of rich assholes." He hesitated, rolling his lower lip between his teeth. "Except for my grandparents, who raised me. I mean, they were rich too, but not as asshole-ish as all the others."

"What happened to your parents?"

"Nothing. They were just too busy being rich assholes to take care of their kid." His tone made it clear he didn't want to talk about it, so I stopped with that line of questioning and tried another.

"How did you get to be so good with weapons?"

His crooked grin returned at that. "Military academy, if you can believe that."

I couldn't. "No way! You?" I reached out and twirled a lock of his golden hair in my fingers. "With this hair and your attitude? I'm gonna need proof."

"Reaper might have a picture somewhere," he laughed. "But yeah, I had the pressed uniform without a speck of lint on it, shiny black shoes, and an even shinier flag pole up my ass."

"What was that like?" I was still trying to reconcile the free-spirited, crafty Gunner I knew with growing up at some prestigious academy.

"In the early years, about what you would expect," he sighed. "Lots of rules, long days of classes. Cliques and petty drama. Girls trying to get away with the shortest skirts as possible. That part wasn't bad, but I hated it overall. I lived for the weekends and breaks away from that place."

"You didn't fit in?" I asked.

"Nah, it wasn't that," he smirked. "I was popular enough, just thought everyone else was stupid and fake. But on the weekends, I could take off my stuffy school uniform and trade it for leathers and a motorbike."

"Ah," I said, understanding. "After you met Reaper and Jandro."

"Yeah, bailed them out of jail with my parents' money during my sophomore year." He chuckled. "I'm certain they never noticed it missing."

"And after you were done with school?"

"More school," he grumbled with an eyeroll. "Only this time, the Collapse was looking more and more like a reality. So my parents enrolled me at the finest military college money could buy. I was expected to become a general, an adviser at the Pentagon or some shit, I dunno. They had connections and could pull strings."

"What was that place like?"

"Night and day difference from my high school," he said. "It was basically a boot camp. Drill sergeants yelling at me at four in the morning to get out of bed. Push-ups and running every day. I learned how to field strip an M4 rifle within seconds. I'm telling you, baby girl, it was so much harder than prep school, but..."

"You liked it," I completed for him.

"I fucking loved it," he admitted. "Could've done without dickwads breathing down my neck, but I loved handling firearms and learning how they worked. I got engrossed in military tactics and strategy. I just," he sucked in a deep breath. "I didn't want to follow orders for some politician, you know? Be part of a system that was driving this country into the shitter. When Reaper told me he was making a real MC, I had to make a decision."

I smiled at him. "And are you happy with the decision you made?"

He leaned forward, folding his arms on top of mine along the back of the chair, and rested his chin there with a smile.

"I used to wonder about the *what-ifs* a lot. I was offered a job in DC when I finished school. Great pay, benefits package, the whole nine. But lately?" He shook his head, his eyes locked onto mine. "I wouldn't want to be anywhere but here."

JANDRO

"You think she's done yet?"

"I swear to God, I'm gonna waterboard you if you don't shut up," Reaper grumbled.

Hades growled in agreement, taking a moment to look away from the street to narrow his black eyes at me.

I sighed and folded up the rag I was using to clean the bike parts strewn out on the patio coffee table. Reaper sat across from me, cleaning a few of the guns we kept stashed around in case of an attack.

"She's bringing Gunner with her," I said, watching carefully for his reaction.

The president barely batted an eye. "So is he hers, or not?"

"I dunno. They were all close in the pool the other day."

"I saw." Reaper stubbed out his cigarette in the ashtray. "She hasn't said much to me about him, so I'm not pushing it for now."

"Same here," I agreed. "But it's pretty telling that she wanted him during her tattoo and not us, don'tcha think?"

"Gettin' jealous, 'Dro?" Reaper glanced at me with a wry grin as he reassembled two Glocks.

"Not exactly." I rubbed my chin, trying to explain it. "Like I know they're into each other. I'm not bothered by that. But it's a special moment for her. We're her men, not to mention the leaders of the club she's getting a tattoo of, and she doesn't want us there?"

"What she said makes sense," he shrugged. "I don't like seeing her in pain, and it would stress her out. You'd be bouncing off the walls and probably fuck up the tattoo."

"You don't think there's something else to it?"

"No." His voice was stern, and he eyed me squarely. "I take her at her word. That's what trust *is*. That's how this whole thing works." He drew a circle in the air between us. "If you think she's up to something and treat her like she is, that's a quick way to send your whole relationship crashing to the ground."

I leaned back, scratching both hands over my scalp as I tried to calm whatever the hell was going on inside me. "I just wanted to *be* there. Not because I don't want her alone with him, I just wanted to support her doing this. I took it like a man when she told me to leave, but—"

"Your ego was bruised." Reaper lit up another cigarette. "You wanted her to choose you for something, and she didn't. Get ready for a lot of that, especially if she adds him in."

"I guess," I frowned.

"This shit's not easy, 'Dro," Reaper exhaled a cloud of smoke. "You can't treat it like being with one person. This isn't like if your girl gives some lame-ass excuse to not see you, and you've got reason to be suspicious. Mari is just telling all of us what she needs while going through this, and that happens to be Gunner. It's nothing against you, bro."

"I s'pose you're right." I looked at him. "That shit never gets to you? If she wants someone else and not you?"

"Sure it does," he shrugged. "But I know what it means and how to handle it, because I saw how my dads did. And you know what, dude?"

"Huh?"

He pulled the cigarette from his mouth and grinned. "It makes it so much sweeter when she wants you, and you alone. Everything you worry about just goes away when she's right here," he brought a palm to his chest, "and you remember that she really *does* need you. She needs what only you can provide."

"Damn." I reached for the smokes to light one up myself. "Thanks, Dr. Rory."

"Shut up." His face morphing from blissed out to scowling was the funniest shit I'd ever seen. I'd have to tell Mari about it.

Hades suddenly lifted his head with a soft whine. With his nose pointed down the street and ears pricked forward, he was the first to notice someone coming our way. Gunner's laugh floating down the street made my heart leap. Finally, she was done!

Reaper and I jumped up from the patio furniture at the same time, following Hades to the pool gate. Mari and Gunner were a block away, walking side-by-side toward us with Freyja a few feet away. Gun's hands were shoved in his jean pockets with Mari's arm linked around his.

The contact could have been either friendly or flirtatious, but seeing it caused something to tighten in my chest.

Reaper opened the gate to let Hades out, and Mari's arm pulled away from Gunner as the giant black dog ran toward her. He reared up and hugged around her waist with his front paws, his usual greeting to her lately, while she laughed and wrapped her arms around his neck.

"Hades, down!" Reaper bellowed, but the command was unneeded.

He dropped all four paws back to the ground and walked at Mari's side, looking up at her with all the love and adoration a dog could.

The tightness in my chest didn't let up as she entered the gate to join us.

"Hi *guapito*." Mari grinned at me first and slid her hands around my waist.

My heart skipped a beat. "*Hi bonita*." I leaned down to meet those plump red lips tilted up to me for a kiss. "How do you feel?"

"A little sore, but fine." She rested her cheek on my chest, and only then did the tightness begin to soften. "Watch out for my upper back, that's where it is."

"Can I see it?" I led her by the hands to the couches to sit down, Reaper and Hades following closely after. Reap smirked at me knowingly over the top of her head. Smug bastard. He was right—she came to *me* first. She needed *me* now.

"Shadow just did the outline." Oblivious to our silent exchange, Mari plopped down on the couch and pulled her arms out of the sleeves of her top. "I'm getting the rest of it filled in in two weeks."

She lifted her shirt, turned her back to show me, and I couldn't hold back the awe I felt at the sight of it.

"Holy...shit." Holding the sides of her waist, I leaned in to examine Shadow's work more closely. "My boy really outdid himself. Reaper, look at this fucking work of art."

"Mm..." I didn't even notice he'd been lip-locked with Mari until I looked up. She turned on the couch to face me, giving her back to Reaper, and let out a content little sigh as she leaned on my shoulder.

Mine. All fucking mine.

"You like it?"

"It looks amazing on you." I stroked a hand down the side of her cheek. "After that's done, you should get my name right here." I dragged a finger just underneath her collarbone.

"You get my name first," she shot back, laughing.

"You joke, but I just might," I warned her. Name tattoos weren't really my thing, but I could get a butterfly as a symbol of her. Shadow could make it look badass and not girly.

"So, it wasn't too bad, sugar?" Reaper leaned in and dropped a kiss to the nape of her neck.

"No." She turned to kiss him over her shoulder, but slid her legs over mine to remain solidly in my lap. "Some spots were more intense than others, but it was fine. I was good to keep going, but Shadow said we were at a good stopping point."

"How was *he?*"

I had to admit that part of my reluctance to leave was due to what happened the first time they were alone together. They ended up having sex because he mistakenly believed I sent her over for that reason. He knew better now, plus he'd seen her in her office since then. Mari was sympathetic to his trauma and his many issues with socializing, which was sweet. But a small part of me was still uneasy about them together in close proximity. I just wasn't sure what made me more nervous—his potential to misunderstand something and cause her harm, or her pushing too hard in trying to help, and triggering something dangerous in him.

Ninety-nine percent of the time, Shadow wouldn't hurt a fly. But that one percent usually meant no survivors. The man lived at two polar opposites and knew nothing of the spectrum in between.

"He was...really good." She sounded surprised herself. "I think he even cracked a joke with me."

I stared at her. "Really?"

"Yeah, he made fun of Gunner for being a pussy during his tattoo."

"Highly uncalled for." The blonde man in question draped his long arms and legs over the lounge chair across from us. He shook his head disappointedly, but his eyes were full of humor. "Totally unprofessional."

"Other than that," Mari chuckled, "he just did his thing, didn't talk much, like usual. Except for checking in with me about pain and discomfort and stuff. It was really sweet, actually."

"He got her a towel so she could comfortably rest her arms on the back of the chair," Gunner scoffed. "What a princess."

Mari threw my soiled cleaning rag at him. "You used that armrest more than me!"

"I didn't say *you* were the princess." He batted his eyes at her dramatically.

"See what happens when we leave you alone?" Reaper chuckled, returning to cleaning his guns.

"I have such great taste in men, don't I?" Mari teased him.

"You do in one, at least." I pulled her more into my lap, stretching her legs over mine to the other side of the couch. Now that she was all mine for the moment, I was going to savor her.

"Hmm, the same one who cooks me fresh eggs and plies me with good tequila," she grinned, grabbing my chin. "I definitely hit a home run here."

"You want me to help wash you later?" I ran my fingers lightly over the center of her back, just under her tattoo. "You'll need to keep the new ink clean and moisturized."

"Bath time is *my* domain," Reaper barked. "You can rub her down with lotion afterward, though."

"Shit, man. Who gave you the monopoly on bath time?"

"No one," he grinned. "I took it for myself."

"Hmm." Mari looked between us, amusement in her eyes at how we bickered over caring for her. "Maybe you can wash my back, and Reap can do my front?"

"I'm fine with that idea." My fingers dragged across her sides. "As long as we get to switch."

"Works for me," Reaper muttered with a shrug.

"Okay, for real?" The exclamation came from Gunner, who stared at us from across the coffee table. "This is how y'all work shit out?"

Reaper cocked an eyebrow at him. "How else are we supposed to work shit out besides talking about it?"

"It's just...weird to listen to. Like you're a family splitting chores."

"That's basically what we're doing," I pointed out. "Only it's no chore to make our woman more comfortable after getting needles in her skin for two hours."

"Okay, tell me this." Gunner rested his chin in his hand. "How are you okay," he directed at Reaper, "with her being all up in *his* lap?"

"I had her to myself this morning," Reaper shrugged. "'Dro gets up early to go to the shop, so we get to lay in together."

"Then she has lunch with me." I wrapped around her tighter.

Gunner kept his bewildered eyes on Mari. "And what about after you're all done for the day?"

"We split time between both houses," Mari answered. "The evenings are usually all three of us. We have dinner, talk, and wind down for the evening together. But we make sure to have alone time, too. We've established a cozy little routine."

"We sure have." I dragged my lips from Mari's ear to her temple, and felt her completely melt in my arms as a result. The insecurity in my gut melted away, as if it were never there.

Reaper was right, as usual. Sharing a woman was tricky to navigate, but she held the wheel and steered us true. One woman could only do so much to keep multiple men happy. I had to trust her, to believe she was genuine in her feelings, and had all of our best interests at heart.

"But what about..." Gunner's question trailed off, but he raised his eyebrows pointedly.

"Gun, if you never heard of a threesome, I regret ever letting you into my fucking club," Reaper growled.

"Of course I know about threesomes!" Gunner snapped. "But...all the time?"

"No, not all the time," Mari answered. "If I want to be alone with one of them, I'll say so. I try my best to keep it equal, but honestly?" A rosy blush filled her cheeks. "I love it best when all of us are together."

"You're getting spoiled." Reaper leaned over and kissed the back of her shoulder.

"And that doesn't bother you either?" Gunner asked him. "Seeing your best friend and your woman in bed together?"

"Not a damn bit." Reaper set his gun and cleaning supplies down, resting his forearms on his knees. "Bottom line, I want my woman happy, whether it's from me or another man. This way, I know it's from someone I trust. Someone who'll love and protect her if anything happens to me."

"Don't talk like that," Mari scolded, reaching over to smack his arm.

"I'm just saying it's another benefit to what we have, sugar. Especially if we take on General Tash in the near future. I'll be at ease knowing you'll be looked after, no matter the outcome."

I decided to steer the conversation back to a less ominous topic. "The sex thing isn't as weird as your mind makes it out to be, Gun. Yeah, I love this woman. Yeah, I watch my best friend nail her until she's creaming all over his cock. One does not invalidate the other."

"They try to make it all about me," Mari groaned like she was complaining, although nobody missed the smug grin on her lips. "But I make sure nobody gets neglected either."

I nuzzled her neck and kissed her there. "You're too good to us."

"That's why we put up with you," Reaper added, playfully swatting her hip.

"I just..." Gunner ran both hands through his hair, tilting his head up to the sky with a long breath. He stayed like that for a while before resuming his gaze on the woman at the center of all of us.

"I want to be with you, Mari," he said in a rush of breath. "I tried to fight it, but that only made me want you more. I love that you trust me when you're scared and I want to be someone that's there for you. I just," he paused, his eyes filled up with only her, "I just don't know if I can handle *this.*"

A long, heavy silence fell over us. Reaper and I exchanged a glance and a mutual shrug. We answered all his questions, said all there was to say. If none of that was enough, maybe Gunner wasn't cut out for this. That was fine, but he couldn't keep being Mari's emotional support person if that was the case. It would be too close, too intimate.

Our woman stared at him with a gaze that reflected his. They only saw each other in that moment, and I wondered what was going through her head.

"I guess there's one way left to find that out, Gunner." She stood, grabbed my hand and then Reaper's. "Let's go home."

"Oh...kay?" I stared at her, my ass still glued to the couch. "What's on your mind, *bonita*?"

"We're going to bed." She turned her head to look at Reaper, then the man sitting across from us. "And Gunner's going to watch."

MARIPOSA

All three of them snapped their heads in my direction, shocked at what I just said. But my eyes were only on the blonde man sitting across from me.

"Why?" Gunner's tone was quiet, curious. He looked calmer than the two men standing on either side of me, squeezing each of my palms in a death grip.

"Because I told you two weeks ago," I replied. "We could take this slowly. You could ask us whatever questions you had on your mind, and we've answered them honestly. But at some point, you have to make a decision."

"I know, Mari. But what's that got to do with watching you all have sex?"

"To see if you can *handle it*, as you put it. Because this is a regular part of our relationship. And until you're there to experience it for yourself, you'll have no idea how you'll react to it."

Jandro chuckled darkly at my side, leaning in to whisper, "Smart girl."

Reaper's face remained stony on my other side, his signature resting scowl revealing nothing about what his thoughts were.

"Um, okay." Gunner shifted uncomfortably in his seat. "You're right, I guess."

"After tonight," I swallowed thickly, trying to conceal my own nerves, "there's no more dancing around this, Gunner. You're either with me or not. I want to be with you too, but I—"

Each of my men squeezed my hands reassuringly as my throat tightened up. It didn't matter that Gunner was the third man I had feelings for. I was giving him an ultimatum, and it was just as difficult as if he was the only one I wanted. If I said my whole piece, I'd have to follow through, no matter the outcome. My heart had already cracked from him pushing me away before, and I had to risk that pain again if he said no. But having Reaper and Jandro's support made a world of difference in strengthening my spine.

"I can't keep waiting and hoping for you to say that you want this. *All* of this." I lifted my hands to show how Reaper and Jandro held me, clasped between them. "So after tonight, you're either telling me yes, or," I pulled in a shaky breath, "or any other answer is a no."

Gunner watched me speak the whole time with rapt attention. His jaw clenched just before he rose to his feet.

"Okay," he breathed. "I'm in."

"Hold up." Speaking for the first time, Reaper raised his index finger. "I have one rule."

Gunner's eyes shifted to him. We all waited with bated breath.

"You don't touch her." Reaper's voice had the sharp edge of a growl that heated my core. "You do nothing but watch. I don't care if you jerk off, but no one except *her* men touches her in the bedroom. Am I clear?"

"Crystal," Gunner nodded.

With that, Reaper led the way through the pool gate toward his house. He tugged me by the hand and Jandro followed after me, with Gunner bringing up the rear. Once out in the street, Reaper released my hand to wrap an arm around my shoulders. He pulled me in close and murmured close to my ear, "You sure about this, sugar?"

"Not really," I admitted. "I just didn't know what else to do."

"It's probably the only option left to get a straight answer out of him," he said. "But it could go badly. If he's not cut out for this, it could fuck with his head."

"Well, he's agreed to it. That must mean something, right? That his gut instinct wasn't to shoot it down."

"Maybe. We're about to find out." His hand slid down my back, gliding gently over my tattoo and following my curves until he grabbed a handful of my ass. "You ever been watched before?"

"No." I pinched his side to make him let go of my ass, wondering if Gunner saw. "Have you?"

"Nope." He shot me a lopsided, cocky smirk. "I think it's a first for everyone involved."

The moment all four of us walked into Reaper's house, Jandro insisted we all take a shot of whiskey before heading up to the bedroom.

"I'll have two," Gunner grinned, following him into the kitchen.

"Make yourselves at home, why dontcha?" Reaper grumbled, but he pulled my body flush to his, nuzzling my neck before kissing under my jaw.

"Can I get wine instead?" I scratched over his scalp, making him hum against my neck. The vibrations of his voice traveled all the way to my toes.

"Nope. Won't work quick enough." Jandro emerged from the kitchen, holding shot glasses for me and Reaper.

"This better be the cheap stuff." Reaper tossed his shot back and handed the glass back to Jandro. "And make sure Gunner's not draining my whole handle."

"I heard that!"

"Waiting on you, *Mariposita*." Jandro gave me a naughty look. "Don't make me pour it in your mouth."

With a sigh, I knocked the whiskey back while trying in vain not to taste it. "Ugh, blech."

The guys laughed at the faces I made as I thrust the glass back at Jandro. "You love *añejo,* but not this?"

"Ugh, yes. Can I please wash this taste out with some wine?"

"Here you go, baby girl." Gunner was already heading over with a half-full glass for me with a smile that made my heart skip a beat.

"Thank you, Gun." I smiled back appreciatively and covered his hand with mine as I accepted the glass.

What? I silently asked Jandro and Reaper's glares. *The no-touching rule is just for the bedroom.*

"Hurry it up, sugar." Reaper playfully tilted up the bottom of my glass.

"What're you in such a hurry for?"

"You really need to ask that question?" His green eyes were devilish as his hand snaked around to grab my ass again.

"You can have me whenever you want." I teased, playing with the henley buttons on his shirt. Okay, that whiskey shot might have been gross, but it definitely got me relaxed and loosened up fast.

"And I wanted you ten minutes ago," he growled.

I finished my wine while the three of them looked at me like a pack of hungry dogs. Two of the hungry stares, I was used to. And the third one spurred a new thrill of excitement up my spine. I only hoped he found enjoyment, not despair, at what we were about to do.

Reaper pulled me into a ravenous kiss the moment I set my empty glass down. Whiskey tasted so much better when it was on his tongue. He was already hard, his cock thick and rigid against my hip. What kind of dirty fantasies had he been thinking about while we were all trying to calm our nerves?

The world beyond Reaper's skilled lips and tongue melted away, until I felt the firm pull of Jandro's fist in my hair. With gentle guidance on the base of my skull, Jandro turned my face to his. His pillowy lips devoured mine, soothing the roughness of Reaper's kisses a moment earlier.

Not even a second later, the heat of Reaper's mouth latched onto the exposed side of my neck. I whimpered against Jandro's lips as his best friend nibbled and sucked on my tender flesh, marking me as his.

Both men started pressing in on me, caging me between two hard bodies and rapidly accelerating heartbeats.

"Fuck."

Neither of my men said that. Their mouths were occupied.

I cracked open my eyes, sliding my lips across Jandro's cheek to look over his shoulder. My gaze locked onto Gunner's stare as I teased the VP's earlobe with my teeth. Blue eyes watched my every move, not missing a single detail. Gunner's lips parted, and he wet them with his tongue as he watched.

"Bedroom," Reaper growled at the nape of my neck, his hand returning to mine to tug me up the stairs.

"Thought you'd never say that," Jandro purred, sneaking a fast kiss before Reaper pulled me away.

For a moment they seemed to forget all about Gunner, who trailed after us a few feet away up the staircase. But as the three of us stumbled, kissed, and groped our way into the bedroom, Jandro turned and told him, "Close the door behind you. No animals allowed."

Reaper seized that opportunity to wrench me out of Jandro's grip with a devilish grin. He picked me up from the back of my thighs, allowing me to wrap them around his waist as he carried me to bed.

"Careful with her back," Jandro scolded as Reaper dropped us both down to the mattress.

"I know, asshole." Reaper's voice was muffled by my skin. He had already lifted my shirt up and was dragging his rough, delicious kisses across my belly.

My fingers dug through his dark, rich hair before sliding down his neck and over his wide, muscle-bound shoulders. I tugged up on his shirt until he had to pull his lips away to bring it over his head.

Jandro, already shirtless, sat next to us and gave Reaper a playful shove. "Don't be greedy. Me first this time."

Reaper grumbled a complaint, but pressed a kiss on my navel as he moved away to let Jandro take his place.

"Hi, gorgeous," Jandro grinned, placing a smoldering kiss on my hip as his fingers dug into the waistband of my pants.

"Hi, handsome," I returned, scratching over his much-shorter hair.

My eyes lifted to find Reaper and Gunner in the room, while Jandro dragged my pants and underwear down my legs, chasing every inch of exposed skin with a kiss.

Gunner sat in the armchair in the corner of the room, his foot propped up on the opposite knee. With his elbow on the armrest, his fingers rested on the side of his face as he watched us, eyes rapt with attention.

Reaper stood a few feet away from the bed, bottom lip sucked between his teeth as he unbuckled his belt and yanked down his zipper.

A pulse of heat flooded my core just as Jandro removed my pants and underwear. Reaper's hand slid down the firm planes of his stomach and disappeared into his boxers as Jandro kissed his way back up my body, holding my legs apart.

Reaper's arm and chest flexed as he stroked himself beneath the fabric, smirking at me as he hid himself from view. Jandro's kisses reached the inside of my thighs, lighting me up with shivers as I watched Reaper tease me.

"Look at you, *bonita*. So fucking soaked already." Jandro cupped between my legs, soothing the needy ache building inside me with the pressure of his palm. He glanced over his shoulder with an amused look. "Is Rory putting on a little show for you over there?"

"Shut up. Hearing you talk makes me soft." But Reaper's stance was relaxed, his smirk still present and cocky as he continued to stroke himself. "You want me, sugar?"

"Yes please, president," I whined, loving the soft groan from his throat when I addressed him by his title.

"Where?" he demanded in a husky growl.

"Down my throat. Now please."

His smirk widened into a delighted grin. He liked to ask me where, to give me the illusion of control. But we both knew he held me like putty in his hands. Whether he held me gently or with an iron grip, I knew he would never let me fall.

He shoved his jeans and boxers down his thighs, letting his cock bounce free, just as Jandro pulled his hand away from my pussy and replaced it with his mouth.

My hips lifted off the bed with a moan at the sudden onslaught of sensation. Jandro sucked my lips into his mouth, tongue gliding up and down my slit to drink from me. He clamped one hand on my waist, the other hurriedly making off with his pants.

Reaper, now gloriously nude, kneeled onto the mattress and made his way toward my head. Across the room, Gunner didn't appear fazed by either of my guys getting naked. His eyes only roamed over me as Reaper pulled both my shirt and halter top underneath over my head.

"Her back," Jandro murmured through a kiss on my clit.

"Shut the fuck up, and put your mouth to good use. I would've made her come twice by now."

"I'm fine," I laughed lightly, scratching down the back of Jandro's neck. "My back is still pretty numb. And what you're doing feels wonderful."

"Good." Jandro lifted his head to look at me as he slid one finger inside my slick channel. "I like to warm my girl up nice and slow."

"Mmm..." I squirmed when he slid a second finger in, his tongue returning to dance lazy circles around my clit.

Meanwhile, Reaper grabbed a pillow and positioned himself to kneel slightly next to and behind my head. He gently lifted my shoulders up and slid the pillow between the back of my head and his thigh.

"So considerate," I cooed, gazing up at the powerfully-built man towering over me.

"Mm-hm. Suck me, sugar."

I held in a laugh, wrapping my palm around the thick base to stroke his rigid length to the tip.

"So bossy," I said in a poutier tone, darting my tongue out to flick the sensitive underside of his crown.

"Sugar..." He growled it out like a warning, but I heard the edge of desperation in his voice. One of the rare moments the balance of control tipped in my favor before I gave it all back to him.

I drew his swollen head into my mouth, swirling my tongue around it as I continued pumping his length with my hand. His sexy moans amplified the effects of Jandro's mouth and fingers working me down below.

"Damn, our girl loves sucking cock. She's squeezing like crazy around my fingers."

"Fuck yeah she does," Reaper agreed, stroking down my neck and over my sternum to palm my breasts.

I couldn't see him, but I still felt Gunner's eyes on me, almost as heavy as a physical touch. What was he thinking? I hoped my body didn't look weird in this position and completely turn him off. My guys showered me with attention and bantered like no one else was in the room. They didn't seem to feel the prickle of self-consciousness from having an observer.

"Hurry up and make her come. I need to fuck her." Reaper pinched my nipples, eliciting a muffled squeal from me as Jandro's tongue lashed my clit at the same time.

"She's a squirmy little thing today," Jandro laughed.

"You're too fucking chatty today."

"Yeah?" Jandro's tone was playful. "Help me out."

Reaper's weight shifted under my head and I felt the pillow get removed as my head returned to the bed.

"Keep my dick between those pretty lips, sugar. I'm showing Jandro how it's done."

With his knees on either side of my head, he started leaning down over my body toward my legs. In doing so, his cock slid further and further down my throat. The next thing I felt were his rough hands on my inner thighs. He splayed them open, leaving me completely exposed, as he pinned my legs down to the mattress.

"There. Now eat her out like she's your last meal."

Jandro's mouth descended on me with ravenous hunger and I had nowhere to run. Each swipe of his tongue felt like a jolt of lightning, his fingers inside me beckoning me closer and closer to the final strike.

As if that wasn't enough, Reaper began thrusting into my mouth.

I could hardly breathe, both from having my mouth stuffed *and* chasing an orgasm at lightning speed. I needed to move, for one of them to ease up because everything was so, *so* fucking intense. But the intensity just built and built and built, until it was painful. Searing, blinding, and then an explosive release.

Reaper withdrew from my mouth and I gulped in a gasping breath of air. Convulsions and my pounding pulse wracked my body. I thought

I heard him say, "You're okay, sugar," but he sounded so far away. But I felt him stroke my hair and neck so I knew he was near.

"Holy shit."

I turned my head as the room started coming into focus. The proclamation came from Gunner, leaning forward in his seat.

"Your face was turning so red, baby girl. I thought you were gonna pass out."

"We don't need your commentary." Reaper hauled me up and hugged me to his chest. "We'd never do anything to hurt her. She just loves tag-teaming stuff sometimes."

Gunner's eyes fell to me, as if he was waiting for confirmation of Reaper's statement.

Still panting, I leaned my head back on Reaper's shoulder, smiling as I kissed his neck. "That was probably the craziest orgasm I ever had."

"You're welcome." Jandro was now sitting up against the headboard, with one arm behind his head, the other gliding up and down his cock.

My mouth watered as I gently untangled myself from Reaper and crawled across the bed to him. "You look delicious enough to eat."

He grinned appreciatively. "*You* certainly were."

I angled my body next to him, some of my awareness back on Gunner's voyeurism and giving him something pleasing to look at. From the corner of my eye, I saw Gunner's hand move. I resisted the urge to look over, leaning over to kiss Jandro instead.

"So beautiful when you come." Jandro cupped my face and pulled me in closer, fingers skimming from my shoulder down my side.

I slid a hand over his thigh, teasing him like he did with me. His kisses grew hungrier, frenzied, as I massaged his balls, and all around the base of his dick, without touching him directly. I heard Reaper's dry chuckle behind me, the weight of his hand stroking my back just under my tattoo. He knew I was getting Jandro back for that slow, teasing buildup.

The man in question tried closing my hand around his cock and groaned when I smacked him away. Jandro loved to tease, but didn't bask in control like Reaper. He'd sit back and wait for me if I made him.

Making a slow trail of kisses down his chest, I did just that. And I loved every hitched breath from his lungs on the way down. He squirmed like I did when I reached the head of his cock resting on his belly, and kissed it too. I placed soft kisses all along the hard length of his shaft, enjoying the twitches and grunts from him.

"You're so evil," he moaned, his body wound up tight like a spring.

I giggled, finally ready to give him some relief, and flipped my hair out of my face. Jandro held my hair back for me, and with my unobstructed vision I saw Gunner stroking his palm down the front of his pants.

Our eyes stayed locked on each other as I slid my lips over Jandro's silky crown. Gunner bit back a moan, rubbing harder at the bulge tenting his pants.

Take it out, I begged him with my eyes. *I want to see you.*

He didn't though, and the need to see my beautiful, golden man naked became a deep, greedy ache.

Because he *was* mine. He became mine that day he got captured with me, just so I wouldn't be alone.

Hell, he was mine since that first moment at the service center in Old Phoenix.

Reaper slid into me then with one long, powerful thrust. My eyes slitted halfway closed from the sudden fullness, but I still watched Gunner through my lashes. Reaper's cock driving into me eased the ache deep in my body, but I still wanted more.

Tension knitted Gunner's brow, his blue eyes sharp with desire. His cheeks flushed pink, ragged breaths left his chest. I wanted to see ecstasy on his face. I wanted to watch his pleasure ascend and release, and to be the cause of it. I wanted him to know how much he was loved.

"Fuck," Reaper rumbled behind me, each thrust a crash of flesh and power. "So fucking good."

My moans echoed over Jandro's dick, my mouth wet and slurpy and sliding all over him.

"I'm not gonna last if you keep screaming on my cock like that," he choked out.

That only made Reaper laugh and fuck me harder.

With a few strategic swipes of my clit, I was done for. The orgasm crashed over me like a wave, nearly making my knees give out. Just as my pleasure crested, Jandro's salty warmth spilled into my mouth.

I lapped him up, licking and sucking him clean, as he shivered from the aftershocks.

"You're my fucking dream woman," he murmured woozily, hauling me up for a kiss. "I love you."

"*Te amo,*" I smiled, panting against his plush lips.

He excused himself to the shower, leaving me alone with Reaper and Gunner. Only then did Reaper take notice of our voyeur.

He turned me to face the man in the chair, and began slow, rocking thrusts into me from behind.

"Do you like Gunner in here, sugar?" His fingers curled into the hair at my scalp and pulled.

"Yes," I gasped, my body already quaking under his dominance.

"What do you want him to do?" Reaper's voice was calm, steady, just like his thrusts, rocking himself into my body. But there was no denying the simmering power just beneath the surface.

"I want to see him," I moaned, heat tightening in my belly at the thought. "I want to watch him come."

Gunner's mouth dropped open and the sexiest sound escaped his lips. I needed to hear that sound again. In my ear, against the most sensitive parts of my skin.

"Well?" Reaper mused. "You going to give our girl what she wants?"

Gunner stilled. He didn't move a muscle. Fear began creeping into my mind, killing my buzz. After staying through everything that just happened, was he still going to pull away?

He stood from the chair and my breath caught in my lungs.

Then a rush of air returned, my heart pounding, as he shrugged off his cut and peeled off his shirt. He licked his lips, hands going to the button on his jeans as he took long strides toward me.

Reaper's thrusts intensified, bringing soft whimpers to my lips as Gunner stopped at the edge of the bed and pulled his length from his pants.

Unsurprisingly, his cock was just as beautiful as the rest of him. Long, thick, and veiny. My tongue lolled out, aching for a taste, despite Reaper's no-touching rule.

Gunner sucked in a hissing breath as he squeezed his dick through his fist, eyes rapt with attention as Reaper fucked me. He looked so sexy, a golden god pleasing himself at the sight of me, a mere mortal.

Heat coiled between my legs, my limbs shaky with fatigue. Another orgasm was only a few thrusts away and then I'd be down for the count.

"Jandro was right," Gunner rasped, his whole body rigid.

"About what?" My head swam. I could barely get the words out, I was going to explode.

"You're so beautiful when you come."

Reaper's cock flexed hard within me, then the last few crashes of his body on mine sent me hurtling over the edge. He spilled inside me moments later, muttering curses and dirty nothings as his forehead touched my back.

My eyes found Gunner again just as his hand became a fast-moving blur, his moans so hot and unrestrained. The first spurt of come landed on his chest, the next on his stomach. He stroked and squeezed again and again, wringing himself out with hot grunts and breaths, until his pleasure slowly ebbed away. His eyelids fell to half-mast, blue eyes still fixated on me as his abs flexed with effort of his breathing.

"I'd get you a towel," Reaper panted, "if Jandro wasn't in the shower."

"Didn't really think this through," Gunner laughed breathlessly, holding his jizz-covered hand away from his body.

"I'll get you one," I muttered, rolling off the bed.

"If you can still walk, I clearly didn't fuck you hard enough," Reaper snorted.

I wobbled a little, but managed to get my feet underneath me. Using the wall for support, I just made it past the bedroom door when a rapid pounding came from the other side.

"Who is it?" I called.

"Me!" Noelle screamed from the other side. "Your orgy better be done, 'cause I need you!"

"What's wrong?"

"It's Tessa," she answered. "Her water broke and she's going into labor!"

MARIPOSA

I threw clothes on in a frenzy, explained to the guys what was happening in some rushed, nonsensical words, and ran out the door.

"I'll meet you there, I need to grab supplies from my office," I told Noelle, my breath whooshing out of me as I gripped the banister. All the sex still had me wobbly.

"Okay! What do I do while we wait?"

"Have Big G start a pot of boiling water. Keep track of the time between her contractions. Tell her to breathe and that I'll be right there."

We reached the street and split off into opposite directions. I did a double-take as I noticed Freyja's fuzzy black form running after her. I had no time to dwell on it, though, and sprinted to the medic's office.

After getting what I needed and pushing through Tessa's front door, chaos waited for me on the other side.

Tessa was up and walking around, pacing back and forth as she rubbed her belly and sucked in deep breaths. Noelle was further back, in the boys' playroom next to the kitchen. She had a hand on each boy's shoulder as they sat on the floor, listening to her intently. I heard,

"Mommy's going to be okay..." but the anxiety in her own voice betrayed her.

A pot of water boiled on the stove, beginning to spill over the sides in sharp hisses.

Big G hovered over his wife, following her pacing and pleading with her to sit still, lay down, anything. When he grabbed her arm and she flinched, I stepped in.

"Okay, that's enough." I used my best medic's voice and set my bag down on the couch. "Big G, I'm gonna need you to take the boys upstairs to play. Maybe even go to someone else's house."

"Fuck that, I ain't leaving!" He turned on me, stopping right in front of my shoes and leaning down into my face. "You might be a medic, but you ain't my family. I'm not missing the birth of my son."

"You are doing nothing but stressing out your wife," I shot back. "For fuck's sake, you've done this twice already. Don't you know walking around is normal?"

His teeth gritted hard with a non-answer. Tessa pitched in for him.

"He wasn't here for the first two," she huffed. "He was off on rides, begging Reaper not to leave him out of all the pussy they were going to drown in."

"Well, I'm fuckin' here now and I'm not leaving! And for real, shouldn't you be lying in bed or something?"

Tessa slapped a hand to her forehead, then clutched at her side with a pained cry. Big G and I ran to her at the same time.

"Sit down for a minute, Tess. Try to get comfortable. When was your last contraction?"

"Um—"

"Baby, let me carry you upstairs. You really should be lying down, right?"

"Oh my god, just go away!" she screamed at him. "Mari's right, you're just stressing me the fuck out." She turned to me, her face in a grimace of pain. "About ten minutes ago, I think."

"No way! You're really gonna listen to this bitch?"

"Watch it," I growled under my breath. "You want the president, *and* the VP, knowing you're disrespecting me?"

His scowl was venomous. In truth, I felt bad for him. Despite coming up short in the father and husband categories, he didn't outright deserve to miss the birth of this child. It was unfortunate that he *thought* he knew best, and kept ruining it for himself as a result.

"Take the boys upstairs and I'll bring the baby to you when she's here," I relented.

She? Why did I say that? Tongue must've slipped.

He finally conceded, with a scathing look, and backed away. "Boys!" he hollered at his sons. "Grab some toys, let's go upstairs and give Mom some space."

"Is Mommy hurt?" the youngest asked with wide eyes and a wobbly lip. "Why's the baby hurting her?"

"She'll be fine." Noelle hugged him, turning him to look away from where Tessa groaned and huffed from the couch. "Nurse Mari is taking good care of her. We gotta let her do her job, okay?"

He nodded and accepted being swept up into his father's arms. When the boys finally left the room, Tessa released a deep sigh.

"Thank you," she whispered. "Maybe I'll get to deliver this baby in peace."

Her relief was short-lived as another contraction ripped through her. My hand flew to my own stomach. I swore I felt the shooting pain in my own body, along with something else that seemed wrong.

"She's still breech, isn't she?" I pressed my fingers around Tessa's pelvis. "Your contractions are still far enough apart that we can try to turn her before she starts moving."

"Why do you keep saying *she*?" Noelle asked. "Know something we don't?"

"I don't know, sorry. Can you get that boiling water and bring it here with some clean towels?"

When Noelle scurried off to the kitchen, Tessa grabbed my hand and squeezed. "I thought I still had a few more weeks. Is something wrong for the baby to be coming early?" She stared at me worriedly.

"My estimation could have been off," I told her. "Plus, we were going off your previous experience and the expectation of a boy. If it is a girl, she's probably a bit smaller, which is why you'd be farther along than I thought."

Noelle returned with the water and towels. I grabbed a washcloth to dab at the sweat on Tessa's forehead.

"And even if the baby is early, she—it's active and healthy. We might take some extra precautions, but we're close to full-term, regardless. I got this, mama. I promise you."

"And the breech position?" she huffed. "What if we can't turn her?"

"Then I'm going to have to pull her out as fast as possible, so she'll be able to breathe. I may have to make an incision, but I *will* get her out, Tessa. I promise you."

She nodded sharply, eyes hard and determined. "Cut me wide open if you have to. Just make sure the baby's okay."

"Rowwr?"

All three of us looked around for the source of the tiny sound. Freyja jumped onto the couch, seemingly out of nowhere, and rubbed her head against Tessa's belly with a loud purr.

"Hey there, little friend," Tessa cooed, scratching between the two triangular ears. "Thanks for helping me out last time. Are you here to do it again?"

Freyja answered with a meow, running the full length of her body along Tessa's side.

I immediately noticed the ease and relaxation settling into Tessa's body. "How do you feel?"

"Good," she breathed. "Still, you know, feeling like a watermelon is splitting me in half from the inside, but the pain isn't too bad now." She glanced down at Freyja. "You're pretty damn magical, kitty."

"Okay, good." I shot her a reassuring smile. "I'm gonna try to turn the baby around now, okay?"

She nodded and I reached for Freyja to move her out of the way. The kitten yowled and twisted in my grip, slicing me with tiny razor-like claws.

"Ow, what the hell!"

I dropped the cat and she immediately returned to Tessa's side, rubbing hard against her hip and belly with a rumbling purr that seemed to fill the room.

This way, child. Follow me.

The voice reverberated in my head and all around me. I heard it clearly, as if a fourth person was sitting right there with us. It was a feminine voice, deep and rich. Comforting and motherly, authoritative and full of power.

"Oh, she's on the move," Tessa winced, clutching her side and resuming her labored breathing. She gave no indication that she heard the voice. "I think... I think she's turning!"

I swept my hands along her belly again while Noelle wiped her brow and muttered encouraging words. Freyja slid her body along Tessa's left side again, which I could now see was a repetitive, rhythmic motion. Those eyes were losing their wide, kitten innocence and turning the bright, sharp color of green with gold flecks. Endless wisdom stared back at me.

I grabbed my stethoscope to be sure, even though I knew I didn't need to be. Freyja had turned the baby right in the nick of time.

"She's in the right position," I announced, relief filling my lungs as I pulled the ear tips out. "We just gotta let mother nature do her thing."

"Oh, thank fuck," Tessa sighed. "Good thing this ain't my first rodeo, but holy shit am I gonna need a drink."

"I'll get one started for you," Noelle squeezed her shoulder before getting up. Her green gaze caught mine just as she turned away, and that look made my heart stop. She didn't look anywhere as relieved as Tessa or me. What was that about?

Her smile returned however, as she came back to the living room with a round of tequila shots for us once the baby arrived. As we worked with Tessa through her labor, I forgot all about that look.

Roughly four hours later, Noelle supported Tessa in a squatting position as her daughter arrived, headfirst, into the world. It was a beautiful delivery, one that nearly brought tears to my eyes.

Thanks to experience and sheer female bravery, Tessa barely pushed at all and allowed her body and gravity to do the work. All I did was wait with a clean, warm towel to catch her daughter. I cleared her airways when her head popped out, and seconds later, I held a tiny, newborn human in my hands.

I did nothing but stare at her for a moment. It felt like a lifetime ago that this was all I wanted to do. To humbly assist in an event so beautiful and divine—the first meeting of mother and child.

After the Collapse happened, and then had my license to practice ripped away at the final moment, I never thought I'd have the chance to do this.

But the Steel Demons gave it back to me. Reaper gave it back to me.

I cleaned off the baby and wrapped her in a dry towel, before giving her to Tessa.

"Do you want Big G to cut the cord?" I asked when the baby settled in at her breast. "It's tradition for the father to cut it, but it's up to you."

"Noelle can do it," Tessa whispered without a second thought, then snorted. "She's practically my sister-wife anyway."

I handed Noelle a clean scalpel and she did the honors with a big grin on her face. "Time for shots!"

Noelle held Tessa's shot since her arms were full of baby. We clinked glasses, then she poured the alcohol down the new mother's throat.

"Ugh, that burns so good," Tessa coughed softly. "I'm never getting knocked up again."

"If you want," I broached cautiously. "I can stick a birth control implant in your arm right now. Won't take but a minute."

"Do it," Tessa whispered, her eyelids lowering to half-mast. "I might pass the hell out first, but do it anyway."

When the baby finished eating, Noelle took her tenderly from Tessa's arms to meet the rest of her family upstairs.

"You know what you're gonna name her?" I extended Tessa's arm and marked the spot to insert the birth control implant on her bicep.

"I'll have to think about it," she laughed softly. "I was so convinced she was going to be another boy."

Her brow knitted when the implant stuck under her skin, but she otherwise didn't react. "You're good for three years," I told her.

"It's not safe out there for girls," she mumbled as if she hadn't heard me.

"Hey," I squeezed her shoulder. "But she *is* safe, because she's in here. And if she ever goes out there, she's got two big brothers and an army of men to protect her. No one will even get away with looking at her funny."

Tessa nodded, her eyes droopy and tired. Freyja purred loudly and kneaded at the blanket covering the exhausted mother's legs. I reached over to give those fluffy ears a scratch and got my hand headbutted in return.

"I think our work here is done, Freyja." I kissed Tessa's forehead and adjusted her pillows and blankets. "Congratulations, honey. I'll come check on you tomorrow."

With the little black cat at my feet, I walked back to Reaper's house in a daze. I barely remembered the walk at all.

"That you, sugar?" Reaper called from his study when I entered the house. "We're in here."

I paused at the open doorway, my pulse thrumming at seeing Gunner still here. He grinned at me, sitting in one of Reaper's leather armchairs with a cigar and a glass of whiskey. The room was hazy with smoke.

"How'd it go?" Jandro approached me, examining my soiled scrubs. "Everything okay with Tessa? The baby?"

My resolve shattered and I burst into tears. Three men rushed me at once, but it was Reaper who pulled me into his chest, arms creating a fortress of security around me as he soothed and shushed me.

"What is it, babe?" he murmured over my chest-wracking sobs. "What happened?"

"Nothing," I blubbered.

His palms pressed to the sides of my face, making me look at him while someone else rubbed my back.

"What do you mean, sugar? Why are you upset?"

"I'm n-n-not." I hiccuped, and a hysterical laugh bubbled out between my sobs. "I delivered a baby!"

He stared at me like I lost my mind.

"She's perfect, beautiful, healthy," I gasped. "Ten fingers, ten toes, all there. Such a strong cry, and she latched right on to eat. Freyja even turned her from a breech position."

I was rambling, crying, and laughing like a madwoman, but I didn't care. There was no putting a lid on this pure, unbridled joy coursing through me. I did it, I delivered a perfect, healthy baby!

"So you're okay?" Reaper asked me skeptically. "You're just...really happy?"

"Yes!" I cackled, wiping at my eyes. "It's been my dream since I went to school. I never thought I'd be able to do it, but now..." I circled my arms around his neck, sinking deep into those green eyes. "I did because of you."

He smirked then cupped my chin and kissed me deeply. "I can't take credit for making *this* dream come true. But I'm glad everything went well."

Jandro's plush lips pressed to the nape of my neck, his arms enveloping my waist. "Proud of you, *mi Mariposita.*"

My heart swelled to the point of tears gathering in my eyes again. How did I go from hanging by a thread to a life full of purpose and love?

Someone came up to the side of me and kissed my temple. Gunner looked down at me with his dazzling smile and sky-blue eyes.

"Congrats on a successful delivery, baby girl. And if it wasn't obvious," he pressed his lips to my ear, "I'm all in. I'm yours and you're mine."

MARIPOSA

"I need to talk to you."

Noelle's look was stern, similar to the one she gave me while Tessa was in labor. I'd forgotten about it until now, the morning after.

"What's up?"

Noelle jerked her head to her bedroom, indicating I should follow. Her lips pressed into a tense line at the sight of Freyja right on my ankles, but she didn't comment.

Larkan was just putting on a shirt, smelling shower-fresh as we entered her room. The mess of sheets and pillows all over her bed indicated either restless sleep, or a highly enjoyable night.

"Hey, Mari," Larkan greeted me with a friendly smile as he pulled the shirt down over his torso. I caught a flash of a hickey low on his abs before he covered up.

"Hey, Lark," I returned, trying to keep my smile hidden. *A fun night indeed, then.*

He grabbed Noelle possessively, pulled her close, and pressed a deep kiss to her mouth. They murmured low, parting words to each other, then he released her with a swat to the ass, flashing me another smile as he passed me on the way out.

"I take it that's going well," I mused after his footsteps hit the bottom of the stairs.

"Yeah." Noelle's face was flushed, her green eyes shining. "He's great. Perfect, even. It's all coming true."

"What is?"

Her smile fell again. She wrung her hands as she watched Freyja jump on the bed and began kneading her paws into the mattress.

"Has Reaper told you anything about our brother?"

"A little. He told me about how he died. When he took me to see the place you all grew up, he told me he came back and found you while everyone else was gone because of...some feeling Daren had."

"Daren was different." Noelle chewed her lip, still watching my cat make herself comfortable on her bed. "He knew things before they happened. But it wasn't like a good thing. He got headaches, had seizures. Our parents worried about him a lot."

"Noelle, do you want to sit down?" I wasn't sure what she wanted to tell me, but I got the sense it was heavy and important.

She lowered herself onto the edge of her bed, a few feet away from Freyja, and hugged a pillow to her chest.

"This is going to sound completely fucking nuts, but..." she took a deep breath, "Daren still talks to me. In my dreams."

A beat of silence passed between us.

"You heard the voice yesterday, while Tessa was in labor," I said. "Didn't you?"

She nodded, relief etched in her features. "It was your cat that spoke, or rather, the god that inhabits her." She swallowed. "I've heard Hades and Horus too."

My heart pounded. Finally, someone who understood how downright freaky all of this was. Reaper and Gunner played it off like, *no big deal, weird shit happens sometimes.* And to some extent, I could get behind that too. But Noelle's confession added a different angle I never thought of before.

"You think this has to do with Daren?" I whispered.

She nodded, reaching for my hand. Her fingers shook in mine. "He talks to me from...wherever he is, because Reaper won't listen to him. He shuts it down every time Daren tries to reach out. Maybe because it's still painful for him, the guilt over how he died. So Daren talks to me, because I let him in."

"What does he tell you?"

A dreamy smile crossed her lips. "That he misses us, but he's happy. He's not in pain anymore, he's let go. He's free of the pain his human body gave him. He's...outside of the boundaries of time now, so he can see the future much more clearly than before."

"Noelle?" I gave a gentle squeeze of her hand, trying to bring her focus back. "What's that got to do with the animals, er, gods?"

"He hasn't said this straight out, but I think when he was alive...fuck, this is nuts. I think they were all *inside* him."

"Inside him?" I repeated.

"Like how they're inside the cat," she nodded at Freyja. "The dog, the falcon. Using them as vessels, somewhat. Like, one and the same, but also separate."

I gaped at her. "All of them? Like how many?"

"I don't know, but I'm almost certain that's why he was different. He always talked about how his body didn't *fit* right. That his head felt too crowded. He would scratch himself bloody in his sleep sometimes. And then when he died—"

"He was free." I began to understand. "And the gods were set free."

Noelle gave a sad smile, her eyes welling up with tears. "I'd never tell Reaper this, but I think Daren was ready to go. Either *they* told him it was time or he just couldn't take it anymore. He just sounds so much more at peace now."

"I'm glad." I squeezed her hand.

"The parts of the future he tells me, though," she shivered, "they're scary, Mari. I'm a bitch that can laugh in the face of death, but what he says makes me so worried. The club is about to change, Mari. As a whole, all the way down to the individual people within it."

The air in the room went cold. Noelle's gaze hovered just over my shoulder, and I had no doubt she saw something, or *someone* that I couldn't.

"You're going to get your heart broken," she told me in a strained voice. "And not just by one man."

"What? No." The faces of my three men flashed through my mind. It wasn't possible.

"It will tear you apart," Noelle went on. "Make you question everything."

"No," I repeated.

They wouldn't hurt me, not to that degree. My guys made me want to burst from how happy they made me. Reaper was doing so much better. He talked to me when he was frustrated, instead of shutting me out. Jandro never wanted anything except to make me laugh. And Gunner, my sweet beautiful man. Our love story had only just begun.

"But," Noelle's eyes fell on Freyja, who lay stretched out on her bed like she owned it, "the goddess of love will guide you when you feel like you can't trust your own heart. That's what my brother told me." Noelle's green gaze returned to me. "And Daren has never been wrong."

My chest ached, like my heart was already bracing itself for irreparable damage.

"Who's going to do this to me?" I asked, my throat going dry. "And how, other women? Is someone going to..."

I couldn't bring myself to say the word, but my imagination took me there. In my head I saw the shadowy apparition, the figure who called himself Hades, leading a man in an SDMC cut down a hallway to a light at the opposite end.

No, I couldn't lose one of them, or any of them, like that.

"Tell me," I begged in a soft whisper when Noelle didn't answer.

"Hey, there you are."

My head snapped to the doorway, where Gunner's smile shined like the sun. Horus puffed up in a ball of feathers on his shoulder.

"Guess how many supply runs I got today, baby girl?"

"Um," I blinked, trying to act normal. "I don't know."

"None." His grin went sideways in a cocky, adorable way. "Which means I'm taking you out."

"Out?"

"Yeah, for a ride." He glanced up at Noelle. "Unless you're busy."

"Nah, get gone!" Noelle plastered on a smile and flung her hands at me in a shooing motion. "We were just having some girl talk."

"By the look of those bedsheets, I'm sure you had *lots* to talk about," he teased her.

"Pft! I don't even want to know what my brother's bed looks like, now that you're roped in."

"I'm more of a headboard breaker, myself." Gunner's tongue slid along his lower lip as his gaze returned to me. *Lord have mercy.* I had a feeling he was going to be trouble, in the best way.

"Where are you taking me?" I added a flirtatious tone to my voice as I rose from Noelle's bed, trying to shove down the unsettling feeling from what she just told me. I waited so long to call this man mine. After everything we went through and overcame, would he really hurt me again?

"Somewhere fun and educational," he smirked.

"Meow!"

We both looked down, watching Freyja rub herself between his ankles with a loud purr. "Don't worry, little one." He reached down and scooped her up. "You're coming too."

"She is?" I stared at him.

"We'll figure something out." He flipped her over belly-up, holding her like a baby. "For all we know, she can keep right up with the bikes like Horus and Hades."

"She's barely left my side, so I guess we'll find out."

He scratched the cat's head while Horus tilted his head to peer down at her from his shoulder.

"Get your gear on, baby girl." Gunner leaned in and kissed my forehead. "We'll take off when you're ready."

"Okay," I smiled at him, hoping the freedom of the open road would release my fears. "I should let Reaper know where I'll be."

"While you're at it," Gunner stepped closer, bringing his lips to my ear, "I'd love to bring you home tonight. Just you and me. I know you haven't seen my place properly yet, and," his eyes dropped shyly, "I just want some time with you. Naked or not."

My chest finally started to relax, the tension melting away to all the warmth and safety I felt with this man. It couldn't be him to hurt me. Never him.

"That sounds amazing."

His smile lit up the darkest depths of my soul as he set the cat back down on the floor, then touched a chaste kiss to my lips.

"I'll bring the bike around," he said. "Meet you out front, baby girl."

I found Reaper in the garage. He was dressed in full riding leathers with the engine idling on one of his bikes, and the garage door open. He had his back turned to me, fiddling with something in his saddlebags. When Hades looked at me, I pressed a finger to my lips and the dog stayed put, grinning slightly.

I snuck up on Reaper and hugged him from behind, feeling his body jerk in surprise.

"Shit, sugar. I didn't hear you." He lifted an arm and tucked me into his side. "Hades," he chastised.

The dog tilted his head, returning his look with wide, innocent eyes.

"Where you off to?" I asked, sliding my hand across his lower stomach.

"Paying a visit to some other MCs in the area. See if Tash's been busy cutting deals elsewhere." He gave a gentle squeeze of my nape. "We're gonna need allies."

"Really?" I looked up at him in surprise. "I thought it was every club for themselves. Two sharks in the same ocean are still enemies, I think was how you put it."

"I know what I said," he nodded. "And it worked for a time. But going up against a general? We're more than just us. And I'm tired of waiting around for Gunner's dickwad uncle."

"Who's going with you?" I asked.

"Slick, Dallas, Big G, maybe a couple other guys."

"Big G?" I raised an eyebrow. "His wife just gave birth yesterday."

"I know, sugar, but he was dying to ride. We're not going anywhere where pussy's on sale, so you don't have to worry about that."

"I'm not, but Tessa needs to rest, feed a newborn every two hours, *and* take care of the boys! Jesus, I'm so pissed for her. I can't imagine how *she's* feeling."

"Dallas sent Andrea to help her," Reaper assured me. "I'm sure she'll be happy to have you and Noelle check in, too."

"I'll make sure Noelle does, but Gunner's taking me out for a ride today." I chewed my lip. "That's what I came down to tell you."

"Oh yeah, where?"

"Somewhere fun and educational, he said."

Reaper chuckled, his hand sliding down my back to cup my ass. "Will I see you tonight?" His voice lowered to that gravelly rumble that drove me wild.

"I told Gun I'd come home with him," I answered sheepishly. "I haven't actually been inside his place, or had any one-on-one time with—"

"You don't have to explain it." He released my ass, rubbing up my back as he kissed my temple. But I already felt the distance in his touch, heard the shift of emotion in his voice.

"I can tell him another time," I said. "If you really want me home, I—"

"Nah, it's fine, sugar." He cupped under my chin and pressed a lingering, sensual kiss to my mouth. "I get you every night. I'm just greedy," he smirked.

I frowned. He was being sweet, but his actions still felt forced. He was disappointed, but would never admit it at this point. Was *this* the first sign of Noelle's warning? Would he leave me over not making enough time for him?

Fucking hell. I started to wish she'd never told me.

"You're sure?"

"Do I have to throw you over my shoulder and carry you to Gun's place?" he laughed. "You *should* have alone time with him. He'll open up to you more than with us around. You'll know for sure if he's got any issues with the sharing aspect."

"You think he still does? After being there with all of us and saying he's all in?"

"I think he's being genuine about that," Reaper paused, scratching his jaw, "but he's going to have more lingering insecurities than me or Jandro. We love it when your attention is focused on us, but me and 'Dro are solid, babe. We trust you when you're not with us. Gunner will try, but this doesn't come naturally to him. He might need a little more reassurance."

I nodded my understanding, reaching on tip-toes as I wound my arms around his neck. "Tomorrow night," I murmured against his lips. "Just you and me."

His smile touched mine as his hands molded to the small of my back. "I'm gonna hold you to that," he said in a playful warning.

"Wouldn't miss it for a damn thing, Mr. President."

REAPER

Talk about getting a taste of my own fucking medicine.

As Hades and I took off out of the garage, I had to remember what I told Jandro only yesterday. So what if Mari was spending time with Gunner? It didn't mean she didn't have room for me.

He was part of us now, and a new, shiny fixture for Mari. It was normal for her to spend the day and night with him. And what I told her was true—he would need more assurance from her than me or Jandro.

In other words, I had to stop being a pussy. My woman would miss me and come back to me. She always did.

Slick, Big G, and Dallas fell in line behind me as we tore out of Sheol. I had to keep my focus, stay at least one step ahead of General Tash. Unfortunately for me, I was completely blind as to what step he was on. He could be plotting world domination for all I knew.

The dipshits of Razor Wire MC and us only had one thing in common—the general used us like pawns in an elaborate chess game. We couldn't have been the only clubs, not for the grand scheme of things he was planning.

An alliance with Razor Wire was out of the question, considering they attacked us at the entrance to our own home. I gave every Steel Demon the authority to shoot a Razor Wire on sight, that's how fucking done I was with them. But not every MC was as slimy as those assholes. There had to be others like us, who lived by a code.

For years I'd heard rumors of just such a club, who called themselves the Sons of Odin. At first I'd written them off as white supremacist fuckheads parading around under a Norse flag, but apparently I was wrong. These guys guarded an area of the northern border, near where the Four Corners used to be—the spot where the old borders of Arizona, New Mexico, Utah, and Colorado all intersected at perfect ninety-degree angles.

That was definitely an area Tash would be interested in, especially if he was successful in stampeding over Gunner's uncle in Jerriton. I'd never heard whispers of the Sons of Odin making trouble for anyone else, so I figured they were worth a visit. I respected any club that handled their shit and kept a tight lid on any drama.

My boys and I went hard on our bikes, kicking up clouds of pale dust as we raced across the landscape. Hades stayed just ahead of me, his running pace leisurely despite our speeds.

Lately it was getting harder for me to obey him without question. Now, especially with Freyja in the mix, I felt the burning need for answers. What was he, and why was he sticking with me? What Mari said about Freyja helping with Tessa's delivery couldn't be a coincidence. Horus being able to hold my two-hundred pound ass from falling off a cliff couldn't be a coincidence. I wasn't ready to believe Noelle's dreams about Daren, but Hades especially had some kind of link with the dead.

That voice he spoke to me with sounded more than ancient. It sounded eternal. And nothing else had scared the living shit out of me more.

Two hours into the ride, Hades threw his head back in a howl as he ran. A chill ran over my skin. No, it went deeper than my skin. I felt an eerie coldness in my bones.

We're too late.

Somehow I already knew, even before the remains of the clubhouse became visible on the horizon.

I signaled my guys to ready their weapons as we approached the burned-out husk of the building. There wasn't even a smell of smoke or charred anything in the air. We were days, maybe even weeks, too late.

Hades stayed alert and guarded as we parked and dismounted the bikes. My hand drifted over my holster, eyes and ears alert to any movement or sound. But it quickly became clear that no one was around.

"Someone fucked these guys up," Big G astutely remarked.

Only a pile of ashes and a few structures, like a stone fireplace and a fireproof safe, remained. The safe door swung open, the inside already looted and empty.

"Tash?" Dallas tilted his head at me, an eyebrow lifted.

"Most likely," I muttered, relaxing my weapon hand. "These boys didn't play ball with whatever Tash had planned. No one else would waste resources on torching the whole place like this. He did it to make an example of them."

"What about the club itself?" Slick asked, his face pale. "Did they get out? D'you think..."

Hades' sniffing through the rubble answered that question soon enough. He dug out a human skull, half-buried in a pile of ash.

"Damn," Dallas breathed, his forehead creasing at the sight. "Poor bastards."

"Fuckin' shame," I agreed, walking through the ashes with care. "Whatever they did, they get all my respect for standing up to Tash. It's too fucking bad they lost their lives in the process."

A dark pit of dread filled my gut. Sheol could be the next ashy ruin if we weren't careful. That didn't mean we'd roll over and give into the general's demands, we just had to think long-term and be smarter, craftier. Tash used MCs because he didn't think like us. He saw us all as lawless road pirates, who'd turn over their favorite child for the right price.

Sure, we played dirty. We fought in ways no uppity general would ever consider. He thought we didn't have the same tactics and strategy as he did, but we had Gunner. With his falcon eyes and military school background, we had the means to meet Tash at every corner. I knew we could play at his level and not be doomed to meet the same fate as the Sons of Odin.

"Pack it in, boys." I turned back toward the bikes, having seen enough. "There's nothing left for us to do here."

"Shouldn't we bury them or something?" Dallas ran a hand over his shaved head. "I dunno if you feel that, man, but this place feels...bad. Not just because they died, but it's ninety fucking degrees out and I'm fucking shivering."

I knew exactly what he was referring to, and couldn't explain it myself. These men were murdered in their home, their safe haven. Probably with their old ladies and children, too. Their deaths were sudden, painful, and unjust. I didn't know if it was their spirits, souls, or anything else hanging around, but this place was drenched in a cold, creepy atmosphere.

"Let's just go, this place is freaky," Big G declared.

"I agree with Dallas. We should pay our respects, somehow," Slick piped up.

"All of you shut up." I was busy watching Hades.

The Doberman was sniffing through the ash-covered foundation and appeared to be collecting remains. He picked up the human skull and placed it next to a cactus just to the side of the ruin. Then he went back and picked up another bone fragment, part of a hand from the looks of it, and placed it next to a nearby aloe plant.

Hades went back and forth several times, finding pieces of the former club members and gently laying them next to their own plants. He didn't just find bones either. One item looked like a charred piece of leather from a cut. Another was a silver ring with a skull on it.

If my guys said anything to me, none of it registered as I watched my dog approach the skull—the first artifact he found, and lay a paw on it.

Rest, he said.

I nearly fell to my knees as Hades walked to the aloe plant and placed his paw on the bone fragment there.

Rest, he said again.

The same voice that boomed at me with the command to reap, now spoke gently to the restless souls taken without warning from this world. One by one, he approached the remnants of their earthly belongings and ordered them to rest. To move beyond the plane of the living.

Slowly, the heaviness and the cold in the air lifted. My guys didn't hear Hades speak, but they noticed the difference in the atmosphere immediately.

Rest, he commanded the final object, a metal picture frame with two men hugging and smiling behind the warped glass.

The last chill down my spine faded away, and nothing was left but a pile of ashes in the desert.

"All right, boys." I held my hand out to Hades, who trotted over and let me scratch his ears. "Now we can go home." With a final glance at the simple memorials over my shoulder, I muttered, "Rest in peace, Sons."

Flying somewhere over our heads, a raven cawed ominously.

MARIPOSA

Ten minutes after seeing Reaper off, I stood next to Gunner and his bike with no clue on how to bring Freyja along. Naturally, she was sitting in my spot right behind Gunner.

"I dunno how you expect to hold on with just your claws." I scratched the base of her tail. "The bike goes pretty fast."

"Maybe she's got like, Wolverine claws," Gunner laughed. "But then she'll slice my seat to ribbons, which would suck."

"Can we stick her in your saddle bags?"

"Don't think she'll fit. They're filled with stuff we need." He still wouldn't breathe a word of what we were doing. "It'll be bumpy and loud in there, anyway. She won't like it."

I picked up the black kitten, turning her belly-up in my arms like Gunner had earlier. "What are we gonna do with you, huh?"

She squirmed, twisting and batting at the zipper on my jacket. When I lowered my arm to put her down, she twisted onto her feet and jumped *up*. Her claw snagged at my zipper pull and yanked it halfway down my chest. Then she jumped again, into my jacket.

"Freyja, what are you doing?" I laughed.

Gunner turned around just in time to see the kitten-sized bump wriggling under my jacket. Freyja finally oriented herself and stuck her head out just above where the zipper opened.

"Well, that's an idea," Gunner grinned with a scratch between her ears. There was no ignoring how close his fingers were to my breasts. "She's secure, protected from all the rattling. The noise probably won't bother her too much."

"You gonna stay put in there?" I looked down to ask her. She licked my chin, but was otherwise completely still. "I guess we're good," I relented, looking back up at Gunner.

He held my gaze as he leaned toward my chest ever so slowly. His lips curved in a tiny, wicked smile as he placed a soft kiss on Freyja's head, his nose barely brushing my cleavage.

Sensation rushed to my nipples, aching for a touch, *his* touch. But he pulled away and returned to face forward on the bike.

"Hold on, girls!" He hit the accelerator, bringing the machine to life with a roar. With a roll of his right shoulder, Horus took off flying.

I slid my arms around his waist, leaving some space between his back and my chest so as to not squish the cat. "Don't I get a kiss?" I teased, my lips touching the side of his neck.

He grinned at me over his shoulder. "If you're good."

The first portion of the ride was short. Gunner pulled up to what looked like abandoned horse stables, just a few miles outside of Sheol. Freyja popped out of my jacket and shook her fur out as we came to a stop.

"Grab the case in there for me, will you, baby girl?" Gunner nodded to the left saddle bag as he popped out the kickstand and swung a leg over the bike.

I unbuckled the top flap and pulled it open. A plain, plastic box sat conspicuously on top, but when I went to pull it out, the box felt like it weighed fifty pounds.

"Holy shit, what's in here?" I huffed, cradling the box against my body.

"Ammo." Gunner opened another case on the bike seat, and held up a matte-black handgun. "We're target practicing."

I shouldn't have been surprised. He did mention teaching me how to defend myself.

"So this is the educational portion of our outing?"

"Might be the fun part too," he smirked, slamming a magazine up into the pistol grip. Sure enough, the horse stalls had been converted into a makeshift shooting range. Metal casings littered the dirt floor. The frames of the stalls stayed intact to designate each range. Walls on the sides and far end had been knocked out, with targets placed in the field behind them at various lengths. Gunner led me to one with a closer target.

He laid the gun on the stall door and patiently explained its parts and their functions. After I successfully repeated everything back to him, he showed me how to load it, then had me do it myself.

I'd always hated the sound of gunfire. It meant there was a chance I couldn't save someone, no matter how fast or efficiently I worked. Invented hundreds of years ago, guns were still one of the most effective ways of killing people, or injuring beyond repair.

But when Gunner aimed the gun at the target and fired two shots through the center ring, none of my old feelings resurfaced. When he handed the weapon to me with an encouraging smile, something else surged through me when I held the weight of it in my hand.

The script had flipped. Now I had just as much power as the next piece of shit who wanted to enslave me.

I lifted the gun, aimed through the sights, and fired two shots.

"Nice, baby girl," Gunner praised. "You're a little jumpy on the pull, but that's all right. It'll go away as you get used to it." He moved behind me, fingertips caressing my arms. "Relax," he whispered. "Put a little bend in your elbows." His touch ran from my shoulders, down the sides of my body, to rest at my hips. "Widen your legs a little more," he added, his voice growing husky.

I shot through several more magazines until my hands started cramping. Gunner adjusted and praised my technique with each reload.

After the last one, he massaged my sore palm between his thumbs and told me that was a good stopping point.

"You feeling alert and full of adrenaline yet?" The gleam in his blue eyes hinted at more surprises.

"What are you scheming next?" With all of the flirty touches and innuendo, I was fired up in more ways than one. If his plan was to take me against one of the stable doors, I certainly wouldn't be disappointed.

He placed a kiss on my fingertips, then released my hand. "Wait here."

Instead of heading back out toward the bike, he headed down to the opposite end of the stables. I watched him spin a combination lock on what looked like a supply closet, and pulled out a set of gymnastics mats.

"Little dusty," he muttered, then went back to the closet and retrieved a broom.

"We gonna be wrasslin'?" I asked, unfolding the mats from their stacked position as he swept them.

"Kinda." The naughty gleam never left his eyes. "If you don't have a gun, you might have to fight close up. We'll have to repeat this a lot so it becomes instinct, but I'll just give you a basic overview today." He put the broom aside and handed me a slender piece of wood carved in the rough shape of a knife. "You're going to use that like an actual weapon."

"Okay." I held it a few inches in front of my body, unsure what to do.

"Stay there. Now," he walked a slow circle around me, "most attacks happen from the back." With incredible speed, he braced one forearm against my throat and the other around my waist. "What do you do in this situation?"

Beg you to fuck me?

"Um, I dunno." His heart kissed my back in steady, calming beats through the solid wall of his chest. His clean, fresh scent, the heat of his skin, everything *him* made it incredibly difficult to concentrate.

"You have a few options," he rasped into my ear. "I have your shoulders, so your arms can't move much. But your legs are free and much stronger."

"I can't kick you in the balls from here."

"No," he laughed. "But look, you can kick my knee joint. Kick it from the side, the direction it doesn't bend."

I lifted my foot and found the side of his knee with my boot. "Right there?"

"Yeah, good. One good kick there will force me to put all my weight on the other leg." The weight of his chest rested heavier on my back as he raised one foot to demonstrate. "Now what?"

"Now...you're off-balance."

"Exactly. That puts you at an advantage, baby girl." The pride in his words made my skin tingle from head to toe. "Bend your knees, lower your center of gravity, then take a big step forward. Shift all your momentum forward hard, like you're about to take off running."

I did as he instructed, which, to my surprise, sent him flying over me to land on his back on the mats. He shot a stunning grin up at me. "Now slit my throat with your knife."

I brandished the carved hunk of wood and drew a line across his exposed neck.

"Good." He rolled up to sit, eyes sparkling. "So what did you learn from that?"

"That I need to use the differences between our weight and size to my advantage." I panted slightly. It wasn't easy throwing such a tall man over my shoulder.

"Exactly!" He beamed with pride. "That's the main principle I want you to learn. You can get away from any guy who grabs you, as long as you can take away his balance and use gravity to your advantage. Finishing him off," he nodded to my wooden knife, "just ensures he won't come after you a second time." He patted my leg and climbed to his feet. "Let's go again."

We went for several more rounds. Each time he grabbed me in several different ways, and gently guided me through finding his weak points, until I had them memorized. After nearly an hour of touching, grabbing, and mock-fighting, my body was fatigued and sore, while craving him like mad at the same time.

"Come on, last one." Gunner hovered over me as my back pressed into the mat. My legs were around his waist and he held my wrists pinned above my head. His hair hung down, tickling the edges of my face. "How you gonna break my hold, Mari?"

"Gun, I dunno," I panted, rolling my head from side to side. Sweat coated every inch of my body. "I'm completely wiped out."

"Last one, I promise," he repeated. "Remember your legs—"

I raised my head an inch off the mat, the only distance I needed to press my lips to his. He shut up instantly, returning the kiss with all the warmth and sweetness I had come to know from him. His hands loosened around my wrists and I seized the opportunity to dig my fingers into his beautiful golden locks.

It was the perfect first kiss, a complete do-over from the harrowing moment I was pretending to be his slave. No one was around to threaten or rush us through this, our lives weren't in danger. At least, not right now. That moment would surely come again, but right now it was just me and the man whose smile captured me from the first moment I saw him.

"I don't recommend doing that with an attacker." His lips, swollen from my kiss, curved amusedly as he looked down at me.

"Hm. I'll remember that." Grabbing the edges of his cut, I rested my head back down on the floor and pulled him down closer.

"Baby girl. Mari..." Gunner's moans were soft and breathy as I peppered kisses under his jaw, trailing down his throat.

"Yes?" I nipped his Adam's apple.

He grinned sheepishly. "I was going to wait until I brought you home tonight before doing this."

"Too bad." I pushed his hair aside and sucked at the crook of his neck. "I want you now."

He let out a heavy groan, running his hands down my sides. I felt him, thick and pulsing against my core already.

"Right here? Where it's fucking dirty?"

"You can still clean me off at your place tonight," I reminded him, grazing my teeth along his earlobe.

"You don't have to keep convincing me," he chuckled, slipping a hand under my shirt.

His mouth returned to mine, tongue and lips caressing as he inched my shirt up over my bra. While we parted so I could take it off, his lips fell to my ribs and belly.

"You looked fucking amazing last night with them." His breath was warm on my skin, kisses shooting pleasure to every nook and cranny of my body. "So beautiful and sexy."

"It didn't bother you, seeing that?" This might not have been the best moment to ask, but I had to know.

He paused, lips hovering over my bellybutton as he looked up at me. "It only bothered me that I couldn't touch you." His mouth returned to mine, tongue diving in hungrily. "I couldn't stand it any longer." His words against my lips became a growl, one hand hurriedly undoing his belt buckle and zipper. "I had to make you mine. I couldn't last another fucking minute without calling you *my* girl."

"But sharing me with them?" I wrapped my arms around his neck, lifting my hips so he could pull my jeans and panties away. "You're truly, honestly okay with that? Because I'm theirs just as much as I'm yours. That's not going to go away, Gun."

"I don't fucking care." He wrapped an arm around my back and hauled me up, unhooking my bra swiftly and pulling it off me.

"Gunner? Ohh..."

He laid me back tenderly on the mat, one hand still supporting my back while the other worked some kind of magic spell between my legs. Two long fingers pressed inside me, the other three somehow teasing my clit from all angles outside. His thumb stroked over the top, while his index and pinky pressed on either side of my pussy. Or at least that was my best guess, it felt so fucking good it was disorienting.

"Reaper was right," he rasped, watching my hips buck from his come-hither motion inside me. "We all just want to make you happy. They know how. I'm gonna try my damn hardest to do the same, baby girl."

"You already do," I gasped, the pleasure hitting me hard. "Oh, fuck!" My orgasm crested without warning, seizing up around his hand.

Gunner's skillful fingers stroked me through, riding the wave of my release and then the aftershocks before withdrawing, leaving me empty. He barely had to move into a position for sex, I was already climbing him.

"I won't let you doubt me." He kissed my throat, pulling my hair back gently to expose more of my neck. "I'll never give you a reason to question how I feel again."

"I never did." I pressed my forehead to his, locking my arms around his neck and my legs around his waist. "Gunner, I never doubted how you felt. You've always been there for me. When you pulled away, you thought you were protecting yourself. It's me that should be making promises." I cupped his cheek, my vision swimming with his large blue eyes, and our lips a hair's breadth away from each other.

"I promise I'll make time for you. I'll never intentionally hurt you. I won't ever make you feel like less than them. Whether I had them or not, I still wanted you. I always did. Gunner, please understand that I'm not adding you to a collection. I want you because you're *you*."

"I know, baby girl." He returned my back to the mat with utmost care, shifting his weight between my legs.

"So don't ever doubt *me*." My lips trembled as I spoke. "Because that won't ever change."

"Mari..."

Together we let out a mutual gasp as he slid into me, slick and effortless, like we were made to fit each other.

"I just hope I can be someone who deserves you," he groaned, framing my face with his forearms.

"You're doing a good job so far." My words were breathless, the air chased away every time he entered me.

He laughed, leaning down to steal more of my breath with another kiss. His movement was fluid, graceful. Gunner made love like he swam through water—long muscles stretching, each breath intentional and heavy. I wrapped my arms around his back, sliding my fingers along the tattoo that matched mine.

Mine, all mine.

My hand slid down to his perky ass, feeling the muscles flex there as I pulled him into me deeper. How did I go so long without this, without him? I needed more of him constantly, always.

He slid a hand under my ass as well, angling my hip in such a way that had my clit buzzing with the impact of his body.

"Gunner, what...yes..." Words weren't making sense. All brain function ceased at the explosive pleasure shooting off where our bodies joined.

My beautiful gunman had to be some kind of magician, moving so hypnotically while his cock hit every nerve ending inside me at just the right tempo, and even the angle he held me maximized my pleasure. How could he be real?

Like the first one, my release came without warning. The crash sent shudders throughout my body, so intense that Gunner had to hold me in place. I was burning up, slick with sweat, and my pulse raced like a rapid drumbeat in my ears. And I could not get enough.

Thankfully, Gunner never stopped. His hand went to my clit this time as he sat up, circling lazily around the center of my pleasure as his hips rolled back and forth.

"Beautiful," he murmured, his eyes dilated and hungry as he watched my breasts bounce.

I grabbed his thighs for leverage, wanting him deeper and harder, more.

"Oh, baby girl," he groaned, zeroing in on my clit. "You're too fucking good..."

His breathing grew ragged, labored over the next few thrusts. The sorcerer of pleasure was finally losing control. He swelled inside me, making me see stars as his thumb strummed its last few magical notes, and we came together in a crash.

GUNNER

"So, how did you get to be so good at that?"

I looked at Mari innocently. "At what?"

"You know what." She kicked me playfully under the table while Horus cooed in amusement from a nearby fence post.

I took a sip of beer to ponder a good way to answer. At the same time I slid an arm around her shoulders, flicking her hair back to admire one of my love bites on her neck.

Mine. All mine.

"I was with someone for a while who taught me a few things."

"I'd say more than a few." Mari sucked at the straw on her margarita. "She gave you the cheat code."

"A satisfactory performance, then?" I smirked at her.

"Highly satisfactory." She leaned against my shoulder. "Ten out of ten, would fuck on the dirty floor of a shooting range again."

We laughed together and I pressed a kiss to her hair. "Happy to be of service."

"Are you happy, Gunner?" She peered up at me. "Really?"

I needed to take my time to answer. Not because I had any doubt, but to really sink into the feeling, like a cool body of water on a scorching day. After we made love at the range, we got back on the bike and headed to this cantina about an hour away. They had a great bar, shaded outdoor seating, and the best taco truck in the Southwest parked outside.

I had a belly full of beer and carne asada. Horus was chilling on a fence post, keeping an eye on us, while Freyja meandered around the patio and made friends with some stray cats. And I had my girl with me. Sure, she'd been on the back of my bike before. We'd had drinks and flirtatious jokes before. But this time, she was really mine.

"I'm happy as fuck," I blurted out like the eloquent bastard that I was. "Everything is fucking perfect right now." I leaned over to steal a sip of her margarita. "Are you?"

"Yeah, I am." She radiated happiness like sunlight, her cheeks still flushed from all the orgasms I gave her.

Not one of her other guys, *me*. She looked every bit as sexy as last night, sandwiched between Jandro and Reaper, but knowing that I alone pleased her today made it a little extra special.

We sat quietly for a while, watching Freyja wrestle with a fluffy grey kitten. Horus made clicks and chirps, as though giving her pointers like some kind of coach.

"How long were you with her?" Mari asked out of the blue.

"With who?"

She tugged on a lock of my hair playfully. "The girl who *taught you a few things.*"

The resurfacing memory brought up an uneasy feeling in my gut. "Jealous?" I chose to deflect, teasing her with a squeeze around her waist.

"Not exactly." She squirmed against my side, the ice in her margarita sloshing. "I mean, I have no room to talk. Just curious, I guess."

"It wasn't really like that, baby girl," I sighed. "She wasn't my girlfriend or anything. We just messed around every so often. We had to sneak around, keep it a secret."

"Why?"

"Well, she was older than me and um," I drained the rest of my beer before finishing my answer. "She was a maid in my parent's house."

Clarity and understanding lit up her hazel eyes. "Oh, I see."

"Yeah." I stared at my empty beer glass, willing it to magically refill. "Long story short, we got caught and my parents sent her away."

"How old were you?"

"Old enough to know exactly what I was getting into," I answered curtly. "She didn't take advantage of me or anything like that. We were just friends for a while before getting physical." I let out another sigh. "Unfortunately for her, I wasn't old enough to think with the right head, and she took the fall for me."

Mari gave my arm a sympathetic squeeze. "Do you know what happened to her?"

"Shipped her off to one of those women's correctional camps, most likely." My tone was laced with bitterness. "Typical move for my folks. Disposing of people who could ruin their image. They didn't even care that she was my friend. I only saw them and her when they hosted parties. They paraded me around like the prodigal son, then forgot about me when the charade was over. So I'd go off to find Beth, and we'd have our own fun. But the son of Hollywood royalty messing around with household staff? Oh no, they couldn't have that."

The whole time I rambled, Mari listened patiently with her head on my shoulder. When I finished, she kissed my cheek and slid her arms around my waist. Even her touch and affection seemed to have healing qualities. It didn't feel great to be dredging up the past, but I did feel lighter. A little less burdened.

"I'm sorry, Gun. Your parents really were assholes." She looked up at me with her chin on my chest.

"That's not even the half of it," I sighed, running my fingers through the ends of her hair.

"Your grandparents, though. They were better, right?"

"Yeah. My grandfather died when I was fifteen, so it was just me and Gram for a while. Grandad's vintage Harley was my first motorcycle. Jandro fixed it up for me."

"Still got it?" Mari smiled at me.

"Yeah, it's in my garage. I take it for short rides sometimes. It's so old now, and I just don't want to ruin it beyond repair."

She snuggled her head into my chest. "I'd love to see it when we get back."

"Sure thing, baby girl." Another quiet moment passed, the two of us just wrapped up in each other. "My grandparents were married for over fifty years. And even until the end, they couldn't stand to be apart."

"Aw, that's beautiful."

"My granddad said," I swallowed thickly, "that he and Gram were like a pair of scissors. When together, they worked perfectly. Separated, they ceased to work at all."

"Soul mates." Mari pressed a small kiss to my throat.

"I guess."

Mari pulled away to look at me. "What, you don't believe in soul mates?"

"I dunno anymore," I admitted. "I mean, this feels right with you. It would feel right if you had a hundred other guys, as long as you still had time for me—"

"Always," she interrupted with a quick kiss to my mouth.

I smiled lazily at her. "I guess the main reason it took me so long to jump in was because I wanted what my grandparents had. They set up this big expectation that there's one person destined for all of us, and life is all about finding your other scissor blade."

"What we have doesn't make that *not* true," she replied. "Your grandparents had something unique, but so do we. So did you and Beth. Just because you're with me now, it doesn't invalidate your time and memories with her." A wicked smile curved on her lips. "Wherever she is, I hope she's well. And I'm grateful for what she taught you."

"Hm, me too," I chuckled and pressed a kiss to her hair. "Especially if it makes me your favorite."

"Nope, I don't pick favorites." Mari shook her head insistently. "It's impossible to choose."

"That sounds like I have to try a little harder," I grinned, pulling her leg over my lap to straddle me.

"Gunner..." She said the first half of my name with a soft growl, like a warning. The second half left her mouth in a decadent sigh as I kissed her neck, pulling her flush against me.

My lips moved lower, tracing the swells of her breasts as my hands memorized the winding curves from her ass to her waist. She writhed in my lap, rolling her core against my dick that was already hardening for her again. I started to wonder if we could really get away with fucking on the patio of this establishment, when a stray glance over her shoulder alerted me to the three massive bikers approaching our table.

Horus screeched, extending his wings to the sides. Freyja arched her back like a Halloween cat and hissed.

I slid Mari off my lap and warily examined the guys on the other side of our table. "Can I help you, gentlemen?"

The big dude in front lifted his chin at me. He had a shaved head, dark beard coating his lower jaw, sharp amber eyes, and was covered in tattoos. The patch on his cut read *Sgt. At Arms*, essentially the same title I had. His road name read T-Bone. But what caught my attention was the raven perched on his shoulder, its glossy black feathers reflecting the sun like obsidian.

"You Gunner Youngblood?" he asked in a low, gravelly voice.

"Depends who's asking." I reached slowly for the gun in my holster, watching every breath of movement he made.

One of the guys behind him stepped up, a taller, lanky dude built similar to me. His head was shaved too, except for a strip of dark hair along the top of his head tied off in a topknot. He went by Dyno according to his patch, and was his club's Road Captain.

"That's him, T. The Steel Demons arms dealer, couldn't be anyone else."

"I'm flattered y'all can recognize me from afar. That still don't tell me who the fuck you dicks are." My hand wrapped around the pistol's grip, finger hovering over the trigger.

The third guy walked up. He had more than enough hair on his head and in his beard to cover both of his friends. I didn't get a chance to look at his cut before he tossed something onto the table.

It landed with a thump and rolled a few times. I braced my arm in front of Mari, not knowing what to expect. Once it stopped moving, I realized it was a leather, drawstring bag. Parts of it were discolored, like dried blood had soaked through.

"A present for me? Aw shucks, boys, you shouldn't have," I sneered up at them.

T-Bone jerked his chin at me again. "Your uncle. He could've used a hand from his family."

The blood drained from my face, as did all bravado, as I stared at the bag on the table. Slowly I reached over and pulled open the top.

"Oh my God," Mari whispered, covering her mouth.

Uncle Jerry's hand had been crudely sawed off at the wrist. Dried blood coated his fingernails and the gaudy, jeweled rings he wore. It was *his* hand, no mistaking it. The same hand that ruffled my hair as a boy and snuck me hors d'oeuvres in napkins from my parents' parties.

It didn't take much effort to school my features. I felt oddly blank. The biker might as well have dropped a pineapple in front of me. Uncle Jerry was never outwardly horrible to me, but he was every bit as manipulative and self-serving as my father. That said nothing of the atrocities he committed while killing and enslaving his way to ruling the Colorado territory.

When I didn't fit my dad's mold of me well enough, he cast me aside. Uncle Jerry, with no kids of his own, then tried to groom me into his perfect successor.

Both of those fuckers failed.

"Where's the rest of him?" I asked impassively.

"His top half might be somewhere down in Texas by now," T-Bone answered in a bored tone. "Cock and balls fed to the buzzards. Other hand probably up in the Dakotas. Oh yeah." He snapped his fingers as though suddenly remembering. "His head's been spiked through on that god-awful fucking front gate to his mansion."

"And I take it you boys did this?" My gaze moved over all three of them, taking in and memorizing every detail.

"We did." T-bone rested his hands on his metal belt buckle, some kind of intricate design in silver that looked like a Celtic knot.

No risk, no reward, I thought as I pulled my hand away from my holster, and held it out across the table to shake his.

"You did me, and the world, a favor." The shock in his amber eyes was palpable as he stared at my hand. "Did he scream and beg like a little bitch?"

"Worse than any woman I've heard." T-Bone's lip curled up in a smirk, but he still didn't shake my hand. "No lost love between you two then, huh?"

"He had a chance to prove he'd help out family when called upon, after the Steel Demons saved his ass from his citizens' first uprising." I let my hand drop to the table. "And he sided with our enemy instead."

"Tash." A muscle jumped in T-Bone's jaw when he said the name.

I stayed silent, choosing not to confirm any details of my club's personal business. This guy would have to draw his own conclusions on whether I was a friend or foe.

He relaxed slightly, his men following suit.

"We'll be seeing you, Steel Demon." The raven on his shoulder cawed in agreement.

They turned and walked, allowing me to finally see the club patches on their backs—a raven with its wings spread out and the words, *Sons of Odin MC.*

MARIPOSA

Gunner pulled straight into his garage and cut the engine. He lowered his feet to the floor while I remained with my arms locked around his waist.

"Are you gonna tell Reaper about those guys?"

"Yeah, I will." He took his helmet off and shook his hair out. "In the morning."

"You sure?"

"Yes, baby girl." He turned in his seat and gave me an affectionate stroke on my cheek. "They're no threat to us. I'm not worried."

He hopped off the bike and started stripping out of his leathers, but I wasn't convinced.

"Why would they do that to your uncle?"

"Probably because he fucked them over." Gunner hung his helmet on his handlebars, then lifted me off my seat by my waist. "Trust me, my uncle was no peach. If those dudes wanted to jump me, they would have. Running into them could be a good thing, actually." He grabbed the edges of my jacket and pulled me into him with a boyish grin. "Now, can we enjoy the rest of our evening together? *Without* talking about other men?"

"Fine," I sighed in mock disappointment, reaching up on tiptoes to kiss him.

He hesitated at the door leading inside, chewing his lip as he turned to me. "Before we go in, I just want to say, don't get freaked out by the stuff I'm into." He rubbed the back of his neck sheepishly. "I never have women over, so it's a bit of a man-cave. Just, you know, it doesn't define who I am, okay?"

"Gun," I laughed, threading my fingers through his. "I don't know if there's much more about MC life that can shock me."

"I guess we'll see," he muttered, pushing the door open. Horus immediately sailed from his shoulder into the house.

From the outside, his house looked like one of the smaller ones in the compound, but the inside was as open and spacious as a cathedral.

The house only had one story, with high arching ceilings and an open floor plan. It resembled a hunter's cabin, with dark wood accents, exposed beams, and a massive stone fireplace. Horus had perched on a hunk of wood mounted to the wall near the ceiling, which blended in seamlessly with the beams.

Gunner had minimal furniture and the space was spotlessly clean. Skylights and huge windows made it seem even bigger, bringing the dark desert wilderness inside. Once I had a moment to admire the house itself, my eyes fell upon what he must have been warning me about.

The wall surrounding the fireplace was completely covered in a display of weapons. My eyes took in the massive assault rifles first, then moved across to the hunting rifles, then shotguns and revolvers—some of which looked to be antiques. He had a small collection of more modern-looking handguns, then blades of every size, shape, and curvature along the far side.

"You already knew I liked weapons," he said. "I'm kind of a collector, too."

"Gun, these are beautiful." I moved closer to inspect a wicked-looking machete-type of blade with a golden handle. The blade itself was inscribed with some kind of pictographs that looked hundreds of years old. "Where did you find these?"

"Here and there," he shrugged. "That one at a market in Tijuana a couple years back. The guy tried to tell me it was Aztec, which is probably a load of shit. I knew it'd look nice on my wall, though. Got a good deal for it."

I dropped down next to him on his low sectional couch, still taking in the artifacts on his wall. "So why the fascination with weapons?"

He propped his feet up on an ottoman, sinking low into the cushions. "I dunno. They gave me a sense of...*control*, I guess. Which I had so little of growing up. Every decision in my life, from the clothes I wore, to the people I hung out with, was predetermined for me based on my family name. It's kind of morbid, but," he laced his hands behind his head, "it's fascinating to me, how many methods we've invented to fight. To defend ourselves."

"To kill people," I said.

"No, baby girl." He looked at me. "I mean it when I say *defend*. Weapons were invented out of the need to survive, and later, for protection. I've never killed anyone unless out of absolute necessity."

"I get that, love, but," I tried to choose my words carefully, so as to not make this an argument, "you can't deny that weapons have been used to achieve terrible things since the Collapse. It's how your uncle and General Tash rose to power, for instance."

"You're not wrong." Gunner smiled gently, humoring me. "But against them, I'd rather have a weapon than not, wouldn't you? To increase your chances of survival, even a little?"

"Sure, I guess."

"This is why me teaching you this stuff is so important." He slid an arm around me, drawing me in close. "'Cause if some small-dicked fucker tries to touch my girl again, I want to give her the power to make him regret laying eyes on her. If I gotta arm my girl to give her a fighting chance? So fucking be it."

I smiled at the protective growl in his words, remembering the surge of power and fearlessness that came from handling the weapons today. It filled me with a deep appreciation that he didn't want to just protect me from danger, but give me the opportunity to protect myself.

I then traced the 2A patch on his cut, which he had yet to take off. "What does this have to do with it?"

"A well-regulated militia, being necessary to the security of a free state,

the right of the people to keep and bear arms, shall not be infringed," he recited.

"Pretty sure that document got shredded when DC got ransacked," I pointed out.

"Sure, it's not law anymore, but the idea behind it is why we're alive and free to govern ourselves." His lips brushed across my forehead. "And so many others aren't."

I nestled my head under his chin. "Do you think life will ever go back to the way it was before? You know, just...normal?"

"Nah." He wrapped both arms around me. "I don't ever want it to, honestly. The cycle will just start over again, and our great-grandkids will be in this same fucking mess a couple hundred years from now. Besides," he squeezed around me, "I never would've met you in a normal, boring life."

"That's true." I placed a kiss on his throat, shifting across his lap to get more comfortable.

Gunner's Adam's apple bobbed as he swallowed. "Can I tell you something kinda fucked up?"

His pulse began to accelerate as I kissed his neck. "You can tell me anything."

"I'm glad the Collapse happened. Not like I'm happy that people died, lost their homes, and rights and stuff. But I hated my life before. Sneaking off to ride with Reaper and Jandro on weekends was the only freedom I had. After everything went to Hell in a handbasket, it was like I could suddenly do anything I wanted. No one had control of anything, which meant my family couldn't control *me*." His nose nudged against mine. "What kind of person does that make me, baby girl?"

I curled my legs up, wrapping my arms around his neck. "It doesn't make you anything, Gunner. You're just a person. Your story is unique, but so is everyone's, in a way. If I could go back, I...I don't know if I'd do anything different, to be honest."

"You could've become a doctor." His fingers lightly grazed over my back. "Delivered all the babies you wanted, get paid lots of money, married some rich guy who'd spoil the shit out of you."

"Bo-*ring*," I snorted. "Being a trophy wife is not for me."

"Yeah, you'd rather run around with a bunch of outlaws?" He

smiled against my cheek. "Deal with knuckleheads like us, when we just make your life harder?"

"Life is hard, regardless," I sighed into his shoulder. "But I think the worse thing would be feeling alone. Not having a friend, family, or even an animal to care about you. That time between leaving Texas and meeting you was the darkest time of my life."

A shuddering breath escaped me. I'd never told anyone this, not even Reaper. Gunner's palm—running up and down my back in a soothing pattern—gave me courage I didn't know I had, to voice a deep fear I never before had put into words.

"I wanted to lay down in the desert and give up so many times," I whispered. "I'd fall asleep alone and hungry, wishing I wouldn't have to wake up. I had nothing. No parents or family left. No friends after East Texas was annexed and everyone tried to flee. I didn't even have a degree to validate my education."

"I'm so glad you didn't," Gunner murmured against my temple, rocking me gently in his lap. "I'm so glad you're here with us, baby girl."

"The only thing that kept me going," I clutched tightly to his shoulder, "was having patients to care for. Sometimes I'd be the only medic for miles, and I couldn't leave people in pain or with treatable injuries. I had no one to turn to myself, but I was *something* to complete strangers. So I couldn't let myself stop. I couldn't let anyone else feel as low as I was."

"You *matter*, beautiful." Gunner spoke each syllable with heavy weight and intention. "Not just because you're a medic, or that you're gorgeous and smart and care so much. You're even more than the sum of those things. You're *you*." He squeezed around me tightly, like I would slip away at any moment. "And you're ours. And you're loved. You're never alone, Mari. I promise you."

I touched the tip of my tongue to his ear, my insides fizzing like a bottle of champagne. "Thank you, but you didn't let me finish."

"Oh, sorry." He grinned, planting a kiss on me. "Go ahead."

"I was about to say," I nestled my head into the crook of his shoulder again, "that I'd go through that all again if I knew the outcome would be this."

"*This* being?"

"Loved. Supported. Beyond any measure that I could ask for."

"You deserve it," he told me, blue eyes shining. "Reaper was right, as usual. You deserve more love than a single man can give." He brushed a gentle caress across my cheek. "I just hope mine is good enough for you to hold on to."

"Gunner." I caught his hand, threading my fingers through his. "That's never once entered my mind. If what I give *you* isn't enough, just—"

"Stop right there, baby girl." He held our clasped hands over my mouth. "You're more than enough. You're *everything*."

He leaned us over slowly, until my back pressed into the couch and he hovered above me. His hands supported my head when our lips came together, while my palm kissed the beat of his heart.

Every kiss and touch throughout that night was heavy with the weight and depth of his love.

MARIPOSA

"Did Gunner tell you about the bikers we met?"

I looked at Reaper over my shoulder, watching his eyes narrow in concentration as he gently washed my back with a damp, sudsy cloth.

"He did." Reaper squeezed the water out of the cloth and hung it over the side of the bathtub. "They must be what's left of the torched club we checked out. Must've not been home when the match got lit."

"You think they're on our side?" Freyja kept peeking at us over the edge of the tub with wide, concerned eyes, so I reached up to boop her nose with a soapy finger. She zoomed out of the bathroom and Hades took off after her with a bark.

"Seems that way, although it's still unclear what they actually want." Reaper reached around my waist, pulling me back to lay on his chest. "I think their little hand gesture was to test Gunner's loyalty, to see how he'd act when faced with his uncle's brutal death."

"Especially if he was away from the rest of you guys," I mused. "Like, in case we had another hidden betrayer. I wonder if they had one of those too."

"It's possible. Tash likes to fuck around with people's loyalty." The bathwater sloshed around our naked bodies as he picked up his whiskey glass from the edge, then held it in front of my face. He laughed at me shaking my head, kissing my hair before he sipped from it. "You didn't develop a taste for it last time?"

"It tastes better on you," I purred, leaning my head back on his shoulder.

"Mm, hang on." He took another sip before pressing his mouth to mine. When my lips parted, expecting his tongue, I got a mouthful of warm, bitter liquid instead.

"Ugh, *Rory!*"

He just laughed and laughed as I coughed and sputtered over the whiskey. The sound of his laughter was deep, throaty music echoing off the bathroom walls as he wiped tears from his eyes.

"Sorry, sugar," he grinned, reaching for me across the bathtub. "That was a lot sexier in my head than real life."

"Hmph," I pouted, but allowed him to pull me back into his arms. "You owe me."

His body went stiff for a moment. I felt his heartbeat accelerate in his chest. "I might have just the thing." He dropped a kiss to my shoulder. "Ready to get out?"

We stood and dried off with fluffy towels. I grinned to myself as I rubbed the towel over my face and hair. Every day that I washed up or got dressed in here, I felt like a princess, not a biker's old lady. Sometimes I still had to pinch myself to realize I wasn't dreaming.

Hades and Freyja watched us from the dog bed in the corner of the bedroom as we made our way out of the bathroom.

"What you lookin' at, perverts?" Reaper muttered to them as he tied the towel around his waist. He seemed nervous, and started rummaging through his dresser drawers in search of something.

"Tessa told me something interesting today." I sat naked on the bed and continued rubbing the towel over my wet hair.

"Yeah?"

"She said this last pregnancy was the most painless out of all of them." I patted the towel over my back where my tattoo had started to itch. "I think it had to do with Freyja being there."

Reaper paused in his rummaging and turned to look at me, brows furrowed. "You think so?"

"I can't remember, but," I rubbed my forehead, "Freyja is a sex and fertility goddess, I think? I read about it so long ago."

"Well, in that case," he grinned wolfishly, "no wonder you can handle all three of us."

"Just barely." I stuck my tongue out at him.

He came over to sit next to me on the bed, holding something just out of view on his opposite side. "I'm glad you and Gun had a good day together, and that he finally got his head out of his ass." He slid a hand around the back of my neck, thumb circling gently. "And when all three of us get up in here? Damn, sugar. You're gonna be wrecked."

"Tell me about it," I groaned, but smiled wickedly at the thought. Getting lost in the hands, mouths, cocks, and firm bodies of my men sounded like utter heaven.

"But I'm glad it's just me and you tonight." Reaper's hand fell to clasp my fingers on the mattress. His gaze darted away. He was nervous again.

"Me too." I leaned in to plant a peck on his lips. "Is everything okay?"

"Yeah," he laughed sheepishly, meeting my gaze again. "I love you, Mari. So fucking much."

"Oh, Reap." I somehow managed to wrap my arms around his neck, despite melting into a puddle. "I love you, too. So fucking much."

"I can't marry you," he blurted out. "Not legally anyway, but I was hoping..." His words trailed off as he showed me the small, velvet box he'd been hiding.

"Oh my God, Reaper." I slapped a hand to my chest. "Is this...a proposal?"

"If you have to ask that question, I'm doing a bang-up fuckin' job," he muttered. "Look, let me do it this way."

He lowered one knee to the floor, and opened the ring box to show a beautiful stone in a dazzling array of colors. It sat in a simple, silver bezel with a twisted rope design on the band.

"Mari, will you be mine forever?" He swallowed thickly. "And only fuck other guys that I approve of?"

The crude second half of his proposal made me giggle, but the fear-some Steel Demons president looked dead serious, if even afraid.

I held the sides of his face and kissed him deeply. "I'm yours forever," I repeated back to him. "It's beautiful, but ring or no ring, I will always be yours."

His grin was equal parts joy and relief. "Put it on, then. I want to make sure I guessed your size right."

I extended my left hand, and he slid the artfully crafted band over my ring finger knuckles with little resistance. It fit comfortably, with a noticeable weight to it. Once on my hand, I noticed the R and M stamped into opposite sides of the stone.

"It's beautiful, Reap." I tilted my hand back and forth to admire the color shifting in the light. "Did you get this at the market?"

"I had a metalsmith there put it all together, but I already had the stone and the setting." He swallowed again, staring at the ring on my hand. "They were my mother's. She used to make jewelry."

"Reaper." I fought back tears as I brought my hands to the sides of his neck, beyond touched at the significance of what he just gave me. "Are you sure you want to give me this?"

"Never been more sure of anything in my life." His green eyes lifted to mine, somehow hard and serious, while filled with so much emotion. "It was my mom's dream, for me to give one of her pieces to the woman I'd give my heart to forever." He laughed softly. "I was such a dumbass. I told her I'd never get locked down, never do something as cheesy as that. But fucking look at me now."

"I like you cheesy," I chuckled. "And I love how you love me. I'll never abuse that, Rory. I was always yours first. I'll love you until the end."

For once, he didn't balk at me using his birth name. For once, I wasn't making fun of him. He must have understood I was speaking to the man his mother named and raised, the person he was before becoming Reaper, the Steel Demons president. I loved them both—who he was before and now. They blended into each other to make an incredible, complex person—one capable of loving and caring so deeply, while striking fear in the hearts of all who threatened him.

One did not cancel out the other. And I loved it all.

"Mari," he groaned, hands sliding to my waist as his torso moved between my legs. "In a world that has gone so fucking wrong, you are the one thing that's right."

His kiss was warm, a soothing balm without its usual rough, biting edge. The weight of him leaned me back on the bed, and his hand was quick to support my head on the mattress. A quick shimmy of my thighs around his waist made his towel drop. His naked, freshly bathed skin covered mine with a delicious heat.

When his mouth moved to my neck, I stared at the ring on my hand. It was mesmerizing, shifting greens and pinks as it caught the light. And it looked so perfect and regal on my hand, which now rested on his shoulder.

"I love this stone," I whispered, dancing my fingers on his skin. "What is it?"

"Watermelon tourmaline," he answered, lips between my breasts.

"I'm honestly relieved that you didn't give me a diamond." My hand flattened and sailed down the wide muscles of his back. "Always thought they were kind of boring."

"Huh. Mom said the same thing." His rough, calloused touch swept over my flesh, bringing my nipples to hard, aching peaks. "She liked stones with colors and flaws. Depth. Hidden character, she called it."

"Funny." I sucked in a breath, sensation pulsing through me as his teeth and tongue grazed over my nipples. "I like my men the same way."

His laugh sent ripples of goosebumps along my skin. "That's why you're so perfect for us."

He made it as far down as my navel before I touched his cheek. "Come back up here."

"Not happening, woman. You know my rules." He smiled lazily, dragging his fingers down my belly, teasing toward my entrance.

As tempting as it was to lay back and let him work his magical tongue and fingers, tonight my body called for something different.

"Would you believe me if I said I didn't feel like coming half a dozen times before you get inside me?"

"Hmm." He pretended to think. "No."

"Reaper," I sighed. "Will you please come up here?"

He slid up my body with a frown, green eyes hovering above me while his cock rested on my hip. "Something wrong, sugar?"

"No, my love. Not at all." I wrapped my arms around his neck to pull him down. "Kiss me."

His arms slid around my back, the heat and weight of his whole body lowering gently as his mouth pressed to mine. Our lips moved against each other, tongues caressing and penetrating, a perfect prelude for what we were about to do. I shifted my hips underneath him, nudging my thighs up so his silky head kissed my entrance.

"I can't fuck you before you're warmed up," he groaned, forehead heavy on mine.

"Reaper, I'm warmed up every time I look at you."

He kissed the bridge of my nose with an amused huff. "On top of everything else, you're good for my ego, too."

"I just want to feel you inside me," the confession came out with a light whimper. "I want to come wrapped around you. I want to look at you and feel you on top of me."

He paused, looking at me with curiosity. Then a corner of his mouth quirked up as he dragged one finger down the length of my body.

"My dirty girl wants to make love to me, is that it?"

"I know. Kinky, isn't it?"

His finger found my core, nudging his cock out of the way so he could touch me. He dipped inside, releasing a groan at the discovery of how wet I already was. The pad of his thumb circled lazily around my clit as he pressed another finger into me, stroking my pussy in a way that brought my hips lifting off the bed.

"Reaper," I whined.

"I know, babe. Just checking you." His grin was wolfish as he withdrew his hand, aligning his hips with mine again. "I don't think I've done this before."

"Huh?" I stared at him.

A deep kiss pressed me down into the mattress. A full-body shiver wracked me as his cock slid across the aching wetness between my legs.

"You're a lot of firsts for me," he admitted, settling over my body. "The first woman I really loved. I loved your mind first, I think. Then this smart little mouth." He traced my lips with his thumb before skimming down my chest. "Then your heart."

"Not my body?" I gasped jokingly.

"Of course I love your body." His hands ran down my sides as he stared at me reverently. "But have I really loved you with *my* body before now?"

He slid into me in one fluid stroke, clutching my hair in his fist to keep our gazes locked. All the air felt shoved out of my lungs as my head leaned back, my hips raised up for more.

"You know why I love making you come so much?" Reaper locked both hands in my hair, his body rolling over me with the slow, intentional penetration I'd been craving.

"Because...you love me?" I was half joking, half unable to form a coherent string of words.

He was right. I never felt him like this before either—stretching and filling me with such relentless care.

"Because I'm selfish." His forehead lowered to mine, lips hovering a hair's breadth away from a kiss. "I want to please you so fucking good, you'll never have a reason to leave me."

Noelle's premonition crackled through my head like lightning, just as his mouth fell to mine, and his cock hit new depths within me. Reaper's lips dragged to my neck with a groan, his shoulders flexing with restraint. He wanted to unleash that dominance, that strength and power he usually fucked me with. But he kept his thrusts slow, pressing all the way into me before slowly withdrawing.

He can't be, I thought, a cry on my lips as he filled me up again, lingering there before pulling his hips back. He couldn't be the one to break my heart. Everything he did was for me—my happiness, my safety. But if not him, then that meant...

I pushed the thought away, turning my hand so his mother's stone in my ring caressed his cheek.

"I'll never leave you," I panted in his ear. "Even if you don't give me ten orgasms a day, this ring is never coming off."

"Mmm." His mouth found mine for another kiss. "What's a good number then? Eight? Nine? How much slack are you willing to give me?" His serious face morphed into a devilish smile as he cupped one side of my ass, angling my hip higher.

"I mean... fuck!" He kept up the deep, slow tempo, but my clit was buzzing from the new friction. "Don't make me think of numbers right now."

"What would you rather think about while I'm so deep inside you?" he grunted out. "Christ, you feel so good. I need to love you like this more often."

My reply was a mix of wordless moans, gasps, and whimpers as the pleasure built, coiling like a spring where our bodies conjoined. Fingers dug into hard muscle. Flesh and heat collided and broke apart, again and again.

"What was that?" Reaper chuckled into my ear, his voice raspy and ragged. "Do you want more of this from me, sugar?"

He swelled inside me, pulling a scream from my throat.

"Worshipping you," he groaned, his control unraveling with every breath. "Revering you. Loving you. With every inch of me."

My climax crashed over me, sending ripples of shivers from my head to my toes. Reaper did the opposite, his body stiff as he held me twitching in his arms, until his release spilled with a heavy groan. He melted over me, a heavy blanket of heat with a rapid pulse that matched mine.

I licked a bead of sweat from his neck. "That," I panted, "is definitely worth repeating."

SHADOW

Why do you do this to yourself, my son?

"...what...?" I rolled over in bed, not ready to wake up. Sleep had become so pleasant now, and I wanted to stay there for a little bit longer.

I showed you the sky. I gave you my sight. Why do you continue to shroud yourself in darkness?

I cracked an eyelid open, squinting against the tiny strip of sunlight peeking through my blackout curtains. It was so reminiscent of my only view of the outside world from my tiny dungeon years ago.

No, the light wasn't coming from that. Someone was in my room. A tall figure, with wings spreading out to either side of him. The light was a glare reflecting off of something gold he wore, some kind of collar or chest plate.

I couldn't make out details, like his face or clothing. Sleep still held me in a warm embrace, my vision murky through slitted eyelids.

"Who's there?"

Hades will not take you prematurely, so there's no need to lock yourself in a dark coffin every night. The figure sounded like he was sneering. *You have as much right to the sky and sunlight as anyone else. You didn't know when I gave you my gift, but you must know it now.*

"Who the fuck are you?" I growled through gritted teeth.

You know who I am. I'm Horus.

The tether of sleep snapped and I jolted upright, wide awake. My room was empty. Somehow I knew it would be. He never spoke to me when I was fully lucid. And he had never explicitly told me his name before.

Horus, like Gunner's falcon. Was that why his bird came so close to me that time on the roof? I couldn't understand it, so I didn't bother to try.

Pushing the sheet back, I got out of bed and crossed the room to my window in two long strides. I snapped open the blackout curtains, the sunlight flooding my room making me squint a little.

The sun was already high and people were going about their days. Since taking the sleep medication, I'd been sleeping in later and later. I never knew that sleep could feel good. I'd begun to crave it after a long day, instead of drinking myself into a stupor to avoid it.

I showered and dressed quickly, hoping Jandro left coffee in the kitchen. He was always an early riser, and was likely at the shop already.

"Meow!"

I paused in drying my hair with a towel, cocking my head. Either that was something in the house squeaking or—

"Meow!" This time the sound was followed by scratching at my bedroom door.

It only took me cracking my door open for Freyja to squeeze through the gap and begin climbing up my pant leg.

"Good morning, funny kitten."

To my surprise, the greeting tumbled out of me without me having to think about it. With no other people around, I didn't have to worry about being socially inept.

I plucked the cat off of my jeans when she reached my thigh, carefully dislodging her tiny, needle-like claws. "Your human must be near," I added, more to myself than the animal.

Carrying the kitten in my palm, I left my room and started toward the stairs. Mariposa was already halfway up and shot me an apologetic look.

"Damn it! I'm sorry, Shadow. I'm going to have to put a harness on her or something."

"It's all right." I met her on the stairs and held the kitten out to her.

"She's really taken a liking to you." Mariposa picked up the cat with both hands, her thumbs sweeping over my palm. "The moment I walked in, she zoomed right up to your room."

I didn't know how to respond to that. Freyja's green eyes were glued to me, even as Mariposa scratched her head.

"She's a funny little animal. I really don't mind," was all I could think to say.

Mariposa smiled at me, turned to walk back down the stairs, and paused. "So how are you this morning?"

I realized she wanted to walk down alongside me, so I sucked in a breath and followed her steps. "Uh, I'm good. Quite good. And you?"

"Same. You're still sleeping well?"

"Yes, thank you." I debated telling her about the lucid dream right before waking up, but decided against it. I knew it wasn't from the sleep medication, but wasn't sure how else to explain it. "Are you looking for Jandro?" Something squeezed inside my chest as I asked, like I was secretly hoping for a certain answer.

"No, I know he's at the shop." She turned to me, setting Freyja on the floor when we reached the bottom of the stairs. "Today's my second tattoo session, right?"

"Oh! Right, yes." I hadn't forgotten, not at all. In fact, I'd been counting down the days until it was time to tattoo her again. I just never expected her to be the one to bring it up. I figured her men would have to cajole her into sitting down with me to finish it. But here she was, first thing in the morning, looking bright-eyed and excited.

And pretty. So fucking pretty.

"If you're busy today, I can come back later."

"No, no. Today is fine," I assured her. "I'll just get some coffee, clean and set up, then we can get started."

"Want me to clean while you start the coffee? Jandro took the whole pot."

"Of course he did," I muttered. "But no, you don't have to clean for me."

"I'm just excited to get started," she laughed lightly. "I'll do it right, I promise. I know a thing or two about sanitizing."

I stood frozen, unsure how to feel about her cleaning my tattoo area. Mostly, I was floored at the fact that she was offering to help.

"Um, if you really want to—"

"I'm on it."

She went straight to my desk and pulled the spray bottle of bleach solution out from a drawer. With a few quick sprays onto a paper towel, she proceeded to wipe down the chair she would be sitting in. Before she had a chance to catch me staring, I abruptly turned and headed into the kitchen to start the coffee.

On my way back, I made sure to grab a clean towel from the guest bathroom for her armrest.

"What do you think?" She stepped back, and held her hand out to my spotless tattooing station.

"Looks great. Thank you."

As we sat down and I began prepping my tattoo gun and ink, I realized with the exception of Freyja, we were truly alone. While in her medic's office, I was forced to think of her in a professional capacity. But now it was just the two of us in my house, and I would have to touch her.

We hadn't been truly alone like this since *that* day.

"Where's Gunner today?" I hoped my tone was casual.

"Off on a supply run." I tried not to watch as she piled her hair into a topknot to keep it out of the way. "Is that okay?"

The question caught me off-guard. Her expression was concerned when I glanced up at her.

"That he's off getting supplies? Um, yes. I'm not sure I follow."

She smiled a bit sheepishly, lowering her gaze to her lap. "I just don't want to make you uncomfortable by coming here alone."

"You don't," I blurted out before I could think.

Her eyes lifted back to me, lit up with surprise. "Really?"

I nodded, heat filling my face before I turned back to my tattooing supplies. "You never have, to be honest."

"So we're okay, then?" she asked hesitantly. "To be unchaperoned, I guess," she added with a nervous laugh.

Her question bewildered me. No one had ever been so concerned with *my* comfort before. What was this feeling? She had a way of bringing up all kinds of sensations I never felt in my body before. I couldn't name what was swirling in my chest right then, but I found myself trying to hide a smile.

"I'm fine with it, as long as you are."

"Good," she beamed, looking genuinely happy. I couldn't completely understand why, but I liked seeing her happy, regardless.

I took a minute to adjust the voltage through my power supply, averting my eyes when she removed her top layer shirt to give me access to her back.

"How does it look?" She spun around in the chair to face away, wearing the open back top she had on last time. "It itched like hell, but I tried my best not to scratch it."

I glanced up. "Looks good." I swallowed, clenching my fist on my thigh. "Really good, actually. You took good care of it while it healed."

"Thanks." She tossed me a smile over her shoulder. "I think having a good artist helped."

Mariposa's back was smaller and leaner than most clients I'd worked on before, and I had to adjust the design as such. The Demon flowed surprisingly well over the contours of her body, accentuating her feminine curves, while also sending a clear sign to outsiders who she belonged to.

Fuck, I was staring again.

"Ready?" I asked when there was nothing left to stall me.

"Whenever you are."

I took a deep breath and laid my gloved palm flat on her skin, much like she did to me *that* night, and began to work.

Several minutes passed with the buzzing of my machine as the only sound. Mariposa sat like a rock, even when I added shading directly over her spine. She really was an easier client than most men I worked on.

"Can I ask a question?" She glanced back at me, her head resting on her arms.

I lifted my foot from the pedal, making the buzzing stop. A sharp claw of anxiety gripped my chest. "Um, sure."

"For a tattoo artist, you don't have many tattoos. Any reason for that?"

I released the breath in my chest and put my foot back on the pedal. An innocuous enough question, but one I'd still have to answer carefully. "My skin doesn't hold ink well because of all the scar tissue. Lines get blurry faster, and it just doesn't look good. Otherwise, I'd probably be covered."

"The Demon you have doesn't look blurry. Did you do it yourself?"

I paused, lifting my foot again. She only saw my chest tattoo because of what we did. Or rather, what *I* did to *her*. I didn't even know anymore if it was a mutual act or not. All I knew was that it couldn't be repeated. Talking about it seemed to be off the table too, so why go there?

She's just making conversation about tattoos. Don't be a dumb fuck.

"I did, using a mirror and drawing it backwards. I don't have a lot of scars in that spot, so it turned out okay."

She didn't need to know my lack of scars there was because of the proximity to my heart. A blood sacrifice wasn't any good if it stopped spilling blood. They didn't cut me on the neck for the same reason.

Another few minutes of silence passed between us. As I worked, I felt the tension settling into her body, the subtle shifts and the urge to fidget.

"Do you want to take a break?" I asked her.

"I'm okay." She watched me again over her shoulder as I reached to dip more ink, her eyes following the length of my arm.

"You want to ask me about them, don't you?" Again, the words came out of me without thought. That seemed to be happening a lot today. Usually, I struggled to get words out.

"Do *you* want to talk about them?"

I looked at the crude handiwork decorating my forearm. Years upon years of scars weaved a pattern of distorted flesh. I wavered between disgruntled acceptance of my scars, and seething disgust. It wasn't really about my appearance, though. Most people had some amount of scars. What I hated the most was never getting the chance to be normal. The scars were a constant reminder of how I was shaped and molded into the socially-stunted freak I was now. I didn't know how to be anything else. I never got the opportunity.

"No, not particularly." I resumed shading Mariposa's tattoo, trying to filter out everything else but the artwork.

"Then I won't ask."

That too, made me pause. I could tell she was curious, and appreciated that she didn't push. The only conflicts I ever had with newer club members were with those who got too fucking nosy about me. I knocked Big G on his ass once years ago, after multiple warnings to stop getting in my face. No one asked nosy questions about my past or my scars again after that.

We continued on with little words between us, mainly me checking in on her pain level and her assuring me she was fine.

"How did you get into tattooing?" she asked at one point.

I took an extended pause to refill ink. The questions she asked were so simple, so entry-level to normal people. But I felt the need to answer in a particular way in order to keep...whatever this was between us. Talking to her gave me a sense of ease and comfort that I didn't want to end. Socializing was not my strong suit, but even I knew certain subjects were off-limits for casual conversation.

"I was, um, not formally educated," I began, returning my hands to her back. "I didn't learn how to read and write until a later age than most. So drawing pictures was how I expressed myself, how I communicated."

"That's really cool, actually."

A small surge of pride welled up in me, before quickly deflating. Of course she would think that. She didn't know any better.

"I started drawing with a stick in the dirt," I went on. "When I had access to pen and paper, I used that. I learned about tattooing in prison from another inmate. He showed me the stick-and-poke method, which was all we had. After Jandro and I left, he rigged up my first machine for me."

My voice sounded strange coming out of my own head. When was the last time I talked so fucking much? Probably never. But the words poured out of my mouth like a waterfall, and the smile over her shoulder grew wider as she listened. I started to feel like I'd tell her whatever she wanted to keep that smile going. Even the sordid details of my past I never told anyone before, if she wanted to know that.

"That's really amazing, Shadow. Did you design the Steel Demon logo too?"

"Yes, I did." I tried to keep my eyes focused on her skin, but couldn't resist meeting her gaze again just to see if that smile remained. "Reaper told me what he wanted, and I gave him a few rough sketches based on that. He picked the best one, in my opinion."

"Your *expert* opinion," Mariposa corrected me with a soft laugh.

"Hmm, maybe. I don't know."

"I do know. You're great at what you do, Shadow. Not just with the artwork itself, but you have a good bedside manner."

I pulled away to stretch my hunched-over position, mulling over her words. "I'm not sure what that means," I admitted.

"It's a medic term," she explained. "A medic's visit, or a tattoo, can be an uncomfortable experience. But if we can make the client feel at ease, less worried or uncomfortable, we can transform the experience into something good." Again came that smile over her shoulder. "That's what I mean by bedside manner. You've made my first tattoo a painless, fun experience, Shadow."

"I...I'm glad." My throat worked uselessly, my pulse going crazy as I processed what she was telling me.

She was...enjoying this? Not in spite of me, but *because* of me?

"Are you okay?" Her brows furrowed slightly.

"Yes! Yes, sorry. I—" I shook my head, nearly running a hand back through my hair, before I remembered and stopped myself. "It's just no one's ever told me that before."

"Someone just did," she smiled.

We continued on, Mariposa insisting she was good every time I checked in. Finally, I lifted my foot from the pedal and set my machine down. With a clean cloth, I wiped all the remaining excess ink from her back.

"I think we're done." A tinge of longing crept from my chest into my throat. "Go ahead and take a look."

Mariposa stood and stretched with a soft groan. I jerked my gaze away, the combination of that sound and the fluid movement of her body sending heat straight to my dick.

"Shadow, I love it!" She looked over her shoulder in the mirror, swaying her hips and shoulders to look at the tattoo from different angles. "Seriously, it's so badass!" She twirled until she faced me, her smile bigger than ever. "I'll have to come back to you for more."

"I'm glad you like it." I peeled my gloves off, sounding nonchalant, but the inside of my body sparked and buzzed like fireworks in a beehive. "And you know where to find me if you'd like more."

She took one step toward me, opened her mouth to speak, and promptly crumpled to the floor.

"Mari!"

I rushed over, not even realizing I'd used the shortened version of her name, and knelt at her side. "What's wrong?"

"Well, that's embarrassing." She let out a sheepish laugh and leaned to one side, bracing a hand on my arm.

"Are you hurt? Should I get Jandro?" Panic tightened around my heart like a vice. Jandro would be the best person to help. Gunner was gone, and Reaper would definitely kill me.

"No, no. I'm fine." She laughed again, this time nearly leaning her head on my shoulder. "I think I just stood up too fast after sitting for so long. I felt my leg going to sleep, but didn't think it would give out on me."

"So...you're not injured?"

"Just a bruised ego," she snickered. "As a medic, I should know better." She tilted her head, and this time it did touch my shoulder. "Sorry to worry you."

"I'm just glad I didn't—I mean, glad you're okay."

She let out a huff of breath, still laughing at herself. "You're sweet, Shadow."

More feelings erupted in my chest, foreign sensations I didn't have words for. Needless to say, no one had ever called me sweet before, either.

A slight turn of my head would bring my cheek in contact with her forehead that was still resting on my shoulder. Even such a small movement felt too close, too intimate. I'd seen her men touch her in such a way, which meant it was wrong for me to do.

But I never saw her put her head on anyone but her mens' shoulders before either.

"Can you stand?" I asked.

The confusion and anxiety about this close contact made my chest ache, even though I liked feeling the weight of her head on me. I liked the delicate scent of her hair and seeing her smile up close.

"Yeah, I think I'm good."

She lifted her head, but kept her hand on my arm. I closed my hand around her elbow to steady her as we rose from the floor together. And then, all contact was gone. The few feet of distance between us felt like a barrier that I dared not penetrate.

"I'd really appreciate you not telling anyone about my little spill." Her face flushed red, the embarrassed smile lingering.

"What little spill?"

The joke worked and she laughed, the pretty sound filling up the empty space in the house. I felt it almost like fingertips over my skin. I didn't say it out loud, but I'd also never breathe word of her head on my shoulder, her hand bracing against my bicep. Maybe it was wrong, but I wanted to keep those small moments of touch to myself. Just like how I selfishly recalled the feelings of her hands on my chest, her knee on my fingertips, and the silky warmth of her pussy wrapped around me. I lingered in that forbidden memory more than I would ever admit.

"Shadow, I'd like to tell you something." Mariposa clasped her hands nervously in front of herself, chewing on her lower lip.

Her nervousness made my anxiety dial up to an eleven. Could she tell what I'd been thinking about just from looking at me?

"Yes?"

"I just want to say," she took in a deep breath, "that I'm proud of you."

"Proud of me?" I blinked. "For what?"

"For everything," she breathed. "You taking steps to treat your sleep issues, and trusting *me*, a woman, to provide the medication. For cutting back on the destructive drinking, which is going to do wonders for your health. For talking to me, tattooing me, everything! I know it hasn't been easy for you, but you're taking all these new experiences in stride." She glanced down at the floor before looking back up at me. "I figured you don't have many people saying this to you, so I just wanted you to hear it from me. You're doing great, and yeah, I'm proud of you, Shadow."

I was stunned, rendered completely unable to do anything but stare at her. *She* said all of that to me? This woman, with her shifting brown-green eyes, the smile I couldn't get enough of, and the strands of dark hair falling out of her bun to caress her graceful neck?

This woman—so warm, captivating, and beautiful that three Steel Demons fell hopelessly in love with her, said she was proud of *me?*

The softest breath of air from her lips could have knocked me to the ground.

"Please say something," she laughed nervously.

"I don't—I just—" I stammered uselessly, the words out of my grasp. I forced a swallow and a deep breath. "Thank you. I don't know what else to say. It...It means a lot to hear you say that."

Her smile returned, and my heart truly stopped when she took a few steps toward me, shattering the barrier between us like it was nothing.

"Is it okay if I give you a hug?"

No amount of deep breaths and mental preparation could bring words to my mouth in that moment. I wasn't supposed to touch her at all, but that got blown out of the water because of her fall, never mind her tattoo. A hug was a completely foreign gesture to me, but that meant nothing in the grand scheme of things. Men hugged each other. Adults hugged children. It wasn't harmful. Not sexual. I understood logically that it was a platonic thing, but I never in my life had that much of my body touch another person.

But I wanted to.

Only with her.

My mind screamed *yes,* but my throat and tongue froze up. So I jerked my chin down in a sharp nod.

She came to me slowly, small hands skimming across my ribs to land gently on my back. Her head turned to rest one cheek in the center of my chest. Then, with a light squeeze of her arms, pulled her body flush against mine.

My hands stayed low at my sides as I just stood there, soaking up the most physical contact I ever had with a woman, or anyone.

The front of her body felt soft pressing into me, her cheek bringing a soothing warmth near my heart. Her hands moved with gentle pressure on my back, pulling forth a sensation that was so good, so intense, I wanted to release it with a moan.

"You can hug me back if you want to," she said in a small voice.

My attention returned to my arms at my sides. I knew hugs usually meant both people wrapped arms around each other, but what if I did it wrong? Plus, I had to be careful with her fresh tattoo.

Tentatively, I brought one arm around the back of her shoulders, just above the tattoo. She didn't seem at all fazed by my scars touching her, even tightening her arms around me when I used the weight of that arm to press her gently into my chest.

Mindful of her fresh ink, I kept my other arm lower, ultimately deciding to wrap it around her waist. With both arms, I returned the light squeezing that she initiated.

So this was my first hug.

I closed my eyes and willed my body not to shake from everything running through me.

REAPER

I rapped my knuckles on Jandro's door while Hades sat like a good pup at my side. It was hard to look at him lately and remember that he wasn't just my dog, my most loyal companion and friend. There was some higher power at work here, using me for some divine purpose. Was that toothy smile mocking me or was this being in a dog's body truly happy to follow me around and guard my loved ones?

I questioned everything now. How he seemed to understand everything I said. The way he guarded Mari so fiercely, and even the circumstances of how I found him. After Mari told me what happened as Tessa was in labor, I couldn't bury my head in the sand any longer. I needed answers now.

"Shadow," I greeted the large man who pulled the door open. "Just the person I wanted to see."

His dark eye, uncovered by his hair, blinked at me in confusion. "Me, president? I...wasn't expecting you. Did I forget about something?"

"No. I apologize for dropping by unannounced, but I would like your help with something. May I come in?"

He pulled the rest of the door open and stood aside for Hades and me. The dog wandered in first, giving Shadow a cursory sniff and huff of approval before moving on.

The first thing I noticed upon walking inside, aside from all of Jandro's mechanic shit, was Shadow's desk with a sketchbook and his disassembled tattoo machine.

"Oh, hey, thanks for doing such a badass tattoo on Mari. It looks fucking great on her and she's already talking about wanting more."

Shadow cleared his throat and, unless my eyes were tricking me, even seemed to blush. My old lady had that effect on people, so it didn't concern me. If anything, I was pleasantly surprised she was able to have a positive effect on him at all.

"Of course," he muttered, closing the door behind us. "She's a good client. I'm glad you're pleased with it too. So what can I help you with?"

"You still have all those old books?" I asked. "There's some...ancient knowledge I want to look into."

That piqued his curiosity. "How ancient do you mean?"

"I'm not sure," I admitted. "Possibly thousands of years. I want to know about gods. Pre-Christian, all that pagan shit."

Shadow nodded and led me through his side of the house. "I may have some old books that used to teach about this kind of subject matter. Any particular pantheon?"

"Pardon?"

"Pantheon," he repeated. "Different cultures used to worship multiple gods. A grouping of gods worshipped by a single society is called a pantheon."

I stared at him as we walked into a small room lined with bookshelves. Each shelf was near-bursting full of books.

"How do you know all this shit?" I asked him.

Shadow scanned the titles on the shelves. "After we settled here, I asked Gunner to find me books on every subject that used to be taught in schools." He glanced at me over his shoulder. "I was never truly educated, as you know. I figured this way, I could learn some of the things I missed."

"It's an impressive collection," I mused, eying one shelf that was all about US military history. "Maybe we can use these to educate the kids when they're old enough."

Shadow coughed with surprise. "If you think they'll be useful, I'll be happy to loan them out. I have multiple copies of a few things."

"I'll talk to Andrea. She homeschools their little ones now. I bet she can make a curriculum for when they're older, too." I scratched my jaw. "But to answer your original question, no. I don't know what pantheon I'm looking for."

"What about names of gods? Any in particular?" Shadow began pulling books from shelves and setting them on a side table.

I swallowed, meeting the bright eyes of my dog. "Hades, Horus, and Freyja."

Shadow looked at me again with surprise. "You all named your animals after gods without knowing their origins?"

"We didn't name them. They told us their names."

This wasn't information I planned to spread to the whole club, but I trusted Shadow. Maybe he didn't have an animal bond, but with his inhuman strength and uncanny ability to see in the dark, I'd place all bets on him being something not-quite human as well.

Just as I thought, he seemed surprised, but not more than that. After a bit more shelf-scanning, he placed an impressive stack of books onto a side table. "These are all the books I have on ancient mythologies. You can look for the names of gods in the index in the back."

I grabbed the first book off the top of the stack, which was on the Aztec religion. One flip through the index told me I wouldn't find anything useful in there. The names of the Aztec gods were no less than twenty letters long and used too many Xs and Zs.

"They're not in this one." I set the book aside and moved onto the next one—Greek mythology.

Something about it rang a bell. Was it Mari that asked me if I took Hades' name from a Greek myth?

My pulse shot up as I scanned down the list of names in the index.

"There it is!" I declared, before running my finger across to find the page number.

"All of them?" Shadow asked me.

"No." My hands were damn near trembling as I flipped to the section in the book. "Just Hades."

And of fucking course. Hades was the god of death and ruler of the underworld.

"The gates of the underworld were guarded by his three-headed dog, Cerberus," I read aloud, before sliding my gaze over to *my* Hades. The damn mutt was goofing off, rolling around on his back on the floor.

"I found Horus," Shadow announced, showing me another book. "The falcon-headed god of the sky."

"For the Greeks too?"

"No," Shadow shook his head. "The ancient Egyptians." He sucked in a hard breath and nearly dropped the book he was holding.

"What's gotten into you?" I asked.

"There's...a story here." He shoved his hair back, odd-colored eyes moving rapidly over the page. "Horus battled with another god, Set, and lost his eye in the process." A hand floated up to the scarred side of his face. "I didn't lose my eye, but was blinded before being able to see with it again."

I looked back down at my book, reading more thoroughly on Hades rather than skimming like I just did. What I read legitimately made me drop the book. "Fuck me, this shit is freaky."

"What?" Shadow stared at me.

I looked back at my dog, still acting like a fool on the ground, twisting on his back with his tongue lolling out.

"Hades kidnapped his wife, Persephone."

The dog finally rolled over to his belly, barked once, then grinned at us.

"She was his prisoner at first but," I shook my head in utter bewilderment, "they eventually fell in love."

"Like you and Mariposa," Shadow breathed, voicing the connection I didn't dare say myself.

"What the fuck is happening here?" I raked my fingers over my scalp.

"Freyja." Shadow picked up another book and frantically flipped through it. "What can we find out about her?"

I went over to Hades and kneeled down to his level. "Anything you want to say about this?"

No response, but a big doggy smile, naturally. Still looking through the book, Shadow let out an amused huff.

"What'd you find?" I asked.

"Freyja drove a chariot pulled by two cats," he reported. "And she slept with four dwarves for some rare necklace."

My stomach turned in on itself. Clearly, Mari having a cat companion was no coincidence.

I recalled Noelle telling me her dream, supposedly from Daren, that Mari would love four men. So aside from me, Jandro, and Gunner, she would bring in one more. I couldn't even speculate as to who that was —there were no other men I trusted enough to be with her. It wasn't even the mysterious fourth person I was concerned about—but the other part Noelle told me.

That if I killed one of Mari's lovers, she'd never forgive me. So typical of Daren's uncanny ability, to give me a warning with no context whatsoever. Not that I believed my dead little brother was actually communicating with Noelle. Hades' amused smile and head tilt seemed to disagree with me, though. Like this vessel of an ancient god, or whatever the fuck, could actually hear what I was thinking.

"Anything else?" I rose from the floor, turning my back to the dog as I meandered back to the stack of books.

"She's the goddess of erm, love, lust, beauty, sex, and fertility." Shadow appeared deeply uncomfortable with all of those words. "She takes half of those slain in battle to her heavenly field."

"What happens to the other half?"

"They go to Valhalla, Odin's hall."

"And what pantheon is this?"

"Norse mythology."

"Gods from three different pantheons, all right here," I muttered under my breath. "How the fuck does that make any sense?"

"I'm not sure." Shadow held his chin, eyes darting over the open books spread out in front of us. "I wonder if it even matters."

My eyes narrowed at him. "What do you mean?"

"Death, the underworld," his finger tapped down on the section about Hades, "The sky and sun above," the finger moved to Horus's book, "and between the two, life and love." His fingertip made a small caress over Freyja's depiction. "What do they all have in common?"

"I don't fuckin' know," I groaned, rubbing my forehead.

"All these...human experiences were personified by ancient cultures. Deified, you could say. They were given a name, an image, and were worshipped."

"So?"

"Every ancient culture had a deity associated with death, the sky, and with fertility and beauty. Their names are different and they may be depicted slightly differently, but they're all the same ideas." Shadow approached another bookshelf, scanning the titles before pulling out one particularly ancient-looking volume. "I read about something called a collective unconscious by this psychologist in the early nineteen-hundreds."

"Give me the watered down version, if you will." My head was already spinning.

"Okay, so," Shadow paused in his rapid page-flipping. "The collective unconscious is this *something* that connects all humans. It's what unites us, in a sense. We're fascinated with death, we get, er, anxious about being accepted, we seek out, uh, love and partners—all of that is part of the human experience. The theory is that it's the collective unconscious that drives those desires."

"Okay," I sighed, rubbing my temples. "What does that have to do with gods?"

Shadow closed the book and put it back on the shelf. "Well, one theory is the collective unconscious is the divine part of humanity."

"I'm not following," I admitted.

He cocked his head toward the table where the open mythology books laid. "Did those ancient cultures create their gods, or were the gods inside them all along?"

"Fuck me. You really expect me to answer that?"

"It's just something to ponder. We can't prove whether the collective unconscious is real or not. But if they just made gods up, they would be more unique to that culture. We wouldn't have divine beings associated with love, death, and whatever else across *all* cultures."

"So say, the god of death," I turned toward my dog, who cocked his head at me, "he exists across all of humanity, all cultures. He's just given different names."

"That is the basic theory, yes."

Glancing back at Shadow, I tossed him a smirk. "You're a lot smarter than you put off, dude. I had no idea you knew half of this history-psychology shit."

"Ah—um, thank you, President."

"It's Reaper," I reminded him. "You earned the respect of calling me by name a long time ago." Crossing my arms, I turned in a slow circle to take in his library again. "Mari would get a kick out of this, I bet. She likes research, pursuing knowledge and all that."

"She's welcome here anytime," Shadow said, his dark eye brightening.

"Really?" I didn't hide my surprise. "Her presence doesn't bother you like other women, huh?"

"No, I uh..." A deeper shade of red crept up his face as he stammered. "I'm comfortable around her. It felt strange at first, but I think she's helping me get better at this in general." He gestured a hand between us. "You know, talking. Socializing."

"You have been more talkative lately," I observed. "Not a Chatty Cathy by any means, but I've noticed the change, Shadow. Your whole demeanor is more confident around people now."

"Thank you, Pres—ah, Reaper."

A sudden growl from Hades startled us both.

The dog lunged for the window, hackles raised and teeth bared. A deep coldness settled over me. I hadn't seen him act like that since Mari was kidnapped at the market.

"What is it?" I followed him to the window to look, but saw nothing amiss.

Hades barked menacingly, then abruptly whined, rubbing a paw over his snout.

"Do you smell that?" Shadow cracked the window open.

I felt it in my throat first, like someone shoved sandpaper down my gullet, then saw it outside.

"Shut all the windows!" I rasped before a dry cough overtook me, my lungs already heaving for fresh air. "Do you have gas masks?" My eyes started to water, like someone rubbed peppers into them.

"I'll get them." Shadow coughed into his arm before running out of the room.

Outside, I watched the small canisters rolling over the street, releasing dense, fluffy smoke that burned the inside of my lungs and made my eyes water. Tear gas. Someone was attacking us *again*.

And then an explosion knocked me off of my feet.

JANDRO

I pulled the garage door down with a heavy clank of metal on concrete. Wiping my brow, I locked it securely before heading down the driveway.

Mari would be at Tessa's house until later, checking on her and the baby, while helping around the house, so I meandered to the front gate where I knew Gunner would be posted.

He and I were always cool, though not especially close. We disagreed more often than not, but respected each other enough to not start shit. Because of our differing opinions, Reaper often listened to us in equal measure. He balanced both of our viewpoints before coming to his own conclusion.

Reaper had always been my brother. I knew him almost as well as myself. In contrast, my friendship with Shadow grew out of him having no one else to help him lead a somewhat-normal life. So even though I knew the big guy for the shortest amount of time, I felt closer to him than Gunner.

Now that Gunner was part of our little love-rectangle, I felt an inkling to spend more time with him. Just to kick back as a couple of dudes who loved the same woman.

A screech and the feathered bullet flying over my head alerted

Gunner to my approach. Or more likely, he saw me coming from down the street as soon as I closed the garage.

"Vice president," the posted guards mumbled in greeting as I approached the front gate.

"Just come to bullshit with your boss," I announced, shielding my eyes to look up at Gunner, sitting on the edge of the brick wall surrounding our compound.

The blonde Demon jerked his head at me in invitation to join him, a black cigarette between his lips. "Come on up, VP."

I grabbed the wrought-iron bars of the gate, hauling myself up and scooting onto the pale, sandstone bricks next to him.

"Smoke?" Gunner held his soft pack out to me.

"Sure. Thanks, bro."

He lit us both, then leaned back to address his posted guard. "Y'all nosy fucks can keep an eye on shit over there." He pointed at unguarded areas of the perimeter to the guys who'd been coming in closer to smoke, chat, bullshit.

They returned to their posts and Gunner exhaled a white cloud of smoke. "They're bored," he sighed. "Nothing's come near us for weeks. They're getting lazy, but I can only bark so much if I don't know what we're guarding against."

"You been rotating shifts?" I blew smoke out through my nose.

"Yeah, as much as I can. Problem is, we just don't have enough people for a compound this big. I can't exactly have guards twenty-four seven, then give 'em a week off for R&R."

"Reaper being extremely selective about who joins has only been good for the club," I reminded him.

"Yeah, I get it. This place is just kinda big for our britches, don'tcha think? We've got like what, ten empty houses? Mari's office was just a storage closet before Reaper made it a mission to get a medic."

"It's what we got. We'd be fools to give this place up." I took another drag. "Me and Shadow don't run into each other at home if we don't have to. I even got room for my chickens."

Gunner huffed out a dry laugh, exhaling smoke. "You and those damn chickens."

"They're great, dude. Low-maintenance care, free eggs. They walk around like funky little dinosaurs. Chela even jumped into my lap the other day."

"They make a great snack for falcons," he grinned.

"You keep that damn bird away from my girls. Plenty of ground squirrels and shit for Horus to eat."

"Yeah, yeah."

I flicked ash off the end of my cig. "So how are things?"

He lifted an eyebrow. "What *things* are you referring to?"

"You know, things in general." I blew out more smoke. "With the new woman in your life, for instance."

"She hasn't told you everything?" His voice revealed some surprise.

"Nah. Mari tends to keep the one-on-one stuff private. Not *everything* has to be shared, you know."

Gunner turned a thoughtful gaze to the horizon. "I guess I didn't really think about that part."

"I didn't either, 'til just now, really. Lots of things to learn and discover about sharing a woman." Now finished with my smoke, I stubbed it out on the rock wall. "So how *are* you handling it?"

He didn't answer for a time, just smoked pensively while watching the horizon like some damn romantic cowboy. "Good," he answered finally. "Like, I'm kind of amazed at just how good and easy it is to be with her."

"See?" I nudged his arm. "I told you, dude. It's not always easy, of course. Especially now that she has three of us to consider. But she's got a way of making you feel like the only man in her life, right?"

"Yeah," he admitted. "That whole day we spent together, I kept feeling like I had to hold onto it. To savor being alone with her because it would come about so rarely."

"Nah. Even when we're all together, her connection with each of us is pretty special. It takes getting used to, but it's worth it."

"I'm starting to see that." He barked out a laugh as he tossed his cigarette butt. "Listen to us fucking saps. I'm glad I told my guys to go away."

I looked over both shoulders to make sure no one was in earshot, but still lowered my voice. "Now, be honest. What did you think of the whole group bedroom scenario?"

"Huh, I forgot you were in the shower so you missed the ending." He rubbed a hand down his face to hide his smirk. "Honestly, it was fucking hot, man. She wanted to watch me finish myself off, so I got closer to her. Reaper was pounding her and, well...I made a fucking mess of myself."

"Atta boy." I slapped his back. "Other dicks in the bedroom don't have to be weird, if you don't let them."

"Guess not," he chuckled before a stern mask took over his face. "Be right back," he muttered, then his eyes rolled back until only the whites were visible.

"Aw, fuck," I grumbled, grabbing his arm to prevent him from tumbling over the wall. "This can't be good." I looked up in search of Horus, knowing Gunner was looking through the falcon at that very moment.

His blue irises rolled back into view less than a minute later, as did the control of his body. "We need guns and gas masks," he hissed, climbing down the wall. "We're about to be attacked."

In disbelief, I looked out at the empty, silent desert beyond our walls. "Gunner, what the fuck?"

But he was already running along the perimeter, whistling loudly and yelling to the guards, "Rifles up, fuckers! Goggle and mask up! This is not a drill! Our enemy is airborne!"

They sprung into action, following their captain's orders, but looked just as confused as me.

"Gunner, where—"

Something small and metallic whizzed by my head. Another hit me square in the back and clattered down the wall to the ground. A dense, white smoke began pouring out of the canister. By the time I felt the stinging in my eyes and throat, it was too late.

Hundreds more of the tear gas canisters sailed over the walls, seemingly out of nowhere. Coughs and cries of confusion filled the air. Even without the burning in my lungs and eyes, visibility was reduced to nearly nothing as smoke filled the air.

I scrambled off the wall, covering my nose and mouth with my shirt as I headed for the clubhouse. We needed guns. We weren't getting choked and blinded for no fucking reason. I had to reach the armory.

Half-blinded by tears and stinging pain in my eyes, I spotted my woman running to rush out of the clubhouse while I, and a dozen others, crowded the doorway to rush in.

"Jandro, what's happening?" Mari moved away from the door, flattening herself against the wall to let the stampede of people through.

"Attack," I rasped through my body-wracking coughs. "Smoke and tear gas. Keep everyone insi—"

A deafening *BOOM* rocked the building, knocking me off my feet and directly into her. Hysterical screams from outside made my blood run cold.

"You okay?" I turned my head to cough into my arm, which I braced against the wall to not crush her.

"Yes, but we need to help those still outside!"

"Follow me," I coughed. "Armory."

I grabbed her hand and pulled her down the hallway, my sight and breathing only marginally better away from the smoke. Two more blasts went off, rattling the windowpanes and creating even more chaos outside. I could only hope Gunner and his guys were handling it out there.

Our armory was once the cash vault of this ritzy, gated community. Nothing was left in it when we took over the place, but the impenetrable steel and concrete walls made it a great place to store guns.

"You know how to shoot now, right?" I held a rifle out to Mari.

"Um, kind of."

"Good enough. We need you." I showed her how to load the Mini-14, then shoved it into her hands, along with a spare box of ammo.

Next, I pulled out the box of gas masks and dug until I found one of the smaller sizes for her. "Put that on and adjust it as needed. The bottom part needs to seal to your skin."

I found one for me and put it on, grateful that I shaved that morning, as the mask created a seal. At that point, more of the guys started coming into the armory and taking their own guns and masks, their eyes red and noses runny from the gas.

"Make sure the women and kids are safe," I instructed, my voice muffled by the mask. "Have them hide under tables, beds, in closets, maybe. We don't know if they're bombing houses or what."

"It looks like grenades, VP," Slick reported. "Being dropped off by drones."

"Son of a bitch," I cursed. "Then we need to shoot down some motherfucking drones, don't we?"

A chorus of bloodthirsty cheers answered me, their guns raised in the air and red eyes narrowed with vengeance behind their masks. These were the Steel Demons I knew. This attack would not maim us.

I turned to Mari. "Stay by the building to help people find their way in. If you see something flying, shoot it. If you see anyone without a Demons patch, shoot them."

She nodded, but before I could leave, reached out and clutched the front of my shirt in her small fist. "I love you. Be careful."

I wrapped a hand around the back of her head, touching our foreheads together as best I could without my mask knocking into hers. "Can't kiss you now, but I will later, *Mariposita. Te amo.*"

"You better." She stepped back, brandished her rifle in front of her, and cocked it. "Now go."

Damn if I didn't get just a little bit turned on, seeing my woman dressed up like a post-apocalyptic vigilante. I had to give it to her good, after we were done with all this shit.

Leading my guys, I jogged out of the building into the war zone outside. You'd think there was a forest fire nearby, the smoke hung thicker than coastal fog. The air through my respirator was now just mildly irritating, rather than choking.

"Spread out," I commanded. "Stick to walls and what you can see. Don't run out into the smoke unless you see someone who needs help. If you do, send them back to Mariposa."

"Drone! Three o'clock!" Slick raised his rifle in the air and fired off a shot. A choking, sputtering sound like a dying engine roared above us until a white object crashed into the street ahead of us.

"Wait, wait, wait!" I screamed at my guys who started running toward it.

My instincts were right. The crashed aircraft exploded, sending burned metal and melted plastic flying in all directions.

"Nice shot, bro." I clapped Slick's shoulder. "Be careful where you're shooting, though. Make sure no one's close by or under. That goes for all of you."

They gave me an affirmative and we kept moving. My eyes strained through the smoke that never seemed to clear up. White drones camouflaged well against this bullshit. Fucking Tash thought of everything.

I saw no signs of Gunner, so he and his guys still had to be at the front lines. My stomach clamped with worry, but I couldn't get to him just yet. I had to make sure no one in the residential areas was still out, possibly hurt and unable to move.

Keeping my head ducked low, I crept along the sidewalk toward my own house. Another blast sent my ears ringing, and I covered my head and face against a shower of dirt and rocks. The grenade had gone off in the small hill beyond the retaining wall next to me.

I scanned the smoke-filled sky, listening for the telltale buzzing of the drone through my ringing ears. Only by chance, I saw it as it swerved to head in another direction, and took it down with two shots. The white aircraft didn't explode on impact, which told me these things were only carrying one grenade at a time.

"Jandro!"

Two dark figures ran toward me, their features so obscured by the smoke that I didn't recognize them until they were right next to me.

"What the ever-loving fuck is going on?" Reaper roared behind his mask.

Hades hunkered down close to his side, an extension of his human master. Shadow loomed over all of us, his hair pulled back so the mask could seal to his face. The big guy's odd-colored eyes focused skyward.

Another blast went off and the three of us crouched low on the other side of the retaining wall. Shadow raised his rifle and fired off one shot, picking off the drone I had no idea was there.

"You can see through this shit?" I asked him.

"Not well," he admitted. "I can make out rough shapes in the smoke, though."

"I want his fucking head." Reaper was practically frothing at the mouth, rage in his eyes like I'd never seen before. "Tash is right outside our walls, I just fucking know it. He's sitting back and smiling. I want to hear him scream."

"Bro, take a breath." I clapped hard on Reaper's shoulder to get his attention. "We're blind right now. We've got to stay calm and get our people out of the way of these blasts. Then we can go after him."

Hades barked suddenly and took off running, his black fur becoming little more than a shadow in the smoke.

"Someone's in trouble. Mari!" Reaper bellowed.

"Stay back." I shoved a hand against his chest. "I just came from there. I'll get her. You two keep picking off these drones, and sweep the residential areas."

I took off after Hades before he could argue. Reaper wasn't in a good state of mind right then. His obsession with bringing Tash down got in the way of his rational thinking. If he saw Mari in trouble, he'd positively lose it.

A blast knocked me to my knees. Hard asphalt bit into my palms, but the harrowing scream up ahead made the sting feel like nothing.

"Mari!"

I hurried to get my feet underneath me, but felt like I was moving through sludge, no matter what.

Dark shapes lay motionless on the ground up ahead and I still couldn't move fast enough. *Not her*, I begged whatever powers were listening. *Please not her.*

"Jandro, help!"

Her voice. Raspy and full of terror, but it was hers.

I dropped to the ground, only seeing her. "Why aren't you at the clubhouse? I told you to stay there!"

"It's Dallas!" Mari sobbed. "He blocked the blast from hitting them. Help me, I can't move him."

Only then did my gaze drop to the motionless figure on the ground. The cries underneath the limp body were barely discernible through the ringing in my ears. Together, Mari and I turned him over, rolling Dallas off of his two hysterically sobbing children underneath.

"Hey, guys." I tried to keep my voice calm as I moved between the kids and their father's body. "I need to get you inside, okay?"

"Dad!" Avery, his daughter, shrieked. "Why's Dad not moving?! I want my dad!"

Blocking their view with my arms, I looked at Mari over my shoulder. Leaning over Dallas, her hands were slick with blood as she searched for a pulse. When she caught my gaze, she gave a tiny shake of her head, her eyes glittering with tears.

Fuck.

Fuck everything about this.

"Daaaad!" the kids wailed, pushing on my arms as they tried to get around me.

"We need to get you guys inside," I repeated, numbness taking over me.

Dallas was dead.

No fucking way, how could we lose *him?*

Hades' growl pulled me back to the present. He grabbed Dallas's son by his shirt and started yanking him back toward the clubhouse.

"Mari, get them inside."

"We can't just leave him out here—"

"We can't leave *them* unprotected either. Go!" An increasingly loud buzz alerted me to another approaching drone. I jumped to my feet to make a shield over them, scanning the sky with my rifle ready. "Get them out of here! Get somewhere safe!"

"Jandro, look out!"

I didn't feel the blast. First I was on my feet, looking for the drone through the smoke. Then I was either falling or flying, maybe both. And then nothing.

Blackness surrounded me, like I was floating in a pool of ink. I felt weightless, even bodiless. I tried to move my fingers and toes, but couldn't feel them in this space.

"Fuck no. Am I dead?"

Was I actually speaking, or just thinking? I couldn't tell.

If this was death, how fucking boring.

I just hoped Mari and the kids were okay. The guys would take care of her. Poor Dallas. Would I see him here? It didn't seem like anyone else was here but me.

Something appeared to shift and materialize in the blackness. I couldn't see clearly, but I could make out the rough shape of a man in front of me. He had no discernible features, but the solidness of his presence was a small comfort in this weird, floating blackness.

"You shouldn't be here," the figure said in a deep masculine voice, almost with an air of snobbery.

"Well, excuse me," I huffed. "I didn't exactly intend to stumble in here, wherever the fuck this is. Death? Hell? Some signage would be helpful, you know."

"Neither. You're close, though." The figure seemed to cock its head to the side, like a dog. "But it's not your time, Jandro."

"Sweet. Send me on back then." I tried to ignore how unsettling it was that this figure knew my name.

"I can't *send* you anywhere. You have a choice to make—fight and live, or give up and pass on. Mariposa is doing everything in her power to save you right now. The least you can do is fight for your own life."

How the fuck was I supposed to respond to that? I was hanging by a thread, and my girl was probably scared shitless.

"Who are you?"

Not that I could see anything, but I *felt* like the figure smiled.

"I'm Hades."

"Hades?" I repeated. "Hades, the dog?"

"Part-time dog. Full-time lord of the underworld."

"...What...the..."

"I suggest you make your decision soon, Jandro. I would hate to open my gates to you prematurely. Unless," he paused, his tone changing as if talking to someone else, "you'd be interested in taking him, dear? He did fall in battle, after all."

A second figure materialized, this one definitely feminine. Like the masculine one, I only saw the rough outline of a waist and hips to die for. She may have had long hair, I couldn't tell. If the weight of their presences didn't feel so heavy and real, I would've been convinced I was hallucinating.

Fuck, for all I knew I *was* hallucinating. Didn't mean it wasn't real on some level.

"No, darling, I can't take him," the feminine figure protested. "It's far too soon. He's too young and handsome."

"Precisely what I was saying," Hades muttered.

"And who are you, the tooth fairy?" I asked. "An angel?"

The feminine figure chuckled, and I swore soft fingertips caressed my cheek. "Perhaps you'll recognize me with this sound?"

A rumbling purr filled the air, the fingers on my cheek now digging in like tiny claws.

"Freyja?" I whispered, dumbfounded.

"Oh, *Alejandro,*" she murmured, with a perfect Spanish accent. "You have so much love to give, beautiful children to make. You're a fighter, handsome. Fight for what matters. Don't let go yet. We'll be here when you're ready."

"Wait," I protested as both of their presences started lifting away, like anchors being pulled up. "I can't feel shit! How am I supposed to fight?"

But no answer came. Both of them were already gone.

SHADOW

"Like hell I'm going wait and see if my wife is fucking dead!"

Reaper was like a rabid dog, face twisted behind his mask with a murderous expression. I always knew he had a temper. Anyone could see the rage he carried just below the surface. In situations like these, he always unleashed it on his enemies. It was one of the reasons our club had a reputation for such violence and ruthlessness.

But today our enemy was invisible, and his rage was aimed at whoever stood between him and his woman.

"Shadow, if you don't let me go, I fucking swear I'll shoot you. She needs me!"

"Jandro has her," I reminded him, tightening my grip on his cut. "President, we need to spread out. Once everyone's contained, we need to get on the rooftops. Get above the smoke so we can—"

A nearby blast sent us crouching to the ground as pebbles and debris showered down on us.

"Fuck, I think that was my house." Reaper waved his hand in front of his face, trying to clear the smoke, to no avail. "Noelle might be inside."

"Go." I slapped his shoulder. "Check on her. I'll swing around to the front of the compound."

"Find Mari. Please," he begged. "I need to know she's okay."

"I will, president." Truth be told, I too found myself concerned about the pretty medic.

It shocked me, this burning need to see for myself that she was unharmed. I never worried about Jandro, he could take care of himself, but he was the only other person I cared about to an extent such as this. A woman I barely knew now occupied more of my headspace than my best friend of several years. This worry was unsettling.

I took off in the opposite direction as Reaper, with only the few feet of road ahead of me as my guide. The rough shapes of roofs and street-lights all looked the same in the dense fog. And with the sun blocked out, it was impossible to tell which direction I was going.

I jogged blindly down the street, trying to listen for the drone propellers, but these aircraft were nearly silent. They had to come into my line of sight before I shot them. I took down three as I ran, all with their grenades already released. Fuck, this was bad.

How long had Tash been planning this attack? Since I shot down that first drone weeks ago? Earlier?

A loud blast stopped me in my tracks. I crouched low, covering my head, my ears ringing. That one was close, probably no more than fifty feet away. The harrowing scream that followed it pushed me to my feet.

"Jandro!" a woman's voice wailed. Mariposa's voice.

I pumped my arms and legs hard, sprinting toward her voice at top speed. My heart felt like it was going to burst from my chest, and it had nothing to do with how hard I was running.

Dark shapes on the ground slowly became clearer as I got closer. Some shapes were frantically moving, others lay eerily still. "Who's there?" Mariposa waved her hand in front of her face as Reaper had, her hair wild and tangled.

"It's me, Shadow." I reached out and touched her shoulder, not real-izing it until I felt her arm trembling under my hand. "Are you hurt?"

"No, but—"

Ear-splitting cries cut her off, coming from the ground near my feet. I took my hand from her shoulder and looked down. Two children huddled together, screaming, next to two motionless bodies.

"Jandro!" I lowered down, laying my rifle next to my barely recognizable friend. An overwhelming burning smell nearly gagged me through my mask.

"He's got a pulse, but it's faint." Mariposa yanked the children close to her, picking up the girl first, then holding tightly to the boy's hand. "We can't waste any time! Can you carry him to my office?"

I grabbed Jandro's limp arms and threw them over my shoulder, letting his torso slide down my back until I could hold him around his waist and legs.

"Who's the other one?" I asked Mariposa, rising to my feet.

"Dallas." She led the way back toward the clubhouse, fighting against the children who were trying to run back out to the street.

"Is he...?"

She gave me a single look that told me all I needed to know.

"I'll go back for him," I told her, shifting Jandro higher on my shoulder.

"Thank you, Shadow. Fuck, I'm really glad you showed up."

"Me too. What happened?"

"Give me a second," she huffed, pulling open the clubhouse door and yanking the kids inside.

I held the door open with my free hand, blocking the entrance with my body as Dallas's children fought, kicked, bit, and screamed at Mariposa.

"Can you take them, please?" she nearly tossed the girl in her arms to a small group of women huddled inside. "Wait until the Demons say it's safe before you take them to their mother."

Finally free of them, she ran back to me, leading me down the hall to her office.

"Dallas shielded the kids from getting hit with a blast. Then Jandro came to help, and he shielded us from another one."

"Will he survive?"

Fear was the feeling I was most familiar with. I feared pain, confined spaces, and the flashbacks that assaulted me without warning. I recognized fear in the faces of most people who looked at me. But never before had I feared losing someone I cared about.

"He will." Mariposa wasn't afraid. She was tight-lipped, determined. Maybe even angry. She reminded me of Reaper in that moment, holding back a storm with sheer will. "I'll drag him back to life, even if I have to go all Dr. Frankenstein on him."

"I like that book," I muttered, ducking in the doorway to her office to not further injure Jandro.

"Yeah? You like to read? Lay him down on his stomach for me, please."

I lowered myself to the level of her table, while she slid him carefully off of my shoulder. "Yeah, try to read anything I come across, really."

"Jesus Christ." Mariposa's attention was back on the man she loved, lying face down on her table. "Why'd you have to do that, *guapito*? I love you, but you're such a dumbass."

"Do you, um..." I watched as she cut away what little remained of his clothes, exposing the charred, raw flesh of his back. "Do you need me to do anything?"

Her eyes lifted to mine. Maybe it was the shock of everything going on, but I no longer felt uncomfortable with her looking at me.

"Can you get Dallas, please? Wrap him in a sheet and put him somewhere until, you know, until we can..."

"Yes, of course."

"Be safe out there, Shadow."

"I will, Mariposa."

I'd moved bodies before, but never one of my own brothers.

Dallas and I weren't close, but he was a good man, and a good Demon. I didn't know if there was any social etiquette to treat dead comrades a certain way, but it felt wrong to just drag him along the ground.

I found several dark sheets and wrapped him up tightly in the street. All the while I watched for more drones, and shot a few more down that came close. Most of our people seemed to be safely inside, but the drones kept coming. The teargas seemed to be dissipating now. I could see clearer, but the chemicals still itched the hell out of my eyes and sinuses.

When I finished wrapping Dallas's body, I slung him over my shoulder like I did Jandro. I placed the body in one of the empty rooms in the clubhouse and locked the door. Mourning him would have to wait.

Once he was secure, I went back down the main hall to check on Mariposa and Jandro.

"How is he?" I asked from the doorway.

She looked up from examining his back with a grim expression. "Not good. I've got fresh blood going into him, but his pulse is still weak. I can barely detect a breath. And that's got nothing to do with his burns—"

Her voice cracked and she quickly wiped her eyes with her sleeve. My chest ached at seeing her emotion. I wasn't the only one who cared about him. She loved him, and carried the burden of trying to save his life.

"He'll pull through." I walked in to stand next to her. "He's stubborn as hell, he won't let this stop him. And you're a talented medic. He's lucky to be in your hands."

She gave a weak smile. "Thanks, Shadow."

I thought of the hug she gave me. Would it be appropriate to hug her now? People hugged to comfort each other, didn't they? My fingers itched to reach out to her, to ease the worry on her face.

"Where are the others?" Mariposa asked, turning back to Jandro. "Have you seen Reaper and Gunner?"

I closed my fingers at my sides. "Reaper was checking on his sister at home when I found you. I haven't seen Gunner, but I assume he's with his guards at the front gate."

"Can you check on them for me? I should get multiple stations set up in case there are more injuries." She looked worriedly around her small office. "God, I wish I had clones of myself."

"I'll head to the front gate now." I retrieved my rifle from my holster, checking it for ammo. "I'll let your men know you're safe."

"Thank you, Shadow." Relief softened her features slightly, which eased the ache in my chest.

I looked down at Freyja, who was nuzzling Jandro's hand that hung down from the table. "Watch over your human, little one."

I had barely turned to leave when crashing sounds came from outside. Mariposa and I braced ourselves, but it didn't sound like grenade blasts.

"Stay here. Lock the door," I instructed, cocking my rifle.

Silently, I moved out into the hall with my weapon raised. Keeping it against my shoulder, I pushed the clubhouse door open and surveyed the outside. Visibility was much clearer now, I could see all the way down the street.

And three drones hovering in the air.

I took aim, curling my index finger around the trigger, when the one I set my sights on suddenly jerked to one side and dropped sharply in altitude.

"The fuck?"

Out of nowhere, it simply dropped out of the sky and crashed to earth. The two others did the same, one after another.

"Yo, you seeing this?" someone yelled.

I looked to the left to see Reaper running up the street toward me.

"She's fine," I told him before he could ask. "But Jandro's badly hurt. She's in her office with him."

He nodded, the relief palpable on his face. "What do you make of this?" He gestured toward the sky.

"That they're crash-landing all of a sudden? I have no idea."

The president clapped my shoulder. "I think the worst of it is over. Gunner's on his way in. Cover him at the gate, will you? We'll be with Mari."

"Yes, president."

Gunner ran past me, not a minute later, on my way to the gate. "Thanks, Shadow. A lot of the same shit, just dropping out of the sky for no reason. Keep your eyes peeled, though."

I climbed the metal rungs embedded in our perimeter wall and squinted at the landscape beyond our once-safe home. Broken drones and their parts lay strewn across the desert like some kind of robot cemetery, but nothing else seemed amiss.

"See anyone out there?" I asked Benji.

"Not a damn soul," he spat. "Some of the tear gas didn't make it over the wall, so we got faces full of it. Then, still nothing once it cleared. It was like some damn robot uprising. 'Til their batteries went out."

"That's impossible," I muttered.

The tear gas cleared up hours later, with no drones coming back to life. Near dusk, I took my mask off and filled my lungs with sweet, fresh air. In the last sliver of sunlight, I spotted movement that made me look closer.

Three figures approaching on motorcycles, with a black bird flying above them.

MARIPOSA

"Good fucking damn it, Jandro."

I wiped my face with my arm, tears and snot making a mess on my sleeve. But I couldn't stop. I wouldn't stop until I saw a fucking heartbeat on that monitor.

"Clear!" I yelled before pressing the defibrillator paddles on his chest again.

His body jumped with the jolt of electricity. But the monitors still displayed a flat line. His kissable, pillowy lips were turning blue.

"Fine, Jandro." I set the paddles aside and ripped off my gloves. "You want to play that way? You're just going to make me even more pissed off for when you wake up."

I went to my cabinet and pulled out the small glass jar of adrenaline. Ripping open a fresh needle and syringe, I stuck the lid and withdrew the highest safe amount to give a human without throwing them into cardiac arrest.

Safe was an iffy word when it came to shooting pure adrenaline, but I was desperate. We already lost Dallas. I wasn't about to lose one of my men.

"I love you," I told Jandro's lifeless body stretched out on my exam table. "But I fucking hate you right now." With that, I stuck the syringe directly into his elbow and shoved the plunger down.

Nothing happened right away, so I started up CPR on him again.

"Mari," someone said from the corner of the room. Probably Gunner, I didn't know. I had to fucking focus.

"Shut up," I responded, counting through my chest compressions before breathing into Jandro's mouth again. The butterfly necklace he gave me hung down from my throat, brushing against his chin.

Not a single cell in my body was ready to give up. I would not lose him. I'd break every single rib giving him CPR, before I let him go. But as I kept pressing down, kept giving him my air and trying to jumpstart his heart, the cold grip of fear started to creep in.

Just as I started feeling lightheaded and completely out of breath, the man on the table pulled in a ragged, desperate gasp of air.

The heart monitor beeped to life, almost too fast as Jandro choked and coughed, his body bringing in much-needed oxygen. I slid to the floor, completely drained of energy and also limp with relief. Someone pulled me back up, a solid chest and strong arms wrapping me in a hug. Leather and cloves filled my nostrils as kisses swept across my face.

"You did it, sugar." Reaper's voice was choked with emotion. "You're a fucking lifesaver."

Someone else had pulled the oxygen mask over Jandro's face, his breaths still deep and pained, but steadier as he regained consciousness. His pulse slowed gradually as blood returned the color to his face.

He pulled the oxygen mask from his mouth and looked at me.

"How long have I been out?" he rasped, barely over a whisper.

"You weren't breathing, and had no pulse, for nearly two minutes," I replied flatly. "You've sustained third degree burns on your back from the grenade. You've lost a lot of blood, required a transfusion, and might have brain damage from your lack of oxygen."

Jandro's eyebrows lifted. Most of his body was numbed from anesthesia, but he still had strength to move his head.

"You don't look too happy to see me, *bonita*."

I snapped.

Pulling myself out of Reaper's embrace, I took one long step to the VP's side, and slapped him hard across the face.

To say he was stunned would be an understatement. His jaw dropped as he clumsily raised a partially-numb hand to his cheek.

"Hey, hey." A hand squeezed my shoulder, and Gunner's soothing voice brushed across my temple. "Take it easy, baby girl."

He brought my temper down a couple notches, but I was still focused on Jandro, seeing him through red-tinted vision.

"It stops with this, Jandro." I willed my voice not to shake. "You're not taking bullets for me anymore. You're not blocking grenades with your body anymore. I need you *alive,* you fucking idiot, don't you understand?"

No fucking way in hell would he break my heart by dying on me. I wouldn't allow it. Fuck Daren's prophecy. I didn't even notice the tears spilling down my cheeks until Reaper wiped them away with a rough thumb pad.

Jandro just shook his head at my demands. "Not happening, beautiful. It was either me, or you and the kids. I wasn't about to let you or them take any force of the blast." He shifted, trying to get comfortable in the makeshift hospital bed. "Why the fuck are all of you in here anyway?" He scanned the room, seemingly noticing Reaper and Gunner at the same time. "What happened? Is it over?"

"Yeah." Reaper scrubbed a hand down his face with a sigh. "It went on for a while after Mari got you in here and tried to stabilize you. We kept picking off drones, and they just kept coming. That was, until..." He looked to Gunner, like he couldn't believe the next part of the story himself.

"Until they all just started dropping out of the sky." Gunner crossed his arms, looking just as puzzled as Reaper. "Like their controllers got switched off, or ran out of batteries or something."

Jandro stared at him, wide-eyed. "All at the same time?"

"No, but one after another pretty quickly. It was freaking weird. My guys are out combing the surrounding area right now. They couldn't have been controlled from far away."

"Did we lose anyone else besides..."

A dark, somberness fell over the room. I couldn't bear to say Dallas's name either, to refer to him in the past tense. Out of all the Steel

Demons men, he was probably the most innocent and least-deserving to be killed in such a way.

"No." Reaper's face was grim, and he couldn't bring himself to make eye contact with anyone. My heart ached for him. I knew, as president, he took Dallas's death as his personal responsibility.

"A few minor injuries, but that's all." I picked up speaking, where Reaper clearly couldn't. "The effects of the tear gas have started to wear off. It was standard law enforcement stuff. Nothing causing permanent damage, thankfully."

"Do you know how Dallas...what the cause was?"

I let out a sigh, exhaustion hanging over me like a massive load on my shoulders. "His spinal cord was severed in multiple places, which was the most likely cause. He also had massive internal bleeding, which would have killed him if the spinal damage hadn't." My gaze dropped to the floor, my head feeling incredibly heavy. "There was nothing I could do."

"Did he go...painlessly?" Gunner and Reaper both looked up at Jandro's question, as if they needed to know this too.

I nodded, trying to turn my exhausted mind away from the image that would haunt me forever. Dallas running out to shield his kids. The blast knocking me off my feet. And he, in its direct path, falling limply on top of his children. He was dead before he hit the ground.

"It was over fast," I assured my men. "He didn't suffer."

They all nodded, that morsel of information a small comfort to them.

"We need to hold a memorial for him," Reaper muttered. "A big one, with the highest honors of our club. One on par with Daren's." He scoffed dryly. "Both of the Steel Demons who've died, did so protecting others. Funny how shit works out like that." He turned to look at Hades, who'd been sitting quietly in the back of the room, as if the dog would offer an explanation. But none came.

A heavy knock pounded at my office door, rattling all of us. Reaper and I exchanged a glance.

"This is your domain, sugar. You decide if you want people in here or not."

"President." I recognized Shadow's rough, but oddly soothing voice from the other side. "I'm bringing news that we've detained three men found outside the walls."

"Come in, Shadow," I called.

The door opened, and the large man quickly filled the remaining space in the small room. Freyja, who'd been curled up asleep on my stool, woke up at the sound of his knocking, and after a quick stretch, trotted over to her favorite human. Shadow picked her up without hesitating, tucking her against his chest with his forearm as he scratched her head with his other hand.

"Hey man," Jandro greeted tiredly. "Do you have General Tash waiting for us with a bow tied around his head?"

"No. I don't know how to tie a bow." Shadow actually had to raise his voice to speak over Freyja's loud purr. "And it's not the general, regardless. It's three men from another MC."

"Great," Reaper growled. "More of the general's puppets. I hope you broke a few of their fingers? Got them started on at least thinking about talking. How many do you estimate were out there in total?"

"That's the thing," Shadow answered hesitantly. "They said they're alone, that they weren't part of the attack. They came to the front gate and allowed themselves to be detained willingly."

Everyone in the room stared at him. Except for Freyja, that is. Her eyes closed softly with blissed out relaxation in Shadow's arms. There was no place she'd rather be.

"Did they have patches?" Gunner's question cut through the silence. "What's their club name?"

"Yes. They call themselves the Sons of Odin."

Gunner and I looked at each other, clearly recalling the same three men who approached us at the cantina with his uncle's severed hand in a bag. Reaper also rocked back on his heels with surprise.

"Did one of them have a raven?" Gunner asked.

Shadow cocked his head, still scratching Freyja idly. "I spotted a black bird flying over them as they approached, yes."

"All of you, out." I made a shooing motion toward the door. "Question them. Find out what you need. I have to keep tending to this one." I jerked my head at Jandro.

Reaper chuckled, while Gunner beamed at me with a radiant smile.

They each kissed me, while Shadow reluctantly slid a very sad-looking Freyja out of his arms. Once they were gone, I put on a pair of fresh gloves and slid a hand behind Jandro's shoulder.

"You should be good and numb back here now, so let me check out this burn."

"Yes, ma'am," he groaned, using his little remaining strength to lean forward.

I pulled away the gauze I'd drenched in antibiotic ointment and did a closer inspection of his back.

"How bad is it?"

"Pretty bad," I admitted. "You're going to have extensive scarring. You might need skin grafts. I'm going to need to keep you on IV antibiotics for at least a week. I already gave you a tetanus shot while you were out, but the risk of infection is still high. You'll need to let me know if you get a high fever."

He looked at me over his shoulder. "You really mad at me, *Mariposita*?"

"Pissed," I snapped. "The last thing I need is any one of you dying on me."

He scratched his head. "I was really only gone for a couple minutes, huh?"

"Yeah. I wasn't about to quit, but I started getting scared that you might..."

"Not come back?"

"Yeah," I sniffed, picking hunks of dead tissue and debris out of his back. "And that would've sucked even worse, 'cause I'd never get a chance to let you know how pissed I was."

Jandro laughed softly. "I'm sorry to piss you off, babe. But I'm not going to stop protecting you. I don't care if I come out on death's doorstep, or end up looking like Shadow—"

"Okay first of all, that's rude," I growled. "He's your friend. He carried your ass in here while I wrangled Dallas's kids. Second of all, there's nothing wrong with how he looks."

"I didn't mean—"

He flinched with a hiss, then stilled. I had most likely probed closed to a nerve with my tweezers. It was impossible for the local anesthesia to reach absolutely everywhere. His back was such a mess regardless, I no longer could tell where I had numbed him or not.

"You're right," he finally voiced softly. "That was messed up of me to say. Sorry, babe. My head's all messed up." He leaned forward, placing his head in his hands. "I keep thinking I saw, or rather *heard*, Hades."

"He was barking his head off for a while," I mumbled absently, steadfast on my task. The stainless steel pan nearby was quickly filling up with dead chunks of Jandro.

"No, I mean like, *speaking* to me. As a person."

I froze, my tweezers hovering in midair. The memory of a man-shaped apparition sitting at the end of the bed came to the forefront of my mind.

"What did he say?"

"That it wasn't my time yet." Jandro raised his head, resting his chin on his hands. "He told me I had a choice—let go or fight. He would open the gates for me if I let go, but it would be too early." My highly-medicated lover turned to look at me over his shoulder, pupils wide. "Then Freyja shows up and agrees with him. How much oxygen did I have to lose to see that shit?"

"Freyja?" I squeaked. "*My* Freyja talked to you?"

"Well, not your cat. It was some lady. But all I could see was a rough outline, like through fog."

"What did she say?" I demanded, moving in front of him. "What *exactly* did she say, Jandro?"

"Um," he scratched his head. "I had a lot of love to give and beautiful kids to make, so I couldn't die yet. Something along those lines."

"Love and fertility," I realized, muttering the words under my breath.

Reaper had to know about this. I knew he went to see if Shadow had any books on the gods who seemed to present themselves to us. It was right before the attack and I didn't have the chance to ask if he found out anything. Even without knowing, I had no doubt that Jandro really did communicate with Hades and Freyja on the brink of death. I suspected it for weeks, and this confirmed it.

Gods were talking to us. And protecting us.

"*Mariposita,*" Jandro cooed, reaching for my hands. "What's wrong? You look like you've seen a ghost."

I let out a sheepish laugh, closing my fingers around his. "I don't even know how to begin to explain this to you—"

"Something's watching out for us, huh?" he whispered. "Something bigger than us. And they came to us through those animals following you all around."

I blinked at him. "How did you—"

"Reaper doesn't keep anything from me. I've noticed the strange things here and there. Plus," he smirked, "I talked to the source myself. How many guys can say that?"

"Reaper and I have heard Hades," I admitted. "I've heard Freyja only once. Guess I'm just waiting for Horus to say hello now."

"Yeah, he was strangely absent from the conversation," Jandro mused. "But yeah, don't ask *how* I know, but they were real, Mari. I joke about losing oxygen, but they were as real as you or me."

"And if it weren't for them," I leaned in close, "you might not be here now to hear how pissed off I am."

"Still, huh?" he chuckled. "I take it you don't want to practice making some beautiful kids right now?"

"No." I moved to his back and picked up my tweezers, resuming my cleaning of his burn.

"No? Your goddess said we should!"

"Don't care. Still mad."

"That's alright, babe." He turned, aiming a kiss at me. "You can hate-fuck me later."

GUNNER

I twirled my favorite hunting knife in my fingers as Shadow led us down the hall. Horus clicked his beak, talons squeezing into my shoulder. I swore I could feel his frustration, or maybe I was just projecting my own.

He barely flew during the attack—the tear gas was too thick even for his vision. He was able to get above the smoke clouds, but still couldn't chase the drones that were in the thick of it. My fly boy was almost as blind as we were, and I knew that pissed him off.

Those drones had to have infrared sensors on them. That was the only explanation as to how they were able to drop grenades so close to people. Thankfully, my guys were ready and had plenty of cover. Their ears would be ringing for a few days, but that was a blessing compared to what Dallas got.

Fuck. I stopped my knife twirling and tightened my grip on the handle. Losing him was huge, a wound that the Steel Demons would feel for months, if not years. I barely thought about Python, but Dallas was just a good dude. It didn't feel fair. Why couldn't it have been Big G?

Reaper stopped Shadow and I a few feet away from the holding room where the Sons of Odin were being kept.

"Tell me exactly what happened," he instructed the big guy.

"I was overseeing the scouting team, as you ordered," Shadow reported. "As the smoke cleared, I saw three men approaching the front gate on bikes. They claimed they were not part of the attack, but happened upon it and stopped it. We stripped them of their weapons, cuffed them, and I came straight to you."

Reaper listened intently with his arms folded. After Shadow finished, he looked toward Hades as if waiting for some input from the dog. Whether he got it or not, he continued on to the holding room with me and Shadow right behind him.

"Well, let's meet our saviors, or see if they need to meet their maker. Gentlemen?" He pulled the door open and stepped aside, allowing Shadow and I inside first.

"Youngblood," T-Bone's familiar, gravelly voice greeted me. "Good to see you again, although this isn't the welcome we expected from the Steel Demons."

Reaper ignored him. "These the ones you met at the cantina?"

"Yeah." I studied all three of them, sitting with their arms and legs cuffed to metal chairs. "These are them."

"Where's that pretty little brunette you had with you?" T-Bone was in the mood to be a loudmouth apparently. "Gotta say I'm disappointed she's not in the welcoming committee—"

My knife was in my hand. And then it wasn't. No one saw a thing until the *thunk* alerted the whole room that my blade was half embedded in the wall directly behind our new guests.

And a small cut on T-Bone's cheek began to bleed.

"Sorry, I didn't catch that. You want to ask about our woman again?" I gestured between me and Reaper, who was trying his damn hardest not to smile.

All the bravado dropped out of the Sons right then. Their jaws clenched, throat muscles working with nervous swallows. It was one thing to give *me* shit, but disrespecting our president's property was not a road they wanted to go down. In all likelihood, they'd probably heard stories about Reaper's kills, including Python.

"Didn't mean nothing by it," T-Bone backpedaled. "She ain't my type, anyway. Youngblood, on the other hand..." He trailed off, eyes taking me in appreciatively from head to toe.

It didn't completely surprise me. I got that look from women, as well as men on occasion. What I didn't expect was T-Bone's two club brothers to slide narrow-eyed gazes over at him. It looked like jealousy.

"Enough," Reaper snapped, grabbing an empty chair and spinning backwards to sit in front of them. "Y'all are gonna tell me how you just *happened* upon our club while we were in the middle of an attack."

"Like I told your big friend there," T-Bone nodded at Shadow, "we weren't part of it. We stopped it. You're fucking welcome, by the way."

"How convenient," Reaper sneered. "How'd you do it? And for that matter, why?"

Hades growled at his side, showing his teeth off to the captives. Horus screeched on my shoulder, spreading his wings threateningly as he leaned forward. Shadow stood with his hands clasped in front of him, ever the loyal sentry. I swept my arms back by my sides, showing off the silver gleam of the 9mm under my cut.

Forget the good cop, bad cop routine from the movies. We were all fucking bad.

T-Bone didn't look scared, though. He just dropped all the cockiness and decided to give it to us straight.

"I saw you, Reaper," he began ominously. "At the remains of our clubhouse."

"Did you now?"

"I saw the little memorials you made with the personal objects. You paid respect to my fallen brothers and I thought, that's a man I can ally with. We're all that's left." He jerked his chin to indicate the three of them tied up. "And we need all the help we can get to rebuild."

"Why'd you confront me with my uncle's hand?" I demanded. "Did that have anything to do with your place burning down?"

T-Bone leveled his gaze at me, a predatory smile growing on his face. "Oh, it has *everything* to do with it."

"Don't leave us in suspense now," Reaper growled.

"Governor Youngblood reached out to our main employer, Governor Vance—"

"Of what territory?"

"Four Corners," T-Bone snarled. "Ain't a big territory, but it's essential. Blink and you'll miss it."

"And what do you do for this governor?"

"The usual shit," T-Bone rumbled. "Patrol and protection. Inspection and oversight of trade. Do you want me to get to the point, or not?"

"So you're a good lap dog to politicians," I sneered. "Sure, go on."

"It's not like that." Dyno, the road captain, spoke up for the first time. "Vance doesn't do those power games. His trade is fair, he doesn't keep slaves, and no one goes hungry in Four Corners. But everyone wants a piece of the good thing he's got, so he employed us. Paid fucking well, I might add."

"So he loaned you to Uncle Jerry because...?"

"He gave us the choice," T-Bone picked up again. "It was a temporary contract with a fat payout. We'd been itching to ride somewhere new, break up the routine, so we said why the fuck not?"

"Did Vance know Gunner's uncle?" Reaper asked.

"Not well, I don't think. They'd never done business before, to my knowledge. It sounded like Vance was open to a trade agreement if our contract went well."

"I see," Reaper mused. "Go on."

"So we ride to Colorado—"

"Jerriton," I mumbled.

"Whatever. We get there, and this guy is living like a king. He's like Tony Montana, or some shit."

"Tell me about it." I rubbed my forehead.

"He had a lot to say about you," T-Bone's gaze narrowed at me. "It was pretty clearly a delusion, but he was convinced his golden nephew would fill his shoes one day. The heir to the Youngblood legacy."

"And you probably saw by my reaction to his severed hand, that I want no part in that shit."

"Let's hurry this shit up," Reaper sighed. "How did y'all go from working for him, to cutting his hand off and getting your place torched?"

"Right. The job itself went without a hitch. We escorted a general's troops up from the south—"

"New Mexico?" I barked. "They call it New Ireland, now?"

"Fuck, if you don't quit interrupting me. Yes, New Ireland."

I slapped my palms together and looked pointedly at Reaper. I fucking *knew* it. Uncle Jerry thought he was getting a cut of that land, but Tash would fuck him over, just like he did everyone else. Under the guise of being allies, Tash had invaded my uncle instead.

"Go on," Reaper implored T-Bone.

"Yeah, we finished the job. Went to collect our pay." He sucked his lip between his teeth. "Fucker wouldn't let us leave."

"Wouldn't *let* you?" I repeated. "How does an MC worth its salt *let* someone else control where they're going?"

"Your uncle took us prisoner," Dyno spat. "Those troops we escorted barricaded him in that mansion. And he ordered *his* people not to let us out of our wing. We'd be shot on sight if we were let out."

Reaper and I exchanged another long, narrowed glance. It felt like sheer, dumb luck that Uncle Jerry let me walk away when he did. Maybe because I came alone, and one biker wasn't enough of a personal guard detail. That, or some small part of him still cared about his family enough to let me make my own decisions. I'd never know now. But if I had gone up there at a different time, maybe with more guys to back me up, we might have met the same fate as the Sons of Odin.

"What did my uncle want from you?" I asked when the Sons fell silent.

"Who the fuck knows?" T-Bone groaned. "Our muscle, our connections to Four Corners' wealth, probably. All we knew was, we wouldn't make it home until we fought and clawed our way out."

"How did you get out?" Reaper leaned forward in his chair.

T-Bone gave a smug little grin at the question. "We had ears in the trees and eyes in the sky."

Horus clicked his beak. Hades' ears pricked forward. Us three humans all looked at each other, knowing what that meant without needing to say anything.

"Anyway, we took out our guards and slipped out in the dead of night," Dyno said. "Found your uncle's bedchamber, removed that lying tongue of his, and took our parting gifts," he added with a sneer. "We made it home to the clubhouse after two days. The next day, us three rode out to the Four Corners capitol to report the fuckery to Vance. After that, we rode home to a pile of smoking ashes."

"Our president, VP..." T-Bone choked up, the muscles at his throat working hard as he swallowed. "All our men, their women, kids. Fucking boarded up inside." He sucked in a ragged breath through clenched teeth. "I'm just hoping they died quickly."

Silence fell over the room. Reaper watched the three of them struggle to keep it together. Our loss of one man was a heavy weight in all of us. I couldn't imagine if we lost the entire club.

"I meant what I said the other day," I told T-Bone. "You did the world a favor by taking care of my uncle. But he was a minnow, and General Tash is a shark. I imagine you took out some of those troops you escorted when you escaped?"

T-Bone nodded, his gaze down at his shoes. "Grudge here picked off a couple of squadron leaders. He's good at the silent assassin stuff."

He jerked his head at the man with the long hair and beard, who'd been completely silent. Come to think of it, he didn't say anything at the cantina either.

"That'll do it," Reaper said softly. "Any slight against the general and you're living on borrowed time."

"He was probably hoping to use them after getting my uncle to surrender," I pointed out.

Reaper nodded his agreement. "We'd been working with Tash, until we fulfilled our usefulness a couple months ago. He turned one of our own against us and tried to take us out. We escaped, but it's been a shit-show of trying to stay ahead of him ever since. We lost one good man in the attack today."

"My condolences." T-Bone actually sounded sincere. He sighed tiredly. "We were hard up trying to figure out what the fuck to do. After meeting Youngblood here, we decided to swallow our pride and see if y'all would offer refuge to some homeless strays." He let out a bitter laugh. "Just our luck that we'd roll up to find fucking drones bombing your place."

"How'd you stop them?" Reaper's knuckles were white on the edge of his chair. Finally, the question we'd all been waiting for.

"Found a few small teams of well-camouflaged asswipes. First waves were close, only about a hundred yards from your wall. They triggered the launchers that tossed the tear gas over. Must've buried those things ahead of time in the dead of night."

"Shit," Reaper and I breathed in unison.

Our night vision was our biggest weakness, and that fucked us. Horus was a daytime predator, so while we saw every blade of grass moving when the sun was up, there was no way we could catch everything at night.

"Second waves were about a quarter mile out," T-Bone continued. "They controlled the drones. Pretty fancy setup, too. And so well-concealed, we almost missed 'em."

"But you didn't." Reaper peered at him shrewdly. "How?"

"Like I said, scythe-man," T-Bone smirked, noting his patch. "Ears in the trees. Eyes in the sky."

"Long story short," Dyno cut in. "We killed them, destroyed the controllers, saved the day. Want to stop treating us like the bad guys now?"

Reaper tented his fingers in thought for a few moments, then stood from the chair. "Take off the restraints, but they're staying in here for the time being." As Shadow walked up to unlock their cuffs, the president turned to me. "Bring these guys some food and water, then put people on their door. Twenty-four hour shifts."

"You got it, Reap."

As I turned to leave, a snarl and a curse made me pause.

"Fucking Demons," Dyno hissed, rubbing at his wrists, now free of restraints. "We save your fucking asses, tell you our whole story, and you *still* treat us like prisoners?"

"Easy, Dyno." T-Bone leaned back in his chair, his posture relaxed. "We had to decide if trusting them was worth the risk. Let them make the same decision."

"Listen to your sergeant," Reaper warned.

With that, he followed me out the door, with Shadow bringing up the rear.

MARIPOSA

"This is fucking humiliating," Jandro moaned.

"You want me to get a wheelbarrow?" Shadow huffed, bouncing Jandro higher in the piggyback position he carried him in.

"No, that's even worse! Mari, why won't you let me walk?"

"'Cause I shot you up with local anesthesia everywhere, and I don't know the extent of your nerve damage," I explained, not for the first time. "If you stumble and fall, you could end up worse for wear."

"I'd much rather stumble around like a *borracho*. Shadow sucks as a ride."

"I'm happy to drop you on your ass if Mariposa says I can."

"No," I huffed. "Your fucking ego is not giving me extra work to do tonight."

"But you *love* taking care of me," Jandro goaded.

I ground my teeth, still fighting the residual anger at his stupid act of bravery. "Don't push your luck."

I pushed open his front door and held it open for Shadow to follow through. The large man carefully lowered his friend to the couch. Freyja had already jumped up beside Jandro, waiting for him to settle so she could find a place to curl.

"Stop!" I yelled, letting the front door close. "Don't move."

Jandro froze, propped on his forearm as he was about to lie down. "What now?"

"Lie on your stomach, not your back." I gestured for him to roll over. "Nothing should press on your burn, aside from the bandages. Plus, it's gonna hurt like a bitch when the anesthesia wears off."

He flopped onto his stomach with a heavy groan. "How long do I gotta lay like this? I'm not a stomach sleeper."

"Until you're mostly healed. At least a few weeks."

"A few *weeks*?! What if I suffocate when I'm facedown?"

"Figure out how *not* to!" I pinched my forehead, turning to Shadow. "You see what I have to deal with?"

He actually cracked a smirk. "Welcome to my world."

"Want to trade places?"

After such a long, awful night, on top of Jandro going from human shield to whiny baby, I couldn't resist some lighthearted banter. Imagine my pleasant surprise to find Shadow receptive to it, not a twitch of discomfort on his face.

"Sorry, medic," he returned. "He's all yours."

I released a dramatic, disappointed sigh. "Well then, maybe you can help me dispose of his body, if it comes to that."

Shadow's mouth twitched as if fighting laughter. I wished he would just let it out. I would've loved to hear that sound, just a single moment of uncontrolled joy from him.

"That, I can probably help with," he played along.

"I'm hurt," Jandro moaned, watching our exchange. "My roommate and my woman, plotting against me before my very eyes!"

"So do what your medic says without bitching." I sat down next to him, leaning over to kiss his least-damaged shoulder. "And we won't have a problem," I added in a sweet voice.

He let out a wordless moan into the couch cushions, while I peppered his face and shoulders with kisses to let him know I was kidding.

"Hey." He lifted his head abruptly. "Has anyone told Andrea what happened?"

Something tight and uncomfortable squeezed around my heart. "I've been fixing you up all day."

We both looked to Shadow, who gave a small shake of his head. "I was with Gunner and Reaper, talking to the Sons of Odin."

"Someone should check on her." Jandro's hands closed around the edge of the couch cushion. "Fuck. I don't know if *anyone* knows about Dallas yet—"

"I'll tell her." I stopped his movement with a hand on his arm. "She needs to be the first one to know."

"You don't need to carry that burden, *bonita*," Jandro said softly. "Find Reaper and get him to tell her."

I shook my head. "He's got enough on his plate. Besides, I checked Dallas's body myself. She should hear it directly from me, before someone else has a chance to give her wrong information."

"Why you always gotta be right?" Jandro sighed. "Shadow, go with her."

"No, that's okay—"

"Babe, don't fight me on this." All the humor was gone from Jandro's voice. "We still don't know for sure how safe it is. I'd feel a lot better if Shadow was with you."

I looked at Shadow's dark, looming figure still standing in the middle of the room. "Do you mind?"

"Not at all," he said quickly, then hesitated. "I'll stay back a bit when we reach her house. I don't think Andrea likes me."

"Why?" I demanded with genuine disbelief.

Jandro disguised a laugh with a cough.

Shadow's eyes slid to him before returning to me. "I think it's because I scare her children. I, uh, accidentally made her son cry once."

Jandro looked like he was dying to tell the story, but my mood for fun and humor had vanished. I was about to tell someone the worst news they would likely ever receive.

"Let's get this over with." I started for the door.

"Hey." Jandro grabbed my hand at the last moment, tapping his lips as he pulled me back to him. "*Beso*."

I lowered onto the floor next to the couch to kiss him deeply, all the tension and anger draining out of my body. I savored the kiss of my living, breathing man—holding onto the warmth pulsing from his mouth to mine and shutting everything else out.

At the end of all this, I still had my man, and Andrea didn't have hers.

"Te amo," I murmured, my lips refusing to lose contact with his.

"Te amo, mi Mariposita," he whispered. "Hurry back to me."

Now the last thing I wanted to do was leave, but I forced myself up, and headed for the door where Shadow waited.

Andrea lived only four houses down, at the end of the block. We began our walk together in silence as cool, quiet darkness settled over the day that had been so chaotic.

"Thanks for coming with me." I hugged my arms around myself, even though it wasn't that cold. A memory of the man walking alongside me, his arms around me in a hug and my head in his chest, flashed through my mind.

"It's no problem," Shadow answered. His gaze was fixed straight ahead when I glanced at him, long strides keeping pace with my hurried steps. "How, um, how's your tattoo?"

"It's fine. You know, itchy."

Neither one of us seemed able to hold a conversation to distract us from the one about to happen. Andrea's house loomed up in front of us a long, tense minute later, and yet all too soon.

We stood at the bottom of her driveway, where Dallas's lifted truck was parked.

"You okay to stay back here?" I asked Shadow.

"Yeah," he swallowed. "If you don't mind. I don't...I don't want to make anything worse for her."

"That's awfully considerate of you." I forced a smile and exhaled quickly. "Okay. Wish me luck."

"I'll be right here," he promised.

I walked up the driveway, each of my feet feeling like lead. As I raised my fist to knock, I silently prayed that she already knew, that I wouldn't be the one to shatter her whole world.

She opened the door right after my knock, looking confused and worried, but that was all.

"Mari! What the blazes is going on? We got the order to stay inside and hide. Is it over now? Where are my children?" Her dark hair, streaked with a few gray strands, was held up by a red bandanna. Bright blue eyes, lined with a few crow's feet, peered at me for answers. Answers I didn't know if I'd be able to give.

"There--there was an attack," I stammered out. "From the air. Drones dropping grenades. The kids are safe. They're at the clubhouse with, uh, Martha, I think."

"Oh, thank God!" She pressed a palm to her chest and leaned against the doorway. "They're at the clubhouse, Elise!" she yelled into the house.

"Told ya our boys would keep the babies safe!" Another woman walked up to the door, someone else's wife I didn't know as well. "Is the coast clear? Can we come out?"

"Andrea," I started, fighting the closure of my throat, the desperation to not hurt her. "I came to tell you about Dallas."

The smile dropped from her face as she straightened up. "Did my silly old man get himself hurt?" She tried to laugh, but it came out hollow.

"I'm—I'm *so* sorry..."

She stepped closer to me, grabbing my shoulders, though I barely felt it. "Tell me the truth, hon. Is he hurt bad?"

I tasted blood from biting the inside of my cheek so hard. "He...he didn't make it. There was nothing I could do. It happened so fast. I'm sorry, Andrea."

She didn't make a sound, but her friend behind her gasped. "Oh no. Andy..."

"My husband's dead?" she demanded.

I nodded, my whole face sore from trying so hard to keep it together. "It was instant, painless." Like that made the situation any better. "He saved the kids from getting hit."

That last bit of information seemed to be the trigger. Andrea released a choked cry, her knees buckling underneath her. I moved in to support her, but her friend was already there.

"Oh, Andy. I'm so sorry, honey..." Her friend's tears fell freely, soaking Andrea's red bandanna as she held the new widow's head to her shoulder.

Dry, heaving sobs wracked Andrea's whole body. Pained moans

escaped her, like she was dying herself. Her body slumped against her friend, all strength gone.

"Come sit down, honey," her friend sniffed, dragging her to the couch. "Oh my god, I can't believe he's gone..."

I reached forward and pulled the front door closed, then stepped numbly down the driveway. My purpose was fulfilled and I was no longer needed.

It occurred to me that I'd never had to do that before. Sure, patients had died in my care, but it was on war-torn battlefields. I had to report the deaths to generals and lieutenants, but never loved ones.

Deaths were tragic, but common enough in my field that I became desensitized. I knew since the beginning that my skills could only go so far, and I never expected to perform miracles.

But Dallas...I never wanted so badly to wave a magic wand and make him reappear, alive and well. He would never be a nameless corpse in a mass grave. I only knew him briefly, but he was *someone* to me. And someone more to Andrea, his kids, and the men I loved.

It hurt. I hated that any of us had to lose him.

I met Shadow at the end of the driveway, barely aware that I had walked at all.

"How'd it go?" he asked.

I didn't want to freak him out by being emotional, but I couldn't hold it in anymore. All my resolve was gone in speaking those few sentences to Andrea.

A sob escaped, painful and ugly as it dragged out of my chest. I tried to tell him I was sorry, but another one came out. And then the tears blurred my vision.

"Mari—?" Shadow moved as though to touch my shoulders, then stopped himself. "Shit. I'm sorry. Can I—"

I didn't give him a chance to finish talking. I just squeezed my eyes shut against the tears, as my forehead pressed into his chest. The sobs heaved through my lungs as I cocooned my arms between my body and his.

Not a moment later, his arms wrapped around my back and held me tightly.

MARIPOSA

Every Steel Demon wore somber expressions, their hands clasped in front of them. The only sounds floating over the desert were Andrea's soft sniffs and cries. Noelle and Tessa stood on either side of her—each of them rubbing her back and arms. Tessa gently bounced her sleeping daughter strapped to her chest.

Dallas looked like he was sleeping. I knew nothing about preparing a body for burial, but I cleaned him as best I could, and dressed him in his favorite leathers. He was laid on a tarp on the ground, next to the hole dug that morning. His hands were folded on top of his broad chest, like I'd often seen him when he laid on the patio couches during the parties.

But this time his head wasn't in Andrea's lap, her gentle fingers massaging over his scalp, nor were his kids climbing all over him like a jungle gym. He was going into that hole in the ground. And he wasn't coming back.

I held onto Reaper's elbow, listening with my head bowed, as Gunner stepped up to recite a prayer from his worn-out Bible. His grandmother's, he told me right before the funeral began.

I found myself latching onto innocuous details like that. Jandro stood on my other side, solemn face to the horizon. On the other side of him, Shadow's dark eye kept looking skyward. I realized he was watching Horus circling above us.

The passage Gunner read told of sacrifice and faith, of the peace brought upon Dallas's soul now that he was in his final resting place.

Next to me, Reaper's muscles clenched.

When Gunner finished, Reaper gently removed my hand from his arm. He slowly went to stand in the middle of the semicircle his club made around Dallas's body.

"You all probably know I wouldn't have prepared anything to say, even though I felt I should." His voice was rougher than usual. He barely got any sleep the night before, just fitful tossing, turning, and getting up to smoke on the balcony.

"The truth is," he let out an exhausted breath, "there's nothing I can say that'll make this any better." His eyes lifted to address his club. "Dallas shouldn't have died. He's gone because I failed to protect us. Don't!" He raised a hand to silence the arguments ready to burst from twenty open mouths. "I ain't gonna make this a pity party about me. It's about *him*, and what he left behind."

Reaper lowered his hand, resting it on his hip. "Dallas is someone we should all strive to embody. He was a true Steel Demon, living by the code we uphold," he paused, "and dying by it." He turned to look at the body in question. "He ran straight into the path of danger, of death, to protect what mattered most." His eyes lifted to Dallas's two children, clinging to Andrea's legs. "His future. His legacy."

Reaper rubbed the back of his neck, almost sheepishly. "I've asked every one of you, when initiated into this club, if you'd be willing to do what Dallas did. And every one of you has told me yes. You *meant* it. That's why you wear the patch and ride next to me. I take your oaths seriously. But—"

His jaw clamped down, and I clasped my fingers together hard, fighting the need to run over, to hold him to me and let him release his grief. I understood now that it had to wait for a private moment. In front of his club, he had to be the strong, infallible president.

"But it doesn't make it any fucking easier when it actually happens," he forced out through clenched teeth.

I blinked back tears and released a shaky exhale. Jandro rubbed his palm into my lower back.

"I'm not changing your oaths." Reaper's eyes scanned the men standing before him. "I'm not saying this fucking hurts too much to happen again, because it will. I'll do everything in my power to prevent losing another brother, but I only have so much control. We *know* this is a risk of the life we lead. So I want you to ask yourselves honestly," he lifted his chin. "Do you still want to wear the Steel Demon on your back, knowing you could be the next one in the ground?"

The wake following Dallas's burial was just as somber, if not more so, only with alcohol. Everyone poured a bit of their first drink out for their fallen brother, but no one seemed able to muster up the good cheer to celebrate his life. His loss brought a dark cloud over a sunny, warm day.

I wiped at the sweat trickling down my neck, eyeing the empty pool. But it didn't feel right to strip out of my floor-length black dress. I piled my hair up in a bun and my upper back was bare, save for the thick layer of sunscreen over my tattoo. I wanted to make sure it was visible today, even though it was still healing, to show my support for Reaper in case any of the other guys started having doubts about their oaths.

As everyone milled around the patio, I stayed by his side, touching him in small ways. His face remained stony as he chatted with his men, but his thumb stroked over my ring every time he held my hand. When I wasn't looking at him, I watched the sun move slowly over the sky, counting the moments until we were alone and he could let his guard down.

Toward the end of the day, as people finished paying their respects and began to head home, he tugged me toward Andrea.

"I'll need your help with this," he murmured, brushing a kiss across my forehead.

"What do you need me to do?" I whispered.

"Just be with me," he sighed and squeezed my left hand, caressing over the ring again until he kneeled in front of Dallas's widow. Releasing his hand, I took a seat next to her on the couch.

"Andrea."

Her tears had stopped hours before, but her face was still puffy. Eyes vacant. Her fingers were limp as Reaper took them in his hands.

"You'll always have a home with us, if that's what you want," he said gently. "You don't have to decide now, but you and your children will always have our protection. Just say the word and the Demons are yours."

I rubbed my palm along her back. Understandably, she didn't react to Reaper or me.

"My sister can stay with you," he offered. "My dog is here to guard you at any time. If any of the men try to...to crowd you before you're ready, just let one of us know."

Andrea lifted her hands out of Reaper's grip, and leaned away from my embrace. "Thank you, Reaper," she said flatly. "If you don't mind, I'd like to go home now."

"She fucking hates me." Reaper slammed his heavy glass tumbler on the kitchen counter and poured a generous amount of whiskey into it. "As she should."

I walked up behind him, and he stilled at my light touch on his waist. Turning my head, I laid my cheek on the center of his back as I hugged him from behind.

"She's heartbroken," I murmured. "The love of her life is gone. She's going to see him every time she looks at her children. Sure, she probably blames you for some of it, but that's part of her grieving."

Reaper turned to face me, his body stiff, but he didn't remove my arms from around him.

"Have you ever lost someone you loved? Someone you thought would always be there?" His voice was still rough from lack of sleep and chain smoking, which made the question sound like a harsh accusation.

"You know I have," I retorted. "My dad. And then my mom. I don't even have the closure of knowing if they're really dead or not."

"Closure," he snorted, like the word amused him. "A whole fuck-ton of good that does to make you feel better."

I stepped away, letting my hands fall to my sides. He clearly wasn't about to let his guard down tonight, to spill out his grief and sorrow in my arms as we fell asleep together. He was wounded by grief, by ego, and by the pressure he put on himself to protect and lead.

Those wounds were not something I could heal right then.

"You know what's fucked up?" He took a deep swallow of whiskey. "I never told Andrea I was sorry. I wanted to, but," he turned back around, pouring more into his glass, "I fucking hate those words. They're just so hollow. They don't *mean* anything."

"But you mean them." I placed a hand on his arm, watching the internal conflict he struggled with.

"More than anything," he whispered, head bowing low. "Daren at least knew what was coming. He made that choice himself. But Dallas... it's all wrong. He should still be here."

Reaper gently removed my hand from his arm. "You should spend the night with one of the other guys, sugar. I'm not going to be great company for a while."

He was right, but the statement still stung. "I don't want you to be alone."

"I won't be. Hades'll be with me."

The dog raised his head from the floor at the mention of his name. He looked calm and regal, paws stretched out in front of him as he observed us.

"I'll be with Jandro," I told Reaper. "I need to keep an eye on his burn, anyway."

"Okay." For a moment, he looked like he didn't want me to leave. Longing and love softened his features as he leaned in for a kiss.

"Do me a favor?" I murmured against his lips.

"Anything." His arm on my waist tightened slightly.

I pulled back to see his whole face clearly.

"Let your brother in," I whispered. "Let Daren talk to you. He communicates only with Noelle because you shut him out."

I slid out of his embrace before he could ask any more, not that I'd be able to tell him anything that Noelle hadn't said.

Before leaving I knelt down next to Hades, scratching over his velvety fur. "Take care of him," I whispered. "He needs you now."

The dog, or god within, didn't respond with words. I didn't know what to expect, but it wasn't the weight of a warm hand on my shoulder. Even so, a sense of comfort washed over me, and I bowed my head in a silent thank you.

JANDRO

"What did he do?" I stared at Mari as she walked in, even though she didn't meet my eye.

I saw it in her posture, though. In the way her shoulders slumped forward, and the pinched tightness of her brow.

When she didn't answer me, Gunner backed me up. "What happened, baby girl?" He was sprawled on my couch, boots up on my footstool. I didn't have the energy to tell him to take his damn shoes off.

Mari dropped her supplies on the coffee table and sat down next to me. "Nothing, he's just," she sighed, peeling away the gauze on my back, "being Reaper."

"Dallas's death doesn't give him an excuse to be an asshole." I ground my teeth against the odd sensation of my injury.

It didn't hurt exactly, but I felt a weird pinching and pulling, like my muscles were too tight. Sometimes an area would seize up or suddenly go numb. Mari said it was because my nerves were damaged, and my brain was trying to communicate with what was no longer there.

"He wasn't being an asshole," she protested, inspecting my burn closely. "If I insisted on staying with him, it might have gotten to that point, though."

"Good thing you didn't," Gunner remarked.

I tossed a smile his way. "You're starting to get the hang of this group thing, huh, bird boy?"

"Yeah, whatever." He flung a hand at me, but an adoring smile crossed his lips as he watched our girl tend to me.

"How's it lookin' back there?" I could only turn my head so far to look at her. My neck muscles felt like they'd been shortened by several inches.

"Good," she muttered, dabbing something all over my back with a gloved hand. "Really good, actually. You're healing faster than I thought you would." Then, in a lower breath to herself, "I don't know why that surprises me anymore."

"When can I ride?" I dropped a kiss to her shoulder.

"Getting *way* ahead of yourself, *guapito*. I don't even want you out in the sun for at least two weeks."

"Two weeks?!"

"Do you know if anyone has a humidifier?" She started pressing fresh gauze onto my back. "Your skin needs to stay hydrated to heal."

"I got parts in the shop. I can make one."

She gave me a wide-eyed stare before laughing softly. "Of course you can."

"Maybe a better question is," I dragged my lips from her shoulder to her ear, "when can *you* ride?"

I felt the grin at the edge of her jaw. "Well, my seat still works, doesn't it?" Her fingers trailed up my thigh and I never felt so alive since coming back from the dead.

"Even if *that* burned off, I have another place for you to sit." My tongue darted out, dragging along her earlobe with my teeth.

"I don't know how you can be in the mood right now," she sighed, though her grin never faded.

"It's easy when I'm right next to you." I pressed a slow, smoldering kiss to her jaw. "And after the last couple of days, I think we could all use some feeling good."

"Am I included in that *we*?" Gunner rested his chin in his hand as he smiled at us.

"Yes," Mari and I said in unison. "And you're not just watching this time either," she added.

"That took convincing," I squeezed her knee with a chuckle.

She looked at me, face etched with concern. "I still don't want you to—"

"Put pressure on my back. Yeah, yeah, I know." An idea struck me right then. I stood her up, spun her around, and smacked her ass in Gunner's direction. "Gun can take you lying down. I'll be standing."

She gave me a coy look over her shoulder on her way to the bird boy. "Shadow's not home, is he?"

"Don't really give a fuck if he is." I followed like a predator, staying one step behind her as she lowered into Gunner's lap. He grinned like he won the fucking lottery as she leaned toward him. "Hey, baby girl."

"Hi, handsome," she returned sweetly, before kissing him.

I don't know how he did it that one time with all of us, just watch her without touching her. That could never be me. I needed contact with my woman like I needed air to breathe.

While the two of them had fun, I did the work. Gunner kissed her, and I lifted her clothing up and out of the way until they littered my living room floor. My dick punched a hole in my jeans as he kissed every inch of newly exposed skin. Our girl sighed so sweetly, still reaching behind her to feel for me.

"Not going anywhere," I promised her, my mouth against her nape. "Just work on him for me."

Her attention returned to Gunner, getting him out of his clothes while I stepped back for a moment. I pulled apart my belt buckle, letting my jeans fall as I choked my dick in my fist.

I lasted for all of about five seconds watching. Her feet hit the floor —calves, thighs, and mouthwatering pussy on display, as she worked Gun's pants down to his knees. When she bent over to draw him into her mouth, I couldn't stand it any longer.

Her pussy called to my tongue like a magnet. I descended on her like a starving man, holding the back of her thighs in place with both hands.

She made those sexy little moans around Gunner's cock, while her sweet wetness coated my tongue. Gun was being noisy too, cursing and grunting as she took him down her throat. Hearing him was kind of hot too, I had to admit. Not that *he* did anything for me, but knowing our woman was so good at what she did. Mari was meant to be pleased by multiple men. I couldn't thank whatever higher powers enough that I got to be one of them.

"I need to be in you," Gunner groaned.

Mari's panting breaths and soft whimpers told me her mouth was free. "Jandro," she whined.

"Mm-mm." I smacked her cheek to the right side of my face. I wasn't done feasting.

"Please—ah!"

Her sweet begging got cut off by kissing sounds. I rolled my tongue through her flesh, sucking her decadent lips into my mouth. She was drenching my face, thighs quivering with her oncoming release. I loved this part so much. When she was so close to the edge, practically in tears from nearing the crest of her pleasure.

Reaper liked making her come fast and often. I liked to take my time and draw it out of her slowly. And now that he was too busy being a moody bastard to boss me around, I was gonna make her come my way.

"Jandroooo," she whimpered louder.

I pulled my face away, looking around her ass toward her head.

"Yes?"

Her beet-red face was on Gunner's chest, her whole torso draped over his legs. He just smiled down at her, so beautiful and frustrated. His hands petted her hair and stroked her back.

"Please let me come."

Her hand slid down in a desperate instinct to touch herself, but Gunner snatched it and held her forearm against her back.

"He'll take care of you, baby girl," he whispered soothingly, dropping a kiss to her forehead. "Just let him."

"Listen to your man." It pleased me more than words could say that Gunner went along with it. We discussed nothing beforehand, but he instinctively knew his role—to soothe her while I tortured her.

I took my time returning to my work, leaving a sizable bite mark on her ass before devouring her tender flesh again. Her clit begged for attention and I held out as long as I could before giving it. She couldn't even stand anymore, her legs draped on the couch on either side of Gunner, before I sucked that sweet pleasure button into my mouth.

Her release was instant and beautiful, sweeping her from head to toe in shivers and convulsions. I drank my fill of her orgasm, letting her ride my face through the aftershocks.

Gunner was enough of a good sport to wait until I pulled away before he seated her on his dick. She was still exhausted, just slumped against him while he moved beneath her.

"Sorry, I..." she trailed off breathlessly, head heavy on his shoulder.

"Baby girl." He cupped her face in his hands, forcing her to look at him. "Don't ever be sorry for feeling *that* good."

I hid a smile behind quickly wiping my face with a hand towel. He really did get it. It took a hell of a time getting him here, but he really did fit in seamlessly with us. And most importantly, he treasured her.

Gunner held onto Mari's face, his eyes locked on hers as he kept rolling his hips beneath her—putting in the work while she caught her breath.

It didn't take long for her to take the lead, using his shoulders for leverage as she bounced on his stiff length.

"Hold on, hold on." He grabbed her waist, holding her poised above him before she could sink back down. "My turn for a breather," he said with a sheepish smile. "You just feel too good."

I didn't say a word, just came up behind her. I took her hips from his grip, and sank into her in one long stroke.

"Ohhh..."

Her moan was equal parts surprise and unabashed pleasure. She looked at me over her shoulder and that beautiful, sex-flushed face told me all I needed to know.

She loved fucking both of us.

I pounded her hard, holding nothing back as I watched that perfect ass bounce off me. The moment I started feeling close, I pulled away so Gunner could have her back.

Fuck, I could do this all day. Maybe I really did die because my idea of heaven was this right here.

Gun braced his arms around her back, holding her to his chest and moaning into her neck as her second orgasm squeezed around him. She barely came down, before he lifted her off again.

"Too good. Too fucking good," he moaned. "Feels like I'm fucking fourteen years old again."

"Don't let it get to you, man," I said, sliding in again. "We can't always be studs."

My cock felt as heavy and solid as iron. I was already getting close again too. Rather than pull out, I slowed down, drawing out my thrusts as my thumb rested just over Mari's ass.

"You like having both of our cocks, *bonita*?" I circled my thumb around the tight ring of muscles I had yet to touch, just to gauge her reaction.

"Mmm!" She had taken Gunner back in her mouth, bobbing on him greedily.

"Would you want us both at the same time?" I pressed directly on her ass now, just pressure without inserting.

She answered by clenching around my dick in another orgasm, one my stamina was powerless to resist.

"Fuckkk..." I drove into her with a crash, her pussy closing around me like it would never let go.

Gunner's fists closed in her hair and his head threw back in a hiss as he emptied himself into her mouth.

Now I had some sense of what Mari felt like after coming. I could barely stand, and I rested my forehead on her back.

She released Gunner from her mouth, head in his lap as she looked back at me with a woozy smile.

"Yes," she breathed.

"Yes, what?"

"Yes, I want you both at the same time." She hid her face for a second, like there was anything left to be shy about. "It would be a first for me, though."

I made my way to the couch, a monumental effort after my soul had just left my body via my dick, and almost forgot to not roll onto my back.

"We'll work up to that," I panted, stroking her face. "Another time."

REAPER

"We have to move."

I placed my elbows on the table, my head in my hands. At my side, I felt Hades' nose nudge against my thigh. Across the conference room, I felt the weight of the eyes of my men as heavily as boulders.

On some level, I knew it would come to this. Hell, I probably knew it deep down from the first attack. Tash knew where we lived, where we stored our resources. And each attack was only escalating. We couldn't afford to be here for his next attempt.

The more I thought about it, the more I became certain that the Sons of Odin's clubhouse was a warning to us.

"Reaper."

"I heard you, Jandro," I snapped, dragging my fingers through my hair. "But where?"

He couldn't shrug because of that fucking burn on his back, so he lifted his hands, palms up. "We might have to do the nomadic thing for a while. We've done it before."

"Not with this many people," I argued. "Not with a zoo of animals and a newborn baby, for fuck's sake. We need a place to settle."

"And what's stopping Tash from finding that place, too?" he countered. "Reaper, our people are not safe anywhere. The safest place we'll be is on the road. Because then we can see the general coming."

"Everyone here understands the risks of rolling with an MC," I said. "Safety is never guaranteed. But we're not simple thugs on wheels anymore. We can't just drag everyone behind us constantly. We have a responsibility to those we're protecting. "

"Believe me, I know." Jandro raised a palm to placate me. "We have something *worth* protecting now. But settling can happen later. Who knows, maybe we can move back here after we're done with Tash. But not before then, it's too risky, man. The next attack could end you or me, or one of the kids. We don't want *any* more losses if we can help it."

But Death will come anyway.

Did I think that? Or did Hades say it to me?

My dog rested his chin on my knee, staring up at me with those big dark eyes. Wherever that thought came from, I felt deep in my bones that we hadn't encountered all of our losses yet. We could make all the right moves, but we were still gnats that the general swatted at. No true threat, just pests he had to clean out.

"I get what you're saying 'Dro," I rubbed my forehead, "but how are we supposed to coordinate an attack on Tash when we're constantly on the run?"

"Depends on where we ride and who we meet along the way." He lifted his chin, swiveling from side to side in his chair. "How'd the talk with the Odin guys go?"

"Fucking peachy. They're going to be three more mouths to feed from the sounds of it. Three more bodies fucking using up our resources."

"So you trust them?" he pressed. "You're letting them stay?"

"I haven't decided yet," I admitted.

He nodded in the direction of Shadow and Gunner. "What was y'all's take on 'em?"

"I don't see any reason to treat them like prisoners," Gunner shrugged. "It's not their fault Tash and my uncle fucked them over. We don't have to be all buddy-buddy, but us and the Sons are on the same side as far as I'm concerned."

"Shadow?"

"They've suffered a great loss at the hands of our mutual enemy." The usually silent man voiced his opinion without much prodding, which was noticed by everyone in the room. "Now we've lost a brother too, and risk losing everything as they did. I think they're the best allies we have right now."

I lifted my weary eyes to the room. Sleep hadn't come easily lately. "Any objections?"

No one said a word.

"Settled." I smacked my gavel on the table, but my heart wasn't in it. "I'll let 'em out after church. Now how the fuck do we plan a move?"

The discussion was primarily between me, Jandro, and Gunner, with the occasional comment from another one of the guys. Gunner knew the surrounding territories best, all their trade routes, conflict areas, and most attractive places to settle. An hour later, the conference table was covered in maps with a dozen of us leaning over it, and no agreement reached.

It all felt pointless, anyway. Even with the most recent maps only a few months old, borders could have been redrawn since then and areas of peace turned into war zones. We might as well just ride out to wherever the horizon took us. A tempting proposition, to be honest.

"Fuck this shit." I threw my hands up, storming out of the room after going around in circles.

We'd have time to squeeze in one more Fight Night before getting the hell out of dodge, but I wanted to spill blood right fucking then. I wanted to call Dallas back from the grave and shove my fist straight through his jaw. I wanted to yell all the grief in my lungs into his face, and tell him never to die on me again.

I almost went home. If I couldn't fight, I'd drink, smoke, and fuck my woman. But I almost forgot I had prisoners to release.

Turning in the hall, I found Hades already heading toward the Sons' room. He sat by the locked door, waiting for me with wide, expectant eyes.

"Still ain't saying shit to me, huh?" I withdrew the ring of keys from my pocket and unlocked the door.

He only licked his lips and grinned as we stepped into the room together.

T-Bone was doing push-ups on his knuckles in the middle of the floor. Grudge did squats nearby, carrying Dyno on his shoulders.

"President." The sergeant at arms climbed to his feet, panting slightly. "How good of you to visit. Did you bring cookies?"

I gestured an arm behind me, indicating the open door. "You're free to move about our compound as you see fit. The central clubhouse has a kitchen, the medic's office, gym, and conference rooms. There's an empty house on the corner two blocks down that you're all welcome to share." I reached a hand down to scratch Hades' head. "It probably goes without saying, but I'll say it anyway—don't trash the place and don't take more than you need from our stores. You're fucking guests here. We can rescind our hospitality at any time."

"And what a gracious host you are," T-Bone smirked. "You have my word that we won't be a nuisance."

"Sounds like we're still prisoners, with a slightly bigger cage," Dyno huffed, climbing down from Grudge's shoulders.

"Oh, believe me. You are free to go any time you wish," I snarled. "I'll even have my boys roll out a carpet for you. A proper fucking send-off."

"Easy." T-Bone halted Dyno from coming at me with a gentle tap on the man's chest. The touch lingered there, affectionate in a way I didn't miss, before returning his attention to me.

"Times are difficult now, even more than before," he continued. "I understand why you're all still hesitant to trust us. So I'd like to put an offer on the table."

"Not interested," I snapped.

"Hear me out, Reaper." He took two cautious steps toward me before Hades released a low, warning growl.

"We don't know each other nearly enough to be making offers," I retorted. "I'm being generous enough, just opening my home to you."

"And we appreciate the hospitality, don't get me wrong." He paused, eyes flicking down to Hades before returning to me. "But word floating on the wind says y'all ain't staying here for much longer."

My blood turned to ice in my veins. My fingers clenched into fists at my sides. I just might get my goddamn fight in after all.

"How do you know that?" I took a step forward, seething that he had private intel from my church meeting not an hour earlier. "Who the fuck do you have spying on us? Church is sacred. You should fucking know that, *Sergeant.*"

"A little birdie told me," T-Bone sneered.

The next thing I saw was my fists curled into the worn leather of his cut next to his neck. Dyno shouted something and tried to come at me from the side, but Hades blocked his path. T-Bone's bald head slammed against the window on the wall behind him. I slammed him clear across the room and the rage in my blood still simmered, barely satiated.

"Now that was awfully quick," I hissed, inches away from his face. "Your welcome has been withdrawn. The three of you can kindly get the fuck out."

"Before you do that," T-Bone said in a rushed breath. "My offer was for the Steel Demons to stay in Four Corners. I guarantee you'll have the hospitality of the governor himself, for giving us refuge. It'll be safe for your women, kids, everyone."

"I don't want shit from you—"

"I listened to your meeting through my raven, Munin."

My grip on his cut loosened slightly from pure shock. "...What?"

"I can see and listen through my bird like I'm in his head. That's how I saw you all pay your respects for my people at our clubhouse." He sucked in a breath, shoving my hands away as I just stared at him dumbly. "You can't be that surprised, Reaper. I know your captain has the same ability with his falcon." He nodded down at Hades, who still had his teeth bared at Dyno. "And I'd bet both my nuts that dog is something otherworldly too."

"Why?" I fought to keep my focus on that anger, but it started to dissipate. "Why use your animal to fucking eavesdrop?"

"It's a standard cover-your-ass move when you've been locked up here for three days already," he retorted. "If y'all were planning on killing us, we would've liked a heads up."

As pissed as I was, I couldn't blame him for listening. After sweeping the area, we found the bodies dressed in General Tash's insignia and broken drone controllers. The Sons' story had checked out, and we hadn't exactly treated them with the best hospitality.

"Your raven," I repeated in a dumbfounded whisper, having never considered that gods could come to anyone other than me, Mari, or Gunner. "He told you his name?"

"Yes." T-Bone's voice was now low with reverence. "Munin was one of Odin's two ravens. The other was Hugin, who had chosen our president. We believe Hugin returned to the afterlife with him."

"My old lady," I breathed. "She has a cat called Freyja."

The thirst for violence was completely gone from my system now, replaced by sheer awe. I stepped back to give T-Bone some space.

"Freyja and Odin share the responsibility of taking slain warriors home," T-Bone said, the tension draining out of his body. "We believe our men are with Odin now. Maybe the man you've lost is with Freyja."

"But I also have Hades," I nodded to my dog. "Lord of the underworld of a different pantheon. And Gunner has Horus."

"Ah," T-Bone smiled. "You have quite the cultural mix under one banner."

"I still don't know what any of it means," I admitted. "I literally looked them all up in a book three days ago."

"That's the thing about gods," T-Bone chuckled. "You never really know what they're getting at, not until it clicks into place."

"Right. Still fuckin' waiting for that part."

He stroked his beard, watching me curiously, if even appreciatively, then folded his arms across his chest.

"I think the gods led us to find each other, Reaper. Don't you agree?"

"I dunno about all that." I headed back for the door, Hades at my side. "So you've got good timing and a special bird. Doesn't mean you're any more trustworthy than before. Not until I see the proof with my own eyes."

"So, you kicking us out of this place or not?" The demand came from Dyno, arms crossed as he leaned against a wall.

I paused in the open doorway, glancing down at Hades. Again, nothing. Not a word or even a feeling. My dog looked back at me, but apparently no one else was home.

"You can stay for now," I answered. "But trust goes both ways, all right? Listen in on me again, I'm slicing your bird into three parts, which I'll feed to the dog, cat, *and* the falcon."

The house was dark when I got home, which meant Mari was still out tending to Jandro, or one of the other injuries from the attack. I flicked on a light, surprised to find Freyja sleeping in Hades' dog bed.

"Why aren't you with your human, rodent?" I knelt to rub her exposed belly, earning a palm full of teeth and claws for my efforts. "Suit yourself," I muttered, heading to the kitchen in search of alcohol.

Three full drams of whiskey later, I realized it was a bad idea to drink alone. But by the time I reached that point, I couldn't stop. Alone, with no one to watch me, my mind went down a road it hadn't in years. I learned to soften up around Mari, but this was beyond even that.

"Fuckin' Dallas," I slurred, dragging my fingers down my face. "Why the fuck..."

His blood was on my hands, a wrongful death that never should have happened. While at the same time, he was a hero. A martyr. Selfless and pure. He'd become a Steel Demon legend, one that our grandchildren would talk about. Everyone would remember him fondly, as a man who was loyal, protective, and warm.

"Dallas!" I barked to the empty kitchen. "Why the fuck did you have to die? It coulda been, I dunno, fuckin' Big G, an' that woulda been fine."

An idea went off like a lightbulb in the drunken haze of my brain, and I nearly missed the floor when I slid off the barstool. Moving clumsily from the kitchen to the living room, I looked around for Hades.

"Hey, dog!" I called out. "Hades, lord of the underworld, whoever the fuck. I needa talk to ya."

A disgruntled bark whipped my head around to the dog bed, where the massive Doberman and black cat cuddled together like old friends. I was too drunk and focused on my mission to notice how strange that was, and stumbled closer to the animals.

"Hades." I lowered myself to the floor, faithful whiskey bottle in hand. "We're friends, right? Partners and all that. Well, I need you to do me a solid." I took a swig from the bottle. "Bring Dallas back."

The dog actually narrowed his eyes at me.

"Come on," I urged. "You know he shouldn't have died. He's nothing like the ones you have me reap."

Hades had the balls to yawn, poisoning me with a face full of dog breath.

"Damn it, Hades!" I pounded the floor with my fist, my desperation turning to anger. "He was a good man, all right? He had kids that needed him, a wife he loved. He never even looked at another woman. He didn't deserve this."

The dog blinked, but otherwise remained expressionless.

"What kind of fucking god are you?" I seethed. "You're just sitting there mocking me! You have me reap for you, and I'm fine with that. But I ask you to spare one innocent man and I get nothing? I haven't heard anything from you in weeks!"

You do not make demands of me, Reaper.

The voice knocked me back. Pure fear gripped my heart in a cruel fist and refused to let go. I wasn't even a man anymore, but a lowly, undeserving animal. I felt smaller than when my fathers yelled at me as a boy.

I rule the dead. Hades' face remained unchanged, dark eyes staring at me with an eerie calm as his voice reverberated through all of my senses. *I do not control life and death. I owe you nothing. You are a tool, an instrument for my bidding. But you are human, and even you do not wield absolute power as my reaper.*

"Some fucking god you are," I muttered.

Hades barked, his teeth snapping within an inch of my face. His lips and ears pulled back, snarling at me like he never had before.

All that research and you still understand nothing.

"Then explain it to me!" I cried out. "What are you? What's the fucking point? What do you want from me?"

Another menacing snap of teeth caused me to flinch.

Death is neither right nor wrong. It simply is. You cannot control or undo it. Once your species stopped dragging its knuckles, you became obsessed with death. How to prevent it, how to use it as a weapon. You obsessed so much about something you could never control, you gave it a face. A name. You gave it a story.

I leaned back to rest my palms on the floor, still hopeless to reconcile my dog's face with the sound of this voice rattling through my ribs and teeth.

In an ironic turn of events, Hades yawned, *humans gave life to the concept of death.*

"So what, this is all in my head?" I stammered out. "You're just a figment of my imagination, even though Mari has heard you? Even though Gunner has flown through Horus?"

We are manifestations of the divinity within all humans. The dog licked his lips. *Humanity may have brought me to life, but I am very much real.*

Every answer only led to more questions, more *hows* and *whys*. They ran laps in my head, stringing together into gibberish. Mari's curiosity seeped into me, but it only made my head hurt. I wanted to undo everything and go back to never questioning my dog's abilities or what he was.

"My brother." I didn't know why those words were the ones to leave my mouth, but it made sense as soon as they hit the air. Thinking of him was the only spot of clarity in the garbled mess that was my mind. "Daren. Can I talk to him?"

You can, if you are open to receiving him.

The voice that answered was softer than Hades'. It was feminine and almost sweet. Instead of the sound vibrating my bones and organs, this felt like a warm caress on my skin.

Freyja stood and stretched, arching her back like a bow. Sliding her body against Hades, she settled between his front paws with a loud purr.

Your brother is with me. As is your fallen brother-in-arms.

"Why you?" I blurted out, quickly adding, "No offense." It occurred to me too late that these were *gods* and I should have probably groveled or offered one of Jandro's chickens or something.

But Freyja didn't seem offended. *Their deaths were sacrifices. Selfless acts of love.* Her sharp, feline eyes fixated on me. *Rest assured they are at peace.*

"Can I talk to Dallas too?"

No, I'm sorry. She stepped off the dog bed and walked toward me. A cat-goddess purring loudly and rubbing on my leg was the last thing I expected, but a small, almost minuscule, sense of ease washed over me from the contact. It was like a small piece of my grief lifted and evaporated into thin air. And not just the grief for Dallas, but the long-time festering guilt I held for Daren's death.

Dallas is not gifted like your brother, Freyja explained to me. *He cannot communicate from beyond. But his children, the products of his love, will feel his spirit. So will their mother, even after her heart mends and she falls in love again. Their memories of him, their joy in this present life, give him peace.*

My eyes couldn't stop moving from the cat to the dog, to the rafters in the ceiling, to the air in front of my face. The voices seemed to be coming from everywhere. I might have been well and truly losing it, but at least I wasn't the only one. It was time to face the music.

"So what am I supposed to do?"

Freyja answered first.

Protect your people, especially the children. Love your woman with your whole being. And when her heart opens to love another, do not refuse her.

I narrowed my eyes in confusion. So Noelle had to be right. Mari would have a fourth man, but who else would there be after Gunner? He was the last of the men I trusted with Mari's heart, let alone her body.

A low, rumbling growl pulled my attention back to Hades. He stared at me squarely, eyes bright and ears erect. I sucked in a breath, bracing myself. I knew what was coming.

When I give the order, you will not disobey. You will reap.

MARIPOSA

I released my breath while squeezing the trigger once, and then pulled again to squeeze it a second time.

"Nice double-tap, baby girl!" Gunner beamed at me.

"Did I get it?" I lowered the gun and squinted at my target.

"Pretty close. Your groupings are getting closer, see?" He came up behind me, resting his chin on my shoulder as he pointed out my shots.

"Hey, they are!"

"All it takes is practice." A kiss landed on my cheek, followed by the warmth of his arms around my waist, hugging me close. "You'll be nailing those bull's-eyes in no time."

"I have a good teacher." A smile formed on my lips as I turned my head, nuzzling against his mouth. It felt good to smile again, and my falcon boy turned out to be right about target practice releasing frustration.

Not that I could pinpoint the cause of my frustration. Reaper shutting me out again? Maybe. Nearly losing Jandro to him being a hero? Possibly. Having to leave the first place in years that I called home? Likely. Myself, for not being able to save Dallas's life, however irrational it was? Even more likely.

"I heard you're sleeping with your teacher." Gunner nuzzled my neck, his grin teasing on my sensitive skin. "Bad girl."

"What can I say?" I leaned my head back on his shoulder, reaching up to grab handfuls of that gorgeous hair. "I like working for extra credit."

His warm laughter cut off abruptly. When I looked at his face to see why, his blue irises had just returned from rolling back in his head.

"We're about to have some company," he muttered, reluctantly untangling from me.

"Who?"

"The Sons." He became preoccupied with checking and reloading the magazines of our guns. "They're not close enough to hear us yet."

"What's your take on 'em?" I picked up my favorite handgun and began reloading it myself.

Gunner's face brightened as he watched me do it just as he had instructed me. "I dunno yet. I don't *dislike* those guys, just don't know 'em well enough to say. Offing my uncle definitely puts them in a pro column though."

"Are they going their own way when we leave? Or coming with us?"

He clicked his tongue. "Sounds like they're coming along. They don't exactly have anywhere to go."

Heavy footsteps crunched over the rocky ground as the three Sons of Odin approached.

"Mornin'," greeted T-Bone, accompanied by a caw from the raven on his shoulder.

Freyja, who'd been scratching one of the fence posts, arched her back and hissed in reply.

"Don't mind my cat," I grumbled, glaring at her like I would a petulant child. "Good morning."

"She's protective of you," T-Bone said with a small grin of understanding. "And I'm a stranger. No offense taken."

"Can we help you boys?" Gunner's hand slid possessively around me, resting low on my hip. I bit my lip to hide my smile, the touch making my insides dance and flutter.

"Just going around being neighborly, making our introductions," T-

Bone remarked. "You two know us already, so figured we'd check out the target practice."

"We haven't formally met the third of your trio." I lifted my chin at the quiet one hanging in the back. I'd yet to hear a word from him, or the Sons mention his name. He reminded me of Shadow.

"That's Grudge," T-Bone turned to acknowledge his silent friend. "He ain't much of a talker. Prefers to listen and observe."

The tall guy, Dyno, lifted his eyebrows slightly as if daring me to talk shit. To ridicule or write off his friend for being different.

But I just shrugged and looked past the two men in front to address him directly. "Fair enough. Nice to meet you, Grudge." Then I returned to loading my handgun.

The raven fluffed his feathers and let out a cackling set of caws that sounded like laughter. T-Bone and Dyno visibly relaxed.

"So," T-Bone eyed the arsenal of weapons laid out before us. "What's the Steel Demons weapon of choice?"

"We like our rifles here." Gunner leaned on a fence post, relaxed and in his element. "Handguns while riding, 9mm usually. Sometimes automatics. Me and a couple of the guys are into knife-throwing, too."

"You put scopes on these bad boys?" Dyno broke off from his pack, meandering over to admire Gunner's collection with a closer look.

"Nah," my blonde demon answered with a smirk. "Me and Shadow especially don't need 'em. We train all the guys to shoot without scopes, because you're more likely to use them as a handicap. Without em, you'll learn to be more accurate using the eyes God gave you."

Grudge followed Dyno to admire the guns and nerd out with Gunner, while T-Bone bumped into me with his elbow.

"Mind if I share your target, little lady?" He pulled a matte-black handgun from his holster and set it down next to mine, followed by a series of magazines of all different sizes.

"Suit yourself." I felt Gunner's eyes on me from several feet away. If T-Bone so much as looked at me wrong, I knew my man's weapon would be drawn faster than any of us could blink.

And that was *if* I wasn't faster while right next to the big sergeant at arms.

"You can stop thinking about shooting me. I'm a fucking gentleman," he chuckled, slapping his first magazine into his gun. "Besides," he lifted his weapon, tattooed arms extended straight in front of him, "pretty as you are, you're not my type."

He fired off a series of rounds, each trigger squeeze relaxed and controlled. I saw his first bullet hit the golf-ball sized red center of my target, but none after that. The center hole just got bigger as each subsequent shot chipped away at the cardboard. I'd only ever seen Gunner shoot that accurately.

"Nice work," I said, keeping my voice light. "And by not your type, you mean...?"

He popped the release on his mag, shooting me a playful grin. "I like dick almost as much as you do, Mrs. President."

Heat flooded my face, having nothing to do with the desert sun. I had suspected that T-Bone swung that way. More out of a gut feeling than anything he actually did. Neither he, nor the other two Sons, looked at me the way men usually did. Even with the protection of my men around, it was a relief not to be the object of yet another heavy stare.

T-Bone looked down to load another mag, his playful expression falling, turning distant and somber.

"I loved my president, too," he murmured, before raising his weapon and firing off another dozen rounds.

"I'm sorry," I whispered when his gunfire ceased. "I can't imagine going through what you did."

"Y'all might go through it just the same if the Demons don't get their asses in gear." His mouth closed abruptly, lifting a quizzical eyebrow at me. "Sorry, I dunno how your club handles women knowing their business."

"Reaper and the guys tell me everything." I double-checked my own weapon and raised it to take aim. "I'm the medic. I clean them up after business is handled, so I kind of need to know everything."

I squeezed my trigger to release my shots, going slower than T-Bone's rapid fire and checking my aim in between each round.

"Looks like you're becoming quite capable of handling business yourself," he remarked. My grouping made a small pattern just above his bullseye on the target.

"That's my girl!" Gunner hollered from further down the range. He and the two others took turns with long-distance targets and shotguns.

"I'm getting there," I smirked at T-Bone.

Reaper was still passed out on the couch when I returned home, the empty whiskey bottle on its side on the floor next to him. Hades lifted his head from the dog bed, releasing a soft whine as I came over to stroke his head.

"No change, huh boy?" I whispered, allowing him to lick my hand.

Freyja immediately hopped up next to the dog, kneading a soft place on the bed with her paws, before snuggling up to his side.

"Aren't you two the cozy couple?" I remarked as I made my way over to the facedown man stretched out on the couch.

"Sugar?" he groaned as I lifted his head, turning his cheek gently to lay on my lap. He rolled over to face upward with his eyes still closed, but hummed as my fingers dragged over his scalp.

"How bad is it?" I asked.

"Mmph." His brow pinched as he rubbed his forehead. "Seven out of ten. Been worse."

"I'll get you some Tylenol and water."

"No, stay." His arm went around my waist to hold me before I could stand up. "I love you, Mari."

My chest fluttered and I leaned back into the couch. My ring caught the sunlight through the windows, twinkling like a star as my fingers dove through Reaper's dark hair.

"I love you, Rory." My hands moved down to massage his neck.

He moaned at my touch, eyes slitting open. "What have I done this time to make you say my dipshit birth name?"

My fingers stopped moving, contemplating for a moment. "Nothing, really. I guess I'm just worried about you."

"Worried why?"

"I've never seen you hungover like this, for one. I don't like that you didn't want me around after Dallas's memorial. But," I placed a finger on his lips to ensure he'd let me keep talking, "I get it. You're in a tough position with losing Dallas, as his president and friend, plus moving, the attack, and dealing with the Sons. I'm not angry, love. I just want you to be okay." My fingers returned to kneading his shoulders and neck. "You carry such a burden all the time, but you don't have to do it alone."

He let out a deep sigh that deflated his whole chest. "I know, babe. I told you to leave because my head wasn't in a good place after the funeral. I didn't want to hurt you by saying something fucking stupid again."

A surprised breath escaped from my chest. Reaper tilted his head up to look at me, eyes green and clear, while mine filled with tears. I thought I knew before, but now I was certain.

It wouldn't be him. This man would never, ever break my heart.

"Sugar, what's wrong?"

"Nothing." I smiled and wiped my eyes before he could reach them. "You're just the best and I love you."

"I'm not the best." He took my hand and kissed my wrist, his fingers playing with the band of my ring. "That's why you have other men, to love you when I'm a fucking dick."

"I love you even when you are a dick," I laughed.

"And that's why you have my ring." He kissed the underside of the band, then laid my palm flat over his heart as he looked up at me. "I called you my wife to Shadow during the attack, when I didn't know where you were. It just slipped out in a panic, but it's true, Mari. We might not be bound together by any law or god, but you're *mine*. You'll always be mine."

"I bet we know of some gods that'll approve," I chuckled, raising my gaze to the dog bed. Hades was curled around Freyja, both fast asleep.

"Ain't that right." Reaper wrapped a hand around mine on his chest, his thumb stroking over my palm. "I have a lot to tell you about what Shadow and I found." He pinched the bridge of his nose, eyes squeezing shut. "Soon as my head stops fucking pounding."

"Let the medic take care of that." I leaned down to kiss his forehead, and blinked droplets of tears onto his skin.

I blinked again, the tears rolling freely down my cheeks now. Reaper sat up, a protective hand cupping the back of my neck to pull me into him.

"Something else bothering you, my love?" he asked tenderly.

"I just..." A ragged breath sawed out of me, taking all of my strength with it. I leaned heavily against my husband, melting into his calming heartbeat and gentle strokes of my hair. "I just miss Dallas."

His arms squeezed around my back, lips raining soothing kisses on my face and hair.

"I do too."

MARIPOSA

"**R**emember what I said." Scooting off the bed, I gave Jandro a light swat to his ass.

"You'll pin me down under a bike and have your way with me?" he murmured, facedown in his pillows.

"No," I laughed. "No rolling onto your back allowed."

"*Si, mami,*" he answered sleepily, before I crept out of the room to let him rest.

His healing was going well, and I was hoping he might not need skin grafts after all. The damage still limited his range of movement, however, and he wasn't likely to sit with his arms forward on a bike for a few weeks. Thankfully, Reaper decided to hold off on moving until his VP was in riding shape. It would give us time to figure out the logistics of uprooting so many people, and allow us to say goodbye to our home.

I headed downstairs, following Freyja as she scurried down fearlessly. She went straight for the sliding glass door to the backyard, paws up and eyes wide on Jandro's chickens.

"You be nice to them," I told her, sliding up the lock. "They're not for you to hunt."

I cracked the door open and she squeezed through the gap to dart outside. But she bypassed the chickens completely, running straight to the workout area.

"Damn it, cat." I muttered under my breath, my face heating up. "You are absolutely shameless."

Shadow was doing a set of bench presses when Freyja jumped on his thigh. He paused for a moment when he felt her, then carried on with his set like normal. His labored breaths and soft grunts of effort made my pulse quicken. The worst part was knowing that he had truly no idea how hot it was.

Displeased at being ignored, Freyja decided to walk up his thigh and settle on his stomach. She proceeded to knead him, paws moving rhythmically up and down as she purred up a storm. I could hear it all the way from inside the house.

Shadow finally set the bar on the catches and rolled up, holding her gently against his torso.

"Hello again, kitten." He cradled her like a baby in the crook of his arm, scratching her cheeks and chin as her eyes closed in bliss.

His shirt was off, chest muscles flexing as he petted her. With his long hair tied back, I got an unobstructed look at his face for the first time. A long, deep scar cut through his eye, stretching from his forehead to his cheek. My throat closed up uncomfortably. It was a miracle he still had that eye at all.

That scar didn't match the rest of the ones on his body. Whoever made it had taken out something personal on him, wanted to hurt him with more than just a surface level cut. Someone wanted to maim and disfigure him. But by all accounts, Shadow seemed perfectly capable of seeing with both eyes.

I could never imagine wanting to hurt the large man playing with my kitten. He was now curling his fingers into her belly, laughing softly as her claws and teeth dug into him. The evidence was written into every inch of his skin that this man had been hurt deeply, and for many years. Perhaps more than anyone else I ever met, he needed to be loved.

And that scar on his face did nothing to slow the fluttering of nerves that happened now, and whenever he was nearby. If anything, it only amplified my body's response to him.

I turned away from the sliding door, busying myself in the kitchen before he saw me. A few minutes later, I was entranced by a packet of Mexican hot chocolate mix when he came inside, still holding Freyja.

His shirt was back on, hair loose and pulled forward over the scar, the iris of his pale eye peering at me through the dark strands.

"Hi, Mariposa." He greeted me first, no longer trying to hide while I sought him out to say hello or good morning.

He set the cat down gently on the floor, where she proceeded to wind around his ankles.

"Hi, Shadow." Despite his dark, serious demeanor, I always felt like smiling around him. "Congratulations, I think you have a new cat."

He let out a dry laugh, watching Freyja rub all over his feet like a shameless hussy. "She's not mine. I still haven't figured out why she likes me."

I bit the inside of my cheek. *I can think of a few reasons.*

"You, ah, ready for this move?" My fingers crinkled up the hot chocolate packet, like the sugary brick was the key to breaking the tension between us.

"I think so. Excuse me, can I get past you?"

He closed the distance between us in one long stride, and my senses filled up with the warm, earthy scent of him.

"Oh yeah, sure! Sorry." I crossed the kitchen in a leap, like a gazelle.

"It's okay." He pulled open the cabinet that had been right above my head and brought down a tall glass. I openly stared as he filled it with water from the faucet and drank deeply.

Yeah, I'm thirsty too.

"I'll have to leave most of my books behind in the move," he said, oblivious to my ogling. "But my tattoo equipment should all fit on my bike. I'll just need someone's truck to hold my solar charger and generator so my machine can have juice."

"Are you doing a lot of tattoos before we leave?"

"I have designs in the works for a couple of the guys, but no, not many." He set his empty water glass in the sink. "Why?"

"If you have time, I," my shoulder crept up bashfully, "think I decided on my next one."

"Oh yeah?" A dark eyebrow lifted, as did the corner of his mouth, just slightly. "What did you decide on?"

"Something that portrays that I'm a medic," I said. "To you know, signify this time in my life if there's ever an end to this war, or the Collapse altogether."

Or, if my body is found before it all ends, someone will know what I did.

Shadow nodded. "What kind of design did you have in mind?"

"I was thinking just the word *Medic* with a red cross on my arm, like the armband the combat medics used to wear in the old wars."

Shadow tilted his head in thought, lips pursing in a way that was almost cute. The thought of kissing him sent my insides fluttering. How would he respond to an affectionate touch? Something more intimate than a hug. I wasn't even thinking of any part of him under his clothes, appealing as those areas were. No, I wondered about kissing that scar on his face, the one part of him he adamantly didn't want me to see.

"Can I show you something?" he asked, quickly adding, "If you don't mind."

I imagined pushing his hair away, letting my fingers trail over the hidden side of his face. "Of course you can."

He turned and left the kitchen, carefully stepping over Freyja sprawled out on the floor. She looked at me and then at him as if to say, *why aren't you pouncing on him? Do I have to do all the work?*

He returned moments later, flipping through a book, before he turned it around and held it out to me. "Have you ever seen this?"

I took it from him, studying the symbol on the open page. "I don't think so. What is it?" The image was of a staff with a snake wrapped around it. My first thought was that it would look right at home on a motorcycle jacket.

"It's called the Rod of Asclepius," Shadow said. "It's associated with the Greek god of healing and medicine. And it was a medical symbol before the onset of the Collapse." He took the book back from me and closed it, seeming embarrassed all of a sudden. "I just thought you might like to see it. You don't have to—"

"Shadow, wait." My hand caught his forearm as he turned to put the book away. "I *do* like it. It's a cool symbol with a lot of history." I smiled at him. "And I bet it would look better on my arm than a blocky red cross."

"I—I thought so, too." He hesitated, glancing down at my hand on his arm. "But it's up to you. It was just an idea I had when you said a medic tattoo."

"You have good ideas." I allowed my hand to drop from his arm. "I'm glad you showed me. Let's do the Rod of Asclepius instead."

"You're sure?"

"Positive." I wanted to hug him again to reassure him and show my excitement, but I settled for smiling and clasping my hands behind my back. "When can we do it?"

"Um, well." He reached up to rub the back of his neck, his massive bicep flexing. "I can draft a few designs this afternoon. You can pick your favorite tomorrow, and we can get started right after that, if that works for you."

"That works perfectly," I grinned. The urge to hug him was so intense now, my fingers tightened almost painfully around each other behind my back.

If it was anyone else, I wouldn't have hesitated. But I didn't want to push my luck, nor his precarious comfort zone with me.

"Great, good." He lifted a booted foot to gently remove Freyja, who clung to him like velcro again.

Somehow that silly cat eased the tension between us, while shamelessly demonstrating exactly how I wouldn't mind touching him.

Again.

I shoved down the stubborn memory, so vivid, but in a closed-off part of my mind like a distant dream. It never should have happened, and everyone treated it like it never did. But there was no forgetting how the space inside me stretched when it filled with him, nor the heat and texture of those scars under my palms. Scars I itched to feel and explore again.

"Tomorrow, then," I practically skipped out of the kitchen, restraining my own hands behind my back. "I'll be over in the morning to change Jandro's bandage."

"Okay." He licked his lips, flexed arm falling to his side. "It'll be fun to draw. I'll come up with something you'll like."

"I know you will." I forced myself to turn toward the door, despite wishing I could lean my head on his chest again, and this time press a palm to his face. "See you then, Shadow."

"See you, Mariposa."

EPILOGUE
REAPER

I rolled to my side and found her there. Beautiful and looking like an angel in her sleep. Jandro had scooted near the bottom of the bed, using Mari's thighs as a pillow. Apparently that helped him to sleep while lying on his stomach.

On the other side of me, Gunner slept near the edge of the bed, his long arm hanging down to the floor.

Taking care not to disturb any of them, I scooted off, grabbed my smokes and headed for the balcony. Hades and Freyja waited there for me, their black fur turned silver by the moonlight. My hands were already shaking as I pushed open the doors, and stepped out into the cool, night air.

Of course the moon was full. It never looked so eerie and cold before.

I stuck a cigarette in my mouth and lit it with a trembling hand.

I *had* done this before, and not too long ago, even though it felt like an eternity. But I never meant it. This time I had to.

No matter how badly I wanted to dive back into bed and pull my woman close.

"What's it like?" I asked.

Freyja wound herself around my ankles, her purr floating up to me.

It's like a dream, she answered. *But it's just as real as you or me. The hardest part for humans is trusting that it's real.*

"Can he—can he hear me right now?" I stammered.

Yes, he always has been able to.

My throat tightened, all the incidents of me cursing what he did running through my head. Every single time, both privately, and to Noelle and Mari, he knew. Never more did I yearn to walk away from this, but I kept my feet rooted to the ground. If he already knew the full gamut of my emotional state, then I had nothing left to hide.

I had to face what I spent a year shoving down. The demon that haunted me the most was the one thing I swore, then failed, to do— protect my family.

And I just wanted another chance to talk to someone I missed so much.

"I don't know what to do," I confessed.

Just begin speaking to him as if he were here, Freyja said. *Because he is here.*

I took a final long drag on my cigarette before tossing it away.

"Okay, Daren," I began. "We're long overdue for a conversation. So let's talk."

HELPLESS

STEEL DEMONS MC BOOK FIVE

Prologue

GUNNER

TEN YEARS EARLIER

My father came across as an unassuming man. If he paid attention to you, it made you feel like the only person in the room. Jonathan Youngblood could be warm, non-threatening, and a good listener. My mother said I had his smile, and when I got excited about something as a kid, my eyes would light up with the same brightness as when he used to look at her.

Used to.

I noticed from an early age that his smiles were never directed at her anymore, but his teeth and eyes shone brightly for pretty new fixtures—the socialites who came to his parties, daughters of his business partners.

It was jarring to me, seeing my father giving my mother the cold shoulder at their events. Mom held onto his arm, nails manicured and diamond jewelry throwing light all over the place like disco balls. Her smile was just as fake as his.

In contrast, my grandparents, who I spent more time with, only had eyes for each other. Gram would cackle with laughter, smacking Gramps' hand away when he pinched her behind as she walked by. They had touched all the time, bantering and bickering with smiles on their faces. Until Gramps passed away when I was thirteen, they slept in the same bed every night, and always retired to their bedroom together.

I couldn't remember a time when my parents ever went to bed together. One of my earliest memories was being carried by my nanny as I watched my parents walk to their separate, opposite wings of the house for the night.

All of these contrasting views rifled through my brain as I sat across from my father in his office. There were no family pictures, no touches of warmth or humanity in this space. Just polished wood and leather with the occasional shiny metal surface, reflections of him and his ego.

A massive taxidermy rhinoceros head jutted out from the wall behind him. The animal was completely extinct now, with no subspecies left except for those in zoos. Dear old Dad and his cousin, a US Senator, paid a fortune to hunt the last six wild rhinos remaining. He laughed at the activists, the public outcry, and the woe from environmentalists. This motherfucker was *proud* to have a direct hand in wiping an endangered species off the planet. That's the kind of man he really was underneath the smiles.

I kept this all in mind as I stuck my fingers between my neck and my shirt collar, the silk tie feeling like it was strangling me, while I waited for him to begin this charade.

Sometimes, even behind closed doors, he found it amusing to play the part of a father.

"General Arros sent me your final marks from McAlister today." Jonathan Youngblood folded his hands on his desk as if speaking to a business associate. "All perfect scores, as usual."

I frowned, shifting in my seat. "Grades don't come out until next month. I turned in my final project this morning."

"Don't be foolish, Gunner. You know the power I have over the entire academy board." A self-satisfied grin pulled at his lips. "You know the benefits of being a Youngblood."

I propped my elbow on the arm of the chair and lowered my head into my hand. I actually worked my ass off at McAlister Academy, and not just because I woke up doing push-ups at 4:30 am every day. I actually studied. I paid attention in class. Military history, battle strategy, it all fascinated me. I begged my teachers, and even met with the headmaster, to grade and evaluate me based on my own effort, not what my dad slipped them under the table. They all assured me they did, but apparently being in Jonathan Youngblood's favor was more appealing.

Dad began pouring a glass of Scotch—only one of course, for himself. This was a success for *him*, after all. I fantasized about breaking the bottle over his inflated head and gulping down the expensive booze myself.

"You'll receive a call from the Pentagon in two weeks' time," he said. "They'll offer you a job as a junior strategist. It's just above entry-level, you see. I couldn't place you in a higher-level position without... arousing suspicions." He chuckled, like that was a cute joke. "Keep your head down, do your job, and the pieces will move in your favor."

He paused to take a drink, swallowing while he looked me over, as if inspecting merchandise. "You'll be flying out to D.C. the following Monday. I suggest you prepare in the meantime, such as getting a haircut."

I scoffed, running a hand back through my buzz cut that had grown shaggy. During the last few weeks of the semester, I said 'fuck it' to my weekly haircuts. I was fucking sick of them.

"Yeah, about that..." I let my arm fall back down to the couch. "I'm not taking the job."

It was Jonathan's turn to scoff, not that he was surprised. He even humored me with a smile as he poured himself a second drink. "Don't be ridiculous, son. And sit up straight, you look like a fucking delinquent."

I slouched further down into the chair, spreading my feet wide on the floor, adding insult to injury. Only then did I see the first hints of cruelty he displayed when he didn't get his way. The pulse in his neck, the steely coldness in his eyes. Dad was used to me rebelling, that was why he sent me to live with my grandparents. If a five-year-old who poured ink all over his favorite ottoman while the nanny was distracted could be considered a rebel.

After that, he enjoyed toying with me when I said no. When I didn't want to come to his parties so he could show me off like a prized pig, he sent men over to Gramps' house, who punched and kicked me in the stomach until I agreed to come. When I refused to end things with Beth, the maid I was seeing, he sent her away and never told me where.

Like everything else he owned, he loved exerting control over me. He liked seeing me fight back until the moment I caved. But he never truly saw me stand up to him before.

"I'm not working at the fucking Pentagon," I told him. "I'm not cutting my hair. I'm not doing a *fucking* thing you tell me to anymore."

The snarl on his face used to scare me. Now he just looked like a tired old man. "I'm in no mood for your games tonight, Gunner. If I have to lock you in a room, strap you down, and take a razor to your head, I will."

"I'd like to see you try, Jonathan."

He slammed his hands down to push himself up and round his desk, but in the time it took to blink, I was already towering over him. My father's confident motions skittered to a halt, eyes wide with the first glimpse of uncertainty I'd ever seen him express.

"Didn't expect me to move so fast, did you?" I taunted, leaning down into his face. "From sitting like a *delinquent*."

"So you *did* apply yourself to your studies." His gaze roamed over me, as if noticing for the first time that his twenty-year-old son was taller and stronger than him. Shit, he probably never truly *saw* me this clearly in my whole life.

"I did," I breathed softly, squaring my shoulders. "I have to thank you for that, at least. Shipping me off to McAlister was probably the best thing you ever did for me."

"It was," he agreed with a vigorous nod of his head. "Because a Youngblood must always be in power. By the time you're thirty-five, you'll be the perfect candidate for president, son! The Pentagon is just the next step—"

"Yeah, see, that's where you got it wrong, old man." I crossed my arms. "I'm not one of your puppets, not anymore. McAlister didn't just test the limits of my body and teach me military strategy. I learned to think for myself, be my own person." A grin stretched across my face at seeing the rage forming on his. "And I love that, to you, that's the *worst* thing I could've become."

"You are a *Youngblood!*" he bellowed. "You serve no other purpose than to honor and continue our family's legacy! Do you understand? The *only* reason you exist is to follow after *me*."

I spread my arms wide and lifted my shoulders in a shrug. "Well, the world's about to end anyway, so doesn't seem like it would've lasted long. I'm riding off into the sunset instead. And if you try to stop me?" I leaned in even closer, making him shrink back. "I don't want to hurt your guys, but I can guarantee some broken fingers and ribs. Wouldn't want you to waste your money on some hourly workers' hospital bills."

Turning on my heel, I made my way to the office doors, finally tugging the knot loose on my tie. I couldn't wait to trample this whole fucking suit under my motorcycle tires.

"Gunner!" Jonathan called out after me. "You walk out that door, you are dead to me, you understand? You won't see a penny from me. If you come crawling back, begging forgiveness, I will gladly kick your face in myself! See how many maids want to fuck you after you're broke *and* ugly."

"Don't worry, pops." I didn't even spare him a glance as I pulled open the heavy wooden doors inlaid with the Youngblood family crest. "Unlike you, I still have a personality."

I walked out of the room to the sounds of a grown man's temper tantrum, then down the long marble corridor to the front door. The cool night air was like a soothing balm on my skin, a gentle caress after a heated exchange. *I actually fucking did it. I stood up to the bastard and now I'm my own man.*

My jacket and tie were off by the time I made it to my private garage, where the only earthly possession I cared about waited for me. I hit the button on my keyfob and stripped down to my boxers and socks as the garage door lifted. Leaving my discarded clothes and the keyfob on the gravel path, I walked inside and started pulling clothes out the duffel bag I had ready.

Now this was more like it. Jeans and engineer boots. A simple fitted t-shirt and a leather jacket.

Once dressed, I turned to Old Rusty, Gramps' vintage Harley that Jandro restored for me five years ago. I kicked-started the ancient bike as gently as I could, my heart vibrating in my chest as he sputtered to life.

Throwing a leg over the seat, my hands in place on the grips, I felt at home.

I kicked my feet up and accelerated forward, aiming a straight path over the clothes on the driveway. Running over my dad would've been more satisfying, but it was still a rush to grind the costume of my former life into the dirt. As the Youngblood family estate grew smaller and smaller in my rearview mirrors, maniacal laughter escaped me.

One thing I didn't tell my dad, was that McAlister only played a small part in my standing up to him and taking my life back for myself. No, that honor belonged to the two men waiting for me at the end of the property. The two *delinquents* who saw past my family name and wealth, and became my first true friends.

"Took you fuckin' long enough," Reaper growled when I pulled up at the crossroad.

He and Jandro sat on their idling bikes, the machines making gentle, purring rumbles. The cherried ends of their cigarettes lit their faces up in a red, ominous glow. It kind of made them look like demons.

"Yeah, whatever." I beckoned a hand at Reaper, unable to contain the grin on my face. "It's done. So gimme a smoke and let's ride."

GUNNER

Thirty miles outside of Sheol, I slowly rolled through a town that had seen better days. Bullet holes lined the sides of buildings and abandoned cars. Plywood covered up some of the broken windows—those that hadn't been pried off by squatters, at least.

Horus sat perched on my handlebars, beak clicking and eyes darting around, not missing anything about our surroundings. I stroked the feathers on his back idly, ignoring the few remaining residents of this town who were drawing their curtains shut and hurrying into alleyways off the main road. No one wanted to get in the way of the patch on my back.

I pulled up to my destination, a squat, one-story brick building, and cut the engine. Horus flew to my shoulder as I swung a leg over my seat and went to unstrap my cargo.

"Heard you carried Reaper's ass in midair," I scratched under my bird's beak. "Where's my help in carrying this shit?"

He chirped in reply, puffing up and shaking his feathers out.

"Yeah, that's what I thought."

Grabbing the metal case in both hands, I heaved it up off of my bike seat and headed for the front door. Thankfully, Arty left it unlocked today so I was able to push it open with my shoulder. I crossed the stuffy, dimly lit room in two steps and dropped the case with a heavy clang on the counter.

"You're gonna throw your back out, swingin' heavy shit around like that," Arty yelled from his back room.

Behind the counter, his office door was barely cracked. I couldn't see anything through it except flashes of light from sparks, accompanied by the hiss and crackle sounds of welding.

"How'd you know how I swing it, old man?" I yelled through the door.

"I have cameras, dipshit. What'd you bring me this time, your whole damn armory?"

"Nah." I leaned against the counter, eyeing all the new clutter accumulating in his shop. Guns and unique weapons were his favorite, which was why we got along so well, but he also had a bunch of taxidermy animals piled into one corner. Ornate glass bongs littered another shelf and decorative cigar boxes piled up in another.

"Whatcha got, then?"

"A few things," I called back dismissively. "Also a special request, of sorts."

The flash of sparks stopped, and I listened to his groans of exertion through the door as he got off his work stool. When the back door opened, a short, rotund man with frizzy gray hair circling the bald crown on his head peered up at me.

"Special request, eh? What're you damn Demons up to this time?" He shuffled over to his stool behind the counter, climbing up to meet at my eye level.

I pulled open the lid of my case. "Moving, for one. What'll it take for you to liquidate these for me?"

"Aww, Jesus, Gunner." Arty reached in and pulled out one of my vintage revolvers, the beautiful thing polished to a high shine and still in its hand-sewn leather holster. "Don't tell me you're getting rid of these? You're breaking my damn heart."

I raised both shoulders in a shrug. "Can't take it all with me. Keeping my favorites, though."

"Where y'all headed?" Arty began laying my once-glorious weapons collection out on the counter.

"Dunno yet." I scratched my forehead. "Wherever the hell we can go without starting a fucking turf war."

"I take it you'll need fuel, then? And ammo? Standard rounds?"

"That'll work."

He nodded, then peered up at me expectantly. "What was this about a special request?"

I pulled a knife from the hidden pocket in my cut and laid it on the counter, removing the sheath to show the carvings on the blade.

"You ever make jewelry, Art?"

"Jewelry?"

"Yeah, like for a woman." I ran an index finger along the flat side of the blade. "How hard would it be to make this into a pair of earrings and leave the carvings intact?"

Arty patted at his chest until he found his glasses in his shirt pocket. He put them low on the bridge of his nose, then picked up the weapon to inspect it carefully.

"Well, the blade is real silver. That'll make it easy to cut and shape."

"Cool, let's do that."

He looked at me shrewdly over the top of his glasses, mouth tightening into a frown. "Gunner, this knife is somewhere around five hundred years old. You could buy all your wildest fantasies with this thing, and you want it cut into earrings for *one* woman?"

"My wildest fantasies have all come true already," I grinned at him. "So you gonna do it or not?"

"You youngins," he groaned, pinching his shiny forehead. "Always thinkin' with your dicks."

"Honestly, it was never my favorite knife." I shrugged. "I would've thrown it in the box with the other stuff, but my girl likes it. Figured I'd make it into a little keepsake for her."

Arty just snorted, turning the blade over in his hands like it was a precious relic.

"So you gonna do it or not?" I asked him with a harder edge to my voice.

"Yeah, Gun. I got you," he sighed longingly.

"You've got plenty of weapons here to fawn over." I leaned both forearms down on the counter and snatched one of his pens and notepads. "Now here's what I'm thinking for the earring design."

With the load on my bike now twice as light, I made the ride home in half the time. I felt a lightness in my chest too, picturing Mari's face when I gave the earrings.

Knowingly or not, Reaper and Jandro set a precedent with their gifts to her. She only took off her necklace and ring in the bath or for work, and I wasn't about to be the odd man out that *didn't* have something for her to wear. I just hope that she liked what I came up with.

As the Steel Demon flag waved at me on the horizon, I sat upright, relaxed on my ride, taking one hand off the handlebars to rest at my hip. Only a few more runs to liquidate assets, and then I wouldn't have this homecoming view again.

For nearly four years, we had called this place home. I never expected it to be ours forever, but having to leave had crept up on us sooner than expected. And just when I found someone I could make a permanent home with.

The thought of Mari brought my hand back to the grip, the machine accelerating with a gentle thrust between my legs. After spending so much time pushing her away, I stuck to her like velcro now. I soaked up every beautiful laugh, sigh, and kiss, and then took every opportunity to fill her up with more. There was no undoing the hurt I caused her already, but I swore I'd never be a source of pain for her again.

Horus screeched above me, his shadow running along the ground just to my left. As we approached the gate, I glanced up just as he dived. Wings folded back, he hurtled through the air, almost faster than my eye could follow. I squinted, watching him, and slowing the bike down as I met up with Benji at the front gate.

"Welcome back, captain. Your bird hunting?" He shielded his eyes as we watched Horus's missile-like form together.

"Shouldn't need to. He ate this morning."

I spotted Horus's target as soon as the words left my mouth—a black-feathered bird roughly the same size as him and nowhere near as fast. Panic stole my next breath as the realization hit me.

"Oh shit! Is that T-Bone's bird?"

"Sure as fuck is."

We both whirled around to find the Sons of Odin Sergeant at Arms staring at us through the gate. Unlike Benji or me however, he didn't seem at all concerned about his raven becoming a snack for my falcon.

Tattooed arms crossed as T-Bone leveled his gaze at Benji. "Mind if I have a word with your captain?"

The kid scurried away without a breath of argument. I wondered if he'd run to get Reaper or Jandro. If T-Bone was out for my blood, I wasn't about to go down without a fight.

He leaned in close to me, wrapping his hands around the wrought iron bars that separated us. "Haven't been inside your bird's skull in a bit, have ya?"

I bristled at the question, a knee-jerk reaction. I wasn't used to people knowing about my ability to see through Horus, much less meet someone who could do the same thing.

"I don't fly and ride," I huffed. "Been on the bike running errands all morning." My head cocked to the side. "You don't seem all that concerned, though. Confident your raven is still alive? It's been a minute."

A grin tugged at his lips. "See for yourself, Youngblood."

The dude was testing me. If his ability was anything like mine, he lost control of his body while seeing through his raven. He could stab me through the gate right now if I *saw for myself*.

Except for the few times Horus seemed to pull my consciousness into him himself, which I had no control over, I only looked through him when alone or with those I trusted most.

I still didn't know T-Bone from Adam, but he and his two fellow Sons proved to be trustworthy at every opportunity so far. The Sons of Odin killed my uncle—something he deserved, but I'd probably never have the balls to do—after he violated their contract and kept them prisoner. They stopped a drone attack on us, then allowed themselves to be detained, tied up, and questioned by us. All the while, dealing with the loss of their clubhouse to a fire that spared no one.

So even my skeptical ass was willing to put a tiny bit of trust in T-Bone's hands.

My eyes rolled back, my consciousness leaving my body as easily as a breath. The next thing I saw was the entire compound from five hundred feet in the air.

I was light as air and just as free. No dead prey in my talons weighed me down. A black blur caught my eye and then Horus was diving again.

No, don't kill that bird! I yelled silently as the wind rushed past my feathers.

Horus ignored me, zeroing in on the raven like a target-locked missile. The bird cawed and beat its wings hard, but it was no match for the sky's fastest predator.

Stop! Stop!

My, our, *his*, talons stretched out, wings spreading out to brake hard. One more second and those glossy black feathers would be in our reach.

Ah—fuck!

At the last possible moment, Horus twisted in midair. We veered off course, wings spread wide and floating on the momentum. Chirps and screeches left my beak, Horus's happy sounds. The raven followed me, cackling as we began to fly in tandem.

Like a slingshot, my awareness slammed back into my human body. I grabbed onto the gate for support through the vertigo, blinking my eyes rapidly while T-Bone looked at me expectantly.

"They're...playing," I breathed, when I finally found my feet under me.

"Like a couple of kids on the playground," T-Bone chuckled. "What do ya make of that?"

"I think," I grinned back, "you should open this damn gate and I'll pour you a drink."

MARIPOSA

"What in the fucking hell is this shit?" Jandro's voice floated all the way through the house from the backyard. "Foghorn, what the fuck did you do?"

Sitting together at his home tattoo station, Shadow and I exchanged a look. We could do that comfortably now, look at each other without that bolt of terror in his eyes or the apprehension in mine.

Everything to do with the tall, scarred man, from small talk to eye contact, was easier now. We went from no words exchanged, fear and distrust on both sides, to sitting comfortably in close proximity. As comfortable as one could be while receiving a tattoo, anyway.

The fear of crossing his tripwire-like boundaries had evaporated at some point, although I was still careful about touching him. I only did so when it was absolutely necessary. To be honest, it was more about me not feeding the simmering tension I felt in his presence than it was about making him uncomfortable.

The gentle pressure of his hand on my arm only exacerbated my blooming crush on him. It amazed me how he had no true awareness of how sweet he was. He inked the outline on me so carefully, dark brows knitted together in concentration. Even now, he asked several times if the pain was too much.

The Rod of Asclepius, an ancient symbol of medicine, on my arm was nowhere near as painful as the Demon covering the top half of my back. Plus, all my tattoo jitters disappeared the moment he first touched that needle to my skin. I cherished this new warm, friendly territory with him, and the age-old dilemma of potentially ruining the friendship if I pursued more, took over the forefront of my mind.

"I should probably see what that's all about," I said apologetically as Jandro cursed up another storm from the backyard, this time in Spanish.

"I think you better." Shadow's lips curved in the echo of a smile as he set his tattoo gun down. "We can stop there for today."

Looking down at the fresh black outline on my arm, I tried, and failed, to swallow my disappointment. "But we just got started."

"You're bleeding a little." He wiped gently at my sore, freshly inked skin, the contact stinging. His uncovered eye brightened as it returned to my face. "Had a bit to drink last night?"

I stared hard at him before breaking out into a grin. "What's this I hear? Are you *teasing* me, Shadow?"

"No. I never tease." Still, his lips quirked up again as he taped a thin bandage to my arm. "I'll make sure to finish it before we move. But no drinking the day before."

He didn't cap it off with a *missy* or *young lady*, but the playful sternness in his voice said it all.

I bit back my laugh as I stood from his chair. "Whatever you say, boss."

He huffed, snapping off his gloves before organizing his supplies. "I'm not your boss."

"Hey so, uh..." I raked my hair back, feeling like I was thoroughly killing the mood as I lowered my voice to a near-whisper. "How are *you* doing with the whole drinking thing?"

His hands paused as he looked at me slowly. "Good, I think. I have a few with the guys now and then, but I've still cut way back."

"Still sleeping well?"

"Yes." His gaze dropped. "Thank you."

"Just checking on you." I resisted the urge to touch his massive shoulder as I scooted past him toward the backyard. Aside from starting my tattoo today, we'd had no physical contact since I cried into his chest outside of Andrea's house. "If I'm being too nosy, just let me know."

"You're not," he said, so softly I almost didn't hear before sliding open the back door.

"What's going on, *guapito*?"

Jandro was shirtless out in the direct sun, raking up chicken manure. I crossed my arms and gave him a piercing stare from the doorway. He *knew* I didn't want him pushing his range of movement, nor exposing his back to the sun, while his burns were still healing.

"I thought you were getting tattooed," he said, pointedly ignoring my glare.

"I thought you were following my care instructions," I retorted.

"Babe, look." He turned around, showing his back to me. "Am I high, or does this shit look almost fully healed?"

My mouth fell open at the sight of him, and I stepped off the porch to get a closer look.

The healing tissues were still tender and red in many areas, but the top layer of skin had definitely hardened in record time. None of his muscles or deeper skin layers were exposed to the elements anymore. He'd have a large burn scar covering most of his back, but I'd never seen such accelerated healing in my life.

Wait, yes I had.

Hades, back at the Sandia outpost after I pulled the shrapnel from his flank.

"Do you feel this?" I poked Jandro between his shoulder blades.

"Ah. Little tender, but yeah."

"What about here?" I poked two more spots on his back and received the same confirmation. Without warning, I slapped his fine ass so hard that my palm stung.

"Ow!" He rubbed the spot I hit, spinning around to face me. "What'd I do?"

"Your nerves have reconnected!" I laughed, grabbing his face and reaching up on tip-toes to smack a kiss on his lips. "You didn't have any feeling in those places when I touched them two days ago."

"Well, shit." He returned my grin, pulling me in by the waist for another kiss. "My girl fixed me up good, huh?"

"Not me," I shook my head. "It's all your body. This healing is ridiculously fast. You're at least two weeks ahead of where you should be."

We looked down at the same time to find Freyja winding around our ankles. She met our eyes with a green gaze, bumping her forehead against Jandro's shin with a loud purr as she weaved her body between our legs in a figure-eight pattern.

"After my narrow brush with death," Jandro's forehead slid against mine, "I'm not about to question things that are supposed to be impossible."

"Someone's watching out for us," I agreed, nudging the black cat with my foot.

"A few someones." Jandro rolled his shoulders back, then his head around his neck. "Still feels weird, though. Like I'm a snake in a new skin."

"That's basically what it is," I said. "I'm amazed you didn't need skin grafts. You should still keep it covered when out in the sun and moisturize—"

"I know, bossy medic," he chuckled. "I just came out for a couple minutes. I felt like a caged rat inside all the time."

"So what were you yelling about earlier?" I asked. "I could hear you all the way from inside the house."

His cheerful face fell into a scowl that I barely recognized on him. "Come look at this."

He led me to the chicken coop, which he'd built out of scraps from his auto shop and leftover lumber soon after bringing the birds home. It wouldn't win any beauty contests, but, knowing him, it was solidly built.

Foghorn, the rooster, and two of the hens, I think Leti and Chela, milled about outside the coop. As Jandro approached, Foghorn stuck his neck out and crowed loudly at him.

"Yeah, I got my eye on you, cocksucker," Jandro pointed at him. "I know what you did."

"What the hell?" I followed Jandro around to the back of the coop. "Did he hurt one of them?"

"No, worse." He leaned down and opened one of the nesting box doors. "Look!"

The third hen sat in a clean nest of hay. Nothing seemed unusual until Jandro reached in and pushed some of her feathers aside.

"Oh my God!" My hands pressed to my chest as I saw four tiny beaks and beady, dark eyes peering out from under the mother hen. "Baby chicks! Jandro, they're so cute!"

"They're gonna grow up and multiply," he groaned, slapping a hand to his face. "Not thrilled about transporting more animals as we move, but I guess we'll have more to eat soon."

"What?" I stared at him in horror. "No! They're your pets!"

"Mari, we're gonna end up with a flock of five-hundred if we don't do something."

"Then get the eggs as soon as they're laid. It's not Foghorn's fault, he's just going off of instinct."

"Yeah, it is," he muttered. "Damn cock fertilizing my eggs."

I snorted, earning a sheepish grin from him. "That came out wrong."

"Sure it did." I patted his arm. "Congratulations on the new babies, *papi* Jandro."

"It's not me, it's that motherfucker!" He pointed accusingly through the coop to Foghorn on the other side, strutting around proudly like the pimp he was.

"What are you gonna name them?" One of the chicks wandered out from under its mother, and I reached out to pet its fuzzy down feathers.

"I can't name them or else I'll get attached," he groaned, extending a finger to pet another one that emerged. "Seriously, we'll probably have to trade some of them for supplies while on the road, if you won't let me cook 'em."

"I guess that's better than watching them die with us," I sighed.

"You're already attached," he teased, pressing a kiss to the side of my head.

"How can I not be? They're so cute."

"Yeah, just wait 'til the males grow up and start competing with King Foghorn over here." Jandro rose to his feet, pulling me with him. "Guess I should let you get back to your tattoo."

"Shadow told me we'd pick it up another day," I sighed. "Those *anejos* last night thinned my blood enough to make me bleed during the inking."

"So?" Jandro lifted an eyebrow.

"He said no drinking the day before," I shrugged. "I assume it interferes with his work."

"Never heard him give anyone that stipulation before." Jandro scratched his head. "But whatever. What are you up to now?"

"I say we get you," I poked his chest, "back inside before you burn and undo all that healing."

"Hmm, now that you mention it." I heard the grin in his voice as I turned back toward the house, Jandro following me with his fingertips on my waist. "I haven't gotten anywhere near enough sexual healing."

I giggled while sliding the door open, his plush lips already teasing the back of my neck. "That is a bold-faced lie. You get all of that in spades."

"That's the thing, *mi Mariposita.*" His mouth skimmed from my neck to my ear. "I'll never get enough of you."

Jandro was fast asleep a half-hour later, lulled into utter relaxation by me rubbing healing ointment into his back. He looked incredibly adorable hugging a pillow, lips parted slightly. I knew he'd never say it outright, but he seemed to relish his afternoon naps. He protested at first when I told him to take time off from the shop, but a sensual back rub with soothing balm shut him right up.

As luck would have it, the three remaining members of the Sons of Odin MC were competent bike mechanics and eager to make themselves useful. With the three of them helping out Slick and Larkan, Jandro wouldn't even fall behind on his work while he recovered.

I slipped out of the bedroom quietly, Freyja following me with a high tail and her loud purr still rumbling.

"Do I have you to thank for that?" I cocked my head toward Jandro's sleeping form as I closed the door softly behind me.

Which part, the healing or the deep sleep?

The warm, omniscient voice made me stop in my tracks. It came from no discernable direction, but stroked over every inch of my skin like a hug. *Oh, don't look so bug-eyed. You've heard me before.*

"Guess I wasn't really expecting an answer." My feet started moving again, heading downstairs with my companion cat goddess at my side. Shadow was nowhere to be seen, which left the whole bottom floor empty except for me and Freyja.

I answer when a question piques my interest enough. Which is more than what can be said for Hades. She ran ahead of me and jumped up on the couch. Despite the complete lack of human gestures, I knew it was an invitation to sit and have a conversation.

"I thought you and Hades were practically the same." I lowered to the couch, keeping a few feet of distance between me and the cat.

Goodness no, child! What ever gave you that idea?

"Jandro said," I frowned, "when he was...unconscious, that you and Hades talked to him. You both convinced him to keep fighting and not let go. And from what Reaper explained to me, you're both gods of death from different pantheons."

Did it feel weird to be speaking those words out loud as part of a conversation with an actual deity? Abso-fucking-lutely. Did I still care about how crazy and unexplainable this all seemed? Not in the slightest. In the months of my life with the Steel Demons, I had seen and experienced too much to write it off as anything else.

Hades and I represent different aspects of one of humanity's many mysteries—death. And that's where our similarities end. His culture made him masculine, a stern overlord of a dark, cold afterlife, so that is the lens through which humanity perceives him.

"And how do we perceive you?" I asked.

The cat rolled onto her back, twisting her spine as she looked at me. I didn't *hear* laughter, but got the sense that she was amused.

You tell me, Freyja challenged.

I thought for a few moments. "Feminine," I began. "Nurturing, affectionate, independent."

Yes, go on. Say what's really on your mind.

I waffled over which adjectives to use. "Sensual. Loving."

Also sexual. The amusement bled through her voice. *And fertile. I represent the sacredness that is femininity. Both a woman's gentleness and her fierce strength.*

"That's why you were with Tessa," I realized. "You eased her pain and turned her baby while she was in labor."

I was always with her, Freyja said lightly. *As I was always with you. Just not always in this form. The gods are the tether that bind humanity into one universal existence.*

"So why are you here now?" I asked. "In a cat's body, with a voice? Why was I pulled to find you?"

Humanity is on the verge of breaking beyond repair, Freyja's voice turned solemn. *It is not just your civilization that has collapsed, but your collective spirit. To turn against each other as you have, you destroy yourselves. And if humans fall, so shall gods.*

SHADOW

I left the house silently before Mariposa made it to the backyard, closing the door behind me without a sound.

Her bleeding was a lame excuse to stop the tattoo, but there was no way I could tell her the real reason. Not that I *ever* wanted to stop. I made the Rod of Asclepius as large as she would allow me on her arm. Once finished, it would be a great piece with lots of detail.

I couldn't help but feel like a thief. Her smiles, her warmth, her time —none of it was meant for me. So I stole it. I wanted to steal every second she sat with me. The soft laughs and the glances, I collected every one and kept them tucked away in my memories like a dragon hoard. She may have thought she gave them to me willingly, but the fact remained that we were never meant to share anything between us.

She had three men who gave her everything she needed. I was never supposed to be the one who held her as she cried into my chest.

Hands shoved deep in my jeans pockets, I headed down the street toward the clubhouse while my fingers itched to wrap around a bottle and drink. When the urge came on strong like this, I knew the outcome would be one I'd regret. So I ignored the alluring thirst for numbness, bypassed the kitchen and headed for the stairwell.

It was the middle of the day, not anywhere close to sunset yet. But the first view of the sky from the roof eased the tight clamping in my chest just slightly. The air was cooler lately and I welcomed the chill on my skin.

I leaned over the balcony and allowed the breeze to blow my hair freely. No one could see me up here. It was one of the few places I didn't have to hide.

Around *her*, I wanted to hide everything. Everything that was wrong with me, I wanted to bury and shove away. Being around her made me feel like all my faults were on display, out in the open to shame me. I made sure to keep my facial scar hidden, and to speak at appropriate times. I never cared about being normal before. Now I wished for nothing else.

But at the same time, she made me feel normal—despite my freakishness being painfully obvious to me. I felt like I could grow an extra head and she would just smile and ask me how my morning was.

Her warmth and kindness shined an ugly spotlight on how fucked up my upbringing was. The pain from a blade slicing my skin used to be the only physical contact I ever knew. After touching her during a tattoo or our few brief hugs, my skin felt like it was starving for more contact.

I'd never felt anything remotely like that before, like I *needed* to feel the touch of another person.

Violence and alcohol used to be my drugs of choice. I kicked them, but found a new addiction in Mariposa, and couldn't begin to understand it.

Horus and the raven, Munin, circled each other in midair, diving and chasing each other. Watching them distracted me from my own thoughts, at least for the moment. Their aerial acrobatics must have done the trick, because I didn't even hear the Son of Odin walk up until he was right next to me.

My pulse shot up but I didn't react. Distracted or not, no one had been able to sneak up on me in a long time.

The silent man to my left was the one they called Grudge. His hair was pulled back into a ponytail at the base of his skull. The wiry whiskers of his beard nearly reached the top of his chest. I'd only ever seen Dallas with a beard that rivaled that one.

I gave him a nod of acknowledgment but otherwise ignored him.

He kept his distance and seemed to be up here for the same reason I was —to get away from everybody else.

Commotion on the pool deck drew my attention below. Gunner and T-Bone walked up together from the front gate, talking and laughing. Those two seemed close lately, but Gunner was always good at making friends.

The smell of fry batter hit my nostrils. It was nearly lunch time, and we were trying to use up our perishable food before moving. If my senses were correct, fish tacos were the main menu item today.

Just as I was debating heading down for a bite, a nudge at my arm nearly startled me out of my skin. Fuck, I'd have to learn some things from this Grudge guy. I thought I was silent, but he took it to a whole new level.

Turning to face him, I saw that he held a small pad of paper out to me, which was what had touched my arm. Written across the paper were the words, *Sisters of Bathory?*

Fuck.

Fuck. Fuck. Fuck.

I felt like a child again as I stared at him, the shadows deep in my psyche rising up to darken the sky and sun that I found freedom in. It had been nearly a decade since I'd seen or heard the name of that community.

"You too?" My question came out a choked whisper.

Grudge gave a single, tight nod. He pointed at my arm, indicating my scars, then hovered that same finger in front of his face and opened his mouth.

The man had a small, moving muscle in his lower jaw toward the back of his throat, but nothing where his tongue should have been.

"Holy fucking shit."

He closed his mouth and nodded.

"But," I narrowed my eyes, "I was born there, and the only male they kept long-term. No one else survived. I would've remembered you."

Grudge quickly wrote across his notepad, *NV, outside of Old Vegas. You?*

"Here in Arizona," I answered. "I don't know where, exactly. The community got invaded by the National Guard and they sent me to a mental health ward at a prison."

"Hm-hm-hm!"

Grudge seemed to be laughing, but it was hard to tell from the limited amount of sound he could make. He pointed his pen at me, then at the notepad to ensure I was watching. Slowly, he wrote the word COMMUNITY in large, all capital letters across a fresh sheet of paper. Then he took the pen in his fist and dragged it through the word, making deep black lines across the letters.

He dragged the pen back and forth until the word could barely be seen underneath. Then underneath, he slowly wrote the word CULT.

"I know," I sighed. "Trust me, I'm still catching on to how fucked up they were. Especially after finding a brotherhood like this." I allowed myself a small smile. It was getting easier to do. "I guess we lucked out in some ways, Grudge. I didn't even know Bathory had other locations."

He nodded and flipped to a fresh page in his notepad. *Nothing wrong with your "mental health", yeah?*

"No," I shook my head. "I don't understand a lot of things, but nothing's wrong with my brain. The medic hasn't given me pills for that, at least."

Grudge made his odd chuckling sound again. *Medic's pretty. Yours, too?*

"No, she's not mine." Tightness enveloped my chest and throat in a painful grip. "She's the president's, VP's, and Gunner's, who you've met."

You two are close.

"We're...friends." The word felt strange in my mouth, but I knew it would be the one Mariposa used to describe us. "She's the only woman I'm comfortable around. You know, considering..."

I trailed off, no need to elaborate. Grudge nodded to show that he understood. I could barely wrap my head around the fact that another man had been subjected to the same life as me, and lived to talk about it.

"How did you get out?"

It was the first question that left my mouth, although dozens more piled up in my brain. He couldn't have been a blood bag like me, but why else would they keep a male alive? Why remove his tongue? Grudge wasn't all scarred up like me, but my torturers never felt the need to silence me. I had a feeling they enjoyed my screams, and had become dissatisfied when I stopped feeling pain, stopped reacting to anything they did.

They would never kill me, so a big reason for my silence was to spite them.

Grudge chuckled again, the pen in his hand moving quickly. *A longer story than I got paper for. T and D can tell you, though.*

"They're good men, huh?" I asked. "Helped you make sense of the outside world? Made you feel more normal, useful, like you had choices and a purpose?"

"Mm." Grudge nodded sharply. *Learned what trust meant. Loyalty. Respect. Being a person.*

"Being in a brotherhood," I agreed.

He laughed again and continued writing. *Wouldn't call 'em my brothers. Love them, but not like that.*

I looked at him. "I'm not sure what you mean."

Smirking, he huffed out an amused breath. *We're brothers like you and the medic are "friends".*

"I don't *lov*—" My mouth clamped shut as my face burned. I couldn't even bring myself to say that alien word.

No, that definitely wasn't why the need for her touch had replaced my drinking habit. I was just a shell of a man, trading one vice for another to escape the past. It definitely wasn't the reason I purposely ended her tattoo sessions early, just to ensure I'd see her again. I was nothing but a thief, stealing time and attention from a woman who would never be mine.

Grudge gave me a knowing look. *Tell her how you feel.*

"There's nothing to tell." I shook my head. "Even if there was, she has *three* men. All of which know how to actually be with a woman."

You a cherry?

"No," I sighed. "Just service girls, that's it." *And her, who I was never supposed to have.* "I know what hole I'm supposed to go in, but nothing beyond that."

"Hmm." Grudge just stroked his beard as he smiled at me, laughing at some internal joke I wasn't privy to. *Some advice?*

I shrugged. Whatever he wanted to tell me wouldn't apply to my situation, as nothing would ever happen between me and Mariposa. But being able to listen and relate to someone who'd been through what I had was not likely to happen again in my lifetime. He understood me. And in my situation, that was incredibly rare.

He thought for a moment before returning to his notepad. *Be yourself. Don't hide who you are. Not even from her.*

The bitter scoff left my mouth before I could contain it.

"I appreciate it, Grudge. But I still have no idea who that person is."

MARIPOSA

I stared at the cat long enough for her to grow bored of me and begin grooming herself.

"So we're on the brink of a full-fledged apocalypse, huh?"

Yes. Not exactly the nuclear meltdown your fictional stories presented, is it? Freyja's tail flicked. *Although the political unrest and slaughter of citizens is not far off.*

"So where do you come in?" I asked. "Have the gods come to save us?"

Oh, we were always here. You just stopped listening. She yawned, revealing more teeth than I ever remembered seeing in a cat's mouth. *As for the saving business, that's on you to do yourselves.*

"Then why *are* you here?"

To remind you. Her sharp, feline gaze returned to my face. *Me, specifically, I'm here to fuel the love stories. I'm the magic you feel in the smiles of children. The celebration of life. I'm here to kindle the flames of desire, to accelerate that muscle beating in your chest. I'm here to remind humanity of the beautiful vulnerability that happens when you give yourself to another. And when a life ends due to a selfless act of love, I reveal my true form and guide that soul to peace.*

I sank into the couch, small moments with my men over the last few months flickering through my mind like a highlight reel. Everything, from a sweet touch and tender words spoken, to the roughness and heat that my body craved with the most primal desires.

"So how many thanks for my three-way love life do I owe you?"

None. An amused chuckle laced the goddess's voice. *I only steer with gentle guidance. I do not manufacture what is already there. The success of your relationships has everything to do with your compatibility, and the strength of your human hearts. However,* Freyja walked across the couch to me, bumping my hand with her forehead, *I sense some resistance in regards to a certain tattoo artist.*

"Shadow?" His name burst out of me so loudly that I straightened up and looked around to make sure he was really gone.

The sexual attraction is palpable. Your care and affection toward each other is clear. You have clearance to take another lover. So what stops you? She lowered to her belly next to me, tucking her front paws in toward each other as she stared at me expectantly.

How to explain why I didn't pursue a man who nearly drank himself to death to avoid nightmares? Who, when he *did* have nightmares, was uncontrollably violent to the point of needing to be locked in his room?

The answer seemed obvious when putting his most glaring flaws at the front and center of my mind. But I couldn't ignore what the medic in me knew—those flaws were only symptoms, not the cause.

Even thinking of him purely as a patient, without feelings clouding my judgment, I knew kindness and compassion were the best measures to counteract the root cause of his issues. To be treated as a person and not something *other.* He just needed practice and exposure to forge new neural pathways in his brain—pathways that told him women were just people too. That we weren't so different.

What Shadow *didn't* need was me selfishly projecting my own desires onto him. Of course I was attracted to him on a deep, primal level, but as his medic, I was also responsible for his well-being. To pursue things physically or romantically, especially while he was healing and still learning social norms, would only be looking out for *myself.*

"I don't want to scare him." It seemed to be the easiest way to sum up my feelings to Freyja. "His trauma with women runs deep and I don't want to trigger anything that could set him back."

His ability to adapt is stronger than you give him credit for. The cat goddess almost sounded like she was chastising me. *You don't need to be a god to see that he doesn't associate you with his painful past.*

"I don't even know if he likes me like that," I said. "He's easy to be around in just a normal context, but I have no idea what's going on in his head."

He doesn't know how to express his desires, because these desires are not something he's ever felt before.

My eyebrows lifted. "So he does like me?" I felt like a teenage girl gossiping with a friend.

Your presence soothes him. He finds comfort in you. He's finding it easier to communicate in general, now that he's realizing he won't be punished simply for existing.

A twisting pain rolled through my chest. "What happened to him?"

The cat blinked slowly at me.

That man has wounds only love can heal.

I stepped out to Jandro's front porch after that bizarre conversation, then turned to close the door behind me. Freyja acted completely normal, so nothing alerted me to the figure behind me until I felt arms wrap tightly around my waist and throat.

"Break my hold, baby girl." Gunner's warm breath tickled my ear.

"And slam you straight into this door?"

"Well, pretend to."

I tapped the side of his knee with my boot, just hard enough for him to feel, then drove my elbow back toward his gut before surging my weight forward. He followed my momentum, catapulting over me until he slapped a palm against the door.

"Nice job!" His smile beamed through the hair in front of his face before he raked it back. "You're getting faster, babe. Don't forget, you can also swing a fist down to hit 'em in the crotch. That might be more effective than the elbow."

"I'll try it next time," I grinned coyly, running my hands up his shoulders. "Thanks for the warning," I directed down at Freyja.

She stared back at me, then began licking a paw.

"Your kitty's smart, she knows I gotta train you to react on your feet." Gunner's hands laced at my lower back.

"Mm-hm, I'm sure that's what it is." I gazed up at him, playing with the hair at his collar. "Where's Horus?"

His sunshine-bright smile nearly split his face. "I'm glad you asked. He's doing an errand for me."

"An errand?"

"Let's go to the pool." He slid his grip from my waist to my hands, tugging me in the direction of the clubhouse.

"Gun," I started to whine, but followed him nonetheless. "It's getting too cold to swim."

The fall and winter months seemed to get colder every year in the Southwest. Back in Texas, I hadn't noticed much of a difference in climate, but in recent weeks I felt the humidity creeping up, which seemed unusual for Arizona. Maybe it had to do with the oceans being closer than they were fifty years ago.

"We're not going swimming, baby girl." He tugged me to his side, throwing the arm with our laced hands over my shoulder. "What we are doing is making a dent in the booze and perishables to lighten our load for when we move."

"I can't drink too much," I protested, "Or I'll bleed through my tattoo session and piss Shadow off."

Gunner's sky-blue eyes narrowed at me. "Since when does Shadow care about a little blood during a tattoo? I bled like hell through mine. Hell, I'm pretty sure I was drinking *during* my session."

"You're the second person to ask that question," I muttered. "Anyway, what's this errand Horus is doing for you?"

"You'll see." The wily grin never left his face. "You hungry? They're frying up fish tacos to use the last of the stuff."

"I am, actually."

Jandro and I hadn't had our usual lunch dates together since he got injured. Most of my time was spent tending to his burn and making sure he rested enough.

Freyja ran ahead when we reached the pool deck, and I could quickly see why. Hades had his back to us, sitting like a good boy, looking up at Reaper for a piece of food. After moving in closely behind tables and chairs, and then some strategic butt-wiggling, she pounced on him.

Hades yelped and whipped around, but she had already taken off to hide under one of the couches. Reaper saw the whole thing and laughed so hard he nearly choked and started coughing.

"Careful, or you'll need mouth-to-mouth," I said as Gunner and I walked up.

"Are you suggesting I shove things down the wrong pipe more often?" The president cleared his throat and grinned lazily as he drew me into his lap on the deck chair. "Hey, old lady."

"Hey, old man." I circled my arms around his neck, curling up against the hard planes of his body. "Chew your food or I'll look at getting you a set of dentures."

"Watch your mouth or I'll put something in there to keep you quiet," he returned, low and rumbling, with his thumb on my lower lip.

I melted like an ice cream cone under the sun. No one else could get away with talking to me like that. It would be crude, disrespectful, annoying, and definitely *not* hot. But coming from Reaper, the quiet threat of dominance revved me up like the roar of his bike.

And he knew it. The delighted hum from his chest was like a purr as he placed a smoldering kiss at the corner of my jaw.

"Gunner's up to something," I mumbled the first thing to pop into my flustered brain.

"I know."

We both watched the blond demon make his way through the taco line, piling fixings onto a plate of tortillas while grinning and chatting with the others milling about the patio. He and T-Bone seemed particularly chummy today.

"Are you in on his scheme?" I dragged my fingers along Reaper's scalp, admiring how my ring caught the sunlight through the dark strands.

"Nope," he chuckled, picking up his whiskey from the side table. "But he's got a shitty poker face. He's grinning bigger and dopier than usual."

I let out a frustrated groan and nuzzled my forehead into the side of his neck.

"How's Jandro?" Reaper's fingers skimmed across my back in a hypnotic pattern.

"Good. Better than good, even." I lifted my head to look at him in the eye. "He's healed super fast, weeks ahead of schedule."

"Like Hades did."

I nodded. "That, I still can't explain. But I think Freyja being around helped this time." I blew out a breath. "Not that that's a real, medical explanation."

"It might be. Just not one that you're satisfied with, medic." Reaper's teasing expression turned thoughtful. "So we might be able to move sooner than we thought. We're liquidating shit fast enough." He chuckled at my whining groan. "I know, sugar. But the sooner we're out of here, the safer we'll be, away from Tash's eyes."

"Have you decided where we'll go?"

His mouth tensed. "Still working on that part."

I rested my head on his shoulder again, my fingers running over his chest in a way that I hoped was comforting. Gunner meandered back to us after a few moments of quiet. He held a plate out to me, then quickly pulled it out of reach when Reaper made a grab for it.

"I was gonna give it to her," Reaper laughed.

"Like fuck you were." Gunner stayed out of arm's reach, then jerked his chin at me. "Come here and let me feed you, baby girl."

I smiled against Reaper's neck and kissed him there before standing up. "Can't say no to that."

"Get, woman." He swatted my ass and stood after me, heading toward the kitchen, presumably to refill his drink.

Gunner laughed lightly with a small shake of his head. "Still throws me for a loop."

"What?" I followed him to a small table near the pool, just outside the overhang.

"That the president's girl is also my girl," he grinned. "And he doesn't want to slice my dick off and feed it to me over you."

"And you're still okay with seeing us together?" Reaper warned me that Gunner might need some extra reassurance about our relationship, considering he was resistant to the idea for so long and wasn't familiar with a multi-person dynamic.

"More than okay." Gunner squeezed my knee under the table. "I thought it would be harder, like I'd have to figure out how to tolerate it. But I actually really like seeing you with them."

"You do?" I folded up my tortilla around its filling and took a cautious bite of my overfilled taco.

"Yeah, it's like Jandro said," he mused thoughtfully. "It's weird how *not* weird it is. I just love seeing you happy and taken care of. And when you're with me—" His eyes flicked away from my face for a moment, then back to me. "It doesn't diminish anything between us. When we're together, it feels like I'm the only guy in your life."

"Aww, Gun." I reached for his face, leaning over the table to kiss him just as a screech and a whoosh of air warned me to duck my head.

"Shit, Horus!"

Gun pushed his chair back to the sounds of thumps and ruffling feathers. I looked up to see that Horus had crash-landed on one of the couches, and everyone on the patio had ceased their conversations to see what had happened.

"Is he okay?" I rushed over to where Gunner had picked him up and inspected his wings.

"Yeah, he's fine." He looked sheepishly at me. "I guess he didn't expect you to touch me right then. It's hard enough grabbing onto my shoulder with only one foot."

I stared at him. "Why would he grab you with one foot?"

Gunner looked down at the bird on his lap, now seeming nervous. Everyone was still staring. "Because," he sighed, "he was supposed to land on my shoulder and then hand you this." He lifted Horus to show that the falcon held a small box in his talons.

A jewelry box.

A giddy laugh escaped me as I gently took the box from those fearsome claws. "This was his errand?"

"Yeah," Gunner frowned. "Tried to have it all planned out and romantic—"

I leaned in, kissing him to the sound of whistles and cheers from our spectators. "You're the sweetest man ever. Thank you."

His smile touched mine, one hand reaching up to stroke my cheek. "You haven't even seen what I got you."

"Doesn't matter." I kissed him again. "You're still the sweetest." His face was flushed, throat working nervously as I sat back and opened the lid on the box.

"Gunner!" I gasped and looked up at him with my mouth open. "Are you serious? Are these..."

"From the dagger on my wall, yeah." He swallowed again. "It didn't mean that much to me, was too old to be used as an actual weapon. But I knew you liked it, so—"

This time, he saw the kiss coming. My ears recognized Reaper's sharp whistle, the only hint that there was a world outside of my gunman's beautiful smile.

"They're perfect." Both of us were smiling too hard to really kiss properly.

"Put 'em on," he whispered, his grin reaching up to his sky-blue eyes.

The earrings were shaped like two daggers, the sharp end pointing down with a slight curve like the original weapon they came from. The silver had been polished to an almost mirror-like finish, while the carvings had been etched and blackened to show them more clearly.

It felt like putting on a unique kind of armor as I slipped the hooks into my earlobes. I realized the gifts of each of my men represented the nature of my relationship with them. Gunner helped me find my own strength. Jandro filled my life with laughter and color. And Reaper's devotion promised I was never alone.

"They look amazing on you." Gunner's eyes moved from my ears to the butterfly necklace at my throat, his gaze then lowering to rest at the ring on my finger. "All of it does. It's a complete set."

"Because I'm completely yours." I was all but crawling over him now, him leaning so far back he was nearly reclining on the sofa. "I love you." I made sure to say it low enough that none of our audience could hear.

His grin, however, was telling enough. "Love you so much, baby girl."

My next kiss did send him lying back, Horus squirming to get out from between us. Gunner grabbed my upper arms to pull me closer, and a throbbing pain shot up to my right shoulder.

"Ow!"

"Shit, sorry." He released the bandage covering my newest tattoo. "Forgot that was there for a second."

"It's okay."

The ache throbbing up my arm was a stark reminder of Shadow, how the tattoos were his own, unique kind of gift. Not in the same way as my guys, but...

I pushed the thought away and melted deeper into Gunner's kiss.

REAPER

The maps in front of me blurred into meaningless squiggles and lines. I rubbed my eyes, leaning back in my chair with a groan. Trying to decide on a route for the whole club was tedious enough, but after a full belly of tacos and maybe a *little* too much whiskey, working on anything was a chore.

I couldn't help that last drink though, not after seeing Mari and Gunner all wrapped up in each other. Before giving her my ring, I thought about having Hades give it to her. Although entertaining to watch, that crash-landing by Horus made me feel good about my decision *not* to have animals involved in my proposal.

In any case, I was glad to see that Gunner had fully embraced his place at Mari's side, symbolizing his devotion with a gift in the same vein as me and Jandro. An extra celebratory drink was the only logical thing to do.

Celebrating could never last, as I knew all too well. Mari went to check on Jandro and bring him food, Gunner rode off to liquidate more supplies, and I came back here to my study. To stare at fucking maps again, and try to guess the least dangerous route through the desert, to some unclaimed place we could settle. Away from General Tash and his spies.

Naturally, I'd rather be doing just about anything else. So when a knock came to my study door, I welcomed the distraction. Hades, in a food coma of his own, barely acknowledged the sound—just an ear twitch from his sprawled out position in the dog bed next to my desk. At least I knew whoever was at the door posed no threat.

"Come in," I called.

The door swung open and I regarded my visitor with cool indifference from across the room.

"Prospect," I greeted, refusing to address Larkan by his name. "What can I do for you?"

"President," he returned just as coolly. "Mind if I sit?"

I gestured to the armchair across from my desk and watched him stride over to it. The kid was not lacking in confidence, I'd give him that. It was him who gave us the information that Tash turned against us. I thought he was just a rat at first, flipping on his employers in the hopes we'd spare his life. It turned out, he was an accomplished marksman and bike mechanic, and had wanted to become a Steel Demon since he heard about us nearly a decade ago.

I was man enough to admit my first impression was wrong, and we took him on as a prospect. If he continued being loyal to us, he might even become a fine Demon one day. Only when Larkan sat down did I notice the nervous swallowing of his throat.

"President," he began. "I know I haven't been with this club long, but I want you to know you have my steadfast loyalty and respect—"

"Skip the ass-kissing, prospect." I waved my hand in a *move along* motion. "Just tell me what you need."

His throat worked again, Adam's apple bobbing as he swallowed his nerves.

"I came to ask your permission to make Noelle my old lady."

My gut feeling told me this was about my sister, but I felt no victory at being proven right. Instead, I felt the heat of my temper curling under my skin, shaping my hand into a fist. I beat Larkan's ass at the last Fight Night for being too damn handsy with my sister, and the fucking kid just seemed eager for more.

"No."

He had the gall to look confused. "No?"

"I'll be clearer—absolutely fucking not."

Larkan sucked in a breath, his own hands curling into fists at his sides as he fought to control his own temper.

"With all due respect, Reap—president, I love her."

"I'm sure you do." I reached for my cigarettes and stuck one in my mouth. "I don't give a shit."

"President, I—" He stopped himself and tried again. "I'm not new to this. I've been committed to a woman before, faithfully. I have and will continue to treat her well. I'm not the kind of guy who will—"

"I'm sure you're a fine man, Larkan," I said. "I'm not refusing on the basis of your character, but on the simple fact that you're just a prospect, and she's the president's sister. By club law, you're not worthy of her. Not until you're a fully patched-in member."

Knowing better than to argue, his lips clamped shut while I lit my cigarette. In all honesty, I had no doubt he'd be a full-fledged Demon within a year. The right time to patch him in would be at my discretion, sometimes preceded by nomination from one of the other guys. But he would only receive that honor if he breathed and bled Steel Demon loyalty, not because he was in love with my sister.

"Was there anything else you needed?"

Larkan sighed, unclenching his fists on his knees. "I was hoping you might be willing to look past club politics and see what really matters."

"Keep talking along those lines," I pulled the cigarette from my mouth and pointed at him with it, "and I guarantee you'll never earn a fucking patch. You've got some big, heavy-swinging balls to come in here asking *me* to circumvent the laws of *my* club."

"Noelle wants this too." Larkan's jaw set, hard and determined. "We've talked about this and want to be together, officially."

"And you know why she's not here?" I didn't give him a chance to answer. "Because she's not a fucking fool. She already knew what I would say. Let me guess," I paused for another drag off my smoke, "she tried to talk you out of coming to see me. Told you it was a bad fucking idea."

His face told me everything without having to say a word.

"If you really love my sister," I said, not bothering to hide my smugness, "you might want to listen to her more." I tapped my cigarette over the ashtray. "You can leave now."

He walked out without a word, and moments later I was stubbing out my smoke and rubbing my eyes while groaning again.

I needed space. Open road and fresh air. Sitting here would just keep me stewing over young punks who wanted what they hadn't earned yet. After sparing Larkan's life, giving him a home, and an opportunity too. Thinking any more about his ungrateful ass would leave me sour for the rest of the day if I didn't do something.

Hades' ears perked up as I scraped my chair back noisily. He got up from the dog bed with a few lazy stretches and followed me out of the study and into the garage.

I hit the button to open the garage door, and turned the ignition on my favorite steed as light from the outside world filled the room. I didn't notice the booted feet standing in my driveway until the garage door was waist-high. At first, I thought Larkan was still hovering around and squared up toward the door. If he didn't get the message with words, I'd teach him another lesson with my fists. At this point, I didn't care about waiting for the next Fight Night.

But the garage door continued rolling up to reveal one of the Sons of Odin standing on the other side.

"Dyno." I lowered my fists cautiously to my sides. "What are you doing here?"

"President." The tall, slender man noticed my stance and did not appear the least bit threatened. "I was on my way over for a quick word, but looks like you're heading out."

"Seems I'm popular today," I sighed, walking toward him so as to not yell over my bike idling. "What do you need?"

"Just to say thank you, and uh, apologize." He scratched one side of his shaved head, a few dark strands coming loose from the topknot at his crown. "I didn't appreciate your men tying us up, nor you keeping us locked in a room for three days, but I understand your caution. And aside from that, you've been a very generous and hospitable host. So, I thank you and I'm sorry for my earlier remarks." He stuck his hand out and waited.

After a moment to collect myself from the surprise, I clasped his palm in mine and shook it firmly. Now there was another lesson in respect that Larkan could afford to learn.

"Apology accepted." I released Dyno's hand and crossed my arms as a thought came to me. "You got anywhere to be right now?"

"Ah, no." He looked puzzled. "Why?"

I jerked my head toward my rumbling steed in the garage. "Ride with me."

"Me?" He raised a hand to his chest. "You're sure, president?"

"I was gonna go alone to clear my head, but someone with a fresh perspective might be even better." I shrugged and turned toward my bike. "Come or not. S'up to you."

Five minutes later, I was roaring out the front gate with Hades at my side and Dyno right behind me. For a moment, I regretted not dragging Mari out with me. The sun was just starting to lower, casting long shadows and bathing everything in a golden light. The sky would explode into colors in a few short hours, before being swallowed by dusk.

I thought of how I woke up in bed that morning, the first thing I saw was her turning her hand over as she admired my ring.

"Still like it?" I had murmured groggily.

"Of course I do." She looked over at me with a sleepy smile. "I love it."

"Still love me?"

She pursed her lips together and her look became playfully stern. "What do you think?"

"I don't know." I pulled the sheet back and rolled over, tucking her beneath me where she fit so perfectly. "Tell me," I whispered, kissing my favorite spots to elicit those soft sighs and giggles. "Show me."

"I love you, Rory," she told me with the sweetest whimpers while we did serious damage to the headboard this morning.

It was hard to believe I'd have a lifetime of those mornings ahead of me. Plus a lifetime of sunset rides to take with her, my wife. As long as I found my club somewhere safe to resettle.

That last thought was sobering, like a face full of ice cold water. I leaned forward on my bike, accelerating hard, knowing Hades and Dyno would stay with me.

The three of us cut across the landscape, leaving a trail of dust behind. Originally I didn't have a destination in mind, but with Dyno joining, I led our small, merry band to my favorite place to think.

A half-hour of riding took us to a ridge overlooking what was once the Hopi Indian reservation. We cut our engines, the silence of the land swallowing the roars of our bikes. Dyno looked over the ridge, his foot on a boulder as I poured water for Hades from my canteen.

"Did you realize our old clubhouse was on Hopi land?" he asked.

"Suppose I didn't," I muttered, joining him to look over the expanse of red rock down below.

"Here, the markers are obvious." He pointed out the stone dwellings that remained of the tribal homes. "But when you ride up directly from the south, everything on that end's been destroyed."

"How does that work, having a Norse-devoted MC on tribal land?"

Dyno shifted his gaze toward me. "The Hopi were never a warring tribe. They were peaceful, harmonious." He released a scoff. "Guess it doesn't really matter. Most of them fled or were killed when General Tash rolled through."

"You grew up on the reservation," I realized.

"My mother's family was Hopi," he replied. "Our clubhouse used to be a visitor's center for tourists. Our president, Bash, and T-Bone, suggested it so my home with the club would be near my ancestors."

His throat worked, jaw clenching as his gaze jerked back to the landscape.

"I'm sorry for what happened," I said. "That's just further proof that Tash is right outside our door, and we've got to get our people to safety."

Dyno sucked in a shaky breath and nodded, quickly composing himself.

"Four Corners is your best bet," he said. "There's not much there yet. You'll be living rougher than you do now, but it's well-defended and safe."

"And people have rights?" I asked skeptically. "No slave labor? Human trafficking?"

"That shit's strictly forbidden. If you're worried about your women and kids, you don't have to be. Governor Vance runs a tight ship, but he's fair. The Sons can vouch for him personally."

"It's not that I don't believe you. I'm just reluctant to trust anyone with enough power to call themselves a governor. Or a general, for that matter."

"We know Governor Vance's general too. He was a border war conscript who escaped his assignment, and now serves Vance willingly to keep the peace."

"Hmm," I mused, scratching Hades' ears. "I'll believe it when I see it."

"So you'll go?" Dyno's eyes brightened with curiosity, hands resting on his belt buckle.

"I'll pitch it to the club at church. This is something we should vote on." I cocked my head at him. "You and your boys are welcome to sit in and make your case. There will be questions, I'm sure."

"We'll be there." Dyno looked out to the stretch of desert once again. "If you all do this, you'll have to go around the reservation, up into Utah. We know the area pretty well and can scout ahead for you."

"And what about when we show up at Four Corners' door?" I asked. "Is the benevolent governor going to welcome us with open arms? Somehow I doubt that."

"We'll vouch for you, too," Dyno assured me. "We've done dozens, if not hundreds, of contract jobs for Vance. He's solid. He doesn't have any preconceived notions about MCs like some rich folks do." Dyno clapped a hand on my shoulder. "Once he sees how well you look after your people, I don't think he'll have any issue letting you stay."

"It'll be temporary," I reminded him. "Until we find someplace permanent, that's ours alone."

An eyebrow lifted. "When do you think that'll happen?"

I lifted my water canteen to my lips. "When General Tash is wiped off the map."

MARIPOSA

I fumbled blindly in the dark, woken up by my bladder screaming at me to be emptied. Reaper's chest was usually a solid wall behind me, but tonight it wasn't there at all. Carefully maneuvering around Gunner and Jandro, loosely piled around on the mattress, I made it to the bathroom in time.

After finishing my business, I paused, standing next to the bed and allowed my eyes to adjust to the darkness. Jandro and Gunner both splayed out on their stomachs, their back muscles rising and falling with their steady breaths. As tempting as it was to fall back asleep in the cuddle pile, I felt a nagging need to know where Reaper was.

I found him on the balcony just off of the master bedroom, leaning over the railing wearing only his jeans, and a cloud of cigarette smoke surrounding him. But he wasn't alone—Freyja and Hades lounged on the floor nearby. Neither of them looked surprised as I shrugged a robe on and pulled it closed around my waist. Reaper's head cocked at the sound of my bare feet padding over to him.

"What are you doing up, sugar?" he asked, his voice rough.

"Got up to pee and saw you were missing." I slid a hand along his lower back and he lifted an arm to tuck me into his side. "What are you three doing?" Freyja's tail flicked playfully, and Hades padded over to lick my hand.

"I think these two are just making sure my dumbass doesn't fall over the railing," he laughed dryly.

"What are you doing, then?" I laced my fingers with his hand draped over my shoulder.

"What you all said I should do." The words came out softly as a whisper, but with a bite of frustration. "Trying to let my brother in so we can talk."

I squeezed his hand. "And?"

"Nothing," he growled. "I think Daren's given up on me. Or more likely, I'm a fucking idiot for trying to talk to a dead man."

You are not truly letting him in. Freyja's voice hit us both at the same time. *You are allowing your doubts to create barriers.*

"I *am* trying, okay?" Reaper grumbled. "Of course I have doubts. I haven't talked to my brother since he fucking *died* in my arms."

Would it help to remind you that death is not an end? Freyja rubbed her head against Reaper's leg. *It's a transformation. A new chapter for the soul. Daren isn't gone. He's on a different plane of existence.*

"Sounds like a bunch of horse shit to me."

This is what I'm talking about. Freyja's voice seemed to sigh with exasperation.

"Well, what are you doing out here?" I ran a hand up his back, fingers digging into the knots of his muscles. "Noelle said he comes to her in dreams."

"According to them," Reaper's hand flung out to indicate the animals with us, "I should talk to him while I'm awake, to let him know I'm listening. He's supposed to respond in my dreams after I go back to sleep."

"And nothing?"

He shook his head. "I've been having a bitch of a time falling asleep as it is, with the move, Dallas, everything. So I keep coming up here to clear my head, get shit off my chest, and—"

His arm tightened around me with a sigh. "There's so much I want to say to him, but it feels stuck. It's not that I doubt him being out there, but everything I say feels forced. Like I'm fucking faking it, 'cause I am."

"You're too hard on yourself." I brought our linked hands to my lips and kissed the back of his palm.

"I'm not hard enough, sugar." He squeezed me harder with the confession. "Dallas died within our own walls. That never should have happened."

"There was nothing you could have done. You had no way of knowing what would happen." I leaned my weight into his side. "No wonder Daren can't get through, your mind is all over the place. You're not focusing, love, except to blame yourself."

"One of the things I do best," he grumbled.

I released our hands and moved in front of him, blocking his view of the compound and surrounding desert as I looped my arms around his neck.

"Come back to bed." I lifted onto my tiptoes and pressed a kiss to his frowning mouth.

"I probably shouldn't. I'll just keep you and the guys up with my tossing and turning."

"No, you won't." I traced his collarbone in the dark, my finger following the length of bone to the hollow of his throat. "If you don't fight me for once, and relax."

Even in the dark I saw his smirk, and a soft huff of breath left his mouth. "What are you scheming, sugar?"

"I'm good at following your rules when you set them." My finger dragged slowly between his pecs. "Now I'm asking you to follow mine."

"And what rules do you have for me?" His voice turned husky as my hand drifted down his abs to rest at the waistband of his jeans.

"To relax." My thumb flicked at the button on his pants. "To lie back and let me do everything that *I* want to you."

"Hmm." Heavy, calloused fingers pushed my hair aside to caress my neck and shoulder.

"And when I'm done with you?"

"Yes?" he mused, thumb on my lip.

"You will go right to sleep. No touching me or getting me off."

"Not fuckin' happening, sugar."

"Reaper, come on." Only while arguing with him, attempting to assert myself and take control, would I find myself pleading. "You need to sleep. You need just a few hours of having *nothing* run through your mind."

"Maybe, but I ain't about to be a damn pillow prince to get it."

"Just tonight," I begged, rubbing my palm shamelessly against the front of his jeans. He was getting thick and hard with each passing second, so I knew he wasn't completely opposed to the idea. "Let me take care of *you* for once."

His head tilted up, facing the star-filled night sky as he blew out a breath. "Fine."

"Oh yeah?" I wrapped my arms around his waist, bringing my chest to his. "I thought for sure you'd take more convincing than that."

"Don't push your luck, sugar." He tapped a finger to my nose. "Or I might change my mind."

I could have skipped with giddiness as I led him back inside. A smile stretched across my face, but I bit my lip to halt any noises tempted to escape. Our sneaky footsteps to the bed, and Jandro and Gunner's deep breaths, were the only sounds in the room.

Careful to avoid the two sleeping men, Reaper sat on the edge of the bed and pulled me roughly into his lap.

"Hey!" I whispered harshly. "This wasn't the deal. I call the shots, remember?"

"Just let me kiss you first." His mouth was already dragging a fiery trail along the side of my neck. "And let me take this off."

He reached for the lapel of my robe, aiming to slide it off my shoulder, when I grabbed his hand. "No. I see what you're doing, *Rory*."

"What?" He feigned innocence, but his shoulders shook with the laughter he kept inside. "You want to please me. I'm pleased by seeing you naked."

"You're trying to be sneaky." I pulled on his bottom lip with my teeth. "*I'm* doing the seducing here, not you. Now lay back."

"Damn bossy wife," he sighed while my insides turned to jello at hearing him call me that. But he obeyed, lacing his fingers behind his head as his back hit the mattress between Jandro and Gunner, somehow still passed out. "Go ahead, have your way with me."

I remained straddling his thighs, loosening the robe so the sleeves fell just past my shoulders. Most of my chest and the swells of my breasts were visible, the lapels making a long V down to my navel. Reaper tried to look passive, but I could feel how his eyes watched me, cloaked in darkness with only slivers of light. Leaning over his stretched-out torso, I kissed him full of tongue and heat, while pinning his wrists in place—a wordless reminder not to touch me.

He groaned softly into my mouth, hips shifting beneath me, but otherwise remained still. My kisses trailed down his neck, moving leisurely over the lines of ink swirling across his chest. I held onto his wrists until my reach was fully extended, with my mouth near his navel. As I moved lower, my hands mapped down his body where my lips had just been.

I felt him hot and pulsing against my cheek by the time my fingers reached his zipper. As I started pulling it down, planting kisses on his hip bones and lower stomach, his caress of my arms had me yanking the zipper back up.

"No touching," I whispered.

"Fuck, sorry." He placed his hands back under his head. "Feels wrong not to touch you."

"Be quiet or you'll wake them."

"Yeah, yeah."

I unzipped him again and worked his jeans down his legs, watching the tension in his face and how his arms flexed with restraint. For a moment, I considered binding his wrists with his belt, but not even I had the patience to go without touching and tasting him for too long.

His cock rested on his lower stomach, angling to the left as I kneaded his thighs. My thumbs moved in steadily toward his balls, massaging all around his base without touching him directly.

"Sugar, please..."

A grin split my face as I leaned down, lips hovering over his stiff length. "Hm, I like hearing you beg." How many times before had he told me the same thing? Payback was sweet.

Reaper let out a growl of frustration, tilting his head back toward the far wall. I would have bet anything his fingers were curled into a white knuckle grip on his hair. Only then did I give him any relief.

I dragged my tongue in a long, slow trail, starting at his balls. His shaft pulsed under my tongue, smooth skin over concrete hardness, growing hot at the contact. When I reached the base of his crown he sucked in a sharp hiss, then moaned as my lips slid over him and took him within.

I circled my tongue around his head first, my hand wrapping around his base to assist. My other hand wandered up and down his body shamelessly, if even cruelly. Just feeling my man, the way his breath stuttered, how his muscles bunched and stretched in response to my touch, gave me pleasure too. I was still getting so much out of this, even while focusing on him. But I could see how much difficulty he had in not touching me in return.

"*Fuck*, Mari..."

My mouth slid down his shaft now, swallowing his head as my hand worked him from the bottom.

"Sugar, let me kiss you. Please."

I slid my free hand up his chest, finding his lips with my fingers as I continued dragging my mouth up and down his cock. He kissed my hand like a man dying of thirst, desperate to lick and nibble at any part of me that he could reach.

"Can I touch you with my hands? Please?"

"Mm-mm." I shook my head no as I pulled my fingers away from his mouth. Releasing his dick with a pop of my lips, I glided both hands along his shaft, now coated with my saliva. "Was this your plan? Go along with me, then beg to get your way? You're not as resilient as I thought, Mr. President."

"I have no resolve at all when it comes to you." His breaths were ragged, voice taut with the tension winding up in his body.

"You always need to be in control." I planted a small kiss on his hip. "Relax and let go for a little bit."

"I can't *not* reciprocate when you're doing that to me. I'm going fucking crazy here, I have to please you too."

"Trust me." I ran a palm up his body again, lowering my mouth to lick at his crown again. "I am pleased."

"Ugh, not enough," he groaned as my lips sealed around him again.

With my head down and mouth at work, I paid no mind to the

movement on the bed, figuring he was just squirming and thrashing as I sucked more of his thick length down my throat. When a hand grabbed my breast, I released him with a gasp of air. Ready to scold him again, I blinked with surprise in the darkness to see Reaper's hands still clasped behind his head. But he wore a cocky smirk, and the two sleeping bodies of Jandro and Gunner were no longer sprawled on the mattress.

A familiar pair of soft, pillowy lips dragged a kiss along my neck. "Put that dick back in your mouth, *bonita,*" Jandro murmured as his hand found its way inside my robe.

"You traitor," I whimpered, my nipples aching as he rolled them between his fingers.

"What? You didn't want *him* to touch you, so he's not." He leaned in, his head nearly resting on Reaper's leg, to suck the sensitive peak into his mouth.

Before I could protest, the cool breeze of someone lifting my robe from behind sent a shiver wracking through me. Gunner let out an appreciative hum as his skilled hands roamed my backside. He kneaded the back of my thighs, cupped my ass, and then I felt his mouth press against the hot molten core between my legs. All three guys seemed to revel in the satisfaction of my moan that followed.

"This is so not fair," I complained, while pushing my hips back into Gunner's face at the same time.

"Do we look like we care?" Jandro dragged kisses alongside my ribs, his palm smoothing over my spine.

Gunner hummed his agreement, grabbing the sides of my ass as he buried his face in my pussy. I was already slick from playing with Reaper, now my golden man's skilled tongue was dangerously close to getting me off first.

"You seem a tad distracted, sugar." Reaper cupped my chin in his hand, his grin still cocky. "I thought you wanted to please me."

I stroked him from base to tip, squeezing his hard flesh. "How did you plot this out?"

"I didn't, I swear." He was terrible at looking innocent. "They woke up and saw what was happening. I can't control what they do."

"Uh...huh."

My noise of skepticism came out more like a moan. Gunner had just inserted a finger into me, his thumb rolling across my clit while his mouth continued to do magical things to my pussy. Jandro started kissing the nape of my neck, his hands still sweeping across my waist and breasts.

"Gonna finish what you started?"

I glared at Reaper. "Shut up and put your hands back where they were."

"Yes, ma'am," he grinned.

"You move a single finger, I'm stopping entirely." It was an empty threat. Infuriating as he was sometimes, he never left me unsatisfied. And he knew I would never leave him blue-balled.

"Mm, sure," he chuckled.

I descended on him again, taking him deeper down my throat than I had yet so far. With the other two awake now, there was no point in staying quiet. My head bobbed and my hips rolled, moaning loudly with every stroke of Gunner's fingers inside me.

"Holy fuck." Reaper's hips bucked underneath me. Jandro pulled back my hair as his teeth dragged over my earlobes and neck.

My stifled moans grew whining and desperate as pleasure coiled up tightly in my core. I made wet sucking sounds with my mouth as well as my pussy, Gunner hitting the perfect spot over and over, as Jandro teased all my nerve endings into a frenzy.

"Oh yes, yes, yes," came the husky whisper behind me. "Come for us, baby girl. You're so close."

I closed around his fingers in a rushing, sudden release. The convulsions of my orgasm rolled over me in hot waves just as Reaper spilled into my mouth.

"Fuckkk," he panted, fingers curling in my hair as I swallowed, squeezed his balls, and pumped my hand to drain him. I didn't even care that his hands were free now.

Gunner lapped me up, just as I did to Reaper, until we were a sweaty, panting pile at the foot of the bed. Jandro was the first to scoot back up to where he was sleeping and pulled me with him.

"Goodnight, bonita," he whispered with a fast kiss to my lips, then arranged his pillows for sleeping on his stomach.

Gunner slid up behind me, tilting my face to plant a kiss on my forehead. "Goodnight, baby girl."

"Night, guys." My eyelids were already drooping, searching for Reaper before I completely passed out.

He laid right in the middle, hands rested on his chest with his mouth parted softly. Deep, even breaths became gentle snores.

I crawled over to lay a soft kiss on his forehead before whispering, "Good night, my love."

JANDRO

"Tell me this. How the shit does he expect me to pack up a whole damn bike shop and fit it in the bed of a pickup truck?"

Shadow bent over his desk in the corner of the room. He didn't reply and likely hadn't even heard me, deep in drawing some tattoo design. It didn't really matter, I was just venting and talking to no one in particular.

"So we've unanimously voted on Four Corners, but aren't making it a permanent stop until we scope the place out. Fair enough. I understand we might be continuing on to fuck-knows-where and we gotta pack light for the road. But where does Reaper expect me to store all my tools and shit? And on top of that, I've got like a dozen chickens to pack now!"

A grunt floated over from the desk.

"He asked if I can bring the lift! The fuckin' two-ton hydraulic lift that took us three days to get here from down the road! Like sure, I'd love to hold on to that thing, but are you fucking kidding me?"

"So don't bring it," Shadow muttered distractedly. "We'll prop bikes up on blocks like before if we need to."

"That's what I'm saying! Reaper's all," I lowered my voice and added a growl to imitate him, "Oh, don't over-pack, bring just the essentials, like all the fuckin' machinery in the shop and my fuckin' mahogany coffee table."

"He didn't say anything about a coffee table."

"I know, man. I'm just picturing him trying to load that thing onto his bike as a taste of his own medicine. I bet he would too, he stole that out of some governor's office."

Shadow's shoulders shook with a light chuckle, but he otherwise remained steadfast on whatever he was working on. I didn't like to hover over his tattoo work, but curiosity got the best of me and I walked up to lean against his desk. He stopped immediately, straightening up with a stiff back, but didn't try to hide the design.

"Still tweaking Mari's design, huh?"

He had four separate sketches of her Rod of Asceplius arm piece, each the same base design with slightly different variations. One had smoke and flames billowing out from behind the snake. Another had the snake and staff emerging from a rose with a small butterfly on the petal.

"I just keep getting different ideas," he shrugged. "I want to make sure she gets something she likes."

"Like you do with all your clients?"

"Yes."

"Shadow." I cocked my head, giving him an intent look.

"What?"

"Bro, I saw your line work after her bandage came off. She was hardly bleeding at all."

"Yeah, well, I just didn't want to—"

"Come on, dude. Be straight with me." I crossed my arms. "I'm not mad. I know you two are on friendlier terms now. But is it more than that? Do you *want* it to be?"

He met my eyes for the first time since starting the conversation, and I was surprised to see it wasn't the confused, deer-in-headlights look when I usually asked him an uncomfortable question.

"I don't know," he admitted. "I don't know if that's what I want, what she wants, or even if I did know, what that would feel like."

"You like her, though."

He nodded carefully. "I like being around her. I enjoy it when she's here and it feels...strange when you're all at Reaper's house."

"You miss her," I said, the realization becoming clear. "You...long for her when she's not around."

"I...I think that's what it is, yes."

I released a sigh, lowering my head to pinch my brow. On one hand, I was glad to learn Shadow felt something toward a woman besides fear, resentment, and defensiveness. He was miles ahead of where he was just a few months ago, and it was all Mariposa's doing. On the other hand, why did *she* have to be the first woman he developed feelings for?

I wanted the big dude to be happy, to have good experiences with women, but he was still years behind the curve emotionally. He'd make mistakes, like we all did, back when we were young dumbasses chasing girls for the first time. And I didn't want Mari to deal with any of that. She deserved better than that.

Maybe after a few years, when he got some real experience under his belt and had some time to mature, we could see about bringing him in our relationship. That was of course, assuming Mari felt the same way. Not to mention *if* Shadow would be able to handle a multi-person relationship. Gunner never had any trouble charming women and he almost missed out because of his own biases.

"I won't *do* anything, Jandro," Shadow said in a voice that was almost pleading. "I know what's off-limits and I'm not crossing that line. Really, what I enjoy most is talking to her."

That was exactly what I was afraid of. He was more emotionally attached to her than physically. I couldn't pinpoint what concerned me more, the emotional intimacy developing between them, or the physical act that had already happened—the proverbial elephant in the room.

"I trust you, man. I really do," I said. "But she's *my* woman and I'm feeling this protective...shit right now. Like my hackles are raised, but I can't pinpoint why. You won't hurt her physically, I know that. I believe that you won't touch her. And I'm not opposed to y'all becoming friends, I'm just..." I scratched at an itch on my chest, scrambling for words that got the point across, but weren't cruel. "I'm concerned about your lack of experience, I think is what I'm trying to say."

Shadow's posture didn't change, but I sensed the deflation in him, like air out of a balloon. His attention returned to the sketches at his desk.

"I understand. I'll finish her tattoo, and then I won't take up any more of her time."

"Dude, I care about you," I sighed. "And you've been doing great at being more social and all. But I love her, and—"

"You don't need to explain, I get it. I'm still behind in those areas. It's not fair to you, the other guys, or Mariposa. I won't overstep."

"I'm not saying *never*, you know. I'm jus—"

"It's okay. I'd like to finish this now, if you don't mind."

"Sure, yeah," I sighed. "Guess I gotta see about getting a lift hooked up to someone's truck."

With that, I took my leave, not feeling any better about getting that off my chest. If anything, I felt like an even bigger asshole.

MARIPOSA

"Good morning, Shadow!"

"Good morning, Mariposa."

I frowned a little. Shadow seemed distracted. He was getting better at eye contact and some semblance of a smile when we greeted each other lately, but today he mumbled it all while turned away, clearing his desk for tattooing.

He was the second man today who'd apparently got up on the wrong side of the bed. Reaper had slept well, but woke up in a foul mood. Three more nights had passed with no dreams or any contact from Daren, and he was getting frustrated. Seemingly satisfied that they'd given him enough guidance, the gods had also gone silent.

Freyja wriggled out of my arms to dart over to her favorite person, headbutting Shadow's leg hard before winding all around him like a furry black rope.

"Hi, Freyja."

He reached down with one hand to give her a cursory pet along her back, but she wasn't having that. She jumped into his lap and got between his arms as she lifted onto her hind legs. Her front paws rested on his chest as she rubbed her cheeks on his neck and chin, purring up a storm.

"Just when I thought you couldn't get any more clingy," I sighed, taking Shadow's other seat. "Let the man work."

"I don't mind."

He never did. Setting his tattoo machine down, he curled his fingers into Freyja's fur on the sides of her neck. She stretched up higher, leaning her head back for more of his touch and undivided attention. Shadow huffed out a chuckle at her reaction and scratched her more vigorously.

I'm getting jealous of a cat, I realized, watching from my chair.

Touch was such an uneasy subject with him. Coaxing him into speaking to me, treating me like any normal person, was one thing. But physical contact could go from harmless and platonic to so much more. A wandering hand during a hug could easily turn into something else. Freyja said he needed love to heal, but was escalating touch okay to do? As much as the physical chemistry crackled from my end, I didn't want to do anything that confused him, or worse, that was unwanted.

He placed Freyja on the floor and, apparently satisfied with her daily Shadow fix, she shook out her fur and walked off with her tail high.

"I didn't have a single drink yesterday," I told him with a playful tilt of my head. "I hope you're proud."

He nodded, but otherwise didn't tease back like he did at our last session. "Ready?" he asked me with a shy glance.

"Yep." I forced a smile, shoved down the feeling of rejection, and scooted my chair closer. The heat from his large body seemed to engulf me even though I was still a couple of feet away. Or maybe that was the battery for his tattoo machine.

"I, um, came up with a few more background ideas, if you'd like to see."

He seemed nervous today, and I wondered if something happened. Did he accidentally say or do something that Jandro had to correct?

I waited until his gaze met mine and gave him my best reassuring smile. "Hell yes, I do. I always want to see your ideas."

His shoulders softened a little and he opened up his sketchbook to a spread showing variations of my Rod of Asceplius piece.

"Oh, wow." I scooted closer and leaned over until I was sitting right alongside him. My eyes bounced all over the pages. "I don't know what to choose."

"You don't have to choose any," Shadow murmured softly. "We can always fill the background in later—um, fuck!"

"What?" I snapped my gaze to look at him, brow pinched and jaw clenched. "Something wrong?"

"No, sorry. I, um…" He sat back, rubbing his forehead and teeth grinding in obvious distress. After a quick breath, his eyes flashed open, focusing on me for the first time that day. "If that's what *you* want. Getting the background filled in later, I mean. Only if you *want* to get tattooed by me again later."

"I mean, I can probably decide today after a minute to think." I watched his body language with curiosity. He seemed conflicted about something. "But I definitely want to get tattooed by you again. Why wouldn't I?" I smiled again, it seemed to make him feel better. "You're my favorite artist."

"I'm your only artist so far. You do have other options, you know."

"Why would I go to anyone else? I like *you*."

Three simple words that didn't hold nearly as much power as *I love you*, but in this context they felt heavily weighted all the same. My heart sped up and I wondered if Shadow picked up on the multiple meanings of those words. I liked his art, and I liked *him*.

"This doesn't bother you?" he asked. "Spending so much time with me?"

The question made me lean back in shock. "Of course not, Shadow. Why—" I stopped myself from demanding an explanation from him, reminding myself how outcast he'd been all his life, and still was.

He wasn't used to people spending extended time around him, and didn't need to explain his feelings of otherness to me. I realized he needed to *unlearn* what he'd always known and start at a new baseline—having a friend who simply enjoyed spending time with him.

"I like just sitting with you. Talking to you," I said. "I love the tattoos, but honestly, I'd sit and chat with you while doing nothing."

"You *would*?"

"Yeah. We can just have coffee and let Freyja climb all over you. We can talk about books, the weather, whatever we want."

"What would your men think about that?"

I crossed one knee over the other, folding my hands in my lap. "I think they respect me enough to let me talk to, and form friendships with, whoever I damn well please."

The color deepened in his cheeks. "I just don't want to make anyone uncomfortable. Or put strain on your relationships with them because of..."

What we did.

His words trailed off, but I knew exactly what he referred to. My cross-legged position tightened at the memory of him filling and stretching me, the way he watched me as if hypnotized, but otherwise never touched me.

Heat flooded my skin, bringing a rush of sensitivity to the surface. My pulse pounded in my lips, gaze falling to the large hands still wrapped around his tattoo machine.

"See, I've made you uncomfortable already," he said, his voice pained.

"No," I said in a rush of breath, my throat tightening. "You haven't. I..." I raked my hand back through my hair, for a moment wondering how truly inappropriate it would be to run over to Reaper, get his approval, then run back and hop on Shadow right then.

"Whatever comes up between me and the guys is on us to work through," I said. "What, um, *happened*, was acknowledged and moved on from. I won't deny that it's awkward," I added with a forced laugh. "But we can't undo it. We can just move forward. And I'd like to do that by being your friend, Shadow."

I had told him this before. But like most people facing trauma, he needed gentle reminders of safety. He needed to know that I genuinely wanted this, and wasn't just giving empty promises.

Did he need to know about my ever doubling-in-size crush on him, and ridiculous sexual attraction? That was still up for debate. And putting my own desires aside for a strong, foundational friendship that made him feel safe, could only be a good thing.

"I...would like that with you, too." His eyes flicked to my face before adding hesitantly, "as long as it doesn't cause any problems. I don't just mean with your men, but I know I'm still learning socially—"

"Shadow, you have more social grace and tact than *many* people I know." I leaned forward and, after a moment's hesitation, placed a hand over his. "As far as I'm concerned, you're not behind socially on anything. You watch people, you learn and adapt. Considering we're in a *motorcycle club*, I'm a bit shocked you're as well-mannered as you are."

"You think I'm well-mannered?"

"You *are*," I laughed lightly. "There's no thinking about it. I've never heard you say anything rude or in bad taste. Your mood is more even-keeled than Reaper, and you've definitely never stuck your foot in your mouth like Jandro or Gunner."

He stared at my hand on top of his, dwarfed by his large palm. With the tiniest, hesitant movement, his thumb lifted to brush over the edge of my wrist. "No one's ever told me anything like that before."

I fought down the urge to touch more of him, keeping my hand still as I smiled. "That's what I'm here for."

"It's like..." He trailed off again, leaning back in his seat as he began to slide his hands out from under mine.

"Tell me," I urged through the ache in my chest as I sensed him retreating. "Don't be afraid to express yourself, Shadow. I *want* to know what you're thinking. This is just between us."

He touched the tips of his fingers together, resting his forearms on his thighs. With a deep breath, he began again.

"Everyone is always telling me I'm improving. I'm doing better. I've come so far." He swallowed. "Which is nice, I guess. But all of that implies that I'm still not good enough. I'm not there yet. I'm not *normal* yet." His fingers laced together. "Like you said, I keep watching people to make sure I'm not being weird. I read psychology, history, all of that, to learn how normal people behave. I exhaust myself trying to remember everything, only to keep hearing the same things. 'You're doing better, Shadow. You've improved so much.' You're the first person to tell me that—" He pulled in another breath, this one shakier, as he looked at me. "That I'm already good enough."

I leaned into him, my hands finding their way to his again, fingers nestling into wide palms that were surprisingly soft. If he didn't hiss in a breath of surprise at the contact, I can't say that I wouldn't have kissed him.

"You *are* good enough," I breathed, lips inches away from his. "As you are, right now. There is absolutely *nothing* wrong with you, Shadow."

His gaze dipped lower to our conjoined hands, moving his lips further away, but his forehead touched softly to mine. Slowly, his fingers unlaced from each other and closed around mine, thumbs rubbing down the backs of my palms.

"Thank you, Mariposa."

"You can call me Mari, you know."

"I like saying your full name." There it was, that glint of humor and personality dying to come out. "Saying longer words helps me practice speaking."

"You're a natural at it already." I leaned away and he released our hands.

His touch felt like it remained on my skin and I wondered if that moment felt anywhere near as intimate to him as it did to me.

"So." The confidence in him had returned, eyes bright and hints of a smile on his face as he turned back to the sketches on his desk. "Did any of these appeal to you? Or did you want something different?"

Biting back my own grin at his lifted mood, I leaned over his desk again. "Hmm, I kind of like this background," I pointed at a sketch with swirling smoke behind the snake, "and this kind of detail on the scales. Can you combine them?"

"Of course. That's easy."

I sat back in my chair, trying not to beam too hard as Shadow held my arm steady while he cleaned my already-started tattoo with an alcohol wipe. He didn't hesitate in touching me this time and I hoped that would only continue.

For his own comfort, not for your thirsty ass, I reminded myself.

We sat together in companionable silence as he worked on me, much like my first tattoo. I enjoyed this with him too. With my three guys, everyone was always chattering on about something. I'd almost forgotten how comfortable silence could be, too.

"Can I ask you a medical question?" Shadow said—completely unprompted—when my line work was done and he prepared the colored inks for the scales of my snake.

"Shoot," I answered.

"I guess I'm wondering," he mused, "if there's a medical reason why I can't feel pain."

"Ah." I tilted my gaze up toward the ceiling to ponder. "Most likely there is. Is it everywhere on your body, or just certain areas?"

"Yes, everywhere."

"All types of pain?"

"Um, yes. I think so."

"That tells me it's neurological," I said. "Your brain shut off the signals from those nerves for some reason, probably to protect you in some way."

He finished pouring the small pots of ink and turned to me, looking unsure of himself again.

"Something wrong?" I asked.

"I only feel it during those nightmares," he confessed. "I feel everything vividly. But while I'm awake, I only feel my skin coming apart, the blood spilling. All of the other sensations, but never *pain*."

"It sounds to me like your brain is trying to process your past trauma when you're asleep. And the feeling of pain is closely linked to that. But when you're awake, it gets buried again, to protect you."

"Protect me from what?" he muttered with a frustrated growl that was oddly adorable. "If it weren't for those pills you gave me, everyone would have to be protected *from* me."

"This isn't my area of expertise," I admitted. "But in simplest terms, when people confront their trauma before they're ready, it can make things worse. They can become depressed, harm themselves, or attempt to take their own lives. So sometimes the brain sort of locks traumatic memories away to prevent that from happening."

"I remember everything that happened to me," Shadow said. "And I can remember what pain feels like, if I focus on it. I just...wonder why it left and never came back."

"I don't have an answer for that." I looked at him sympathetically. "I'm sorry."

"That's okay." He returned to tattooing me, the buzz of his machine filling the silence between us.

"Maybe not right away, but at some point," I said softly, "you might want to talk to someone about what happened to you."

"No," he shook his head. "I don't like thinking about it, much less talking about it."

"I don't know if it would bring the pain sensation back, but the sleeping pills are only a band-aid on your nightmares."

"They work for me."

"They won't forever," I insisted gently. "You'll develop a tolerance, and another bad habit, if you're not careful. But if you want the nightmares to go away for good, you have to work *through* what's causing them."

Shadow paused to set his machine down and wipe away the excess ink on my arm. "I just want to move on. My past isn't something I ever want to return to." His gaze flicked up to mine for a moment. "The present is so much better."

MARIPOSA

"What a shame to have to leave this all behind." I walked around Reaper's study as if noticing it for the first time. Glass cases held mementos and artifacts like elk antlers, a skull carved out of quartz, and motorcycle parts. A heavy, wooden bookshelf held maps and weathered volumes.

"It's just stuff." Reaper moved behind me, fingertips skimming over my waist. "It can all be replaced." He pulled a slim, leather-bound journal from the shelf and tossed it onto his desk. "We'll need that. All the Steel Demon MC laws are in there."

"Have you made copies?" I opened the cover to find an ink drawing of the Demon grinning up at me from the title page. Shadow's work, most likely.

I traced the horns with a finger, picturing Shadow bent over this book as he sketched the symbol of his one place of belonging.

"Hard to do these days," Reaper sighed. "Can't find a fucking copy machine in working order anywhere, let alone a camera or a scanner. Jandro started copying it by hand, but got bored of that quickly."

I chuckled at the thought. "He just needs something complex, like a puzzle or an engine to keep him stimulated."

"Yeah, I don't blame him. No one is exactly lining up to volunteer. Gotta keep the book safe in the meantime."

I moved to the closed wooden box on his desk, running my hand over the varnished lid. "What's in here?"

Reaper cleared his throat and placed his hand next to mine on the lid. "My mom's journal, plus a few of her gemstones and other jewelry pieces." His hand moved to cover mine, squeezing gently around my fingers. "I still haven't brought myself to read it."

I pressed a kiss to his cheek, wrapping my free hand around his bicep. "She might want it back from you someday."

"That's what I tell myself, even though it sounds delusional," he said. "I feel like if I open it, I'm admitting that she's gone and all I'm reading are memories of her."

I turned to face him, sliding my arms around his neck. "You're a good son to keep hoping," I said. "And to hold on to her things."

He reached for my hand again, gazing at me with such warmth and love as his thumb caressed over my ring.

"I've never touched anything in that box since Noelle and I left that place," he whispered. "Not until I knew I had to give you this."

The kiss that followed was cut short by a soft knock at the open study door.

"Yes?" he barked.

"Um, is this a bad time?"

"Tessa!" I untangled myself from Reaper and rushed over to let her in. "Of course not. Come in and let me hold that baby!"

She sent a bashful smile in Reaper's direction before holding her daughter out to me.

"Oh yes, come here, little lady!" I took her gingerly, supporting her head. "Did you decide on a name?"

"Vivian," Tessa beamed. "Aiden, my oldest, picked it out. We're calling her Vivi."

"Well, you're awfully calm, Miss Vivi." I watched her wide, blue eyes move around the study. "Not giving your mama any trouble, are you?"

"She's really good, actually," Tessa admitted. "Easier than my two boys were, by a mile."

"I gotta say, sugar," Reaper leaned over me to look at Vivi, resting his chin on my shoulder, "You look good with a baby in your arms."

"Yeah, right," I huffed. "Right before a massive move, perfect time to get pregnant."

"I actually wanted to talk to you, president." Tessa lowered her eyes meekly. "About, um, a family matter."

Reaper straightened, peering at her shrewdly. "What's going on?"

"Should I leave?" I asked, looking between both of them. "I'll watch the baby while you two talk."

"No it's alright, Mari." Tessa clasped her hands nervously in front of her. "Please stay. I'm glad you're here, actually."

"Do you want to sit down?" Reaper turned the armchair facing his desk toward her. When she nodded and accepted the seat, he knelt next to her. "What's on your mind, Tessa?"

Her eyes flicked to me for a moment before returning to my husband. "I want to separate from Big G."

I couldn't say I was surprised, but took in a sharp breath all the same.

"Has he hurt you?" Reaper asked. "Or the kids?"

"No, not physically, anyway." Tessa looked at me again. "I think you know this has been building for a while, but it all kind of came to a head last night."

"What happened?" I held Vivi against my shoulder as she sucked on her fist.

"I've been spending a lot of time with Andrea," Tessa explained. "You know, just helping out while she grieves. Big G wasn't happy about being left alone with the boys for longer than usual. So I started bringing them with me to hang out with Andrea's kids, and to give him a break. Then G got mad about none of us being home."

"Fucking Christ," Reaper grumbled.

"I was going to bring dinner over to her last night and, um," she swallowed, "he wouldn't let us leave the house."

"Oh my God, Tess." I went to stand next to her, rubbing her arm and shoulder as I looked at Reaper. "That's awful. He can't be allowed to do that."

"He started screaming at me in front of the kids," Tessa's voice shook. "Blocking the doorway. He didn't touch me, but I was *scared*."

Reaper took one of her hands between his, as though trying to calm the tremors running through her. "Would you be alright with living at Andrea's for a while?"

Her eyes widened, blinking like she couldn't believe what she was hearing. "Um, yes. Yes, I would. She was even asking if I wanted to stay in one of her spare rooms..."

"I'll have Gunner and some of his guys move your things from Big G's house. The kids, too. Only the essentials, though. Whatever you're taking with you on the move."

"And," she breathed, "what about after we're moved?"

"That'll depend on where we end up," Reaper sighed. "But I'll keep guys posted on you if you feel unsafe. No one will force you to be near him, if you don't want that."

"He will want time with the kids, though," I pointed out. "And as much as I hate to admit it, he has a right to."

"I'm not even thinking that far ahead." Tessa rubbed her forehead. "I just want some fucking *space* for a couple weeks. To help my friend. To remind him of what it's like to *not* have me there doing everything."

"You have our support," Reaper assured her. "No matter what you decide. Whether you're with him or not, you're one of our own, Tessa. You're raising three baby Demons, after all."

"In more ways than one," she muttered, then gave Reaper a relieved smile. "Thank you, Reaper. Honestly, I wasn't sure how this was going to go."

"This is the first time it's happened in the club," he admitted. "But it's not right for him to scare you and trap you in your house. I don't think any of the guys would disagree."

Tessa rose from the chair and held her arms out to take Vivi back from me. "Again, thank you."

"Go on straight to Andrea's," Reaper said. "I'll have Gunner and his guys escort you back to gather your things."

She nodded and left the study quietly, with a small smile back at me. Reaper and I just stood there for a moment, sitting with the weight of what she told us.

I broke the silence after a heavy few seconds. "Are you going to do anything to Big G?"

"I'll talk to him." Reaper rounded his desk in search of his cigarettes and lighter.

I stared at him. "That's it?"

"What do you want me to do, sugar? She said he didn't put hands on her. He was acting like an asshole. Guess what, he *is* an asshole. That's not news to anyone." He stuck the black cigarette in his mouth, but didn't light it, choosing to flick his Zippo open and closed instead. "Hopefully the mere threat of losing his woman and kids is enough to make him act right." He finally lit the smoke and dragged deeply, exhaling with a dreamy smile.

"What's that look for?" I asked.

"Just thinking about you holding that baby." He approached me, grabbing my shirt at the waist with his free hand to pull me closer. "When are we gonna make some, sugar?"

"No sooner than three years, when my birth control expires," I said. "And this," I snatched the cigarette from his hand, taking a quick suck before returning it to him, "can *not* be around me while I'm pregnant."

"Hm, making me give up my vices already." His eyes danced with amusement, bringing it back to his lips.

"Do it outside. On the balcony, I don't care. But the second I find out I'm pregnant, I can't be inhaling your smoke."

He grinned, turning to ash out the cigarette in the glass tray on the desk. "A lot can change in three years, sugar. That's plenty of time to kick a habit."

"We'll see." I crossed my arms, the skepticism plain on my face.

"Now whiskey, on the other hand," he pulled me into his chest by my belt loops, "I draw a line there," he said with mock seriousness.

"We'll talk when you're up at all hours of the night, changing diapers and bottle-feeding," I retorted.

"Have you forgotten you have *three* men?" he laughed. "We'll be rotating shifts, baby. You won't have to do a thing but whip these gorgeous tits out."

He pawed at my breasts, leaning down to kiss my chest with a groan while I laughed and shoved him away. "You animal."

"Seriously, sugar." He stood upright, wrapping me in a protective embrace. "I want a family with you, and I'm here for all of it. Late nights, exploding diapers, projectile vomiting, banshee screaming, the whole thing."

I laughed, nuzzling into his chest. "Okay, at first I thought a baby sounded nice, then you said all that, and now I'm having second thoughts."

"Ah, come on. It'll be fun." He stroked my back, resting his chin on top of my head. "Can you imagine Jandro with a kid? Or Gun?"

"Jandro will never let the fun stop," I groaned. "He'll be like the big brother figure. I can see Gun taking on the daddy role well."

"And me?"

"You?" I laughed, tilting my face up to kiss under his jaw. "I worry for any girls we have. You'll terrorize every single boy that looks their way."

"As I rightly fuckin' should," he growled. "If they're anything like you, they'll put me in an early grave."

"Like me how, a pain in the ass?"

"That, too." He leaned down, lips hovering over mine as he kept me locked against his chest. "But I was thinking if they were anywhere near as beautiful."

Just when I thought I became used to him looking at me like that, the fluttering in my chest overwhelmed me. I got bashful, burying my face in his neck with a playful thump of his chest. "Stop."

"Never." He caressed my nape, massaging circles into my hairline. "Really, though. Is it something you want, too?"

I nodded, my face still hidden from him. "I want to meet the people you and I would create," I whispered. "I want to teach them about what went wrong with us, our parents, and grandparents. How their generation can do better."

"Me too." His lips brushed across my forehead. "You know what else?"

"Hm?"

"Thinking of you with a big, pregnant belly, growing my kid inside you," he whispered, "it's so fucking hot. Damn, it's making me hard right now."

"Reaper!" I slapped his chest.

"Just being honest," he chuckled, hands drifting lower toward my belly. "Three years feels like a lifetime from now. But I'll take that time to build a better home for us. A place where all of us can raise families in safety."

I lifted an eyebrow. "And?"

"And," he sighed. "Give me time to cut back on smoking."

REAPER

"How's it look from up there?"

Gunner blinked, his irises returning to focus on me. "About what you'd expect," he sighed. "A mass exodus."

I could only imagine. I didn't need a bird's-eye view to know that a long trail of vehicles stretched out behind me. Some stayed on bikes, but much of the club piled into their trucks and RVs to haul their families and belongings. We had to stick together, so we'd be making one hell of a caravan once we hit the road.

Fluttering in the wind, the Steel Demons flag slowly lowered down the flagpole at our front gate. That was the moment it hit me, like a sucker punch to the gut. This place wasn't our home anymore. Someone meticulously folded the flag and held it out to Jandro for safe-keeping. He took it carefully, to store it with his things.

One day, she'd fly again.

Mari walked up to me, securing her helmet with a frown, then settled onto my rear seat without a word.

"What is it?" I ran my fingertips up her thighs.

"Keep guys on Big G," she said. "Apparently he's done being on his best behavior. Tessa and the kids are riding with Andrea in Dallas's truck, and he's making a big stink over it."

"I'm on it." Gunner made a wide U-turn and headed toward the back of our long line of vehicles.

I squeezed Mari's knee, watching the sliver of her face visible through the helmet. "Ready, sugar?"

"No," she sighed. "I don't think I'll ever be ready to leave this place."

"We'll find our home." I leaned in and kissed the bridge of her nose. "Our permanent home."

"I know. It's just hard." She touched my arm. "Now or never, I guess."

I gave her knee a final squeeze before settling in front of her, revving up my bike for the long road ahead. My woman's arms came around me with natural ease. With one loud whistle, Hades zoomed ahead as a black blur. I kicked the bike into motion and, after taking a final look at my former home in the mirror, drove away from the gate for the last time.

The first day was uneventful. As Dyno had suggested, we took the long way around the Hopi reservation on our way to Four Corners. Stops were frequent, as expected with fidgety children and vehicles that had been sitting in driveways for a year or more. Jandro and Slick kept busy, running back and forth to check tire pressure, change oil, or add coolant for whoever needed it. By the time night fell, it seemed like we barely made any distance at all.

So much for our once-nomadic lifestyle. When the Steel Demons were just six to ten single guys—plus Noelle—making the open road our home was like second nature. Now, we'd gotten used to staying in one place, and it showed. It didn't bother me like I thought it would. Sure I felt nostalgic about the old times, but I wouldn't trade what I had now for anything.

By day two, most people had gotten into the swing of being on the road again. With the vehicles getting tuned up as needed the day before, we didn't have to stop as frequently. But just the fact that we were a grouping of roughly fifteen vehicles felt like we went at a snail's pace.

"How many members did the Sons have before?" I asked T-Bone during a pit stop.

"Oh, about twelve I'd say." He stroked his beard, the loss still clear in his eyes. "We were a small club, but mighty."

"Sometimes that's better. A small, tight-knit circle."

"You're pretty lucky though, Pres." He looked out over the span of people eating, talking, and children and animals chasing each other. "You've got a lot of people who will follow you anywhere. Not because you force them or they're scared of you, but you're just a natural leader."

"I get that a lot," I sighed. "Sometimes I see it, sometimes I don't."

"They trust you." He looked at me, the raven on his shoulder eyeing me as well. "The Sons cycled through a few presidents in our time, so I've seen all kinds. Bash was a rare breed." He went silent for a moment, staring out at nothing. "I see a lot of similarities in your leadership styles. He wasn't a perfect president, but he was a good one. As are you."

"We'll see."

Hades growled, his nose pointing behind us. A woman's shriek and some kind of commotion spurred us into turning around, hands on our holsters.

"The fuck is your big man doing?" T-Bone said.

"Fuck me with a fucking rusty spoon," I muttered under my breath "Not this shit *again*..."

With Hades at my side, I stormed over, aiming to head off Big G who was walking away from a screaming, distraught Tessa, who was following and yelling after him. He held an infant car seat in one hand, swinging it at his side as he walked. The baby was clearly distressed, if the wailing coming from inside the carrier was any indication.

Mari was quickly at Tessa's side, supporting the distraught mother as she stared venomously at Big G's back.

"G, stop!" Tessa sobbed. "*Please* give her back."

"I'm fucking tired of this shit!" Big G spun around, the baby carrier swinging dangerously fast in his hand. "You don't wanna be with me anymore, fine! But you can't have *our* fucking kids all to yourself!"

"You fucking Neanderthal, she's an *infant*!" Mari yelled. "She needs to stay with her mother!"

He jabbed a finger in my woman's face, looking seconds away from exploding. "And I'm tired of *you* sticking your nose where it don't belong, medic."

"Say another word to my wife, G," I kept my hand over my gun, "And you'll lose that finger, plus whatever else I feel like shooting off."

He glanced over, noticing me for the first time. By that point, all the commotion had drawn the whole club's attention. Gunner and Shadow pushed their way through the crowd to back me up, while Jandro stepped between the women and Big G's outstretched finger.

"Let's all just calm the hell down." My VP stretched his hands out to his sides to put distance between the two parents. "Everyone," he made a shooing motion with his fingers, "mind your business. This doesn't concern you all."

Once people quit rubbernecking, I let my hand fall from my weapon. "G, you want to tell us what's going on?"

He turned to me with a huff. "Vivian is *my* daughter too. I've barely seen her since she was born. The boys are one thing, they can come and see me as they please. But it's not fair for my...*ex*," he spat the word out, "to keep my newborn away from me just because *she* decided to move out."

"Vivian is three weeks old," Mari shot back. "She needs to eat every two hours. This isn't about fairness, but your baby's survival!"

"I can feed her!"

"She's breastfed, you idiot!"

"Don't call me—"

He lunged forward but Jandro's palm collided with his chest.

"Stay back," the VP warned. I wasn't concerned. G was bigger than him in every dimension, but Jandro was a more skilled fighter. Not to mention, Gunner and I would let all hell break loose if he came within spitting distance of Mari.

I was just dumbfounded as to what his thought process was, if there was any processing going on in that big melon at all. What did he think snatching the baby would accomplish?

"I'll let you see her whenever you want," Tessa sniffed, pushing against Mari's arm. "Just please, *please* give her back." Big G doubled down, stepping away as he swung the car seat behind his back, making Tessa whimper. "Please stop doing that, she's not strapped in."

"I have rights to my own kids," he insisted.

"Big G." I stepped forward, Gunner and Shadow silently moving with me. "Give the baby back."

"She's *mine*!"

"That is an order from your president," I continued. "If you do not comply, you're out of the club."

His eyes nearly bulged out of his head, they went so wide. "You're not fucking serious!"

"Do I look like I'm joking? Look at you, swinging that thing around. You think that baby's safe with you?"

"Look, we'll find you guys a mediator," Jandro said in an attempt to de-escalate the situation. "So you can work out visitation, custody schedules, whatever. But this is not the right way to do it, G."

"Give the baby back to Tessa," I ordered. "I will not repeat myself."

Big G's hand clenched around the arm of the car seat, and everyone stiffened. The last thing we wanted was for this to turn violent, but we'd given him plenty of warning.

In the time it took to blink, Shadow went from his position at my back, to squarely in Big G's face. Now those two were much closer in size, with Shadow a few inches taller. He also had the benefit of being fucking intimidating, even to grown men.

"The president gave you an order," he said, inches in front of Big G's nose, hands resting on his belt where we all knew hidden knives sat at the ready.

With Big G distracted by Shadow sizing him up, Gunner snuck around and plucked the car seat from his hand.

"Hey!—"

"Don't," Shadow warned, his body eerily still, but ready to strike if needed.

Gunner went behind me to hand the baby back to Tessa, who let out a sob of relief.

"Escort them back." I nodded to Jandro and Gunner, who began walking away with the women immediately. "Stay with me a moment, Shadow."

"Yes, president." He resumed his post at my back, leaving me to face a raging Big G.

"This is not the first time your impulsiveness has landed you in hot water," I told him. "First you accuse Gunner of betraying us, now you're kidnapping—"

"She's *my* fucking kid too!"

"Yes, I heard you the first five times," I snapped. "And after what you just did, I don't see why Tessa *should* trust you with the kids."

"I'm their fucking father! I have the right to see them!"

"And what if that baby fell out and hit her head while you were swinging her around?" I barked.

He stared me down, jaw clenching, without an answer to my question, which just pissed me off even more. Hades stepped forward and growled, showing off his teeth.

It wasn't like me to get so involved with my men's relationships, but Big G was getting under my skin in a major way. Maybe I was getting a soft spot for kids, not only due to thoughts of starting a family with Mari, but because the Steel Demons future was so up in the air now. Children were the only small hope for a possibly better world.

And if it had been Mari, sobbing and distraught because someone took our baby away—well, that someone wouldn't be standing, nor in one piece. Big G was lucky. Maybe I'd allowed him to be too lucky.

My eyes slid to Hades, the answer immediate.

You will not reap. His life is not yours to take.

"This is your last warning, G," I said, turning to walk away. "You step even one toe out of line, that cut on your back is going up in flames."

MARIPOSA

I didn't know what to expect once we crossed the border into Four Corners, but a long, noisy stretch of construction zone was not it.

The smell of fresh asphalt hit my nose as our vehicles gradually slowed. To my left and right, men in hard hats poured concrete foundations, sawed through fresh lumber, and assembled that lumber into frames for buildings.

Some structures looked brand new, while others appeared to have stood before the Collapse and were being repaired. I watched one man power washing long window panes on the side of a tall building, three stories high. As we came around a gentle bend in the freshly-paved road, my chest tightened at the sight of the word HOSPITAL on the adjacent side of the building.

We came to a stop about a quarter mile later at a four-way intersection. A man held up a stop sign as he waved a group of children to cross in front of us. Some of them wore backpacks and held the hands of adults leading the way. Once they crossed safely, the man lowered the stop sign and waved us through.

I lowered my chin to Gunner's shoulder and pressed my lips to his ear. "Did you see that?"

"Yeah." He took one hand off of the handlebars and squeezed my fingers at his stomach. "It's surreal to see something so normal."

I recalled Reaper talking about wanting a family before we left, and a flutter of warmth spread throughout my chest. Maybe here, if we decided to stay, we'd be able to make it happen.

The ride to the governor's house was a few more miles, with more stops along the way for crossing traffic. The whole place was teeming with activity. If not working construction or crossing guard, people had food vendor booths set up along the road. I spotted a few food trucks, and one guy had even dug a pit in the ground and was roasting a whole pig.

When the head of the pack finally stopped, it was where the paved street abruptly became a dirt road and a barricade blocked our way. Ahead of us, T-Bone leaned over to speak to Reaper, his hands gesturing and pointing. At Reaper's nod, T-Bone signaled for everyone to turn right onto a narrow, older road that hadn't yet been paved.

A clearing was carved out on the side of this road and T-Bone led the way, parking his bike under the shade of an overhang.

"We go on foot from here," he explained, after everyone started pulling in and cutting their engines. "They're paving the road up to the governor's house today, so we're supposed to stay off of it. We can take a short walk up this hill, though."

"Gunner and Mari with us," Reaper called, swinging a leg over his bike. "Shadow and Slick, guard the bikes. Make sure no one wanders off or gets body-snatched."

Freyja wiggled out from her cocoon inside my jacket, then darted over to Shadow and hopped up into his empty bike seat. He smiled amusedly, reaching down to pet her.

T-Bone chuckled, wiping his mouth free of water after a sip from his canteen. "You saw those kids crossing the street, right, Pres? I assure you it's safe here."

"You can assure me all you fuckin' want. I'm still not taking any chances." Reaper cupped my nape, turned my head to plant a smoldering kiss on me, then released me and continued on. "Where the fuck are we supposed to stay here? I didn't see a single building that looked finished."

Gunner smirked at my side, then held my hand as we, Jandro, and the two other Sons followed T-Bone and Reaper up a gently sloping hill.

"There are housing developments going up on the side streets," T-Bone said, pointing further down the road we'd just parked on. "Houses with bigger plots of land for farming and raising animals are that way." He pointed in the opposite direction.

"Need one of those." Jandro came up to sandwich me between him and Gunner, grabbing my hand to kiss my palm. "Space for Foghorn and the girls."

Gunner puffed out his cheeks and began making soft clucking noises, earning a smack on the back of the head from his VP.

"Is the hospital in use?" I called ahead, ignoring their shenanigans.

T-Bone looked over his shoulder at me, slowing his pace enough for me to catch up. "It's in rough shape, was raided during the Collapse, but it's slowly getting organized into working order. Four Corners has one doctor and a few medics working on-call for emergencies, but no full-time staff yet. They mostly treat construction accidents so far."

"Why *is* there so much construction?" Reaper wondered out loud.

"Governor Vance calls it 're-investing'," Dyno answered. "He poured his personal wealth into rebuilding people's homes and essential businesses after everything was looted. But if people wanted to stay here, they had to work for it."

"Every person coming into Four Corners must take on a job," T-Bone picked up. "Some kind of trade, skill, or service they can offer. The governor isn't picky about what that is, as long as it serves the community in a non-harmful way."

"What about people with physical disabilities, who can't do manual labor?" I piped up. "What about girls running away from those camps that brainwash them? Don't tell me the governor turns these people away."

T-Bone looked at me with an endearing smile. "There are many more job opportunities here than just physical labor. Someone could tutor or babysit children. They need cooks, cleaners, servers, couriers, all kinds of jobs. If someone has no discernible skills, they're sent to the library to enroll in courses and assess what their strengths are. If they're interested in a trade, but have no experience, they can become an apprentice. Everyone is given an opportunity to succeed here."

I listened with rapt attention as he explained, trying to keep my excitement in check. This place seemed to have all the markings of a good, fair community being built from the ground up.

"You're really selling this place hard, despite not living here." Reaper did not sound as optimistic.

"Ah, you know how it is, Pres!" T-Bone laughed. "Guys like us can't be contained by a quiet, normal life. We need adventure and freedom. And sometimes, we like to play more than work."

"We probably *will* be staying here for the foreseeable future, though," Dyno chimed in. "Until we start doing some rebuilding ourselves."

The humor drained out of T-Bone's face, sadness and guilt replacing it. Losing his club and someone he loved weighed heavily on him. He reminded me of Reaper in that sense.

Dyno stroked an affectionate hand up his sergeant's back and T-Bone leaned into him, winding his fingers almost absently into the other man's ponytail. Their affection was brief and, on the surface, hardly more intimate than two brothers or friends. If I didn't have my gut feeling, and T-Bone hadn't explicitly told me he liked men, I never would have assumed anything about the touch.

Gradually, the hill we climbed flattened out to a grassy field. Two long rows of soldiers in desert camouflage uniforms marched to our left, their faces solemn as their drill sergeant shouted orders.

"Vance's general is highly organized," T-Bone commented, noticing our gawking. "We'll probably meet him later. Four Corners is a target for other governors looking to increase their wealth and infrastructure, so General Bray is tough on his militia to defend the borders. But the soldiers are compensated well and have support systems in place, so morale remains high."

"They'll need the absolute best army they can put together," Gunner said next to me. "I guaran-fuckin'-tee you General Tash has already set his sights on this place. He has the two biggest territories bordering to the east."

T-Bone's shoulders went rigid at the mention of General Tash's name. "You may want to sit in on some meetings between Vance and Bray, Youngblood."

"Highly doubtful," Gunner retorted. "I'm just a road pirate looking for a place to lay my head down at night."

"Um, did you forget about right here?" Jandro reached over and groped my breast that was closest to Gunner.

"Get your mitts off me." I slapped his hand away. "We're about to meet a *governor*."

"I didn't, but you're always hogging 'em," my blond demon laughed. "I'm more of an ass man when it comes to pillows though."

"I'm done with you two," I huffed, breaking away from between them and walking up to squeeze between Reaper and T-Bone.

"Oh, you want to walk with the adults now?" my smirking president chuckled, drawing me into his side with an arm around my shoulders.

"It's been a long couple of days," I sighed, leaning my head on him.

I was not in the mood for my men being overgrown children. Gunner and Jandro's playful antics didn't normally bother me, but on top of being sore, dusty, and exhausted, we were about to meet a powerful man. Governor Vance would decide whether we stayed here for the time being or hit the road again early tomorrow morning.

"I know, sugar." Reaper brushed a kiss along my forehead. "This really couldn't have waited, huh?" The question was directed at T-Bone.

"If y'all were some small-fry club of nobodies? Maybe," he grinned. "But everyone here has seen, or at least heard of, those patches on your cuts. Vance probably already knows you're here, and the longer you stay without any clarity on whether you're friend or foe will make the citizens uneasy."

"At least that's what General Bray told us," Dyno added, "when he ordered us to bring any supposed allies directly to the governor if we returned to Four Corners."

"So you're protecting your own necks, first and foremost," Reaper concluded. "Following orders even though you're not citizens, so you can keep your cushy escort and protection contracts with the governor."

"Yeah, and?" T-Bone's eyes heated, his jaw jutting out in challenge to Reaper's statement. "What else are we supposed to do? Our friends and family are gone. We don't have a home, and now you don't either. We're not taking you to a prison cell for fuck's sake, we're just being transparent about who we're bringing into the territory."

"I would appreciate more transparency with *me*," Reaper returned with an eerie calm. "I'm trusting my whole club with you, following you here."

"I haven't kept anything from you. Are you not familiar with the idea of self-preservation? Do I have to tell you my personal motivations for everything I do? No, president."

"Guys, cool it." T-Bone and Reaper had started to lean into each other, and I forcefully pushed their shoulders away from the other man. "Let's just meet the governor and get this over with so we can get some fucking rest."

The two men gave each other stink-eyes, but otherwise quit arguing and continued walking in silence. Once at the edge of the grass field, a gravel road took us through some kind of orchard. The trees were young saplings, with some people walking through the neatly planted rows to adjust stakes or prune leaves.

"Apple trees." Dyno answered the question on my mind before I could voice it.

T-Bone cleared his throat. "The governor's house is just on the other side of the orchard."

Surprise washed over me at the sight of the oversized cabin beyond the orchard. It was big and luxurious, no doubt, but a fraction of the size of Reaper's mansion back in Sheol. Dark wood paneling gave the home a rustic feel. Porches wrapped around the ground floor and upper level, and a stone chimney jutted straight up against a slanted roof. It was a nice house, but the furthest possible image from where I expected a governor to live.

The only indication that a politician lived here at all was the two armed soldiers guarding the front porch leading up to the door. There wasn't even a gate around the house.

T-Bone raised his hand in greeting to the guards and received a sharp nod in return. "Wait here," he muttered, and walked up to speak to the guards alone.

It was a short conversation. Only a few seconds passed before the guards shifted into at-ease positions and T-Bone nodded back at us to follow.

Our small group walked up the porch steps to stand in front of two heavy wooden doors inlaid with glass. The doors pulled open from the inside and a young man wearing glasses and a suit smiled at us across the threshold.

"Come in, come in! I was hoping to see Sons of Odin faces again, good to see you, T-Bone!" He clasped hands with the large sergeant at arms and shook enthusiastically.

"Josh, we have some guests with us." T-Bone turned toward us with an arm outstretched. "This is Reaper, president of the Steel Demons MC, his old lady, Mariposa, vice president. Jandro, and captain of the guard, Gunner."

"A pleasure." The suited man nodded at each of us, sandy blond hair flopping into his eyes. "I'm Josh Lemon, Governor Vance's secretary and chief of staff."

"Nice to meet you," I offered with an elbow jab to Reaper's ribs when none of my men said anything.

A couple of wordless grunts came out of them following my greeting. Overgrown children, the lot of them.

"Where's the rest of your crew, at the B&B?" Josh turned to face T-Bone.

"No, uh—"

"We have," Dyno cut in with a hand on T-Bone's shoulder, "a lot to update the governor about. Can we see him right away? It's been a long ride and we'd all like to rest."

Josh sighed and pushed his glasses up the bridge of his nose. "The governor is eager to see you as well, and also has lots to update you on. He has a job for you, and I'm afraid he won't let you rest for long."

"Fair enough. We're happy to stay busy after a bit of proper R&R."

The secretary shook his head. "This is a personal matter to Governor Vance. He would let Four Corners crumble before delaying this any further. You *must* take this job, and it must be carried out immediately."

"What the fuck's so important?" T-Bone demanded with a cross of his arms.

Josh glanced at us with a nervous clench of his jaw before answering the question. "His daughter's been kidnapped."

MARIPOSA

T he whole second floor of the cabin was essentially an open loft, I realized, as Josh led our party from the foyer up the stairs. A collection of antlers and taxidermy animals like coyotes and elk decorated the sloping walls. I even spotted a jackalope perched on a shelf.

Our group was tense after hearing Josh's news regarding the governor's daughter. "I really hope we don't get roped into this shit," Reaper grumbled into my ear.

I pinched his side, urging him to be quiet, as we walked over a Navajo-style rug toward the far end of the second floor. A bay of windows looked out over more construction sites and people going about their work. In front of the windows, a disheveled middle-aged man sat at a heavy wooden desk, looking distraught.

Josh cleared his throat politely. "Governor, the Sons of Odin have returned. And they've brought guests with them who...may be able to assist with this matter."

Reaper made a noise of disagreement and I jabbed him with my elbow.

The man at the desk lifted his face from his hands, his eyes bloodshot and features looking haggard and exhausted. He clearly hadn't slept or eaten well in the past few days.

"T-Bone, Dyno," the governor rasped, a weary smile lighting up his face. "And even you, Grudge. It's great to see you all. Thank God you're here."

"We're sorry to hear about Kyrie, Governor," T-Bone said in response. "You've been good to us over the past few years and we're happy to help in any way we can."

Reaper thankfully bit his tongue that time, but I didn't miss the hiss of breath and his jaw clenching.

Governor Vance's watery eyes fell to us. "Who are your friends?"

"Governor, it's my pleasure to introduce the Steel Demons MC." T-Bone pointed us out and gave our names, just as he did with Josh. "They're looking for a new place to settle and have a club of around 25 at the bottom of the hill."

Reaper cleared his throat. "If you would allow it, governor, we'd like to stay temporarily to see if Four Corners is a good fit for us. My club has excellent mechanics, cooks, carpenters." He nodded at me. "My wife here is a skilled medic. I'm sure we can contribute to the development of your territory in exchange for a temporary stay."

I took a moment to bask in his praise and him calling me his wife before stepping forward.

"We are very sorry to hear about your daughter, governor. All of us will pray that she's found soon, safe and unharmed. We're extremely grateful for your generous hospitality in the meantime. Please let us know if there's anything we can do." Returning to Reaper's side, I felt him fuming and caught Gunner trying to hide a grin.

"I know you." Vance tilted his head as he peered at Reaper. "You're the one who rides with a hellhound at your side."

"You mean this one?" Reaper leaned down to pat Hades' head, the dark four-legged guardian never making a sound. "He's no hellhound, just a hell of a runner."

"And you." Vance's gaze fell upon Horus perched on Gunner's shoulder. "You're some kind of shaman with that bird. I've heard stories that you turn into a bird yourself."

My golden demon huffed out a chuckle, his smile wide and relaxed. "Just tall tales, governor. I'm a trained falconer, nothing more to it."

"People have said the same things about our ravens," T-Bone added with a shrug. "Now regarding the matter at hand, the Sons of Odin are yours, governor, but—"

"I need *them*."

Vance lifted a weary hand from the desk, finger pointing shakily at us. I only then noticed the empty liquor bottle on the corner.

"They...they use some kind of witchcraft. Some Indian Great Spirit magic. They can find my daughter, bring her back to me safely."

"Um, sir?" Josh cut in nervously. "I understand your worry, but you've been up for several days. Perhaps you should rest."

"I can't! Not until she's home! Oh God, to think of what they're doing to her..."

"Sir, if I may remind you." Josh rounded the desk, placing a comforting hand on the governor's shoulder. "We know who she's with, and that she hasn't been harmed."

"Well, fuck," Reaper muttered under his breath. "What the hell do you need us for?"

"They sent a picture, but how do we know she's really okay? Jesus, my poor baby..."

"Sir, if you don't mind," Josh reached across the desk and hit a button that made a brief buzzing sound, "I'll brief T-Bone and our guests on the situation while you take a shower and maybe sleep for a few hours, okay?"

Three women in simple, matching dark-blue uniforms politely slid past us to attend the governor. House staff, by the looks of it.

"If you could please wash him up, see that he eats soup or something, and make sure he sleeps for a bit." Josh pinched his brow, just above his glasses, as the women surrounded Vance and gently eased him out of his chair. "Give him a sleeping pill if you have to. Thanks, ladies."

We all stepped aside to allow them down the stairs, when Vance twisted in their grip to look back at us.

"Save my daughter, Steel Demons," he begged, weakly fighting against the women practically dragging him down the steps. "Save her and Four Corners is yours. A home, a place of refuge. An army..."

With that final word, his body slumped against his caretakers who buckled under his weight. The governor's lips continued to move as they dragged him across the first floor, mumbling what appeared to be his daughter's name, at my best guess.

"I am terribly sorry about all that," Josh huffed. "She's his only child and her mother passed away, so he's been all out of sorts since she was taken."

"Nothing to be sorry for. His reaction is understandable." T-Bone swallowed, his jaw tight, and I watched his expression with curiosity. He'd never mentioned having children, but appeared to be the one in the room who empathized most with the governor.

"You are welcome to sit down. Um, I apologize for not having enough seats." Josh looked around the room awkwardly, with only a loveseat and a couple of armchairs in the office area.

"That's all right. We ought to head out and find somewhere to crash for the night." Reaper started to turn, gently guiding me in the same direction with a hand on my back, but I resisted.

"Wait. I want to hear this."

"Sugar." He narrowed his eyes, but didn't seem angry, just tired. "Why?"

"We might be able to help. I can, at least, if she has any medical needs."

Josh cleared his throat, which became a cough at the glare from Reaper. "I would suggest you stay for this, just to listen. The governor did ask you specifically."

"And I'm *politely* refusing to be part of this," my husband growled. "The governor's all bent out of shape, anyway."

"Reaper," I chastised.

"I have my own people to take care of. I ain't gonna ride all over fuckin' kingdom come just for some girl."

"A few minutes," I pleaded. "I just want to listen."

He blew out a long breath. "Fine." He wasn't even in the mood to say, *but you owe me*, in that teasing smirk, so I knew his patience would only hold out for so long.

When I turned back around, the Sons of Odin were already squished up into the loveseat adjacent to the desk. Dyno was practically sprawled across T-Bone and Grudge's laps.

"You know where she is, you said?" T-Bone began.

"We know who she's with, not necessarily the location," Josh corrected. "There's a newer territory north of here, Blakeworth, and their governor's family has been trying to kiss Vance's ass ever since they established power, about three years ago. They've attended nearly every diplomatic event here, bringing lavish gifts for Vance, Kyrie, and staff."

Careful to avoid colliding with antlers or taxidermy heads, I leaned against the wall to listen.

"For the past year or so, the governor's been not-so-subtly trying to arrange a marriage between his son and Vance's daughter, Kyrie."

A scoff puffed out behind me. "What is this, the Middle Ages?" Gunner muttered.

"How old is Kyrie?" I asked.

"Nineteen this year," Josh replied. "Governor Blake's son, Malcolm, is twenty-four." Josh's eyes nervously darted around the room. "Just between us, I think Kyrie might have gone willingly."

"Hardly a fuckin' kidnapping then, is it?" Reaper spat. "She's a fucking adult."

"Reaper," I growled. Jesus, he really did not have anything resembling a filter today.

"We have reason to believe she was manipulated into leaving," Josh continued. "She's an adult, yes, but young and impressionable. She's also had a rebellious streak, as young women with protective single fathers tend to have."

"What makes you think these people have nefarious plans with her?" Dyno asked. "What if they're just two rebellious youngsters who genuinely want to be together?"

Josh's lips tightened into a thin line. "Ever since the Blake family came into power, we've had an increasing number of refugees coming in from the north. A big part of Blake's talks with Vance include deals for repatriation. They also want to contract labor from us, because so few people are willing to stay in his territory."

"What do the refugees say?" Jandro's tone sounded odd when he was so serious.

"About what you'd expect," Josh sighed. "Long hours of unsafe working conditions for little pay, or no pay at all. Food rations are barely enough to keep people healthy. Armed police patrol the streets and beat people for the slightest infraction. Very little is being done in the ways of education, housing, and general safety."

"Let me guess," I ventured. "No reliable medical services, or very poor ones at that."

Papers crinkled and shuffled as Josh's fingers tightened around the documents on the governor's desk.

"Birth control is outlawed," he confessed with a grim expression. "Blake says it's a temporary measure to help boost their population, but..."

A heavy scratching cut into his words, and all heads turned to see Grudge scrawling on a notepad. T-Bone rested his chin on the silent man's shoulder to read the message, then looked up at Josh.

"How is Blake justifying the working conditions? What excuse does he give for people leaving?" he read aloud, while Grudge looked on expectantly for the answer, lips pursed slightly in determination.

"From what I've overheard," Josh rubbed his forehead, "Blakeworth is a hot spot for oil and natural gas, which is what most of the workforce revolves around."

"It's tough work," I said with a nod. "I grew up in an oil-rich area in Texas."

"Right, so Blake kept saying that his people are soft and they're not used to hard work. That they're just lazy, entitled, and need to be corrected."

"Hence why he wants labor from Four Corners," Jandro realized. "He sees all the progress going on here and wants it for himself."

"Motherfucker sounds like Hitler," Gunner breathed. "I wouldn't be surprised if he was running labor camps and shit."

The whole room nodded their silent agreement while Josh rifled through more documents on the governor's desk.

"So it's reasonable to assume Kyrie is *not* in good hands," the secretary muttered, pulling out a folder and opening the top cover. "But a messenger delivered this three days ago, and that's what really sealed it for us."

He passed the folder to T-Bone, whose eyebrows shot up the

moment he saw its contents. Dyno and Grudge peered over eagerly to see, their faces morphing into knitted brows and narrowed eyes.

Once all three finished looking, T-Bone glanced at us, then at Josh as he held the folder limply in his lap. "Can they see this?"

"Of course."

T-Bone crossed the room, holding the folder out to Reaper and I with a grim face.

"Oh my..." My hand flew to my mouth.

"Jesus," Reaper bit out.

Jandro and Gunner looked over from next to and behind me, letting out similar curses.

A photograph of a young, willowy blonde woman was paper-clipped to a letter that appeared to have written on a typewriter. In the photo, the woman sat barefoot on a filthy concrete floor with her knees to her chest. Her arms, pale with distinct purple bruises from rough fingers, wrapped around her knees, her head buried under her arms with only one eye peeking at the camera.

Underneath the photo, the letter said:

Dearest Governor Vance,

It has been a pleasure getting to know you and your darling daughter over the past couple of years. It's easy to see why you dote on her, why you're so reluctant to let your little bird fly from the nest. Unfortunately, birds with under-developed wings most often fall prey to predators who will eat them without a second thought.

Don't worry, Vance. Kyrie has merely been transferred from one cage to another. She has not yet been eaten, in any sense of the word. Her current cage may not be as gilded as yours, but in time, she will learn to appreciate it and forget all about the glossy veneer of her former prison.

Especially if she finds a reason to stay. Such as, if she finds herself with child, and as a result, must agree to marriage if she does not wish to end up as trash in the gutter. These events will happen regardless, dear Governor, but if you would prefer to have more input on the timeline, and thus, extended time with your daughter, you will agree to lend Blakeworth two-hundred contracted soldiers, and one-hundred contracted laborers.

The contract length and terms shall be decided by my father and I, with no input from Four Corners. Any attempt to renegotiate these terms will be considered a refusal, and you may find yourself grandfather to the heir of Blakeworth before your next birthday.

Either way, congratulations are in order. We look forward to your response in one week's time. Any delay in receiving an answer will also be considered a refusal.

Your humble servant,
*   Malcolm of Blakeworth*

"Who in the fuck does this chode think he is?" The disgust was clear in Jandro's voice.

"The crowned prince of Doucheville," Gunner scoffed. "He writes like he actually believes the sun shines out of his asshole."

"Vance has been a wreck ever since seeing this," Josh said tiredly. "He does not want to give in to their demands, naturally. Losing two-hundred soldiers and a hundred laborers will devastate us here. And if we agree..."

"You don't expect to get those citizens back," Reaper filled in.

"If Blake sets the terms of the contract and does not allow any negotiation," Josh shook his head. "They'll be trapped there as indentured servants, most likely. Escape will mean risking death. We can't sacrifice three-hundred people like that. It'll be sending them to slaughter."

T-Bone leaned his head back with a groan, rubbing a hand over his shaved crown. "How far's the border from here?"

"About five-hundred and fifty miles."

"So at least a day's ride, probably two if we want to be stealthy."

"Then we still gotta find out where she is," Dyno said. "We'll have to do some interrogation, send Munin out. But even if we get her location relatively quickly..."

"We'll have to ride out early tomorrow at the latest," T-Bone concluded. "Before that sick bastard fuckin'—" He shook his head, unable to complete his thought when he looked over at us, chin lifted. "What do ya think, Demons? Feel like riding in and being fucking heroes?"

"No."

Reaper answered before any one of us could voice an opinion, ignoring my bewildered stare at the side of his face.

"I wish you all the best in getting the girl back, but I've got too much on my plate. If Governor Vance doesn't want us sticking around, I respect that. We'll rest up, and then keep moving. We'll be sure not to overstay our welcome."

"Reaper!" I hissed.

He ignored me and turned to leave, heading down the stairs.

GUNNER

Mari was pissed. And not in the cute, adorable way.

"Reaper, stop." She marched after him, breaking into a jog to keep up with his storming out of the governor's house.

Jandro reached for her shoulder. "*Bonita*—"

"Not now, Jandro."

He lifted both hands away and looked at me with a shrug, walking a few steps back to trudge alongside me a few paces behind the arguing married couple.

"What do you think?" he asked.

"That I need a drink," I sighed. "And a night in a real fucking bed." I reached up and tapped my hand on Horus's talons. "Go."

He spread his wings and launched himself off of my shoulder. Once he got high enough he'd be able to see the club where we left them.

"Agreed on those points. What about *this*?" Jandro gestured ahead to where Mari kept after Reaper, demanding that he talk to her.

"I can see both sides," I admitted. "This isn't our business to get involved in, and we do have our own people to look after. Refusing to help doesn't make us look good to the governor, though. And we might need him in the future."

"And it pisses our woman off that we're not stepping up to help someone," he added.

"That, too."

We caught up to Mari and Reaper on our way down the hill, catching their heated back-and-forth conversation.

"I don't understand," she was saying. "We have plenty of capable people who can do something to help. Why are you refusing this?"

"I'm not sending any of our people to some fascist territory where they'll be beaten to death if caught." Reaper turned abruptly, holding his index finger up in Mari's face. "I'm done with this conversation."

"No, you're not." She batted his hand away, not even flinching. I couldn't help the swell of pride inside me. She really was becoming fearless. "What about the girl who's already there, already a hostage? She's alone and scared. What if that was me?"

"It's *not* you, so it doesn't matter," he growled. "It's an awful situation, but I can't save every girl in trouble."

"You can save *this* one!"

"She means nothing to me, so why should I?!"

"Okay, okay." Jandro wedged his way between the two of them, who looked moments away from literally tearing into each other. "Let's all take a breath. Reap, you need to chill."

"I *would* chill if people would get the fuck off my back."

"She means something to someone," Mari muttered, still glaring daggers at him. "She's a human being. That should be reason enough."

"Okay, sugar, that's fair. But I can only be stretched so thin."

"It doesn't have to be you. You have an entire club—"

"Who I am still responsible for. It's on *me* if something happens to them. Jesus, fuck, I don't want to go in circles like this."

"Come here." I wrapped a hug around Mari from behind, partially to comfort her, partially to hold her back from lunging at Reaper, which she still looked eager to do.

"If I can say something..." Jandro looked between the two of them, still poised in the middle. "Gunner mentioned we might need the governor in the future, Reap. Refusing to do this doesn't swing anything in our favor."

"He also mentioned his army," I reminded them. "Which we'll need if we're taking on Tash directly."

"Who knows if he'll stick to that?" Reaper argued. "Politicians lie. He's a delirious old man offering up whatever he can think of. But once we do our part, who's to say he'll do his?"

"Rescuing his daughter will give us leverage," I reminded him. "He'll owe us. When it comes down to brass tacks, I'll remind him of that. I'm sure there's more we can bring to the table once we get a better lay of the land."

"Fuck." Reaper turned and started back down the hill to the rest of our people at the bottom.

"Talk, Reap." Jandro moved to his side while Mari and I followed, my arms still around her. "What's on your mind?"

"What's on my mind is that we're basically homeless, with no defenses, and the most vulnerable we've ever been," the president growled with a glance over his shoulder at Mari. "We have more to lose now than ever before. I just think we should take care of ourselves now, before others."

"I hear you," Jandro nodded at his side.

Gripping my forearms wrapped around her chest, Mari leaned her head back on my shoulder. "What do you think? We can't ignore the fact that this girl needs help, right?"

"I don't like it, but I get what Reaper's saying." I took a nip at her earlobe at her disappointed groan. "Go easy on him, baby girl. He's not being heartless. It's a hard decision for him, even if it doesn't look like it. He's choosing what's most important to him."

Mari grumbled, her anger now at a more adorable level, all the way to where our vehicles and people waited for us.

"Meeting go well?" Slick asked with a jovial grin, which quickly faded at a closer look at Reaper and Mari's faces.

"Let's find some place to fuckin' eat and spend the night," Reaper said in a non-answer. "No one goes alone, pairs or groups only. They probably can't accommodate all of us in one place, so we'll have to split up. Prospect!"

Larkan straightened up, but his hand clamped tighter around Noelle's waist. "Yes, president?"

"Come with us. When we've found a place, go around and tell everyone where we are in case someone needs us."

I closed my eyelids, slipping into Horus for a brief moment. He was perched on a tree with a clear view of us and half the town. He'd be able to track everyone, plus our vehicles, until it got dark. Then we'd need someone with better night vision to take over.

Something bumped my shin. Freyja. The black cat seemed to read my mind as she wound herself around my boots with a calming ease.

You're safe here, I thought I heard her say.

"Shadow." Jandro nodded at his tall, silent friend. "Come with us."

With that, club members began splitting off into the town on foot. Reaper and Jandro led our small group, followed by Mari and me, Noelle and Larkan, and Shadow bringing up the rear.

Exploring on foot proved to be the wisest option, despite wishing I could roll through on my bike. Streets and sidewalks were narrow, with tons of blocked areas for construction zones, even off of the main roads.

"They're really rebuilding from the ground up," Mari observed as a crane slowly lowered some kind of pipe into a hole in the street.

"Makes you wonder how badly this place got fucked over," I said.

Her hand found mine, slim fingers lacing through. "Makes you admire how resilient people are."

I kissed her forehead as we walked past the construction zone, squeezing my arms tighter around her. That was my girl, always seeing the best outcome in every situation.

We came upon a bed-and-breakfast and piled into the small lobby. The plump old woman behind the front desk looked frozen in terror at the leather clad bikers in her establishment, until Mari and Noelle pushed their way to the front.

"Hi, do you have three rooms available? With one big enough for four people?"

After a few surprised blinks, the owner breathed a sigh of relief and began to explain her options to the women. Looking around, the place was charming, clean, and smelled freshly painted. I peered out the window to the vegetable garden alongside the building.

"That's what I want." Jandro pointed over my shoulder to the chicken coop against the back fence. "Only mine's gonna be even more dope than that."

"If we stick around, I bet you can sell your extras to this lady."

"Extra eggs? Or you mean...?"

"Chickens themselves. I heard you have quite a virile cock there, buddy."

"Shut up." He smacked my shoulder. "But that's a good idea. That way I can keep my population under control without upsetting," his eyes darted to the side, "you know."

"We got rooms," Mari announced. She eyed me and Jandro turning innocently away from the window. "And Mrs. Potts here says there's a bar with an open grill down the road. We can barter for food there or bring our own."

"Thank fuck." Reaper was the first to storm out of the place. "Let's go."

After the rest of our club squeezed into the bar an hour later, followed by the Sons of Odin, I had a hunch there weren't yet many fun places to go in Four Corners.

"Reaper!" T-Bone walked in with a grin on his face, arms spread wide, with his guys flanking him on either side. "You owe me big time now, Pres. I just saved your reputation in the Four Corners territory."

"I don't need you to save dick." Reaper's arm lifted, gesturing the Sons to our table. "But if you bring a full bottle over, I might be willing to hear you out."

While T-Bone went to the bar, Dyno and Grudge grabbed chairs and dragged them to us, the latter pulling up beside Shadow. The scarred man nodded at him in greeting and leaned over to say something over the din of the bar.

"Whoa," I muttered to myself. "Shadow's making friends."

"It's great, isn't it?" Mari watched for a moment over her cocktail.

The two men's communication consisted of Shadow speaking and Grudge writing on the notepad he always carried around.

"Yeah, good for him," I agreed.

T-Bone seated himself next to Reaper at the head of our table, holding a bottle out for our president to examine. "Heard you like the good stuff, Reap."

Reaper gave the bottle an approving nod and gestured for the man to pour. "I'm listening."

A hush came over our group as we all leaned in to hear what T-Bone had to say.

"Dyno, Grudge, and I are riding out in the morning to save the girl—"

"Thank you," Mari cut in smugly, with a scathing look at Reaper.

"—and we convinced Josh and Vance to give you the benefit of the doubt. Josh seemed convinced the governor would've ordered the army to march your asses out of the territory if you didn't lend a hand in this rescue."

Jandro and I exchanged an *I told you so* look from across the table, but Reaper didn't seem fazed by that news.

"Fine by me. We can ride on tomorrow morning."

"You better not." T-Bone sucked his teeth following a long swallow of whiskey. "Because I told them we'd work together on this rescue."

Reaper looked moments away from punching him in his face. "That's what you told them, but what's it really mean?"

T-Bone threw back another shot. "We've got this handled, but I need one man from you. Two at the most. Can you swing that?" When Reaper didn't answer, he pressed, "We'll sing your praises and give you all the credit when we get back. The governor will host you, and your officers, at a dinner and give you everything you need to fight Tash. I'm giving you vengeance on a silver platter here, Pres, and you'd be a fool to refuse it."

"Why?" Reaper wasn't threatened by T-Bone, but still didn't fully trust him. His body language said it all—arms open and draped carelessly over his chair, but eyes narrowed in suspicion. "Why would you do that for us?"

"Because you have the manpower, brains, and resources to strike

Tash where it hurts." T-Bone's voice wavered with emotion. "You can topple the king looking down at us from his tower, but *we* can't. Our goal is the same, but we've already been wiped out. If my whole club was here to back us, I wouldn't be asking you for shit. But they're gone. *You* still have a chance."

Reaper kept silent, but the suspicion lifted away from his eyes. His whole expression softened as he took in the weight of what T-Bone was saying. Before he could respond, Larkan abruptly stood.

"I'll go, president."

"Sit your ass down, prospect," Reaper growled.

"Yeah," Noelle hissed through her teeth at her boy toy. "What the fuck are you doing?"

"No, I should do this," Larkan insisted. "I'm not even a Demon, so you're not sacrificing anyone important by sending me." The prospect shrugged his shoulders. "If I don't come back, it's no skin off your nose, Pres. If I do?" He leveled his gaze at Reaper. "Maybe then I'll be worthy of a patch."

"He's got a point," Jandro weighed in, slouching low in his seat.

It took Reaper only one dram of whiskey to make up his mind. "Fine. Shadow, you're going too." He fumbled for his cigarettes and a light. "Because whatever happens, I know for a fact you'll come back and tell me accurately what happened."

"Yes, president." Shadow didn't seem to feel one way or the other about the situation. He did his job without question, and was therefore the perfect pick.

With a jovial grin, T-Bone clapped Reaper on the shoulder. "Thank you, Reap. We can't fucking lose with two Demon riders with us. We'll be in and out with the girl in no time."

The matter seemed settled until Mari spoke up. "I'm going too."

"*No!*"

The three of us were loud enough that the whole bar fell silent. Lookie-loos at other tables craned their necks to see what got our hackles raised.

"Hey, all y'all mind your own business!" I snapped. When the peering eyeballs were gone and the background noise resumed, I grabbed Mari's chin to make her look at me. "Baby girl, I love you, but are you out of your fucking mind?"

She pulled my hand away with an icy glare. "No, I'm not. But the girl might need medical services that shouldn't wait for a two-day ride." She looked at the Sons over the table. "Do any of you know CPR? First aid? How to set a broken bone or treat an infection? If so, then fine, you don't need me." Her gaze swept over Shadow and Larkan. Her questions only met with blank stares, she looked back at me. "I'm going."

"Like *fuck* you are," Reaper roared.

"I'll be fine. The guys won't let anyone come within a mile of me. Especially with Shadow there."

It was hard to tell with all his hair hanging in front of his face, but I swore the big dude blushed and tried to hide a smile.

T-Bone cleared his throat. "If I may add something to the little lady's defense?"

"No, you fucking may not!" Reaper stared at him, incredulous.

"Go ahead, T-Bone," Mari implored him with a loud slurp on her straw.

"The governor's daughter will likely feel better about coming with us if she sees another woman in our company." He gave his beard a thoughtful stroke. "I mean, we'll tie her up and throw her on a bike if it comes to that, but we'd get out a lot easier if we didn't have to. 'Til we get her home, she'd just feel like she was being kidnapped again."

"Excellent point!" Mari was getting louder the more she drank. "I'll make the girl feel safe. The whole thing will go a lot more smoothly if I'm there."

"Sugar?" Reaper leaned as far across the table as he could without standing up. "Be quiet. You're not going."

"We've got the majority of the club here, right?" Mari looked around. "Let's put it to a vote."

"This isn't church," Reaper hissed. "We aren't voting on shit."

"Who thinks I should go on the rescue?" Mari bellowed.

Everyone at the table, save for the men currently sleeping with her, raised a hand.

Jandro grabbed Dyno's arm and brought it down to the table. "Y'all don't get to vote on our business. Neither do you, Prospect, or Noelle!"

Reaper's sister just shrugged and lifted her arm higher. "I want Mari watching out for my man. But I draw the line at her kissing his boo-boos."

"Don't worry, Nellie. Even if I wanted to, I bet Shadow would snitch on me."

"What?" Shadow looked confused for a moment, until Mari tossed him a smirk that almost seemed flirtatious.

"Don't fuckin' matter anyway," T-Bone laughed, leaning his chair back. "Y'all are outvoted. Your woman is ours for at least two days."

MARIPOSA

I fell into bed with the room spinning slightly. The guys shoved the two queen beds together to make one gigantic bed in the middle of our room. I was tired enough to fall asleep almost immediately, but it became clear Reaper wouldn't let that happen.

Smack!

"Oww!" I rolled away, clutching the side of my butt he'd spanked harder than ever before. "What the hell?"

"I oughta tan your hide for that stunt you pulled." He sat in a chair and kicked off his boots, then slid his cut from his shoulders, but otherwise didn't undress for bed. "At least one of us should be with you at all times. What the hell are you thinking volunteering to go off with men that aren't yours?"

"Is that what you're mad about?" I asked, still rubbing my stinging cheek.

"One of us can still go with her," Jandro cut in from where he lay on the other side of me. He could lie comfortably on his back now, and looked delicious in that position with his fingers laced behind his head. Too bad Reaper was ruining the moment by looking for a fight.

"You all need to be here," I told him. Reaper *was* right about that, at least. "You two need to lead the club and keep order, and Gunner needs to keep an eye on things with Horus." I turned my gaze back to Reaper, anger burning in my chest. "I don't like what you're insinuating by me going off with other men. What exactly are you worried about?"

My husband sighed, scrubbing a hand down his face. "That's not what I'm saying. I trust the men, and I trust you. What pisses me off is you undermining me. I'm still president, sugar. You cannot call a vote on club business. In fucking public, no less."

The anger withered down to guilt. He was right, I'd stampeded over him when I shouldn't have. At the time, it felt lighthearted and fun. Everyone was drinking and laughing. We had compromised on the mission and came to a solution. Now, with him sitting there looking all disappointed in me, it sank in how seriously he took it.

"I'm sorry." I reached over the edge of the bed for him. "I didn't mean anything by it. I just saw an opportunity to help and went for it."

He looked at my outstretched hand, then back to my face, face stony and unreadable.

My hand dropped over the side of the bed as I rolled onto my back, letting my shirt ride up my torso. "Can I do anything to make it up to you?"

A beat of silence passed before he rose from the chair, standing over me as his gaze drifted over my body. I was only in panties and a T-shirt, my breaths already shallowing with deep rises and falls of my chest as I waited for him to do something.

Make-up sex with him was always intense, rough, and passionate. I hated when we got into arguments, but those animalistic sessions afterward were on another level. We kept it only between us though. I wasn't sure how he'd respond with Jandro and Gunner in the room.

"I have to punish you," he bit out finally. "On your belly."

I rolled to my stomach, core and thighs clenching in anticipation of what was coming next. Reaper reached out, fingers trailing gently over the backs of my thighs. When the spank came down on my other cheek, I was ready. My fists curled around the sheets as I bit down my whimper.

He smacked the other side, heat cracking on already tender flesh. Alternating sides, his palm switched between soothing and cruel, rubbing over my sore bottom before slapping down hard again. When I couldn't hold in my cries anymore, he stopped.

"Gunner." He nodded at my blond demon across the room, but I didn't know what he was ordering. "Jandro."

The VP slid across the bed to me, remaining stretched out on his back. "Straddle me, *Mariposita*."

I lifted up and slid my weak knee to the other side of Jandro's torso. He pulled me down for a kiss, sweet relief after Reaper's punishment. Much gentler hands roamed inside my shirt and down my sides, bringing sighs of contentment to my ragged breaths.

"Take her shirt and panties off," came the harsh order.

Jandro obeyed, pulling my top over my head to discard in a corner of the room. I brought my legs together briefly so he could hook his fingers in my underwear, dragging them down to my knees. I shimmied them down the rest of the way and kicked them off when they reached my ankles.

Once naked, I straddled Jandro again and looked up at Reaper, still fully dressed and sitting next to the bed.

"Come here." I reached for him again, my lips parted and already longing to taste him.

"No." His expression was aloof, smug, even cruel.

My hand lowered slowly, the shock slicing through me with a sharp pain. He didn't want me?

I willed my lip not to tremble. "Why not?"

"Because that's your real punishment, sugar." He cupped my chin with just his thumb and forefinger, not allowing any more touch. "You can't have me until you come back."

"What?" I cried. "I'm not gonna see you for two, maybe three, days!"

He shrugged. "Should've thought about that before being so eager to go."

"Reaper, please!" I looked down at the man under me, then Gunner standing on the opposite side of the bed, hiding something behind his back. "Guys, come on!"

"Sorry, baby girl." Gunner walked slowly around the bed until he stood behind me. He was shirtless, jeans unbuttoned and hanging low on his hips. "We follow our president. In the bedroom, he's your first man and sets the rules for the rest of us."

Traitor. I glared at him. After all the time he spent resisting our whole dynamic, now he decided to just fall in line?

"Don't worry, though." Gunner's playful grin returned, his arms giving nothing away to what hid behind his back. "We have a surprise for you."

"What—ow! Hm!"

Jandro pulled me down with a fist in my hair, silencing me with a rough kiss. His hips moved underneath me, his length, hot and thick, rubbing through his boxers against my lower belly.

I jumped with a shriek when something cold touched my pussy, and whipped my head around at the sound of Gunner's amused chuckle.

"Relax, baby girl." He sat at the edge of the bed, rubbing the cold thing against my soaked core, and pressed a kiss to my lower back. "It is a punishment, but you'll still enjoy this."

"What is it?"

I breathed out a soft gasp as he pushed it inside me. It felt heavy and quickly warmed up with my body temperature. Gunner's eyes heated, breaths coming out in soft puffs as he gently fucked me with the toy. Then he pulled it out and showed me with a triumphant grin.

A silver, metallic butt plug.

Crack!

"Ah!"

Reaper's punishing spank came out of nowhere, but neither of the guys seemed surprised. They must have planned this, in some way or another.

"Give that to me and play with her, but do not let her come until I say so."

Gunner handed Reaper the plug without another word. My eyes locked onto those predatory green eyes as Reaper stuck it in his mouth. His cheeks hollowed out as he sucked my juices off the metal toy like it was an ice cream cone. Our stares remained locked, even as Jandro moved me up and down over his length, and Gunner's thumb massaged circles around my ass.

My pussy closed around nothing and it bordered on painful. It felt completely unfair that he got to taste me, without even touching me himself, and I wouldn't feel any part of him for days.

And it hurt the worst, knowing that was the whole point of this.

Reaper pulled the toy from his mouth, the metallic surface now shiny with his saliva. He reached with it, circling the pointed end slowly around my nipple.

"If you were any other woman," he said softly, dragging the wet, heated metal across my breast. "If you were just some club bitch that didn't matter to me, do you know what I'd do to you for undermining me?"

The heat and wetness from the toy on my skin didn't hurt, but the lack of touch from him was painful. He brought it back to his mouth, wetted it again, and continued his torturous path to my other nipple. It could almost feel like a tongue, but wasn't soft enough, wasn't *him* enough.

"I bet you'd actually fuck me," I ground out at him. "If I was just some whore that mouthed off."

He laughed lightly, dragging the plug along my sternum now. "No. I'd use my belt on you, for one. Not just my hand." Pulling the toy away, he reached behind me and dipped it into my pussy again a few times, then returned it to his mouth. "Mm," he moaned around my taste. "And I wouldn't wait to punish you privately in a bedroom. I'd tan your ass raw, out there for everyone to see."

Jandro sucked in heavy breaths beneath me, his shaft pressing hard on my clit as he kept rolling me back and forth on him. I bit the inside of my cheek to fight the building pleasure, knowing Reaper would punish me further if I came without his permission. Behind me, Gunner squirted a generous amount of lube onto his fingers, then returned to playing with my ass.

"Fuck!" I gasped as he pressed through the tight ring of muscles.

It was a completely different sensation, a stretch with a bit of a burn, but not altogether unpleasant. Gunner's finger worked through gently, his thumb still massaging around in a circle to relax me. I was relieved he was the one back there, the perfect person to work with me through something new and uncomfortable.

"You're safe, baby girl," he reminded me in a whispered kiss on my back.

It didn't feel bad, but my pussy was the one aching for attention, needing to be filled. I had soaked Jandro, who shoved his boxers down and slid me up and down his length with ease now. His clenched jaw and grip on my hips told me he was barely hanging on to his own control.

"If you were any other woman," Reaper continued, my skin trembling under the heat of the plug now, "after I was done spanking your ass, I'd make you crawl naked across the room, in front of the whole club. Ass in the air, on hands and knees, all the way over to me, while I sit and watch like this." He sat in the chair and leaned back, knees open and inviting. "And like a good girl, you'd suck me dry for everyone to see."

My lips parted, mouth watering at the sight of the bulge pressing through his jeans. I wanted to be right there, as he described it. On my hands and knees, between the long muscles of his thighs. Worshiping or controlling him, the power dynamic didn't matter as long as I could touch him. My fingers curled into Jandro's chest, his touch was soothing, but I still ached for the man who was punishing me.

"You're really not going to touch me until I come back?"

A muscle feathered in his jaw, the only shift in his demeanor. Just as quickly as it happened, he reeled the control back in. "I might give you a goodbye kiss tomorrow."

"Reaper," Jandro groaned beneath me, sliding me off of his shaft so I sat on his legs. His dick pulsed and his balls were tight and snug up against his base. He was already close.

"Take a break, but do not make her come," Reaper snapped. "Here." He handed the plug back to Gunner, who dragged the now-cooled metal through my sex again.

Jandro slid out from under me to lean against the headboard while Gunner played me—one hand in my ass, the other stroking my greedy pussy with a toy that didn't hold a candle to what I wanted. I needed my men, all of them. I wanted fresh memories of their touch and warmth while I had to be away from them. Reaper *knew* how badly I wanted him and used that information to fuck with my mind.

"Please..." There were no words for what I was begging for. I needed someone inside me, but I would've cried with joy if Reaper would just touch my face. Just gave me a kiss. Just told me I was being good.

"Come here, *bonita*." Jandro beckoned me forward and I crawled eagerly up the bed to him, just as Reaper had described .

Warm, hazel eyes drank me in as he cupped the sides of my neck, looking at me with adoration before he kissed me, passionate and languid.

"Beautiful," he murmured with another luscious tug of my lips. "You're a pain in the ass sometimes, but you're ours and we love you."

"I'm gonna miss you." I nudged my nose against his, angling for more of those pillowy lips.

"We'll miss you too. *All* of us," he said pointedly, hands caressing down my chest. "Someone's just more upset and worried about you leaving."

I knew that, but hearing him say it was comforting. Reaper, the most protective and dominant of them, was frustrated—both sexually, and with the helplessness of being unable to protect me for a few days.

Jandro's soothing touch reached my breasts, rolling over my nipples as he kept sucking luscious kisses from my mouth. I became painfully aware of nothing in my pussy or ass now, and arched my back with a wiggle of my hips, hoping Gunner would do something about that. Instead, I got two more punishing spanks from Reaper's palms.

He's making sure you'll feel him, all right, I realized as Gunner's hands smoothed over the stinging flesh. *You'll feel him on every bump and piece of gravel on the road tomorrow while you're on someone else's bike.*

Pressure returned to the tight ring of muscles around my ass, and I knew it wasn't a finger this time. More lube aided the plug in sliding through the entrance, filling me deeper and wider than before.

"Good, baby girl?" Gunner's hands and lips caressed up my back.

"I want you there," I whimpered, twisting around for a kiss.

"Not yet." He nuzzled my neck, wrapping his arms around my middle. "You're not ready. We'll get there, though."

Gunner slid around from behind me to kneel next to Jandro, who still reclined against the headboard. My breath was stolen for a moment at how gorgeous they looked next to each other. Jandro's dark tan and beefy muscles contrasted with Gunner's leanness and fairer complexion.

I grabbed Gunner's waist, holding him for balance as I scooted up Jandro's legs to rest on his dick again.

I was so wet, my body so needy for affection and touch. And this was just the beginning of Reaper's mind game—his punishment for undermining him and for leaving him.

Jandro looked at him, still sitting to the side of the bed, fully dressed. The cool, collected puppet master of this scenario. I'd do anything he wanted just for the hope of him touching me.

"Go ahead." Reaper lit a cigarette and crossed his arms. "You can only make her come once though, so make it count."

I leaned forward, angling my hips as Jandro grabbed the base of his dick. He slid into me in one deep thrust, our mutual moans reaching the rafters in the ceiling. Everyone staying at the B&B would probably hear us, but I didn't care at that point.

Bracing one hand on Jandro's chest, I turned Gunner's hip toward me for easier reach. I found a rhythm with my hips first, grinding back and forth on my Latin lover, before leaning to the side to take Gunner in my mouth.

"Oh, baby girl," he groaned, fingers digging into my hair as he slid over my tongue, long and heavy.

I let out a satisfied hum, taking my two thick cocks deeper with every swallow and rock of my body. The plug in my ass added a new sensation, like Jandro filled my pussy even more with the added pressure. I leaned into it, rolling down to take him deeper and pressing the end of the plug between my body and his.

"Don't let her come," Reaper growled from the other side.

I lifted my hand from Jandro's chest to flip him off, earning a laugh from the man underneath me. To my disappointment, he lifted my hips up to reduce my friction.

"Boss's orders, Mariposita," Jandro groaned beneath me.

"Fuck him," I growled, lips resting on Gunner's pulsing crown while I took a minute to stroke him.

"That's not allowed either," my golden man chuckled above me. He stroked my cheek tenderly, turning my gaze up to his hooded blue eyes. "Can't say I'm mad about it, though, when I have you like this."

I leaned against his hip, resting my head there while my fist slid up and down the long, beautiful cock jutting out from his body. His breaths were loud, echoing around the room with the furious pulsing of my heartbeat.

Jandro took control beneath me, his strong grip on my waist as he drove up inside me. He filled me deep with long strokes, feeling even thicker with the plug's fullness in my ass. I teetered on the edge of release, but tried to steady my breath and whimpers. Maybe I could get away with more than one if I controlled my reactions.

Reaper's gaze was heavy over my shoulder. He loved seeing me pleased no matter what, so not touching me wasn't as bad for *him*, as long as my other two did their jobs. But only letting me come once? That had to be some kind of punishment for himself, too.

"Baby…"

Gunner couldn't even finish saying my pet name as my lips sucked a trail from his hip bone to his balls. He stiffened like concrete in my hand, his fingers tightening against my scalp as I licked and sucked the most tender parts of his body. A sharp inhale, that I knew didn't belong to him, reached my ears. My chest swelled with satisfaction as I ignored the surly president watching the show. Two could play at this game, and I wanted him to know what he was missing.

"Not gonna last if you keep that up," Gunner rasped in a rush of breath.

The confession just encouraged me even more, keeping one hand on his balls as my lips returned to his crown, tongue flicking the sensitive underside. Jandro's thrusts into me continued relentlessly, my clit crashing into his body with every impact.

Forgetting everything else but the sensations of my men filling me and pleasing me, I moaned around Gunner's dick as I pressed down against Jandro, matching him thrust for thrust. There was no stopping my release now, and I wanted their pleasure as much as my own.

My orgasm closed around Jandro like a vice, aided by the weight and pressure of the plug in my ass. He gasped with the rush of his own release, fingers curled into my flesh as he stiffened beneath me. Gunner's salty taste filled my mouth a moment later, his moans dragging heavily out of his chest as he flexed and twitched between my lips.

We untangled into a slick, sweaty pile. Gunner carefully removed the toy, but it wasn't him who came over to gently clean me with a damp washcloth.

Reaper shut off the lights before I could react, leaving the guys to fumble blindly for their sleeping spots in the bed. His shadowy form made the bed dip under his weight. The calloused touch of his palm opening my legs made me shiver with aftershocks. Cool softness pressed to the heat at my core, making me gasp.

"You're touching me," I panted.

"I know," he said, all anger and bite gone from his voice.

He dragged the washcloth all around my tender pussy first, before moving to my ass and wiping up any excess lube. When he stood and went into the small, adjoining bathroom, I wasn't sure whether to expect him to return to bed or not.

I turned on my side, facing away as I snuggled up to Gunner. Already half-asleep, he rained kisses down on my cheeks and forehead. The water faucet in the bathroom ran as I settled my head on Gunner's shoulder, my leg draped over his.

Clothes rustled behind me, and then the bed dipped again as bodies shuffled and moved around. I didn't turn around to see who'd snuggle up to my back, as much as I wanted to.

The broad arm wrapping around my waist felt like a shield, protective while sometimes unyielding. Cloves and whiskey filled my senses, and I melted with relief into the broad chest at my back.

"Sleep well, sugar," Reaper murmured in my ear. "You've got a long day tomorrow."

SHADOW

I *need to get laid.*

The thought wasn't one that came to me often, but with the sounds of Mariposa and her men through one wall, plus Larkan and Noelle from the other, it didn't leave room for much else to think about.

I popped a sleeping pill and chugged down a glass of water. While waiting for the pill to kick in, I double-checked my weapons. My shortest knives were under the pillow I was sleeping on, handgun under the other pillow. My daggers were under the bed, carefully placed with the handles out so I could reach them at a moment's notice. And my favorite rifle was tucked between the mattress and the headboard.

Anyone who broke into my room and searched for weapons wouldn't be able to find them without waking me first. Such was my standard procedure for sleeping anywhere that was unfamiliar.

When all weapons were checked and I had nothing else to do, I shucked off my shirt and kicked off my boots to the sounds of sex through the walls around me. Once undressed for bed, I reclined on the mattress, propping my pillow up against the headboard.

Someone mentioned there was a brothel in this territory. I briefly toyed with the idea of paying for some company, but quickly dismissed it. None of the service girls I'd slept with had ever really done anything for me. They were just there, convenient.

And the one person I actually wanted to spend time with was already busy next door.

You'll have her company for the next two days, though. Without *her men.*

The thought sent a flutter of nerves through me, and not for the first time that night. It sounded like a dangerous rescue mission, nothing I couldn't handle, but I was usually focused to the point of being robotic for these kinds of missions. Now I couldn't stop thinking of everything *but* the objective, my thoughts bouncing around like tennis balls.

I wondered if Mariposa and I would get the chance to talk over coffee, like friends. Like she suggested before the move. Would there be an opportunity to hug her again? Would she want to ride on the back of my bike?

That last thought sent a rush of heat to my dick so abruptly I groaned, my hand moving down my torso toward that annoying organ. I never exposed my back to anyone. It was why I always rode in the rear, why I always faced the door when inside a room. And I sure as fuck never had a woman ride with me.

I wanted to, though.

As long as it was her.

Even just as friends, I could trust her at my back. I wanted to take that chance. I wanted to know what it felt like.

I closed my eyes and my fist at the same time, willing my thoughts to stop bouncing all over the place, my cock to calm down, and to go the hell to sleep. But her soft voice continued to murmur through the walls, with deeper voices responding. I knew I should dig through my bags for my earplugs, but I couldn't stop listening.

I couldn't stop wishing she was here with me.

It was purely selfish. It wasn't like I could give her anything. I couldn't please and satisfy her like her three men did on a daily basis. I'd probably make a fucking fool of myself if we ever ended up in a physical situation again. *Not that we ever would, but...*

I might've been rock hard for her, but I couldn't help that response. All I really wanted was for her to be here next to me.

Lost in my own fantasies, the small, dark blur completely startled me when it jumped on my bed. The knife under my pillow was in my hand and pointed at the thing in the blink of an eye. Freyja just lowered herself into a seat as she stared at me from across the blanket.

"What are you doing here?" My gaze moved to the locked bedroom door. "How'd you get in?"

I can't tell you all my secrets now, a feminine voice that definitely wasn't my own floated softly through my mind. *I have a reputation to protect. Cat-like reflexes will mean nothing to humans if you learn my ways, Shadow.*

My hand with the knife lowered slowly to the mattress. "You can speak too. Like...like..."

Like Horus, yes. And Hades. Although those two are particular about who they speak to. Hades is not yet concerned with you, though I see Horus has taken you under his wing. The cat's green eyes dilated, her gaze growing darker. *He's touched you, and I can see why. You poor, lonely creature.*

"What...do you want?"

This didn't at all seem like the animal who purred endlessly, who rubbed herself all over me, and allowed me to pet her. No, there was something unsettling and...*human* in the way this cat looked at me. Her mouth didn't move, but the voice could only be hers. I heard with my ears and from a place deep inside me.

I'm here to give you permission, since you won't give it to yourself.

"Permission?"

To think of her. Lust after her. Talk to her and touch her if you feel the urge. Hell, even touch yourself at the thought of her.

"What?" Heat and shame filled me, my hands jerking away from my own body as though I couldn't trust myself. "I don't want to—why would I—"

You do want to, son. And that's all right. The cat walked across the bed toward me, a loud purr starting up from the small animal. *No one polices your thoughts, your wants, and desires. You're not hurting her or anyone else. So do not feel guilt or shame for feeling the way you do.*

Her head bumped against my hand, the side of her small, furry body following to press along my side. The contact made the panic in me subside just slightly. Freyja had a similar calming effect to Mariposa.

"What do I do?" I whispered to whatever wisdom inhabited the animal. "I can't stop thinking about her. I want to touch her every chance I get, but I—"

You're terrified, I know. But you must take some risks, son. Take a leap of faith. She is a gentle woman. If you fall, she won't drop you painfully.

"But I don't want anyone else," I said. "It feels like I'll never find anyone like her if I fail, but I feel like a fucking idiot for even thinking I have a chance."

That is the poison you've heard all your life, dear one. You know in your heart it isn't true. What did she herself tell you? These men you ride with, what do they tell you?

The cat stared at me expectantly, like she really wanted an answer.

"That I'm good at what I do. My loyalty is unwavering. I'm an asset to the club, and I'm, um, a good tattoo artist."

Yes, what else?

I looked down at my hands, remembering Mariposa's fingers wrapped around them just a few days ago.

"She told me I'm already good enough as I am. That I'm already a better man than many out there, better than others she's known."

And does that sound like someone who considers you beneath her?

"No, she's nothing like—like them."

My chest tightened as I fought memories of my past, feeling like cold blades trying to cut their way to the forefront of my mind. Mariposa said I'd have to confront them one day to truly beat them. But I was perfectly fine with keeping them locked away for as long as I lived.

You won't grow as a human unless you face what terrifies you.

I stared at the cat, unsure if she was reading my mind or referring to taking a chance with Mariposa.

Try something tomorrow. Share a part of yourself. She wants to know more about who you are.

"She does?" My heart leaped. "She told you that?"

The rhythm of Freyja's purr changed abruptly, sounding almost like a laugh, but the cat said no more. She jumped off my bed and disappeared.

I laid back against my pillow and closed my eyes, my body heavy with the sleep medication now settling into my limbs. They were either finished next door or I was already too far under to hear. But I returned to that feeling, the one that made my thoughts bounce around knowing I'd spend at least two full days with her.

I think this means I'm excited, was my last thought before drifting off.

The sky was still dark when I woke up, the coldness of right before dawn settling into my room. I pushed back the covers and rose from bed, already wide awake and eager to start the day.

Walking around my bed on bare feet, I was unsurprised to find I was alone—no cat trapped in here with me, despite never opening the door last night. I splashed cold water on my face and wondered if Freyja's pep talk last night was some kind of hallucination from my sleeping pills.

You know it wasn't. Your own brain would have never encouraged you like that. Plus, it wasn't the first time. At this point, it was hardly unusual for anyone in the SDMC to hear voices.

I dropped down to the floor and started a quick workout routine, hoping it would calm my nerves. Since joining the SDMC, I'd never spent extended time away from the majority of my brothers, and that gave me a mixture of excitement and nervousness.

Jandro taught me how to function in the real world, and I leaned on him heavily in the first few years of my freedom. Lately, I'd started to wonder if I was outgrowing the routine we established. I could talk to people without him prodding me now. I might even be able to talk to a woman besides Mariposa, if a situation called for it.

I held myself up at the top of a push-up, clenching my jaw as I slowly lowered down. Jandro almost felt overbearing lately. Not that I wasn't grateful for his help in getting by, but with each passing day, I was starting to feel like I didn't need him for that anymore.

Whenever we found a permanent place to settle, I might even like to try having my own home.

The sun just started to rise as I finished my workout and took a quick shower. After packing a few necessities in my saddle bags, I left my room to enter a still quiet common area of the bed-and-breakfast. Everyone's doors were closed and I couldn't detect any movement—none except for the man already at the coffee pot.

"*Buenos dias.*" Jandro seated himself at a table with a full cup. "You're up early, man."

"Yeah." I'd forgotten he was such an early riser. "Wanted to make sure I was prepared for today."

"Mm-hm."

I felt him watch me as I headed for the pot myself and filled a clean cup, then meandered to the same table and sat across from him.

"What are you up to today?" I brought the steaming, dark liquid to my lips.

"Exploring Four Corners, probably." He leaned back and stretched, lacing his hands behind his head. "Try to keep my mind off missing the hell out of my woman while she's gone."

"Mm." I nodded with a swallow of coffee, like I understood how that felt. If it was anything like the ache I felt whenever Mariposa wasn't around, I knew it well. "I'll make sure nothing happens to her. You have my word."

"I know I do." He didn't seem relieved, but continued to peer at me from across the table. "You think it's gonna be...difficult for you?"

I nearly choked on my next swallow. "Difficult how?"

"You know."

I placed my mug down on the table. "I don't, Jandro."

"You've slept with her before. Now you're going to be in close proximity again, without any of *us* there for days."

The hard, familiar clamp of anxiety tightened around my chest, as it always did when someone insinuated that I did something wrong. But I felt more in control this time. Now, I felt confident that I might not actually screw up like I was expected to.

"You know I wouldn't do anything behind your back, Jandro. And I'd never put Mariposa in a situation where she'd be frightened like that again. We've both gained a lot of trust in each other."

His eyebrows lifted. That wasn't the answer he was expecting. While Jandro meant well, I realized he was used to ordering me around. Both because he was vice president, and also because I was once meek, scared of my own shadow, and didn't know any better.

"Not behind my back," he repeated slowly, weighing each of the words. "Do you really mean to say…"

"It's Mariposa's decision too," I said, which made his mouth drop open. "I don't know if she wants…anything with me, or just to be friends. But I'm grateful to her and value her in my life, regardless."

Jandro rocked forward in his chair, placing his palms down on the table. "Shadow, dude. We've talked about this before—"

"You told me I'm inexperienced, which is true. But I'm not dumb, and I'm not a bad man."

"I never said—"

"No, but you think I'm not good enough for her." I sucked in a breath that was almost painful to take in. My chest felt like it was going to explode, but I had to finish saying my piece. "Which is fair enough, Jandro. But that's ultimately not your decision. It's hers."

His mouth abruptly closed and opened again with surprise, before stroking his chin with his hand.

"I suppose you're right." His expression turned a bit embarrassed. "I just want the best for her, you know. But she's her own woman, and I do love that about her." He looked toward his bedroom door, still closed, with silence behind it. "One of my best friends is already with her. I suppose it's not too weird if another one joins us."

"I just want you to know that," my grip returned to the coffee mug, "I appreciate everything you've taught me about the world. And now I'm at a point where I think I'll be okay managing on my own."

He nodded sagely at that. "I respect that, Shadow. Hell, I might've held your hand on some things for too long. But I'm glad you're feeling more confident now. It's a good look on you, bro."

"Thanks." I hid my heated face behind another large swallow of coffee.

"I trust you out there, in every respect," he said. "And while I'm gonna be counting the seconds til she comes back, I trust Mari too. So, if you still get those moments where you feel…skittish, let's say, just know that you can trust her too." My oldest friend gave me a solemn look across the table. "Remember that, man. She'd never hurt you."

"I know." I set my now-empty coffee cup down on the table. "But thanks for the reminder."

MARIPOSA

"All set, little lady?"

T-Bone was in a cheery mood, whistling a tune as he approached me with a cup of coffee in his hand.

"Almost," I assured him, rummaging through my supplies.

"Yeah, yeah. Take your time, get your goodbye smooches."

Chuckling to myself, I double-checked my medic bag, securing all the side pockets but left the main compartment open for Freyja to jump in. She was getting goodbye pets from the guys on the front porch of the B&B.

I made my way over to them, sliding my arms through the straps. My heart skipped a beat when Reaper's green gaze leveled on me. I woke up this morning with tender, bruised butt cheeks, and felt every square inch of fabric as I pulled my pants on.

"Sore?" His lips quirked amusedly.

"A little," I replied in a snippy tone. "You still mad at me?"

He sighed, staring at me longingly from head to toe. "I'm gonna miss you too much to be mad."

We moved toward each other at the exact same time, closing the short distance with enough momentum to crash into each other. We collided, the force strong enough to knock me back if he hadn't grabbed my bag straps to hold me in place. The kiss came down with equal force, his tongue invading my mouth like he'd never get to taste me again.

Coffee, leather, and clove cigarette filled my senses. It was early morning and I knew he hadn't drank yet, but I picked up that hint of whiskey on his tongue, too. I clung to his shirt, sucking on his lower lip as though my life depended on holding on to every one of my husband's flavors.

The kiss came to a slow, gentle ending, but our mouths never fully separated and our hands continued to hold the other person.

"I'm gonna miss you too," I breathed against his mouth. "And I'm sorry about yesterday."

Reaper released my straps, his hands gliding down my sides to hug around my waist. "It's forgiven, sugar. I think you were adequately punished last night." With a wicked grin, his palms slid down to cup my ass.

I winced, shifting in his grip, much to his amusement, as he kneaded my sore flesh. I was definitely going to be feeling every single pebble and pothole throughout the ride. And yet despite it, I craved his hands on me and his cock filling me up. This romantic goodbye felt wholly unfair since he deprived me of him last night.

"No time for a gentle quickie?"

"Nope," he chuckled. "Nice try though." His touch slid back up the front of my body, shamelessly running over my breasts before he cupped the sides of my neck. "I love you, sugar," he breathed, nose nudging mine. "And it's gonna be so fucking good when my wife comes back home to me."

Another rough, biting kiss felt like the fresh hit of a drug high before he tore himself away.

"Be safe, old lady." His forehead nuzzled mine. "Don't let these dickwads get themselves killed, either."

"We'll be back before you know it." I stood on tiptoes to steal one last kiss from him. "And I love you too, old man."

Reaper stepped back with an amused smile, making room for Gunner and Jandro to come up to me.

"*Oh, Mariposita,*" Jandro sighed, pulling me into him to wrap me in a bone-crushing embrace. "I don't like this at all. Frankly, I'm scared to death," he whispered into my neck.

"Shadow won't let anything happen." I wrapped my arms around his neck. "Just don't jump in front of any explosions until I get back."

The VP groaned his displeasure, squeezing around me tighter as he peppered kisses to my neck and cheek.

"You can fight and shoot now, baby girl," Gunner reminded me, with a kiss on the back of my head. "You'll be fine."

I spun in Jandro's arms to face my golden man. "Finally, a vote of confidence."

He grinned, cupping my chin with a gentle hand as he lowered an incredibly hot, languid kiss to my mouth. Our chemistry buzzed through the contact of our lips, but he didn't deepen or speed it up. It was Jandro who pushed my hair aside and sucked at my nape, leaving me gasping and writhing between them.

"You two are evil together," I whined.

"Hurry back, then." Gunner moved his lips to my ear. "So all three of us can fill our woman when she gets home."

Right then was the moment I almost decided to stay. But I swallowed the hungry need to feel all my men at the same time, and looked out toward the packed, revving bikes, ready to go. I was about to see a new territory, spend time with new friends, without my men hovering. And Reaper was right—it would be so much sweeter after some time away.

The Steel Demons president had the Sons of Odin, Larkan, and Shadow in some kind of group huddle. I couldn't hear him over the bikes, but it sounded like he was barking instructions. Or threats. Probably both.

T-Bone caught me watching and winked over Reaper's shoulder. When the group broke up, Reaper turned with his back ramrod straight and chin high. I smirked as he approached and grabbed me around the waist for a final, *final* kiss.

"What did you tell them?"

"That I'll skin every one of them alive and let Hades feast on their organs if you get so much as a scratch on you."

"Figured it was something like that." I pressed my hands to the sides of his face. "I *will* come back to you. My place is at your side, love."

"I know you will." His palms squeezed around my shoulders. "I need you with me, sugar."

We parted slowly, our hands the last to disconnect. As I walked up to the men waiting by their bikes, Larkan came over to me with his chest puffed out.

"Mrs. President," he declared. "It would be my honor if you rode with me at the start of our trip."

I smiled, catching the glances of the other guys. T-Bone and the Sons were trying, and failing, to hold in their laughter. Shadow glanced over quickly but looked away, preoccupied with tying something down on his bike. I had intended to ask if I could ride with him, but Larkan beat me to the punch, and he looked so hopeful.

"Larkan, the honor is mine." I accepted his outstretched hand.

"Fuck," Dyno spat. "I owe you a beer, Grudge."

His silent, long-haired comrade grinned smugly as he snapped dark goggles over his eyes.

Freyja jumped into my backpack just as I got my helmet on and settled into Larkan's seat. With a final look back at everyone as we took off, I realized this was the second time I rode off on a man's bike to somewhere unknown.

Hopefully it would turn out just as successful as the first time.

The landscape became greener, lush with dense trees and rolling hills as we rode north. Instead of desert heat and sand blasting my face, cool, damp air made my skin dewy.

The Sons of Odin led the way, followed by Larkan and I, then Shadow bringing up the rear. I stared at him shamelessly in Larkan's mirrors, now that I couldn't be caught.

It baffled me that Shadow had no idea how hot he was. He always hid part of his face, but now the wind whipping his hair back showed a strong jaw and prominent cheekbones. The scar cut through his eyebrow and part of the beard on his left cheek, and the presence of it only made me want to touch his face and kiss him there. Freyja's words echoed in my mind. *He has wounds only love can heal.*

At this rate, Shadow would be confident enough to talk to any woman soon. Maybe he would find love in Four Corners, or wherever we ended up.

The closer and friendlier we became, the more I wanted that person to be me.

A few hours into the ride, the road took us from smooth asphalt to potholes and gravel. Every bounce of Larkan's tires felt like Reaper's hands on my sore ass all over again.

Thanks a lot, Reap. Your spanking did what you intended.

I gritted my teeth and didn't realize I was clutching harder around Larkan's waist until he tapped my fingers.

Reaper. My protective, ruthless husband. How would he feel about something developing between me and Shadow? I was also surprised Jandro hadn't said anything to me yet, considering how close the two of them were. He got an eyeful of Shadow doing my second tattoo, and had to know we were closer than before.

We stopped twice briefly for piss breaks during the day, then made our final stop for the night once the sun began dipping over the trees. Larkan, Shadow, and I all found our own spots to put our things down, but the Sons worked together as a single unit, like they'd done this hundreds of times before.

Grudge dug out a fire pit and began setting up logs and kindling. Dyno set up their bedrolls and shared tent, and T-Bone checked all his weapons.

"What do y'all Demons want for dinner?" the sergeant asked with a grin. "Bet I can take down a buck before it gets dark."

"No, get something light." Dyno shook out a blanket. "We'll be in and out tomorrow, right? Don't need to carry half a buck along with a girl."

"On that note," I leaned against my pack, stretching out on my own blanket with Freyja at my side, "is there a plan for tomorrow? Josh mentioned not knowing where she actually is."

T-Bone nodded, his smile faltering. "I have some ideas, but let's eat and relax first." He checked a rifle before cocking it and leaning the barrel over his shoulder. "Settle in and I'll find us something *light*." He gave Dyno an affectionate shove before walking off toward a densely wooded area.

A half-hour later, Grudge had a cozy fire going and the two Sons cuddled up while waiting for their third to return. A pang of longing hit me at the sight of them, knowing I wouldn't be sandwiched between my own men tonight.

Larkan caught me staring wistfully and nodded in my direction with a smile. "Yeah, I'm missing my favorite snuggle partner too."

I returned his smile. "For what it's worth, I really hope Reap patches you in soon. You deserve it, and you and Noelle are already official in every way but the title."

"Yeah," he sighed, tilting his gaze up toward the stars. "It's cheesy as hell, but the Demons, her—it feels like my destiny, you know? Even though I thought I was gonna fucking die when I ran into all of you."

"I thought the same thing when Shadow tied me up and put me on Reaper's bike." I laughed, tossing a glance over to the man in question. "Remember that?"

"Yes," Shadow huffed with air of amusement. "And I was just following orders." He poured something from a flask into two mugs, then squeezed lime wedges over the drinks before dropping the fruit in. "Vodka tonics?"

"Sure, if you're offering." My insides fluttered as he handed one mug to me, the other to Larkan.

"Sorry I don't have ice, and it's not the same as that tequila you like."

He remembers, I realized. *And pays attention.*

"It's tasty," I assured him, smacking my lips at the lime's tartness and bubbles of the tonic water. "You can sit closer to us if you want."

Shadow eyed Larkan and my tents set up right next to each other, while his bedroll and bike were several paces away.

"Um, if you're sure."

"Man, if anything, I should be the one on the outskirts," Larkan said. "I don't have a patch or nothin'. Hell, I should be the one getting food and making drinks too."

"Normally you would be," Dyno called from across the fire. "But we're leading this mission and luckily, you're not our prospect."

"Consider yourself on vacation." I elbowed Larkan playfully. "My guys aren't here to boss you around."

"Yeah, but is their old lady gonna tell on me?" He grinned.

"My lips are sealed."

While we bantered, Shadow dragged his stuff closer to us and settled down on my other side. Now I was sandwiched between two men again— neither of which were mine, and only one I was entertaining the idea with.

Freyja couldn't be more pleased at Shadow setting up next to us. She rose up from my blanket and crossed over directly to his, climbing up his torso to rub her head directly under his jaw.

"Hello again, kitten," he chuckled, stroking a hand down her spine. "I guess you're not really kitten-sized anymore. You're getting bigger."

Larkan choked on his drink. "Dude, a cat is one thing, but never tell a woman that."

"Why not?"

"It's just not what they ever want to hear." He poked me in the arm. "Help me out here."

"Not all women are the same, Lark." I poked him back. "But generally speaking, yes. Most women aren't happy to hear it if they're gaining weight."

"I used to be rail-thin, much thinner than Gunner." Shadow scratched Freyja's cheeks with both hands. "But I gained weight quickly and got a lot stronger as a result. I was happy to get bigger."

I almost couldn't believe what I was hearing. Not that I couldn't believe Shadow was ever thin, but the fact that he was sharing something about himself, unprompted. I wanted to curl up on his chest like the cat and listen to anything and everything he had to say.

"Yeah, same here," Larkan nodded, oblivious to the fact that there was anything groundbreaking about this conversation. "Lifting did wonders for my confidence. I think getting bigger is a different mindset for us guys, though."

T-Bone emerged from the brush a short while later, holding up three dead pheasants like they were trophies. "Dinner time!"

Each person had plenty to eat with half a bird. Grudge set up a spit and turned them over the fire with careful precision, while T-Bone informed us of his plan for tomorrow.

"We should leave the bikes hidden just outside the territory border and go in on foot. Ah, thanks, man." He accepted a drink from Shadow. "Their big thing is cheap or free labor, so one of us should pose as a foreman and the rest as laborers."

"You mean an overseer with slaves?" I asked.

"If you want to be technical, yes." He looked over at Shadow. "You could play the role well. All those scars, avoiding eye contact while staying observant. It'll keep people from messing with us."

"I don't know." I wrinkled my nose, feeling defensive for him. Shadow had been exploited enough. "This feels...gross."

"It's fine," Shadow shrugged. "I'll do it if it helps the plan."

"Right, thanks." T-Bone nodded appreciatively. "So we know the area roughly, but none of us have actually been *in* the territory. We're just going off what Josh told us. We have to get the lay of the land. Find the right people to talk to."

"How likely are we to really do this in one day?" I asked. "They're probably not keeping her out in the open, right? And how big is this territory?"

"Right now, the bulk of the action is in the one big city right on the border." Dyno unfolded a map and laid it out on a rock. "They're in the process of making it into a shiny metropolis. The rest of it is open land for drilling oil. If we go through the heart of the city, act like we're looking for work, we should be able to see where the governor and his family hang out. If we can capture him, the son, or someone close to them, we might be able to find out where the girl is. If we're *really* lucky," he looked up at all of us, "she'll be out in the open with them. But that's only if it's public knowledge that she and the governor's son are betrothed."

"According to Josh, the governor takes daily strolls through his square," T-Bone picked up in a mocking, posh accent. "To survey the blood, sweat, and beatings that build the foundation of his great territory."

"Sounds like a piece of fuckin' work," Larkan observed. "But potentially easy to grab, which is good for us."

"Mari, as a woman," T-Bone looked at me apologetically, "your role to play should be someone's whore or wife. I'll let you pick, but it's essentially the same—"

"Don't speak unless spoken to, and do so quietly. Smile sweetly. Dress modestly, but not in a way that hides my femininity. Don't invite ogling from men. Don't try to act smarter than men." I rolled my eyes while rattling off the list.

"I guess you'd know it better than any of us," Dyno said sheepishly.

"We got pamphlets handed to us constantly while I was in nursing school," I explained. "The new governors had been working on getting women out of medicine for years, telling us what our roles should be instead. They couldn't even be original. It was all straight out of the 1950s."

All the guys, except for Shadow, gave me guilty looks. He appeared curious, if even confused.

"Sorry," T-Bone offered. "If you're not comfortable—"

"It's fine, I'll do it," I said with a wave of my hand. "It's all about getting the girl out. And you're right, we should play convincing roles to not bring suspicion. It's a good plan."

Grudge stood up to check on the cooking food while T-Bone scrubbed a hand over his beard. "If no one has any objections to this, then eat up and sleep well. We ride out early for another couple hours before we reach the border."

Shadow and I returned to our spots with bowls of roasted pheasant and rice, while Larkan remained chatting with the Sons across the fire.

"I didn't know that, about how they tried to control women back then," he muttered, digging into his food. "It's not in any of the history books I've read."

I washed a mouthful down with more of his deliciously bubbly vodka tonic. "It wouldn't surprise me if they cut it out of the books published in the last decade or so. They burned and deleted all the ones about feminism itself. Wouldn't want to give modern women any ideas."

"How did you learn about it?"

"My parents told me," I said. "They told me about their grandparents. How women couldn't even vote almost two-hundred years ago, back when we could actually choose our leaders. They couldn't get divorced, get paid the same wage, or control their own money for a long time, either. It was like that and worse going back hundreds, even thousands of years."

"That...explains a lot of my upbringing." He drank deeply from his own mug. "The anger toward me and other men. I never knew the true reason for it. Now I have an idea."

I gripped my mug and food bowl painfully tight so as to not drop them. He seemed relaxed, completely at ease to be talking about himself with me. His long legs stretched out in front of him, crossed at the ankles and his back propped up on his saddle bags. Of course the picture wouldn't be complete without Freyja at his side, eyeing his bowl of pheasant.

He was opening up by his own choice, and not while under any distress. After how withdrawn he was when I first met him, did he have any idea how groundbreaking this was?

"Nothing justifies what was done to you," I said. "Hurting you, keeping you isolated—no one with a normal amount of anger does that to another person. It's completely wrong, and I'm sorry you were a target of that."

Shadow didn't answer for a few moments, but just ate his food quietly. Once finished, he set his bowl aside and turned toward me, making my heart jump.

"Thank you for saying that, Mariposa." He reached into a saddlebag pocket and pulled out the orange bottle of sleeping pills. "Hope you sleep well," he added, shaking one into his palm.

"You too," I answered, lowering my back onto the ground. I glued my eyes to the starry sky, because if I looked at him it would feel too much like we were lying next to each other. "Good night, Shadow."

SHADOW

I wanted to stay alert on the road, so I only took half of a sleeping
pill. The fire died down not long after Mariposa went into her tent
for the night. Like me, the guys preferred sleeping under the stars.
Unlike me, the world around them went dark at night, and they kept
solar lanterns on low power nearby so they could still have some sight if
needed.

I dozed off for a couple of hours, waking up with a start and my
heart pounding. Looking around quickly, my surroundings told me
whether or not I went "ape-shit" in my sleep again, as Jandro put it.

Much to my relief, everything was in place and the others were still
in their bedrolls. Even after Mariposa started me on the pills, I'd wake up
paranoid that I'd destroyed my room again, or worse, hurt someone. So
far it hadn't happened, but overnight rides like this made me nervous
about it. That was why I also made drinks before bed, to knock out my
subconscious a little more.

Anything to keep the monster at bay.

Mariposa alluded that I needed to confront the source of my nightmares in order to be truly free from them. That I should talk to a brain
doctor when I was ready. The thing was, I wasn't sure if I, or a doctor,
would survive the full brunt of what lurked inside me.

Taking a pill, having a few drinks. That was an easy solution I felt comfortable with.

I went to the fire pit and knelt down to blow on some embers. Just enough heat to make some coffee would suffice. Carefully disassembling Grudge's meat spit, I replaced it with a grate and a metal percolator.

Something caught my eye just past our camp as I waited for my coffee to heat up. Several bright white things, roughly shaped like stars, stood out against the muted tones of the landscape. I squinted over the fire, my hand drifting to my holster as I saw more of them emerge slowly out of apparently nothing. They seemed to cluster on rocks or tree trunks, dozens of them in one place.

A memory struck me like a fist to the chest, one buried under years of loss, loneliness, and so much blood.

But this one didn't hurt. This one didn't send me spiraling into darkness and fear. The memory surfaced like a seedling breaking through the soil. It was from *that* time, but I was still here. I was okay, and witnessing something I never thought I'd have the chance to see again.

"...Shadow, is that you?"

I turned to see Mariposa halfway out of her tent, rubbing her eyes.

"I'm sorry. Did I wake you?"

"No, I'm just a light sleeper out here, and woke up smelling coffee this time." She grinned sleepily, making my chest ache. I wanted to hug her to me again, to feel her head resting over my heart. "What are you doing up?"

"I only took half a pill because I wanted to be alert. It'll be dawn in a few hours anyway." I took the percolator and began pouring the coffee. "Would you like some? Or are you going back to sleep?"

"Oh, I don't think I'll be getting any sleeping done." Wrapped in a blanket, she came over and plopped down next to me, her knee brushing my leg. "Thank you."

We sat quietly, with only crickets and the crackling of embers filling the silence between us. I kept my eyes on the white star things hovering in the distance, growing brighter by the minute. I was just about to take a closer look when Mariposa woke up, but I didn't want to leave her by the fire alone.

Freyja's crackling purr floated up from my opposite side, her head rubbing along my thigh before looking up at me with those knowing eyes. She didn't need to say anything this time. The voice in my head was my own.

Take a risk. A leap of faith. The worst she can do is say no.

I spoke the words before I lost the courage to do so. "Would it be all right if I showed you something?"

Mariposa's gaze flicked over to me in surprise, the fire embers lighting up her irises.

"Sure."

She said it with no fear, no apprehension, and my body soared with lightness.

"It's just on the other side of the camp. I can see it from here."

I rose to my feet first, waiting for her to follow. She looked up at me, sitting cross-legged on the ground with a tiny smile pulling at her lips. After a final swig of coffee, she set the mug down and raised a hand toward me.

"Help me up?"

I wondered if she could hear my pulse. It thundered in my ears as my hand reached to clasp around hers, pulling her to her feet.

"Thanks." She left her blanket on my bedroll, and removed her hand from mine to dust herself off. "Lead the way."

I turned, walking past the sleeping Sons of Odin and toward the bright white things. If I was right, it could be a nice moment to share with her. That was assuming she didn't think this was dumb or—

"Shadow, wait!" Mariposa called from a few paces behind me. "I can't see anything. I didn't bring my flashlight."

"Oh, sorry." I went back to her side, shame burning my face. "I forgot."

"It's okay," she laughed lightly, wrapping a hand around my bicep. "You can be my night-vision. Just tell me if I'm about to trip over something?"

"Of course. I won't let you hurt yourself."

We began again, side by side. She squeezed gently around my arm, leaning on me slightly as I told her to step over various rocks and branches in front of her feet.

"Is this okay?" she asked at one point. "Me holding on to you like this?"

"Yes, it's okay." *More than okay.*

My other hand itched with the desire to cover her fingers, to feel what it would be like if they laced through mine, like I saw her do with her men. I kept that arm stiffly at my side.

"What are those?" She could see the white things now, bright as star-shaped diamonds clustered on boulders. "Is that what you're showing me?"

"Yes." My heart pounded with recollection, the familiarity of those shapes and their brightness back when I knew nothing but darkness. "They're flowers."

The blooms attached to scrambling vines that covered the boulder in a complex net-like structure. It was a cactus plant, the vines covered in spines, and looked altogether unremarkable, if even ugly without the blooms.

But the flowers, they were breathtaking.

"Oh my god!" Mariposa leaned forward, pulling me with her hand still around my arm. She looked back at me, the white flowers practically casting a glow on her face. "These were in your sketchbook, that pencil drawing."

"Yes," I admitted, cringing at the memory.

I didn't know she'd come over, and had left my sketchbook open. She asked about it, and I slammed the book shut while telling her it was nothing. I had drawn the flower that morning in a half-asleep daze, the memory murky and fleeting. Not crystal clear as it was now.

"It's beautiful." Mariposa turned back to gaze at the long, thin petals, the spines circling the base of the flower like a crown. Some of them rivaled the size of sunflowers, nearly as big as her face. "What does this flower mean to you, Shadow?"

"It's called, um…"

My voice threatened to leave, to retreat into silence where I risked nothing, shared nothing, and closed myself off. But I didn't want to do that anymore, not with her. I forced myself to speak.

"It's called Night-blooming Cereus," I said. "It blooms once a year, and only at night."

"Amazing," she breathed, eyes moving all around the various blooms. "So this is a rare opportunity, huh?"

"Yes." Her observation was correct, but I could only bring myself to look at her instead of the flowers. Even wide-eyed and bedheaded, I never saw a more beautiful woman in my life.

Her gaze turned to me, a smile curving at her lips as her hand slid from my bicep, fingers trailing down my arm, to my palm.

"Thank you for showing me," she said. "This is really special."

"I..." I cleared my throat, still fighting past my instinct to retreat. "I thought you might like to see them."

"So you've seen them before." She said it as a statement, not a question.

"Yes." Her fingers skimmed over mine, and I allowed my hand to close around hers. "A long time ago. It's one of my few good memories of um, before joining the club and everything."

"Will you tell me about it?"

Some of the flowers had already begun to close, their blooms incredibly short-lived, but nothing diminished the radiance of the woman standing next to me.

"I...met a man." The memories were desperate to pour out of me now, but I held back on the grisly details. None of that deserved to be heard. "When I was a boy, maybe eight or ten years old. He was a plant scientist, a uh..."

"A botanist?"

"Yes, that. The only thing he had on him was a small book of his field notes. He showed me what he'd been researching when he, um, was placed with me."

If Mari was confused or annoyed by my vague details, her face gave no indication. She just held my hand, circling her thumb inside my palm.

"He was researching these types of flowers?" she asked.

"Um, yes. He said it was strange for them to be growing this far north. They're native to Mexico and Central America. So to see them in Arizona, either they had adapted to the drier climate, or the climate itself changed to become more habitable for them."

I was rambling now, my nerves getting the best of me. Here was where the memory started turning dark, where the horror that followed didn't deserve the light of day.

"You saw these blooms with him?" Mari moved closer to me, standing directly between my feet. The side of her body started to lean against mine with soft warmth and pressure. A light touch skimmed across my back, resting on the far side of my waist. "That must have been magical to see, especially as a kid."

"It was." I lifted my arm to rest it on her shoulders, spreading my fingers on the opposite hand to allow them to twine with hers. She kept me in the good part of the memory, and I was grateful for that. "He woke me up one night and told me to look out our, um, window. It was at a weird angle and I couldn't see well in the dark then, but I saw something white and thought it was a ghost. Or a fallen star."

Mari chuckled, resting her head on my shoulder as her arm tightened around my back. Her fingers laced through mine and gently squeezed as she watched the quickly-fading blooms.

"He was so excited," I went on. "He'd been wanting to see one of them bloom for months. Their growth cycle was all different up here and he kept missing them when going out in the field."

"And he got to share something meaningful with you." Mari turned in toward me, her chest now against mine, and her cheek resting on my heart. "That must have been nice."

"It was."

The blooms had completely faded, but the last thing I wanted to do was move from this spot. Her body pressed against me, my forearm around her upper back, and our hands entwined at our sides. I just wanted to keep this feeling, both the physical sensations of her, and what surged through the deepest parts of me. But I should have known it was foolish to even think about keeping this.

Mari pulled away slowly, her cheek that had been pressed to my chest more flushed than the other.

"Thank you so much for telling me that, for showing me this." Her arm slid away from my back. "We should probably head back."

"Yes," I grunted, already longing for the warmth and softness of her again. "Of course."

She continued holding on to my hand as we walked back, her other hand wrapping around my forearm as I led us back to camp.

"What happened to him?" she asked quietly when we were almost there. "The botanist."

My throat closed up when I heard the question, the dark emptiness wanting to drag me under until I was alone and cold again. It was familiar, a twisted type of comforting when faced with an uncomfortable question.

But talking to her, giving her small bits and pieces of me, felt good, even if doing it was strange and scared me to death. I liked the warmth better than the coldness, and I wanted to hold onto that.

"He died the next day."

"I'm sorry." She squeezed around my arm, hugging her body to it with her temple on my shoulder.

"Thank you. Me too."

One day, a long time from now, I might be able to tell her the rest of it. That I heard his screams until his throat gave out, and his blood rained on me through the cracks in my cage.

MARIPOSA

Shadow and I stayed up talking over coffee when we got back, about small, innocuous things. I learned his favorite color was orange. Not because he liked to wear it, but because it reminded him of sunsets. He seemed very curious about why I was passionate about helping people, even total strangers. I found it difficult to articulate a reason, aside from feeling like I was meant to do it.

A few hours later, the others roused and the sun was just emerging from behind the trees. Larkan took a long look at me and my blanket sitting on Shadow's bedroll, but thankfully didn't comment.

"Mind if I ride with you?" I murmured quickly to Shadow before Larkan could swoop in.

Freyja meowed and wrapped herself around his ankles, looking up with a pleading kitten stare, as if she was backing me up.

He rolled up his bedroll and turned to his bike to secure it, but he couldn't hide the pink flush creeping up his face.

"Sure, if you'd like to," he muttered.

After a quick breakfast and packing everything up, we hit the road. I couldn't even see over Shadow's shoulder without lifting my butt from the seat. My hold around his waist was light, casual, just like with Larkan. But with this driver, I had to seriously restrain myself from squeezing around him and nuzzling my face into his back. He was like a brick wall I was desperate to turn into a soft, pliant place to cuddle.

I saw a glimpse of that side of him last night, and with every touch or hug it felt like we were disassembling this wall together, brick by brick. But I wanted him to feel safe in this process. He could still be strong without a wall built around him.

This ride was much shorter, and the landscape quickly changed again. Trees and lush greenery gave way to felled logs and barren ground. Pumpjacks in the distance moved in their slow, methodical rhythm, positioned over oil wells underground. And just beyond them...skyscrapers?

By my estimate, we were in what was once known as Wyoming, maybe roughly in the northern Colorado-western Nebraska area. But the shiny glass and metal buildings in the distance looked reminiscent of New York City or Los Angeles, both of which had been evacuated and then leveled to nothing decades ago.

T-Bone led us down a barely marked side road just as we passed the oil wells. He came to a rusted, barely-standing barn when he cut his engine and turned to us.

"We'll leave the bikes in here," he said. "No one will tamper with them."

"Are you sure?" I looked at the structure skeptically.

"Trust me, little lady." He grinned as the sound of wings fluttered, his raven temporarily blocking the sun before landing on his shoulder with a *caw!* "Your men ain't the only ones who got their connections. Our things will be safe here. But once we're in the city limits," he nodded at the buildings, "I make no guarantees about our safety."

"Just another day in an MC then," I sighed.

Dyno laughed. "She gets it, T."

We filed into the barn, parking side by side along one wall. Shadow got off as I unsnapped my helmet and shook my hair out. When I swung my leg over to follow, he took me completely by surprise when he placed both hands on my waist and lifted me off of the bike.

"Why thank you, sir," I laughed when my feet touched the ground, my insides bursting in a mass of flutters.

For a moment, he looked utterly terrified. "Was that okay to do?" he whispered. "I'm sorry if I—"

"It's completely fine," I assured him, clasping his arms just above his elbows. I wondered if his heart was racing like mine. "Just unexpected, that's all."

"I wasn't thinking. It just came to me and I—"

"Do it again next time." I patted his arm before turning to secure my helmet to his handlebars. "That was fun."

"Oh. Okay."

He, Larkan, and I came into a group huddle to decide who would be playing what roles when we entered the city. After taking a look at the changes of clothes everyone brought, it was decided Larkan would play the foreman looking for a contract, and I would be his wife. Everyone else would be laborers.

The guys were polite enough to turn around while I changed into the one dress I brought as a just-in-case measure.

"Feels fuckin' weird to not wear a cut," T-Bone complained, rubbing at his shoulders.

"Okay, I'm good," I announced, smoothing my hands down the skirt in hopes that it would hide my motorcycle boots.

They all turned slowly, and it was Dyno who let out a long whistle.

"I am so fucking glad Reaper isn't here," he chuckled. "We would all be dead just for looking at you."

"Oh, stop," I grumbled.

It was a simple black maxi dress, which thankfully wasn't cut into a halter top like most of my clothes. My back was covered, which meant my SDMC tattoo was hidden. But the Rod of Asclepius on my arm wasn't.

"Is this gonna be a problem?" I asked, pointing to the tattoo.

"Maybe just keep that arm facing me," Larkan suggested. He had brought a white collared shirt and looked the cleanest, most upper-class out of all the guys. "You should be on my arm pretty much the whole time, anyway."

"Alright, are we good?" T-Bone's eyes darted over all of us. "Any questions?" When no one answered, his raven cawed and flew toward the open barn doors. "Stay close to each other. Eyes and ears open."

We hailed a cab just outside the border, instructing the driver to drop us off downtown. My stomach churned immediately upon entering the city limits. The streets were shiny and pristine, without a speck of dirt in sight. The skyscrapers looked like sculptures of glass and metal that defied gravity. The few trees and plants were perfectly-manicured topiaries, without a leaf or flower out of place. It felt like stepping into the future, but also wrong somehow. Like this glittering, beautiful city was just a mask for something much uglier.

The people walking on the main street alongside us looked like extensions of the city. They wore expensive clothes with crisp, precise tailoring. Women wore heavy makeup, most looked like they had plastic surgery, and each hairstyle and color was more extravagant than the last. The road didn't have many vehicles, but the few that did pass us were sleek sports cars in flashy colors. By all accounts, these people and their lifestyles looked like perfect images to envy. But my whole body screamed with warning and distrust.

"This whole place," Larkan leaned close to my ear, pretending to be an affectionate husband whispering sweet nothings, "it feels fucking fake."

My thoughts exactly.

"Look down the alleys," T-Bone muttered behind us. "That's where the real people are."

I plastered on a smile, holding tightly to Larkan's arm while my head swiveled around like I was sightseeing. But I made sure to peer down the narrow walkways and side streets branching off the main road.

Hidden in those dark corners, people crouched low, watching the passersby warily. Some sat on the ground, others leaned against the walls of the building. More sat on trash cans and dumpsters. I spotted what looked like children, teens, adults, and even elderly people sitting out of sight. Everyone was thin, dirty, and silent. None of them dared to step foot onto the glossy main road.

"How many people do you think," Dyno kept his voice low, "came here because it was supposed to be this wealthy, beautiful place? Next thing you know, you're eating out of a dumpster."

"Look at the servants." I pressed a smile to Larkan's cheek, playing up the part of the doting wife. "The ones following the rich people."

Across the street, a wealthy couple walked arm-in-arm, while a more simply-dressed man walked behind them, eyes down and arms full of shopping bags. They passed by a restaurant, where patrons sitting on the patio loudly berated a waitress with dark circles under her eyes. She flinched as one of the men pawed at her arm.

"Fuck this place," Larkan muttered under his breath. "I bet all these rich fucks are related to the governor somehow, or are in his favor for some shady shit. People like this don't want anyone outside their circles getting a piece of the pie."

"Focus," T-Bone growled at him. "Look, there's City Hall. Let's see about getting a contract or a permit or whatever the fuck we need."

Our small group approached an intersection and waited for a small cluster of vintage Lamborghinis to pass before crossing. In that time, the couple with the servant behind them had crossed and were coming toward us.

"Can I spit on that bitch?" Dyno mumbled.

"No," the remainder of us told him in unison.

"Damn, I really want to ruin her makeup."

The woman, her eyes an unnatural turquoise color under lashes as long as my pinky finger, took no notice of Dyno or the other Sons, but seemed very interested in Shadow.

"Now that's an exquisite specimen," she purred, reaching out to run a hand along his arm.

"Don't touch him," I snapped without thinking.

She pulled her hand back, her filler-injected lips parting in a soft gasp. "I apologize, I didn't realize he was yours. Excellent taste, I must say. A build like this comes with good breeding. Shame about all the scars. I imagine you got him at a discount?"

She looked at me expectantly with those fake crazy eyes, and I realized she expected an actual answer. The urge to spit on her as Dyno had suggested was incredibly tempting. I even felt the saliva begin gathering in my mouth, but reminded myself I had a role to play here.

"He's worth every penny," I told her smugly, wrapping tighter around Larkan's arm. "Perfect the way he is."

"Well, aren't you a charitable one." I imagined she would have wrinkled her nose if it weren't for all the Botox in her face. "Do I know you? I don't believe I recognize you."

"We're new to the territory," Larkan cut in, casting a glance my way. "Looking for some labor contracts. You'll have to forgive my wife, she's a bit possessive of our erm, specimens."

"Ah, welcome to Blakeworth!" The woman's male companion spoke up for the first time, a forced smile on his face.

The woman didn't even bother hiding her displeasure. "Contracts are in high demand here," she said in the snobbiest voice I'd heard since high school. "You're better off renting your muscle to those of us who are already...established in the territory." Her unnatural gaze slid appreciatively over Shadow once again, who looked unnerved by the attention.

"I'm sure we'll find the most profitable methods for our needs," Larkan turned us back in the direction we intended to cross. "Good day to you."

"Good job in keeping your cool," I told him, taking a final look back at the couple and their poor servant struggling to carry all their belongings. "I was this close to spitting on her, like Dyno said."

"Me too," Larkan sighed. "At the Sandia outpost, I guarded tons of rich, pompous assholes. Guess I learned to emulate them."

"You're playing the part of a rich asshole very well." I patted his arm.

"Thanks," he smirked before glancing at our "laborers". "One of you, get the door for me and my wife," he requested loudly.

"Bitch," T-Bone snorted, jogging around and ahead of us to grab the frosted-glass front door of the city hall building. "Sir, Madam." The sergeant-at-arms did a dramatic, sweeping bow as he held the door open for us. Everyone was fighting to hold in laughter.

Thankfully, the person at the clerk's desk looked relatively normal, and not like a rich asshole. Although it made sense that a member of the territory's elite class wouldn't be working a desk job dealing with the public.

"Can I help you?" they asked, peering through thick-rimmed glasses.

"Yes, please." Larkan smiled charmingly as he approached the desk, and I released his arm. "I understand the territory is in need of labor for the oil fields, and my team here is looking for work. Can you walk me through the process?"

The other guys hung back while Larkan chatted with the clerk, and I did my best to look like I was meandering through the lobby out of boredom. Clasping my hands loosely in front of me, I looked down demurely at the pattern of tiles under my feet.

They were polished to a high shine and a little slippery, like this place didn't get enough foot traffic to build traction into the floor. That, or they were excessively cleaned by the territory's biggest asset—human labor.

The echoey sound of footsteps scuffling away brought my gaze up. I looked just in time to see three people disappear through a door, dragging mops and buckets behind them. Blakeworth's elite seemed adamant that their working class remain unseen and unheard.

I wandered toward a long window that stretched to the multiple floors above. The view showed more of the city below, indicating we were at the top of a hill or valley. More skyscrapers stretched so tall from the district below, it was hard to get a sense of the natural landscape.

One building, though, drew my attention more than the rest.

There was nothing remarkable about it—just another glass and concrete monstrosity, but it felt like my gaze was pinned there. Distantly, I was aware of Freyja rubbing around my ankles.

A small black bird seemed to be circling the building, going multiple times around the same floor. My stomach dropped as I turned to look at the guys, and saw T-Bone supported between Dyno and Grudge. His eyes had rolled back in his head so only the whites were visible, and he was twitching. Smartly, they had turned him away from the clerk Larkan was still talking to.

Heart drumming in my chest, I made my way back to them, still trying to look calm and bored. When T-Bone's irises returned, they focused on me and he nodded.

"She's in there," he mouthed.

Dyno coughed once, an apparent signal to Larkan who leaned up from the front desk.

"Well, thanks for all your help. We're going to—"

"Oh, one last thing, sir. The best way to seize a governor-approved contract is to attend his mixer and introduce yourself in person. He gives the best work to people who make a good impression on him."

Larkan paused. "Mixer?"

"Yes, he hosts them in the public gardens every week," the clerk smiled. "The next one is tonight."

MARIPOSA

"Is this really necessary?"

"Yes. Now stop grumbling and hold still. Look away." I held Larkan's eyelid open and gently placed the contact lens over his eyeball, then released his lid. "Okay, now blink for me. Does that feel okay?"

"Yeah." He sat up, blinking several times with now fiery orange irises. "How do I look?"

"Almost exactly like these elitist assholes, but we're not done yet." I held up a black tube and Larkan's face paled.

"Is that...?"

"Mascara, yes. All the dudes here are almost as made-up as the women. Now hold still and let me paint those lashes."

"You better not *ever* tell Noelle. I mean it, Mari."

"How do you know she won't like it? Guyliner was hot back in the day, Lark."

He never stopped grumbling and the others couldn't contain their snickering, but he allowed me to apply mascara, a bit of concealer, and some tinted lip balm.

We did a remarkable amount of work in the few precious hours before the governor's mixer. I traded some painkillers for a fancier dress, appropriate menswear, makeup, and colored contacts so Larkan and I could blend in at the mixer.

I sported some glittery, mossy green contacts myself, and piled on more makeup than I had ever worn in my lifetime. I looked and felt like a clown, but judging from the people we'd seen on the street, that was the whole point.

The other guys would stay hidden and scout the building for the best way to get Vance's daughter out. It turned out to be only five blocks from the public garden so they planned to run by if they got her and we'd make a speedy exit. Shadow was quickly taught the hand signals used by the Sons to communicate with Grudge, and we were golden.

"Goddamn, little lady." I couldn't tell if T-Bone was laughing at, or appreciating my new look. "You look some kind of fuckin', I dunno, tropical bird or something."

I quickly penciled in Larkan's brows as a finishing touch. "Should I say thanks, or shut the fuck up?"

He just laughed and turned to the others. "We all ready?"

They made affirmative sounds while Larkan and I straightened up, and I took his arm once again. "Ready as we'll ever be."

"Be safe," Shadow said, looking straight at me. "You won't see us, but we'll be nearby."

My stomach did that fluttering thing as our gazes locked. "You be safe too."

Larkan and I were the first to leave the massive department store dressing room where we'd holed up. The others would wait a few minutes before heading to their destination.

We held our chins high, walking arm-in-arm to the gilded glass elevator.

"Will you look at that," he muttered. "Now that we look like circus freaks, no one's paying attention to us."

"We're like chameleons," I said, giving his arm a playful squeeze.

The public gardens were across the street and we could see the mixer getting started. People dressed just as ridiculously as we were drank flutes of champagne and nibbled morsels of food set out on long tables. Service workers quickly grabbed empty glasses and discarded napkins before retreating out of sight.

"All of these people come to kiss the governor's ass, huh?" Larkan snagged two champagne flutes and handed one to me.

"That's what it seems like." Rather than drink it, I looked around for a place to toss my champagne without getting caught.

The grass felt spongy and plush under my feet. Exotic flowers and all their curious scents surrounded me—those that weren't drowned out by people's perfume, anyway. I wondered if the governor had a Night-blooming Cereus in his collection, if he had the patience to appreciate such a bloom. Probably not.

"I'm Wren, and this is my wife, uh—"

"Butterfly!" I said with my most dazzling smile to the couple Larkan introduced us to.

"Ah. How...*creative,*" the woman said snootily, with a sip of champagne.

"God, I hate these people," I muttered as we walked away, slyly pouring a bit of my drink out on the grass.

"Which one's the fucking governor?" Larkan growled in reply. "I can't tell any of these bedazzled fucks apart."

"There's gotta be something that sets him apart. Maybe he has a separate table? I dunno, keep looking."

We mingled and meandered for another fifteen minutes or so, when I spotted T-Bone walking quickly up the sidewalk across the garden.

"Lark!" I hissed in a whisper, tugging at his arm. "There he is! Let's go—"

T-Bone caught my eye and quickly shook his head, making a slicing motion at his neck.

"Oh fuck, something's wrong." Larkan squeezed my elbow. "Stay here."

I browsed by one of the food tables, trying not to look worried as Larkan got brought up to speed. He returned to me quickly, wearing the same grave expression as T-Bone.

"She's not there anymore," he whispered. "He thinks they probably move her every night."

"Well, shit! Now what do we do?"

"I dunno, but we need to come up with a new plan. It's getting dark and his raven doesn't see well at night. Let's—"

"Excuse me. Have we met?"

Lark and I turned to face an older gentleman who had come up to greet us. He wasn't dressed as flashy as the rest of the guests, but his black suit still had a silky, expensive sheen to it.

"Governor Henry Blake," he said, offering a hand and a polite smile. "Welcome to Blakeworth."

"Butterfly, uh, Jones!" I returned, accepting his hand. "And this is my husband, Wren."

If the clumsy delivery of my fake name raised any alarm bells, the governor gave no indication. "The pleasure is mine, Butterfly." He lowered a kiss to the back of my palm, all while maintaining a creepy amount of eye contact. "I knew I hadn't seen a dazzling creature such as yourself in Blakeworth before. What brings you here?"

Larkan clamped onto my opposite arm, a silent reminder that we needed to go *now*. My mind went blank, scrambling for an excuse to tell the governor.

"We've come seeking an oil contract," I explained through a tight smile. "And we were so looking forward to meeting you at this mixer, sir! You have a beautiful territory."

"Ah, you're too kind. Although hard work has its rewards." He placed his champagne flute on the table, then snapped his fingers at a waiter to pick it up.

What a piece of shit.

"This is such rotten luck, but I'm afraid the drinks have given me a migraine." I pressed my fingers to my temple, furrowing my brow. "My husband should really get us back to our room. It was lovely to meet—"

"Oh dear, I'm so sorry! Please." Rather than give me space, the governor moved in and splayed his hand on my lower back. Larkan's eyes visibly widened at the move. "Have a seat with my family. Take a little pill and see if you feel better. I'd hate for us to miss a business opportunity due to a little headache."

"My wife suffers from migraines regularly, I'm afraid," Larkan stepped in. "It's really best for her to lie down and rest."

"Nonsense! You know how women exaggerate these things. Let's all have a seat. I'll make some introductions you do not want to miss, and if Butterfly here isn't feeling better in a bit, you can say your goodbyes."

The governor was smooth, persuasive. Lots of tiny signals flashed at me through his words and body language. He didn't take no for an answer, and seemed desperate for us to not leave. But there was one other tidbit I fixated on.

"Your family's here, sir?" I continued playing up the migraine, squinting my eyes as I rubbed my temples.

"Yes, my wife, son, and soon-to-be daughter-in-law are all under the gazebo there," he pointed across the gardens.

The gazebo was covered in dense vines, something elegant, like ivy. A warm light radiated from inside it, but it was impossible to tell who was inside from this angle. We never saw her. That was why we didn't know.

Larkan released my arm as I turned to look at him, trying to not give anything away in my face. Forcing a smile, I lightly pushed him away. "Wren, would you be a dear and fix me plate? I just might need something in my stomach."

He nodded tightly, looking between me and Blake. "Of course. I'll be right back."

"Ah, you must be one of those women who doesn't eat much to keep her figure." The governor pulled me tightly against him as he led me to the gazebo. "I know I speak for all men when I say we appreciate the sacrifice, but if only it didn't contribute to those pesky headaches of yours."

"Yes," I said through gritted teeth, following his lead. "It's an unfortunate side effect."

"Watch your step, dear. Don't trip."

It was only one step. I swallowed the desire to tell him to fuck off, but plastered on a smile for the curious glances from his family members.

"Everyone, this is Butterfly Jones. She and her husband are new to Blakeworth. Butterfly, this is my wife, Eva, my son, Malcolm, and Malcolm's fiancee, Kyrie."

"A pleasure to meet you all." I allowed my gaze to rest on governor Vance's daughter for a single extra moment. "Congratulations on your upcoming nuptials. I wish you both much happiness."

Kyrie's eyes shifted downward after a small, forced smile.

"Don't be rude," Malcolm chastised. "What do you say?"

Kyrie flinched, then said softly, "Thank you, ma'am. I'm very excited."

"She's from another territory," Malcolm huffed with an eye roll. "So you'll have to excuse her rudeness."

"Oh, it's all right." Remembering I was supposed to have a migraine, I quickly took a seat next to Kyrie, and groaned softly as I rubbed the side of my head. "I'm from a different territory too. It might be the, uh, elevation here that I'm not used to."

"Where are you from?" Blake's wife, Eva stared down the length of her nose at me.

"East Texas." I figured the simplest answer was an honest one. "Or, Texahoma as it's known now."

"Ah, so you are new to our heightened elevation." Blake had sat down next to his wife, but with some distance between them. He kept staring at my legs, like he wanted to be close enough to touch them. Ew. "Has General Tash gotten that shithole under control yet?"

The question didn't register until a few seconds after I heard it. "I'm sorry, what?"

"Ah, nevermind. I should have known women have no ideas of these things. Malcom, have you heard?"

"The general's moving west, not east," his son scoffed. "He's crushing the vermin way south of us first, in New Mexico and Arizona. Outlaw gangs on motorcycles are out of control."

While the men talked, I leaned back against the ivy-covered frame of the gazebo, looking outside for any sign of Larkan. There was no indication of him, or any of the guys, so I could only hope he was able to relay the new intel successfully. In the meantime, I had to let Kyrie know I was here to help, and that she could trust me.

"Guess your husband went off to chase some fresh tail," Malcolm taunted, watching me.

I glared at him, hoping it would pass off as headache-induced squinting. Poor Kyrie. This territory was full of Grade-A Assholes, from the top all the way down.

"So what else is new?" I quipped with a playful smirk.

"See there?" He swatted Kyrie's thigh, which could have been harmless, had she not jumped in her seat. "A woman who knows her place. Men have to spread their seed, you see. It's in our nature."

I wanted to hug her. To sit between her and him, anything to keep him from touching her. But I had to stall, had to just play along, until the guys figured something out.

I opened my clutch and dug through it, pretending to look through my makeup items when the soft pack of tissues gave me an idea. Twisting open the lipstick, I quickly wrote, *4C, here 2 help* on the tissue. Heart pounding, I folded up the tissue and flipped open my compact. While I pretended to check my face, my eyes darted around again in search of the guys.

Come on. Where the fuck are you all?

Clicking my compact shut, I slid it back into my bag and turned my palm over with the tissue still in my hand. Turning to Kyrie, I gave her my best friendly smile.

"That's a gorgeous engagement ring! May I?"

"Um, sure."

While the men dismissed us as empty-headed vessels gawking at shiny objects, she allowed me to hold her hand for a closer look at her ring. I pressed the tissue into her palm as I inspected the rock, making a big show of admiring it. Without missing a beat, her thumb held the tissue in place, and my heart soared.

"That's um, a pretty ring you have too," she said, discreetly unfolding the tissue in her lap.

"Oh, it's all right." I tilted my hand with Reaper's ring on it, a pang in my chest from missing him. The shifting colored stone covered me from catching her eye as she read my note. "It's a starter ring, from before my husband had any money. He promised me an upgrade when he got his big oil contract."

"*If* he does," Blake corrected me from across the gazebo. "I'm very selective about who I offer contracts to."

"As you should be, governor."

"Your husband has not impressed me so far, and seems to have gotten lost," he sneered. "Lucky for him, I enjoy looking at his wife very much."

"I'm very flattered, sir." My fingers clenched in my lap, but I forced my posture not to change. Next to him, Eva threw back a full glass of champagne, and I didn't blame her. How could anyone stand to be around him sober?

"You should be. Do you know how many prospective contractors throw their wives at me? Nearly all of them. It's standard procedure at this point. But your man wanted to drag you away." His smug grin was infuriating. "Now, I couldn't have that."

"Isn't that so typical of men?" I blurted out before I could stop myself. "Wanting what they can't have."

Oh fuck. Talk about the wrong fucking thing to say.

Governor Blake narrowed his stare at me while my pulse skyrocketed. This was it. I was found out and I'd never see my guys again.

"Of course we do," Malcolm cut in with a snort and a tight grip on Kyrie's thigh. "When you're as rich and powerful as we are, everything comes so easily and life gets boring. But when you go after something forbidden," his hand dragged up to her hip, "it's much more exciting."

"How did you two meet, then?" As long as I was still breathing, I wanted to find out if the sick men in this family would come out and admit to kidnapping and imprisoning people like pets.

"Our families are acquainted," Malcolm deflected smoothly. "Ky's the daughter of a much poorer governor. We did him a favor by agreeing to the match, after all his begging. An act of charity, really, when I had much better prospects in the northeastern territories." He pinched her chin tightly. "Good thing she's nice to look at."

"Butterfly, do you object to men taking what they want?" Blake was still pinning me with a hard stare.

I stared back as aloofly as I could, not bothering to dart my eyes to the sudden motion going on outside the gazebo.

"Even if I had an opinion, it doesn't fucking matter to you, does it?"

His lip curled as he jumped to his feet. "What a foul-mouthed little—"

I stood up and moved in front of Kyrie, my hand now wrapped around the handle of Gunner's small dagger that he loaned me. The silver metal reflected the lamplight and I saw the first look of genuine fear in the governor's eyes.

"Who sent you?" he hissed.

"Doesn't matter." I waved the dagger in front of his chest. "But you're going to back away, right now."

"What do you want, land? Goods?" Blake stared at the weapon in my hand. "We can work something out."

"Dad!" Malcolm had finally caught on to the commotion outside the gazebo. "Something's happening!"

People were running and screaming in my peripheral vision, but I didn't dare take my eyes off of the governor. The guys must have created a diversion of some sort.

"Tell me what you want." Blake raised his hands. "Just don't hurt my family."

I could have laughed. Like he really cared about anyone but himself. He just needed family members for his image.

"Leave her." I jerked my head toward Kyrie. "The rest of you can go."

Blake's mouth tilted up into another smug smile and I realized my mistake. "You're with Four Corners then?"

"No fucking way!" Malcolm bellowed. "I *need* her!"

A loud boom sent all of us stumbling. The gardens were now covered in smoke as armed police filed through, their weapons readied. They didn't look to be pointing at anyone in particular, but that grenade had been meant for someone.

"We'll find you another bitch," Blake reached over and yanked his son up by his jacket. "Four Corners just declared war."

They stumbled out of the gazebo towards the cover of their police. Forgotten, Eva followed with a drunken wobble. I didn't have time to feel bad for her and grabbed Kyrie's wrist.

"You have to come with me!" I pulled her to her feet and started running.

"Is it true?" She hurried alongside me. "You're with my father?"

"Sort of." I whipped my head in all directions as I ran, searching for a familiar face. "We're taking you home. You'll be safe."

I hoped the police would just write us off as panicked women from the mixer running around aimlessly, but I should have known Blake wouldn't let us go that easily. A pair of armed men in matching black uniforms pointed and yelled at us to stop.

"Come on!" I grabbed Kyrie's arm and ran faster, my lungs already burning.

"Where are we going?" she cried, looking back over her shoulder.

"Don't know yet, I'm looking for my people."

A series of loud shots rang out and I dove to cover my head. The momentum sent me sprawling and I thought of Reaper, how I wouldn't be with him for a final time. Gunpowder filled my nose when I hit the ground, and a ringing screeched in my ears. Kyrie crashed-landed next to me and I threw an arm over her to shield her.

My trembling hand moved over her back in search of any blood or bullet wounds, but felt nothing. No more shots came through the ringing in my skull, so I dared to look behind us.

The cops lay dead in the grass.

"Let's go, come on!"

A masculine voice sounded far away, but the rough hand that tugged me to my feet was very close indeed. T-Bone had purple bruising forming around his eye, and a bloody lip. His hands pressed to my cheeks, pupils searching mine.

"Are you okay?"

I nodded, looking back to Kyrie, who was being helped to her feet by Grudge. "This is her. She knows we're the good guys."

"Good. Dyno and Lark are stealing a car. Let's get to the edge of the block—"

More shots rang out, followed by voices yelling. We took off toward the street, the guys pushing us in front so they could have our backs.

"Where's Shadow?" I looked around for him desperately.

"Don't know. He went stealth to pick off these cops." T-Bone ran backwards, he and Grudge returning fire to the cops that chased us.

We ran around trees and jumped over bushes, zig-zagging through the park. Once we reached the sidewalk, I nearly tumbled straight into traffic with all my forward momentum. Following me, Kyrie did the same thing and I pulled her back.

"Watch out!" she shrieked, pointing behind me.

I whirled around to see a massive black Hummer drive up onto the sidewalk, heading straight for us. If it weren't for the driver sticking his head out of the window, I knew I'd have met my death under those massive tires.

"That's our ride," I told her, waving at Dyno in the driver's seat. "Let's go!"

He shoved open a door as we ran up, and I pushed Kyrie inside.

"Mari, get in!" Larkan yelled, firing his own weapon out of the window.

"We can't leave without Shadow!" I hid behind the open door, looking through the dark glass as T-Bone and Grudge made their way to the vehicle.

"I'm sorry, hon. We can't fuckin' wait around." T-Bone stood in front of me as a shield, helping return fire.

"There he is!" In a bold move, Larkan stuck his torso out of the passenger window and waved his arm. "Shadow, come on!"

Through the smoke and gunfire, I saw him. And then I didn't. Holy shit, he was fast. He made his way to us, taking cover from gunfire under the plants and patio furniture, swift and powerful like a black jaguar in the jungle.

"Don't return fire, we'll cover you!" Larkan yelled, aiming his weapon.

Shadow picked up speed, making a break for it as he sprinted across the grassy lawn. My chest began to relax with relief. He was so close! Just a few more yards and he'd be right here.

"Bro, look out!" T-Bone screamed at the top of his lungs, waving his arms frantically. "Take cover!"

"What? What is it?" I demanded.

Shadow suddenly fell forward and I screamed. Fear and confusion rose in equal amounts. I didn't hear a shot, so why had he fallen?

He sprang to his feet quickly, so I thought he must have tripped. Then he fell again and I saw them—arrows sticking out of his back attached to long ropes. I followed the lines with my eyes to the top of the gazebo, where the shooters were hidden by dense tree covers.

I realized with horror they must have had some kind of crank or pulley system, because despite Shadow's fighting to move forward, they were pulling him back.

SHADOW

I *bet this fucking hurts on normal people.*

I fell to my knees again, bending over to keep my weight low and forward. If I stood up, they could pull me straight back off my feet and potentially embed the arrows deeper.

My hands swept over my hidden pockets, but all my knives were gone, embedded in various people's throats and hearts. It became too chaotic earlier to retrieve them. Bracing one hand on the ground, I reached back, feeling for an arrow shaft to snap, but just my luck, they were both out of my reach.

A harsh pull on the ropes sent my knees sliding backward on the ground. Fuck, this was bad. These arrows hit me deep, and were probably barbed in some way to stay embedded in my flesh. Sick fucks and their torture devices.

"Shadow!"

Something else hit me from the front, but this was warm, soft, and had small hands wrapping around my neck.

"Mariposa?" What the fuck was she doing? I *saw* her get in the car. "You can't be out here, it's not safe!"

She ignored me, reaching over my shoulder for the arrows. I felt a weird pulling and jerking motion on my back. "Shit, I can't break them! They're too solid."

If I wasn't on my knees already, I would have fallen to them. She ran out here to save me. She was too good, too perfect, and she could *not* be captured by these people.

"Stop." I grabbed her arms and brought them back between us. "Run back to the car. Now."

"No." Her hands flew over her dress, searching herself. "Shit, I must have dropped my knife. You don't have any of yours?"

"No, I don't—ugh, fuck!"

The ropes pulled me back another foot.

"Shadow!" She was crying now, and panicked. Her fingers curled into my shirt, forearms braced against my chest. "I'm not letting them take you."

I wrapped both arms around her back, shielding her in case any one of these fuckers dared to take a shot. Using all my strength, I walked my knees forward to reclaim some ground. The ropes went taut, and while it didn't hurt, I swore I could feel my muscles tearing.

"Mari." I wasn't sure when exactly I started using the shortened version of her name, but it felt right now. "If they capture you, it's going to be a lot worse for you than it is for me."

"I don't care." Her fingers grazed my cheeks, stroking over my scar. I felt her shaky breaths over my nose and lips. "I'm not leaving you behind."

"I'll be fine. They can't hurt me, remember?"

"That doesn't make it okay to leave you."

We slid back again a few inches, and she clutched onto me tightly with a whimper. Her forehead rested on mine, the salt of a wet tear falling to my mouth. I realized then I was holding on to her just as tightly. I didn't want to be taken. I didn't want to lose my club, my only friends. And I never wanted to let her go.

But their hooks were already in me, literally, and she deserved so much better than to be dragged into whatever awaited me.

I dared to do something I'd never done before—touch a woman's face. Cupping her soft cheek, I looked into her watery, red eyes. She was still wearing the fake eye-color lenses, but I still saw her underneath them.

"Thank you for everything you've done for me," I told her. "I'll never forget any of it. But you have to let me go."

"I won't." She shook her head defiantly, her forehead still brushing mine. "You're not alone anymore. I won't let you be."

My fingers curled into the fabric at her back, holding her tight with what remained of my fading strength for this last moment.

"Then I hope you forgive me for this."

I shoved her away as hard as I could.

Mari stumbled back several steps, arms windmilling for balance before she fell back. Her mouth still open in an O of shock, she jumped to her feet and started toward me again.

"Run!" I roared at her, no longer resisting the ropes pulling me back. "Get back to the car!"

Shots were already popping off and she bent low, covering her head. While ducking to protect my own head, I saw the massive black car driving through the garden. Dyno mowed down hedges, bushes, small trees, and crashed into toppled patio furniture to get to her.

Hurry. Hurry.

I barely noticed that my ropes went slack. I was heavy, so I figured the cops just took a break from their pulling. But then someone grabbed my arm with a hand much bigger and stronger than Mari's. I looked up to see Grudge's impatient expression, his mouth growling with wordless screams to *fucking move.*

I rose to my feet, following his lead with no time to question it, and bolted toward the car. I must have lost a lot of blood or something, because my body was going much slower than I was telling it to. Grudge kept pulling on my arm as we ran. The glint of something metallic in his other hand must have been what cut me free.

My vision was going blurry, unfocused. I felt like I was swimming through fog and getting nowhere.

More hands grabbed me, shoved me. I was in a dark place again, great. Oh no, this place had windows that were just tinted dark. And Mariposa was here. She touched my face and her mouth moved. My body felt like it was being tossed around, despite staying stationary. I couldn't figure out if I was sitting still or moving, and multiple voices were yelling.

Cool water touched my lips and I opened my mouth for more, just like when it rained over my dungeon and I drank only what I could catch on my tongue. But this water flowed freely, cool and satisfying to my parched throat.

I wasn't sure how much time had passed when Mari came into clear focus, her finger pulling up on my eyelid.

"Shadow?" Her makeup and contacts were gone. Now it was just her normal, beautiful face etched with concern. "Are you with us?"

"Um, yes."

The car was dark and silent, Dyno driving on a dirt road with the headlights on the lowest setting. Next to him sat Larkan. In the next aisle sat Grudge and T-Bone, sandwiching the small blond woman we came to rescue. Mari and I were alone in the backseat.

"You were in shock," Mari explained. "I think you still are, but at least you're lucid now."

"Where are we?" I peered out of the dark tinted windows at the endless, dense forest rushing past us. Not a single light of the city was to be seen. Good fucking riddance.

"Only about a hundred miles in the wrong direction," Dyno called up from the front seat. "We had to zig and zag all over kingdom come to lose the cops. We're damn lucky this beast had an extra full gas can, 'cause we'll need to loop back around to grab the bikes tomorrow."

"The plan is to camp tonight, head for the bikes early tomorrow, then hit the road hard, back to Four Corners." T-Bone stretched his arm along the back of his seat, casting a glance down at the woman next to him. "Then deliver this little lady back to her father, safe and sound."

The woman didn't move or reply. I wondered if she felt as Mariposa did when we first took her, or if she already knew she wouldn't be harmed.

"I'll get these out of you tonight." Mari's hand glided over my back, and I realized just how closely she was sitting.

Her leg pressed against mine, with one hand on my arm and the other gently prodding the pierced area of my back. If I focused on how ragged and shitty my body felt, I could ignore her breast pressing against my arm.

Mari's mention of the arrows did succeed in drawing attention to how tight and seized up my back felt. Sleeping would be a bitch, if I managed to sleep at all.

"Grudge."

The man sitting in front of me turned and looked over his shoulder.

"Thank you, brother."

He nodded his chin down sharply. "Hm."

Dyno took the Hummer off the road for another hour before we finally stopped for the night. My legs felt stiff too, as we piled out of the car.

"Girls can sleep in the car," T-Bone said, walking around to the trunk. "We ain't got much else for shelter. I'll try to hunt us some dinner. Y'all get a fire going and watch your fucking backs. If *anything* moves that's not one of us, shoot it."

He took what he needed and headed out into the wilderness, while the others started up a fire. Mari led me to sit on a fallen log and had me turn away from the fire so she could see my back.

"I can't do much with limited supplies," she grumbled, rummaging through her bag. "But I can get those out and close you up until we get back."

"I trust you," I said, bracing my hands on my knees and staring into the dark woods. I could just make out T-Bone creeping low and silently.

"Thank you." Mari squeezed my arm and got to work. Her scissors snipped away at my shirt and I heard her soft laugh. "This is the second time I've had to cut your shirt off of you. Maybe you should just stop wearing them."

"You don't want that," I grunted, helping her pull the fabric away and down my shoulders. "I'm not much to look at."

She was quiet for a moment, then I heard gloves snapping and her rummaging through her items again.

"That's not true, Shadow."

I didn't know how to answer. Was this...*flirting?* If so, I was completely out of my element and better off not saying anything. I just sat still as she gently prodded around my wounds.

"These are definitely barbed and they've torn like hell through your muscle tissue already," she reported. "I'm going to have to make a few small incisions—"

My eye caught the glint of a metal blade, a sharp edge in her hand coming to slice me again.

"No!"

I jumped up from the log, spinning to face her as I backed away. What was I thinking? I never exposed my back to anyone. My heart drummed in my ears, while my chest and throat closed up. I was suffocating, sweaty, small, and weak. The floor was coated in my dried blood.

"Shadow! What's wrong?"

"Don't come near me!"

I backed up against a tree trunk. No, a cold brick wall. Mari's face looked concerned, and then morphed into the face of the woman who haunted me since my first memories formed. She was sitting right there, taunting me as she painted her face in my blood. She dragged one bloody finger into her mouth and moaned with her lips around it.

I shut my eyes, feet kicking out in front of me to scoot further away, but I was trapped. I was always trapped.

"No more cutting, please..." My head shook from side to side, as if that would make the grotesque vision go away. "Don't cut me anymore. I didn't do anything..."

"Shadow, listen to my voice." A pair of hands held the sides of my face, keeping my head still. "You're a member of the Steel Demons MC. You're among friends right now and you're not in any danger. No one is going to hurt you."

"Don't cut me." It was Mari's voice I heard, but I couldn't trust my eyes to open and show me it was really *her* there. "Don't cut me, please."

"I want to help you, Shadow. I want to make you better."

"Okay, just no blades. No cutting, please."

"Shadow, I need you to trust—"

"I do. I can't explain it, but I can't...just please don't cut into me. Don't cut my skin, don't make me bleed. Just, please..."

A weight pressed down into my lap, like someone laid a warm sandbag across my legs. When the vibrating started, I kept my eyes shut, but felt around with one hand. I felt soft fur and the nuzzling of Freyja's head on my palm. She dialed up the purring even more, until the soft rumbles reached all over my body. Slowly, my throat and chest relaxed. My pulse started to normalize, and I dared to open my eyes.

Mariposa sat between my legs, her face inches away, and her hands still holding my cheeks. Her palms were soft on my stubble and she blinked away water that had accumulated in her eyes.

"Are you with me now?" she whispered.

"Yes." I swallowed. "I'm sorry, I—"

"Don't apologize." She shook her head, thumbs caressing over my cheekbones. "Don't ever apologize for what someone else did to you."

"But I scared you."

"You worried me for a minute. But I'm glad you're back." She pulled in a deep, tired breath. "In regards to your back, I need to make incisions to extract the arrows with minimal damage. I could pull them straight out, but that will shred the hell out of your muscle and skin. Your mobility is already affected, and I don't want to injure you worse."

"It's okay. I won't feel it."

"That's not what I'm worried about. They could still get infected. You'll have a longer recovery time while those tissues heal." Her hands lowered from my face, trailing for a brief moment over my collarbones until they rested on top of mine, on Freyja. "You believe that I would never want to hurt you, right?"

"Yes."

Her tongue darted out to wet her lips. "And you trust me to know what I'm doing in a medical sense?"

"I do."

She swallowed, her eyes cast down to our touching hands and the cat before looking back up at me. "And you know that I—I care about you. A lot. I don't like seeing you hurt. I would have been devastated if you were captured. You're not just my patient, but my friend. So everything I do is with your health and wellbeing in mind, okay?"

My pulse skyrocketed again, but for different reasons than before. I ached to find the words that echoed everything she said, with the same simple eloquence. But my words were gone, as they often were with flashbacks. And the poisonous part of me I fought so hard to keep buried, whispered to my brain for the first time in months.

She's lying, like all women do. She'll watch your blood spill and take pleasure in your suffering. And you'll let her, because you're a sad, submissive little animal in a cage. Doesn't matter how far you ride on that bike. You're always caged and you can never escape.

"Shadow?"

"Yes," I bit out, harsher than I intended. If only grinding my teeth could crush the voices and darkness I fought tooth and nail to silence. "Yes," I repeated—softer with a deep breath. "Thank you for being my friend."

Her brow furrowed, noticing my discomfort. She squeezed my hands. "If I keep talking to you, will you let me use my scalpel to get the arrows out?"

Trust.

A new voice stepped in to join the ensemble cast in my head.

Trust, it repeated. Warm, familiar, and feminine. *Love is not possible without trust.*

"Freyja," I realized.

You know what you have to do, son. The cat rubbed her head on my hand. *Step into your fear. Show it how brave you are. Show this woman that you trust her.*

"She's talking to you?" Mari scratched near the base of the cat's tail.

"You didn't hear her?"

Mari gave a small smile. "Not this time. Whatever she's saying must be only for you."

I removed the cat from my lap, grimacing at the stiffness taking over my arms already. If I didn't do something, I might not be able to drive my bike.

"Okay," I turned back to Mari. "You can make your, um, incisions. Whatever you need to do."

She searched my face. "You're sure?"

I took one of her hands, a gesture that seemed normal and comfortable between us now. Her fingers opened and I laced mine between them.

"Keep talking to me? So I know where I am, and...who you are. It's not that I don't trust *you*, I just..."

She squeezed my hand, leaning forward until her forehead touched mine again. Her other hand stroked lightly down the side of my neck. Such a simple touch felt too good to be real.

"I know, Shadow." Still holding my hand, she pulled away with a warm, gentle smile. "Come back to the fire."

I followed her lead, my hand never leaving hers until the last possible moment.

MARIPOSA

I woke up with my back aching in at least ten different places. My neck didn't fare much better. Stretching with a groan, I forgot that I slept in the backseat of the Hummer until my fist hit the seat in front of me.

"Shit," I whispered, hoping I didn't startle Kyrie.

My worries were for nothing I realized, as I sat up and saw her poking the charred logs from last night's fire. With one shove of the heavy car door, I stepped out into the chilly morning.

"Trying to get it started?" I asked, pulling my arms close around me.

"Um, yeah. Seeing if there were any embers left." She gave me a sheepish look. "I've never been all that outdoorsy."

"That's all right. Here, let me show you."

I tip-toed over to Dyno, sleeping curled up with his back to us. All three Sons of Odin were cuddled into a puppy pile to stay warm for the night. Dyno's head never even twitched on T-Bone's chest as I carefully pulled the lighter from his pants pocket.

"The thing about traveling with bikers," I said to Kyrie, tossing the lighter once in the air, "they're always carrying gasoline in one form or another."

She helped gather pine needles and sticks for kindling, then I set up a triangle of fresh logs and lit them up.

"How are you holding up?" I asked her. "I was so exhausted after helping Shadow last night. I'm sorry I never checked on you."

"That's okay. I'm fine." She extended her palms to the growing flames. "Just can't believe this is really happening. I thought I'd never get out." She shook her head with a heavy sigh. "I thought I actually wanted to marry him. I'm so stupid."

"Hey, you're not," I insisted. "That whole family is a bunch of manipulative pricks. They took advantage of you."

Kyrie sucked her lip between her teeth, her hands wringing in front of her. "Do you really think they'll declare war on Four Corners?"

"I wouldn't put it past them. But we'll deal with that when it happens. Right now, our priority is getting you home safe."

She nodded, her worried expression relaxing slightly. "How did you end up with these guys? No offense, but you seem...a little less feral, I guess."

"None taken," I grinned. "It's a long story, and I certainly never thought I'd end up in a biker gang. Life has a funny way of dumping you right where you belong." I reached out and placed a hand on her forearm. "These are good guys, you can trust me on that. They're rough around the edges, but they don't use people like those pricks we took you from."

She looked over at the Sons, still wrapped up in their cuddle pile. "They actually look really sweet like that."

"They are sweethearts," I agreed. "Armed, dangerous, and foul-mouthed sweethearts, but sweethearts nonetheless."

Kyrie's head swiveled across the fire, where Shadow and Larkan slept a few feet away from each other. "Are you one of their uh, old lady? Is that the right term?"

My chest squeezed with the aching memory of last night. Shadow's fear of my scalpel, his trauma rearing its ugly head. And then when he finally allowed me to remove the arrows. He trembled the whole time, but he *let* me. I couldn't even put into the words the amount of trust that must have taken.

And then afterward, when he laid down to sleep, it almost physically hurt me to leave his side. I wanted to stay near him the whole time, to soothe and reassure him. To show him I understood how difficult it was to face such a lifelong fear. That I was so proud and did not take his trust in me lightly.

"No," I answered Kyrie, watching Shadow's deep breaths. "Larkan, the smaller one, was posing as my husband, but he's kind of my brother-in-law. Shadow and I, we're," I swallowed, "we're friends. My men are actually all waiting for us in Four Corners."

"Men, plural?"

"Yeah," I smiled sheepishly at her. "I have three husbands."

"*Three?!* What?"

"My first husband, it's um, part of the culture he grew up in. For one woman to be with multiple men. It's normal for him. He introduced me to the idea, and his best friend was all for it. My third was a little more resistant, but he came around."

"That's, wow." Kyrie went back to staring at the fire. "I've never heard of anything like that."

"I didn't either before meeting them. It weirded me out too, at first." I grinned. "But it has its perks."

"I can imagine," she snickered.

We heard moving and rustling behind us, and turned to see the Sons untangling as they roused.

"Mornin', ladies," Dyno yawned. "Mari, I'll take my lighter back."

"Damn it. How'd you know?" I tossed it back and he caught it in midair.

"You're not the first person to lift my shit while I'm sleeping." He scrubbed his face. "Did y'all make any coffee?"

"No time." T-Bone's voice was gravelly as he sat up. "We gotta get movin'. Mari, can you wake up your guys?"

"On it."

As I walked toward Larkan and Shadow's sleeping spots, I heard T-Bone ask Kyrie, "You hungry, little lady?"

Larkan woke up with just a small shake to his shoulder. I went to rouse Shadow with more caution, remembering how Jandro had to lock him up at night because of his violent nightmares. I advised him not to take a sleeping pill last night, considering we had to be up in a few short hours.

Shadow looked peaceful, if a bit pale. His face was softer in sleep, without his perpetual glower. I stroked the back of my fingers against his cheek. He seemed to like it when I touched his face. If only he knew how many times I thought about touching him like this.

He stirred but didn't wake. His face turned, the soft bristles of his beard leaning into my hand. I lifted a finger to push his hair back, exposing the deep scar carving through his cheek, eyelid, and brow. He was fucking beautiful, and I couldn't stop staring.

"Shadow," I whispered, my thumb stroking over his cheekbone. "Time to get up."

He rolled to his side, my hand now trapped between his cheek and the ground. His arm reached out, coming close to resting on my thigh before it stopped and jerked back.

"Ugh," he grunted, eyes now blinking awake. "I'm stiff as a fucking board." His head lifted and I slipped my hand out.

"How do you feel, aside from that?" I watched him roll up to sitting, one of his hands skimming over the cheek I just touched, before he pulled his hair forward to cover it.

"Fine, I think."

"Can I see?"

He turned his back to me, allowing me to lift his clean shirt up to his shoulder blades to examine the wounds. I frowned and huffed out a breath. They didn't look good. The flesh puffed out and looked discolored between the stitches I made last night. Infection was setting in, but there wasn't much I could do until we got back to the bikes.

"Do you feel weird at all?" I fished my small bottle of alcohol from my kit and poured it over the wounds. "Nauseous? Too cold or too hot?"

"No, I don't think so. It itches a little back there, but I can't even reach them."

"Good." I pulled his shirt down, resisting the urge to skim my hands over the many scars on his back. "Don't rub up on anything to scratch them. They're infected, but I don't have antibiotics to give you until later."

"I'll be fine. Thank you, Mari."

I sighed and reached out to squeeze his shoulder. It was easy to fuss and fret over him, but when not staring down the face of his trauma, he was so stoically calm. "I know you will. And you know what?"

"Huh?"

"I like it when you call me Mari."

It was another three-hour, bumpy, off-road drive, going around the Blakeworth city before we reached the barn where the bikes were stored. I half expected them to be stolen, all our belongings looted, but everything was as we left it.

Shadow, however, continued to look worse.

He was pale and sweating, moving slowly as he walked his bike out of the barn. I had agreed to ride back with Larkan, but now that feeling returned, the urgency to never leave the scarred man's side.

"Shadow?" I approached him warily. "Are you sure you can ride?"

"Don't have much of a choice, do I?" he grunted, struggling to get his cut over his elbows.

"Here, let me."

His arms stilled at his sides while I grabbed the soft leather, pulling it over one massive bicep to rest at his shoulder, and then the other.

"Thank you."

I took the opportunity to touch his face, his eyes half-closing at the contact. It would have been sweet, even intimate, if his skin didn't burn against my palms.

"Shadow," I gasped, pressing a hand to his forehead. "You have a fever. Let me—"

"There's no time." His palms were clammy as he removed my hands by the wrists. "Blake could still be looking for us."

"I'd feel a lot better if you weren't riding," I frowned, noticing how heavily he leaned against his bike. I wondered if he could even fully stand. "I know you've got manly pride or whatever, but can't you link up with one of the guys?"

"And leave my bike here? We have no way to haul it."

"Mari, we've got to go!" Larkan hollered over the revving of his machine.

Shadow flung a hand weakly in his direction. "Get going. I'll be fine." He sounded like he was trying to convince himself more than me.

"Okay, well just take this." I grabbed my bottle of prescription-strength ibuprofen and handed him two tablets. "They should help with the fever and muscle stiffness."

"Thanks." He didn't smile, but his gaze was warm. "You can take care of me all you want when we're home."

"Oh, good. Because you don't have a choice in that matter." I squeezed his hand around the pills before backing away. "Please ride safe. I'll be watching you in the mirrors."

"I'll guard your back," he said softly. "Always."

I left his side with a sinking feeling in my gut. *We're not going to make it home,* my thoughts whispered. He really needed more rest and proper care, but we couldn't stay here. We had no other option but to ride hard to safety.

After securing Freyja in my backpack, I climbed on behind Larkan and immediately checked his mirrors. Shadow had none of his usual grace and confidence as he sat astride his bike. He moved slowly, painfully. Even if his brain couldn't feel it, his body was reacting to the damage he took. My stomach knotted even tighter as we took off.

We took a different route home, T-Bone leading the way through a mix of forests and open fields. Kyrie clung to his waist, her blonde hair streamed out behind her like a comet. The landscape was pretty, but I couldn't bring myself to enjoy it. My thoughts were only on the injured man riding in the rear.

Shadow seemed to be holding on fine, much to my surprise. I had to remind myself how strong and capable he was. He had already survived so much. As hours passed, I started to relax. We weren't stopping, so I couldn't physically check on him, but every mile he stayed on that bike was a good sign.

When late afternoon turned the landscape golden and striped with long shadows, my stomach was cramping from hunger. My thighs and butt ached like they did when I first started riding. T-Bone's bike began to slow, and buildings started popping up on either side of the road. I lifted the visor on my helmet and blinked several times, certain that it had to be a mirage.

"I know this place," Larkan yelled to me over his shoulder. "We're way off-course from Four Corners, but this town is Toquerville. It's neutral territory, so nobody owns it yet. We'll be safe to stop here."

T-Bone seemed to have the same idea as he slowly rolled through on the dirt road. He pointed out things to Kyrie, but I couldn't hear what he was saying. Hope soared within me when I saw an apothecary sign on one of the buildings. It was dusty and didn't seem to be open at the moment, but I might be able to treat Shadow's infection here.

My eyes slid back to Larkan's mirror. Now that we were moving slower and the bikes were closer together, I could see Shadow clearly. He was bent low and forward over his handlebars, pale as a ghost and grimacing. His hair was slick with sweat, clinging to his forehead, and his breathing looked labored.

Holy shit! How was he able to ride for the past eight hours like that? Panic gripped my chest, but before I could say anything Larkan suddenly picked up speed, following T-Bone's acceleration through the town.

I patted Lark's shoulder. "Where are we going?"

"I dunno. Just following T's signal."

"We need to stop. Shadow looks really sick."

He turned a corner, following the bikes in front along a side street, and I lost sight of Shadow.

"Lark, slow down! He can't see us anymore."

Thankfully he slowed, and I twisted in my seat to look behind me.

The whole world seemed to slow down as Shadow came around the corner, his bike turning too sharply.

The motorcycle spun off in one direction, his body flying lifelessly the other way, and I screamed.

MARIPOSA

I hit the ground while Larkan's bike was still moving, and painful jolts shot up to my knees. He yelled something after me, but I ignored him. I ignored everything that wasn't the man lying motionless on the ground.

"Shadow!" I knelt at his side, feeling desperately for a pulse in his neck.

When the beat throbbed weakly under my fingers, it was a small relief. He could have a head injury or broken bones now, on top of his infected wounds.

"I need a hospital!" I cried out. People were standing around gawking on the street. Where the fuck were the Sons? "Hey!" I yelled in the faces of onlookers. "Where's the hospital?"

"We don't have one, miss. I'm sorry. A doctor comes through sometimes, but he left yesterday."

"A room with a bed, then!" I screamed. "He's hurt! He needs to rest. He needs—"

"Shh, Mari." Someone grabbed me by my shoulders, shaking me gently. "There's a service center at the end of this road. We'll get him there, okay?"

T-Bone's voice was calm, his eyes sharp. Seeing him quelled my panic slightly.

"He can't ride," I whispered. "He shouldn't go anywhere for several days, maybe even a week or more."

"That's okay. We'll figure something out. Grudge, can you help me get him up?"

The silent man slid his hands under Shadow's shoulders and lifted.

"Careful with his head." I reached out, supporting Shadow's neck to minimize movement.

After I determined that he hadn't broken any bones, the Sons and Larkan carried Shadow down the street to the service center. Some people still rubbernecked, but most lost interest in the spectacle after the crash. When the guys finally carried him to a room and laid him on a clean bed, I snapped into nurse mode.

"I need boiling hot water, alcohol, and clean towels. Can someone ride down to the apothecary and get bandages, syringes with needles, and any antibiotics that end in -cillin, -cin, or -cline."

"Can I do anything?" Kyrie piped up.

"You can ask the kitchen for soup, broth, and drinking water. He's probably going to be on a liquid diet for a few days."

"What about you?" Dyno looked at me sharply. "Mari, you need to rest, too. You look like you're about to fall over."

"Just get what I asked for. Now, please." I was already cutting away Shadow's shirt. Hunger pains could wait if he was dying. "I'll be fine."

Everyone filed out of the room, except for Grudge. He made a noise that sounded like a harsh "Huh!". I looked at him and he tilted his head toward Shadow, pointing at the unconscious man with his thumb and a wry grin.

"You saying I sound like him now?"

Grudge nodded, pleased that I understood.

"Guess that's why we get along so well," I sighed. "Help me turn him over?"

We carefully rolled Shadow onto his side so I could access his back.

"Fuck," I hissed after lifting his shirt. "Those look even worse. I've never seen infection set in this fast."

Grudge made a gagging noise and went to the window as I finished pulling Shadow's shirt off. I didn't blame him, the smell was worse than the stitches looked.

"I'm sorry, Shadow," I whispered, grabbing my scalpel and dousing it liberally with the rubbing alcohol I had left. "I have to cut you again."

The others started returning just as I cut the sutures free and began draining the pus from the wounds. T-Bone and Larkan retched, quickly joining Grudge at the window. Kyrie, surprisingly, had no reaction at all.

"Here's some soup you can just heat up when you're ready." She placed the containers by the bed. "And here's a cold sandwich for you. I didn't know what you liked, so I just had them put everything on it."

"Thank you." I didn't even look up from poking through Shadow's infected flesh.

"Please don't talk about food," T-Bone begged, swallowing another dry heave. "Dyno went to the apothecary. He should be back soon."

"Thanks. I know it stinks, you guys don't have to stick around."

Their footsteps were little more than background noise as I sterilized Shadow's wounds as best as I could. A friendly squeeze came down on my shoulder.

"We're all on this same floor if you need us," T-Bone said before leaving.

Only Grudge remained, and he seemed in no hurry to leave. I didn't mind that he stayed. He certainly wasn't in the way. Concern etched his face as he watched me work on Shadow.

"You and him have gotten close, huh?" I asked.

"Mm," he nodded, moving to sit at the opposite end of the bed from me.

Shadow wasn't bleeding badly, so I opted to not stitch him back up. Air flow was important to fighting the infection, and it could possibly fester under his skin if I closed him back up. So I covered his wounds with sterile gauze and rolled him onto his back.

"Help me prop him up a little?" I asked Grudge.

Together, we scooted him up toward the headboard and I stuck a pillow under his head, making sure there wasn't a lot of pressure on his upper back. Only then did I pause to just take a breath. Dyno came in to drop off the supplies I ordered and quickly left, his face turning green at the smell lingering in the room.

Grudge came around and patted my shoulder, then pointed to the container with my sandwich in it.

"Guess I might as well," I laughed. "Make sure you eat, too."

He nodded and pulled his notepad from inside his cut. *I'll be back. Will watch him w/you.*

"Thank you," I expressed sincerely. Having an extra pair of eyes on Shadow would honestly be huge for my peace of mind. "I'll be here."

He gave a thumbs up before heading out the door. I tore open my sandwich and wolfed it down, my eyes glued to the man in the bed.

They could be brothers, I realized. Shadow and Grudge had the same long black hair, glossy like raven feathers. The same dark eyes and quiet, observant demeanor. Since the Sons first came to us, those two seemed to gravitate toward each other.

My sandwich gone far too soon, I washed my hands thoroughly, then dug out my thermometer. I ran the sensor across Shadow's forehead, and my heart sank when his temperature read 103.

"You poor thing," I murmured, running the back of my hands over his cheeks.

I opened the window, the evening air quickly chilling the room, then wet a washcloth to run over his face and neck. His skin erupted in goosebumps despite being drenched in sweat, and he finally, finally opened his eyes.

"M-mari..."

"It's okay, you're safe." I clasped one of his hands, the other continuing to drag the wet washcloth over his neck and the top of his chest.

"I'm c-cold..."

"I know, love. We need to bring your fever down." The pet name I usually reserved for my men slipped out, but it didn't faze me. He needed this care. He needed to feel loved.

Shadow dragged a hand along his taut stomach, following the lines of scars there. "Think I'm gonna be sick."

I found a trashcan just in time, and he heaved his guts over the side of the bed. He hadn't eaten all day, so it was mostly dry heaves.

"Try drinking some water for me." I held the glass out for him to take a few weak sips. He threw that up not a minute later.

"I'm s-sorry..."

"Stop." I ran the washcloth down his back. "You have nothing to be sorry for."

"I feel like shit," he moaned. "Like I got run over by a truck."

"Well, you did fall off your bike."

He coughed and spit into the trash can, then allowed me to wipe his mouth. "I'm no Steel Demon if I can't even sit on a bike."

"Stop. I don't want to hear that shit. Are you done?" At his weak nod, I pulled his shoulder back to help him recline in bed again. "You're hurt. Your wounds are infected. I'm amazed you lasted on the bike as long as you did."

"This has..." he took rapid shallow breaths, as if he'd been running for miles, "...never happened to me before."

"Well, thank fuck for your strong immune system. But I wonder if those arrows were covered in something. Some kind of bacteria or poison. Infection set in awfully fast."

As I filed through the list of antibiotics in my head, Shadow leaned over the bed again to dry heave into the trash can. I discarded the towel and asked Grudge for a new one. As Shadow's back heaved with ragged breaths, I mopped the towel over his feverish skin. The jagged map of scar tissue stretched with each breath he took. He looked completely exhausted by the time he sat up again.

"Please try to drink something." I ran the cloth over his forehead and neck. "I'd give you IV fluids, but I don't have the right supplies."

"Can't...keep anything down."

"I know it's hard, but please try for me."

He accepted a few small sips of water when I held the glass out to him. A full minute passed and he made no move to vomit.

"Good." I forced a tight smile.

"Why...are you taking care of me?" His eyes followed my every movement, still sharp as a falcon's despite the weakness in his body.

"You know why." I dug out my stethoscope and wiped the ends with alcohol.

"Tell me." His gaze rested on my face as I placed the dial over the dark tattoo on his chest. "I want to hear you say it."

"Stop talking and just breathe normally, please." His heart was beating rapidly, way too fast for a resting heartbeat. But his lungs sounded clear, which was a positive sign. "I'm taking care of you because of this." I pressed a finger to the grinning skull on his chest, the tattoo we shared, that he put on me with his own hands. "We both have a duty to the SDMC. Yours is to be an assassin. Mine is to be a medic."

I put the towel aside and scooted closer to him, my hip nudging against the outside of his thigh. He didn't move away like I expected, maybe out of weakness, or maybe the fear of touching me really was gone.

"But you're also my friend." My hand closed around his. "And I don't like seeing you unwell. I'm taking care of you because I want *my* Shadow back."

I didn't intend for the possessiveness to slip out, but didn't panic when it did. A calm settled over me instead. This man and I shared something unique, we had all but said it to each other in those exact words. Still, this was the first time I dared to speak aloud, claiming him as mine. In saying it, I realized I was ready to. This time, I wouldn't worry about being unfair to Reaper, Jandro and Gun. I knew what I wanted, and what I was able to give.

If Shadow realized the implication of what I was saying, his sickness didn't allow for him to dwell on the thought. He hugged himself, broad arms wrapping around his chest. "C-can't stop...shivering. I feel like... like I'm falling in and out of sleep."

"Lay down and rest." I got up from his side, moving toward the far end of the bed. What was between us didn't matter right now, anyway. He needed to get better first. "I can't give you a blanket, I'm sorry. You're already too hot. We need your temperature to come down."

He scooted down from the headboard and didn't object when I started unlacing his boots. I pulled them off his feet and placed them next to the door. Returning to his side, my eyes lingered on the silver button at the front of his jeans.

"Shadow? Are you okay with me taking your pants off for bed?"

He didn't answer right away, and I thought he'd fallen asleep. Then the weakly whispered, "Yes," floating up to me made my heart pound.

I unsnapped the button and pulled down his zipper, working to be as clinical as possible as I pulled the denim down his muscular thighs. I jerked my gaze away from the deep V-lines in his hips, the snug, black boxers outlining a thick bulge. *He's sick. He's my patient right now,* I reminded myself.

Something else caught my eye and I found myself looking out of sheer curiosity. A tattoo was on his upper right thigh, the ink blurred by scar tissue and faded to a bluish gray color. It was a band of symbols, small pictographs of some kind, stretching about five inches across and no more than an inch tall.

He never mentioned having other tattoos, although I didn't really ask. I did recall him saying that the scar tissue made it difficult for ink to keep over time. Why did those symbols look so familiar, though?

I kept thinking about it as I tidied up the room. Grudge came back a half hour later with more food and some books. Shadow tossed fitfully in and out of sleep. I kept sponging cool towels over him, and finally relented when he asked to cover himself with a sheet.

His fever kept bouncing between 101 and 103. I kept going through his symptoms in my head, looking at his back wounds, and re-reading the labels on the antibiotic bottles. His symptoms were generic enough that it could literally be any kind of bacteria, but the medicine would only work on certain strains. To give him the wrong one could mean bad side effects and wasted time as his infection worsened.

I explained all this to Grudge, who listened with attentive, curious eyes. Neither one one of us seemed eager to sleep, so he just watched over Shadow while I paced around the room.

"Hieroglyphics!" I blurted out after an exhausting, silent few hours.

"Hm?"

"The tattoo on his thigh," I said. "I undressed him for bed and saw symbols inked there. They looked familiar, but I didn't know from where. Now I remember seeing them in an ancient history class in high school, years ago."

Grudge smiled wolfishly. He didn't have to gesture or write anything down for me to know what he was thinking.

"I was *not* getting up to anything!" I told him. "He needed to rest and still had pants and shoes on."

The silent man chuckled and held his hands up in a defensive posture.

"I like you guys," I blurted out next. I was so exhausted, but not allowing myself to sleep made my mouth seem to disconnect from my brain like I was drunk. "The Sons are good allies. You saved us out there, and you guys have never steered the Steel Demons wrong. So, thank you."

Grudge glanced down at the floor, a smile still on his lips. He pulled out his notepad and quickly scribbled out, *Feeling's mutual. Feel bad S got hurt, though.*

"Nobody could have seen those fucking harpoon arrows coming," I told him. "And you cut him free. So, thank you for that. I'll make sure Reaper knows you saved one of us."

It's what friends do.

I gave his arm a friendly squeeze and went back to my worried pacing.

Freyja climbed in through the window at some point during the night and curled up in the bed next to Shadow. Her presence seemed to calm his fitful tossing, turning, and mumbling, but his fever never came down past 100.

I can help you put him under the shower, Grudge told me as dawn started creeping through the windows.

"Maybe, but," I rubbed my forehead, well past exhausted at this point, "it's not super high anymore so it's not life-threatening. The fever serves a purpose, it's trying to fight the infection in his body. If we keep bringing it down, the infection could run rampant. My instinct is to let it run, but..."

Something else nagged at me. My gut was trying to tell me something, I just didn't know what.

Shadow rolled to his side, seeking a cool spot on the sweat-soaked sheets. Taking a seat on the bed, I looked at his back for the hundredth time that night, noting the purple bruise-like discoloration spreading out from his wounds.

"I'm sorry, love." The endearment slipped out again while I touched his shoulder, and I seriously considered brushing a kiss along the scar running under my hand. "I don't know what to give you to help you."

It's sepsis.

That word clicked into the knowledge in my head like a puzzle piece. Freyja stared at me from the other side of him, but I couldn't be sure that was her voice. It felt like my own, but I was too tired to pay attention.

Even so, I knew what to do now.

I headed for the door and went out into the hallway. Picking the door on my left at random, I knocked with a heavy fist.

"Hold on!" T-Bone's gravelly voice called from the other side.

I pounded again. There was no time to wait. I heard the latch unlock, and pushed the door open just as he zipped himself into a pair of jeans. A blond service girl in the bed covered her chest with a sheet. Next to her, a naked Dyno slammed a pillow over his lap.

"Uh. Morning, Mari." He smoothed his hands over the pillow in an attempt to look casual.

I lifted an eyebrow at T-Bone in question.

"What?" he responded. "We like variety sometimes."

I shrugged. I thought women weren't their type, but it was none of my business. The girl didn't look mistreated, at least. On the contrary, she was panting slightly with dreamy, dilated eyes. Apparently, they'd been in the middle of something.

"How far is Four Corners from here?" I asked.

"Um." T-Bone scrubbed a hand down his face, shifting his thinking to the correct head. "Five-hour ride. Maybe four if we push it."

"I need you guys to ride back and bring some supplies here for me. I'll give you a list. My guys will know where my stuff is and what's what."

T-Bone shook his head. "We're not leaving without you. If Reaper doesn't have eyes on you, I'm as good as dead."

"Shadow isn't fit to travel and I'm not leaving him." I crossed my arms to show that I wasn't budging. "The bacteria has infected his bloodstream. He's getting worse, and I need specific equipment as soon as possible."

T-Bone sighed, casting an apologetic glance to the couple in his bed. "Well, we're not *all* leaving, then. You shouldn't be alone here."

"Grudge can stay," I said. "And Larkan. Reaper will want one of our own with me. But you and Dyno need to get Kyrie back and tell my guys what I need. Then at least one of you needs to come back here with my stuff as soon as possible."

"All right." He nodded, running a hand over his shaved head. "All right, we'll just, uh, finish getting dressed. Make me that list."

"On it."

I went back to my—or was it Shadow's?—room to find him thrashing around in bed, with Grudge struggling to restrain him. The silent man looked up at me with confusion etched in his eyes, but thankfully this wasn't a violent nightmare. Now that I knew the cause of his illness, the symptoms of disorientation and confusion weren't too alarming.

"Shadow, it's Mari." I pushed back the dark hair over his face and placed my hands on his cheeks. "You're safe, love. You're going to be okay."

"Mari?" His eyes were barely open, just slits, while his head moved around as though in search of me.

"Yes, I'm right here." I stroked his cheekbones with my thumbs and pressed a kiss to his clammy forehead. "I'm always here."

He stopped struggling, sinking limply into the mattress. I nodded at Grudge to let him know it was okay, and he climbed off the bed.

"Mari..." Shadow's hands stretched out in search of me. I held one in mine and let his other hand rest in my lap. "Why...why are you always here?"

"Because I'm taking care of you, silly." *And you're mine.*

"No, I mean..." he twisted in the bed as if trying to get comfortable. "Why are you always *here*?" His chin lifted, his feverish gaze pointed toward the ceiling. "In my head? I can't...I can't get you out. You're always there."

My heart drumming wildly, I brought his hand to my lips and kissed the lines of scars over his fingers and knuckles. This beautiful, battered man had been hurt so much and never encountered love a day in his life. Even just the slightest glimpses of it, he didn't know what to do with.

But I would show him. I'd give him what he didn't even know he hungered for, and never make him want for it again.

"Probably the same reasons why I can't get you out of mine," I answered.

REAPER

"Hey." Jandro smacked me with his bag of chicken feed. "Gun's coming back."

I sat up so abruptly, the cigarette nearly fell out of my mouth. Looking toward the hill where Governor Vance's house sat, I saw Gunner barreling down the narrow street on his bike, hair streaming out behind him. Jandro and I went out to the front porch of the B&B to greet him, both as eager as kids on Christmas for any news.

My heart sank at the sight of Gunner's grim expression when he pulled up.

"What happened?" I demanded.

"Don't know. They're still about two miles out." He climbed off of the bike and released a heavy breath. "It's just two riders—T-Bone and Dyno. With a blond girl I assume to be Vance's daughter."

"*What?!*"

Jandro and I rushed at him at the same time. I couldn't speak for my VP, but my blood was already simmering. We fired questions rapidly.

"That's it? Are you absolutely *sure* it was just them?"

"You didn't see Mari at all? Or Shadow? Maybe he was riding further back?"

"Hey, back the fuck up!" Gunner shoved both of us out of his face.

"I'm just the messenger, all right? I know what I saw, and I did not miss shit. It's just those three and no one else."

"They better have a good fucking explanation," Jandro glowered.

"Well, they'll be here in a minute and then we'll find out."

"There is no explanation," I seethed. "There is no fucking excuse to leave our woman—and two of our men—behind on a fucking rescue mission in some fucking slave labor territory—"

"Reap, calm down."

"Fuck you!"

I wanted blood. I didn't care if the Sons had a direct hand in leaving Mari and my guys behind, or they had to make a tough choice in rescuing the girl, none of it. All my people being left behind was the worst possible scenario I could imagine. Oh fuck, what if they had to trade hostages? I'd happily watch T-Bone's bald head turn red as a tomato, then purple while I fucking throttled him—

You will not reap.

My head snapped down and to the side, where Hades sat calmly next to my leg. His head tilted up, dark gaze meeting mine as his nose brushed the side of my hip.

"Well, aren't you full of useful advice," I glowered at him.

Their lives are not yours to take. You will not reap the Sons of Odin.

"We'll see about that, dog." I stepped off of the porch and headed into the street to meet the Sons at the edge of town.

Jandro quickly caught up to me. "What did Hades say?"

"I'm not allowed to kill T-Bone and Dyno," I grumbled. "So let's just hope that means Mari and the guys are okay. 'Cause if they're fuckin' not, I don't give two shits about defying an ancient god."

My eyes slid down to Hades trotting calmly at my side, seeing if he'd have any more commentary. But except for the soft panting from his mouth, he kept silent.

The Sons were just cresting the hill when we made it to the base. Dyno veered off toward the governor's house, the young blond woman clinging tightly to his back. T-Bone continued down the gentle slope to the bottom where we waited.

"Where are they?" I demanded before he even came to a complete stop on his bike.

"Safe and unharmed." He tried to sound reassuring as he cut his engine.

"That's not what I fucking asked."

"Reap." Jandro went to touch my shoulder, but I shook him off.

"Don't fucking touch me. I'm not gonna repeat myself, T-Bone."

"They're in Toquerville. A neutral town about five hours from here."

"Why?"

"Shadow took a bad hit and fell off his bike. Mari's fine, but Shadow can't ride and she won't leave his side. Grudge and Larkan are watching over them."

"Wait, what?" Jandro spoke up. "You're saying Shadow took a hit? *Our* Shadow?"

T-Bone nodded. "Arrows with ropes attached. He got hit in the back."

"Jesus," Gunner blanched. "They fucking harpooned the guy."

"Mari said something about an infection. She needs stuff from her medical kit and gave me a list." T-Bone looked at each of us. "And she needs someone to bring it back to her. Said it was urgent."

"I'll go," the three of us said in unison, like a bunch of stooges.

"It should be me," Jandro said. "Reap, the club needs their president. Gun, we need you and Horus to keep eyes out. I'll bring her stuff to her."

"Probably for the best, as much I want to go," Gunner said. "You know Shadow the best, anyway. If he's that sick, he'll probably feel better with you around."

"Reap?"

"Yeah, fine. You go," I muttered. "T-Bone, sorry for almost biting your head off."

"It's nothing, Pres. I completely understand."

"No, I wasn't finished." I stepped closer to him, getting into his personal space. "If you come back a second time without my people, I won't give you such a warm welcome."

"Understood, president." He didn't swallow or shrink back, which I had to give him credit for. He knew his place with me, but wasn't a pussy.

"You got that list?" Jandro broke in.

T-Bone fished a folded piece of paper from his cut pocket and handed it over.

"Chill out for an hour or so while I put this together." Jandro smirked at him. "Hope your *cajones* can handle another long ride in the saddle today."

"Nothing to worry about, VP," T-Bone chuckled, caressing a hand over his bike seat. "My baby knows exactly how to handle my goods."

"All right, then. I'll see you in a bit."

"What does she need?" The question came from Gunner, but we both looked over Jandro's shoulders as he unfolded the list.

"IV bags, sterile tubing, tape, needles," Jandro muttered, going down the list as we walked back toward the B&B. His head lifted as he refolded the paper and shoved it in his pocket. "While I got you guys, I should mention something about Shadow."

"Isn't there always something with him?" Gunner chuckled.

"I'm pretty sure he has a thing for Mari. And I think it's reciprocated."

"Wait, what?" Gunner grabbed his shoulder. "You serious?"

"Inside." I jerked my chin toward the B&B's front door just up ahead. "Let's talk in private while you get Mari's stuff together."

Hades led us up the front porch, earning head scratches from Mrs. Potts, the B&B's owner who was sweeping across the patio.

"Such a sweet dog you have," she beamed at me.

"Thank you, ma'am," I muttered as we made our way inside.

Our room had been tidied and cleaned. Thankfully, my cigarettes remained untouched on the side table. I avoided looking at the bed, well, beds pushed together, as I sat in the armchair and lit up. The nights had been too fucking long. Too fucking lonely without her in it.

Gunner leaned against the windowsill while Jandro grabbed Mari's assorted bags and started laying her medical items out on the bed.

"All right, talk. Mari and Shadow, really?" Gun crossed his arms, looking more agitated by the minute. It didn't entirely surprise me. He was the new guy to our arrangement.

"Yes, really." Jandro pulled out the list and laid it next to the items on the bed. "You can't tell me you've missed all the time they've spent together. He pretty much admitted to splitting up her tattoo sessions so he could see her more."

"What makes you think *she* likes him?"

"She hasn't really said anything about it, but it's not like she's avoiding his attention either."

"She was bringing him into the conversation the night before they all left," I pointed out. "Not quite flirting, but getting there. They're more comfortable with each other than they ever have been."

Gunner turned to me, his brow pinched. "What do you think of this?"

"What do *you* think?" I countered. "You're part of this too, Gun. What are your instincts telling you about them being together? I don't mean your knee jerk reaction, like when you first thought about sharing her. I'm talking deep, gut instinct."

He paused, stroking his chin as he thought about it. "I'm not against it, *per se*. I just have a lot of questions. Basically, why him? What does she see in him? I mean I like the guy, of course, he's a Demon through and through. But he *is* different. Is he going to be good for her?"

"Those are good questions to have," I nodded at him. "It's our responsibility to look out for her. Sometimes women see things through rose-colored glasses and miss red flags. It's up to us to see those clearly." I looked to Jandro. "You know him best. Your thoughts?"

He had been placing Mari's needed items in a small pile at the foot of the bed, and paused when I addressed him.

"I was worried at first," he admitted. "Like, I love the guy. He's my brother, and he's done so much better since she's been around. But I could tell he was still really attracted to her, and spending more time with her after, *you know.*"

Of course we knew. That time they fucked, early on in our relationship. Shadow had misread the situation, and Mari felt a whole storm of confusing things. What she made abundantly clear from that situation though, was her loyalty to me. Once she was calm and reassured, that incident was able to show her that sexual fidelity was not a requirement of mine. She even admitted to enjoying it with him, despite acting only out of self-preservation at first.

"I was worried about his lack of life experience, mainly," Jandro continued. "He doesn't know what to do with a woman besides stick his dick in her when it's offered. I'm damn certain he's never been in love before, probably never even had a crush before Mari."

"I think that's what's bugging me," Gunner said. "He doesn't know how to treat her. Or the subtleties of giving and taking in a relationship. Is he gonna act like us at sixteen years old and just expect to get his dick sucked all the time?"

"See, that's what I thought." Jandro pointed across the bed at him. "But is that really true? He's been through shit the three of us could probably never fathom. When he's not working out or drawing, he's reading history and psychology shit constantly. He's desperate to understand people, and he's fully aware that he's different. He doesn't act entitled or immature in any other way, so why assume he's gonna be that way with her?"

"Mari makes him feel normal," I pointed out. "Because she treats him like anyone else."

"Okay, but how does he make *her* feel?" Gunner argued. "What is *she* getting out of this, is what I want to know. And furthermore, what's she lacking with us that she's seeking out with him?"

"Careful with that line of thinking," I warned him. "You'll go in a downward spiral real quick."

"So explain it to me, then. Since you're the expert."

"Mari hasn't come to me about this yet, so I don't know what's going on in her head. But all people are different. Everyone has *something* that isn't present in others, at least not in the same way. Shadow has something that attracts her, which doesn't mean she's unhappy with us."

Gunner blew out a long breath, shoving his hair back. "I guess that makes sense. I just figured three dudes would be enough, you know?"

"She's meant to have four of us." I let my hand fall off the armrest, stroking down Hades' back.

"How do you know?"

"I just do."

"All right, well," Gunner sighed. "What are the boundaries to this? Do you think they're fucking?"

"She wouldn't do that." Jandro was now sweeping up Mari's personal items from the bed and putting them back in her duffel bag. He paused with a sigh, holding a lacy black thong in his fist. "Damn, I miss her."

"Says the fucker who gets to see her in a few hours," I growled, before addressing Gunner's concern. "No, she wouldn't fuck him without our explicit approval. He's probably too fucking sick anyway. But they've probably gotten closer, emotionally."

Gunner let out a pained sound. "I don't know if that's better or worse."

"It's better," I assured him. "She doesn't have sex clouding her judgment."

Jandro came around the bed and patted him on the shoulder. "Don't get yourself twisted in knots over it. She might be attracted to him, but she loves *us*. She won't jeopardize that, especially not after you got her all worked up with that toy in her ass."

The blond demon gave a wolfish smirk. "I think it was Reap that did the working up."

"What I do best." I ashed my cigarette. "Don't forget that Shadow is loyal to us too, in every way. He's probably the Demon I'm most proud of and trust the most, aside from you two."

"That's true," Jandro agreed. "Shadow is almost hyper-aware of his behavior because he doesn't want to fuck anything up. He won't do something that he feels wrongs us, or jeopardizes the club."

"So, what do you think?" Gunner returned his gaze to me. "You're just good with this?"

"I never said that," I shot back. "I'm a little surprised, but like 'Dro mentioned, the signs were there. They're getting closer, but for all we know, it may just be as friends. We still don't know how Mari feels about everything, and this is ultimately about her. As far as bringing Shadow into our fold, I'm cautiously optimistic. It's not who I would expect, but Mari could certainly choose worse."

"On that note." Jandro smoothed out the bedspread after packing Mari's supplies. "You had eyes on Big G lately?"

"Always," Gunner answered. "He's staying away from Tessa for now. Andrea and Noelle are helping to be a buffer between them."

"Good." Jandro pocketed Mari's list and shouldered the pack with her supplies. "I'm packing a lunch and heading out, *chingados.*"

"Kiss her for me," Gunner sighed wistfully. "Fuck, I can't wait til she's back."

"Smack her ass for me," I pitched in. "See if she still feels anything from two nights ago."

"Sure thing, you domineering fuck." Jandro rolled his eyes as he headed for the door. "Don't worry, guys. I'm not coming back without our girl."

MARIPOSA

"You found some, Grudge?"

The silent man nodded, producing a small flask from his cut pocket. He held it out for me to inspect. I unscrewed the cap and took a whiff, the unmistakable burn of rubbing alcohol hitting my nose.

"Perfect, thank you." I ran out of my small stash, and only had one needle and set of tubing until someone came with the rest of my stuff, hopefully tonight.

Grudge held his pad of paper out to me. *What are you going to do?*

"The infection is in Shadow's bloodstream," I explained. "And I don't want to give him the wrong antibiotic, or a useless one, against the strain he has. We have no way of knowing what he has without a lab to test it. So the next best thing is bleeding him out."

His dark eyebrows pinched together as he listened.

"We drain the infected blood out of his body," I said. "Which will prompt his body to speed up the process of creating new, fresh blood cells to fight the infection."

Won't losing blood make him weaker?

"I won't drain him too much." I looked at the bed, where Shadow continued to toss around restlessly.

Sometimes he slept for an hour or so, but kept waking up disoriented and confused. He could only eat and drink in small amounts before becoming nauseous. Touching and talking to him seemed to soothe him the most.

"Sepsis can go bad very quickly," I said to Grudge. "The best I can do for him right now is to literally get that infected blood out of his body."

What about a blood transfusion? If you drained him and he got fresh blood from another source.

"That might work, once someone gets here with my supplies and we find a blood type match," I sighed. "But Shadow's blood type is rare. Partial matches are okay, but a perfect match is ideal. And since he's AB+—"

Grudge's eyes suddenly widened as he sucked in a sharp breath. He tapped his chest repeatedly.

"You?"

"Hm!" He nodded emphatically, continuing to point at himself.

It took me a few seconds, but finally clicked into place. "*You're* AB+?"

He nodded again, a grin pulling at his lips.

I shoved a hand through my hair, which had to resemble a tumbleweed at this point. "Well, damn. We still have to wait for someone to get here, but that...makes things a lot easier for us."

Grudge chuckled on his way to Shadow's bedside. As he grabbed Shadow's shoulder in an affectionate way, I took a moment to look at the two men more closely. Same dark hair. Same quiet, observant demeanor. Grudge wasn't nearly as broad or tall as Shadow, but their builds were similar. It was hard to tell from his much longer beard, but I'd bet money on them having similar facial structures too. And the two of them having the same rare blood type? That felt like too many coincidences.

"I think you two are brothers." My exhaustion still had me blurting my thoughts out like a drunken sorority girl.

Grudge looked at me, unfazed by my observation. He pulled out his notepad and wrote a slow, thought-out response.

I think we are too. It explains our similarities, and also how we're both different from other people. He paused in thought before writing more. *There's a lot we know about each other that only the two of us understand, that we've never breathed a word of to others. T & D don't even know everything about me.*

"Did you both grow up in the same type of environment?"

He nodded, elaborating on his notepad. *Different locations, but yes. The same abusive cult of women.*

"I'm sorry, for what you both went through."

Not your fault, M. You're one of the good ones. He's lucky.

"I'm sure he doesn't feel like it right now." I ran a hand over Shadow's forehead and cheeks again. He was warm, but not burning up at the moment. I estimated his temperature to be somewhere between 99 and 100. "We should drain him a bit now."

Just tell me what to do, Grudge quickly scrawled out.

For now, he had to do little more than hold a bowl to catch Shadow's blood when I pricked him. I wrapped a strip of gauze around Shadow's arm below his bicep and tied it off tightly to find a vein.

"Please don't thrash on me, love." I leaned over him, brushing a kiss across his forehead. "I'm trying to make you better."

He mumbled wordlessly, moving his head back and forth a bit, but otherwise didn't resist.

"Ready, Grudge?"

"Hm," he nodded.

I inserted the needle and watched the dark blood wind through the tube to empty into the bowl in Grudge's hands. The coppery smell filled the air and I imagined the infection flushing out of Shadow's system into that bowl. It didn't work like that, but aside from this, positive thinking was all I had left at the moment.

"Okay, that's about a half pint," I said. "Let's stop there for now."

I removed the needle from Shadow's arm and bandaged the insertion spot while Grudge went to throw the contaminated blood away. When I went to sit down at the edge of the bed, it was Grudge gently shaking my shoulder that made me realize I dozed off.

"Jesus, sorry..."

"Mm-mm." He shook his head, lips pressed into a thin line, and pointed to the other side of the bed where Freyja sat curled up.

"I'm fine, really. We should wake him and see if he eats—"

"Hmm!" Grudge wrapped a hand around my shoulder and gently pushed me toward the empty side of the bed. Then he released me and made a shooing motion.

"Okay, fine." My eyelids were already drooping again, and that pillow did look super comfortable. "I'll rest just for a few minutes. Can you make sure Shadow eats and drinks something?"

"Mm-hm." He was already pulling an extra blanket down from the closet to cover me with.

"Thank you..."

I surrendered to the fatigue and let it pull me under.

The room was dark when I woke up, with only a dim lamp on the bedside table providing light. I was warm. Hot, even. Almost too warm, until I realized where I was. The pillow under my head had been replaced by Shadow's chest.

Somehow I migrated across the king-sized bed in my sleep, and found myself nestled into his side. His arm draped over my back, hand settled in the dip of my waist. His sleeping face was calm, his breaths deep with the steady rise and fall of his chest. I had abandoned my blanket and the sheets were a twisted mess at the foot of the bed, likely kicked away in his thrashing.

I lifted my cheek from his warm skin to just marvel at the long stretches of scars and muscles on him. Sure, I'd touched him, seen him before, but not like this. He was like a map of an unknown continent I couldn't help but want to explore.

Not wanting to startle him, I skimmed a light touch with my fingertips to his waist. Deeply asleep, he didn't respond. I slid my hand with a slow drag across his stomach, his abs flexing with each breath. His skin was surprisingly soft, the scars little more than light texture on my palms. My hand inched up the solid planes of muscle to his chest, coming to rest over the Steel Demons tattoo a few inches away from my face.

His heartbeat was still too fast for my liking, but his fever didn't feel any higher. And at least he was resting.

"Hey, *Mariposita*."

The voice coming from the armchair in the dark corner of the room made me jump. I instinctively searched for my knife before my brain caught up.

"Jandro!"

I crawled to the bottom of the bed and ran around Shadow to attack-hug my man, who'd been watching silently.

"Fuck, babe." He squeezed me tightly to his chest, face buried in my neck as I wrapped my arms around his shoulders. "Fuck, I missed you."

"When did you get in?" I pulled back just enough to smack a kiss on those plush lips I missed so much. "Why didn't you wake me?"

"A couple hours ago." He held the back of my neck to kiss me deeper. "And you looked comfortable," he chuckled against my lips.

Our kisses were full of relief and longing. Every sip and tongue flick was passionate and savoring, dragging out the moments we didn't get to have over the past few days.

"How is he?" Jandro dragged the question with a kiss along my temple, loosening his hold on me, but never letting go.

I rested my head on his shoulder, my gaze returning to Shadow. "Better, but still not great. Did you get everything?"

"Yeah, it's all there." He nodded toward a duffle bag on the floor against the wall. I waited for him to make a comment about me cuddling up to Shadow, but it never came.

"Thank you, *guapito*." I hugged around his waist and pressed a grateful kiss under his jaw. "Where did Grudge go?"

"He's next door, resting up with T-Bone."

"I'll leave him be for now, then. But I'll need him for this blood transfusion." I untangled from Jandro and went to dig through the bag.

"Transfusion?"

"Shadow needs non-infected blood and Grudge is a perfect match," I explained. "They're probably brothers. Or biologically related somehow."

"Huh." Jandro rubbed his chin. "Never noticed it before, but you're right."

"Help me with this IV? And I should drain him again."

Together, Jandro and I set up the IV drip along the headboard. Shadow woke groggily when I stuck the needle in the back of his hand.

"Hey man, welcome back," Jandro grinned at him. "Heard you took a hit and couldn't believe it. Had to see for myself."

"Jan...dro?" Shadow blinked several times.

"He's really here," I assured him with a hand to his arm. "Rode all day to help me take care of you."

"I wouldn't go *that* far," Jandro joked, then playfully thumped Shadow's shoulder. "It's good to see you, bro. I'm glad you're okay." He leaned over and kissed my neck. "That you're both okay."

"What's this?" Shadow turned over his hand with the IV needle attached.

"It's giving you nutrients," I said. "At least until you can keep food down, okay?"

He nodded. I noted that he didn't seem to be triggered by needles, only blades.

"I'm not sure if you were awake for this, but it turns out Grudge matches your blood type," I said. "So if it's okay with you, I'll take another pint of blood or so from you, then Grudge can donate his blood to replenish you. I think it's your best chance to beat the infection."

Shadow paled slightly. "You'll take blood, how?"

"With a needle and tubing. Just like when you first donated, remember?"

He nodded, relaxing against the headboard as he sat up. I caught myself staring when the muscles in his arms jumped. For as sick as he was, he didn't look one bit weaker.

"Okay." His odd-colored eyes lingered on my face. "I trust you."

"Thank you." I squeezed his hand, a gesture that Jandro did not miss. "Ready to get started?"

"Yes."

Jandro made a very capable nurse, as it turned out. He lifted the spirits of everyone in the room, without goofing off too badly. Seeing

Shadow in the shape he was in was probably a sobering experience. Grudge came back soon after I started taking more blood from Shadow. Once I collected about a pint, Grudge rolled up his sleeve and offered his arm without hesitation.

All-in-all, the procedure was simple, and easy to do with the right equipment. Almost immediately after receiving Grudge's blood, Shadow began looking healthier and more alert.

"I think I can manage a shower," he said, after all was said and done. "I feel gross."

"If you can stand, great." I watched him warily swing his feet to the floor and push to standing. "But you should still rest tonight. We'll see how you feel in the morning."

As he took a towel and clean clothes to the bathroom, Jandro turned to me. "I'll go downstairs and see about getting us our own room."

"Oh, sure." I leaned over to kiss him swiftly. "I'll just be cleaning up."

It didn't take long for him to return. "No vacancies," he reported. "These fucking small towns, I tell you."

"Oh, okay." My eyes darted around the room. "Shadow should keep the bed. There a might be a cot folded up in the closet if—"

"Mari, don't be silly." Jandro approached me with a curious expression. "The bed's big enough to fit all three of us."

I watched him, trying to get a read on his expression, while he did the exact same thing.

"I know you saw me," I said, my eyes locked onto his. "Why don't you just come out and say what's on your mind?"

Jandro's gaze flicked up to the bathroom door behind me, the shower still running, before looking back at me.

"Has anything happened that I should know about?"

"Nothing beyond what you just saw."

He folded his arms, one hand stroking the stubble on his chin in thought. "Do you want to be with him?"

Like the man we were talking about, the answer wasn't simple. It wasn't just about what Shadow or I wanted, but his comfort level. Maybe an affectionate friendship was enough for him, and there was no need to escalate anything. Maybe, like Gunner at first, he was not into the idea of sharing a woman.

"Or is it just a physical attraction thing?" Jandro tilted his head when I didn't answer right away.

"It's more than that," I said. "But I'm not sure what to tell you, because he and I haven't even talked about it. We're *just* getting comfortable with each other."

A boyish grin spread across his face. "I see. So you're just crushing on each other hard and pretending not a damn thing is happening. Fuck, that's adorable."

The shower shut off and my pulse jumped.

"I want to get to know him better," I said in a quick, rushing whisper. "As a potential partner, but not just physically. I want to take things slow, so he's never uncomfortable."

"But you *do* want his dick. You're imagining it right now, I can see it. You have dick-eyes."

"Jandro," I whined. "Please don't be embarrassing."

"Oh, *mi Mariposita*," he laughed, drawing me into his chest. "You're the cutest thing ever, and that's why I love you."

SHADOW

The hunger pangs rippling through my stomach woke me up. I wanted to eat an entire cow, and wash it down with a freshwater pond. But something was holding me down.

No, wait...

I lifted my head to assess the weight on top of me. It was Mariposa, sleeping on my chest.

She looked so pretty, my breath felt momentarily trapped in my lungs. Her cheek rested on my pec, parted lips nearly brushing my sternum. Her arm draped across me, hand resting on my opposite side like how she usually hugged me. Somehow, my arm ended up wrapped around her back with my hand resting on the side of her hip. I found it hard to believe we just ended up this way in our sleep, but how else could it have happened?

I lifted my other arm, propping it up behind my head so I could see her easily. Her eyes moved under her closed lids as she slept, dark eyelashes occasionally twitching. She sucked in a deep breath and stirred, her arm holding me tighter, but she didn't wake.

Taking in the details of her face, I struggled to remember the past day or two. Last night I felt better, more lucid than before. I felt good enough to shower and walk around a bit. Before that was a lot of feeling awful with hazy memories. I was either freezing or sweating my balls off. Thirsty, hungry, and weak, but unable to keep anything in my stomach. My body felt fatigued and stiff, like I wanted to sleep for weeks, but then I was too hot, cold, or nauseous to sleep.

Physically I felt miserable. I had no idea if I was sick for weeks or mere days. But for the first time ever, I had no fear of dying alone and discarded while being sick. Because Mariposa was always there.

Through the feverish haze, her face was the only thing I saw clearly. It might have been real or hallucinated, but I sometimes heard her voice telling me I was safe and okay. Once in a while I felt her hands holding mine and her lips on my forehead. That had to be just the fever dreams, but even so, I knew she would heal me. Even at a subconscious level, I knew she was safe, capable, and cared about me to some extent.

Looking at her now, her body glued to my side and resting on me so sweetly, I didn't just feel healed from the infection. This trip, this time we got to spend together, made me feel like something deeper inside had healed. Where there was once anxiety and shame, I now felt warmth and ease.

I was still fucked up. I would never be the same as other people. But a small something within me had shifted. My past didn't have the power over me it once had.

Mariposa sighed and began stirring some more. I lifted my arm away to give her space to move. Her cheek dragged along my chest, lips brushing my skin as she pulled herself away. That sensation, along with her hand sliding across my stomach, hit me with a rush of heat and desire. I wanted to draw her back into my side and taste how those lips felt on my own.

"Morning." Mari rubbed her eyes as she rolled to the center of the bed.

"Good morning."

She smiled groggily and warmth bloomed in my chest. Saying good morning became our daily ritual. She used to force it on me, saying it when I dreaded hearing the words because I was expected to answer back. When I finally did answer, she never stopped. Eventually I looked forward to seeing her, to having the opportunity to say two insignificant words to her. It was never insignificant to me, and I wondered if she knew that.

I just then noticed Jandro sleeping on his stomach on the far side of the bed. *Oh yeah, he got here yesterday too.* He accumulated some serious scars of his own, from the burns on his back. And yet Mari still loved him...

Don't start wishing for that. Be satisfied with what you have already.

"How do you feel?" She sat up and stretched, exposing a sliver of belly under the hem of her sleeping shirt.

"Better." My stomach protested loudly. "Hungry."

She grinned, scooting toward the foot of the bed. "I was hoping to hear you say that. Let's start you with soup, then see about introducing solid food."

While my soup heated on the hotplate, she checked my temperature and other vitals. "Fever's gone," she reported, then picked up her stethoscope. "Breathe for me." She pressed the dial to my chest and I looked down at her fingers so close to my skin. "Your resting heartbeat sounds back to normal. Lean forward for me." Once I did, she took one glance at my back and let out a soft gasp. "I guess I shouldn't be surprised," she muttered. "All signs of infection are gone and the arrow wounds are closing up beautifully. If you're feeling up to it, I don't see why you couldn't ride home today."

"Really?" I started looking at her, then four points of soft pressure on my legs drew my gaze down. "Good morning, Freyja." The cat chirped as she walked up my thighs, purring hard when I went to scratch the side of her face.

"She never left your side." Mari gave an affectionate scratch at the base of the cat's tail.

"Neither did you." I returned my gaze to the stunning woman sitting next to me, the healer of not just my body, but the toxic parts of my soul I once thought were beyond repair. "Thank you, Mari. For everything you've done for me."

Her smile was lighthearted, but the air between us felt tense and heavy. "I'm just so glad you're better. I hated seeing you so unwell." She looked down from my face, eyes traveling slowly down my torso.

It only hit me then how exposed I was. Sunlight poured in through the windows, so she could see *everything*.

I'd felt self-conscious of my scars before, but never like this. Every doubt I thought I'd conquered fought and clawed its way back to the forefront of my mind. She was kind enough to not treat me like a freak, but I'd always be something *other*, a curiosity. It didn't matter that our bodies found each other during sleep and seemed to fit so well. In her eyes, I'd never be held in the same regard as her men.

And that hurt me more than I ever expected.

I wanted to wipe my skin clean, to erase everything that designated me as *other*, just to have her look at me the same way she saw them. But I was helpless to alter the past that left its marks permanently on me. In that moment, all I could do was find a shirt to put on.

Mariposa blinked, her cheeks flushing a delicate pink as her gaze returned to my face. "I'll check your soup." She stood abruptly. "Watch out for Jandro. He's rolling toward you and will try to smother you with cuddles."

I decided to stand too, much to Freyja's dismay, but it was funny to watch Jandro roll completely off of the bed to the floor.

"Fuckers." He rubbed his face, grumbling at Mari's cackles.

"We need to set up guardrails for you," she cooed.

"You know I can't be near an edge. Usually you or Gunner is there to stop me."

Mari wouldn't let me have solid food until I finished all of my soup. Once she was satisfied, she had Jandro bring up toast, eggs, and bacon from the kitchen.

"Don't eat too fast or you'll feel sick again," she warned me.

"It's so cute to see you fussing over him," Jandro teased her over his coffee.

She glared daggers at him, but otherwise didn't respond.

T-Bone, Grudge, and Larkan joined us for breakfast a bit later. The moment I saw Grudge, a strange urge pulled in my chest, which I ultimately decided not to question. I went up to him and pulled the silent man into a hug.

"Thank you," I muttered. "For helping Mari, and for giving me your blood." He looked stunned when I pulled away, and I was sure everyone in the room looked the same. Shit, maybe that was the wrong thing to do?

"Don't get used to that." I brushed it off with a wave of my hand and went to return to my food. But Grudge's chuckling laugh escaped and he thumped me on the back.

Once everyone finished breakfast, it was clear we all had one thing on our minds—heading home.

"You owe for the paint you scraped off in your spill," Jandro jabbed my arm. "Lucky for you, nothing was badly damaged. Your bike just looks ugly now."

"Yeah, yeah. I'll pay you back for the paint." I downed the rest of my coffee, eager to feel the speed and power of my machine under me again.

"Do you hear this shit?" Jandro was pointing at me, but looking at Mari and the Sons. "'*Yeah, yeah*'? Dude hit his head and woke up with Reaper's fucking attitude. Mari, bring the old Shadow back. We don't need two Reapers."

Mari nearly choked on her own coffee. "It's not his fault you become an uptight dad when it comes to taking care of their bikes."

"An uptight dad?! *Dios mio*, you're supposed to be on my side."

"I am, I just love giving you a hard time." She grabbed his jaw to kiss him, and an odd sensation stirred in my chest.

It felt sharp, like how I remembered pain felt when I was being cut. But it wasn't because she was kissing *him*. I'd seen her being affectionate with her men plenty of times before. Maybe it was just cementing in the knowledge that she'd never see me that way.

Thankfully, T-Bone seemed just as antsy as me to hit the road. As Mari and Jandro joked and dawdled, he collected our dishes to return to the kitchen downstairs. "Meet you all in the garage," he called on his way down.

I collected my few belongings and followed after him.

The open road and my bike felt like the final pieces of healing that I needed to be one-hundred percent better. Once I settled into my seat and felt the rumble of the engine beneath me, I remembered how I felt *more* than human while riding, not sub-human. The motorcycle became an extension of me, carrying me with speed and strength no one had with just two legs. And when we pulled into Four Corners at the end of a long day of riding, I was elated to be seeing a sunset again.

As we pulled up to the B&B and parked, I felt the desire to point out the sky to Mari, to just watch and enjoy it with her. Maybe, like with the Night-Blooming Cereus, share for the first time why they were important to me. But she was already off in search of her men.

"You're back!"

I turned to see Dyno walk up, clapping T-Bone and Grudge in a three-way hug. The three of them kissed and muttered affectionate words to each other, while I busied myself with removing my saddlebags from my bike.

"Shadow!"

I looked up. "Yes?"

"Come have a drink with us." Dyno tilted his head toward the bar up the street. "Since the other Demons are busy, you can hear updates first." He waggled his eyebrows. "It's official business from the governor. Trust me, you want to hear it."

"Uh, okay." I had nothing better to do, and rather than fatigued from the ride, I felt amped up and energized.

I set my things in my room, then returned outside to follow the Sons to the bar. Dyno seemed completely unable to wait until we were actually sitting and drinking to start talking.

"You got anything nice to wear, big guy?" He faced me, walking backwards down the sidewalk. "And I don't mean like, nice leathers, but *nice*. Fancy shit like a suit or something."

A sense of dread crept over me. "Do I look like I do?"

"Didn't think so," he laughed. "It's all good, I was just curious. Vance has tailors and seamstresses and shit, though they'll probably need a whole bolt of cloth for you."

"What exactly would these things be needed for?"

We reached the front porch of the bar. Dyno grabbed the door and held it open for us as he explained.

"The governor's throwing a dinner party in honor of us bringing his daughter back safely. It's gonna be one of those big, grand ballroom type of things. Dignitaries and officials from allied territories will be there. Other important assholes, I dunno. Yo, a bottle of whiskey! Shadow, what're you drinking?"

"Um, whiskey's fine."

Dyno slapped my chest as we made our way to a table. "We're heroes now, dude! Aren't you stoked?"

"What are we supposed to do at parties like this?" I asked. "I barely know how to be around people as it is."

"Relax, man." T-Bone had his arm around Grudge's shoulders, tangling his fingers in the silent man's long hair. "You're around people right now. Hell, you're hanging out with *us*! And you barely know us compared to the rest of your crew."

"I like you guys better than some of the Demons," I admitted. "And I can be in places like this," I gestured around me to the bar, "without much issue. It's ballrooms and important people who are complete strangers that I'm unsure about."

"Important people are just like normal people." Dyno pulled an empty chair over and stretched his legs over it. "Although, we might get a lot of weird questions from these fucking politicians because they know jack shit about our lives."

"They want to live vicariously through us," T-Bone smirked. "Like all we do is ride and fuck chicks. It's no big deal, Shadow. Just wear the fancy threads, drink the good shit, smoke the Cubans, and enjoy yourself."

"I'll try."

The whiskey bottle placed on our table called out to me to finish it, to numb the anxiety and retreat into the dark recesses of my mind. I knew if I did, I'd find another bottle and finish that one too. And then maybe another, however many it took to wrap myself in that protective layer of numbness.

But now I felt stronger in ignoring that seductive call. I managed to challenge myself before, when I trusted Mari to cut the arrows out of me. I hadn't felt that scared in years, and for a moment, thought I might not survive it. But I did.

I was changing. The meek, silent man who once clung to Jandro as his only friend was someone I didn't recognize anymore. Now I could hang out in a bar with other guys, hug a woman I cared about, and talk to her without issue.

When looking at it that way, a dinner party no longer sounded like the worst thing in the world.

I might even survive it.

GUNNER

They looked like ants marching through the dust, but we knew it was them. I urged Horus to fly closer, just to make sure.

He sailed overhead, the details of the riders becoming clearer as he approached. There was no mistaking Jandro's tricked out ride in the middle of the pack, or Mari wrapped around his waist. Shadow rode a few bike lengths behind them, while T-Bone, Grudge, and Larkan guarded the front.

My human body was moving before my consciousness slipped back into it, and I nearly tumbled over the small table.

"Watch it, bird brain," Reaper growled.

"They're heading back," I said. "Maybe three miles out."

He looked up from his maps. "All of them?"

"Yeah, everyone."

The president slammed his palms victoriously on the wood surface as he stood up. "Fucking finally."

It felt like they took three hundred hours to travel three miles. We stood anxiously outside of the B&B, our temporary home, while the roars of their bikes grew steadily closer.

My heart went nuts at the sight of them with my human eyes coming down the street. I bounced on my toes, eager to see my woman's smile and taste her kiss again. Reaper stood like a monument next to me, his emotions on a tightly-held leash.

When Jandro pulled up and Mari threw her leg over the bike, Reap was on her in a flash. Her helmet went crashing to the ground as he shoved it off her head and grabbed her nape for a rough kiss.

"Lark, Shadow." I nodded at our guys who were also dismounting. "Glad to see y'all back in one piece."

"Glad to be back." Larkan looked around, in search of Noelle most likely. "That territory was fucking weird."

I looked back at Reaper, still wrapped around Mari and playing tonsil-hockey with her like they were in their own little universe. Jandro saw me and laughed. "Give them a few seconds. He deprived her, remember?"

"Yeah, and whose fucking fault is that?" I crossed my arms.

Mari finally came up for air and looked at me, a dreamy smile on her face that made my heart leap. "Gunner!" Thankfully, Reaper released his hold and allowed her to come over to me.

"Baby girl."

I took her face in my hands and kissed her sweetly at first, but that single taste awakened just how badly I missed her. I pulled her sweet curves flush to me and devoured her mouth just as Reaper did.

"Never leave us again." The taste of Reaper's cloves and whiskey on her dissolved quickly, and my tongue found her sweet, feminine flavor underneath.

"I won't." She pulled at my shirt, nails scraping over fabric and skin as she devoured me just as hungrily.

A growl ripped from my throat as she nipped my neck, hands roaming under my shirt shamelessly. Meeting Reaper's eyes over her head, I knew we had to be briefed on what happened, but fuck it. Everyone was home and alive. It could wait.

Reaper walked up behind Mari, pinning her against me with his own body against her back. Dragging his fingers through her hair, he raked the dark strands away from her ear to growl, "Inside." Then he nipped at her earlobe and released her.

He didn't have to tell me twice. I pulled her by the hand to our room in the B&B, leaving it open for him and Jandro before I lifted her up. Knowing where I was headed, she wrapped her legs around my waist, arms around my shoulders.

"Fuck, I missed you." She let out a soft gasp when I pressed her back to a wall.

"Baby girl." With my hips anchoring her to the wall, my freed hands roamed my woman's gorgeous body. "You're about to find out *exactly* just how much I missed you."

I got her topless before the other two got there, Jandro nearly tripping on her discarded bra before he locked the door with a definitive click. "Remember to share, Gun," he smirked.

"Whatever, asshole."

I was too busy remembering how many tongue licks was the length of Mari's neck. And how far my hands slid up her ribs until her perfect tits filled my palms. My cock ached as it rubbed against her spread-open center. I could feel the heat from her there and it drove me fucking wild. Before she became mine, I hadn't fucked anyone in months. Now, I could barely go three days without her before turning into a rutting animal.

Mari's feet slowly touched to the floor and the other guys were on her like animals themselves, diving in to consume her. She shrieked with laughter as Reaper tossed her over his shoulder and onto the bed, swiftly removing her boots, and stripping her jeans and panties from those long legs. He wasted no time in pulling her thighs apart and diving in to give her sweet cunt a long, sucking kiss.

"Fuck." I palmed my cock through my jeans, trying to ease some pressure as I watched her thrash under his tongue. Jandro started tearing his clothes off and so did I.

He crawled on the bed toward her head, sliding a thigh under her head for support as he caressed down her body. Already panting, Mari had one hand on the back of Reaper's head between her legs, the other reaching up to find Jandro. He held her wrist, kissing her palm, when her gaze found me with a lazy smile.

"Don't tell me you're going to sit back and watch," she breathed, before shuddering as Reaper slid a finger into her.

"Not a chance," I grinned back, heading for the nightstand. She watched as I pulled the drawer open and took out the bottle of lube and toy we used last time.

"I don't want that this time," she panted, thighs clamped around Reaper's head.

I lifted an eyebrow, stroking down my length with an idle hand. "You don't want anything back there at all, or...?"

"No, I do." Her lips parted with breathy moans, tongue darted out to wet her lips as she watched me touch myself. She wanted me so bad and it was so fucking hot to see. "I want you. All of you."

Reaper released a long moan, his mouth still fixated to her pussy. He kept one hand clamped down on her waist, the other busy below his own waist to free his cock.

"You sure about that, baby girl?" I picked up the plug and held it next to my shaft. "You did good with this last time, but there's still a size difference."

"Quit showing off, bird boy." Jandro leaned over her to pull a pert nipple into his mouth, then released it with a loud sucking noise. "We all know you'll make it good for her, so get your ass over here." His lips wandered over her breasts and sternum as he spoke, hands following closely behind.

"Well if Reaper ever stops hogging her down there, who knows if I'll get the chance." I walked around the bed, tossing the lube in the air once before crawling to the other side of her. I brushed off Jandro's remark, but internally I swelled with pride. My biggest hesitation about being Mari's was not knowing where I'd fit, not knowing how or where she needed me. Now that I knew, I was going to put my heart and soul into giving her exactly what she saw in me—feeling safe and secure, especially in the face of doing something scary or new.

Jandro shifted to the side, kissing down her shoulder and left breast to make room for me. Mari turned her head, kissing me eagerly with soft pants and whimpers that grew increasingly desperate for release. Reaper took his time with her orgasm for once, eyes closed and savoring her, dining on her pussy like it was the finest meal he'd eaten in his life.

I ran my fingertips over the swell of her breast, dragging over her nipple and ghosting a feather-light touch on the underside. When she turned her head to kiss Jandro, I traced over the same movement with my tongue. The VP and I made a game of it, alternating who kissed her lips and her luscious body.

She was quivering on the razor's edge of release for minutes before Reaper finally sent her there with a vicious tongue-lashing. Her hands curled into my hair, nails raking across my scalp while Jandro smothered her cries with kisses. Reaper licked her through the crest of her pleasure and the aftershocks before he finally sat up, lower jaw coated her in arousal as he pulled his clothes off to join the pile on the floor.

"My turn," I announced, sliding down toward her legs. "You guys sit back."

"Gunner, I need a minute," she panted, limp like a noodle when I rolled her to her stomach.

"Don't worry, baby girl." I propped her up until she was on her hands and knees. "I'm just gonna play with you 'til you're ready to come again."

She was so wet, pink, and pretty with her ass in the air. Knowing how sensitive she was, I resisted the urge to take a long lick up her entire slit. Instead, I smacked both palms on her ass, making her jump as she took Jandro and Reaper's cocks in each fist.

"Don't distract her too much." Reaper's growl turned into a low purr, running a hand along her neck and upper back as she stroked him.

"Just getting her warmed up for the fun part," I promised, massaging down the backs of her thighs.

"I'm already having fun," Mari giggled, before her lips made soft sucking and kissing noises.

Jandro groaned, leaning his head back until it met the headboard.

"Baby girl." I brought my mouth even closer to her delectable pussy, knowing she could feel my breath on her tender flesh as I spoke. "We've barely gotten started on your fun."

Running my hands over her ass and thighs, I began with just kissing around her swollen lips, lapping up her sweet nectar without touching her directly. Already, she deepened the arch in her spine, pressing back into my face for more. I grinned against her flesh, and sucked a hard kiss right where her thigh met her butt cheek.

"Fuck." Reaper smacked his head back on the headboard now, while

Jandro took in deep, ragged breaths. Both of their eyes fixated on Mari, hands touching her anywhere they could.

I brought my mouth to her pussy, taking light sucks and kisses of her lips while avoiding her clit. Moving my hands to her lower back, I massaged lightly and moved down until my thumb grazed the tight ring of muscles.

"Mmm!" Her mouth was full of someone—Reaper, by the looks of it, but her reaction to me was immediate.

She wiggled her hips, pressing back eagerly into my face, and my dick flexed with need. She wanted *me* back there, where she never had anyone else before. I couldn't get over the high that she trusted me so completely, to ensure she'd enjoy it and not make it painful. Another part of me reveled in the fact that she chose me to do something more dirty and taboo.

I'd always been the sunny, good-natured, smiling guy. Chicks always went to Jandro or Reaper if they wanted something more depraved. So knowing Mari not only trusted me, but saw me as capable for things like this was an amazing fucking feeling.

Dipping my tongue into her pussy, I felt around on the bed until I found the bottle of lube. I flipped the cap open with my hand and poured a generous amount directly over her ass. Massaging the slippery liquid all around her hole until my fingers were coated, I started inserting them one by one, always pausing to gauge her reaction.

Once I was up to three and started moving them in and out, she came up gasping for air, both hands still working the others' cocks.

"How is that, baby girl?" I sat up, pouring more lube over my fingers as I worked them in and out of her ass, then pressed a kiss to her back.

"It's...a lot." She lowered her head with a sigh, resting her cheek on Reaper's lap.

"Want me to stop? Or back off?"

"No, just keep doing that. It doesn't hurt, it's just intense."

I dragged my other hand over her pussy, finally coming to that hard little pleasure button of hers. Separating two fingers, I slid them back and forth on either side of her clit. "How's this?"

Her head threw back and a shuddering moan escaped her, the reaction making me grin like a madman. Reaper smiled down at her too, watching her fingers curl into his thigh and her eyes pinch shut as she rocked back on both of my hands.

"Gonna come for us again, sugar?" He stroked her face tenderly. "Gonna get yourself all nice and relaxed so you can take one of your men in your ass?"

Her thighs quivered with the effort of staying up and I knew she was close. I kept my hand on her pussy still, letting her rock back between my fingers to get what she needed. My other fingers kept stroking in and out of her ass, getting the muscles stretched and used to having something back there.

"Holy fuck, you're so perfect," Jandro moaned. She had returned to him, head bobbing and slurping loudly as his hands tangled in her hair.

I dipped my face between my hands, desperate for another taste as she grew wetter from her approaching orgasm. Her pussy was so sweet, I could never blame Reaper for taking his time down here. She rocked harder between my fingers, her muffled moans with her stuffed mouth still reaching the ceiling.

She came with shudders wracking all over her body, her knees giving out beneath her. I followed her down to the mattress, my fingers still stroking the inside of her ass while my mouth chased her pussy for a taste of her orgasm. She ground against my hand, now flat against the mattress as I licked her.

I pulled both hands away from her then, just to give her a break from all the sensations while she caught her breath. But I couldn't stop touching her completely, and laid alongside her to plant kisses down her spine.

"Hmm hi, love." She gave me a dreamy smile, eyes all hazy from pleasure as she touched my face.

"Hi, baby girl," I grinned back, scooting closer to reach her lips. "I love you."

"Love you." Mari returned my kiss, warm and sweet, before pushing up to her hands. She crawled to Reaper and leaned in to kiss him. "Love you." He tried to hold her there for longer, but she leaned over to kiss Jandro next. "And I love you."

His flushed skin and giddy smile echoed what we were all feeling.

She loved all of us, and we felt it, as sure as we felt this bed beneath us. Nothing about this was disjointed or unfair. This one woman somehow made three bikers want to please, satisfy, and hear those words from her like it was all that mattered. She was incredible for that alone, and for so much more.

"You're our world, sugar." Reaper cupped her chin and pulled her back to him, love and adoration in his eyes. "Don't leave us again."

"Never." She accepted his demanding kisses this time, melting into him as he pulled her forward until she was straddling his lap.

He moaned into her mouth, hands digging into her ass as she rolled forward. Her pussy dragged along his length, leaving a trail of wetness from base to tip. I spotted her wicked smile as she pulled back to tease him with no entry.

"Sugar," he growled a low warning.

She finally paused, her entrance hovering over him. Still, he wrapped an arm around her waist, crushing her to his chest so she wouldn't move, then surged up to impale her.

"Oh, fucking god, I missed that..." He caged her in with both arms, forehead on her shoulder as he pressed into her with long strokes. Her arms went around his neck, mouth against his ear with her soft whimpers.

This looked intimate, something between only them. Jandro and I hung back, giving them space for a few moments, until Mari looked over her shoulder at me.

"Come here, Gun."

I scooted forward, running a hand down her back as Reaper's hold on her loosened. She turned to Jandro then, pulling a deep kiss from his mouth before kissing down his chest.

My fingers trailed down the cleft of her ass, circling her tight hole. "Still want this, baby girl?"

"Mm-hm..." Her mouth was stuffed with Jandro's cock again, a hypnotizing sight, better than any porn film.

Reaper paused in his thrusts and slid down the bed, allowing me better access as I placed a knee on either side of Mari's feet. I lubed up my cock first, letting the head rest on her ass while I stroked the slippery liquid up and down my length. Her eyes were on me as she took long sucks of Jandro.

"Feel this first, babe." I reinserted my slick fingers in her ass, earning a moan from her as she began to move on my hand with Reaper inside her pussy.

"Mm, you feel tighter." His hands swept forward and I heard the wet sucking sounds of his mouth on her nipples. "But I bet you want more, don't you?"

"Mm-hm." She illustrated this by pushing back harder on my fingers.

I chuckled, pulling my hand away and resting my cock head on the same place. "Who am I to deny our girl what she wants?"

With a hand on her lower back to steady her, I poured more lube on her ass and my head, then began pressing through her tight entrance. A few inches in, she released Jandro from her mouth with a gasp.

"Oh god, that's..."

"Breathe, sugar. Relax."

I added more lube, pulled back until I was nearly out, then slowly pressed forward again. She hissed in a breath and shut her eyes tight, hands balling into fists in the sheets.

"Talk to me." I leaned over her back and brushed kisses over her shoulder blades. "Good, bad? Pain or no pain?"

"Just...a lot." Her eyes cracked open at me. "It's intense. I feel so full."

"You are." Reaper kissed her. "Full of your men's cocks."

"Not *all* of them," Jandro smirked. His cock laid across his lower stomach, slick with her saliva.

"Easy, 'Dro. Give her a minute."

"I know, I'm just correcting your statement."

"Move on us if you feel like it." I kept smoothing my hands up and down her back, planting kisses on her spine and shoulders. "We'll stay still. You take what you need."

She wrapped so tightly around me, all my baser instincts urged me to move, to thrust and feel the grip of her body send pleasure through my dick. But she chose me for this because keeping her safe and unafraid was my number one priority.

A tightening of pressure made me hiss in a breath, but I kept still. Only my hands moved across her skin, reminding her I was here. I realized it was Reaper rubbing her clit, making her pussy flutter and respond to his touch. I felt the same response in her ass and it was incredible, almost making me forget where I was.

As Reaper coaxed another orgasm out of her, she did start moving. I sank my teeth into my lip, holding my breath as her twitches and movements of pleasure shot heat and intensity down the length of my dick. I wondered if this was what she feeling—so much, but so fucking good.

Gradually she made her movements bigger, riding Reaper as she pressed back onto me. I felt his cock move through her and it was fucking wild. From the look on his face, he felt her more intensely too, and like me, was struggling to keep his control on a leash.

When she leaned over to take Jandro back into her mouth, Reaper and I took over. We found it easiest to alternate our thrusts—as he sank into her pussy, I pulled out of her ass. It was fucking surreal, almost like I wasn't really there, but in someone else's body, watching. But how incredible she felt every time I slid back in was a hot dose of reality.

This was my life, pleasing and protecting this woman with two other men, in a world where others would use and discard her.

I leaned over until my forehead touched the tattoo on her back, the one that matched mine. Lost in the rhythmic, mounting pleasure, my body felt weightless. She grounded me, kept me right where I wanted to be.

"You feel amazing," I rasped on her shoulder.

"Fuck yeah, she does." Reaper watched her with rapt attention, and I knew he was just as concerned about her pleasure and comfort level as me. His green eyes were hooded, fixated on her like she was the drug we needed to feel an ounce of anything good.

Mari matched us in our movements now, her sweet ass bouncing off my hip bones as we crashed together, slamming down on Reaper as he drove up into her, and stroking Jandro into ecstasy with her mouth and fist.

It was amazing to watch and feel. We all came at her from different angles and positions and, with just a bit of adjusting, she took it all like she was made to be shared by us.

The pleasure was taking full control of me now, filling every pore in my body with a delicious ache. Every movement through her, every sound she made, and even hearing the other guys moan, loosened the threads of my control and I drove harder, deeper into her ass to chase it.

She got louder, her holes squeezing around us as Reaper sped up to match me.

"Oh fuck, that's so hot." Jandro squirmed as he watched, his body under the mercy of her mouth. "Fuck her good, guys."

Her moans turned to long, drawn out whimpers as Reaper and I drove into her again and again. I tried to listen carefully through the pulse pounding in my ears for any sounds of pain, but she rode us just as hard as we did her. Her hands clamped down on Jandro's thighs as she took him down her throat. I grinned at the sight of our greedy, dirty, perfect girl. The pleasure, the heat, the sensations of us filling every one of her holes was possessing her too.

"Oh, come for us, sugar."

Reaper's voice was barely more than a raspy whisper, like he smoked a whole pack of cloves in an hour. Sweat slicked across his skin from effort and restraint. He felt for her clit again, strumming it with a barely-controlled frenzy to get her off before we did.

She let out her loudest whimper yet before her ass closed around my length like a vice. Judging from Reaper's strangled moan, her pussy did the same to him.

"Fuck! Fuckkk…"

It took every last drop of my remaining control to fuck her through her orgasm, her ass pulsing with the tight convulsions that wracked her whole body. I couldn't hold out through her aftershocks though, and pleasure zapped through my whole lower body as I spilled violently into her. Through the thin wall separating us, I felt Reaper empty into her too, sending another jolt of sensitivity throughout my whole body.

We slid out of her with slow care just as she lapped up Jandro's release, licking the panting man's cock like an ice cream cone.

I fell to my side on the bed, utterly spent and blissed out. Mari stretched out long between me and Reaper like she was just waking up from a nap.

"How was that, baby girl?" I skimmed my fingertips down the side of her body, still helpless to keep myself from touching her.

"Intense," she breathed with a bright smile. She looked ready to face the day, save more lives, maybe. "But so, *so* good."

"Worth repeating?" Reaper kissed her shoulder, a wolfish grin on his face. "With me in your ass next time?"

"I'll fight you for that, Reap." Jandro moved around our stretched-out legs to rest his head on Mari's lap, his usual spot.

She smiled lazily, running her fingers over Jandro's scalp. "I just love feeling all of you at the same time. It really solidifies how good we all are. Together."

Reaper kissed her first, then Jandro slid up to take his kiss from her, and then finally me. I held her chin between my fingers as I sipped love and affection from that beautiful mouth.

It was wordless agreement from all of us, because the way she said it was perfect. There were no more words to accurately describe the feeling as we snuggled in closer to her on all sides. Contentment settled over me as I closed my eyes and just sank into this feeling.

Together. Us.

MARIPOSA

"You couldn't have told me *before* our crazy sexathon?" I huffed, rubbing the towel over my wet hair.

I wasn't really upset, though. I just didn't expect to attend a fancy dinner party in the company of the governor, while still feeling the ache of all my men inside every part of me.

"Really, *bonita*." Jandro hugged me from behind, smacking a kiss on the crook of my neck. "When it comes to you, or being in a room full of peacocking politicians, where do you think our priorities lie?"

"Well, at least I got to soak in a long bath before the tailors came looking for us."

I turned to the dress hanging on the bathroom door. It wasn't quite a ballgown, more like a knee-length cocktail dress that hugged my form. Still, it was finer than anything I'd worn in years, maybe ever.

Governor Vance's tailors balked when I asked for the back to be open, but with my insistence, they made it work beautifully. Running my hand over the silky material, I smiled inwardly at the thought of all these politicians and dignitaries seeing a biker gang's tattoo on a woman in an expensive dress. We were honored guests and undoubtedly expected to play nice for the evening, but the tattoo would serve as an important reminder.

MC women had to be just as strong as their men to survive, albeit in different ways. I earned my tattoo, just like the men did. Hopefully it would remind the governor and his associates that outside his world, where women were little more than dolls to be dressed up and traded around, there were others like me who weren't so helpless.

Now, we were in his home by invitation. Our working relationship was off to a good start, but it wouldn't take much for our completely opposing worlds to clash. We would show him respect, but he had to return that same courtesy. Tattooed women and all.

I had to hand it to Vance's tailoring staff. Reaper and Gun told me about the dinner party after our sexathon, then a well-organized team of people with garment bags, measuring tape, bolts of cloth, and fabric shears knocked at our door. They got us fitted into semi-formal clothes that slid on like gloves within hours, before moving on to the rest of the party.

I thought I heard protests from Shadow's room as they measured and fitted him, but tried to keep my excitement in check. A party like this seemed like it was absolutely *not* his thing, but I really wanted to see him in a suit.

Once my hair was dry enough, I took the dress off the hanger and stepped into it. The built-in bra was snug and supportive without being too restricting. Reaper had looked like he wanted to murder the seamstress who measured my chest, but I was glad they sewed this in. It accentuated my shape nicely, and allowed my back to be completely bare without a bra strap ruining the look.

The guys wore slim-fitting slacks that paired well with their riding boots, and white button up shirts tucked in. They picked out blazer jackets to wear, but chose to forgo ties. Jandro was already undoing the top buttons on his shirt and pushing his sleeves up.

"Okay, as hot as you look like that," I folded his collar down and pressed it smooth, "this is a look for after the party, not before or during."

"I'm just making it easier for you to rip it all off me later." He ran his hands down my sides and took a step back. "Jesus, you're so fucking stunning."

Reaper came over from getting himself situated in the mirror. He had the top buttons undone too, teasing a bit of the ink under his neck, but he at least kept his sleeves intact. "I fucking swear, sugar, you're making it even more tempting to skip this whole thing."

"Not fucking happening." I imitated his tone, enjoying his smirk as I came over to run my fingers over the exposed skin of his throat. "You need this time with Vance, president. To have his attention as an equal, for the wellbeing of your club."

"It doesn't matter what I say, Mrs. President." He ran a hand along my side, following my waist to my ass. "With you on my arm, I know exactly where his attention will be."

"I'm sure we can steal her away to prevent any distractions." Gunner walked up to check himself in the mirror, looking dapper as hell. He'd shaved, and brushed his hair back neatly so it fell to his collar in soft, uniform waves. Not only were his shirt buttons and sleeves intact, but he even added a pocket square to his blazer. Rather than his engineer boots, he wore a pair of polished brown loafers.

In his usual biker getup, it was easy to forget he came from money. But right then, he looked every bit the polished, private academy graduate. The others noticed too.

"You clean up nice, Gun." Jandro reached out like he was going to mess up Gunner's hair, but the blond demon shot him a scathing look.

"All of you do." I placed Gunner's earrings in my lobes, then adjusted Jandro's necklace at my throat. Reaper's ring sparkled under the bathroom lights as I finished touching myself up. "I'm going to be the luckiest woman at this party."

"These stuffy old farts aren't gonna know what hit 'em." Gunner slid an arm around my waist and placed a delicate kiss on my earlobe.

"Are we ready to go and get this over with?" Reaper hovered impatiently by the door. "They said the governor would send a car."

The guys spilled out into the B&B lobby, while I hurried to finish setting my make up. I heard the familiar voices of Larkan and Noelle floating in, then my heart jumped at the sound of Shadow's low rumble.

He's coming too! Be normal. Act natural.

What was natural and normal with him anymore? Treating him with polite distance? Hugging him or kissing his cheek? With closer friendliness, like with the Sons of Odin now? Something shifted between us since the rescue mission, and Jandro spoke aloud of what I tried and failed to shove down.

I wanted him. I wanted to sit and talk with him just as badly as I wanted to curl into that huge, strong body. I wanted to help him face his fears, to feel his strength like an impenetrable shield. I wanted him to know how amazing love could feel.

My whole body thrummed with nerves as I forced myself to quit stalling. I shoved some items into a clutch purse, made a final check of my hair and teeth, then headed for the door.

The tailoring staff politely informed us that animals would not be allowed at the party, so I gave Hades, Freyja, and Horus final pets before leaving the room. If I wasn't already nervous enough, I turned out to be the last one ready. Everyone stopped chatting to turn and look at me.

"Holy shit, girl!" Noelle held her arms out. She wore a simple, but elegant, white toga-style dress that made her red hair and colorful tattoos pop. "Are you ever not fucking stunning?"

My face reddened as she leaned in to kiss my cheek. "Thanks, Nellie."

She held tightly on to my arms, her lips lingering near my ear. "Thanks for watching out for my man," she whispered. "I knew he'd be in good hands with you."

I returned her affectionate squeeze. "He watched out for me. He's a true Demon and you should be proud."

She released me with a beaming smile, returning to Larkan's side as he slid a possessive arm around her shoulders. They looked as adorable as ever, but my gaze slid over to the largest man standing with us.

Shadow's broad chest and arms filled out his suit in a way that made my knees buckle. His slacks could barely contain his muscular thighs, and if he turned around, I'm sure the same would go for his ass. Like Gunner, his hair had been brushed back and fell over his shoulders in soft waves. He'd clearly run his fingers through it, as evident by the strands pulled forward to cover the scarred side of his face.

He looked uneasy, and completely out of his element. But none of that took away from the fact that he just looked wildly masculine and beautiful. He would be even more irresistible if he didn't see himself as so ugly and unworthy.

I made a decision right then. Jandro knew, so the other guys had to as well, to some extent. If Shadow didn't know, I hoped it would be made clear to him soon.

With a smile, I crossed our small circle to Shadow's side. "You look so handsome." Even in heels, I had to stand on tiptoe to reach his face. Slowly, to not catch him off guard, I brushed away a strand of dark hair to kiss the scar on his cheek.

Everyone's eyes felt heavy on my back, but I ignored them, stepping back after the brief kiss to give Shadow space.

"Um, thank you." He looked equal parts stunned, confused and terrified. "You look...very nice."

"Thank you." I put him on the spot, so I didn't expect to get a compliment back. I just wanted him to know what I saw when I looked at him.

Reaper's dry chuckle rumbled in my ear, followed by his firm hand on my lower back. "Ready, sugar?"

I nodded, following his lead out to the front porch.

Two large black SUVs waited for us, Governor Vance's staff wearing dark suits as they held the doors open. The short drive took us into the heart of Four Corners. I thought at first that the event would be at Vance's cabin home, but our rides pulled up to a sprawling pre-Collapse building in the middle of the city.

The driver opened our door, with Reaper taking my hand as he stepped out. Jandro and Gunner followed, framing me protectively on all sides as we walked up the stone steps. A quick glance over my shoulder told me Shadow followed a few paces behind, as usual. More staff members pulled open heavy glass doors for us, and I could only blink in awe at the inside of the building.

The outside had been completely understated, if even unremarkable. But the inside had a beautiful dome ceiling as one big skylight, showing the early evening sky darkening above the chandeliers. Tall archways led to various spacious rooms for different functions. One was clearly a smoking lounge, another with drinks and hor d'oeuvres. Another room appeared to have a live band with a dance floor and its own private bar. The main banquet appeared to be straight ahead, and also the largest room, with a single long table elegantly set with dinnerware.

It was all very classy and clearly expensive, but was worlds different than what we saw in Blakeworth. There was a timeless, simple wealth to this place. It wasn't flashy, nor overtly trying to show off how rich the governor's family was. This place looked like anyone could dress up for a night and have a good time here. As nice as everything was, there was no clear class divide between people, and I found that comforting.

"Mari!"

I turned to see Kyrie floating elegantly through one of the archways. The fear and anxiety in her eyes was gone, only warmth shining through.

"Kyrie!" I reached out to clasp hands and kiss cheeks with her. "I barely recognized you. You look amazing."

"Yeah, damsel in distress isn't a great look on me," she laughed.

I squeezed her hands and leaned in a little closer. "You sure you're okay to be here?" I whispered. "You just got back yesterday."

She returned my hand squeezing and gave me a reassuring smile. "Trust me, I'm good. All I wanted to do was go back to my normal life, and this is exactly what that is." She laughed lightly and spread her hands. "The life of a governor's daughter isn't for everyone, but it's the normal I know."

"Fair enough." I released her hands. "But if you need anything, even just someone to talk to, let me know."

"I'll do that," she said earnestly, before her eyes drifted over the men flanking me on all sides. "Now will you, uh," she cleared her throat, nerves creeping into her voice, "introduce me to your, um, husbands?"

"Of course! Where are my manners?" I slid my left hand around Reaper's bicep, my colorful ring flashing against his jacket sleeve. "This is Reaper, president of the Steel Demons motorcycle club." I wrapped my opposite hand around Jandro's arm. "This is Jandro, vice president and mechanical genius. The pretty one standing behind me and grinning at you is Gunner, captain of the guard."

Gunner laughed lightly, my assumption obviously correct as I felt his soft kiss on the back of my hair.

"You met Larkan and Shadow," I continued. "And the gorgeous woman on Lark's arm is Noelle, my sister-in-law."

"We are not her husbands, I just pretended to be one," Larkan winked, earning a playful smack on the arm from Noelle.

"It's a pleasure meeting you, Kyrie." Reaper's voice was warm and smooth as honey. "We're glad you're back safely, and grateful to your father for allowing our stay in Four Corners."

Kyrie's eyes dropped under Reaper's heavy gaze, her cheeks flushed pink. I knew exactly what she was feeling—these men were just as hot as they were intimidating to those who didn't know them. It was the same intensity I felt the moment they burst into the Old Phoenix service center, which felt like an eternity ago.

"The pleasure is all mine." She composed herself with a bashful smile. "Mari quite literally saved my life. The Steel Demons are welcome here for as long as you choose to stay."

"We appreciate the hospitality," Jandro said charmingly.

Kyrie lifted her chin to acknowledge Shadow behind all of us. "It's good to see you feeling better, sir. I'm glad you could come."

He blinked in surprise at being noticed. "Um, thank you. Mari is the best at what she does."

Warmth filled me as I tried to keep my smile in check. I secretly loved that I wasn't the only woman to acknowledge and validate him. He might need more than just me to boost his confidence.

Kyrie's hand went to the pendant at her throat, a large tear-shaped stone with swirling colors in shades of red and white. I noticed Reaper's eyes fixated on it too. It was definitely a unique statement piece.

"Have you guys seen Dyno and the other two?" Kyrie asked as she looked around.

"They're coming, but may be a bit late." Shadow surprised everyone by answering her calmly. "Grudge needed some convincing to attend, so they're working on him."

"Well with you here, hopefully he feels better seeing a friendly face," Kyrie smiled politely at him. "Can I offer you all some drinks and appetizers? Everyone is just kind of milling about before the first course."

We followed her lead through one of the archways to one of the smaller rooms, which was still as big as the entire B&B we stayed at. I took the opportunity to poke Reaper and tease him.

"Staring at the girl's chest, were you?"

"No, her necklace," he muttered. "It's a lace agate. My mom used to have a bunch of stones just like it. Not many people wear jewelry like that and it just jostled the memory a little."

I rubbed his arm and pressed a light kiss to his shoulder. In turn, he brushed a kiss along my forehead.

The curious and heated stares began almost immediately upon walking into the room. My men subtly pressed in closer to me, my ever-vigilant shields. Gunner swept a hand along my upper back—a possessive, affectionate gesture which also exposed my tattoo. He was telling everyone, in no uncertain terms, that I was claimed.

"You must be the biker crew everyone's been talking about," a portly, older gentleman greeted with an extension of his hand.

Reaper's nostrils flared, but he accepted the handshake. "One and the same. I'm Reaper, Steel Demons president."

"Ah. Well met, R-Reaper." The man smiled uneasily. "I guess we'll find out tonight if the stories about you are tall tales or true?"

"If I'm in the mood to divulge," my husband returned coyly. "A good whiskey usually helps."

"Oh, please sir, come this way!" Another middle-aged man swept his arm toward the bar. "I promise you've never seen a whiskey selection like this. Do you care for cigars, Reaper?"

I chuckled and removed my arm from Reaper's when I saw his eyes light up. "Go on. Indulge in your smoke and booze."

"Keep close, sugar." He kissed my cheek and headed for the bar to peruse the selection.

Governor Vance's associates made more introductions and small talk with us, polite enough to not stare at me too much or ask probing questions. I struggled to remember all of their names and titles—every one was a John or a David and their titles were things like Minister of Finance and Secretary of Development. The Sons of Odin finally showed up, and the difference in Kyrie's mood was like night and day.

She nodded and listened politely to one of the older men rambling about something to her, then completely tuned out when T-Bone,

Dyno, and Grudge walked into the room. Dyno's eyes lit up at her too, then he bit his lip with a silent nod to acknowledge her. T-Bone winked at her in greeting, but seemed preoccupied with Grudge, who looked like he wanted to bolt back out into the street.

Shadow also noticed his distress, and my stomach fluttered when he went over to greet his silent friend. He didn't just protect people with his strength, but also his softness. If only he could see that in himself.

"Yes, unfortunately General Bray couldn't make it," one of the men said to Jandro, cutting into my thoughts. "His wife isn't feeling well so he stayed home to take care of her, even though they have house staff. Completely devoted husband, that one."

"As a husband should be." Jandro's arm tightened around my waist. "But we'll look forward to meeting him another time. Gunner's our strategist and I'm sure they'll have lots to talk about."

A tuxedo-clad waiter strode into the middle of the room at that moment. "If I could have everyone's attention," he projected his voice. "The first course is about to be served, if you would all follow me to the dining room."

MARIPOSA

Governor Vance waited for us at the entrance of the main dining hall. He accepted a kiss on the cheek from Kyrie before addressing me and my guys.

"President," he greeted Reaper jovially. "And Sons," he turned to T-Bone. "As my honored guests, I've marked your seats near mine at the head of the table."

"Thank you, governor. You're looking well."

Reaper followed him down the length of the long table, one hand in mine, the other holding a tumbler of whiskey. Jandro and Gunner trailed after me, while the Sons and Shadow walked up the other side of the table to sit across from us. I couldn't get over how endearing it was that Shadow stuck so close to Grudge.

"It's wonderful what restful sleep and the peace of mind of having my daughter back will do," Vance returned.

He did look much better than that sorrowful, shell of a man we first met in his cabin. His eyes were bright, and he'd just gotten a fresh shave and a haircut. He looked across the room to Kyrie, who was further down the table chatting with Larkan and Noelle. She kept sneaking glances down toward the Sons, but her father's attention had returned to my husband.

"Please, sit. Make yourselves comfortable." Vance dropped into his seat at the head of the table. "What whiskey did you select, president?"

"I like this twelve-year from, what was it?" Reaper dipped his nose in the glass. "Big Sky Distillery. Your friend told me it's the only above-board distillery running since the Collapse."

"Ah yes, still wild country up there in Montana," Vance grinned. "Not much has changed that far north."

"I hope this doesn't make you think I keep my business strictly legal," Reaper smirked.

"Wouldn't dream of it!" Vance laughed. "Working with the Sons has taught me to ask either the right questions, or none at all."

"Smart man."

The conversation paused as everyone leaned back to allow servers to place salads in front of them. My eyebrows lifted as I watched Reaper place his napkin in his lap, then reached for his salad fork. I wondered if my guys would eat like they were raised by wolves in a place like this, but it seemed I had nothing to fear.

"My daughter has taken quite a liking to you, ma'am," Vance nodded at me before his first bite of salad. "From what she tells me, you were the one who conducted the actual rescuing."

"You can call me Mari, sir. And thank you," I smiled at him. "I just had to get near her and stall for a distraction. I couldn't have gotten her out of there without the men providing firepower and muscle."

"She's being modest." T-Bone grinned from across the table. "She pulled a knife on Blake and his son, then put herself between them and Kyrie. And then they made a break for it when armed guards started shooting."

"My word." Vance leaned back in his seat, looking at Reaper. "I know things work differently in MCs, but I can't imagine sending my wife into danger. Medic or not."

"I tried to stop her," Reaper chuckled. "But we also work democratically, and I was outvoted. It's ironic that the women came out unscathed, while my best fighter nearly died."

"Ah, yes. I was told. Remind me his name?"

"Shadow, he's the big fucker—er guy, right there."

Vance leaned over his plate. "Excuse me, Shadow?"

His head jerked up from reading something on Grudge's notepad, eyes wide with confusion. "Um yes, governor?"

"A toast to you and your bravery." The governor lifted his glass, prompting everyone at the table to do the same. "The injuries you sustained on this mission were not in vain. I'm forever in the debt of the Steel Demons MC and the Sons of Odin MC for returning my only child to me safe and unharmed."

"Daaaad." Kyrie hid her face behind her hands, earning soft laughs from everyone in attendance.

"You're all heroes to Four Corners," Vance continued. "Wherever your travels may take you, you will always have a home here. Cheers!"

He turned to clink his crystal wine glass against Reaper's tumbler, the sound rippling down the table as politicians toasted and celebrated with outlaws. How often did that happen these days?

"I expect you to hold me to that, president," Vance leaned over to talk directly into Reaper's ear. "I want to assure you I'm not making empty promises as a figurehead. I'm a grateful father, who happens to have a bit of wealth and some power. Tell me what you need and I'll make it happen."

Reaper set his salad fork down and swirled the remainder of his drink, ever thoughtful and methodical. "I appreciate that, governor. First I'd like to know, are you concerned about Blakeworth declaring war on Four Corners since they see your daughter as their stolen property?"

"My general has already been informed and is preparing our troops," Vance said lightly. "I'm not especially concerned because of how quick citizens are to desert Blakeworth. I imagine we'll have plenty coming to our side once they see Four Corners as a place of refuge."

"Mari mentioned Blake may be in alliance with General Tash," Gunner jumped in. "Even if Blake's army deserts him, Tash is a force to be reckoned with. He's why we had to leave our previous home."

"I've heard stories about this man, too," Vance mused. "They call him the phantom general around here. He strikes quickly, then disappears and sends others to do his bidding, is that right?"

"Sounds like him," Gunner said. "He tried to use our club as one of his pawns, but we caught on and fought back. One of our best men died in his last attack on our home."

"My deepest condolences," Vance offered. "I'll let General Bray know about this possible alliance. He's very resourceful himself and has his own crafty methods of gathering information. It's a shame he couldn't be here tonight, he's quite the life of the party."

The next course came out, a light and delicate carrot-ginger soup that made me want to drink from my bowl. I resisted, keeping my table manners ladylike as I decided to shift the conversation.

"How is the hospital faring, governor?"

"Oh, it's always short-staffed with so few people medically qualified these days. But Dr. Brooks does the best he can. On top of being the only one trained as a surgeon, he's also running a teaching program in hopes of having more doctors available."

My heart soared at the same time Jandro squeezed my knee under the table. "I don't have a certificate to prove it, but I was trained as a labor and delivery nurse. Plus, learning things on the fly for the past three years. I'd be happy to help in any way that I can."

The governor nodded enthusiastically. "That would be brilliant! Forgive me for not suggesting it sooner. I'm afraid we've grown accustomed to women not taking initiative to such roles in recent years."

"That's all right," I smiled politely. "Maybe it can serve as a reminder to the women of Four Corners that we're capable of more."

"Indeed, indeed."

But I noticed the governor's reservation in that answer, and so did the men sitting around me.

Dyno wiped his mouth with a napkin. "Kyrie sure is born into a fortunate situation. There must be plenty of opportunities for a governor's daughter that not everyone can afford."

Vance swallowed a mouthful of soup, taking the time to choose his words carefully. "She has never wanted for material possessions, not has she had to worry about her education or safety—at least I thought so until recently." He set his spoon down in his empty bowl. "But the unfortunate reality is that there aren't many opportunities for women of any stature, no matter how well educated or financed they are. Unless, and forgive me, I don't like it, but this *is* the truth," he took a deep breath, "she marries another governor or his son to forge an alliance between the two territories."

"So we have come full-circle," T-Bone scoffed. "Back to the dark ages."

"Of course it's barbaric, but it is...the current reality," Vance sighed. "I've never pushed her to marry anyone. Frankly, I'd be happiest if she spent the rest of her days here, safe, unwed, and far away from the eyes of any men." He chuckled, elbowing Reaper. "Once you're a father, you'll understand."

"I do in a way, but my...upbringing is somewhat different from yours, governor." Reaper's fingertips trailed the inside of my thigh. "A girl deserves multiple fathers to protect her, dote on her, and show her examples of what a man really is. When she's a woman, she'll know what kind of treatment to accept, and will choose the best men to please and protect her as an adult."

Vance chuckled politely. "Different worlds indeed, president. But I respect it. And if I may say, Mari, you certainly look satisfied with your ah, *arrangement*."

"I am, governor," I smiled. "Very satisfied."

Jandro started to laugh, then coughed, choking on his soup until Gunner whacked him on the back. Across the table, Dyno and T-Bone still wore surly expressions.

"I'm just curious, sir," T-Bone stroked his beard. "What if Kyrie wanted to marry someone completely below her status? Say, a brick-layer. Or some other tradesman. Would you support the relationship if she loved the guy?"

Vance took a long time to answer. The soup bowls were taken away and the next course replaced it, but none of us were looking at the food.

"My daughter's wellbeing and happiness is what's most important to me," he said finally. "If such a man can give her everything she needs, and provide a good life for her, who am I to tell her no?"

Seemingly placated by that answer, the Sons dug into their meal.

The rest of the dinner conversation was lighthearted. Drinks poured freely and the whole table was soon abuzz with laughter and lively conversation. Plates were cleared and replaced swiftly. I lost track of how many courses the meal was, but was completely stuffed by the time dessert was placed in front of me.

"Help me with this," I begged Jandro, sliding the brownie topped with vanilla ice cream and hot fudge toward him. "I can't eat another bite."

He sliced his fork through and took a heaping mouthful, looking at me like I was crazy for not having any room left.

Dessert was barely finished before the men started putting their napkins on the tables and pulling cigars out of their jacket pockets.

"Won't you join us, gentlemen?" Vance gestured toward the slim case in the hands of a waiter, displaying an array of smoking options.

"Ooh!" I leaned over, spying a slim, feminine-looking cigarillo in the box. "May I?"

Reaper laughed as he made his own selection. "You sure about that, sugar?"

"Just for tonight, while we're celebrating."

Vance seemed caught off-guard, but quickly recovered. "Cigars after dinner is usually a men's tradition, but why not? I have a final gift for the heroes of Four Corners and that certainly includes you, Mari."

"Governor," Reaper coughed. "You have been far too generous already—"

"Nonsense. Follow me to the patio, will you?" Vance turned to see who would be coming along. "Shadow, will you be joining us?"

"Um, I appreciate it, but smoke doesn't always agree with me, governor." Shadow stood behind his chair. "I think I'll turn in for the night. Thank you for the dinner."

"Of course, I'll arrange a ride back for you. Ah, Remy?" Vance called over one of his staff and leaned in close to whisper instructions in the man's ear. It took several seconds, ending with a wink and a slap on the man's shoulder from the governor. "Have a good night Shadow, I've arranged a small gift to meet you back at your room as well."

"Sir, you don't have to—"

"Not another word! You bled for my territory, my family, and it will not go unrewarded. Off with you now, sleep well."

The rest of us stepped out to a cool, picturesque evening through a set of double doors at the end of the dining room. A bonfire was already lit, with patio furniture and another bar outside. Water rippled over a dark lake just beyond the seating area. Moonlight and stars reflected in streaks of silver over the water's surface.

"Mrs. President." Reaper flicked open his lighter and held it in front of my slim lady-cigar.

I smiled, leaning in to puff the other end as the flame embraced it. "Thank you, Mr. President."

He just smirked, the warm glow dancing in his green eyes as he lit his own. We accepted another round of drinks and took our seats next to the governor.

"Martin," Vance called to another member of his staff. "Will you turn on the lights on the other side of the lake?"

"Certainly, governor."

A minute later, warm lamp light steadily grew brighter across the water. A shape took form against the darkness—the form of a house. As my eyes adjusted to the light, I saw it was a two-story cabin, much like the governor's own residence.

"I admit I don't entirely understand your dynamic, except that there's four of you," the governor said. "And that you currently don't have a permanent home. The floor plan is the same open concept as mine, but can be adjusted if you wish."

I sucked in too much smoke and heat burned my throat as I coughed. Someone pressed water into my hands and I drank it greedily.

"Sir," Gunner breathed. "Am I understanding you right? You're giving us…

"A house, yes. You can live in it part-time or full-time, whatever your plans are. I meant it when I said Four Corners will always have a home for you."

A stunned silence fell over us as we stared at the home. Fantasies immediately began flitting through my head. While it had been nice that everyone had their own place in Sheol, a single home for all of us would be so convenient. We'd be cohesive, a real family unit.

I could see Jandro making breakfast with fresh eggs every morning. Gunner watching Horus hunt over coffee as the sun rose. Reaper and I sleeping in and making love before the day began. And Shadow—

My thoughts stuttered before the realization screeched them to a halt. I was getting way ahead of myself, already thinking of Shadow as mine, let alone picturing him in my household. He needed to decide if that was what he wanted, and so did my guys.

"Governor, it's not that we don't appreciate this." Reaper stared across the lake, and I wondered if fantasies similar to mine played out in his head. "But it's not just us. I have an entire club—twenty-five people, including women and kids to look out for. They're spread out in the town now in various rooms and taverns. I can't accept a place like this while my people still need homes of their own."

"I thought of that as well," Vance grinned. "My architects are planning a new development along this lake, I can give you a tour tomorrow. But we're thinking of a community playground, a garden, and around thirty homes, depending on lot sizes. You can all stay together that way, if you'd like."

"Sir," Reaper coughed with a shake of his head. "I don't mean to be rude, but it's too much—"

"Four Corners doesn't have standardized currency yet," Vance clapped him on the shoulder. "So this is how I'm paying you and your men for bringing my Kyrie back to me. Offering a basic human need, such as shelter, is the least I can do. Please," he shook and squeezed Reaper's shoulder a little harder, "don't think the homes come with strings attached. We can draw up a contract if that would make you feel better. But I'm forever in your debt, Reaper. Not the other way around."

"If you would just let me think about it," my husband said cautiously, though still starry-eyed with disbelief. "It's just...a lot."

"We're not used to gifts like this," Jandro explained. "We're used to taking, stealing the things we value most, then fighting like hell to keep them."

"It's not a gift, it's payment," Vance insisted. "Your men risked their lives and returned what's most dear to me."

"No disrespect, sir," Gunner chimed in. "But men like us are also not inclined to trust politicians at their word. I've seen firsthand the corruption brought on by wealth and power because I was born into it. Most outlaws have been a victim to it at some point or another."

"I understand," Vance nodded. "Well, after we have the time to get to know each other, I hope we can come to a place of trust. I think the Sons of Odin would vouch for me."

"It's because of them we agreed to come here." Smoke curled around Reaper's mouth. "They've been loyal to you longer than us and have lost a lot more. If anyone deserves home and community, it's them."

"They're good men. I think of them like my own sons, in a way." Vance lifted his eyes to where Dyno spoke to Grudge in a low voice a bit further away from everyone else. "It's a tragedy what they've endured."

He couldn't see, but I spotted T-Bone talking to Kyrie near the patio doors. Her eyes were wide and dreamy looking up at him, their heads bent together in an intimate conversation.

Reaper followed my gaze over Vance's shoulder and huffed out a quiet laugh. "I'm glad you think so, governor. Keep that in mind for when they do things with no apparent explanation. Bikers are unpredictable, and we mourn our losses in different ways."

"Fair enough," Vance shrugged, either not noticing, or ignoring what we saw behind him. He lifted his drink instead. "To remembering those we've lost and forging new, lasting friendships."

"I can drink to that," Reaper grinned.

SHADOW

I breathed for what felt like the first time in hours. The governor's car dropped me off at the B&B and I was finally alone. Blissful silence was freeing. Spending hours rubbing shoulders with men who wanted to do nothing but talk was suffocating.

But I did it. I made it through the night and lived. Now quiet and solitude were my rewards.

Once in my room, I undressed for bed, kicking my boots off and undoing the buttons on the crisp shirt like they were ropes binding me. I pulled my sleeping pills from the drawer, then sat on the edge of the bed, ruminating on the evening as I untucked the shirt from my slacks.

Mari looked amazing. Every man in the room stared at her like some exotic pet bird and it brought out a bloodthirst I'd never felt before. She wasn't theirs. What right did they have to gawk so openly?

I huffed out a dry laugh to myself, knowing I wasn't any better. At what point did I change? My whole life had been spent in fear and avoidance of women. Now I wanted to gouge out the eyes of strange men over one, as if I had any right to her myself.

Look at me. Pining over an unavailable woman and dining with politicians. You're moving up in the world, Shadow.

I thought back to when Mari first told me she was proud of me. She had that same look when the governor toasted me, drawing everyone's attention to me. I thought I handled it okay, but poor Grudge looked like he was the verge of a panic attack the whole time. Only looking at Kyrie, the governor's daughter, seemed to bring him any sense of calm.

What was it about women that had such an effect on us?

A soft knock on my door pulled me out of my thoughts. Dread filled me at the sound. I had exceeded my limit of socializing. It didn't matter if it was Jandro or someone else familiar, I was done for the night.

The knock came again and I bit back the growl of frustration. Maybe if I pretended to be asleep, they'd get the hint.

"Sir?" a feminine voice called through the wood. "I'm here on the governor's orders."

I was puzzled enough to stand and crack the door open. The woman on the other side had a face caked in makeup, her dress like a second skin as it hugged all her curves. She smiled coyly at me and I remembered.

Fuck.

The governor had sent a gift. And here she was.

"Um, hi."

"Hi," she giggled, tossing a lock of red hair over her shoulder. The color looked fake, like Reaper's sister's hair. "You gonna stare all night or let me in?"

I stepped back from the door and she pushed her way in, closing it with a swing of her hips. Damn it, she was in my space now. A stranger in my room when all I wanted was to be left alone.

My mind raced, wondering how I should get her out, but my body was much slower to move. She walked straight up to me, confident and unafraid as she pressed her chest to mine. That was different. Did I suddenly become approachable? Or was she handpicked by the governor for her boldness?

"What's your name, big guy?" Her hands went to the buttons at the bottom of my untucked shirt, long red nails swiftly finishing the work I'd started.

"Uh, you don't have to do that." I backed away, holding the sides of my shirt closed. I had an undershirt on, so she didn't see the full extent of my scarring yet. As much as I didn't want to sleep with her, I also didn't want to deal with the fear and disgust I'd seen so many times before.

"That's a funny name." She snickered at her own joke, hands coming to her hips. "Well, if you'd rather keep it on or do the honors yourself, it's all good with me, cowboy. I'm Morgan, by the way."

With that, she hiked up her dress and pulled it over her head, now completely naked except for her heels. Like most service girls, she didn't bother with lingerie.

"How do you like it, big guy?" Morgan's voice took on a husky whisper as she stalked toward me. "I could climb you like a tree. You can fuck me against the wall, show me how strong you are."

"Um..." I kept stepping away until it was my back that touched the wall.

"Aw, you nervous?" She reached out and trailed her fingertips from my chest to my waistband. "You seem a little shy. You can lie back and just let me take over. I'm cool with that, too."

She stepped one leg between mine, and just started to rub her thigh against my crotch when I stepped to the side.

"Um, no. No, thank you."

Fuck, why did she have to press against me and get so close? Her presence in the room felt so invasive and I just wanted some fucking space.

"All right," she scoffed, annoyance now lacing her voice. "Tell me what you like, so I have something to work with here."

God fucking damn it. There was no getting rid of her, was there? And how bad would it look if I refused a gift from the governor? I'd have to get this over with, just like I always did.

"You can just, um," I swallowed, "get on the bed. On your hands and knees is fine."

Morgan grinned, heading for the bed like I requested. "See, now was that so hard?"

She assumed the position and waited. I went around behind her slowly, dread sinking into my limbs. My feet felt like lead dragging across the floor. I didn't want to do this, not with her. Not like this.

Glancing up, I realized she faced the mirror—the perfect position to watch ourselves. That made me want it even less.

"Uh, can you face the headboard, please?"

"You're a picky fucking bastard," she huffed, but turned in the direction I asked.

Now I could just stare at the wall like I always did, and not the shame in my own face. I pulled my zipper down slowly, with reluctance. This might be over with quicker if I thought of someone else, the only person I wanted to do this with.

But that didn't feel right either. I didn't want *her* like this. I wouldn't want her facing away from me, just a body to invade. I'd want to see her face, to feel her hands on me. Not that any of it mattered.

Overtly aware of Morgan waiting for me, I began to stroke myself. After a whole minute of trying to get things started, my own hand was failing me. So I stared at the strange woman's opening, spread open and on display. That wasn't working, either.

"Need some help?" She sounded utterly bored.

"No." I ran through every scenario in my head that had gotten me hard before, every one but *that* one.

Nothing did it for me. I knew it the moment I saw this woman standing outside my door. As Jandro put it, I might as well try to shoot pool with a length of rope. Nothing that had previously worked for me could any more. Only *she* did.

I released my limp dick with a sigh, tucking it back into my pants. "I'm sorry. This isn't going to happen."

"Well." She didn't hesitate in sliding off the bed and picking up her discarded dress. "Thanks for completely wasting my time."

"I'll make sure you still get paid," I told her, looking away as she got dressed.

"Uh, yeah," she scoffed. "I better be." She paused once she got her dress on, looking at me from head to toe. "Gotta admit, I'm kinda bummed," she mused, her voice softer. "You look like you could be a good lay if you weren't in your head so much."

Sure, like that was going to happen.

I grabbed the doorknob and swung the door open. "Sorry to waste your time. Have a good night."

"You too, big guy." She cast a coy look over her shoulder as she walked out. "Good luck."

It felt like I couldn't close the door fast enough, and I forced myself not to slam it. My room was blissfully empty of other people again, but my relief was gone. I thought of *her* and my cock stiffened instantly.

I leaned against the door, letting the back of my head hit the wood as my hand cupped over the front of my pants. The room wasn't just empty now, it was lonely. I did want someone here with me, but only if that someone was *her*. I wanted those lips that smiled at me and kissed my cheek. I wanted the only hands that ever touched my bare skin like they desired me.

MARIPOSA

"Holy fuck, I'm exhausted." Gunner laid his head on my shoulder as soon as the car door closed behind him.

"Same here." I ran my fingers through his soft hair, watching blankly through the windshield as we pulled away from the building. "I have a feeling I'll be too wired to sleep, though."

"Right?" Jandro's voice was raspy from cigar smoke. "Just like that, we could have a house gifted to us by the governor of Four Corners? Shit's fucking wild."

"If we're all losing sleep over this, that's a sign we shouldn't accept it," Reaper called from the passenger seat.

"Or you're just looking for excuses not to," I pointed out. "I'm glad you brought up the club, though. Everyone else, like Tessa and the boys especially, need a stable place more than us."

"Yeah, I dunno what to think," Reaper admitted. "I don't get a slimy vibe from him, but I didn't from Tash either."

"Sleep on it." I leaned forward to kiss the back of his shoulder. "Or try to, at least."

The short ride back to the B&B was in comfortable silence. My feet ached once the car pulled up and we stepped out. I couldn't wait to shed this dress and heels.

Under the porch light's glow, I saw the silhouette of a large man sitting in one of the patio chairs.

"Sup, dude," Jandro greeted Shadow as we walked up. "Thought you'd be in bed by now."

He got a noncommittal grunt in reply. "Just felt like some fresh air."

"All right, well," Jandro was already yawning. "Good night."

We slipped inside and quietly made our way to our room. Taking my shoes off was a huge relief, as was getting out of the dress. But I wasn't ready to turn in yet, albeit for different reasons than fantasizing about a home to share with my loves.

"I think I'll sit outside with Shadow for a bit." I pulled on a long-sleeved shirt and lounge pants.

"Okay." Reaper didn't seem fazed as he pulled me in for a kiss. "Goodnight, sugar."

Already falling asleep, Jandro murmured a response in the same manner. It was Gunner who approached me with a tight-lipped frown and a knitted brow.

"What's wrong, handsome?" I wound my arms around his neck.

He ran his hands across my sides, touching his forehead down to mine. "You'll come to bed with us, right?"

"Yes." I kissed him deeply, savoring the rough cigar flavor mixing with his usual bright, sweetness. "I'll only ever go to bed with *my* men." I slid a hand down and grabbed his ass on the emphasized word, and that finally brought a smile to his face. "I love you, Gunner. I'll remind you in any way I need to."

"You shouldn't have to," he whispered, lips on the bridge of my nose. "I'm just being—"

"I will, anyway." I leaned up, catching his lips again with a possessive bite. "Because you're mine, and I'm here to give you what *you* need."

"You do. All I need and more." He sighed, running his hands up my back. "It's just my head being a dumbass. Old habits, you know."

"You're not dumb. This is just strange to you." I pushed his hair back to look into those sky-colored eyes. "So don't let your head talk itself in circles. Talk to me. Talk to them."

"I know." He cupped the back of my neck, thumb massaging gently at the base of my skull. "I love you, baby girl. Thanks for being patient with me."

His kisses were warm and sweet, a gentle rain pouring over my lips and face. This warmth and affection was one of my favorite things about him. My heart was jumping at the chance to talk with Shadow, but he wasn't mine yet. If Gunner needed me, he was my priority.

"Want me to stay?"

"Nah, go hang on the porch with the big guy." He swatted the side of my hip, the easygoing smile returning to his face. "But come cuddle with me when you're back."

"You're sure?" I kissed his throat, licking lightly over his pulse.

"Yes." He grabbed my shoulders and playfully held me an arm's length away. "But not if I let you keep doing that."

"I'll be right back," I promised, dropping a kiss to his knuckles on my shoulder before he released me.

"Mari?" he whispered.

"Yeah?"

Gunner stroked his thumb over his bottom lip as he thought. "Just know that Shadow better appreciate you. He's never gonna find another woman like you, so I hope he realizes what you're worth. If he doesn't, we won't accept him."

So my guys did talk. It was on their radar, at least. Part of me wanted to argue that I could make my own decisions about who I wanted to be with. But I knew how important trust was, not just with me, but between each other. Reaper had already trusted Jandro and Gunner, but Shadow was a bit of an outlier. If I got too deep in my feelings to see clearly, they could have clarity that I didn't. Now I had to listen to their concerns too, because it wasn't just me Shadow would be spending time with.

"I understand, Gun." I closed the distance between us to stroke his cheek. "You all want the best for me, and I love you for that."

He kissed my palm, then playfully shoved me away again. "Go talk to your new boyfriend."

I held back a snort as I left the bedroom, closing the door silently behind me. The whole B&B was quiet and dark as I tiptoed out the front door. But not even being as quiet as possible could get past the assassin sitting outside.

Shadow turned his head as I crept out the front door, the porch light bringing out his cheekbones and deep lines cut into his face.

"Mind if I sit with you?" I asked before moving any closer.

"Um, no." He shifted in his seat, the bench creaking under his movement. "Go ahead."

I lowered down next to him, mindful to keep some space between us. "Couldn't sleep?"

"You could say that." He started to fidget, hand curling around the armrest of the bench. "How was after dinner cigars?"

"Smoky," I laughed. "All the guys are raspy and I'm sure I'll be regretting it tomorrow. But the governor showed us a house he wanted to gift us." I shook my head with a deep inhale. "We're not sure if we'll take it. It feels like too much, but if it was one of our kids we almost lost, we'd probably feel similarly. So we're thinking on it first."

"Congratulations," he said a bit stiffly. "If you do decide to take it."

"We'll see." I lifted one shoulder in a shrug. "There's still everyone else that needs homes. And Reaper's not entirely sure about settling here." I curled my legs underneath me. "How are you liking Four Corners?"

He shrugged. "I'm fine just about anywhere. I wouldn't even mind being nomadic. As long as I can ride and see the sky." His throat worked in a deep swallow.

"I'm sorry you didn't feel up for joining us out back. I didn't know cigar smoke bothered you."

Shadow smiled, a sight as rare as the night-blooming flower he showed me, and just as dazzling to see. "It doesn't. I was just tired of being around people."

"Ooh, naughty," I teased. "The wounded hero of Four Corners dipping out on an invitation from the governor. That takes balls of steel."

"Unfortunately, mine are still fleshy and vulnerable."

He said it with such a straight face, the first peal of laughter burst out of me loud enough to wake the entire B&B. I slapped a palm over my mouth, trying in vain to smother the laughs that followed. Shadow's broad shoulders shook with quiet chuckles as I blinked back tears and tried to compose myself.

"Oh my god," I panted, wiping the corners of my eyes. "I think you leveled past Jandro with that one."

"I learned from the best." He appeared more relaxed now, slouching against the bench, hands no longer fidgeting and his knees wide.

The distance between us was gradually closing, so I took my chances scooting closer until my leg brushed his. His eyes flicked to where our bodies made contact, but he didn't pull away. When our laughter faded to quietness, I voiced the question that had been on my mind for days.

"Can you tell me about your tattoo?"

He looked puzzled for a moment. "This?" His hand hovered over his chest.

"No, this." I touched my index finger once to his thigh, then returned my hand to my lap. "I saw it when you were sick."

"Oh." He returned his gaze out to the road in front of the B&B, his mind somewhere else. "It was the first one I ever did. I wanted to practice on myself before tattooing anyone else."

"Are the hieroglyphs upside down so only you can read them?"

"Yes." Amusement crossed his face as he looked at me. "It's such a shitty piece of work, I'm surprised you could tell."

"I mean, it's clearly roughly done, but it's not *that* shitty."

"I did it in prison," he shrugged. "I worked with what I had, but since this one, I've only gotten better."

"That is definitely true." My next question hovered on my tongue, my heart accelerating for some reason. "Will you tell me what it means?" His brow furrowed, that expression making me backtrack immediately. "You don't have to, of course."

"You *want* to know?"

"Sure I do." I held his gaze, fighting the impulse to push his hair back and kiss that scar again. "I want to know more about you in general."

He stared at my mouth and I wondered if we held the same train of thought. "It means, *the sky is my reason.*"

A simple phrase that clearly held so much weight.

"Your reason for what?"

"For living," he said softly. "When I was confined to my cell, the sky used to feel like another planet, some place far away that I would never reach. I could only see it through a crack in the wall. But seeing it, how the sky changed colors right before nightfall, it gave me a reason to keep waking up again."

My throat felt uncomfortably tight. "You mean when you were in prison?" I asked.

"No," he shook his head. "Before that." He let out a scoff. "Prison was a wonderland compared to that place."

"Shadow?"

"Yes?"

Our eyes locked and I felt frozen in place while also being thrashed around by a storm. My pulse crashed wildly, every cell in my body crying out to touch him, to give him another reason. There was no turning back from this point, and that both terrified and emboldened me.

"I don't want to pretend like nothing happened between us."

His chest lifted with an influx of breath. I remembered the warmth of his skin on my cheek, the gentle rise and fall as I watched him sleep.

"I don't either."

We moved toward each other before the words were fully out of his mouth. His arm lifted and I slid over to nestle into his side, my feet tucking underneath me as I leaned into him. I'd been craving this like a drug ever since the first time, feeling like I was protected by the strongest shield, while also melting into his gentleness and warmth.

Only this time was different, and we both knew it.

I lifted my face to his. He kept his arm along the back of the bench instead of wrapping it around me, his lips hovering close enough for me to taste the soft puffs of breath. Some guys doubted a girl's intentions down to the last moments, and I knew Shadow second-guessed himself plenty. So I decided to leave no room for doubt, and closed the distance between my mouth and his.

Shadow's lips were soft, more pliant than I imagined. But he didn't move, didn't respond to the soft presses of my mouth.

I pulled away for a moment, finding his eyes. "Is something wrong?"

"No. I...just..."

I reached up, finally giving in to pushing his hair away and exposing his beautiful face. "You've never kissed anyone?"

His eyes dropped from mine, stiffness entering his body as he started to pull away from me. That was all the answer I needed, but I wasn't about to let him withdraw this time.

"I can teach you." I wrapped a hand around the back of his neck, gently stopping his retreat. "How does that sound?"

He leaned into my hand on his neck, but didn't pull away further, despite being plenty strong enough. "Okay."

A smile pulled at my lips. God, he was so hot. Sexy, dark, and dangerous, yet adorably innocent. "Okay. Just follow what I do. This is stage one."

I leaned in until our mouths touched again, then pursed my lips to press a closed-mouth kiss on his top lip. He copied the movement on my bottom lip, and it sent a jolt straight to my heart. I had a feeling he'd be a fast learner and that proved to be true. He caught onto the rhythm of exchanging soft pecks after only a few tries.

"Stage two," I whispered, keeping my lips parted as I pulled his top lip between mine.

He released a soft groan as he sucked lightly at my bottom lip, his kiss in perfect sync with mine. My lower half was thoroughly jelly now, while my top half pulsed with heat, with desire I was sick of holding back.

I didn't even have to say stage three. Our tongues simply met in the middle, gentle taps and exploratory licks growing deeper, bolder as this heady rush carried us like a tidal wave. My leg slid over his lap as I came to straddle him. His hands came to my hips, then quickly dropped away.

"Yes, please. Touch me." I grabbed his hands and returned them to me. "I want you to."

A moan came from deep in his chest, our teeth clicking from our hardest kiss yet, as he wrapped one arm around my waist and the other caressed up my spine. I couldn't get enough of his hair, running my fingers through it as my other hand rested on his chest. His heart pounded like a drum against my palm, matching the beat of my own pulse.

"You're a natural kisser," I murmured, pausing for a breath despite wanting to kiss him until I passed out.

Still, he looked puzzled. Uneasy, despite his body language proving he wanted this just as much as I did.

"What's wrong?" I pressed a deliberate kiss to the scar cutting through his eyebrow.

"Why are you doing this with me?" That question and his resulting flinch from my kiss sent a painful ache through my chest.

"Because not only do I like you as a person, I'm also ridiculously attracted to you." I wrapped both hands around his neck, my fingers pressing into the knots behind his shoulders. He still had some stiffness there from the arrows tearing through his muscles.

"How?" Despite his bewilderment at what I said, his hard expression slackened with my touch.

"How can I not be, is a better question." I leaned in to kiss him again, his lips catching and savoring my mouth in a way that sent fluttering down to my toes. "You're strong, you're caring. You're smart and creative. You're loyal and selfless." I rested my forehead on his, letting my mouth hover an inch away. "And you're so fucking hot. Why do you think I stared at you so hard that I spilled beer on your table that day?"

"Because my scars are ugly and make me look like a freak."

"No, love." I kissed between his eyebrows. "Because you were the most handsome man in the room to me."

His hand on my back drifted forward, pushing my hair off my shoulder and gently stroking along my jaw. "You don't mean that."

I leaned into his touch, encouraging him to cup my cheek. "Do you trust me?"

"Yes," he answered quickly. "With my life."

"Then you know I wouldn't lie to you." I brought his hand to my chest, over my pounding heart. "There's no faking this. This is real, Shadow." I returned my palm to his chest, feeling the matching beat of that muscle through his shirt, skin, and the tattoo that bound us together. "It's always been here, and I don't want to fight it anymore."

"Neither do I." His gaze lowered, the arm around my waist running down the side of my thigh.

"But you're still uncertain," I ventured, clasping my fingers over his on my chest. "Tell me why."

"Your men," he admitted, meeting my eyes again. "They...they *know* how to do this. Take care of you, treat you like you deserve." He swallowed. "They know how to...to please you. Why would they share you with me?"

"Oh, Shadow..."

I leaned in, dropping a kiss on his brow. He released a sigh, eyes closing softly, so I kissed each of his eyelids. I kissed his cheeks and his nose. When our mouths met again, his lips were parted, waiting. I melted into his taste, curling up small as his arms came around me in a tight, protective embrace.

When we parted for air, he kissed my forehead, stroking my cheek with his thumb. I expected him to be gentle, maybe even overly careful and a bit clumsy, but these touches damn near brought tears to my eyes. His tenderness sent my heart and hormones running wild and I wanted to drown in it. I wanted to peel back the layers of him with kisses instead of violence, to uncover and protect this man who deserved all the love in the world.

"My men," I whispered, tucking my head under his chin, "care about both of us. They're letting us explore this because they want us both to be happy. Is it so hard to believe that can happen if we're together?" I skimmed my fingers along the collar of his shirt, touching the skin around his throat. "Jandro is your best friend. He loves me. Don't you think he might want this for us?"

Shadow's broad chest rose and fell with each deep breath, his caresses soothing and delicious on my back. If I hadn't promised Gunner I'd come to bed, I could easily fall asleep on him like this.

"I just never thought I'd be good enough." He shifted his weight, but held me in place against him. "Never normal enough, I guess."

I raised my head with a soft laugh. "If I wanted normal, I never would have hooked up with those three in the first place."

"Yeah, I guess you're right." He smiled again and my heart skipped. Jesus, he was just so beautiful.

Our lips touched together again, but I pulled back at the last moment. "You *are* enough," I whispered, bringing my hand to his scarred cheek again. "And whatever you don't know, I'm willing to show you, okay?" I couldn't help the grin that followed. "Although if your kissing skills are any indication, I don't think you'll need much guidance."

"Hm, I don't know." His eyes brightened as he cupped the back of my head. "I think I need more practice."

He kissed me through my laugh, his confidence shining through as he pulled me close. Not a stitch of clothing was removed, and our lips didn't travel anywhere beyond each other's faces. There was an innocence to kissing Shadow that I loved, like we were two teenagers learning the basics. We had already crashed together once and it burned us both. Now, coming together slowly, organically, seemed like a much better idea.

We kissed until my lips felt thoroughly bruised and my eyelids could barely stay open. I must have dozed off for a moment because Shadow was rousing me with kisses in my hair and gentle shoulder shakes.

"Should get you to bed," he murmured with a kiss to my temple.

"Mmhm, I promised Gunner..."

My legs slid to the floor, the rest of my body peeling away from his warmth, his solidness. I didn't like this, the feeling of cold night air with no solid bodies sandwiching me, but crawling into bed would soon alleviate that.

Our fingers intertwined, Shadow led me through the front door of the B&B, through the open front room, and stopped in front of my door. He didn't let go of my hand, and my half-asleep brain considered just dragging him in to snuggle with the other guys.

One day. Not yet.

"So." Shadow stared at our hands, his thumb sweeping over mine. "It'll be okay if I kiss you good morning tomorrow?"

I grinned, leaning my chest against his as I stood on tiptoes. "Only if you kiss me goodnight first."

He grinned back as he bowed over me, bracing his other arm against my back. I would've swooned if he hadn't pinned me against him. In the dark hallway, with his face fully uncovered, long hair falling over his shoulders, and his bright white eye glowing like a cat's, he was every woman's fantasy when it came to late night kisses in the shadows.

The kiss was long, sensual, and lingering. I saw stars as he returned us upright, his fingers reluctantly untangling from mine as our bodies separated.

"Goodnight, Mari." He walked backwards toward his door, eyes never leaving me.

I leaned my head on my door, hand on the knob as I watched him back away. My legs could barely hold me up from fatigue, all the drinks at dinner, and everything this gorgeous man did to burrow his way into my heart.

"Goodnight, Shadow," I breathed before opening the door and quietly slipping inside.

Epilogue
REAPER

The air was warm, the sun pleasant on my face. Desert stretched out in all directions, the sky a perfect royal blue with fluffy clouds. My gas tank was full, so I accelerated and felt the power of the motorcycle kick underneath me. The road was empty and smooth, with no potholes.

That was how I knew this was a dream.

I pulled over at the edge of a canyon, parking under the sparse shade of a Joshua tree. Ancient rock formations stretched out as far as the eye could see, their ribbons of color too vivid to be real.

My instincts urged me to turn around at the footsteps behind me, but I stayed facing forward while the last bit of uncertainty left me.

"Took you long enough, Daren."

"You always were an impatient bastard, Reaper."

I turned slowly, all expectations gone at what I would see standing there.

It was just my brother.

He was still in his riding gear, russet brown hair pushed around by the wind, those cheeky green eyes we shared bright and full of life.

That was what brought my breaths to a stutter, he looked so *alive.*

More than that, he looked fucking good. Nothing at all like the lifeless, pale, clammy body I held as he faded away.

"What's the matter, Reap? You choking up on me?"

"Man, you just..." How could I be dreaming? I could *feel* my throat closing up. "It's good to see you, that's all."

"I'll visit more. Noelle's mind is a little hm, distracted, shall we say?"

"Yeah," I barked out a laugh, still staring at him in disbelief. "Yeah, she's all wrapped up in that guy."

"I saw everything that happened on that mission." Daren hooked his thumbs through his belt loops, propping his foot up on a rock. "Larkan's good people. You should patch him in."

"How did you see everything?"

"Freyja showed me." He smiled lightheartedly. "She's like an anchor that we all come home to. Sometimes I'm tethered to her, other times I'm free to make visits as I please. Like this one."

"They said I had to...to be open to letting you visit me."

"Right. It's a two-way street," he grinned. "Talking animals have a way of opening you up to things, don't they?"

"Heh. I'm a stubborn ass, but yeah, I think it was my old lady's cat that sealed the deal."

Daren's face grew dreamy at the mention of her.

"Mariposa," he breathed. "What a name. What a woman."

"Yeah."

I didn't feel the need to elaborate. If his spirit, consciousness, or whatever was in Freyja's domain, he must have seen plenty. And knew exactly what kind of woman she was.

"You did good, Reap. Mom'll be proud."

Wait. Did he say *will* or *would* be proud? If she was dead, he had to know, right? I opened my mouth to ask, but his face darkened and what he said next made my stomach drop.

"You have to break down the door."

"What?" I blinked. "What door?"

"You *have* to break it," he repeated, his tone grave. "She'll die if you don't."

"Who, Mari? Or Mom? Is Mom okay? Is she with you?"

"It's gonna hurt, man. It's gonna hurt like hell for a long fuckin' time." His brow pinched with pain at the vision he was seeing. "But it's the right thing to do."

Goddamn my brother and his fucking predictions with no fucking context.

"Daren, please." I moved closer, close enough to touch him, but afraid he might disappear if I did. "You have to give me more than that. What's gonna hurt? What door am I breaking?"

"Listen to Hades," he continued as if I hadn't said anything. "No matter how badly you want to, do *not* disobey the command."

"What command?" I demanded, fear now slicing through my veins. "Who is he going to make me kill? Daren!"

But my brother was already gone.

HEARTLESS

STEEL DEMONS MC BOOK SIX

Glossary of Spanish Terms

Mija/mijita: My daughter, a term of endearment that combines the words *mi* and *hija*

Reposado: A type of tequila that has been aged for two to twelve months

Añejo: A type of tequila which has been aged for a minimum of one year, and tends to be the smoothest for drinking

Viejito: Little old man, meant in an affectionate or teasing way

Esposa/Esposo: Wife/Husband

Guapito: Handsome

Bonita: Pretty

Mariposita: Little butterfly

Siempre: Always (can also mean forever)

Te amo: I love you (romantic intention, said to a partner)

Te quiero: I love you (more general intention which can be said to a partner, friends, blood family members, etc.)

PROLOGUE
MARIPOSA

FIVE YEARS EARLIER

"Now this is a surprise." My dad grinned cheekily as he set two shot glasses on the counter.

"I have to take the opportunity while it's here," I said, parking my butt on the stool across from him.

"And here I figured my twenty-year-old daughter would have better things to do than drink with her lame old dad." He twisted the cap open on the bottle of *reposado* and started pouring carefully, shooting me a *dad look*. You know the one. "I could get in trouble for this, you know."

"What, like the militia are gonna peek through our windows, know instinctively that I'm underage, and toss us out into the street?" I rolled my eyes, but neither of us laughed. It wasn't a joke anymore, but a reality.

The latest push from our wannabe governor had been to make drinking illegal for women only. Apparently, it made us unfit to be wives. That crazy old fundie from the newly formed territory of Texahoma had been trying to absorb our county for six months. His utterly insane proclamations weren't laws for us yet, but thousands of others weren't so lucky. So far, Warsaw County's little rebellion had been able to hold the border, but that could change at any time.

Dad didn't respond to my retort, but smiled at me fondly as he sliced limes for our drinks. "So what's on your mind, *mija*?"

He always asked me that when he'd started letting me drink with him, ever since I was sixteen. This was our time to open up, to let me vent without judgment while he listened. My mom would always be a mom to me, but the ever-increasing hostility in our society made me grow up fast. Mom wanted to shield me from it all, so I could have a normal childhood. But Dad took a different approach. He started treating me like an equal and became my friend.

"I, um." I grabbed one shot glass and slowly pulled it toward me. "Carlos broke up with me last week."

"Aw, *mijita*." Dad's smile fell, his eyes warm and sympathetic. "I'm sorry that didn't work out."

"I'll be okay. I just didn't expect it to hit me like it did." My face tensed like I expected tears to come, but I knew they wouldn't. I had cried them all out already. "Like, I knew we probably weren't gonna get married or whatever, but it still fucking sucks."

"I know it does," Dad said. "It doesn't feel like it now, but you'll see it was for the best. Besides," he smirked before putting on his stern dad face, "you should be focusing on school. You don't need some boy distracting you. Your career field is going to make a real impact when you graduate."

"He told me I was *too* focused on school and didn't make time for him," I grumbled. "I confronted him about getting cozy with some girl at a party and he told me *that* shit."

"Even better," Dad huffed. "A boy like that is not worth your time."

"I know you're right, just why does it have to hurt so much? I don't *want* to miss him, but I do."

"Emotions are weird, *mijita*. Hell, people are weird." Dad took a small, thoughtful sip of his *reposado*. "I'm sure this guy cares about you. He probably just wasn't mature enough to tell you how he really felt." Dad put his glass down and suddenly released a sigh that made him look a lot older. "When people can't communicate properly for whatever reason, we sometimes end up hurting the ones we love."

Neither of us said a word, but I knew what we were both thinking about. On his second day home this week, he blew up at Mom over the tea kettle whistling. One minute he was fine, reading the paper and having his coffee. The moment that high-pitched whistle sounded, he started yelling a bunch of nonsense at her, completely unprompted. It was like some uncontrollable violent force had possessed my gentle, mild-mannered father. Mom and I were dumbfounded, and she was most definitely hurt by it.

He calmed down later and apologized, but everything had felt *off* since then. Awkward, like we were walking on eggshells. I attended a seminar on PTSD last semester, and had tried to broach the subject gently with my dad the last time he came home and started displaying symptoms. But he brushed me off, the machismo of his upbringing causing him to refuse to see it as a treatable medical condition.

Only during these heart-to-hearts with our prized tequila, did things seem normal. It was the real reason why I asked for this, for some semblance of normality.

Dad polished off his shot and reached for mine to put in the sink. I cupped my hand around the small glass and brought it closer to my chest.

"One more?"

"Nah, *mija*," he said sadly. "I gotta pack my shit and get ready to leave in the morning."

"Aw, come on, *viejito*. One more shot won't kill you."

"I *am* old," he laughed. "Can't keep drinking with my college-aged daughter no more."

"Dad..." I rolled the shot glass between my hands. "What if you just didn't go?"

His face hardened. "They'll come looking for me and I'll get thrown in jail. You know that, sweetheart."

I slid my glass angrily across the counter to him. "At least then you wouldn't be forced to fight in some bullshit war that doesn't even matter."

"That may be true." He turned and placed the glasses in the sink. "But who's to say I'll survive prison too? And I'd never get to come home and see my girls."

I had nothing to answer that. Of course I didn't want my dad in jail. But I didn't want him out *there* either, fighting for no cause while doing irreparable damage to his mind and body.

He rounded the counter and pulled me into a tight hug, one that made me feel tiny and protected. The type of hug that a little girl burrowed into so the monsters under her bed wouldn't get her.

The monsters were out in the streets now, looting and pillaging. It didn't matter if they were in riot gear or in rags. If they were strangers or familiar faces. The Collapse had changed people. It brought out the worst in them.

"I'm so sorry, *mijita*," he sighed over the top of my head, though I wasn't sure what he was apologizing for. "Your mom and I never wanted you to live in this kind of world. But we're all in this stupid bullshit war, whether we like it or not."

I just let him hug me, let him be my dad. He couldn't save me from anything, but for right now, they couldn't take this away from us.

I didn't know it would be the last time I saw him.

MARIPOSA

PRESENT DAY

Arms, legs, chests, and backs provided solidness and warmth on all sides. I didn't even need to open my eyes to know who was who anymore.

My forehead nuzzled the burn scars on Jandro's back. I kissed them in my half-asleep state, a smile coming to my face at the memory of kissing another man's scars last night.

Jandro didn't stir, still fully in dreamland, but Reaper's arm tightened around my waist. His lips found my ear, pressing a soft kiss there before murmuring, "You awake?"

"Mmm." I flipped over to face him, taking care not to disturb Jandro. Eyes still closed, I nuzzled my head under his chin, kissing his chest while curling up and burrowing into him. "You?"

He was silent for a moment, stroking my back.

"I talked to Daren."

"Hm?" That forced my eyelids open, hands lifting up to rub the sleep and fatigue from my eyes. "When?"

"Just now, before I woke up."

I tried to listen carefully to his tone, to piece together his feelings from his voice, but it was impossible with him speaking so softly. "What did he say?"

"Shit that wasn't good." He pushed himself up from the mattress with a groan, blinking at the pre-dawn light coming in from the window. "Take a walk with me, sugar?"

"Yeah, coming."

We climbed out of bed carefully, crawling over the splayed arms and legs of Jandro and Gunner to get dressed. I pulled on my thickest jeans, wool socks, and a gray flannel shirt. Every day grew colder, and the air before the sun came out was downright chilly.

Reaper got ready in his leather jacket, jeans, boots, and cigarettes, and together we headed out the front door of the Four Corners B&B. Right after stepping off the front porch, we heard the door open slowly again and turned to see who was following.

Hades had pushed the door open with his front paw, and he and Freyja followed us out to the quiet street.

"Can't go anywhere alone," I chuckled as Reaper lit up. "So did he come to you in a dream like," I tilted my head toward the animals, "*they* said?"

"Yeah." He grabbed my hand and started walking, sucking on his clove with the opposite hand. "I was riding and it was too perfect to be real, you know? Perfect weather, full gas tank, smooth road. I stopped to look out at the edge of a canyon and he just walked up behind me."

"Did it feel like you were really talking to him?" I snatched his cigarette for a quick drag. "Or just your brain pulling up memories of him?"

"It was really him, sugar. Well and alive." His eyes brightened on a distant focal point as we walked together. "He said he saw the whole rescue mission in Blakeworth, thanks to Freyja." He looked at the cat over his shoulder with a chuckle. "He's seen you, seen all of us. Sounds like he's into you, sugar. I knew he would be."

"I would've liked to meet him," I said, with a squeeze to his hand.

"I wouldn't," Reaper laughed. "He'd steal you away from me."

"Never." I held onto his arm with both hands, pressing my cheek against his shoulder. "What did he say that wasn't good?"

My husband's smile dissipated, green eyes hardening as he sucked on the last of his cigarette before tossing the butt away.

"I keep running it through my mind and can't even decipher it. I told you his visions were just random bits of information, right?"

"Yeah, that they didn't make any sense without context."

"Right. So he told me I needed to break down the door." A scowl crossed his face. "That 'she' would die if I didn't. Now, is this 'she' Noelle? Is it Freyja? Mrs. Potts? Gods fucking forbid, is it you?" He released my hand and lifted his arm to wrap around my shoulders. "It's driving me nuts that you might be in danger. And that I could—" he swallowed, "I could...lose you if I don't act fast enough."

I slid an arm around his waist, our footsteps on the street the only sounds as I absorbed his words. Breaking down a door could mean any number of things, depending on how literal or metaphorical Daren was.

"Did he tell you anything else?" I asked as we turned a corner.

Reaper looked over his shoulder at Hades sniffing the ground a few paces behind us. "That I had to obey the order when it came, and that it would hurt a lot, for a long time." He squeezed my shoulder, pulling me into his side. "Sugar, I have this bad fucking feeling that I'm gonna have to kill someone to protect you. Someone close to us."

I nodded with a deep breath. For the Steel Demons, killing someone could be business as usual. Or it could be one of our own, someone we trusted, and therefore catastrophic.

We had dealt with a betrayal before, with Python. Another person working against the Demons from the inside didn't seem likely, especially after making such a public spectacle of Python's death. I didn't have a single suspicion about anyone else in Reaper's club. Some people I personally liked more than others, but had no doubts about any of their loyalty. Big G was on thin ice, but he seemed eager to correct his behavior.

We could speculate and walk in circles all day. With so little information to go off of, there was just no way to narrow it down.

"Whatever happens," I looked up at him with my head on his shoulder. "I'm sure it'll be the right choice."

"Daren said something like that too," he muttered, the wheels still spinning in his head. "That it would hurt, but it would be the right thing. God, fuck." He rubbed his forehead. "This shit's giving me a headache."

My hand slid up his back to his neck, where I rubbed the tight knot of muscles. "Do you want to tell the other guys?"

"I don't know if I should," he said. "What if that changes things? He made it sound like I was the only one who *could* do it. I dunno. Fuck, I hate this." He turned to address the animals silently stalking behind us. "Any input you all have would be fucking great."

Hades lifted a leg and pissed on a fence post. Freyja paused to lick her paw.

"Perfect." Reaper turned back around with a snort, fishing for another cigarette.

I held on to his arm again as we continued our walk. "Hades said he was here to guide you and protect me. And I have all of you." My fingers laced through his. "How can anything bad happen to me when I'm loved by Demons and watched over by gods?"

"I fuckin' hope you're right." His finger rubbed affectionately over my ring. "I need something better to talk about. How'd it go with Shadow last night?"

A lightness lifted in my chest, the smile on my face instant. "Good. We talked for a bit and...kissed."

"Kissed?" Reaper coughed. "You mean that guy knows how to do something with his mouth besides suck down booze? Ow!"

"Don't be an asshole," I growled, jabbing my fist in his ribs a second time.

"Sugar, do you know who I am?" He grinned, catching my wrist before I could smack him another time. "I'm kidding, but can you blame me for being surprised?"

"He's a good kisser actually," I said smugly. "And he's...just really sweet."

"*Sweet?* Are you sure we're talking about the same person?"

"There's a whole side of him that is just so tender and gentle," I went on. "I saw moments of confidence that had nothing to do with his killing skills. He laughed and cracked jokes with me. He just held me and didn't try to take anything further than kissing. It was refreshing, honestly."

"So you want someone who will just kiss you without trying to get in your pants?" Reaper squeezed my ass and laughed when I smacked his hand away.

"Not necessarily. I mean, you know how much I love sex."

"Mm, I have some idea." Smoke curled from his grinning mouth.

"But with Shadow, I think I'd enjoy taking it slow. I could work with him to build up his confidence, and really take the time to learn what he likes. What we both like."

"Okay, but it's not like either of you are virgins. Why not just fuck and learn about each other that way?"

I gave him a pointed look. "We did that already and look what happened."

"I know, but it's different now. We're all aware of what's between you two." Reaper flicked some ash away and returned the cigarette to his mouth. "Do you love him?"

My heart crashed against my sternum at the question, my insides heating up in response. Did I?

"I care about him, a lot," was the answer that left my mouth. "But I think it's too soon to tell if it's like...what you and I have."

"Is it really?" Reaper challenged. "You've known him as long as any of us."

"Sure, but my interactions with him haven't been the same as with all of you. I'm still getting to know him beyond the whole 'silent killing machine' thing."

"Fair enough." Reaper released a sigh with an exhale of smoke. "Just keep us in the loop before you make it official, sugar."

"I will," I said with a squeeze of his hand. "I promise I will."

We turned another corner, rounding the block heading back to the B&B. The sun was just starting to come up and Jandro would likely be awake, getting coffee started or feeding the chickens.

The four of us, Hades and Freyja included, walked back in to find both of my other husbands awake and hovering over the coffee pot and breakfast pastries.

"Where'd you go, baby girl?" Gunner was still shirtless, hair up in a messy man-bun, pajama pants low on his slender hips as he pulled me in for a kiss. "I woke up to this dude spooning me instead of you."

"He loved it," Jandro cut in without missing a beat. "He was so impressed by my cuddling skills, he said we should run away together."

"A likely story," I murmured, kissing under Gunner's chin, then sliding over to get my love from Jandro. "We just went for a walk. But it's true, your cuddles are wonderful."

"Fuck yeah they are." Jandro's arms were protective and heavy around my back. "I don't see why these guys can't appreciate it. The Sons cuddle up all the time."

"Because they also fuck each other up the ass," Reaper grumbled, helping himself to the coffee pot.

A door creaked open and my stomach began doing somersault motions. Freyja took off immediately toward the sound with soft, chirping meows. Shadow's footsteps were light, lighter than the murmuring of "Hello, kitten," as he greeted her.

My guys thankfully didn't openly stare, but turned away and busied themselves in conversation, either real or contrived, as I approached the large man holding my cat.

"Good morning, Shadow," I whispered, excited nerves wavering in my voice.

His smile was shy, his gaze downward on the ball of fur in his arms. "Good morning, Mari."

I stepped closer, hoping to convey privacy and a bit of distance from the others as I kept my voice low. "Did you sleep well?"

"Yes, I did." He lowered Freyja gently to the floor then returned upright, eyes now on me. "Did you?"

"I did, thank you." I leaned into him with a smile, my shoulder brushing his chest.

His gaze flickered over me in a thorough reading of my body language. He knew what I wanted, what I gave him permission to do last night. Now it was a question of whether or not he felt comfortable doing it in front of my guys.

My whole upper body burst into flutters when Shadow's hand came to my waist, a steadying, affectionate touch. He leaned down swiftly, neither rushed or slow, and placed a warm, brief kiss on my lips.

I smiled against his mouth, savoring what I could of him before he straightened up. The guys didn't need a full-on PDA to know how things had shifted between us. Longer kisses would be better enjoyed in private anyway.

My hand touched his on my waist, fingers lacing through his. "Are you having breakfast with us?"

"Um." His eyes lifted to meet those of my guys, who now no longer pretended to focus on anything else. "Sure, if that's all right."

"Mornin', big guy." Jandro scooted back and stood from the chair he was in. "Take my seat. I'm gonna collect some eggs."

"Thanks." Shadow moved toward the chair with more hesitation than he did when he kissed me. His eyes darted everywhere, looking for signs of how to behave.

Next to him, Reaper leaned over the maps and documents on the table with a mug of steaming coffee in hand. "Mornin'," he grunted, as though it were any other day. "Shadow, you want to come with me on a tour of the new development with the governor today?"

"Ah, sure." He found an empty mug and began pouring coffee into it. "I mean, yes, Reaper."

"It's a request, not an order." Reaper leaned back in his chair, setting his coffee mug on his knee. "You don't have to if you have something more pressing, but Vance seems keen on showing us this new area he's developing. And I think he's curious about the injured hero of Four Corners."

Shadow bristled at being called a hero, and I couldn't help from running a hand along his upper back, where Blakeworth's arrows came too close to killing him, and down his arm as I took a seat next to him.

"I'll go. I don't have anything else going on." His fingers clasped mine briefly before letting go.

"What are your plans today, sugar?" Reaper lifted his mug to his lips as his gaze settled on me.

"I was thinking of checking out the hospital." I reached for a pastry from the basket in the center of the table. "See if the head doctor has time to give me a tour, or if I can lend my services in any way."

"On that note," Gunner leaned back in his chair next to me, placing one of his feet in my lap, "how do you feel about driving there?"

"Drive?" I nearly choked on my Danish. "You mean, your bike?"

"Not *mine*, but one of the little dirt bikes." He snatched an apple from the basket and tossed it in the air with a grin. "It's about time you learn, baby girl. I'll have Jandro check them over and get you the most reliable one."

I swallowed the lump in my throat nervously. "You'll be there with me?"

"Course I will." He poked his toes into my side. "I'll be in your bitch seat. A little roll reversal, how about that?"

Reaper snorted. "Of all of us most likely to be in a bitch seat."

"You're just sour you didn't get her ass first." Gunner took a loud bite out of his apple, pointedly ignoring my glare. Holy shit, could he not drop details of our sex life out on the breakfast table? In front of Shadow, no less? We just started making out, he did not need to know who had my ass first.

"It's too fucking early for this," I groaned, shoving Gunner's foot out of my lap. "I'm getting a shower first."

He laughed and leaned over to smack a kiss on my cheek. "I'll let Jandro know what we need."

I finished wolfing down my pastry and coffee, then returned my hand to Shadow's shoulder as I stood. He was like a magnet, I just could not stop touching him. He watched me curiously, only slightly shorter than me standing even while he was sitting down.

"You guys have fun with the governor today." My touch slid up his shoulder, fingertips brushing along his neck and cheek.

"We will." His arm came around my waist in a gentle hug to his side. "Enjoy the hospital and riding lessons."

"Will do." I leaned down, only planning for a sweet, brief kiss, but all my lips wanted to do was linger on his.

Who was I kidding? All I wanted to do was crawl into his lap and shove my tongue in his mouth, to feel and explore this mountain of a man with every inch of my skin until I uncovered every mystery about him.

His arm tightened around me, soft sighs escaping him as I pressed kiss after kiss onto the mouth that had learned mine so thoroughly and quickly the night before. He returned every one, sipping lightly with just enough pressure and sensation for me to feel like I was floating.

Reaper and Gunner only looked amused when we finally separated. "Did you forget we were here?" the president chuckled.

"Not another word out of you," I warned, rounding the table to kiss him full of teeth and rough scraping of lips, just how he liked it. My fingers speared through his hair, gripping the dark strands to hold his head in place. Reaper emitted a growl of satisfaction that lit up my core like a match. "Have a good day, love," I whispered against his mouth.

"Yes fuckin' ma'am." He grinned in return. "And hey, listen." His face turned hard, eyes sharp and jaw clenched. "Be careful, sugar. You hear me?"

I stroked my husband's face, pushing his hair back and trying my best to soothe the worried lines etched into his forehead.

"I will," I promised him with another long, lingering kiss.

MARIPOSA

"**S**queeze the brake lever nice and slow. Easy, easy..." Gunner's hand guided mine with steady patience on the dirt bike as we pulled up to the hospital. My stop was abrupt, but not as hard as when I took my first spin around the block and nearly lurched over the handlebars.

"Good job, baby girl!" He patted my sides. "You're getting the hang of it."

"Thanks, Gun." I swung a leg over to stand next to the dirt bike as Gunner scooted up the driver's seat. Freyja popped out of the front of my jacket, shaking her fur out and sniffing the air. "You picking me up for lunch?"

"I *can.*" He leaned over the handlebars with a playful smile. "Unless you'd rather have Tall, Dark and Scarred pick you up? Since you're in the early, getting-to-know each other stages."

A familiar fluttering lit up inside me and I couldn't fight the smile pulling at my lips. Having Shadow like this was new and exciting, sure. I wanted to shout *yes* instantly, but remembered how sensitive Gunner could be about feeling excluded. As wonderful as a budding new relationship felt, I couldn't neglect any of them for a fresh high. Especially not him.

"No." I grabbed the sides of his cut, bringing his mouth to crash against mine. "I want you."

I tasted his smile, and melted into the arms that slid around me. "You sure?"

"Positive."

My fingers extended, tracing the sharp angles of his jaw as I savored each of his slow, sensual kisses. The world outside my golden man's arms ceased to exist for a few precious moments. Our lips barely separated when we parted, soft puffs of breath still mingling in the chilly air.

"Love you," I whispered, dragging my fingers through a stray lock of blond hair.

"Love you more," he sighed contentedly with a final kiss before reluctantly pulling away. "I'll be rendezvousing with Reap and Shadow, see if I can meet this mysterious general soon before I come back to get you."

"Okay." I untangled from him, walking backward to watch him ride off. "I'll be here."

He shot me a heart-melting smile over his shoulder as he turned the bike around, then shot down the road at speeds much higher than he allowed me to drive.

I turned to the hospital doors and walked through, hoping the cool outside air had prevented my face from getting too red. Nothing could be done about my body temperature, though. My guys were just too hot.

The hospital lobby looked clean and well-maintained. Only a few small hints gave any indication that this place had been looted a few years ago. The freshly painted wall behind the front desk covered up some kind of graffiti that was just barely visible. One more coat should be enough. Some of the waiting area furniture looked beat up, as if someone had turned the couches over or thrown chairs across the room.

I approached the front desk, which was empty. Not a soul was in sight on this floor, so I opted to go exploring. Heading for the elevators, I pressed an UP button and was surprised to see it light up. The panel above the doors counted down from five floors, then the door slid smoothly open when it reached my floor. Freyja walked into the metallic box like she rode in elevators all the time.

I hesitated for a moment, then stepped inside, still in a state of awe. It had been years since I'd seen or been inside a working elevator. Luxuries like these ceased to be maintained once the Collapse hit. Now it just had to not get stuck on the way up.

I hit the button for the second floor, stepped back, and held my breath. The door slid closed with a soft *ding* and the sound made a giggle burst from my chest. Who knew an elevator would be such a luxury?

When the doors slid open again to another lobby, this time a woman's head was visible behind the front desk.

"Hello," I called, eagerly stepping out and heading toward her.

She jumped, looking at me with startled, wide eyes. "Goodness!" She brought a hand to her chest. "No one comes through this way, I didn't expect to hear a voice."

"Didn't mean to scare you." I stopped at the edge of the desk. "I'm Mariposa. I came into town last week."

"That's right." The woman's eyes narrowed in recognition at me, but more out of curiosity than suspicion. She was middle-aged and solidly built, with streaks of gray through her carefully curled dark hair that fell to her shoulders. "You're the one who saved the governor's daughter."

"With the help of a few good men," I laughed lightly. "But I'm trained as a medic and wanted to check out the hospital. So far, it seems a bit, ah..."

"Empty?" the woman chuckled. "That's because it is. I'm Rhonda, by the way."

"Well-met, Rhonda." I shook her hand across the desk, noticing her pale blue scrubs were well-worn and carried various stains that lingered after probably hundreds of washings.

A memory hit me of some of the nurse instructors back in school. They wore their old tattered, stained scrubs with pride until they were threadbare. Every rip and stain was like a badge of honor, remnants of someone they once helped.

"If you're looking for the doctor, he's in surgery at the moment," Rhonda said, straightening up.

"Oh, no problem. I don't want to bother him—"

"Good," she smiled. "Because you won't be."

I couldn't resist the smile back. Typical head nurse, stern and quick to put people in their place, but kind once they got to know you. At least I hoped so. It felt like I was back in nursing school, and the nostalgia bloomed in my chest.

"But seeing as there's no one rushing in here with blood pouring out of various orifices," Rhonda continued, making her way around the desk toward me, "I can show you around a bit."

It wasn't until she grabbed a cane and leaned on it heavily that I realized she walked with a significant limp.

"Gunshot, border wars," she grunted out. "Don't know what they're calling it now, but it was at the old Oregon-Idaho border about five years back."

"Sorry to hear that." I picked up my pace as she walked alongside me. Even with a cane, she was fast.

"Heh, I'm not. About time I got a soldier's welcome everywhere I went," she cackled. "And all these nice young men offering me their hands and holding things for me. It's not a bad trade at all." Her sharp eyes roamed over me as we walked down the hallway, my boots and her sneakers an odd mix of sounds.

"I did about three years in the border wars too," I said. "From East Texas to Arizona, just following the battles west."

"You're in damn good shape for being a battle medic," Rhonda observed. She was right—I had no major scars or injuries to speak of from those times.

"I don't know how," I admitted. "I traded pills to get me out of some hairy situations, but even still, I got lucky."

"Someone must've been watching out for you," Rhonda muttered.

Freyja's loud purr sputtered to life as she headbutted my ankle, walking in perfect time with my leg as she rubbed against me.

"Maybe." I smiled. "'Til I ran into a biker gang, and then *they* became those someones."

Rhonda lifted in an eyebrow, taking note of the black cat for the first time. "We don't usually let animals into the hospital, but your little critter sure is stuck to you like velcro. He better not get into anything, though."

"She," I corrected. "And you don't have to worry. Freyja sticks by me and she's great with patients. She's like a," I paused to think of the pre-Collapse term I learned in school, "like a therapy cat."

Rhonda nodded, the gesture stern, like she'd give me one chance and no more than that.

"So, is it true you're married to all of them?" she asked. "The bikers you rode in with?"

"No," I laughed. "I'm committed to three, and... I guess, in the early dating stages with a fourth."

Both eyebrows shot up and Rhonda resumed facing forward with a chuckle. "Oh, to be young and beautiful again."

She took me to a large room at the end of the hall where an actual, real CT scanner sat. My jaw dropped open and I nearly wanted to cry. Hell, I wanted to kiss that beautiful machine.

"How did you get this?" I asked in an awed whisper, approaching the machine. "I thought there were hardly any working ones left."

"Governor Vance bought it himself and had it shipped from over-seas," Rhonda declared proudly. "See? All the words are in German."

"I can't imagine what it must have cost him," I said, shaking my head. "But this is amazing! No more guessing games like out in the field."

"It's quite possibly the only one in the southwest." Rhonda fondly ran a hand over the machine. "And it's helped us save hundreds of lives, that's for sure."

"What else does the hospital have?" I turned back to her, giddiness running through me. "Ultrasound machines? X-rays? How about a lab?"

"Down, girl," Rhonda teased with a chuckle. "We have all of those, yes, but not many, and even fewer people with the skills to use them. Our poor lab tech is always run ragged. He works the longest hours out of any of us and is always behind. We're working on getting more people trained, but you know how it is. Medical professionals don't grow overnight."

"I'd love to help." Excitement continued to brim throughout me despite her *down, girl*. "My specialty was in labor and delivery, but you can put me anywhere that needs the most support. Anything I haven't learned out in the field, I can pick up quickly—"

"Ah, just the person to decide where an eager young medic should go." Rhonda tilted her head down the hallway and I followed her gaze.

A tall, slender man was coming down the hallway with long strides. He wore the iconic, long white coat of a doctor with plain jeans and a T-shirt underneath. Glasses sat on an attractive, friendly face with a medium-brown complexion. What surprised me the most was how young he looked, close to the same age as any of my guys.

"Dr. Brooks, this is Mariposa," Rhonda introduced. "Accomplished combat medic and Kyrie Vance's personal savior."

"Oh please," I laughed, shaking off my surprise at the sight of the young doctor. "It's amazing what a small knife and a huge dose of adrenaline can make you do."

"I've heard you're exceedingly modest too," Dr. Brooks teased me gently with a warm smile, accepting my outstretched hand. "It's a pleasure, Mariposa. I'm sorry we didn't get to meet at the governor's dinner party. We were swamped here."

"That's why I'm here," I offered. "Heard you could use some extra hands and Rhonda was nice enough to show me around."

The doctor nodded, his warm expression turning grave. "Rumors of a retaliation from Blakeworth are already swirling, even an all-out war. We'll need lots of combat medics, and soon. People who can move fast and treat major injuries on the fly."

"You're looking at one." I crossed my arms. "Have you been a combat medic yourself, doctor?"

"Ah, no." He blushed slightly. "I went to medical school in Canada. University of Toronto, to be exact."

"Canada?" I repeated. "Why on earth would you leave Canada for *this* place?" I had been hoping to escape to the great frozen north before running into my guys. It was a major refugee destination that few were actually able to reach.

"Governor Vance reached out to me," Dr. Brooks admitted. "I had recently graduated, just started my residency, and apparently was near the bottom of a long list of candidates he'd called."

Rhonda scoffed. "I can't imagine why anyone else would have said no."

"Right?" Dr. Brooks laughed. "A hospital job in a foreign land in the middle of civil and political unrest. Also, I wouldn't get paid for the foreseeable future, but housing, food, and all basic necessities would be taken care of."

My curiosity got the best of me. "So why did you say yes?"

The doctor straightened. "I wanted to help those who needed it most—the ones without any access to medical care."

"We also take in patients traveling from other territories," Rhonda explained. "Some cross hundreds of miles to get here. They have to be screened by the army at the borders, so we try to have medics posted there in case it's something life-threatening. But it's like Dr. Brooks said," her eyes lifted to him, "we need more people. Badly."

That sealed it for me. I wanted to work here. Their mission matched mine exactly—the same one I'd carried with me since leaving Texas.

"When can I start?" I asked.

My stomach growled as I stepped out of the hospital front doors two hours later. Dr. Brooks and Rhonda had given me an extensive tour, even allowing me to visit current patients and other staff. The time flew by and I hurried out when the tour was all done, hoping I hadn't kept Gunner waiting.

The cold was the first thing that hit me when I stepped outside, a shock to my system after walking back and forth inside for several hours.

Even the landscape looked softer, grayer than this morning. This chill on my morning walk with Reaper had been nothing compared to this. My little flannel jacket didn't stand a chance. I reached down to hold Freyja for some warmth, but she decided to be uncooperative, twisting out of my arms to stay planted on the ground. No motorcycle was waiting for me out front, so I wrapped my arms around myself as I peered down the street.

"What the..." Something was falling on my face, sticking to my eyelashes. I blinked and looked up, holding my palm out for what seemed to be an impossibility.

"It's snowing!" I laughed to no one in particular, spinning in a circle just outside the awning of the hospital entrance.

I was freezing my ass off, but didn't care. Weather patterns had become so unpredictable in recent decades and snow was rare. All my life I'd been used to droughts, freak thunderstorms, flash floods, and even the occasional hurricane in my part of Texas. But *snow!* I had few precious memories of the magical white stuff.

My laughter and spinning continued until I got dizzy, slowing down as the roar of a motorcycle steadily grew louder as it came down the street. I leaned against a parking sign, my surprise apparent as the leather clad rider approached.

"Didn't expect to see you here," I said.

REAPER

The morning sun disappeared behind a blanket of clouds, and the warmth with it, as Shadow and I rode to the City Hall building. I zipped my jacket up to my throat, grateful that I'd dressed for the cold.

"Feels like rain," I remarked as we took up a parking space in front of the building.

"I think it's snow." Shadow stretched and curled his gloved fingers, dismounting his ride.

"That'll be somethin'." I reached into my jacket pocket for smokes, then remembered it wasn't allowed inside the building. My hand dropped with a sigh. I had to start getting used to cutting back anyway.

The governor's assistant, Josh, waited for us in the lobby of the same building where we attended the dinner party last night.

"Morning, gentlemen," he greeted, hands shoved in the pockets of his pressed slacks. Even inside the building, it wasn't much warmer than outside. Heat was expensive, a precious resource, and I knew Governor Vance was conscious of budgets. "The governor is just finishing a meeting in his office, then he'll be at your disposal."

"We're waiting for one more anyway," I said. "Gunner should be on his way back from dropping off our wife at the hospital."

Josh's eyebrow twitched at the use of *our* before he schooled his features again. "Oh, I see. Is Mariposa all right?"

"Fine, just meeting the staff and getting a tour." I inclined my head. "As we are here."

"Yes, of course." Josh clasped his hands in front of him and looked at Shadow. "Did you enjoy the governor's gift, sir?"

The man's face froze, his throat working a nervous swallow. "Um, yes. Please thank him for me. It was very much...enjoyed." He almost appeared to be sweating, despite the cold.

"I'm glad to hear it." Josh turned to a side table with a coffee press and pastry spread. "Help yourself to anything. I'll see how much more time the governor needs." His shiny shoes clacked on the marble floor as he walked away.

"You didn't mention anything about a gift from the governor," I muttered, helping myself to a small paper cup of coffee.

Shadow's eyes flicked to the spread but he didn't move to grab anything. "When I went home last night, he, um," his jaw ticked, "he sent a woman to my room."

"Yeah?" I kept my voice as expressionless as possible while filing this information away. "And did you in fact *enjoy* his gift? Before or after you put your mouth on my wife?"

"I didn't," Shadow insisted, his gaze level on mine. "Nothing happened and I sent her away. She was gone before any of you got home."

I hid my smile behind a sip of coffee. That was exactly what I'd hoped to hear. "Good man." I clapped my palm on his shoulder. "I'm not sure if you're aware of how this works, but while she has all of us, we cannot be with any others."

"I understand," Shadow murmured, turning to look blankly at the mostly-empty lobby. "I wouldn't. I don't want anyone else. And anyway —" He stopped talking abruptly, busying himself with a cup of coffee.

"Yes?" I implored.

"It's nothing, president."

"Shadow." I turned to him. "If we share a woman, we need to be able to talk about things. That's the *only* way this works. If something's on your mind regarding her, please just spit it out."

He wrapped his massive hands around the paper cup, staring down into the dark liquid. "I was going to say, I never imagined having a woman I could call mine, let alone one I could share with men I respect." He swallowed thickly, raising his eyes to me. "I'm not experienced at this, but I'll do my best, Reaper. I only want to do right by her."

The man's odd-colored eyes were starry with daydreams. He cradled his coffee as gently as if it were Mari's hand. It was all I could do to keep from snickering. Shadow was completely and utterly smitten.

And Mari was too. She tried to play it cool on our walk this morning, but I could tell how excited she felt about him. I was a bit taken aback that she didn't want to fuck him right away, but it was cute how she wanted to take things slow. Shadow was a different animal than the rest of us, that was certain.

"Hey! You all still waiting?"

Gunner's voice floated toward us from the entrance, his boots echoing off the high ceiling.

"Governor's finishing some business," I muttered.

"Politicians," Gun scoffed, moving toward the pastry table. "No one's time matters but theirs." He helped himself to a cheese Danish, folding the thing in half before shoving it all in his mouth.

"Mari get off okay?"

Gunner stared at me, the muscles in his jaw working as he chewed his pastry. "I didn't exactly have the opportunity to get her off, but yes, we made it to the hospital and she's fine."

"Ass." I slapped his puffed-out cheek, hoping to make him choke on his food.

The nerves in my stomach that had been twisting all morning remained, despite Gunner's assurance. Daren's warning filled my head like a beacon. If something happened at the hospital, would she be alright? Could I get there in time?

You're going to have to break down the door. She'll die if you don't.

Fuck, I'd be as bald as T-Bone if I kept tearing my hair out over this shit. The easiest solution was to keep Mari home and guarded at all times, but she'd never go for that. I could only do it for so long too, before even my paranoid ass started to feel uneasy about keeping her prisoner. And that was *if* the warning was even about her in the first place. But why would my brother come to me in a dream to tell me about anyone else?

Damn it, Daren. Would it kill you to give one premonition that made sense?

"Ah, sorry to keep you gentlemen waiting."

Governor Vance headed our way from his office wing with Josh in tow. While suited up and sharp as usual, the governor looked slightly disheveled from a few small details that were easy to miss. His voice was a bit hoarse and his tie was slightly askew. His face was flushed, skin dewy. But the most telling sign was the young woman storming away from his office, her blonde braid swinging angrily against her back.

"Daughter troubles, sir?" I inquired casually, although I wasn't just making conversation. I wanted him to know that small details wouldn't slip past me. As long as this politician knew he couldn't cut any deals behind my back, we could have a very productive working relationship.

"Don't get me started," he sighed, wiping his brow with a handkerchief delicately. "Sometimes I wonder if a boy would've been easier."

"We're living proof that they're not," Gunner chuckled.

"Fair enough. Right this way, gentleman." Vance and Josh turned, leading us down a corridor. "I'm eager to show you what I couldn't after dark last night."

We went out another set of doors in the back of the building. Hades waited patiently for us at the back door, seemingly unperturbed about not being allowed inside. To our left, I spotted the patio where we had cigars after dinner. The small lake just off the patio stretched out in front of us, appearing to wrap around the back of the building. The water lapped softly at the shore, choppy and gray with the new winterlike weather.

Governor Vance led us over a quaint wooden bridge that crossed over the narrowest part of the lake. On the other side was a large expanse of land in various stages of development, from the completed house on the water he showed us last night, to work crews still pouring foundations and sawing lumber.

He led us down the freshly-paved perimeter roads first, waving to crews setting up the frames of houses. We stopped to talk to one of the master builders who showed us floor plans of the structures going up. Most of the homes were spacious, big enough for families. Another set of floor plans showed a condo project, smaller spaces for single people and couples without children.

If nothing else, the governor was making sure to cover all his bases. We ventured inward, toward the center of the development where the roads were still dirt and gravel. He pointed out areas where he planned for businesses and schools to go up, and a central square for gatherings and celebrations. According to his vision, this whole area across the lake would become its own city. The territory of Four Corners stretched out far beyond the main city, but was mostly uninhabited desert and ruins. With so many people flocking here, it was a constant race to rebuild fast enough.

"This is going to be a playground for children." Vance swept his arm over a crew of men welding metal pieces together for some climbing structure. "And here, a community garden. Something for the women to do, eh?" He chuckled to himself, the only one to laugh.

"Or the stay-at-home dads," Gunner returned. "That's the life path I'm ready for."

"Mari *might* let you do that," I mused. "If you get any better at cooking than Jandro."

"Shit, I'm fucked. I can barely use a toaster."

"Rich bitch."

"Whatever, broke bitch."

We laughed together while Shadow kept silent. I wondered how he felt about the whole child-rearing thing, or if he gave it any thought at all. The guy probably had zero positive association with childhood or parental figures. All the better that there would be four of us, should Mari decide to bring him into the fold. And if we could all learn to be as patient as she was, maybe we could show him how good raising a family could be.

"You see?" Vance beamed at us ribbing each other. "Your whole club can find home in this community. Your officers could be a neighborhood watch, of sorts, working with the army to keep the territory safe."

"It's got a lot of potential," I admitted, looking around at the half-constructed buildings. "And it's a beautiful dream to have."

"I'm sensing hesitation," the governor pressed gently. "What are your concerns, president?"

"The fact that you're bordered from the north, south, and east by enemies," Gunner answered for me. "At least one of which has a personal interest in attacking you."

"That," I agreed. "It's wonderful what you're doing here, Governor, but we can't help but feel like you're building a future on a very shaky present. Blake and Tash's territories need to be dealt with first, before we make any plans of putting down roots."

"Oh, I don't disagree at all, Reaper. General Bray will be here any moment to discuss plans for securing the borders—"

"Secure borders aren't enough." I shook my head. "We had secure borders at Sheol. They got in anyway with drones and bombs. We need to go on the offensive, governor."

Gunner nodded through everything I said. Shadow stood by with his own silent support while Vance and Josh exchanged nervous glances.

"While I certainly understand your feelings, Reaper, Four Corners is a territory of refuge. Our army is built on principles of protection, of defense first and foremost. I'm hesitant to send soldiers to almost-certain deaths when the vast majority of them came here to ensure safety for their families."

"We want the exact same thing, sir." Gunner clasped his hands in front of him. "I wasn't kidding about the stay-at-home dad thing. I want to live in a world where my wife can do work she loves and I spend my retirement doting on my kids. But none of that is possible if we just sit and wait while Tash and Blake wreak destruction all around us. We have to fight, bleed, and sacrifice for that peaceful life."

"General Bray would agree with you," Vance sighed. "He can tell you himself when he gets here how frustrated he is at my inaction. The army is sharp and well-trained under him, he's just waiting for my command. I know I've had a privileged life compared to you men, but I don't take the responsibility of my citizens' lives lightly. If Bray says we must go to war and you do as well, I am prepared to make that call, but only if there's no other way."

"Is he supposed to get here soon?" Gunner tilted his face up, making note of the sun directly overhead as it peaked through the clouds. "Mari wanted me to pick her up for lunch soon."

"Yes, yes. Anytime now." Josh looked at his watch.

"He has some new recruits he might be spending some extra time with," Vance mused. "A father figure to all the runaways, that one. He demands a lot from his soldiers, but has a soft heart underneath."

"Shit." Gunner rocked back on his heels, looking around in all directions. "She wanted me to come get her, but I don't wanna miss this meeting."

"Shadow," I angled my head toward the large, silent man. "Why don't you pick her up?"

"Me?" His eyes widened. "But if she asked for Gunner—"

"Yeah, go, man." Gunner slapped his arm. "You're her shiny new toy."

Shadow looked between us both as if wondering if this was a test, or a trick. "Are you sure?"

"Positive." Gunner gave him a playful shove. "She didn't want to hurt my feelings, but it was really you she wanted anyway. Go."

"Unless you're just *dying* to listen in on military strategy," I chuckled, pulling out a cigarette.

"Ah, okay. I'll...I'll pick her up from the hospital."

"Don't look so excited," Gunner ribbed. "Get goin'. We'll fill you in on who to assassinate later."

Without another word Shadow turned, walking quickly across the small bridge. I daresay the guy had a spring in his step. The anxiety in my stomach eased just a little. Gunner was a great shot and more than capable of protecting Mari, but Shadow would make a swift kill before the enemy even knew he was there. Our woman was in good hands with him.

"He's, uh," Josh cleared his throat politely. "A bit of an odd one, isn't he?"

"You get used to it," I said, lighting up and taking a deep drag. "He's had it rough but he's good, loyal. And the most efficient killer the Steel Demons has ever had."

"Ah. Good, good." Josh smiled politely but paled a little, swiftly looking away. "Oh, there's General Bray now," he said, sounding relieved.

Gunner and I turned in the direction he looked, spotting the man decked out in a camouflage uniform marching toward us. I squinted through my smoke, feeling an eerie sense of familiarity in the general's posture and the way he walked.

I've seen this man before, I realized. More than that. I *knew* this man, but from where?

"Gun." I leaned toward him, lowering my voice. "Does he look familiar to you?"

He gave a slight shake of his head. "No, Reap. Can't say he does."

"I know him," I growled under my breath. "But fuck if I can remember how."

"Do I need to draw?" His hand was already drifting toward one of his guns.

"Not yet." The general's face was shaded under the brim of his hat, but the width of his shoulders, the mouth set in a firm line--they were all features that poked at long-buried memories.

"General." Vance outstretched his hand. "So good of you to join us. This is Reaper, president of the Steel Demons MC, and his captain of the guard, Gunner."

"It's a pleasure, gentleme—"

General Bray turned to me, his hand outstretched in greeting and his face now clear to me. But it was his voice that finally clicked all the pieces into place.

Both of us froze in disbelief as we stared at each other. His beard was gone, but that was definitely *his* mouth. The brown eyes and bridge of his nose were exactly the same, if a bit more tan than before. He took off his hat with a shaking hand, his dark brown hair speckled with far more gray than I remembered.

He spoke first, a barely audible whisper. "Rory?"

Somehow, I found my voice in the wrangled knot that my throat became.

"Dad?"

SHADOW

I could see Mariposa from up the road, twirling around in front of the hospital, arms out like wings and her mouth open with laughter. A light dusting of snow had just started falling, quickly melting and turning to mush when it hit the ground. But she kicked and danced underneath it like a girl from a Christmas movie.

She slowed her twirling as I approached, leaning heavily on a metal pole outside the hospital. "Didn't expect to see you here." Her cheeks were flushed from her spinning but she hugged her arms close, her flannel shirt doing little against the cold.

"Gunner asked me to come," I said. "He and Reaper were waiting on the general."

Mari smiled, looking down at her shoes as she rubbed her arms faster. "That Gunner. I should have known."

"Are you cold?" I shrugged off my cut before she could answer, then unzipped my hoodie and peeled it off my arms. "Here, wear this." I held my sweatshirt out to her.

She stared at my arm extended out to her, and then to my face. "Are you sure?"

My throat tightened with the familiar fear of wondering if I'd done something wrong. I'd seen old ladies wear their men's shirts and hoodies all the time. Mari wasn't *mine* yet, as far as I understood. Was I being too presumptuous in offering my clothing?

But even if I was, who gave a fuck if I had a jacket and she was cold?

"I'm sure. Take it before you freeze."

"What about you?"

My breath stuttered for a moment at the stark reminder that she cared enough about me to ask. "I'll be fine. Cold doesn't bother me."

She finally accepted the sweater from me and fed her arms through the sleeves. I looked away for a moment to pull my cut back on over my T-shirt. When I glanced at her again, it was all I could do to keep from laughing.

"What's that look for?" she demanded.

"Nothing."

"Shadow."

"Really, it's nothing! I just didn't realize it would be so big on you."

She was swimming in the fabric. Her head floated above the hood at the top like she was treading water, and her legs stuck out of the bottom like skinny trunks on a tree. In the middle, her body was lost in the black circus tent of my hoodie. It was a comical sight, but not in the least bit unattractive. I wanted to pull her to me and warm her up better than any article of clothing could.

"Come on." I scooted back as far as I could and patted the seat in front of me. "Do you know what you want for lunch?"

Mari approached the side of my bike and threw a leg over, settling in front of me until her ass brushed against my crotch. Fuck me. She'd be warmer in front, but maybe for my own sanity I should have told her to sit behind me.

"Can we explore the town for a place to eat?" Her head touched the center of my chest and she looked straight up to talk to me. "We haven't seen all it has to offer yet, and I want to support the locals."

"Sure." I dropped a kiss to her forehead before I could overthink it.

She turned to look over her shoulder in response, lips landing softly on my mouth. I halted my gasp as I returned her kiss, my body still reacting with shock to her affection. It lessened every time though, giving way to that warm, melted feeling that took over whenever she touched me.

The kiss ended slowly, her soft mouth dragging over my beard as she resumed facing forward. Freyja had jumped into her lap and was now cocooning inside my hoodie. "Anything you in the mood for?" she asked, her voice slightly breathy.

You. Always you.

"I dunno." I returned my grip to the handlebars, caging her between my arms. "Just not soup."

"Aww." She leaned her head back on my chest and looked up at me again. "Are you associating soup with being sick now?"

"Probably." I turned us out of the hospital lot and headed down the main road leading through the center of town. "It just doesn't sound appealing."

"No soup, then," she agreed, planting her hands on my fuel tank. "But something hot and hearty would be good in this weather."

The ride was slow, with no particular destination in mind as we checked out the bustling center of Four Corners. It had stopped snowing already and road crews were already raking the slushy snow-and-mud mix off the sidewalks.

"Oh, shepherd's pie!" Mari pointed at a sandwich board outside of a squat brick building. "How does that sound?"

"What is that? I've never had it," I admitted.

"Oh, it's amazing!" She was already wriggling in my seat, eager to get off. *Ugh, don't think about getting off.* "It's a savory pie with a meat filling and mashed potatoes on top. It's *so* good, Shadow. You'll love it."

"Sounds good. I'll try it."

I maneuvered the bike close to the building and looked for a place to park. There didn't seem to be a rhyme or reason to vehicle parking yet, so we found an alley on the next block where a few scooters and motor-bikes sat and decided to take our chances. Crime was supposed to be low within Four Corners, due to the governor's strict entry require-ments. My Harley would be tempting to a thief, but also too big to steal without alerting me in the next building.

Freyja jumped out from under my hoodie and Mari's hand slipped into mine once we got off the bike. I did my best to walk normally while my heart went crazy. She appeared to have no second thoughts about being affectionate with me in public.

Like I was one of her men.

That thought was almost as staggering as her being affectionate with me at all.

"I like your hoodie," she said, bringing the fabric over her nose. "It smells like you."

I looked at her, surprised again. "That's a good thing?"

"Yes," she laughed. "I might steal it, so it feels like I'm wrapped up in you when you're not around."

"You can have it, then." I took my gloves off and stuck them in my cut pocket so I could feel her hand better as I held it. "But what if I want to steal something of yours?"

She gave me a playful look. "You already have my cat."

"That's true," I chuckled, looking ahead to where Freyja waited for us at the end of the alley. "She's lovely, but a poor imitation of you."

"I could say the same for your hoodie."

No words came to me in response to that, so I just rubbed my thumb along the back of her hand. She returned the gesture, squeezing around my fingers lightly.

We turned the corner and walked into the restaurant where the shepherd's pie was advertised. It was a simple, rectangular building with a ceiling almost too low for my head. The tables and chairs were obviously scavenged from other places, spread out with few matching pieces in the dining area. The original counter had been ripped out, but there was a window in the far wall looking into the kitchen. A hand-drawn sign was taped next to the window that read 'Order Here'.

There was plenty of room to sit, with only a few tables occupied. Customers paid little attention to us, keeping their conversations low over their soups and sandwiches. Two chefs cooked over stoves in the kitchen, the closest one looking up and nodding at us as we stepped inside.

"Just holler when you're ready," the chef yelled before turning back to his stove.

He was a stout guy, red-faced with strawberry blond hair. The collar of his chef's jacket was turned up, which was curious, considering the sweltering heat from the stoves. He wiped sweat from his brow before grabbing the handle of a frying pan to sauté his dish. The movement showed a peek of a tattoo on his neck—two straight lines intersecting at the ends—before he readjusted his collar to hide it.

"I hope I have enough to trade for food." Mari dug through her pants pockets. "I always carry a few pills on me but it's not always—"

"Don't worry about it," I said with a light touch to her elbow. "I'll get us lunch."

"Are you sure? I don't mind—"

"I got it, really. Why don't you find us a place to sit?"

"'Kay." She nearly had to jump to kiss my cheek before meandering through the eclectic collection of tables.

I went up to the window, catching the eye of the red-faced chef. He paused his chopping to grab a notepad and a pen.

"What can I get ya?" He tilted his head, making a clear effort to hide his neck tattoo.

"Two shepherd's pies," I said. "Please," I added.

He scribbled it down. "Any sides? Drinks?"

Mari didn't ask for anything else, but I ordered teas for us both.

"Mmkay." The chef looked at me pointedly. "How you payin'?"

I steeled myself with a breath. This could go horribly wrong, but I couldn't continue to be fearful of human interaction. It was always a risk, but lately it felt just terrifying rather than suicidal.

"You looking to get that covered up?" I asked in a low voice.

The chef's eyes widened, his hand immediately clapping to his neck. "What?"

"That neck tattoo you're hiding. You want it covered so you don't have to keep wearing a jacket in a sweltering hot kitchen?"

His hand lowered slowly, but he still looked uneasy. "So, what, you know a guy?"

"You're looking at him," I said. "I'm a tattoo artist. I'll cover that up for you, and do any other work you'd like."

"You will, huh?" He looked me over, taking in my cut and patches. "You with them bikers that just rode in?"

"That's us, yeah," I said. "We're not here for trouble. Just looking for a home like everyone else."

"Stickin' around then?"

"For the time being, yes."

"All right." He rubbed his jaw, nodding agreeably. "Yeah, okay. I'll trade ya grub for ink."

"Good. I'm at the B&B in the northwest part of town. Come by when you're ready and ask for Shadow."

"Right on, man." He ripped my order off of the notepad and stabbed it onto a receipt spindle. "I'll grab your shepherd's pies. They just came out of the oven."

"Thanks."

I scanned the dining room as I waited, spotting Mari at a table next to a window looking out onto the street. A woman with two small children walked by on the sidewalk, and Mari waved to the little girl holding her mother's hand.

"Two shepherd's pies." The mismatched ceramic bowls clattered on the serving window. "I'll bring your teas out in a sec. And hey, man..."

"Yeah?" I grabbed our food, mouth already watering at the sight of the savory filling and lightly browned mashed potatoes.

"This thing?" The chef pulled down his collar to show me the full tattoo. "I was a dumbfuck when I was young, okay? I don't subscribe to any of that shit—"

"You don't have to explain it to me," I told him. "I'm the last person to judge on poor decisions."

He nodded once more, thumping the counter with his hand. "Enjoy your meal, man."

I headed for the table where Mari waited and set our food down in front of her.

"Thank you for lunch," she said sweetly, sliding a napkin and utensils toward me.

"Thank you for telling me about shepherd's pie." I dug in with a fork, watching the steam rise from the piping hot filling.

"If you don't mind me asking..." Mari licked a small piece of mashed potato from her fork. "What did you trade for the meal?"

"Tattoos," I said, sneaking a glance toward the kitchen, then lowered my voice. "The chef has a swastika on his neck. I'm going to cover it up for him."

"Oh." Mari's brows lifted in surprise. "I didn't see that."

"He's hiding it under his jacket. I offered the cover-up on a hunch, glad he took it."

Mari took another bite of her food thoughtfully. "I haven't seen any tattoo shops here yet. You'd probably make a killing if you opened one. You'd have no competition."

"Maybe." I turned it over in my head as I chewed my food. Tattooing and drawing all day would be a dream career for me. My only hesitation was in having to deal with people I didn't know. That part still made me uneasy. But I did gain a possible new client by offering my services to a complete stranger, and that hadn't been so bad.

Mari and I talked lightly until we were scraping the bottoms of our bowls. Fuck, shepherd's pie was good. Maybe I could talk Jandro into making it if we ever settled permanently.

Once finished, we returned our dishes to the serving counter. On the other side, the chef and his partner chopped potatoes, I assumed for more pie.

"Thank you, it was delicious!" Mari called through the window.

"Thanks for comin' in," the chef called. "And I'll be seeing you soon, man!"

"Looking forward to it." Taking Mari's hand, we headed back out onto the street, the now-emerging sun making us squint. Freyja waited patiently for us just outside the front door, apparently having made friends with some doves.

"Can we walk off this food?" Mari rubbed her belly with one hand. "Or do you have to head back?"

"No, I don't need to be anywhere." I was actually relieved that she didn't want to get back on the bike right away. Any opportunity to spend more time with her, I jumped at.

Fingers laced between us, we started a leisurely pace down the side-walk. Freyja followed after us at her own pace, her doves in tow. The next block over was some kind of shopping district. Some shopkeepers worked out of established buildings, while others set up folding tables and canopies.

Mari released my hand to look through a rack of clothing, while I mused over an airbrush artist's display. The artwork wasn't *bad,* just no finess yet. Probably a young artist.

"Alright, mate." Greeting me with a thick foreign accent, the kid nodded at me from his folding chair, dark sunglasses over his eyes and a fat blunt in his hand.

"How's it goin'," I mumbled noncommittally. "You do good work here. Keep it up."

"Cheers, mate."

I wandered over to the next table where Mari looked over jewelry and chatted with the vendor, an attractive older woman with green eyes and streaks of gray in her reddish-brown hair.

"I love that one." Mari pointed to a stone pendant encased in a silver setting. "It matches my ring."

"Oh, so it does!" The jeweler fixed her gaze on Mari's ring, the one Reaper gave her. "Um, may I? Do you mind?"

"Of course not." Mari stretched her hand out for the other woman to inspect.

The woman seemed to go pale as she carefully looked over the stone and setting. "May I ask where you got this?"

"It was a gift from my husband." Mari beamed, wiggling her fingers.

"I see." The jeweler turned to me, a tense smile on her face. "What a thoughtful gift. You must love seeing it on her finger."

"Oh no, I didn't—I'm not, um—"

Shit. My eyes slid over to Mari, who didn't seem at all distressed by the misunderstanding. Her hand wrapped around my arm, fingers resting on my bicep.

"We're together, but he's not the one who gave me the ring. It's part of my husband's culture you see, for a woman to have multiple partners. Everyone involved is aware and consenting."

"I see," the woman repeated, looking no less pale and nervous than a moment ago. "If it's not too personal, can I ask your husband's name?" Her voice wavered slightly.

"It's Reaper," Mari answered. "He's the president of the biker club that came into town a few days ago.

"Well, he has excellent taste." The jeweler brought her hands together, clasping and wringing them. "I wish you all much happiness."

"Thank you so much." Mari smiled politely as we continued walking. Once out of earshot, she leaned her head on my shoulder. "Was that a little weird?"

"I was just about to ask you that."

"Something was definitely off there." She stroked her thumb over her ring, toying with the colorful stone as it caught the sunlight.

REAPER

"Dad?"

I blinked several times, certain that the man standing in front of me couldn't be real. Or alive, for that matter.

"Holy shit." He rubbed his face, staring back at me intently. "Is it really you, Rory?"

"Fuck," I breathed in disbelief. "No one's called me that since—well, my old lady does to give me shit, but—"

"You have a wife?" he asked in an awed whisper. "And you...you lead a motorcycle club?" Only then did he take in my patches, my cut, and Gunner standing next to me wearing the same uniform.

"I, uh, fuck. I guess I should make introductions." I ran a hand through my hair, purposely tugging at my scalp to make sure I wasn't dreaming. "This is Gunner, my sergeant at arms. Gun, this is...my old man."

"My birth name is Finn. Finn Daley." Dad gave a sheepish laugh and awkward wave. "But for the last five years or so, I've gone by Finn Bray. Long story, but I also went by Carter for a little while to escape being detected."

"Carter?" I barked, my anticipation jumping at the mention of my other father's name. "Is he around?"

I regretted the question as soon as it came out. Dad's smile faltered and he gave a small shake of his head. Of course not. He wouldn't be using my second father's name if he were alive and well. But I couldn't stop the questions once they began.

"What about Mom?" I demanded. "Is she okay? What...fuck! What the hell happened?"

Gunner cut in with a friendly squeeze of my shoulder. "We should probably give you some time alone. Right, governor?"

"Oh, yes. Of course." Vance and Josh seemed content to watch the spectacle from the sidelines, but had enough sense to start heading toward the bridge. "Take the rest of the day off, General. Give Alisa my love."

My chest relaxed just slightly. So my mother *was* okay, and still with him.

"I'll join you fellas!" Gunner slid up to Vance's left side, sandwiching the governor between him and Josh.

Good man, I thought. That was Gunner, always rubbing elbows with the powerful people we needed on our side.

Turning back to my dad, we both blew out a long breath and laughed nervously.

"Fuck," we said in unison, and laughed again.

"Holy shit, son. You look good. Little rough, but good." He inspected me from head to toe. "You're a *man*. God, you were what, nineteen the last time I saw you?"

"Something like that." I squinted like he was an optical illusion about to disappear at any moment. "It's been a long fuckin' time."

"How are your siblings?" he asked, crossing his arms. "Still with you?"

"Noelle's good. She's with me," I said, taking a moment to gather myself before dropping the bad news. "Daren...we lost him just over a year ago."

"Oh no." His face fell. "Fuck, that poor kid. Ugh, how?"

"Um, he got sick. A virus, we think." Surprisingly, I didn't feel the need to self-flagellate over his death. At some point over the last few months, I'd been able to release some of the guilt. Plus, I'd just seen him and knew he was at peace.

"Your mom's gonna be devastated." Dad's brow pinched, his eyes lowering with a pained gaze. Daren wasn't his by blood, but none of that mattered to us growing up.

"Were you with him?" he asked. He kept a stoic face but I could see how hard it was for him not to choke up. "How did it happen? When did you get a dog?" He looked down at Hades, nuzzling his hand. "And fuck me, son, where have you been all this time?"

"Got a few minutes?" I angled my head toward the riverbank and pulled out a fresh cigarette. "Why don't we take a walk?"

My father regained his composure and nodded, then promptly shook his head when I offered him a smoke. "Those things will put you in an early grave, son. You don't get to be my age, and running past young punks, when your lungs are all tarred up."

"I never planned on living long anyway," I muttered. "But I'm cutting back. I got a woman now, and we'd like to have kids in a couple years."

"You, a husband!" he laughed, slapping me on the shoulder. "And a dad-to-be, my goodness. Tell me about her! What's her name? Does she have other men?"

"Hang on, old man," I laughed, stunned at how easily we fell into our old banter despite not seeing each other for over ten years. "Let me start at the beginning."

"Holy shit, Ror." My dad scraped his cigarette butt on the ground. He finally took one after I told him about nearly getting blown up at the Sandia outpost. "That's a hell of a few years. And Mari, damn." He shoved me playfully, lines deepening around his eyes as he grinned. "She must be a hell of a woman to deal with a punk-ass like you."

"She is." I pulled out two more cigarettes and held one out to him. "The other guys are good for her. I'm just trying my best."

"You all gotta come over. Lis and I miss having a busy house, and we need to meet our daughter-in-law." Dad took the smoke and went to light up, then hesitated. "But maybe a little bit after I tell her about Daren. She'll need some time, you know."

"Yeah," I said. "Noelle and I have already had a year to grieve. She's got a man too, you know."

"Oh, what's he like?"

"Eh, you'll meet him soon."

I could picture Larkan now, his back ramrod straight as he shook my father's hand and called him 'sir'. He'd be the type of guy to compliment my mother's cooking and do the dishes for her. My parents would love him, and as much as I hated to admit it, he was pissing me off a lot less. He protected Mari on that mission to Blakeworth, and returned her to me without so much as a scratch. The kid deserved a patch, and my respect, for that alone.

"He's her only one? She always did prefer that."

"Yes, and before you ask any more questions..." I pointed at him, cigarette between my fingers. "You've kept me waiting long enough, old man. Your turn to tell me where you've been all these years."

"Alright, alright." He took a deep drag, holding it in his chest for a moment before releasing it out.

"Some militia came to the commune one night," he began. "They were all in black, no insignia, unmarked vans, that whole business we heard whispers of, but never thought it was true. They came in with rifles and riot gear, started pounding on doors and yelling for people to get in the vans."

"Fuck," I said. My cigarette was already halfway gone.

"Noelle was asleep. Carter stuck her in the cellar and told her not to move or make a sound until you came for her. But other than that, no one had time to react. We were outnumbered and they were taking *everyone*, kids and old folks too. No one wanted to provoke these sons of bitches."

"Where'd they take you?"

"Their base, a bunch of old bunkers in Nevada. These guys called themselves the Original Patriots, saying they were trying to restore the country to its former glory, can you believe it? Kidnapping a bunch of families just trying to live peacefully and they call themselves patriots?"

"What did they want with all of you?" I finished my smoke and stuck another one in my mouth, already way past my usual daily amount, but also past the point of caring.

"Different tasks, depending on what they needed to run their camp. Soldiers, cooks, cleaners. They used children to run messages back and forth. We had to do everything we were told, on penalty of death. Some patriots, huh? And they wanted all the multi-husband families separated. It was to repent for our 'sinful ways'," he air-quoted.

"So what'd you end up doing?"

"They deemed Carter and I too old to be soldiers, so we were assigned to be mechanics. On opposites sides of the compound of course, once they figured out we were part of the same household. Your mom was in laundry and cooking for the first two years or so. That was hell. Carter and I barely saw her, and we weren't allowed to talk to her either. Then, uh," Dad paused, looking out over the river as he ran a hand through his salt-and-pepper hair, "Carter got hurt."

"How?" I demanded, anger already boiling in me for what my second father must have suffered.

"Piece of machinery fell on him," Dad sighed. "Broke his leg in three places. I didn't know until days after. When your mom found out, she somehow got hold of a welding torch and made him a cane so he could get around a bit. But his leg was fucked and the poor guy was in so much pain."

"Was there no medic?" I snarled. "Did no one even try to heal him?"

"Only the chosen ones, the Patriots, got medical attention," Dad said bitterly. "We had to repent for some indefinite amount of time before we could have that privilege."

"Fuck." I dragged on my cigarette only to find I had finished that one too. "How long were you there for?"

"Seven years." His voice was heavy with sadness. "We lost Carter after five. His leg got infected and he just kept getting worse. Your mom tried to sneak over to see him whenever she could, but he put a stop to that. He didn't want to risk her getting caught and punished. Last time I saw him, he was feverish, weak. Leg smelled like death." Dad sighed. "He was just gone the next morning. Bed stripped clean."

"You never saw his body?"

"They had a mass grave out in the desert for those that passed. Most likely they dumped him out there, but we'd be shot on sight if we tried to go find him."

"Fuck," I groaned, the desire to smoke completely gone. My stomach turned with nausea instead. "Guess I'm pouring my first whiskey out for Carter tonight."

None of my fathers had been weak men. Finn, my bio-dad, served twenty-two years in the Air Force and retired as a Major. Nolan, Daren's dad, had worked in farming his whole life and was built like a brick house. Cancer had taken him too young, withering him away to nothing within a year when Daren was twelve and I was fourteen. But it was Carter, Noelle's father, who stood like a mountain even when the other two had met their limit.

Never in my life had I heard Carter moan about being in pain. My dads were all roughly the same age, and I remembered Nolan and Finn bitching about aching joints and sore backs when I was a preteen. Carter would just snort and tell them to stop being pussies. They always ran in the early mornings and worked out together, with Carter always pushing himself the hardest.

I looked to Hades, sitting regally on the lawn next to us with his paws stretched out in front of him. His ear flicked in my direction, head tilting to acknowledge the question in my mind.

Carter Daley is at rest, the omniscient voice echoed through me. A brief summation, but one that comforted the agitated churning in my stomach.

"I always thought he'd last the longest, of all of us." Dad nodded, echoing my thoughts while giving no indication that he heard the voice.

"How'd you and Mom make it to Four Corners then?" I asked

"The bunker hideout got attacked by another militia," he laughed drily. "These fucking Patriots thought the Collapse was God calling them to take over, but oh no. It never occurred to them there'd be bigger fish out there. So they were getting their asses handed to them and demanded all hands on deck. Guess they wanted to go out in a blaze of glory. So I grabbed a rifle and made it look like I was headed to the front lines. Instead, I grabbed your mom, stole a motorbike, and floored it in the opposite direction."

"*You* on a motorbike?" I laughed. "Shit, Dad. Want a cut and a patch? You've earned it."

"Hell nah. I ride like a grandpa now that I'm not running for my life."

"So then what happened?" I asked. "You just headed east 'til you ran out of gas?"

"Yeah, pretty much. Ran out of gas maybe fifteen miles or so outside of the border. We kept walking until we saw armed guards and almost ended up running the other direction. But our feet were bleeding, we were starving, dehydrated. Figured we'd either get shot or die out in the desert anyway, so we decided to take our chances."

"And how'd you end up as a general?"

"Well, after a few weeks of recuperating in the hospital, Vance came to see us. Four Corners was a lot smaller then, so the governor liked to personally meet all the refugees. We told him our stories and it turned out he was an Airman too, back in the day. Didn't stay in as long as me, but he knew where I was coming from. Said he needed a leader for his army. Not to fight and conquer like everyone else, but to keep people safe. I told him I was done fighting other people's wars, but I could whip some brats into shape. Five years later, and here we are."

"How do you feel about a war that's likely to still come?" I asked. "Especially with the territory being so prosperous, and now with taking Vance's daughter back from Blakeworth. Tash and that bastard up north have to have eyes on us."

"Oh, we're ready for it, " Dad said with a soft growl. "We're not looking for war, but those seven years opened my eyes, son. People with just an ounce of power are doing terrible things out there, and the less fortunate are suffering for it. We were damn lucky to make it to Four Corners, but not everyone is. How many people do you think collapsed out there in the desert, running from the exact same thing we were?"

"Hundreds," I mused. "Maybe even thousands."

"Exactly. So yeah, I'll take up arms for those who couldn't. And everyone else is just trying to live free in a safe place for their families." His face softened, lips pulling into a smile. "So you're trying to make me a grandpa, huh?"

"Afterward," I said. "When we win, and I can sleep at night without all this shit running through my head."

"I hear you, son." He clapped me on the shoulder, looking out over the lake, which was starting to sparkle from the sun peeking out from the clouds. "We'll get there. Maybe not in my lifetime, but hopefully in yours."

"Better be in yours," I huffed. "Who am I gonna pass my spawn off to when I want to fuck my old lady into next week?"

"Then you have to be ready, Rory," Dad said softly. "Ready to fight like you never have before."

MARIPOSA

"Do you mind dropping me off at the bar up the street? The one that's been renting out rooms on the top floor?" I leaned back against Shadow, tilting my face up to look at him. "I haven't seen Tessa in a few days and I'd like to visit."

"Sure." He kept his eyes on the road, but released one of the handlebars to caress my back as he gently accelerated forward.

Every touch from him turned me to jelly. It was more than just chemistry and the newness of being together. Everything felt more meaningful, knowing how averse to touch he had been when we first met. He placed those fingers along my spine or threaded through my hand because he *wanted* that contact, not because it was expected of him. Knowing it was all intentional and thought out by him made me soak up every piece and hold on to every sensation.

When he pulled up to the bar, I never wanted the warmth of his chest to leave my back, nor his arms to come away from being extended on either side of me.

"Huh, looks like the Sons are here," Shadow noted, nodding at the bikes parked out front. "That's Grudge's ride. Pretty sure the other two are T-Bone and Dyno's."

"Oh, you should stay too then." I stretched up and long behind me to wrap my hands around the back of his neck. "Hang out with the guys while I visit Tess. We can go back home together, if you're up for it."

I expected him to refuse, knowing he had his limits when it came to social interaction. Eating lunch in a restaurant and window-shopping for a half-hour on a busy street would have been enough for one day, I figured.

Shadow stroked my sides, planting a kiss on me with a soft hum as I stared at him upside down. "Maybe I'll stay for a drink or two," he mused.

"You will?" I squeaked.

"Yeah, why not?" He swung a leg off the bike and lifted me out of the seat with a firm hold on my waist. It took a monumental effort not to swoon.

"Come to the upstairs room and knock if you get sick of them." I squeezed his forearm as we walked up the front porch together.

"I should be fine." He pulled the door open and stepped aside to let me through. "Grudge will tell the other two off if they get annoying."

"Well hey there, little lady—Shadow!"

Seated on worn leather couches and armchairs around a coffee table, all three Sons of Odin turned to face the door, mouths pulling into grins at the sight of the two of us together.

"So this has finally happened, huh?" T-Bone gestured between us. "Thought I saw sparks flying between you two on our little Blakeworth getaway."

"Don't you three have jobs or something?" I teased, rubbing my hand over T-Bone's shaved head.

"Hey, it's hard work being on official business from the governor," Dyno piped up. "We require lots of R&R."

"Uh-huh. Hi, Grudge!" I leaned over the back of the couch to hug the silent man around his neck. He hummed a greeting in return and smiled up at me, squeezing affectionately around my arms.

"How are you, brother?" Shadow eased into the seat next to him, accepting the empty glass and pour of whiskey the other man offered.

"Having a drink with us, Mari?" T-Bone lifted the whiskey bottle up to me.

"Later, maybe. I wanted to see Tessa and the baby for a bit."

Dyno cleared his throat. "You might want to, uh," he curled his hand into a fist and made a knocking motion as he clicked his tongue, "knock before you go in there."

T-Bone snorted, trying to hide a laugh behind his drink, his face going red. My eyes narrowed. What had they seen that they weren't supposed to?

"I delivered her baby, Dy," I laughed it off with a wave of my hand. "There's nothing I haven't seen."

Dyno slouched into the couch cushions, hiding a grin behind his whiskey tumbler. "Suit yourself."

I ignored him, turning to run a hand along the back of Shadow's shoulders before heading to the room upstairs. "I shouldn't be long, but come find me if you need me."

"Take your time." He tilted his head up for a kiss and I happily planted a long, slow one on him in front of our audience.

T-Bone immediately started with the wolf howls, and Dyno was quick to join in with barks, howls, and aggressive hip thrusts.

"Just kidding, man. Don't kick my ass." T-Bone smirked as Shadow and I separated. I didn't hear Shadow's reply, but the two jokers burst into peals of laughter that filled up the bar, Dyno nearly sliding off the couch to the floor.

Giggling at their antics, I made my way to the stairs tucked off in the corner of the bar. Freyja ran ahead of me and jumped up the rickety steps to wait for me on the landing. Despite what I told Dyno, I did knock when I reached Tessa's door. Even while sharing a single room with three other people, I still knew the need for privacy. A room to myself was starting to sound downright heavenly.

"Who is it?" Tessa called from the other side, sounding nervous.

"Santa Claus," I snickered. "It's me, Mari."

"Oh! Uh, just hang on a second."

I waited patiently by the door, trying not to eavesdrop as I heard multiple footsteps on the other side. Voices murmured through the wood, not just Tessa's, but another woman's. My mind remained curiously blank until the door pulled open slowly, and it was Andrea, Dallas's widow, on the other side.

"Oh, hey." My voice carried a tone of surprise before I could control it. "Uh, I could come back later?"

"No, no, it's okay." Andrea blushed, palming her neck nervously. "I was just stopping by, and on my way out."

"Okay." I watched her hurriedly gather up her things, large bags full of several changes of clothes and toiletries, as though she had stayed over much longer than she let on. Like she had spent the night, or several nights by the looks of it. "You don't have to leave—"

"No, it's okay! I should get the kids anyway." She hurried out the door, sending a flustered smile over her shoulder at Tessa, sitting up in the unmade bed. "See ya, Tess."

"Bye, Drea." Tessa looked like she wanted to hide under the covers and never come out.

"Hey." I approached the end of the bed cautiously. "Everything okay?"

She raised her hands and flopped them back down over the comforter. "It's exactly what it looks like. You can just come out and say it, Mari."

"Say what?"

"You know." She looked at me with her chin tucked low. "That Drea and I are two women sharing a room. And a bed."

I lifted one shoulder in a shrug. "That's not for me to speak on. But we can talk about it, if you want." I tentatively sat on the far corner of the mattress.

Tess looked hesitant, fingers curled over the bedspread. "Promise you won't tell anyone? Not any of your men, even Reaper. And definitely not my ex-husband."

"Nothing you tell me will leave this room." I moved to sit in front of her, reaching for her hands. "So, what's going on?"

"So I wasn't completely honest with you and Reaper," Tessa picked at the comforter on her lap, "when I talked about separating."

"What do you mean?"

"This didn't just happen out of nowhere. Andrea and I have a...a connection that Big G doesn't like. We have for years."

I nodded calmly. "A romantic connection, I take it?"

"Yeah, I...had feelings for her before, a long time ago, that are kind of rekindling now." She swallowed nervously. "There was, uh, an incident a couple years back."

"A, uh," I cleared my throat, "sexual incident?"

"Not *exactly*, and we didn't cheat on our guys or anything. They were there. It's just, fuck." She slapped her palms to her cheeks too late, they were already reddening. "I'm just digging myself into a hole here."

"Why don't you tell me what happened?" I scooted further up the bed and took her hands, rolling my thumbs over the back of her palms in an attempt to soothe her. "You're my friend, Tess. I won't judge."

"Really?" She looked skeptical.

"Hon, I sleep with, and am basically married to, *three* guys. I'm the last person that should be judging you."

"But...Andrea and I are women. People have been killed for that."

I nodded my head toward the door I had just come through. "I'd like to see someone try. There's at least three men downstairs who would cut through anyone trying to harm you for loving another woman." *Four, if you include mine sitting with them.*

The worry eased slightly in Tessa's brow, a small smile coming to her lips. "The Sons are good allies. They're staying in rooms here too, and have essentially appointed themselves as our bodyguards. They eat with us downstairs, come with us on errands. It has helped to alleviate the gawking and dirty looks."

"See?" I told her. "I can't even imagine what they've had to face. It's sweet of them to want to protect you from that."

"It's amazing," Tessa mused. "They're so openly affectionate with each other. They don't care who sees, they just are who they are."

"They love each other," I said. "And the fact that they're all men doesn't matter, they're fucking adorable together. No one deserves to be killed over that." I squeezed her hand again. "Had you dated women before Big G?"

"I had a girlfriend in high school," she admitted, her worried frown returning. "I loved her, but her family was set on moving away when the Collapse got real bad. We thought it would be safer to break up. People used to yell horrible slurs at us, and anyway," she sighed, wiping quickly at her eyes, "I liked guys too and wanted to start a family. I thought Big G was the person I needed."

"What happened to make him so upset about Andrea?" I asked gently.

Tessa blew out a long breath. "So, there was a party one night, a couple years back in Sheol. Dallas, Andrea, G, and I all went back to their place afterwards. We got the kids set up for a sleepover upstairs while us adults continued drinking downstairs." Her throat worked nervously. "At some point, Andrea kissed me. It was a super quick peck on the lips, practically nothing. We were drunk and being silly. But Dallas was into it and encouraged us to kiss some more."

"And Big G?" I pressed.

"That's what pisses me off so much. He acted like he was into it too." She brought a hand to her chest. "I remember feeling so elated and relieved. Like yes, my husband *does* accept and love me, even though I'm also attracted to women. It felt like a huge weight off my chest."

Anger heated inside me on her behalf. "But that turned out not to be the case?"

She shook her head. "Two-faced bastard. I must have asked him like ten times if he was seriously okay with it. Even then, we kept things pretty tame. Andrea and I made out for a little while, then she and Dallas went off to fuck. As soon as G and I were alone, he did a complete fucking 180."

"Jesus." My chest ached for her. "What a betrayal. I'm so sorry, Tess."

"He berated me, accused me of all these awful things, called me names." Her voice cracked. "It was exacerbated because he was drunk, of course. Not that that fucking excuses it. I trusted him, and it hurt so bad. So yeah, he's always pitched a fit any time she and I happened to be alone. Nothing happened since that night, but he didn't care. Not even the death of her husband was a good enough reason for me to spend time with her, even just as friends."

"I'm sorry, sweetie." I reached over and rubbed her arm. "If Andrea makes you happy, you're much better off with her."

Her face lit up for the first time since telling me her story. "Thank you for being supportive, Mari. It's still tough, you know. She loved Dallas so much, and she's never been with a woman before. We're taking it slow, but it's nice. We're able to comfort each other. Take turns watching each other's kids. It feels so good, being with someone who listens and just *understands* me. Even if it's just a temporary thing, we'll always be there for each other in one way or another."

"That's how it should be," I said with a light squeeze of her hands. "I'm glad you're happy, honey."

"Well shit, I'm glad you are too. You're absolutely glowing!" She leaned over and poked me in the belly. "Got anyone cookin' in there yet?"

"Nah." I slid a hand over where she poked me, just under my navel. "Not for a little while longer."

"Your men must be on their best behavior then, for you to look so blissed out. That, or you got laid just before coming here. In which case, I *highly* resent you knocking when you did."

"Sorry about my awful timing, but it's not that either," I laughed. "I've been seeing someone new."

"Another one? Jesus, woman. There are whores getting less dick than you!"

"We haven't slept together yet," I clarified. "But it feels like that high school kind of relationship, you know? Lots of kissing and hand-holding. Innocent and sweet. It's actually really nice."

Tessa looked confused. "Okay, is Reaper letting you date a barely-legal Four Corners native? Because that sounds like absolutely no one in the SDMC."

I grinned coyly at her. "It's Shadow."

Her mouth fell open, eyelashes fluttering rapidly. *"Shadow?"*

"Mm-hm."

"The big scarred, scary guy who always looks pissed off and doesn't talk to anyone?"

"He's never been scary to me," I said, feeling a little defensive with her assessment. "And he does talk when he feels comfortable enough to do so."

"Wow, guess I've been out of the loop." She climbed out of bed to tend to Vivi who had started to fuss in her bassinet. "How long's this been going on? I thought he hated women."

"Well, we first kissed last night after the governor's party. But before that we'd been slowly getting used to being in each other's company. For months, really."

Tessa settled back into bed to nurse the baby. "Well, he's got to be something special to make you look so doped up with happiness."

"He is." My dreamy smile returned. "He's so sweet in ways I never expected. And to see him come out of his shell, expressing himself and socializing with ease—it's amazing."

"If he's *that* perfect, then his dick is small," Tessa joked. "Or something else is wrong with him. With men, there's always something."

He definitely isn't small. I could recall our first time together with far less guilt now. As for what was 'wrong' with him, it didn't feel right to discuss any of his trauma or his coping mechanisms with her. Especially not as his medic, nor while he was actively trying to better himself every day.

"How are things going with Big G?" I asked. "Is he staying civil?"

"Yeah, now that he knows he's on thin ice with Reaper," Tessa scoffed. "He's damn near father of the year now. Picks up the boys right on time and drops them right off."

"Hopefully he keeps that up, and not just because he has to."

"Yeah." She shifted her grip on the hungry baby. "He still doesn't know anything about Andrea and me, so I'm worried about all his cooperation going out the window if he finds out."

"I understand that, but if you keep seeing each other, it'll have to come out eventually."

"I know that. Believe me, I do." Vivi unlatched and Tess brought her up to her shoulder, patting her back. "One thing at a time though. I'd like to just enjoy being happy for once."

"I don't blame you." I smiled at the sight of her with her daughter, a small twinge of envy running through me. *One day. Not yet.* "Once you've found what makes you happy, you have to hold on to it with everything you've got."

MARIPOSA

"**W**hat do these do?" I picked up one of the metallic contraptions on the table and turned it over in my hand.

"That's a fuel injector," Jandro told me with a smirk. "It injects fuel."

"Don't be a smart ass." I went to swat him but he dodged out of my reach.

Glaring at him across the work table, I set down the fuel injector and spread my feet, poised like a cat.

"Oh, you coming to get me?" He copied my stance, bending his knees and bringing his chest forward like a football player. "Come on, pretty medic."

I faked to one side, then darted around the table in the opposite direction, but he saw me coming. And Jandro knew I was no match for him. I tackled him with a roar and he just laughed, catching me under my thighs as he pressed kisses to my neck.

The feeling of his mouth was electric, as were his strong hands gripping so close to my ass without a second thought. Going slowly with Shadow *was* nice, but there was nothing like the confidence and ease from the men who were already mine.

I locked my ankles behind Jandro's back, squeezing my thighs around his waist as I found his luscious mouth.

"Mm, you can tackle me any time for this," he chuckled, fingers digging into the fabric of my jeans.

"Don't use this as a reason to be more of a smart ass with me." I pulled at his lips lightly with my teeth.

"No promises," he murmured, turning us and parking my ass on the table strewn with bike parts. "Fuck, I want you," he added, spreading my legs around him as he pressed flush to me. "I want you to myself."

"We're alone, aren't we?"

I released his lips to kiss my way to his earlobe, sucking on it until he moaned, then moving on to the warm skin of his neck.

Shadow and I had returned home from the bar an hour earlier, kissed, and went our separate ways. Gunner and Reaper were still gone, and Mrs. Potts, the B&B owner, left us alone for the most part. She remained swift and unseen when it came to cleaning our rooms or refilling coffee and pastries in the common room. Although getting it on out here in the yard probably wasn't the wisest idea, I never got the sense she was spying on us.

"Ugh, no," Jandro sighed, pulling away. "We're not."

"In the room, then." I tugged his cut to return him closer, kissing his throat and under his jaw.

"I see Reap coming down the hill," he said. "Riding fast. I bet you anything he's about to tell us something urgent."

"Fuck, what now?" I groaned, leaning my forehead against his chest. Not that I didn't want to see Reaper. Having him and Jandro in bed would be intimate and cozy too. But he was already worried about me from Daren's message, and I hoped his meeting with the general didn't tell him anything to exacerbate that fear.

Moments later, Reaper's bike roared its way up to the B&B entrance and he quickly waved at us over the fence before cutting the engine.

"Good, you two are together. Stay there, I'm coming over."

"Does he seem happy to you?" I asked Jandro.

"Damn near ecstatic," he replied with a confused frown.

Sure enough, Reaper was beaming as he came out to the backyard with us. He also reeked of clove cigarettes, like he went through an entire pack since breakfast.

"You're not gonna believe this." He was downright giddy, practically giggling with excitement. "My parents are alive. Vance's general is my fucking *dad*."

"Wait...what?" Jandro blurted out after a beat of silence. "Your parents are alive? And they're *here*? All of them?"

Reaper shook his head. "Just Mom and Finn, my bio-dad."

"Carter?" Jandro asked hesitantly.

The glow of Reaper's happiness faded just slightly. "No, they lost him a few years back. I still have to break the news to Noelle."

"Damn, no one's made it this far without some losses." Jandro rubbed a hand over his head. "But dude! Finn and your mom, that's amazing! And he's a fucking general?"

"I know," Reaper laughed. "It's fuckin' wild." He turned to me, a smile lighting up his gorgeous face that I couldn't help but echo. "My parents are alive, sugar. You'll get to meet my family."

"I'm so happy for you!" I held my arms out to him. "And relieved that they're okay. I know how heavily that weighed on you, my love."

A pang cut through my chest. I'd give anything to know if my parents were alive and well, much less in the same town as me. But there was no way I'd diminish Reaper's joy. He deserved to have his family back, something that was so rare after the Collapse tore thousands of families apart. Even more, he could finally be absolved of the guilt he carried.

Reaper pulled me into a tight embrace, his heart hammering against mine. "It sucks about Carter, but fuck, it feels like that weight's been lifted now. A little bit, at least."

"How'd your mom handle seeing you?" Jandro grinned. "I bet she's still hot."

"Fuck off." Reaper shoved his shoulder, but it was lighthearted with no real strength behind it. "I actually haven't seen her yet. Dad and I spent a long time talking, catching up. He wanted to break the news to her about Daren privately, before a whole bunch of us come to see her."

"Oh yeah," Jandro nodded. "That's probably a good idea."

"But yeah, when she's ready, she'll want to see your dumbass for reasons unknown." Reaper shoved him playfully again. "She'll want to meet Mari, of course. Dad's already obsessed with you, sugar." He dropped a kiss to my forehead. "They'll need to see Noelle, who will drag Larkan along, I'm sure. Then eventually, they're going to want to meet all of your men."

"Yikes, that's going to be a crowd," I muttered.

"It's how we do things, sugar." Reaper rubbed the back of my neck. "Big gatherings with lots of hustle and bustle, just like the club parties. You'll be fine. You know almost everyone already."

"You know, come to think of it, I, um." I rubbed my forehead, remembering my lunch date with Shadow earlier that day. "It might be possible that I've met your mom already."

"What?" he gasped. "When? Where?"

"Downtown today, after Shadow and I got lunch. I stopped at a jeweler's table because her pieces reminded me so much of my ring." Reaper's hand wrapped around mine, shaking slightly as he twisted the band. "She seemed very interested in my ring and where I got it from."

"I'll be damned," he whispered.

"Was she hot?" Jandro asked. "You know, for a lady about Mom-age?"

I rolled my eyes. "Yes, Jandro, she was attractive. And—" My gaze returned to Reaper's, the exact same green eyes of the woman I met staring back at me. "Oh yeah, she was definitely your mom."

"Holy shit." Reaper dipped his head back and laughed. "I can't believe this is really fuckin' happening."

"Believe it." I wrapped my arms around his neck. "You deserve this, to have your family back together. No one deserves it more than you."

His grin was wicked as his hands surrounded my waist, fingers caressing my belly. "My family's not complete until I put a little one inside you, sugar."

Jandro pressed into my side, his hand on my back just above Reaper's. "Our kids are going to have living grandparents that actually see them and spoil them. Do you know how rare that is now?"

"You two better stop talking like that." I quickly kissed Jandro, then planted one on Reaper. "I just got back from seeing Tessa, and I do *not* need babies on the brain right now."

"Let's make some." Reaper's voice was already husky, his hand sliding up my ribs to frame the underside of my breast. "Me and Jandro can put twins inside you right now."

"That's...not how it works."

"Oh well, whatever." Jandro's lips grazed the shell of my ear. "I know you can't right now, *Mariposita*, but we can practice."

"Why do I even let you two fuck me?" I laughed, leaning my head back so they could both attack my neck from different angles.

"We have nice cocks." Reaper chuckled, nipping at the column of my throat.

"Aw thanks, Reap," Jandro cooed.

"Sure thing, buddy."

"Nice cocks aside, you two are ridiculous." I planted my hands on the table behind me, relishing in their mouths and hands on my body, shifting from affectionate to passionate.

"You want to do this out here, sugar?" Reaper's hand skimmed over my breast, lightly squeezing before his touch moved on to my shoulder. "Out in the open?" His tone made it clear he had no qualms with that notion.

"I don't care where, but you need a shower first."

His eyebrow lifted. "Excuse me?"

"You stink of those cloves. How many did you smoke?"

"A lot," he admitted. "Dad and I shared my pack while we talked."

"In the shower sounds good to me." Jandro pressed a kiss to the side of my face before dragging his lips to my ear. "We can take turns with your sweet little ass that way."

Reaper made a purr of agreement while I let out a soft gasp. "All three of us in there? Will we fit?"

"We're about to find out." In one quick motion, Reaper hoisted me over his shoulder and started carrying me inside like a damn caveman.

The shower *was* spacious, since we had the biggest bedroom in the B&B. It even had a waterfall shower head with decent water pressure. But none of us had tried to cram in more than one at a time before.

"Kick your leg out for me, sugar," Reaper instructed with a slap to my ass.

I flailed my foot out behind me, hitting the wooden door of our room with a loud thunk to Jandro's howling laughter.

"You got a free hand, dude. Why make her kick it like a donkey?"

"Just wanted to see her do it." Reaper set me down with a laugh and started stripping out of his clothes. The smoke smell was already dissipating, clinging more to his shirt than his skin.

I was slower to undress, not wanting to miss a single moment of them pulling off shirts, tearing apart belt buckles, and exposing swaths of ink, scars, and delicious masculine flesh.

"It's rude to stare, Mariposita." Jandro grinned as he stepped out of his pants and boxers, his thick torso making the tattoos on his ribs expand with every breath.

"I'm a rude girl, what can I say?" I continued to unabashedly drink in the warm tan of his skin, the muscles in his legs, and the broadness of his chest and arms that I loved to wrap myself around.

"Get fucking naked right now," Reaper growled, coming at me from the side with his cock already halfway erect.

"Make me." The challenge was on my lips without thought, my palm wrapping around and stroking his stiffening length.

"Oh, you are a rude girl," Reaper purred like he was pleased, caressing along my neck and shoulder. "You know where rude girls belong?"

He shoved me to my knees before I could come back with another smart remark, pressing his hips into my face. I took him in my mouth just like he wanted, the thrill of his dominance surging in my body.

"Ohh, fuck yeah," he hissed, fingers diving into my hair. "Jandro, come get her clothes off."

I had already gotten started with undoing my pants and taking Shadow's hoodie off. Jandro's hands were indulgent and sensual as he finished the job, running over my body as he kissed my neck and shoulders. I felt him up blindly as I sucked Reaper, my palm finding his lips, chest, then the hard wall of his stomach before finding Jandro's cock.

"Suck him too, sugar." Reaper withdrew from my mouth, turning my head toward his best friend.

Jandro had been kneeling at my level and returned to standing, letting out a deep, satisfied hum as I wrapped my lips around him. "Such a good rude girl," he said with a loving stroke to my cheek.

I would have smiled if my mouth wasn't stuffed. This felt just like how things were in the beginning—the simple contrast of Reaper's rough love with Jandro's tender sweetness. Not that I didn't love Gunner or the slower pace with Shadow, but these two were my rocks. The foundation on which my love for four different, incredible men grew.

I slurped around Jandro's thick head until I needed to breathe, then returned to take Reaper down my throat.

"Ugh, Jesus," he groaned, head tilting back. "Too fucking good."

"So are we nixing the shower? Mm, fuck!" Jandro gasped more curses as I drew him into my mouth again, tongue licking the sensitive underside.

"Nah, let's move there." Both men supported my arms to help me to my feet. "See how well we *fit*," Reaper added with a swat to my ass.

I darted into the bathroom first, leaving them to fight over who came after me first through the doorway. I turned the shower handle and stuck my hand under the spray when an arm wrapped around my waist, pulling me against a solid chest.

"I miss our baths, sugar," Reaper murmured, nipping at the shell of my ear.

"Me too," I sighed, arching against him.

"One day." His mouth made a burning trail from my ear to my shoulder. "We'll have a tub big enough for all of us." He jerked his head to indicate Jandro behind him. "Even this asshole."

"Excuse you, this asshole doesn't stink like a smoke factory, and would like to get in to suds up our woman. Move."

Jandro slid past us into the shower and ripped me out of Reaper's arms to join him under the spray.

"Ah! It's not hot yet!" The water wasn't cold either, but tepid enough to raise goosebumps on my skin as I hugged myself.

"I know." Jandro tugged my arms away and skimmed his mouth over my chest. "It makes your nips nice and tight."

He laved over one with his tongue, soothing the cold, tense peak with the heat of his mouth. Reaper stepped in and closed the shower door behind him, replacing the water running over my back with his hands.

"Wash me, sugar," he said in a seductive whisper before chuckling, "since you think I stink so much."

I turned around slowly, sandwiched firmly between the two of them. We had some extra room, but not much. Reaper's eyes never left mine as I grabbed a loofah and a soap bar from the shelf carved in the shower wall. He was standing directly under the showerhead, so I had to reach around him to lather up the loofah.

Jandro pulled me back toward the far shower wall with a hand on my hip, and Reaper followed, stepping out from under the water.

His gaze was so hungry, so full of fire as I squeezed the loofah over his shoulder first, lathering down his arm before going back up and across his chest. The soap ran down his body in white rivulets, outlining the hard lines of muscles before getting washed away. Jandro used another loofah to wash my back, scrubbing with luxurious pressure from the back of my neck to my ass. Reaper's lips parted as Jandro came around to the front of my chest, squeezing lather over my breasts as he ran his sponge back and forth in a slow zig-zag motion.

I had just reached Reaper's hips, circling the loofah around the base of his cock, which now jutted out, fully engorged, when he tugged me impatiently back under the water.

"You trying to make me fuckin' explode, woman?" He held my jaw and dove down with a harsh kiss, the taste of him cooled by the water running over us. Barely giving me a moment to breathe, he spun me around. "Wash Jandro now."

I leaned in to kiss my other man first, bracing my hands on his chest as I sought out those pillowy soft lips. He indulged me, his mouth as gentle and hot as the water falling over my skin. Lost in kissing him, I squeezed the loofah over his back, massaging it over his burn scars to the sexy moans rumbling from his chest.

His touch returned to my breasts, kneading and rolling while another hand pressed between my legs. I gasped into Jandro's mouth while pressing back onto Reaper's hand, hips wiggling in search of friction.

"Fuck, so wet," Reaper grunted, gliding through my folds. He brought his touch higher behind me, the firm pressure of his thumb circling my back entrance.

"Yes!" I pleaded, arching back further towards him. "Yes, I want you both."

"Climb on, *Mariposita*." Jandro bent his knees deeply and lowered, sliding his hands around to my ass.

I wrapped my legs around his waist, my arms around his shoulders, holding on tight as he straightened up.

"Reap, grab my cock and stick it in her."

"Fuck you, grab it yourself."

Jandro laughed, adjusting his grip on me. "Had to give it a shot."

I clung to him tighter as I felt his wide head nudge my sex, seeking entrance.

"Ohh, yes," we groaned together as he sank in, his hands returning to my ass.

The angle was steep, the friction delicious. I was able to bounce on him with some assistance from his hands. My clit crashed into his body with each downstroke on his cock, and I knew my first orgasm wasn't far off.

Jandro's large hands pulled my cheeks apart as he drove me up and down, giving Reaper plenty to play with behind me.

One hand rested on my back while the other toyed with my ass. He inserted one finger and kept it still, letting me ride it while my pussy rode Jandro.

"More," I begged, stealing a glance at him over my shoulder. "I want your cock in my ass."

Reaper chuckled, his eyes fixated on watching my ass bounce. "Rude girl doesn't even say please." He inserted a second finger and spread them apart, making me gasp and whimper at the stretch.

"Too much?" Jandro nipped a kiss at my jaw, reminding me to communicate my needs.

"No...no, but I'm gonna come soon."

"Come first." Reaper sucked at my nape, rocking his fingers in and out of my hole. "And say please. Then maybe you'll get my cock in your tight little ass."

Jandro lifted me higher to fall harder, the impact sharp and my body already so full. My thighs squeezed his waist, fingers digging into his shoulders as my whole body tightened and shook with my oncoming release.

Reaper's fingers stilled in my ass, sensing me tensing up as he reached around to pull on my nipples.

"Relax and come for us," he commanded, breath hot in my ear. "You're our wife. We've got you."

The pleasure was almost unbearable, tightening like a fist in my body as I reached back with one arm to wrap around the back of his head. Our mouth crashed together in a hard, clumsy kiss.

"I love you." It came out a choked whimper, my breaths ragged with my pleasure so close to cresting.

"Fuck, I love you." Reaper supported my upper back with his chest, fingers still working in and out of my ass as his other arm banded around my chest.

Jandro crashed into me hard once, twice, three more times before my pleasure burst free. My men supported me as I shook and convulsed between them, drawing out my orgasm with kisses and affectionate words.

"Please," I whispered to Reaper, when the peak softened into a dull roar. "Please fuck my ass."

"Let's be real. You never have to say please, sugar." His voice was warm, hands gentle as he secured both of my arms around Jandro's neck. "You know I'm yours. Everything you want from me is yours."

Jandro held my thighs, Reaper spread my cheeks apart and nudged his head against my hole. He pressed in slowly, allowing me to adjust and breathe through every inch.

I rested my forehead on Jandro's, hanging onto him limply as Reaper filled me from behind.

"I love you." I scratched my blunt nails over his head, pulling more kisses from that luscious mouth.

"I know you do," he smirked, bouncing me on both of their cocks and making me cry out.

"Easy, Dro!" Reaper barked.

"It's okay, it's good," I moaned, throwing my head back as I dug into Jandro's shoulders. "Oh God, *so* good..."

Reaper's hands went to my waist, directing the movement carefully while Jandro held me strong, with no signs of fatigue. The way they both surged in and out of me was decadent, so intensely intimate as their bodies pressed and slicked against my skin.

"I love you too, *Mariposita*," Jandro moaned, bouncing me more while sucking a tender kiss on my collarbone. "Fuck, I love you so much it scares the shit out of me sometimes."

"Don't be sca—oh, fuck. Oh God, don't stop!"

Reaper moaned a low curse into my ear, driving harder into me as my muscles tightened around him. My next orgasm came without warning, clasping so hard around both of my lovers that they both cried out after me.

"Holy fuck! I gotta put you down for a sec, babe."

Jandro carefully lowered me to the shower floor, both men slipping out of me as I braced an arm against the wall. Reaper panted behind me, his hand on my hip while Jandro sucked in deep breaths, his cock still erect and pulsing.

"You good?" I shot a smirk at him.

"Yeah, just got close there," He grinned. "I didn't want to come before I got a chance in that ass."

"You up for that, sugar?" Reaper squeezed my waist with a wicked smile.

"I guess I can handle a little switcheroo," I grinned back.

"Let's switch up that water temp," Jandro panted. "I might pass out if it gets any hotter in here and I do *not* want to be in your ass if that happens."

We adjusted the temperature, soaped up all the necessary parts and rinsed off again before Reaper spun me to face him and grabbed my ass with a growl.

"Ride me, cowgirl."

I wrapped around his shoulders and jumped, landing safely in his firm grip as I locked my legs around his back. He sucked my lip in a bruising kiss, swallowing my moan as his freshly washed cock slid into me. I heard the wet sliding sounds of Jandro stroking himself behind me, and wiggled on Reaper in invitation.

"Aw, Jesus," Reaper hissed. "No wonder he almost popped off like a teenager."

"You say that like you're surprised," I teased, using my toes on the wall behind him for a bit of leverage as I rose off his length, then sank back down.

"I'm always amazed by how good you feel," he said. "And this ass is just mm!" His fingers curled into my flesh. "Top fuckin' shelf."

Jandro's soft lips touched my shoulder, the wet skin of his chest caressing my back. "You ready for me, Mariposita?"

"*Por favor,*" I begged, turning my head to kiss him.

His kiss was fast, his gaze lowering to focus on where he was about to press inside me. Slick with water and lube, his head rested at my entrance and began to press through.

"Ah!" I cried at the light sting as he pushed past the first inch. He was thicker than Reaper, but not quite as long.

"Take it easy!" Reaper chastised.

"I am, man. I'm not going any further."

"I'm good, really." I already felt so full and desperate to move, eager to feel both of my men through me again. "Bounce me, please."

Reaper raised and lowered me on him slowly, his arm muscles tight and flexed as he carefully controlled how far I went down. Jandro kept still, only caressing my waist and kissing my back while I adjusted to him.

"More," I pleaded, leaning my head back when the stinging gave way to a delightful stretch. "Please, Jandro. More."

He thrust forward, filling me with another thick inch that had me gasping.

"Sugar?" Reaper prompted, ever watchful of my limits.

"Yes, good, fuck, yeah..."

My grip on his shoulders loosened with my delirious, pleasure-babbling, leaning back on the hard support of Jandro's chest. The gorgeous man in my ass kissed me, tongue licking tenderly into my mouth as his hands swept forward over my breasts.

Reaper's grip remained steadfast on my hips, holding strong as he crashed into my pussy. The guys worked in tandem now, filling and emptying me with rough grunts and wet slaps of flesh. While every thrust was punishing, every caress was caring. They supported me between them, taking and defiling my body while answering every plea for more.

My next orgasm swept them up with me, tipping me over the edge with how they swelled and then spilled into me. Our shouts of release were distorted by the water running over us, and then only harsh breaths as we untangled and leaned our exhausted bodies against the shower wall.

Reaper stood at my back, his forehead heavy against the back of my head like he might fall asleep standing up. Jandro and I faced each other, our pants mingling as our hooded gazes met.

"Sorry we didn't get to be alone," I whispered. "Next time."

He shook his head, his grin spreading. "I know we will, but there aren't many things that can top this, *Mariposita*."

With a quick nudge to Reaper, we all washed off for a third and final time before leaving the now-cold shower.

GUNNER

Governor Vance's meeting room in the City Hall building was humble compared to the grand ones I sat in at McAlister Academy, my old military college. While people like my uncle got fat and rich from their first taste of power while their citizens starved, the Four Corners governor was living lean in comparison.

Aside from when his daughter went missing, Vance wasn't suffering, but he wasn't draped in riches either. I met many politicians who were good at pretending to be humble, to be in touch with ordinary people's needs and made lofty promises to be different from all the slimy puppets before them. I often hoped that they would surprise me and actually be sincere for once. But after they got done shaking hands and delivering emotional speeches, it was always the same story in private.

Even before Horus, I had a knack for seeing things most people missed. I saw leaders lying through their teeth. I heard conversations behind closed doors that contradicted everything they said in public. Reaper was one of the few leaders consistently the same person both in public and private, which was why I chose to follow him.

Governor Vance, I started to realize, might have been another one of those rare breeds. Without the suit he wore, he would have been just another guy across the room laughing at one of Jandro's ridiculous stories.

I learned a few interesting pieces of information straight from the horse's mouth while Reaper was catching up with his dad. Like me, Vance was born into a powerful family. Bred and groomed to be a politician from a young age, thirst for power didn't come naturally to him. He was a helper, and reminded me of Mari in that sense. In his university years, his spare time was spent on projects to provide for the lowest income members of his community.

"You did better than me," I had snickered over a glass of bourbon in his office. "I did well in school, but I also partied. Hard."

"I heard the Youngbloods were known for their debaucherous ways," he chuckled.

I spread my hands in a shrug. "My reputation precedes me."

Vance ended up meeting his wife, Kyrie's mother, at one of these community projects. It was a classic opposites-attract love story. She ran herself ragged working three jobs to support her disabled parents, and had come to a food bank for assistance. He was the son of a US Senator, at the same location to volunteer, and also to keep up a positive image for his family.

"I wasn't a go-getter at that age," he said leaning against his desk. "I was shy, nerdy." He nodded at me. "Guys like you probably would have put my head in the toilet."

"Probably," I agreed.

"But when I saw Val, I just," his eyes went misty, "I *had* to talk to her. Trust me, Gunner, I was not the type of guy to just strike up a conversation with a girl I'd never met before. I was terrified."

"Yeah, can't relate."

"But I pulled it together, introduced myself, and well," he smiled wistfully, "the rest is history, as they say."

"I'm sorry you lost her," I told him sincerely. "The thought of losing Mari, just...fuck, I can't even handle the thought."

"Thank you. Yes, I'm sorry too. Kyrie barely remembers her. And it's painful because I see so much of her mother in her. They're so much alike and our daughter has no idea." He sighed and lifted up his glass. "To our women, eh?"

That conversation told me more about Governor Vance than what he ever said in words. I watched his mannerisms—where he looked and the tone of his voice as he spoke of his daughter and late wife.

When corruption was so easy, and with no system in place to hold him accountable, I was hard-pressed to believe that a governor would ever truly act in his people's best interest. But every doubt I had since first meeting Vance slowly began to erase. He was of a different generation than us, and differing opinions would cause some friction, sure. But he was sincerely good, and that kind of person was a rare find.

I still got that timid vibe from him now that he spoke of in his office, and suspected it to be the reason why he still hadn't taken military action on Blakeworth for kidnapping his daughter. While he was taught to be a leader, it still didn't come to him innately. Luckily for him, he did the next best thing—surround himself with capable people who could advise him.

Governor Vance was hesitant to use violence, but that didn't make him a weak leader. In his interactions with Josh, General Bray, and men of his cabinet from the dinner party, he allowed none of them to steamroll over him. The man had a backbone without a thirst for blood—a rare but highly useful combination.

The more I thought about it, the more I wondered if Horus and the other gods steered us here, to give us the best chance to win against Tash.

As the last person to our meeting arrived, a gangly teenage boy in army camouflage at least two sizes too big for him, we all began to settle around the table.

"Everyone, I'd like you to meet Eduardo." General Bray clapped a hand on the teen's shoulder. "He's a newer recruit, a refugee from the Blakeworth territory. He hopes to be a general one day, so I've taken him on as a mentee. He'll be shadowing me for a while to get a sense of what I do from day-to-day."

My eyes darted around the table as everyone took their seats. Was no one else concerned about a brand-new recruit hearing sensitive information at this meeting? Only Shadow met my eyes before flicking back to the young man sitting next to Reaper's father. But Shadow was suspicious of everyone he didn't know, which didn't mean he shared my concerns. In any case, he chose not to speak up, so I filed my own thoughts away.

"Welcome, Eduardo. Thank you for coming, everyone. Have a seat, please." Vance took his place at the head of the table while everyone got settled.

It was quite the crew of faces. Me, Reaper, Jandro, and Shadow lined one side of the table. The Sons of Odin lined the other. General Bray, his recruit, and a lieutenant sat across from Governor Vance and Josh.

"You're all here because I believe you're key players in Four Corners' defense," Vance began, his palms together on the table. "Every one of you has different abilities, different strengths. I want to utilize every advantage we have to keep the territory safe and our enemies at bay. An army general is not necessarily better than a biker's sergeant-at-arms when it comes to combat."

T-Bone's jaw ticked, clearly put off by that statement for some reason as he pulled his lip between his teeth.

"Blakeworth, and evidently General Tash, have no problem using underhanded techniques for their personal gain," Vance continued. "They've taken someone from all of you, and I'm letting you know that I too, am not above using dirty tactics, as long as it's for the right reasons."

I allowed a small smile. The governor was wise to let us and the Sons in on this meeting. Biker gangs lived and breathed dirty tactics.

"With that, gentlemen, I'll turn it over to you." Vance spread his hands. "Many of you have told me I need to go on the offensive and I listened. Now is the time to start forming a plan of attack."

"If I may, sir." General Bray was the first to speak up, as expected. All eyes turned to the man who looked like Reaper's twin aged by about twenty years. "We're getting more and more refugees from neighboring territories by the day. Blakeworth and New Ireland have much bigger populations than us, but their numbers *are* decreasing. Many of the younger men are enlisting with the army if they're in good health, but that's maybe thirty percent of our refugees. Thinking long-term, we'll need to expand our border to make room for the population."

"Any expansion toward Blakeworth or New Ireland, they'll see as an attack," I pointed out.

"Right. So we need to take care of the problem first. In the meantime, I think we should set up field hospitals just outside our borders, roughly five or ten miles or so. People are dropping dead out there, so we'll save lives and boost our numbers for the long-term."

"Do we have enough medics for field hospitals?" Josh pinched his forehead as he scribbled down notes on a legal pad.

"I'm not sure, but Dr. Brooks and his staff are training them as fast as they can."

"Mari says they have about a half dozen trained combat medics ready, not including herself," Reaper added.

"For an army of roughly a thousand? That's stretching 'em thin," I remarked.

"Not for the army," General Bray corrected. "Not at first. This is just to provide aid to the refugees. And show our neighboring territories that their refugees will get the care they need from us."

"I don't like the idea of field hospitals out there in the open," Dyno piped up. "Who's to say Blake or Tash won't give the order to just blow 'em up?"

"Because *they* will have the option of using them too," Bray said. "The medics and their tents won't have any flags or insignia that show loyalty to Four Corners. It will be there for medical services to anyone who needs it."

"What's this gotta do with an attack plan?" Jandro asked. "I get that you're thinking of growing the army and helping those in need, but what's the first strike? Is it gonna be us, or are we gonna wait for them?"

"We need to send scouts," I said. "The best scouts you have, General, that have the lowest probability of getting captured. Tash has had this advantage on us because we've been blind. We don't know his numbers, what kind of artillery he's packing, nothing. The very first thing we need is information. Then we can plan an attack."

"I agree with that," General Bray nodded at me, and damn if my ego wasn't stroked a little. He was basically my father-in-law, and since my own dad was a colossal piece of shit, that validation from Bray felt good.

"I'm sure you and I can offer some assistance with that, captain." T-Bone nodded at me from across the table.

I smiled openly. Our birds had become inseparable in recent weeks. Even just Horus would be a huge advantage to the scouts with his eyesight, but with him and the raven Munin working together, we could use even fewer humans on the ground and thus put fewer lives at risk.

"We'll talk later, sergeant," I agreed, then swept my gaze between Bray and Vance. "I assume you have topographical maps? Maybe aerial photographs of this region? We'll need a lay of the land before sending people in."

Josh and Bray's lieutenant retrieved maps and laid them out on the table. We poured over them for the next two hours, mainly the Four Corners natives explaining the geography to us who were unfamiliar. By the end of the meeting, my brain was thoroughly muddled and I craved a stiff drink. The work wasn't over, though. T-Bone and I would have to discuss where to fly our birds to oversee the scouts. I borrowed a map and told the Sons I'd meet with them back at the bar where they were holed up.

"Hey, thanks for being here. Gunner, is it?" I turned to find Reaper's dad, General Bray, holding his hand out with a friendly smile.

"Yeah. Uh, thanks for having me." I shook his hand. "Sir." I cringed at my awkward delivery, stuck somewhere between familiar and formal.

He was a general, deserving of respect. My school background demanded that I salute him, but no one around here seemed to bother with formalities. In any case, I had never been an enlisted soldier, despite my education. I lived outside the law now, and in that sense, not even a general was above me. And the fact that he was my president's father added another layer of complexity that I wasn't sure how to handle.

The general just continued to smile as he returned the pressure of my handshake before withdrawing his hand. "You bring up important points and I like the way you think. Looking forward to the next meeting, captain."

"Same here, sir. Thank you."

With a curt nod, he filed out of the room, his lieutenant and new recruit stepping out after him. The teenage kid stared at me with big, empty eyes and I narrowed mine in return. Something was off about him. I'd have to remember to check him out through Horus at some point.

"Hey, Gun." Reaper clapped a hand down on my shoulder, the two of us the last ones in the room. "I gotta tell you something, and I don't want you to be upset."

"What?" I sighed. "The Sons are waiting on me."

My president seemed nervous, a rare look for him. "We're having breakfast at my parents' house tomorrow, so they can meet Mari and, you know, get together as a family and shit."

"Cool, I won't hit the booze too hard tonight," I said absently. "Just let me know when we're riding out."

"Um, that's the thing." Reaper sucked in a breath. "We don't want to overwhelm my mom with too many people because she's grieving Daren. Don't want to put too much pressure on her as a hostess, you know?"

"Oh, that's cool. I get it. So what, it's just you, Mari, and Noelle then? With the rest of the introductions to be made later?"

"Well." He looked more and more uncomfortable with each passing moment. "Jandro is coming too, because my folks knew him from back then. He's like another son, you see. And Noelle is dead-set on bringing Larkan, even though I tried my damndest to talk her out of it."

The pieces finally clicked into place. "So *I'm* the only one excluded?"

"No, Shadow's not coming either. And we're not excluding you, it's just—"

"Shadrow isn't even Mari's," I cut in, my annoyance itching.

Reaper rolled his eyes. "We all know he's going to be, so might as well treat him like he is."

"Does your dad even know you share her with me?"

"Yes," Reaper insisted. "You *are* part of my family, Gunner. He wants to get to know you. It's just a lot of people at once, okay? I promise you that's the only reason."

"Okay, so when? When can it be just us three and Mari with them?"

Reaper spread his hands out and raised his shoulders in a shrug. "I dunno. How does next week sound?"

"Works great." I still sounded bitter but didn't care. Shit like this was why I didn't want to get involved with this group thing in the first place.

Not that I regretted sharing Mari, I actually loved it. But it fucking sucked I had to be the odd one out because of logistical reasons.

"For what it's worth," Reaper fished out his cigarettes and offered me one as we left the building together, "Mari's pissed on your behalf."

"Is she now?" Despite myself, I smiled into my first drag.

"She says you have more of a right to be there than Lark, which is absolutely true. But try telling fuckin' Noelle that."

"Fuckin' families, man." I straddled my bike and made her roar to life, wishing I was going home to my woman instead of talking more battle tactics with dudes.

"I hear ya," Reaper sympathized, sitting astride his own bike as he zipped his jacket up to his chin. "In some ways, you're lucky you don't talk to yours anymore."

"Yeah. I'll see ya later." I pulled out of the lot and rumbled down the road.

He wasn't wrong about that. Leaving the Youngblood life was the best decision I ever made, next to choosing Mari. The Steel Demons had been the only real family I ever had.

I had fended for myself for years and didn't need parents as an adult. Mine had been utterly useless at parenting when I was a child, anyway.

While Reaper's upbringing was far from perfect, he did have the kind of family I always envied. His parents seemed to have a love like my grandparents did, like what I hoped Mari and I had. Something that would withstand the years, growing stronger, deeper over time, rather than fading away.

So it stung, feeling cut out, despite Reaper assuring me that it wasn't the case.

I had to hold on to what mattered—that Mari loved me. She was my wife too, and nothing changed that.

MARIPOSA

Gunner came to bed late that night, long after Jandro and Reaper started snoring. When I asked about where he was, Reaper muttered something about discussing strategy with the Sons of Odin.

I didn't think much of it. My own day had been a long one at the hospital, demonstrating field medic techniques to trainees. Reaper, Jandro, Shadow, and I all had dinner together, and while it was nice to see Shadow feeling naturally included among my men, Gunner's presence was noticeably absent.

My guys didn't seem worried, so I tried not to dwell on it. But after Shadow and I kissed goodnight, and we went to our separate rooms, the bed somehow felt extra empty with only three people in it.

I couldn't sleep a wink, but a sigh of relief left me as I heard Gunner's motorcycle pull up outside. He entered the bedroom with the sounds of someone who was drunk enough to be clumsy, but not stumbling and sloppy.

Thankfully he had enough coordination to undress and slip into the open spot in bed quietly. I rolled over immediately, nuzzling into his skin that was still cool from the night air.

"Where have you been?" I whispered, dragging lazy kisses over his chest and throat.

"Baby girl," he sighed, wrapping around me. "I love you."

"I love you too." My hands slid around to his back, rubbing up and down to warm him.

"Were you really pissed about me not coming to breakfast tomorrow?" He mumbled the words out, lips moving on my forehead.

I sighed deeply, resting my head on his shoulder. "Yes, love. I wish you could be there. Reap's still trying to talk Noelle into bringing Larkan another time."

Gunner let out a soft noise, sounding relieved as he squeezed me tighter. "I knew you would never shut me out."

"Never, love." I kissed him more insistently, finding his lips in the darkness. "I want all of my men with me. But it's not my house or my rules." My fingers stroked the locks of hair falling down his back. "I'm actually really nervous. And I know you being there would make me feel better."

"I love being with you." His voice grew sleepier and more mumbly every time he spoke. "You make me feel like I matter. I must've told T-Bone that like twenty times, but he kept pouring me shots so it wasn't my fault."

I grinned, unable to hold back my chuckle at his confession. "You do matter, love. So much." I pressed a kiss to his Adam's apple. "You keep me safe." A kiss under his chin. "You make my fears disappear." A kiss to his lips. "You make me the strongest version of myself."

He didn't reply, but his chest rose and fell with the steady, even breaths of sleep. Smiling, I turned in his arms and settled on my side.

"There you are, looking all dolled-up and sexy."

I smiled at Gunner's reflection in the vanity mirror, leaning against the door jam with his forearm raised above his head.

"Is it too sexy for the in-laws?" I pulled at the neckline of my dress, hoping it wasn't so low that it was inappropriate.

"Nah." Gunner took a few steps into the room, blue eyes following the lines of my backside. "Not anywhere close."

"And how long have you been spying on me?" I closed my compact and started putting my makeup away.

"Long enough. I like watching you get all made up." He moved the hair draped against my upper back, caressing my neck as he dropped a kiss to my head. "Not that you need it."

"I'm just nervous," I admitted, reaching back for his hand. "Scared shitless, if I'm going to be completely honest."

"For shit's sake, why?" He ran both hands over my neck and shoulders now, massaging the nerves right out of my muscles. "They'll love you, baby girl. As much as we do."

"It's been years since I've met the parents of a guy I'm with, and it's never been as serious as my *husband's* parents. Holy shit, they're already my in-laws!"

"Relax." Gunner's lips rested in my hair, his hands sweeping luxuriously over my shoulders and upper back.

"I wish you were coming," I sighed, melting under his touch.

"Mm." He pressed another kiss into my hair. "You've got this in the bag, you don't need me. Reap's already talked you up a ton to his dad. I bet they're excited to meet their daughter-in-law."

"That scares me even more," I groaned. "What if I don't live up to the hype?"

"It's not hype, it's truth." His hands came over the front of my shoulders, smoothing down my chest and tracing the edges of my dress. "What do I gotta do to make you believe me, huh?"

His touch dipped inside my neckline, a warm palm finding my breast and pulling a gasp from my mouth. "Gunner..."

"What do I gotta do?" he groaned, lowering his mouth to my ear as his other hand wandered down the side of my hip, pulling the fabric up my thighs. "To make you see how perfect you are for all of us?"

"Gun." I turned my head, catching his hungry mouth as it searched for a kiss. There went my lipstick. "Love, I'd love to, but we'll be late."

"Will you?" he challenged, nipping at my lips. "Or will you just be on time instead of early?"

"Reap and Jandro are waiting—"

"Let them wait." He squeezed my nipple between his thumb and forefinger, the other hand diving between my legs to spread them apart. "You're my wife too."

That statement shouldn't have the effect on me that it did, a rising swell of heat and pride that had me grinning and arching against the chair back, angling my head for another kiss. I knew it already, but to hear it from him with such a possessive growl was something else entirely.

Gunner's tongue dove in, claiming my mouth in his little victory as his hand released my breast to settle on the front of my throat. "Stand up," he ordered.

I rose from the chair, bracing my hands against the vanity while he moved the chair out of the way, then slammed the full length of his body against my backside.

"Gun!" I gasped at the heat of his erection pressing against my ass. My breath was short with his hand on my neck, my pulse firing up with anticipation.

"Fuck, you're the sexiest little thing," he groaned, hiking my dress up to my waist. "How do you expect me to control myself around you?" He spanked and groped my ass, grinding his cock against me.

"When did you get so dirty?" I looked at him over my shoulder, catching a rough kiss as he groped my breasts under my dress again.

"Dunno," he laughed, dragging his teeth along my upper back. "When I was fucking your pretty little ass, maybe. You turned me to the dark side."

"As bad as your timing is, I like it." I pressed back against him, rubbing against his jeans in hopes he'd get out of them soon.

"Oh yeah? Let's see."

His grip returned to my neck, holding me firmly while his other hand dipped inside my panties. I squirmed and whined, the heel of his palm grinding against my clit while the rest of his hand stroked and teased between my thighs.

"That's my dirty baby girl." He removed his hand and delivered a wet slap to my ass. "Nice and soaked for me."

"Please, Gunner." I reached back, fumbling for his zipper, only to have both arms held behind my back.

"You want this?" His thrust pressed my thighs against the vanity, rough denim rubbing my ass while his hungry eyes stared at me in the mirror.

"Gun—"

"Or should I make you wait?" He sucked at my earlobe, teeth nipping at me. "Leave you craving me while you're smiling all pretty for your in-laws, huh?"

"Now," I squeaked, wriggling in his hold to grind my ass against his length. "Please, I want you now."

"Fuck yeah. That's my girl." He left a wet kiss on my neck, pulling lightly at my skin. "I'm gonna let you go, but keep your hands where they are."

I nodded, my teeth sinking into my lip as the heat of his hand left my wrists. The sound of his zipper pulling down made me bite harder, a whimper escaping me as his cock fell out and landed on my ass with a soft slap.

"I was gonna bind your hands together with my belt, but *damn*." Hard flesh skimmed over my ass as Gunner leaned back and admired the view. "I like seeing you hold together all nice and obedient for me."

"I can't stay like this the whole time you fuck me," I protested.

"Ah, there's my girl." His hand came around to hold my jaw. "There's her fire. Just do the best you can for me, huh?"

He pulled back, letting his length fall down the globes of my ass until it nestled between my legs. Then he pulled my panties aside, thick cock meeting my tender sex.

"Ride me," he instructed. "Rub yourself on me."

"Gun, I need you inside me."

"Not yet, babe. Just ride that pussy over me first."

I tilted my hips and leaned back, gliding my wetness and sensitive flesh along the top of his shaft. Going forward, I could almost get his head inside me without touching, but not quite. My hand made a slight motion down, just a reflex, and Gunner's strong grip immediately came around my wrists.

"Nope. None of that baby girl," he chastised with a soft laugh. "You do as I say, or I do it for you."

Holding me in place, he did exactly that, gliding his cock back and forth against my sex without penetrating. Wetness coated my thighs and each roll of his head against my clit was unbearable without that thickness inside me.

"Huh," he mused, all calm and collected while I writhed in his grip. "I think you like it better when I do it. Guess I should leave the punishment stuff to Reaper."

"This *is* punishment," I whined.

My worst fear in that moment was him actually making good on his threat to make me wait, to send me off all frustrated and wanting to Reaper's parents.

"Think your dear husband will punish you for making him late?" Gunner taunted, hips driving against my ass. "You think everyone at the breakfast table will be able to smell how wet you are?"

"Gunner, *please!*" I lifted onto my tiptoes, squeezed my thighs, angled my hips— everything I could to fill the empty ache with my limited movement, but he was having none of it. His head met the threshold of my entrance, but he pulled back before I could sink onto him.

"Bad girl," he cooed, sounding too pleased to be truly reprimanding me. "You really want to be defiled before your nice, wholesome meal with your in-laws, huh?"

"I just want *you.*" I leaned my head back on his shoulder, aiming my lips for his neck and cheek. Maybe switching up tactics would get him to stop messing with me and put that thing where it belonged. "Please, love." His pulse thrummed under my mouth and I peppered more kisses along the length of his neck. "I want to be thinking of you while I'm with them. I want to be sore, spent. I want to feel *you* inside my body hours after you're done fucking me. "

The shift from bratty to seductive worked. Gunner groaned, hips stuttering as he released my wrists to dig his fingers into my waist. He ended up bunching my dress in his fist as he *finally* aligned himself with my entrance. Using my dress like reins, he pulled me back as he surged forward.

"Fuck!"

The force of him entering me sent me jolting, palms slapping down on the vanity. I looked in the mirror to see him staring down at where we conjoined, lip pulling between his teeth, my dress balled up in his hand at my lower back. He lifted his gaze, meeting my eyes in the mirror as he pulled out, then sank back in.

"Yesss, Gunner," I hissed, pressing back with his pulls of my dress.

"Fuck, this is the best fucking view," he growled, palming the side of my ass with his free hand.

His thrusts were short, hips barely moving compared to the long pulls of me back and forth on his cock. I was raised on my tiptoes, holding the edge of the vanity counter for support as I rocked along his length.

"So fucking good," he murmured, eyes flicking up to the mirror and down to me riding his length. "My girl is so fucking pretty."

I found myself pressing back harder, eager for his satisfaction and praise as he filled me. Each stroke of him inside me chased a need just outside of my reach. Desperate whimpers left my lips as the smacks of my ass on his hips grew louder, faster.

"Oh yeah, that's it," he said in a choked growl. His hand slackened around my dress until the fabric drifted freely. He shoved it up my back to keep his view, before his grip hooked around my waist.

"Oh, fuck!"

I held on to the vanity for dear life, fighting to catch a breath as he pounded me. The force of his cock stretched and hit new depths inside me, pleasure shooting like lightning up my spine as my legs turned to liquid.

I collapsed forward, chest on the counter and Gunner's heavy hand splayed in the center of my back when I tried to lift up again.

"That's it, baby girl," he panted, swatting my ass once without missing a beat of his punishing thrusts. "Just bend over and take it."

"Oh God, don't stop," I moaned, letting the vanity support my upper body while he crashed into me relentlessly from behind. This new, dirty side of Gunner was refreshing, shocking, and utterly hot.

Knowing my sweet, golden man had a rough side had me wet since the moment he came up behind me.

He always put me first and sought to please me above all else. Not even when he fucked my ass did he let himself get carried away. Every step of the way, he was considerate and careful. Now he was using my body, staking his claim on me. Being selfish. And I loved every rough moment of it.

"Gun," I whimpered, the slaps of flesh nearly drowning out my voice. "I'm gonna come soon."

"Fuck, I'm right there with you, baby." He crashed into me harder, faster, the pleasure white-hot and blinding. "Come on my cock, my sweet little wife."

The way he fucked me drove me to the edge, but his words were the tipping point. I convulsed from head to toe, thrashing to release the pleasure he'd been stoking in me since his first dirty word.

Gunner's hands slapped to the vanity on either side of me with a heavy groan, stroking through the aftershocks as he spilled warmth inside me.

He withdrew from me too soon, sliding my panties back into place and straightening my dress back down over my legs. Ever the gentleman, he pulled me up gently from the counter, straightening the top of my dress and smoothing out my hair with a cheeky grin.

"You good?" he asked with a wicked gleam in his eye.

"Uh, yeah. I think so." My legs were still wobbly, but I could walk without making a total fool of myself.

The grin remained plastered on his face as he threaded his fingers through mine and led me out of the room and to the lobby of the B&B. Jandro and Reaper looked up from the armchairs where they waited.

"You ready?" Reaper grunted.

"Yeah." I was still trying to catch my breath.

Gunner turned to me and placed a slow, smoldering kiss on my cheek. "Have a good morning with the in-laws, baby girl."

MARIPOSA

Reaper's green gaze burned into me as I stepped off the front porch, my legs just as steady as a newborn deer despite my effort to keep cool.

"Goddamn Gunner," my husband swore as he threw a leg over his bike. "Get on. We're gonna be late."

Jandro just snickered, shaking his head as he eased his ride back onto the street.

My mouth wanted to form the word *sorry* on impulse, but I had no true desire to say it. I wasn't sorry in the least. If anything, I was grateful. Gunner had thoroughly fucked the nerves right out of me, leaving me with a relaxed buzz and laid back confidence.

I shuddered at the vibration of Reaper's bike underneath me, my flesh still tender and sensitive.

"Swear to fuck, sugar, if you come on my seat on the way over there..."

"What?" I pressed when he trailed off, squeezing around his waist.

"I'll have to pull over and fuck you on the side of the road, that's what."

"And ruin my dress right before I meet your parents? You wouldn't dare."

"Try me."

"Hey!" Jandro waved his arms. "Are we goin' or what?"

Reaper pulled up alongside him, and I fought the urge to grind into the vibrations and bumps in the road. Tempting as his threat was, I really didn't need to look like we stopped for a roadside quickie. At least Gunner had left me looking mostly presentable.

"Where's Noelle and Larkan?" I yelled in my husband's ear.

"She left early to help them set up," he answered. "Finally came to her senses and left her boy toy behind."

"Well, that's good." Hopefully that would make Gunner feel a little less left out. In the same breath, I slapped Reaper's arm. "When are you gonna patch him in so they can be official? The Blakeworth mission was over a week ago."

He gave me a sideways glance over his shoulder. "That's a conversation for another day, sugar."

I dropped it, keeping silent until we pulled up to a charming ranch-style home. It didn't look brand-new, so must have been one of the few structures left undamaged after the Collapse.

Reaper parked next to Noelle's dirt bike in the driveway, and Jandro next to him. "Need help with those?" I asked, climbing out of Reaper's seat to lean over Jandro's saddlebags.

"Nope." His tone was cheerful as he removed many layers of blankets and padding to reach the gift we brought. "Safe as can be. I got it, babe."

Reaper took my hand, positioning me in the middle as we approached the front door. "Don't be nervous," he said with a brush of his lips to my temple.

I wasn't, until he said that.

He raised his fist to knock and I pulled in a breath, trying to channel Gunner's easy confidence and the strength he saw in me.

Noelle opened the door, a drink resembling a bloody Mary already in her hand. "Finally you all made it. I thought my breakfast was gonna be a liquid diet."

"Nice to see you've been useful," Reaper teased as he led us inside.

"You're *hilarious*, brother." Noelle closed the door after us and waved us through. "They're in the den, we've got a fire going. Looking cute, Mari! Guess the cold's not gettin' to you, huh?"

I only had a leather jacket on over my dress and bare legs. Gunner had left me so flushed and satisfied, I didn't even notice the cold.

"Guess not," I said sheepishly, following her down the hall.

We came to a room filled with cozy warmth, the air thick with aromatic spices. Low couches and armchairs were filled with blankets and pillows. A coffee bar looked especially inviting next to a roaring fire with a cast-iron kettle set inside the flames. Rising from their seats were a beautiful couple in their fifties, one of which was the woman from the jeweler's table downtown.

"Oh my...Rory!" She practically flew at Reaper, and would have slid to the floor had he not swept her up in a tight hug.

"It's me, Ma," he said in an awed whisper. "I'm really here."

She released him slowly, hands skimming over his clothes and face in disbelief before turning to the man at his side. "And is this Jandro? My little *Jandrito*?"

"Hey, Mama Lis," he grinned, wrapping her in a loose hug. "You're still as beautiful as I remember."

While Reaper's mother fawned over the two men, his father turned to me. His face was strikingly similar to his son's, except for brown eyes instead of green, and the white hair that dominated the few remaining dark strands. Finn Daley was also powerfully built, clearly in fantastic shape for a man his age. I guess he had to be, after a long career in the Air Force and now as a general.

"It's a pleasure to finally meet you, Mariposa," he said kindly with a warm smile. Right away I noticed he smiled more easily than his son, with no hint of Reaper's signature scowl.

"Call me Mari, please," I returned. "And the pleasure is mine. Thank you for inviting me to your home."

Reaper's mother turned to me at that point. "Hello again." She smiled sweetly, only her green eyes showing traces of sadness as she reached out for my hands. "So I was right, your husband does have excellent taste."

"In jewelry, at least," I laughed humbly. "I'm so glad to meet you properly, Alisa."

"You're welcome to call me Lis, sweetheart." Her warmth felt genuine, filling the ache I felt over missing my own mother.

"You have a beautiful home, Lis," I said. "And you raised amazing people. Reap—uh, Rory and Noelle have been wonderful to me."

"Well, I certainly can't take credit for the last decade," she laughed, the sound a little forced. "But my goodness, I can't tell you how happy I am to see two of my children alive and well, and even in love!"

"What are the odds?" I smiled back, the pang of longing returning in my chest for a moment before I shoved it down.

"Finn, honey?" Lis looked at her husband. "Will you pour some coffee for Mari and the boys?"

"Mari, yes. The *boys* can get their own," he smirked, turning to the coffee bar. "How do you take yours, Mari?"

"Black, thank you."

"A woman after my own heart," he said, pouring from the French press into a clean cup.

Lis swatted his arm. "Oh stop flirting, she's married."

"So am I." He smacked a kiss on his wife's cheek before handing over my cup.

"Thank you. Habits of being a combat medic die hard," I said, cradling the drink in my hands.

"The Air Force was similar, I imagine. Always had to guzzle the caffeine, then get up and go." Finn squeezed the sides of Lis' waist, gently steering her toward the hallway. "Should we head to the table? I'm starvin', hon."

"Yes, but I'll need your help plating up the food." She kissed him quickly over her shoulder and let him guide her down the hallway.

Their affection was heartwarming, especially after knowing what they'd been through, and how long they had been together.

"We brought eggs," Jandro said, following them into the kitchen with Reaper, Noelle, and I trailing after. "Freshly laid from my girls."

Lis opened the carton he handed to her and gasped softly. "Ooh, these are beautiful." She ran her hands over the assorted colors of shells. "Thank you, Jandro. I didn't take you for a farmer."

"Me neither, but I guess a lot of unexpected stuff happened over the years." His fingers twirled around mine, bringing my palm up to his lips for a brief kiss.

I smiled at him before shooting a glance at Reaper, who was simply beaming at us. While I knew logically his parents had no issues with me having other men, I still didn't want to be inappropriate. Should I pay more attention to Reaper on principle? Or did the fact that they considered Jandro another son nullify that?

"Sit, everyone. Please," Finn said. "Make yourselves at home."

"Can I help with anything?" I asked, remembering my manners.

"Absolutely not." Lis smiled at me from the counter as she chopped fragrant cilantro.

"Mari, do you prefer savory or sweet crepes?" Finn hovered over the small stove with a dish towel over his shoulder, carefully pouring batter into a pan.

"Savory, please."

"Excellent choice," he smiled.

I nursed my coffee at the table while our hosts prepared breakfast. Reaper and Jandro accepted bloody Marys from Noelle, who evidently was quite the mixologist. She and her mother both had cheery expressions on, but there was no mistaking how tired they looked. Lis had just learned of her youngest son Daren's death, and Noelle, her father Carter's.

The mood was light and easygoing while the family talked, so I chose not to bring up condolences. When Noelle sat next to me, I rubbed and squeezed her hand in sympathy. She met my eyes and mouthed, "Thank you." Her lips wobbled only a little before taking another sip of her drink.

"So, Mari." Finn washed his hands and dried them on a dish towel. "How did you have the misfortune of meeting my son?" He shoved Reaper's head playfully, earning a grunt and a narrow-eyed glare.

I bit back my laugh with a smile. His playfulness reminded me more of Jandro than his birth son.

"We had stopped by the same service center in Old Phoenix," I said. "I, uh, provided some medical services there. When my work was done, I didn't have any specific destination in mind. So when his club was leaving, I went with them."

It wasn't a *complete* lie, just an omission of the killing and kidnapping details. Reaper seemed amused by my version of events, sending a lopsided smile my way.

"We heard about the Steel Demons all the way up in Nevada," Finn said as he began setting plates in front of us. "I always knew my boy loved his motorcycles, but never thought he'd become this mythical vigilante figure."

"Admit it. You're proud." Reaper smirked.

His father sat down, holding his thumb and forefinger close to each other in front of his face. "Just a tiny bit."

"So Mari, if you don't mind me asking," Lis said once everyone was seated with a plate of food. "How strange did you feel about taking multiple husbands? Or was it not strange at all?"

Reaper's hand came to rest on my knee under the table, squeezing encouragingly. "It took some getting used to," I answered. "But Re—uh, Rory, was really patient with me and talked me through it. I think what surprised me most was how normal and *right* it felt."

"That's what I hear the most from others." She smiled across the table at me before sliding a glance to her daughter next to me. "Nellie never really saw the perks, and still doesn't, from what I hear."

Noelle huffed, swallowing down her crepe with a slurp of her drink. "Larkan's still just a prospect," she glared daggers at her brother, "and it already scares me to death, all the crazy shit they make him do. I can't imagine being in Mari's position and worrying about *four* of these dicks. I'll drop dead from a heart attack tomorrow."

"Regardless, I'm glad you're happy, dear. I'm excited to meet him." Lis' gaze returned to me. "And the rest of yours, Mari? How long have you been with that man from the market?"

"Oh, Shadow and I are still newly seeing each other," I said, a light fluttering traveling up my body at the reminder of him. "We're taking things a bit slowly, getting to know each other."

"Jandro found him." Reaper cocked his head at his best friend on the other side of him. "The guy was in much worse shape back then. He's a different person now."

"Yeah." Jandro finished chewing his food and wiped his mouth with a napkin. "I did a little bit, got him into the club and all that, but it was Mari that made him come out of his shell by leaps and bounds."

Reaper's parents listened with fascination to the story of Shadow, the heavily censored one that Jandro knew anyway. He didn't betray any personal details like his nightmares or offer speculation on his scars. Everything he said was warm and respectful, as if talking about any other absent friend who'd overcome hardships. Reaper nodded with agreement at certain points in the story and added in his own anecdotes. I was proud and moved by my men, loving their camaraderie and complete lack of jealousy.

"He sounds lucky to have found all of you," Finn observed. "I met a lot of traumatized guys in the Air Force, and the camp where we were held." He looked at his wife, reaching for her hand. "It would be weeks, sometimes months where we couldn't see each other in that place, but I held on knowing Lis was nearby. I feel for everyone who had to suffer alone."

"That kid you brought to the meeting yesterday," Reaper piped up. "He must have a hell of a story. I didn't expect you to bring a new recruit to discuss tactics."

"Eduardo." His father nodded. "Yeah he's a runaway from Blakeworth. Said his family was going to be publicly executed for stealing winter coats, can you believe it? Their police force came to collect the family members, and they shoved him out the back door and told him to run. He got out of the city and was able to hide on a produce truck heading south. Four Corners was a speck in the distance when he hopped off, but he made a break for it and couldn't have ended up in a better place."

"Execution for stealing coats?" Lis repeated, aghast. "I bet they already have a foot of snow up there. Are they really so cruel to people in need?"

"Probably worse than you're imagining," I said. "The people in power up there are awful. Anyone considered lower class is just treated so horribly. I saw it firsthand."

"Ah yes, the daring rescue mission." Finn smiled at me. "You'll have Governor Vance in your debt forever now. The poor man was going nuts at the thought of losing Kyrie. That was the one time he begged me to invade, but the mere whiff of a neighboring army would send Blake-worth into full retaliation mode. I'm glad it was successful as a covert mission."

"Can you blame him though?" Lis asked. "That's his *only* child. If I had known about Daren—" Tears immediately filled her eyes, a shaking hand flying to her mouth. "I'm sorry, I—"

Finn scooted his chair directly next to hers, wrapped a muscular arm around his wife's shoulders and pressed kisses into her temple. "It's okay, hon. My fault for bringing it up." He rubbed soothingly up and down her arms as she cried softly into his shoulder. "We all miss him."

Reaper lowered his gaze to the table, leaning into me slightly as I rubbed his back. "I wish I'd been able to meet him," I offered softly to the grieving family. "And your other husbands too, Lis. I wish I could've..."

Been there to prevent their deaths, were the words I chose not to speak. I could have given Daren the correct antiviral. I could have set Carter's leg and given him antibiotics. Because their deaths were preventable with the right medical care, it was more than tragic. It was criminal that people lost family members to issues that were so easily treatable.

Reaper's fingers clasped around mine, and he brushed a kiss along my forehead much like his father was doing to his mother. "I know you would've saved them, sugar. And I love you for it. Just knowing that gives me so much peace."

"Still." I leaned my forehead on his cheek. "I hate that you lost them. Hate that your family's been hurt so much."

"There's nothing we can do." Lis sniffed and wiped her eyes, leaning away from her husband as she regained composure. "But continue living, honoring and remembering them."

"Cheers to that." Noelle too had shed a few silent tears and wiped her eyes as she raised her glass.

"To Carter, Daren, and Nolan, who we lost too soon to cancer," Finn toasted with his coffee cup. "But at least he passed before seeing how crazy and shitty this world turned out to be."

Lis nodded in agreement, then we all toasted and took a drink silently for their dead loved ones. I thought briefly of my parents again, but dismissed the idea of toasting to them too.

Who knew if my mom and dad had ever reunited, but if they'd died, I had a sneaking suspicion that I would know. The cat always at my side made no mention of seeing them, and until she told me herself, I would continue to hope.

MARIPOSA

Breakfast at Reaper's parents' continued with lightheartedness and good cheer. We ended up staying well past lunchtime, the conversations going on and on until my cheeks hurt from smiling so much. It wasn't an unpleasant time, but I didn't realize until we got back on the bikes how drained I was. The moment we pulled up to the B&B, I hopped off and headed for the backyard.

"Where you off to, sugar?" Reaper called after me.

"I'm just going to hang out with the chickens for a bit." But really, anyone who'd give me a bit of space and not ask a million questions would do. Chickens just seemed like the perfect creatures for the job.

"Okay, but don't leave the B&B," Reaper said. "Not without one of us."

"I know," I huffed with more annoyance than I intended. Maybe it was him being overprotective that was getting under my skin more than anything else. Ever since his dream from Daren, it felt like I could never be alone anymore.

While I escaped the chatter of the B&B, heading for the patio furniture near the coop, Freyja darted off in the opposite direction of the yard.

Shadow must be out here. He could usually be found working out when he didn't have anything else going on. The guys had cobbled together quite the collection of old weights, tires, and various other equipment to exercise with.

It took all of five minutes of sitting and watching chickens peck the ground for me to decide that Shadow was the one person I didn't want space from. As much as I tried to avoid staring, I could still see him across the yard, doing his best to work out with Freyja winding herself around his ankles.

But did he want space from *me*? He was remarkably easy going whenever we were together, affectionate and warm without being over-bearing. If I didn't know any better, I never would have believed he'd never been in a relationship before. He took everything in stride, even when I left him to spend time with my other men. And now it was me wondering if I should go over and see him, or if that would be too much.

Fuck it. My cat has no shame, why should I?

Getting up from my chair, I meandered that way slowly, trying to look casual and not like I was intent on invading Shadow's personal space. Which was exactly what I *wanted* to do, especially right then as he laid back and bench pressed a rusted barbell with concrete plates.

I am too thirsty for my own good. Just his breaths and grunts of effort heated me from inside out. The hard edges of his body, muscles coiling and stretching with his presses, pulled my gaze until I could no longer pretend to casually wander. It was almost a shame no woman had ever truly appreciated that body.

No one except me.

"Watch out, kitten. Coming up."

With a soft chirp, Freyja walked from her seat on Shadow's stomach to his thigh. She balanced on his leg as he rolled upright.

"Hey." Looking up to find me there, he braced one arm on his knee, panting slightly as he pet Freyja with the other hand. "Thought you might be near if the cat was."

"She's usually a good indication of that," I said.

Shadow had tied his hair back in a messy bun that was either hit-or-miss in terms of how good it looked on men. Unfortunately for my thirst, I'd never seen it look better than on him or Gunner. A few strands came loose, falling over his face as he looked down to pet Freyja.

"Here, kitten. You can have my bench." He picked her up gingerly as he stood, then placed her back down where he'd been reclined before, grabbing his T-shirt.

"You don't have to stop on my account." A feeble protest as I watched beautiful lines of scars disappear under black fabric.

"I was just finishing up," he mumbled, gaze turned away as he rolled the shirt down his torso. "How was breakfast?"

"It was good. Just...a lot."

"A lot?" He moved closer to me, straightening his shirt over his body.

"Yeah, a bit emotionally heavy as we took time to remember Daren and Reaper's other father. After that, it was a lot of...smiling and answering questions about my life. Being polite and engaging and sweet, so I can impress these people I've never met before." I let out a sheepish laugh, bringing a palm to my face. "I don't know if I'm making any sense, but I haven't had to do that in a long time and it was exhausting."

"I think I know what you mean." Shadow moved closer to me, close enough to touch but his arms stayed frustratingly at his sides. "I felt like that at the governor's dinner. It was why I dipped out early. Socializing feels like a performance sometimes and it's draining."

"Yes, that's exactly it." I turned to him, wanting to slide my arms around his tapered waist and rest my head on that solid chest. "Reaper's parents are lovely, and I enjoyed meeting them. It was just a big morning and I need to unwind from it all."

Shadow tilted his head slightly, like he was pondering something. "Do you want me to leave you alone?"

"No." I shook my head unashamedly. "I don't."

His face brightened as he reached for me, a tentative touch on my waist that I happily leaned into until his whole palm rested on my side. My hand came to his wrist, stroking lightly up his scarred forearm. His small smile was warm, eyes downcast and shy.

"Do you want to go for a ride?" He leaned down, lips brushing my forehead. "I promise I won't talk much."

I looked up grinning, swimming in the elation of how light and easy things were between us.

"I'd love that," I said, reaching up on tiptoes for a kiss. "And you can talk to me however little or much you like. I never feel exhausted from you."

His mouth pressed indulgently to mine, sensual even as he pulled away, lips hovering. "Same here," he purred. The hand on my waist squeezed gently. "Let me grab a quick shower first."

I will if you let me come in there with you.

Rather than say that, I bit my tongue and reluctantly stepped out of his touch. "Okay, I'll change into riding gear."

As we made for our separate rooms, I wondered how many cold showers I'd need to stop becoming a drooling, panting mess around him.

No less than a hundred, to be sure.

I didn't ask Shadow where he was taking us, nor did he opt to tell me. I wanted to be surprised by the place he chose, without any expectations. This time I sat behind him as we rode out of the city, hugging around his chest as Four Corners' construction projects gave way to wilderness.

The environment out here couldn't seem to decide if it wanted to be desert or forest. Copses of evergreen trees contrasted against bright red and orange sedimentary rock. We were in that in-between area between the Southwest and what was once middle America. I was too young to really know what different parts of the United States were like, back when things were better. All I'd ever known was a culture conflict and ever-increasing tension.

The majestic mountains of Colorado and breathtaking coastline of the Pacific Northwest sounded like bygone fairy tales, as did the party beaches in Florida and rich history of the eastern seaboard.

For better or worse, we were making new history. One that I hoped places like Four Corners would remain a stronghold of, a place to tell the story of Reaper's parents and countless others who escaped unthinkable situations.

Like Shadow.

I rested my cheek on his back patch, squeezing tighter around him while my other hand idly stroked his chest. He still hadn't told me the full extent of what happened to him, the source of the scars lingering on his body and his mind. The biggest clues I got were how he regressed when I tried to cut the arrows from his back after our Blakeworth mission. It broke my heart seeing him so afraid, and knowing some people out there got away with treating him so cruelly.

Curious as I was, I'd never put my own desire for that knowledge above his comfort with me. The most effective way to treat an injury started with knowing what caused it in the first place. If that knowledge wasn't available, I had to do the best I could with what I did know.

Shadow thrived with openness and acceptance. He sought affection and care when he felt safe and not afraid of being judged or punished. I might not have known all the details of his trauma, but I knew enough to foster his healing. I knew not to hold blades near him, and that kissing and touching him in public made him feel more confident. He hadn't tried to hide his scarred eye once since we had our lunch date.

"We're here," he said over the roar of his engine with a light squeeze of my hand.

He pulled to a stop under a large oak tree, dappled sunlight speckling over a grassy knoll just beyond it. Some wild lilies lined the clearing, bright orange speckled flowers like small lamps against the lush, dark greens.

"Oh, Shadow, this is beautiful!" I climbed off of the bike before he had a chance to lift me off. "How did you find this place?"

"Just riding during some free time the other day." He shrugged. "It's quiet. A nice place to be alone."

My whole body lit up at his thoughtfulness. A smile split my face as I reached up to kiss him. "You knew exactly what I needed. Thank you for bringing me here."

"I, um..." He trailed off to kiss me some more, planting sweet pecks on my lips as we shuffled our way to a sunny area.

"You what?" I held on to his forearm, placing a kiss on his shoulder while we found a dry patch of grass to sit.

"I was going to say..." He paused as we sank down together to the ground, eyes shyly cast away. "That I wouldn't share this place with anyone else."

I love you.

The words rang out like a bell in my head and formed a heaviness in my throat. Holy shit, I did. I was in love with Shadow, from every beautiful scar on his skin to the pure goodness in his heart. But my lips remained stubbornly, if even fearfully, sealed. I had to take this at his pace, to not overwhelm him with experiences and feelings that were still new to him.

"You're sweet," I chose to tell him instead, sitting across his legs so I could rest my head on his shoulder.

"You've told me that a few times," he murmured, placing a hand on my knees while the other slid across my back.

Because I'm too chicken shit to tell you I love you.

"Because it's true."

I brought a hand to his cheek, caressing his bearded jaw and cheekbone while staring at his full lips. Fuck, did he have a scar there too?

My thumb ran over the puckered tissue on his bottom lip as he closed the ever-shrinking distance between our mouths. Thick arms pulled me closer, wrapping me in safety as our kisses grew deeper. Lips and tongues pressed insistently, losing their finesse and growing clumsy with desire.

I love you. I want you so bad, my head screamed as Shadow moaned softly into my mouth, his fingers curling into the fabric of my shirt. *Please, make love to me out here. It's beautiful, it's perfect.* You're *perfect.*

But his hands and kisses never strayed. It occurred to me that he might not know how to escalate, given that his experience was limited to transactional sex and making out with me. When we slowed for a breath, I opted to try something new.

I dragged my lips across his cheek, pausing to kiss his scar before pushing his hair back and continuing to his neck.

"Oh! Fuck, that's..."

Shadow's reaction was instant and more satisfying than I could have predicted. Smiling against his pulse, I kissed his neck again, making a small trail from the corner of his jaw to his shoulder as he squirmed.

"That," he groaned again, shuddering under my lips. "Why does that feel so good?"

Fuck, he was so cute. I could not stop grinning against his skin.

"The neck is an erogenous zone for many people," I explained.

"What does that mean?"

"It means," I said, pulling back, "it's a non-sexual body part that you derive sexual pleasure from." I ran a light touch along the side I'd just been kissing. "The blood flow here makes the area especially sensitive."

"I see," he mused, the idea already forming behind his eyes as he pushed my hair behind my shoulder. "Is it an erogenous zone for you?"

"It is." I bit the inside of my cheek to keep my grin in check.

He leaned in slowly, with a few small moments of hesitation, as if waiting for me to stop him. Like that would ever happen. I tilted my head back, baring my neck like those girls in old TV shows asking for vampire bites.

Shadow's lips landed on my neck with a tickling softness, making light presses with a closed mouth like when I first showed him how to kiss.

"Yes, like that," I encouraged him, leaning in. "That feels nice."

His kisses grew bolder, quickly finding how easy it was to suck at a person's neck.

"Hold on, not too hard," I laughed, pulling away. "You don't want to leave hickies."

"Oh no? What are those?" His eyes were bright and curious, staring at my neck like he couldn't wait to take another bite out of me.

What the hell? I wanted him and was feeling bold. Nearly a week of seeing each other and we just got to the necking stage, so I wasn't likely to see his dick anytime soon. Still, I might be able to claim him another way.

I grabbed the front of his shirt in my fist, pulling it down to expose the top of his chest. His gaze remained curious and lightly amused as I pressed my lips just below the hollow of his throat.

"Ah." He let out a small noise of surprise as I sucked hard at his flesh.

"That," I said, pulling back to admire my work, "is a hickey."

He pulled the edge of his shirt down to look at the dark red mark I left on his skin, then stared at me with wide eyes.

"That hurt a little."

"Oh, I'm sorry." I frowned. I should have realized he might not want a bruise on his chest. "It'll fade, and probably faster with some ice—"

"No, it's okay. But I mean it hurt, Mari. I *felt* it."

It took me a moment, then my mouth fell open at the comprehension of what he was saying. "You felt pain?"

"Yes! It felt...sharp. A little hot, although that could have just been your mouth—" His lips clamped shut, a blush rising up his neck.

"And..." I studied his face, trying to get a read on his emotional state. "Are you okay, now that you've felt that?"

"Yeah, just surprised really. I haven't physically felt anything like that in so long. Only during my nightmares, but...it's different." His expression turned playful, a smile twitching on his lips. "Do you think you could do that again?"

"Give you another hickey?" I laughed. "For scientific purposes?"

"Yes." His voice lowered with a light caress to my hip. "Purely for scientific reasons."

"Anything in the name of science." I pecked his lips once before mouthing my way under his chin, taking indulgent nibbles and leaving a trail of kisses down his neck until I reached the space between his collarbones.

"Do it harder," he urged, holding his T-shirt out of the way for me. "Try to make it hurt me."

I giggled at the innuendo in his request before I latched on just below the first mark I made. This time I held his flesh in my teeth, pulling with my lips and lashing with my tongue until my own mouth started to hurt.

"Wow," I remarked, pulling away. "That might be one for the record books."

It was roughly the size of a golf ball, a mottled, dark reddish-purple monstrosity surrounded by more red skin.

"I don't understand it." Shadow released his T-shirt and rubbed at the spot. "It hurt but...it also felt good." He shot me a worried glance. "What does that mean?"

"Maybe your brain has never associated pain with pleasure before." I folded my legs and returned to leaning against his shoulder. "So you've blocked it off when you know the intention is to cause you harm, but the pathway associating it with something pleasurable hasn't been explored until now." I shrugged. "Again, not a neurologist. Just a theory."

"But is that normal?" he asked. "To...enjoy pain?"

"Yes, completely normal." I kissed his cheek, my hand searching for his to hold and reassure him. "It's different for everyone. Some people like a little pain, others a lot. Some not at all."

Shadow's thumbs rubbed back and forth pensively over my hands and wrists. "I think I might like a little. Only from you. And I—" He stopped himself, pausing to think about his words some more. "Even if you liked it, I don't think I could ever bring myself to hurt you."

Why I hadn't melted into a liquid state by then was completely unknown to me. This sweet, beautiful man was just too much.

"I do like a little bit of pain too, sometimes." I propped my chin on his shoulder. "But not all the time. And when I do want it, I can usually get it from Reaper." I stroked Shadow's rough cheek, nudging my mouth toward his. "I like what you and I have."

"I do too." He sighed contentedly, lips skimming over mine.

"And I love—" *you* "—that you can talk to me about what you like. That's important."

His arms came around me, heavy and strong as he pulled me into his chest. "What I like most is just being with you."

My whole damn body couldn't stop fluttering. How could a man with zero relationship experience know the exact words to make me fall so hard?

I knew from Shadow there was no pretense, no flattery or attempt to be charming. He was just telling me what he honestly felt. And it was me, the one with now *four* partners, who didn't have the courage to spit out my true feelings.

Kissing seemed to get the point across well enough, so I let my eyes fall shut and just tasted him. The man knew how to feel out a kiss, and matched my slow, lazy pace, just savoring and tasting.

"Do we ever have to leave?" I whispered, lips pulsing and bruised.

"Eventually," he hummed. "But not right now."

The sunlight had become harsh, almost uncomfortably warm. Being pressed up against a hot man might have had something to do with it too.

"Give me a second. I need to cool off," I told Shadow, scooting away to take off my leather jacket.

"It did get hot," he observed, tugging at the neckline of his shirt.

"This weather is nuts. It was snowing just the other day." I scooted toward a shadier patch of grass and stretched my legs out, crossing them at the ankles while I leaned back on my elbows. My T-shirt had ridden up, exposing a few inches of midriff, but not to the point where I cared. I was sweating there anyway.

"That, um." Shadow was making an adorable attempt to not stare at my body. "That shirt looks familiar."

"I stole it from Jandro, I think." I pulled the fabric straight to get a clear view of the design, now faded and cracked with age. "Looks like an early version of the club logo."

"It is." Shadow sounded pleased. "I screen-printed those shirts years ago. I remember now."

"Oh yeah? I love this shirt. It's my second favorite, next to your hoodie."

Shadow smiled, a rare full one that lit up his whole face. He opened his mouth, then promptly shut it, the smile gone.

"What?"

"Nothing." He averted his gaze.

"You looked like you were gonna say something."

"I was going to ask you a question, but never mind."

"Now you've got me curious." I rolled to my side, propping my head up on my hand. "What is it?"

"Seriously, nothing. Just something dumb that popped into my head."

"*Shadowww*," I whined, letting my head flop down to the grass. "I want to know. Please?"

"I, um." He sighed and raked a hand back through his hair, looking everywhere but at me. "I was going to ask if I could...draw you."

My mouth fell open. "*Draw* me?"

"Yeah, but—"

"Shadow, I would love that!"

Finally, he looked at me again. "You would?"

"Yes, are you kidding? I can't imagine anything more flattering." I grinned hard. "My tattoo artist boyfriend *drawing* me? I'd love nothing more. Did you bring supplies?"

"I always keep a sketch pad and some pencils on my bike," he said. "You really want me to?"

"Yes, if you do." I rolled to my stomach, kicking my feet up. "I can be flash art in your future tattoo shop."

"I don't know about that," he growled, rising to his feet. "A drawing of you on a wall for everyone to see? I'd rather keep you to myself."

I giggled to myself while he got what he needed from his bike. While he was one of the most stoic and easygoing of my men, I liked that small bite of possessiveness too.

"How do you want me to pose?" I asked when he settled back on the grass with the sketch pad on his knee.

"I think, like you were before," he said, his gaze on me now studying and inquisitive. "Lying back on your elbows, ankles crossed. Yes, like that. Can you stay there for a few minutes?"

"No problem," I grinned, glancing down at my still-uncovered belly. "Want me to fix the shirt?"

"No, leave it." He glanced up from his paper with a smirk, the pencil in hand already sweeping across the page.

"Where do you want me to look?"

"Keep looking at me like that."

I was hoping he'd say that. He was fascinating to watch. His gaze was technical, focused, but everything about this was extremely intimate.

Sometimes his eyes would meet mine before returning to his page. Other times he glanced at my body, his hand making long, sweeping movements. Sometimes he made small, fast marks, never erasing anything. I could only imagine how he was capturing me and itched to see it when he was done.

This drawing would be a rare glimpse from Shadow's perspective, I realized. The tattoos he did were a reflection of his clients, but this drawing would be a reflection of *him*. I wanted so badly to know how he saw me.

Neither of us spoke. I didn't dare break the magic of watching him work, and it was over far too quickly.

"It's rough, but I think it's done," he said, straightening up. "I'll clean it up when we get back."

"Can I see?" I was already scooting toward him on the grass, spinning to sit next to him for a peek. "Oh, Shadow!" I gasped.

He drew me in a pin-up style, not quite cartoony, but not entirely lifelike either. The face was definitely me, the nose and lips exactly like mine, eyes large and looking straight at the observer with a coy smile. He redesigned the T-shirt into a crop top, intentionally showing off some belly with killer waist and hip proportions that I wished were real. Legs stretched out long and shapely, hugged by form-fitting jeans with rips in the knees, just like my real ones.

"She's so cute!" I squeaked. "And sexy. She belongs in a magazine."

"*She* is you," he said with a soft laugh on my cheek. "Do you like it?"

"I love it. If this is rough, I can't imagine what cleaning it up will look like."

"It's just me being a perfectionist," he said. "It'll look even better when I add shading and stuff."

My hands wrapped around his bicep, hugging his massive arm. "Aren't you glad I made you tell me?"

"Yes," he chuckled, lips finding mine again. "I am."

JANDRO

The chickens were making their way into the coop for the night when I heard the rumble of Shadow's bike returning with my *Mariposita.*

I rubbed a hand over my head, chicken logistics blurring in my brain. We had a total of nine as of yesterday. This morning I found three more freshly hatched chicks under a mother hen. Damn Foghorn was getting busy.

With the colder weather up here, I'd have to look into some heat lamps that wouldn't hurt the birds or catch the whole coop on fire. If the eggs kept hatching faster than I could collect them, I might even have to make a brooder and bring the smallest ones inside when winter got really cold.

Who the hell was I? Vice president of a biker gang and a chicken farmer? If someone told me a year ago this was what I'd be doing, I would have laughed my ass off.

The bike engine cut off, then Mari and Shadow's footsteps walked through the B&B. Their voices were low, meant only for each other. I listened for the direction of Mari's footsteps as Shadow went to his room, wondering if she still wanted space or would join me outside.

Moments later the rickety back door opened, and my smiling woman crossed the patio to me.

"Someone looks happy." I patted my thigh in an invitation for her to sit.

She parked that cute ass on my leg and wrapped her arms around my shoulders, kissing me deep and hungry, like she missed me.

"Where are the others?" she asked in a soft whisper.

"Out drinkin'." I laced my hands over her hip. "Honestly, I was a little over-socialized from this morning too. Don't blame you for having a little getaway."

"Really?" Her forehead dropped to mine. "I'm not neglecting you?"

"Not for a moment." I took a nibble of her plump lower lip. "Although I would like to take over your next riding lesson."

"Deal," she grinned. "You can show me how to take a bike apart and put it back together too."

"That'll take a bit longer than learning how to ride but," I swatted her hip, "I'm happy to show you what's in my toolbox."

"Don't make this sound like a weird porno," she laughed, slapping my chest.

"Why not? It's the perfect setting for it." The thought of her covered in grease and digging into an engine with me *did* turn me on like nothing else.

"Only in your mind," she teased, fingers swirling with delicious pressure into my neck.

"Fine. I think I'm partial to shower sex anyway." I slid my hands up her back, rubbing into areas I knew would be sore from the ride. "So what were you and Shadow-man up to?"

"Not much, really. Just a ride out to a private place to sit and talk."

She was nervous. Fidgeting. Clearly holding something back.

"Yeah?" I pressed. "That's all?"

Her fingers worked idly at the edges of my cut. I felt her heartbeat speed up through my palm on her back, but stayed patient in waiting for her answer.

"I love him, Jandro."

The relief whooshed out of me in a long breath that became a laugh. "Well, I was expecting much worse. Did you tell him?"

"No." Her eyebrows knitted together, her bottom lip pulling between her teeth. "I don't want to overwhelm him with...you know, intense feelings while he's still getting used to this."

"He's not overwhelmed by you," I said. "Fuck, I'd bet Foghorn's sperm that he's in love with you too."

"But he's never felt like that before, right? What if it freaks him out?"

"He can be a big boy and get through it like the rest of us. Remember, he's got us to lean on too."

She relaxed with that assurance, leaning heavily against me. "Please be there for him. I know you all have your manly pride or whatever, but I want him to know he has someone besides me."

"He always has me, although he doesn't need me like he used to. My boy's grown up." I scratched my head with a laugh. "Fuck, we've all been so busy running around, I just realized we haven't really talked much in the last few days."

"Talk to him," she urged. "Spend tomorrow with him."

"And what if I have plans?"

"I think you can skip cuddling the chickens and yelling at Foghorn for one day."

"I do *not* cuddle them! It's called checking for parasites, I'll have you know."

"If you say so, *guapito*." Her smile brushed my cheek. "You're the best, you know that?"

"Eh, I figure I can place in the top four." I stood up with a groan, keeping her legs wrapped around me. "You want to wait for the others or turn in now?"

"Let's go in." She kissed me deeply, palms cupping my neck. "Can we eat dinner in bed?"

"Hm, Reaper's not gonna like that." I nudged the side door open with my foot as I proceeded to carry her inside.

"Good thing he's not here." Her lips quirked. "We finally got our alone time."

"Perfect," I sighed against her mouth, carrying her through the doorway of our room. "So that means I get dinner *and* dessert all to myself."

It didn't take much convincing to get Shadow to hang out the next day. I invited him to come with me and Larkan to the garage we were borrowing to do our maintenance and repairs. He accepted with his usual grunt, the only change was his insistence to kiss Mari goodbye before she left for the hospital. The big dude joined our lineup in seeing her off like he'd always belonged.

Reaper was taking her today, shooting down her pleas to drive with surly growls that turned down her beautiful smile.

"Just let her, Reap. She needs to learn," I urged.

"Nah, later," he grunted, easing the bike onto the road. "Too much traffic through the city in the morning."

"I did fine with Gunner the other day," she protested.

"Do I look like fucking Gunner? I said no."

"You and me then, *Mariposita*," I reminded her. "We'll do a lesson when you have a free afternoon."

She nodded, setting her chin on the back of Reaper's shoulder with a pout as they rode away. I watched them until they turned the corner, trying to figure out this weird sensation in my gut. Reaper was overprotective on a good day but he seemed over the top with it lately, even for him..

I shook it off, figuring it had to do with war planning and having more at stake now, knowing that his family was here. Clapping Shadow on the shoulder, I headed for our steeds. "You ready, dude?"

"Yeah." He followed me, tying his hair back to keep the wind out of it.

That was new. Every passing day, he seemed to hide his face less and less.

Larkan came up a minute after us, after struggling to release himself from Noelle clinging to him on the front porch. We pulled up to the garage ten minutes later, parking in front of the spare bay that Dave, the owner, let us work out of.

Our prospect was in a surly mood from the get-go, barely saying a word to me while throwing tools around carelessly and grumbling to himself as he worked. Shadow was being a much better helper than him just by replacing a few tires.

"Quit throwing your tantrum like a bitch and spit it out already," I told Larkan from where I lay on a creeper.

"If I do, you'll tell Reaper, so no thanks, I'm good." He proceeded to crank loudly with his socket wrench in a way that would surely strip the bolt.

"Hey, stop." I rolled out from under the bike I was working on and sat up. "What's this about? Your patch?"

"Yeah, my fuckin' patch!" he huffed, throwing the tool on the ground. "I risked my life to protect his old lady, and what do I get? Jack fuckin' shit."

"You'll get your damn patch, man," I sighed. "I hear your frustration, but we have more important shit to deal with right now, like preparing for war."

"I know, but—" He ran a grease-covered hand through his hair, leaving black streaks at his temples. "I wanna marry Noelle before shit gets bad. Set her up in case something happens to me, you know?"

"She'll be fine with or without you," I said. "As the president's sister, she does have some power even if she's not an officer."

"It's not just that, though. Like, I also just want to do it while we still can."

"I hear you, man. I do." I wiped my hands on a rag. "I'll talk to him. See what I can do."

Larkan's jaw dropped and I entertained the thought of shoving the rag into his mouth. "You will?"

"Yeah, but don't expect much. Mariposa has the most sway over him, and I know she's been advocating for you. In all likelihood, he genuinely has too much on his plate to think about club shit right now."

"Hey, a bug in his ear is more than what I could ask for." He picked up his socket wrench, a new ease in his movements as he got back to work. "Thanks, Jandro."

"Yeah, well Shadow and I owe you for that mission too."

Larkan laughed lightly. "Man, if you could be patched in twice,

Shadow sure as fuck deserves that. I still cringe thinking about when they got you with those harpoons, dude."

"I didn't feel it," Shadow answered nonchalantly as he carried two tires to stack against the wall.

"Not even when you got sick?"

"Oh, I felt all of that." Shadow's hand drifted over his stomach as if recalling the nausea and feverish symptoms. "Mariposa made it not so bad, though."

I ducked my head to hide my grin, turning to grab another tool. I didn't even need eyes to see that Shadow was completely in love with her. It was pretty fucking cute how they were both utterly terrified of telling the other how they felt.

"Here's what I want to know." Larkan flipped a wrench in midair. "How'd they fucking hit you? Whenever you come up in conversation, someone always mentions how you're untouchable in a fight."

"They were long-range weapons." Shadow shrugged like the answer was obvious. "It's true, I'm untouchable in close combat. But a sniper can hit me from a distance if I'm dealing with something else up close."

I paused in my work to listen. This was probably the most I'd ever heard him talk to someone he wasn't close to.

"How'd you get to be so good at the close combat stuff?" Larkan asked, his curiosity about the big guy thoroughly piqued.

Shadow bristled, a sign that the real answer was uncomfortable for him. But he humored the prospect anyway. "Having to watch out for myself in prison. I also trained myself to listen for people approaching when I was young."

"You gotta teach me some of that one day." With that, Larkan refocused on his work, the conversation finished in his mind.

Shadow apparently wasn't done yet.

The big dude finished stacking tires and approached the prospect with his hands spread out to his sides. And that look on his face...was he *smiling*?

"Grab a wrench and come at me," he offered. "Here. I'll turn around."

He spun to face the other direction, Larkan glancing at me with a cocked eyebrow. I shrugged and beckoned him to proceed, knowing Shadow would be clued in immediately if he heard any sound.

Deciding to go along with it, the prospect picked up a small wrench to act as a dagger. He stalked up behind Shadow like a cat, careful to not make any noise. But the scarred assassin saw him coming like he had eyes in the back of his head.

Larkan thrust the weapon forward, aiming for a kidney. It was the smart move, rather than swinging high for his head and leaving his body exposed. But it was also exactly what Shadow expected him to do.

At the last possible moment, Shadow pivoted, turning his body in the same direction as Larkan's jab. The prospect's momentum sent him stumbling forward into nothing, giving ample room for Shadow to grab the back of his cut and wrap the other arm around his throat.

"Do a short jab if you're gonna hit me there." Shadow patted his back and released him. "Keep your arm bent and close to your body, so if I hear you coming, you can still get me in the gut or between the ribs." He turned his back to Larkan a second time. "Try again."

"Shank him like an inmate," I hollered. "Short, fast jabs."

The two of them danced around in mock combat for another half hour, leaving me to work alone while I watched and heckled. Not that I minded. Seeing Shadow step up to mentor the prospect blasted beyond my expectations, even after seeing all the strides he'd made in the past weeks.

When the day came to a close and we rode out to the bar, I wondered how many drinks he'd need to loosen his tongue about Mari, or if he'd come right out and spill his guts to me.

"So how are things going?" I asked when we got settled in, me with a beer and him with whiskey.

His brow creased, already suspicious at my digging. "Fine, I guess. Why?"

"Sure, dude," I laughed after taking a long swallow. "You spend the whole afternoon on a romantic getaway and things are just *fine, you guess*?"

Shadow's face relaxed, that smile starting to appear that looked odd on his face at first, but actually suited him. "In that regard, things are good. I think." He pulled down a hefty mouthful of his drink. "They'd probably be even better if I could stop overthinking shit and just relax."

"Believe it or not, that's normal," I said. "I guarantee you, every time a person has started seeing someone they're crazy about, they go nuts with the overthinking."

"You too?" he asked.

"Me, Reaper, *and* Gunner. Fuck, I bet even the Sons felt like that way back in the beginning. They weren't always the cuddly shits they are now. Trust me, dude. It gets easier."

Shadow huffed out a soft laugh. "When I'm not stressing about what to say, or whether or not I should touch her, it *is* easy." He shifted in his barstool, like he was seeking out a touch that wasn't there. "I can be myself and she...*likes* that."

"That's when you know you've got a good thing." I drained the rest of my beer, swatting him on the arm with a grin. "I'm happy for you, man. I had my concerns at first, seeing as she's mine too and all. But I should've known you'd be just fine. You got nothin' to worry about."

I signaled for another drink, sitting back while the bartender poured it for me. My suspicions were confirmed that I'd have nothing to report to Mari. Shadow was just as crazy-nervous-excited about her as she was about him. And that was up to them to navigate. The other guys and I would be here to support them, but it wasn't our job to meddle. Mari and Shadow had to establish their own relationship first, and then we could work him into the bigger group dynamic when he was ready.

At my side, the big guy was clearly deep in his head again, folding and spreading his hands on the bar in front of his drink.

"What now?" I asked him after a few moments of watching.

He sighed, shoving his empty glass away and shaking his head no when the bartender offered him another.

"I don't want to fuck this up, Jandro."

"Well, you can't possibly fuck it up worse than Reaper or Gunner already have," I chuckled. "And she's still with them, 'cause she's a damn angel."

"I should have listened to you before," he went on, rubbing at a spot on his chest.

"Care to be more specific?"

"You know, when…" His face darkened with the flush creeping up his neck. "Back when you were trying to tell me about how to please a woman."

"Oh, that. Yeah, that's up there in the top five, no top *three*, things you should've paid more attention to in Jandro's Life University."

He laughed, an increasingly common sound from him. "One of those life lessons I never thought I'd actually use. But when we were together yesterday—" He stopped abruptly until I nodded at him to continue. "I think she wanted to go further, and I do too, I just…my mind went blank on how to go about it."

"Holy shit, Shadow." I propped my elbow on the bar, rubbing my forehead as I tried to contain my laughter from echoing throughout the whole building.

"What?"

"Nothing, you're just a cute kid in a big, scary dude's body. In any case, you're in luck." I composed myself and let my hand fall to the bartop. "Mari knows you're inexperienced. She's also a big girl who knows how to use her words." I gave him a pointed look. "Talk to her. Invite her to tell you what she wants. Tell her what you want, and let her decide if she's up for it or not. Don't get stuck in your head, dude. She'll want to please you too."

"She already does," he sighed, his gaze drifting as he focused on some memory. "She doesn't even need to do anything."

"Alright, that's it. I'm drawing the line there." I slammed my second beer down and drew a line across my throat, signaling to the bartender that we were done.

Shadow stared at me, puzzled. "What?"

"Too fucking cute. I can't handle that shit." I punched him in the shoulder, making sure he saw my grin as we rose up from the barstools and headed out front to our bikes.

REAPER

"Oh really, now? You've protected my son and daughter-in-law, have you?"

Hades stretched out across my dad's lap, nudging his head into his hand for more petting. Dad laughed, looking very un-general-like sitting on the floor with his legs stretched out in front of him and rubbing my dog's belly. Already eager to be a doting grandpa, he pulled some strings with the building security to let Hades into the City Hall building.

"Yes, you did. That's what a good boy does," he continued as if they were having a conversation. What I would give to see the look on his face if Hades really did answer him.

But the ancient god seemed to lay dormant, only the goofy, drooling mutt with us now. Dad and I were in the City Hall conference room again, waiting for the governor to show up so we could brief him on the scouting missions we set into place.

"Will Vance have a heart attack if he sees his general sitting on the floor?" I remarked from where I leaned over the maps spread out on the table.

"Nah, I've crawled around with his treasurer's grandson before. Can't do it too often though. These old knees quit before I do." Hades rolled off his lap and shook his fur out while Dad climbed to his feet with a groan, grabbing a chair for support.

"How's Mom doin'?" I asked absently, scanning the maps for the routes we established.

"She's alright. You know, hangin' in." He came up next to me and slugged my arm. "You oughta come over more and see her yourself. Noelle's been there a couple times in the last week, but your mom misses her son." Dad gave me a pointed stare. "You're the only boy she's got left."

"Yeah, I know," I sighed. "It's just..." My sentence trailed off, no words coming to me in a believable way. I didn't want to leave Mari out of my sight for even a moment because of what Daren had told me in that dream.

As days passed with nothing happening, my anxiety over it worsened rather than getting better. I felt like I'd been holding my breath for a week and a half, and the moment I let it out, disaster would strike. It was affecting my daily interactions with her and others. I knew I was snapping more, even more short-fused than I usually was. Every time I left her at the hospital or at home with the other guys, I wondered if it would be the last time I saw her. I stared at every door I passed by like a maniac, wondering if it was *that* door, the one I had to break down.

I felt like I was losing it, breaking down every word of Daren's warning in my head hundreds of times. Looking at the faces of the people I surrounded myself with and wondering if they would be the one I had to kill.

"I can understand never wanting to leave that gorgeous wife of yours," Dad chuckled sympathetically. "But she has other men. She'll understand you spending time with family you haven't seen in over a decade."

His voice just got lost in the chatter in my head. I didn't know what to listen to, what was real and what I should ignore. And of course, every time I asked Hades or Freyja to throw me a bone, they stayed completely silent.

Whatever was about to play out, the gods had no interest in interfering. And normally that would have been fine. I did well enough before they came around. But it was the urgency, the understated panic in

Daren's voice saying, *she'll die if you don't,* that scared me more than anything. I'd sacrifice anything—a limb, my sight, my sanity, even my life, for the peace of mind of knowing that Mari would be okay.

When faced with a difficult decision, I always had some inkling of what to do. Sometimes I had to ride to clear my head, or just observe in silence what my instincts were trying to tell me. But the correct action was always there, always made clear once I stripped away all the distractions.

This time? I just felt like a compass needle spinning madly, pulled equally in all directions.

Governor Vance entered the room then, trailed by Josh, bringing my shattered focus back to the meeting at hand. Hades rolled to his belly, stubby tail wagging and puppy eyes on point at the two men who just entered.

"Oh my—shit." Josh startled at the sight of him. "I always forget how big your dog is, Reaper."

"He's friendly," I said with an incline of my head. "You can pet him."

"Maybe later." He gave Hades a wide berth, circling around to the opposite end of the table.

"Come on now, Josh. You're making the poor beast sad." Vance put on a brave face, but I could see his nervousness as he bent down to lightly stroke Hades' head. He got a more vigorous tail-wagging and lick of his fingers for his effort.

"He knows who his allies are." I smirked.

"Smart," Vance praised, scratching him more boldly before glancing up at me. "Is it true he runs alongside your bike for hundreds of miles?"

"Dobermans are athletic dogs. They have good endurance," I answered casually before returning my focus to the maps. "Shall we get started?"

"Please." Vance took his seat next to Josh, folding his hands while he waited for me to begin.

"We've decided on three main points that would provide enough cover for scouts around General Tash's territory." I pointed to the markers on the map. "Because there's a lot of flat ground between here and there, we are recommending sending them through these valleys and canyons. It'll add time to the mission but will prevent them from being seen. T-Bone and Gunner will send their trained birds to assist as well.

"What exactly do these birds do?" Josh peered over his glasses, his hand paused in his note-taking.

"They've been trained to give certain signals if they see certain movements or groupings of people," I said coolly. "We'll teach all the signals to the scouts."

"And what about Blakeworth?" Vance's eyes narrowed at the territory a few hundred miles north.

"It'll be easier to get into, because their focus is on flashing how rich they are, not military tactics." My dad took over, stepping up next to me. "They'll be more alert since Kyrie's rescue, but our scouts heading there can use the same strategy as the Sons did. It'll be as simple as dressing like one of their elite and faking documents."

"You're sure that'll work a second time?" Vance sounded skeptical.

"They'll be checking at every entry-point into the city, but they're an extremely superficial people," Dad said with more than a hint of sneer. "As long as our guys look and act entitled enough, they should get away with it. It's those who appear to be poorer that they're going to take a closer look at."

The door opened and I caught a flash of Eduardo's camo uniform in my peripheral vision. My dad beckoned him over as I continued with the presentation. "Now, we should carry out these missions roughly two weeks apar—"

His life is yours to take.

The once-comfortable room temperature dropped to an icy chill, making every hair on my body stand up. Stunned, I looked at Hades. The dog's whole body was tensed with alertness, his nose pointed directly at my dad's young recruit.

The god had awoken.

"What?" I whispered, fear and confusion locking up my limbs.

Reap what has been sown. His life is yours to take.

"Ah, Reaper?" Vance and Josh peered at me, the puzzlement on their faces a clear indication they didn't feel the cold heaviness of this god's command. "Are you alright?"

My gaze shifted to Eduardo, the skinny teenager staring back at me blankly.

You will carry out my command, came the voice of Hades. *Take his life. Now.*

"What the fuck?" I said numbly, fully aware that I appeared to be talking to myself like a maniac. "Him? He's just a kid—"

You are a human instrument and you do not question me. You obey. Reap. Him. Now.

"He hasn't even done anything! Why would you—"

Eduardo moved faster than I could blink. I only saw the silver flash of a blade before he buried it in my father's gut.

My dad wheezed, his breath laced with pain as he clutched his stomach, eyes wide with disbelief.

"No—"

Either from shock or disbelief at what was happening, I moved too slow. And Eduardo, too fast.

Sharp pain sliced through my ribs, blooming out from a central point as the blood spilled over my palm and fingers. Eduardo's eyes, right in front of mine, were empty, soulless, his face devoid of any emotion as he withdrew the knife from where he had stabbed me.

"Help!" Josh yelled. "Protect the governor! Where is security?"

My knees buckled, head already swimming as I saw Josh scramble over the table to shield the governor from getting stabbed. Eduardo jumped on the conference table, boots stomping over our maps as he walked across the surface and slashed down.

The blade caught across Josh's forearm as he held it up to shield his face, his cry full of fear. My vision blurred, something solid hitting me, which I realized was the floor. Blood soaked my hands and clothes, staining the floor and filling my nose with the smell of copper. Dad had fallen too, his blurry form leaning against the wall with his hands pressed over his wound.

No, not like this, I pleaded. *We cannot go out like this.*

I heard the sounds of a struggle, punches and groans and cries of pain. Blurs of movement flew over the long table, Josh and Eduardo locked in a fight, wrestling for their lives.

"Reaper, do something!" Josh sounded like he was underwater. "He dropped the knife but I can't—agh!"

A thump and Josh went silent, his body eerily still as it draped over Eduardo's. I couldn't see the governor, fuck I could barely see shit. My arm felt like a sack of bricks as I fumbled for my holster, finding sweet purchase on the grip of my handgun.

Eduardo was too busy shoving Josh's lifeless form off of him and the table, sending the governor's assistant to crumble onto the floor in an awkward position. The fucking traitor dared to glance at me and smirk before jumping off the table and landing on his feet like a cat.

I didn't move, worried I'd be too slow and he'd stab me again before I could pull the trigger. My dad's panicked breaths against the opposite wall began to slow and I prayed it wasn't too late. I needed this fucker to turn his back on me, to write me off as good as dead.

I took a painful, rattling breath and coughed, letting the blood from my lungs coat my lips and tongue.

Looking pathetic and close to death did the trick. Eduardo snorted derisively, turned around and lowered to his hands and knees. He began crawling his way under the table, where the governor had hid.

"No, no! Please!"

My arm was so fucking heavy and couldn't stop shaking. Each breath felt like another hundred small knives in my lungs. My vision was going dark and I could barely make out the shapes in the room. There was a very real chance I could accidentally hit the governor if my shots went wide. But it was a chance I had to take.

I raised my gun, willing my arm to be steady and the fuzzy shapes in front of me to sharpen into focus. The governor was about to lose his life and I couldn't afford to wait for a miracle. So, pointing under the table, I used the last of my strength to aim and pull the trigger.

A cry of pain rang out. It didn't sound like the governor's so I kept shooting. I emptied my gun, shooting half-blind until my ammo ran out and my arm fell like a concrete block to the floor.

Hades had been silent and uninvolved through the whole exchange. The black dog just stood off to the side, watching, as if waiting for his chance to step in and escort a new batch of souls to the underworld.

He came over to me after I stopped shooting, while I hung between alertness and unconsciousness. While my surroundings had gone blurry from pain and blood loss, his face in front of mine was the only thing in razor-sharp focus.

You will not hesitate on my command again. When I give the order, you will *obey.*

MARIPOSA

"If you don't have a scalpel out in the field, use anything you can find with a sharp edge," I said to the small group of new medics. "A pocket knife will do, even a shard of glass can get the job done. But you *must* have some way to sterilize it, whether that's rubbing alcohol, a lighter, or a flask of whiskey."

A few chuckles arose from my group, but I kept my face solemn. "It might be funny to think about, but you won't have time to think out there. Whatever you have on-hand might be the thing that saves someone's life. Got one of those little teddy bears on a keychain to remind you of your kids, maybe? Guess what, you might end up dousing it in whiskey and shoving it into a bleeding hole in someone's arm because you ran out of gauze."

The doors burst open then, Rhonda coming in fast and leaning heavily on her cane. "We've got four incoming with multiple stab wounds. One deceased with multiple gunshot wounds."

Stabbings and gunshots? What the hell?

A mix of adrenaline and fear coursed through me as I nodded and turned back to the new medics waiting for my instruction. "You heard her, get your asses to the ER."

We all sprung into action, running down the hallway toward the stairwell. Jogging down the steps two at a time, I tried to stamp down my worry. Multiple stab wounds weren't supposed to happen in a place like Four Corners. Who and what could have caused this?

"Two medics per patient," I instructed, opening a faucet just outside the emergency room doors to scrub my hands vigorously.

Everyone around me did the same prep in solemn silence. Washing hands and putting on gloves, donning masks and surgical caps before heading in to save some lives. I followed after my students, eyes scanning the room to assess the damage when a horrifying realization dawned on me.

Governor Vance was conscious, sitting up and looking pale as the medics cut away his blood-soaked shirt. Forgetting myself, I ran to his side in a panic.

"Governor!" I cried, my voice muffled through my mask. "What happened? Who did this?"

"Oh shit, this is the governor?" a student asked, his eyes going wide.

"Keep working on him, you're doing fine," I said before addressing Vance again. "You're going to be okay, sir. Seems you made off with the fewest injuries."

"Josh!" The shocked man looked all around the room as if searching for his assistant.

Another medic gently pressed back on the governor's shoulders. "Sir, I'm going to need you to hold still and remain calm—"

"I think he killed Josh!" Vance cried out in a panicked sob. "He stabbed General Bray and Reaper too, but—"

"Reaper?" I repeated, my own voice rising with panic. "My husband, Reaper?"

"Reaper shot him. I don't know if he made it, I'm sorry. It all happened so fast—"

I pulled away, frantically looking around the room in search of my husband. Josh seemed to be in the worst shape, Dr. Brooks and another doctor were tending to him along with two of my medics.

"Finn!" I ran to my father-in-law's gurney, making sure to stay behind the medics who worked quickly to slow his bleeding.

"Hey, sweetheart." He smiled, despite looking pained and pale. "I meant to come visit you at work, but not like this."

"What happened?"

"Eduardo," he hissed, grinding his teeth. "Fuck, it's my fault. I was too trusting—"

"You couldn't have known," I said. Now I knew where my husband's tendency to shoulder all the blame came from.

"I'm alright, Mari," Finn insisted. "I've had worse. Go find your man."

"Okay," I nodded, stepping away. "I'll be back to check on you." He was stable, his single stab wound was being tended to quickly and blood bags were being set up for his transfusion. That only left...

Reaper was lying on a gurney, his body still and pale as two medics hovered over him, bloodied and shirtless.

"Talk to me," I snapped, shoving my way over to my husband's side.

"He lost a lot of blood quickly. The weapon nicked the SMA and his lung—"

"Why aren't his transfusion lines set up yet?"

"We're finding out his blood ty—"

"He's O-negative. Grab the blood and set up the drip now."

The medics rushed to follow my instructions while I took over pressing down on his wound. They had already packed it to slow his bleeding, but he was covered in blood from the chest down. It was still wet on his hands and dripping onto the floor. Damage to his superior mesenteric artery explained the heavy blood loss. I'd have to assess the damage to his lung once the artery was treated. The blood around his mouth indicated he'd coughed some up.

"We're getting you topped up on blood, love," I whispered, hovering over him. "You better hang in there, or Hades is about to get an earful from me about bringing you back."

My surroundings melted away as I got to work, checking for liquid in his lungs as his blood drip was set up. Once the coagulants did their job and we got his bleeding under control, I sutured his wound closed while keeping an eye on his vitals the whole time. They never dropped to dangerous levels, but that didn't mean I wasn't going to watch them like a hawk.

Dr. Brooks came up behind me at some point with a pat on my

shoulder. It must have been hours later. The room had been cleaned up, patients were resting, and most of the medics had gone home.

"Take a rest, Mariposa," the doctor told me kindly. "You led the new medics well through their first big ER rush."

"I'll stay, if that's okay," I told him. "This is my husband. And the general is my father-in-law."

Dr. Brooks nodded in understanding. "Governor Vance is sending word to Josh and General Bray's family. Is there anyone you'd like to notify?"

"Yes." I smiled tiredly. "A few people."

"I *knew* there was something fucking fishy about that kid."

"Stop pacing like that." I reached for Gunner's hands from where I sat between Shadow and Jandro. "You'll wear a hole in the floor."

Reaper had woken up a few hours later, opting to share an overnight hospital room with his father. Several of us packed in, bringing extra chairs for everyone who rushed over when they received word.

And it pretty much was *everyone.*

Jandro, Gunner and Shadow rushed over the moment they got the news at the B&B, but not before telling Noelle and Larkan. And course, Reaper's mom rushed over as soon as she got word about Finn. While it wasn't exactly how we wanted Reaper's parents to meet the rest of the guys, all of them being here made me feel supported in light of what happened.

The information sat like a brick in my stomach. Someone had tried to kill the leaders of the Four Corners territory.

"I keep turning it over in my head," Finn sighed, his IV-arm wrapped around his wife who'd climbed into the hospital bed with him. "Fuck, how many meetings had he sat in on? How much did he know and supply to whoever he was working for?"

"Was there any sign of him being a spy?" Gunner asked. "Anything at all?"

"Gun, maybe now's not the time," I said. "They need to rest."

"It's okay, Mari." Finn offered me a weak smile before answering the question. "But no, there was none. I checked his paperwork, like I do all my recruits. No signs of him being pro-Blakeworth regime, and no reason for him to be. He freaking escaped by getting pushed out the back door while his home was raided. Either he's hidden his support for a dictator who ordered the execution of his family or," Finn paused to take in a shaky breath, "or he was indoctrinated here in Four Corners."

I didn't realize I was holding my breath until Shadow rubbed my back, encouraging me to release the air.

"How could any pro-Blakeworth people get in here?" Noelle demanded, leaning into Larkan who wrapped around her protectively.

"The checks at the borders are thorough, but they aren't perfect," her father said. "And you have to remember the relationship between Vance and Blake wasn't outright hostile until they took Kyrie. I wouldn't call it friendly, but the two territories were cordial. There may be some pro-Blakeworth stragglers laying low."

"We have to assume there's more in the territory," Jandro said. "Plotting in secret, fucking cloak and dagger bastards. That kid definitely wasn't working alone."

"We have to find out who gave him the order," Reaper agreed, shifting in his hospital bed.

"I'll get with the Sons and start keeping eyes out," Shadow offered with a low growl.

"I'll alert Demon guards too, but listen. Are we certain it's Blakeworth?" Gunner resumed his pacing, despite my telling him not to. "And not Tash? I mean, he stabbed you two first. Tash has wanted Reaper's head on a stick since the Sandia outpost." Reaper's mom shuddered and Gunner immediately froze. "Shit I'm sorry, Mrs. Daley. I'll watch what I say."

"It's no secret that I'm wanted." Reaper shrugged. "But Governor Vance was the most important person in that room. I think he was just trying to get Dad and I out of the way to get to him." He looked to his father for confirmation.

Finn nodded. "If your biker gang is as notorious as you say it is, I think he would have made sure to finish you off if you were the main target."

Poor Alisa was looking more and more distraught the more her husband and son discussed.

"Alright, guys." I clapped my hands and rose to my feet. "We'll see about discharging you in the morning, and you can discuss the next move then. But right now it's time for the patients to rest." I forced a grin. "By orders of the SDMC medic and president's old lady."

"Are you coming home with us?" Shadow asked hopefully. "Or staying?"

I leaned over to push his hair back and kiss the scar on his eyebrow, and then his lips. "I'm staying here to oversee all the patients' care. I'll be home tomorrow though."

"Good." His mouth lingered on mine, hands brushing my waist as he stood up. "You make sure to get some rest too."

I reached on tiptoes, arms stretching up to wind around his shoulders. "I will."

"I'll take you home, Lis." Jandro helped Reaper's mom out of Finn's hospital bed. "And bring you straight back here in the morning, okay?"

"Thank you, son," she said wearily before turning around to kiss her husband goodbye.

"Don't worry about a thing," I assured her. "I'll be here and I'll have these guys checked on round the clock."

She surprised me by pulling me into a hug. "Thank you, Mari. We're so lucky to have you watching them over them. I leave my boys in your capable hands."

I returned her affectionate squeeze before saying my goodbyes to Jandro and Gunner. The room quickly emptied and Finn fell asleep almost immediately. His injuries weren't as bad, but he was older, and would likely need more time to recover than his son.

Reaper, on the other hand, was wide awake and staring at the ceiling. He barely took notice of me crawling into the hospital bed with him, much like his mother did with his father.

"What's on your mind, president?" I whispered with a small kiss to his shoulder.

"Hades told me to kill him," he replied flatly. "He told me to, and I hesitated. Everyone in that room got hurt because I was slow to act."

"Oh Reaper," I sighed. "Please don't turn this into another situation where you're blaming yourself."

"The moment the kid walked into the room, Hades just *knew*," he went on, staring blankly in front of him. "He knew it was going to happen and gave me the order."

"Do you think this is what Daren was talking about?" I asked.

Reaper's eyelids closed, his head shaking slowly from side to side on the hospital pillow. "I don't think so, but...maybe. I don't know anymore. He mentioned a *she* and it was only men in the room. I'm still going nuts trying to wrap my head around it."

"Stop thinking about it." I brushed kisses from his temple to his forehead. "Just for tonight, and rest for me."

"I can't. Not if you're still in danger."

"Yes, love. You're my hero, but..." I kissed his eyelids, encouraging them to stay heavy and closed. "You saved three people's lives today. Take a night off and protect me after you've recovered."

"Damn you, woman..." His growl had little bite as exhaustion and pain medication finally took him under, his breaths growing deep and steady with sleep.

"I love you, too," I chuckled, planting a final kiss on his cheek before sliding out of the bed and smoothing the blanket over his lap.

Freyja reclined at the end of the bed near his feet, her paws tucked into her body, eyes large and seeing all that I could not. I needed to check on Josh and Vance, but paused on my way out of the room.

"Thank you," I said. "For healing them."

She answered me with a deep purr that echoed throughout the room.

JANDRO

"Where are you going?" Reaper grimaced as Mari changed his bandage. She cleared everyone in the stabbing to go home yesterday, but not even Reaper missed an opportunity to be babied by her. She laid him up in bed in our room here at the B&B, and made sure he didn't have to lift a finger for a damn thing.

"Just the country roads right outside of town," I assured him from where I watched in the doorway.

"Someone else should go with you," he said. "Gunner or Shadow, at least."

"Gun's setting up patrols with the Sons around City Hall," I reminded him. "And Shadow has a tattoo appointment."

"Then consider doing this another time," he huffed. "Mari can learn to ride whenever, preferably when we don't have fucking assassins in the city."

"We'll be fine," Mari told him, cleaning up her supplies as she finished dressing his wound. "And still close by if anything does happen."

"Well, how long you gonna be gone for?"

"No more than two hours," I said. "Just a quick spin, then she'll come right back to dote on you, your Majesty."

Reaper frowned, the lines in his face deepening as Mari cupped his cheek and leaned her forehead on his.

"I need a break, love. It's been an intense couple of days and Josh still needs to be monitored. Just two hours on the bike for some fresh air, then I can get back to my patients."

The tension in his face smoothed just slightly. He brought his hands to the sides of her neck, staring at her for a moment before catching her mouth in a warm kiss.

"You know it's not about that. I just want you safe."

"There are few places more safe than with Jandro on an empty stretch of road," she said, pulling away slowly. "You rest up and don't worry, *Rory*."

"Ugh, fine. Get gone if you're gonna call me that." He swatted her side, prompting her to get up and duck under my arm on her way out of the room. When I turned to follow her, Reaper called out, "Hang on a second, 'Dro."

I approached his bedside in a few steps. "Yeah?"

The hard scowl returned, all the relaxed ease from Mari's presence gone. "Don't let her out of your sight for a second. Not even to check fluids on the bike. That's an order, do you understand me?"

"Yeah, man. Of course, but," I stared back at him, puzzled, "you know she's safe with me. Is this about the assassin or something else?"

He leaned his head back on the headboard, pinching his forehead with a groan. "I don't fuckin' know anymore. I'd much rather she stayed here but if you're gonna go, just do it and get it over with."

"Alright, dude." I turned to leave the room, choosing not to indulge in his overprotective crap today. "We'll see you in a couple hours."

Mari was already in my driver's seat, helmet on and her slim fingers wrapped around my grips.

"Go ahead and turn her on," I said, squeezing in behind her. The bike growled to life after only a bit of protest from the initial spark. That was a small concern. I really had to take cold weather maintenance into consideration up here. "Let her idle a bit and warm up."

After a few moments, I coached Mari through easing back and out onto the road. The traffic was light this morning, despite Reaper's concerns. Vehicles were still few and far between for most citizens, so most of them carpooled or walked the short distance to where they needed to be. Four Corners was still small enough to get to most places on foot, although that wasn't likely to be true within the next few years.

I directed Mari outside of the town limits to the mostly-abandoned country road which had been a highway at some point. She would have been fine in town and probably would learn more navigating city streets, but I did promise Reaper.

"It's all you, *Mariposita.*" I patted her waist. "Take us away."

She relaxed into the seat, cautiously accelerating on the long, empty stretch of road before us.

"Go faster!" I yelled over the engine with a swat to her hip. "I wanna see you make a dust cloud."

"Fuck off," she shot back, but she was laughing. I missed the pretty sound and realized I hadn't heard it in a few days.

I swatted her again, adding, "hyah!" like she was a horse and she shrieked with laughter.

"Stop, you'll make me wobble the bike!" she cried.

"Nah, girl. You're rock steady." But I calmed and settled down behind her. "Here comes a bend in the road. Remember to lean into it."

She took the turns beautifully, each one smoother than the last as she became more confident in her balance and handling of the bike. We took a few laps of the roads looping around Four Corners main city. While she drove, I took a few moments to enjoy the scenery, something I rarely got to do while in the driver's seat.

Gigantic, snow-capped mountains lined the horizon to the north, red rocks and cliffs to the south. *I could get used to views like this,* I realized. I had my doubts about settling in Four Corners when we first ended up here, but even my nomadic heart was getting attached to the little place.

I dropped my chin to Mari's shoulder after our fifth loop, placing a small kiss on her neck. "We gotta head back, babe. Take us home?"

I felt the sigh leave her body, her fingers wrapping around mine at her waist before she turned at the next intersection heading toward town.

"How'd I do?" she asked, her speed decelerating as we approached the city limits.

I chuckled, bringing both arms around her waist and leaving a bigger kiss on her nape. "You were born to ride, *Mariposita*."

"Really?"

"Are you really surprised?" I asked. "You belong to three, almost four men who've made their lives on these roads. I had no doubt you'd take to the bike quickly."

"Oh hey, look." She pointed up ahead where a rusted car was parked on the side of the road, someone bent over in front of the vehicle and looking under the raised hood.

"Probably out of gas or something," I remarked. "Go ahead, let's help out." If I was going to stay here, I might as well be neighborly. Hell, even Shadow was starting to rack up a list of tattoo clients by word-of-mouth, and I didn't have my own mechanic's shop yet.

Mari pulled up next to the car, an unremarkable old sedan that had seen better days. The driver peered at us from underneath the hood, a middle-aged guy in a dark blue shirt. I spotted a bright vest and a hard hat in his passenger seat, indicating the guy was probably off to a construction job.

"Need some help?" I swung a leg off the bike and started toward him.

"If it ain't no trouble." He looked back down at the car in front of him. "It just stopped runnin'."

"Any weird sounds when it stopped?" I asked. "Rattling or clicking?"

"Nah, I don't think so."

"See any smoke coming out from under the hood?"

"Nah."

"Where were you at on gas?"

"Just filled up the tank this mornin'."

I rubbed a palm over my head, shooting an annoyed look at Mari still sitting astride my idling bike. The worst part about diagnosing car issues was having to pull the answers out of the owner like teeth.

"Alright, when's the time you topped off the oil?" I crossed my arms, trying to keep my tone patient.

"Uh..." The guy's hand shook slightly as he wiped at something on his pants. "Not sure."

"Okay, man," I sighed, not wanting to be dealing with this. "I can give you a lift into town, just gotta get my wife home first—"

"Run," he whispered.

"What?" I watched him closely, the tremors now taking over his hands. His pupils became pinpricks, filled with fear.

"I'm sorry. I didn't want to but...just *run*!" He screamed the last word at the top of his lungs, scrambling to the side of his car and ducking down as if to hide.

"What the..."

I whipped around, hearing the low rumble of another engine just as Mari cried, "Jandro, someone's coming fast!"

"Go, go!" I jumped onto the bike behind her, drawing my handgun from my holster. "Head away from town, top speed!"

She accelerated hard, jerking the bike into motion as two figures cut a corner, driving off-road on sport bikes heading straight for us. I cursed under my breath, raised my firing arm and took aim. They'd catch up to us in no time on those fucking crotch rockets.

"Fast as you can go, babe. Don't slow down even a tiny bit," I told Mari.

"I don't want to crash!"

"Better we crash than get taken by them."

The two riders, all decked out in black, had reached our stretch of road and were coming up on us fast. I fired off a shot at the one in front, but it went low, hitting the frame of the bike with a metallic *plink*. Mari was weaving the bike slightly, her balance off-kilter at such high speed.

"I need you to keep her steady for me," I said. "I got them, you can do it."

"Who are they?" she demanded, panic choking her voice.

"Tash's people," I said through gritted teeth. "We're no one important, so they have to be."

Deja vu set in as I turned in my seat, shielding Mari with my body as I took aim at the enemies right on our tail. This was too reminiscent of our ambush from Razor Wire. My dumbass didn't think to bring extra ammo, so I had to be careful with my shots.

The riders couldn't zig-zag much, but they hunched low over their crotch rockets. Black gear on back bikes made it hard to get a clear shot.

The rider in the rear straightened up and began firing rapid semi-automatic rounds.

"Fuck!" I pushed Mari's head down low over the dash, bowing my body over hers. "Don't slow down! No matter what, do not slow or stop!"

"Well don't get fucking hit!"

I decided not to tell her about the burning graze on my calf, my pant leg already wet and dark with blood. It felt like little more than a bad scrape, but I knew that was the adrenaline talking. Mari didn't need to worry about me right then. More than anything, I needed her to just drive.

When the onslaught of bullets finally ceased I returned fire, but the shooter had ducked down, shielded by the rider in front.

Fuck, fuck, fuck. My aim was shit and my shots limited. I was running out of options, especially with two of them to deal with. I'd have to do my damn hardest to make this a two birds with one stone situation.

"Slow down just a touch," I told Mari.

"You said not to!"

"New plan, babe. Just trust me and ease up a little bit. Then when I tell you to," I leaned close to her ear, making sure only she could hear me, "hit it hard, back to full speed. Got it?"

She nodded and slowed as I asked, allowing the crotch rockets to gain significant ground on us. I could practically see the smugness in the riders, thinking we were surrendering. To add to that illusion, I waved both arms above my head.

"Drop the gun, Steel Demon," the first one ordered through his helmet, almost close enough to touch if I reached.

"Okay guys, I will." I lowered my hands slowly, finger well away from the trigger. "Just promise you won't hurt my wife, okay?"

The first one signaled to the rider behind him, who held up his semi-auto again and I sucked in a breath. My leg wound stung, the blood now making a dark trail on the road. *Hades, Freyja, Horus, whoever the fuck is listening, please don't let us go like this.*

"Please," I tried again. "We'll pull right over and I'll go with you, but do not touch her."

The rear rider tapped off a few rounds and more burning pain shot up my leg. I groaned and doubled over, grasping on to the seat to stay on.

"Jandro!" Mari cried.

"We don't need either of you alive, so fuck your demands!"

"Now, Mari!" I yelled.

She accelerated hard and my heart stopped for a moment, thinking I would tumble off. But I held on, squeezing both sides of the bike with my knees as I raised my gun, waiting for the crotch rockets to speed up after us. The shooter copied my movement, raising his weapon and firing off more rounds. An explosion of heat and pain hit my left shoulder before I fired, aiming low at the front rider's tire.

With a loud pop, the rubber shredded and burned. Just as I intended, the bike wobbled and slowed too fast for the rear rider to react. The shooter crashed into his partner with a crunch of metal, my body growing cold and heavy as bikes and bodies skimmed across the road.

"Double back, Mari," I panted, blood now coating the entire left side of my body. "Turn around."

"No! I have to get you to the hospital."

"Turn the fuck around!" I repeated. "We have to make sure they're dead."

I could feel her worry, her intense need to take care of me, but we had to have that sweet nurse and patient moment later. Thankfully, she did as I said and made a wide U-turn. Sure enough, one of our pursuers was stumbling out of the wreckage, dragging a lame foot behind him as he stepped over folded metal and the remains of his friend. His face was still hidden behind the black helmet visor as he raised his weapon.

"Bend down, stay low." I pressed on Mari's back until her chest met the dash, and not a moment too soon. The rider unleashed rapid gunfire on us.

I bowed over Mari to cover her, but her panic and lack of visibility took over. She made us sway to the side, wanting to get away from riding straight into gunfire.

"Babe, brake! BRAKE!" I yelled.

She braked too hard and we were suspended in midair for a split second before hitting the ground hard. I wrapped around her midsection despite the shooting pain up my shoulder, and rolled us away to minimize injury. My eyes shut tight and I thought my teeth were going to crack from how hard I was biting down. Every bump against the ground felt like my leg and shoulder were getting hacked off by a butcher knife.

We finally came to a stop. Her helmet had fallen off and I'd dropped my gun when I grabbed her. The world spun and I was so fucking tired. I'd probably lost a lot of blood. The one thing in sharp clarity was the black figure walking toward us.

"Run." I slid off of Mari and shoved at her side with my good arm. "Get Gunner and Shadow."

"I'm not leaving you!" Her shaking hand fumbled across my chest, reaching for my shoulder to put pressure on the wound.

"*Esposa,*" I groaned, pulling her hand away and bringing her blood-soaked fingers to my lips. "They can either kill us both, or just me. You have to tell the others—"

"Then let it be both of us! Because I am not leaving you here."

"Mari, I'm sorry I don't have time to be romantic, but this is bigger than us. You have to run!" I tried to shove her more forcefully but the weakness was settling into me everywhere now. She barely moved.

Instead she crawled over me, laying on my back to cover me as the black-clad rider approached.

"Mari, don't," I pleaded. My strength was leaving me with every breath, but I could not allow her to die with me out here. Not when she had three other men to love, and a whole town that needed her.

"Do you have another weapon?" she whispered. "Anything at all?"

"Knife. Inside left pocket. But babe—"

She started fumbling over the front of my shoulder, reaching into my cut to feel for the knife just as our attacker tossed his magazine and loaded a fresh one into his gun. If he wasn't so close, I would've made some crack about bringing knives to gun fights.

"Stand up," he ordered Mari, pointing his barrel straight at her.

"Listen, I'm a medic," she said, her voice taking on that calming but authoritative tone as her fingers brushed the handle of my knife. "I can help your friend if he's still alive—"

"He's not. And you're nothing but rotten Steel Demon cunt as far as I care. Stand the fuck up."

"I can help that foot of yours too." She nodded toward his bad ankle, her fingers wrapping around the blade handle. "But if I get up, he's going to bleed out."

"Do I look like I care, bitch?"

Mari began sliding the knife out of my pocket, but my eyes were on that gun pointed straight at my woman. His gloved finger rested on the trigger and that fucking barrel was less than a foot away from her head. Bleeding out or not, I'd spend my last few breaths taking that fucker down if he shot her.

"I'm not gonna ask you again." His trigger finger squeezed just a hair, enough to make my heart stop. "Stand the fuck up."

Mari pressed her knees to either side of my body, her left hand flattening on the ground to push herself up. I felt the knife withdraw from my chest pocket and held my breath. I had no idea what her plan was, but he wouldn't hesitate the moment he saw her holding a weapon. Each second felt like an hour as she slowly rose to standing, my body braced for the sound of the shot. When none came, I turned my head against the ground, squinting up to look.

Mari stood over me with her hands up and no knife in sight. I blinked in confusion, then the fear overtook me as our attacker leaned in and pressed his gun barrel directly against her sternum.

"General Tash wishes the Steel Demons a long and prosperous life," the rider sneered under his helmet.

"No." I thrashed on the ground, reaching for a leg, a kneecap, anything. "No, not her!"

I got a swift kick to my stomach for my effort, the air leaving my body in a violent rush, but it was the gunshot ringing in my ears that felt like the killing blow.

"No..."

I could barely whisper, let alone scream. All I knew was Mari no longer stood above me. *No, no, no. Why, Mari? You should have fucking run.*

It felt like forever before I could get my good arm under me so I could lift my head and look around. The world seemed to go silent, my senses dulling as I scanned the ground for my wife, or what was left of her.

I tracked the movement at the corner of my eye, turning my body painstakingly, slowly. Two black figures seemed to be wrestling on the ground, fighting desperately for the upper hand.

"Mari..."

My vision was going so blurry, I couldn't tell which one was her. I heard her grunts of effort and cries of pain, and ragged breaths and curses that sounded like a man's. I tried to drag myself closer to help, but my own bodyweight was too heavy. I tasted salt and dirt and blood. I couldn't reach my wife. I couldn't save her.

Another shot rang out and the figures went still.

GUNNER

"These dumb fucks," I sighed, dabbing an alcohol wipe at the cut on Mari's cheek. "Getting themselves shot and stabbed days apart. It's shameful, really."

"It's increasing my workload, that's for sure," she sighed. "Okay, that should be good. Now let it dry, then put the ointment on."

She sat on the counter in Jandro's hospital room, legs swinging back and forth like a child awaiting a check up. Her injuries had been minor compared to the VP, who was laid out in the hospital bed, his left shoulder and chest wrapped in gauze, his arm in a sling, and his lower left leg equally wrapped up tight and elevated on a pillow. Freyja sat in a dark loaf at the foot of his bed, green eyes observing the room.

Club members on the fringes of town had heard the gunshots and went to investigate. Members of General Bray's border patrol went to check it out as well. They found the motorcycle crash with two confirmed dead, Jandro nearly dead, and Mari working to slow the bleeding on his leg and shoulder until he could get rushed to the hospital.

Jandro went into emergency surgery immediately, with Dr. Brooks and his team firmly shoving Mari out of the operating room so she could rest and recover from shock. Unsurprisingly, she refused to have any of her own injuries looked at until Jandro was released from surgery a few hours later. Shadow, Reaper, and I rushed over as soon as we heard the news, taking Mari off the hands of the frustrated medics who had been trying to look after her.

"Don't leave us in suspense now, baby girl." I dabbed ointment carefully over the scrape on her face. "How'd you win with a knife at a gun fight?"

"I'm still not sure," she laughed tiredly. "I pulled it out of Jandro's cut when I was on top of him, and tucked it into my waistband like you showed me."

"That's my girl!" I grinned and kissed her temple.

"I stood up with my hands raised and he put the gun right up against me." She touched a finger to her sternum. "I was so fucking scared, I didn't think I'd get to the knife at all."

Across the room, Reaper groaned and scrubbed his hands down his face. He'd bitten his tongue so far, but I knew he was full of pent-up *I-told-you-so*'s. After this, I had no doubt he'd only be extra protective of Mari.

"Then he said, 'General Tash wishes you a long and prosperous life'."

"That fucker," I cursed under my breath. It was what the general said after every meeting back when we traded goods.

"And then Jandro moved." She looked over to the man in the hospital bed, chewing her lip. "Like he was trying to grab his leg or something, and the guy kicked him. I took that as my chance to pull the knife."

"Good girl," I praised, my grin returning. "Where'd you get him?"

"Well I shoved his arm first to get the gun away from me, so I just nicked him here." She dragged a touch along the side of my ribs. "It caught him off-guard and I didn't want him to regain balance, so I jumped on him and we went falling."

"How'd you get the gun away from him?" Shadow asked. He sat next to Reaper against the far wall, but was entranced by her story as I was.

"I honestly don't know." She shook her head. "It's such a blur. I just remember being so desperate to keep the gun away. He had a smashed ankle too, but was still a lot stronger. If I kept wrestling him on the ground, I know he would've been able to overpower me. At some point I just had my finger on the trigger and pulled it. For all I knew, I could've been pointing it at myself."

"You did good, baby girl." I pulled her into me, rubbing her shoulder as I kissed her forehead. "You saved your man, and probably all of Four Corners, again."

"Jandro took care of the first one," she sighed, leaning into me. "If it was just me, I would've kept riding."

Shadow stood and crossed the room in two long strides as Mari pulled away from me. I stepped back to give them space, the two of them in their own world for a moment as Shadow nudged his hips between Mari's legs and placed his hands on her waist.

"I'm proud of you," he said, forehead leaning down to hers.

She tilted her face up to return the contact, a small smile lighting up her face as her petite hands glided over his ribs. "Thanks, love."

I did that thing Reaper always told me to do—check myself for jealousy and try to figure out why. With a woman like Mari, it was most likely my own head trying to find something wrong, rather than anything she was doing.

But I was pleasantly surprised to find none, watching them embrace and kiss quietly. Shadow had been just as worried about her and Jandro, if not more. If the situation had turned out any worse, he could have lost his two favorite people in one swoop. The relief was clear in how his shoulders sagged when Jandro was wheeled out of surgery, and now, leaning over Mari like he wanted to shield her from the world. A world that seemed determined to take us out, no matter where we ended up.

"Gun, what'd you find out about the fucker with the car?" Reaper stood, stretching his arms over his head with a grimace. His stab wound was healing just as quickly as we expected, the fresh scar tissue still itching. Mari had already okayed removing his bandage while we were waiting on Jandro.

"Just some poor Four Corners worker that was bribed," I said. "He swears up and down that he never wanted to be bait in the first place, but they wouldn't take no for an answer."

"They all say that," Reaper growled.

"It's true," Mari piped up. She hopped down from the counter, her arm still around Shadow's waist as she leaned into his side. "He was visibly nervous from the start, and told Jandro to run." She released Shadow to stand next to Jandro's bed, and reached for the VP's hand. "If he hadn't given us a head start, we might not have survived."

"If he hadn't been there at all, you wouldn't have been hunted by those fucks," Reaper spat.

Mari turned her head sharply to look at him. "If they hadn't gotten him, they would've preyed on somebody else. I believe he was a victim in this too, Reaper."

"I'll take that into consideration," Reaper said carefully back to her, his rage clearly on a short leash. I didn't blame him, even if what Mari said made sense. My instinct was always to spill the blood of anyone who hurt my woman, and my brothers.

"You gotta stop doing this, man." I turned to Jandro, trying to lighten the mood. "You, burned up and shot. Reaper almost blown up and stabbed. Shadow harpooned and poisoned. I'm due for something bad."

"Yeah," Jandro mumbled drowsily, proving he wasn't knocked out after all. "'Bout time your pretty face got fucked up."

"Hey, I was *almost* sold into sexual slavery. That shit is traumatizing."

"Right. If you take out the *almost*, I'd believe you."

Rapidly approaching footsteps in the hallway ended our ribbing, with General Bray poking his head through the doorway. "Hey guys. Is this a good time?"

"'Course, Dad."

Reaper turned to give his father a brief hug, but it was Mari, approaching with her arms open, that made the older man's eyes light up.

"Oh, sweetheart." Bray sighed heavily with relief as he hugged her against his chest. "My heart stopped when I heard. I'm so glad you're okay."

"Thanks, Finn," Mari mumbled against his shirt. "Me too."

He released her, sauntering over to Jandro's bedside. "And I'm glad this guy's alright too, I guess."

"Ain't getting rid of me yet," Jandro said.

"You're hard to kill, man," Bray teased, leaning over and squeezing his good shoulder. "But thank fuck you were there." He turned to smile goodnaturedly at me and Shadow. "And it's a damn good thing you guys taught her how to defend herself. It's important, even though there's four of you."

"We should keep her trained." I nudged Shadow with my elbow. "She can learn some assassin tricks from you too."

The big guy nodded in agreement while Jandro groaned from the bed. "Don't give her too many ideas. She'll kill us in our sleep when we're being dickwads."

"By the time I'm done with her," Shadow crossed his arms, a smile quirking on his lips. "She'll kill us on a busy street in broad daylight."

"I already know how to kill you in your sleep," Mari snickered. "And how to make it look like an accident."

"While I'm glad to see you're all in high spirits in spite of what happened—" Finn began.

"Not all of us." Reaper mumbled. That was par for the course for him. He wasn't satisfied with the two riders' deaths. His old wounds with Tash—the first attempt on our lives, Dallas's death, and being driven out of our home—it all had to have been sitting on his shoulders like a massive boulder right then.

Finn walked over and placed a hand on his son's shoulder, sympathy etched in his face. "I didn't just come by to say hello. The attack has floated all the way up to the governor and he wants to meet as soon as possible. Right now, if you can. He's ready for action."

Reaper nodded. "Finally. Mari." He beckoned our wife forward. "You're coming, too."

Her eyes shifted from him to his father. "Are you sure that'll be okay? I should probably stay with Jandro."

"I'm not letting you out of my sight again," the president growled. "Fuck it if the governor doesn't like it."

"I don't see it being a problem," I mused, looking at Finn who answered with a shrug. "Vance gets that we don't leave you out of our business. I don't think he'll say no."

Shadow approached Mari, drifting a hand along her lower back. "I'll stay with him. You go to the meeting."

She looked straight up to meet his eyes. "Are you sure?"

"Yes." He returned her gaze, warmth and adoration in his eyes. "They can brief me later."

They parted with a kiss and a slow untangling of limbs, eyes only for each other until the last moment, when she came to walk between me and Reaper.

"You guys are fucking cute," I teased her as we followed Finn down the hallway to the elevator.

"Yeah, well, so are we." Her fingers slid through mine and then Reaper's on the other side of her as we stepped inside.

Reaper pressed the button for the lobby while I brought the back of Mari's palm to my lips and kissed her there with a grin. "But does he measure up in the bedroom?"

The cut on Mari's cheek deepened to a dark red as her skin flushed. "We haven't made it to that point yet."

"What?!" I looked over her head at Reaper, bewildered.

He shrugged, bringing both of his hands up. "Don't look at me. They wanted to take it slow."

"But...*why?*"

"Because we just *do*, Gunner. It feels right for us."

"You sure about that?" I teased a hand along the back of her neck. "You seem a little frustrated, baby girl."

She just glared at me as the elevator dinged and the door slid open. Finn, who had stayed politely silent during our whole exchange, stepped out first, holding the door open with his arm for us.

"What do you make of this, General?" I asked him. "Did your wife take it slow with one of her men?"

"She did with Nolan," he confirmed with a small smile. "The ah, physical chemistry she had with me and Carter was instant, explosive—"

"Fuck, really?" Reaper released Mari's hand to slap his palms over his ears.

"Lis and Nolan were a slower burn, physically speaking," Finn continued. "Their connection was more emotional, almost platonic at first, like they were best friends. They'd spend hours just staying up late and talking. It might've been weeks before they even kissed."

"That's really sweet," Mari said. "I'm sorry you all lost him."

"Thank you." Finn smiled at his daughter-in-law. "It's been over fifteen years now, so it's not as sharp. But it still hits Lis and I sometimes."

We all piled into the black SUV waiting for us outside. A thread of annoyance started to make a knot in my chest as Finn's lieutenant drove us. Jandro had just come out of surgery. Mari was in danger of dozing off, leaning heavily on my shoulder. The governor had barely given them any time to rest and let the shock wear off before calling this meeting. Tash's forces needed to be dealt with immediately, yes. But the timing of this didn't seem appropriate.

I shoved my discomfort down, wrapping an arm around Mari's shoulder and pulling her closer to me. We'd all make sure she rested well tonight. It was the least our wife deserved.

"Where are we going?" Suspicion laced Reaper's voice.

"To meet the governor, like I said," Finn answered coolly.

"Where?" Reaper demanded again. "We've just passed City Hall *and* his house."

"You'll see, son."

"Dad." Reaper's teeth ground in his jaw. "I'm not the mood for fucking surprises. Can you just tell us what's going on?"

"You'll like this surprise," Finn answered. "Just relax."

Reaper grumbled in his seat, only quieting when Mari lifted her head from my shoulder and turned to snuggle against him.

We drove over the small bridge crossing the lake to the new development on the other side. No streetlights had been erected yet, let alone paved sidewalks, so the SUV's tires rolled over bumpy gravel with just the headlights to guide our way.

The car came to a stop just as our headlights picked up a figure standing in the middle of the road, who I quickly figured out was Governor Vance. It was pitch black outside, the temperature dropping fast, and he was waiting for us in a construction zone away from the main part of town? My suspicion started to match Reaper's, hand brushing the gun at my hip as we started climbing out of the back seat. Everything about this was fucking fishy.

"Mariposa!" Vance beamed at the sight of her, his smile rivaling the brightness of our headlights. "I'm so glad you came out for this, dear."

Reaper's arm shot out to the side, blocking her from getting any closer. "What is *this*, Vance? A meeting out in the freezing fucking darkness?"

"Ah, yes." The governor's eyes shifted to General Bray still behind us. "That may have been a small fib. I wanted you and at least one or two of your men out here for this."

"*This* being what, exactly?" I stepped up to Mari's other side, another shield for her in the event of any danger.

"Josh!" Vance called out to the darkness behind him. "Go ahead."

I heard a series of clicking sounds, like breaker switches being flipped. And then, blinding brightness.

"Ah, fuck!" I brought a hand up to shield my eyes, squinting at the brightly lit house in the distance.

"It's yours," the governor declared. "And this time, I'm not taking no for an answer."

When my eyes adjusted I lowered my hand, blinking as I took in all the details. The house the governor showed us the night of the dinner party had transformed, or expanded at least.

The first story had been widened out from the center—a sunroom lined with windows facing south, and what looked like an additional garage or workshop with a roll-up door on the opposite side. Through all the windows, cozy warm light glowed, lighting up the sparse furniture and fixtures already inside.

"We added two more bedrooms downstairs for three total on the bottom floor," Finn said in our stunned silence, walking up from behind us. "And with the three up top, it should be plenty of room for all of you to have your own space."

"Wha...what?"

"You've been in Four Corners over two weeks already," Vance laughed at Reaper's stunned look. "And have saved us all more times than we can ever repay you for. Take the house. I insist." The governor reached deep inside his coat and produced a set of keys.

"You can't tell us you're good and settled crammed into *one* room at the B&B," Finn laughed, bringing a hand down on Reaper's shoulder. "Take the house, son. Make a life here." His grip squeezed, not letting go as his voice grew heavy with emotion. "Let an old man watch his only son grow old and have his own kids, huh?"

Mari approached the two of them, hugging around Reaper's waist as she stared at Finn with an awed smile. "I bet you orchestrated this ruse, huh?"

"We started building the extension and were gonna surprise you anyway," her father-in-law grinned. "But it was the governor's idea to present it to you now, after what happened."

"I understood your hesitation when you told me the first time," Vance nodded at Reaper. "But after that day in the conference room, and now with what happened to your sweet wife and VP," he shook his head. "Four Corners *needs* the Steel Demons. The house is yours. My trust is yours. And still, it feels like too little for what you've given us."

Reaper looked down at Mari, his arm around her shoulders. "What do you think, sugar?"

"It's a beautiful house." She leaned her cheek on his chest. "Let's take it."

"Gun?" Reaper lifted his gaze to me.

I shrugged, but couldn't stop the grin from spreading across my face. Hell fucking yeah, I was ready to leave the B&B and actually *live* somewhere.

"Whatever the wifey wants."

Mari's excited giggle was drowned out by Finn's laughter as he grabbed my arm and pulled me into a bone-crushing hug.

"Congratulations, son," he said on my shoulder. "Happy to have you in the family."

"Thank you." I returned his hug, leaning into probably the only display of fatherly affection I'd ever received. "Thank you, sir."

"None of that *sir* business," he chided, pulling away. "Well, maybe only when we're at work," he added with a wink.

"We'll throw a housewarming party soon," Reaper said, releasing Mari so she could hug me. "Invite the whole club. Hell, we'll have Larkan's patching in ceremony at the same time."

"Oh, finally!" she declared, her cheek nuzzled against my chest.

"We gotta tell Jandro when he's not all doped up," I said, rubbing warmth into her back.

"And Shadow." Mari's eyes widened like she had mistakenly said that out loud, but didn't take it back as Reaper and I sandwiched her between us.

"Something you want to tell us, sugar?" His tone had finally lightened, arms wrapped around her shoulders from behind as he kissed the top of her head.

Mari held on to his forearm across her chest. "I want Shadow to move in with us," she said, her voice firm.

Reaper and I exchanged a fast look. "Okay," he said. "Does that mean...?"

"He's mine," she answered, gripping his forearm tighter. "I'm keeping him. I...*love* him."

"Alright then." Reaper squeezed her against his chest, planting another kiss in her hair. "He's moving in and picking a room."

"Baby girl." I teased her nickname with a hint of warning, hooking my fingers in the belt loops of her jeans. "You know what I'm gonna say."

Her eyes narrowed at me in warning. "What, Gunner?"

I leaned in close and whispered, "What if his dick is small?"

"You *asshole*!" she shrieked, swatting me. "Don't be like that!"

"Sorry, I had to!" I laughed, blocking her blows with my arms.

"And anyway," she grinned smugly. "I already know what his dick looks like."

"Oh, right," I said sheepishly. "I forgot that...that happened."

"Let's get the fuck out of this cold," Reaper huffed, dragging Mari back to the car. "And celebrate our last night sleeping in the B&B."

"Works for me." I followed them after stealing one more glance back at the house.

Our house.

SHADOW

For the first time ever, my workout felt lonely without an audience.

I set the barbell down after my last deadlift, slightly mystified that I didn't have a cat wrapping around my ankles to watch out for, or the sneaky glances of a woman from the window.

My woman. The thought bubbled up inside me before quickly bursting. *Don't get ahead of yourself. She could still decide that she doesn't want you.*

The night after their meeting with the governor, Mari came back to the hospital in the morning to check on Jandro. She told me to head back to the B&B to rest, and that she'd brief me on what they talked about later. I came back and got a few hours of sleep in my room, then woke up to the whole place being empty. I had no tattoo appointments or anything pressing, so I started my day with a workout like usual.

I could name this feeling now, this tugging in my chest when Mari wasn't around and I couldn't get her out of my head. It meant I missed her.

Getting closer to her only made the sensation stronger.

People being around me used to be an intrusion, their noise poking holes in the shield I wrapped around myself. I couldn't pinpoint when the shift started, it must have happened so gradually, but I started finding myself more comfortable in the company of others. People that weren't her, nor those closest to me in the Steel Demons. I could walk into a room full of strangers and feel...okay. Not *good* by any stretch of the imagination, but like I could survive it.

I headed inside, using my discarded shirt to wipe my sweat before tossing it in the laundry pile in my room. My pill bottle caught my eye on the nightstand. I'd have to get a refill of sleeping pills soon. Those little tablets were one of the biggest reasons I attributed to feeling more like a normal person.

The monster within me, created by years of torture and isolation, had been quiet lately. It might never go away completely, but it had been lying dormant over the past several weeks. I slept through the night without issue, the nightmares starting to feel like a distant memory. I craved Mari's touch and sought it out, rather than retreat into myself. The absence of that dark, oppressive force made everyday life so much less exhausting.

I was no longer terrified of riding out to the hospital to get a refill of the pills, of potentially talking to someone besides Mari, another woman even. If she was there, I might even linger. Talk to her for a few moments, maybe even get a kiss before I left.

A huff of laughter escaped me as I undressed for my shower. I was fucking fantasizing about doing something that used to set me so far back with fear. I had made my own prison, I realized, by feeding into the narrative I'd been told all my life—that I was an evil force upon the earth because I was a man. I deserved to be caged up and cut with blades because men were the reason civilization went into Collapse. Men were the reason so many girls and women were snatched from their homes and rounded up like cattle. I was dangerous and deserved a life of torture simply because I was born.

Even after being taken away and finding my life in the SDMC, I still believed it. No one told me those things anymore, they didn't need to. I told them to myself, because it never occurred to me I could be anything different.

That I might matter to someone.

I turned on my shower and stared in the bathroom mirror while I waited for the water to heat up. The steam on the glass smoothed out the complexion of my skin, softening the textures of scar tissue. If only I could swap places with my reflection.

My fingers drifted up, rubbing over the fading bruises on my chest where Mari had bit and sucked on me there. A hickey, she called it.

I recalled how it felt, the small bloom of pain under the heat and wetness of her mouth that I'd become addicted to tasting. Pain—a sensation I'd forgotten about and hadn't felt in years. The way her teeth pulled at my skin and sent the feeling like small shock waves all over my body. I recognized the sensation but never felt it like that, never thought it could be something I'd crave.

Staring at them in the mirror, I contemplated tattooing over those bruises. Just tracing over the small blotches of purple and red, so her mark on me would never fade.

She'd be willing to leave more on you, if you just asked.

My heart sped up at the thought. Turning away from the mirror to step into the shower, I thought of my conversation with Jandro at the bar the other night. As close as he and I were, I'd never really talked to him like that before. Most of our heart-to-hearts consisted of him talking *at* me, with me doing my best to ignore him.

But this time I listened.

Mari loved him. She kept him and made him hers. I desperately wanted that for myself, and needed all the help I could get with the odds stacked against me.

As well as things were going with Mari, I still felt like I was fumbling around in the dark. The lingering fear of scaring her, or possibly hurting her, halted me from taking anything further physically. Plus the uncertainty from having never done that with someone I actually cared about. I knew how to proceed to the act of having sex, but would never forgive myself if I saw that same fear in her eyes that I'd seen so many times before.

I had to talk to her. Ask her what she wanted. Let her lead me through it like she did with kissing. I just had to remind myself that she didn't hold my inexperience against me. She didn't think I was stupid or ugly. And she would want me to enjoy it too.

Easier said than done.

I finished my shower and had just put pants on when the knock came to my door, heavy and urgent.

"Yeah?" I called, rummaging around for a clean shirt.

"Reaper's calling church," Gunner's voice answered through the wood. "The whole club at City Hall."

I paused in my search and pulled the door open. "When?"

"Right now, as soon as we can get everyone together. Reap's on his way to pick up Mari and Jandro from the hospital now." Gunner's eyes lowered from my face, hovering at my collarbones. "Nice hickeys, dude."

"Shit." I slapped a hand over the marks on my chest, much to his amusement. "Is this about the assassins?"

"Yeah." His expression turned solemn. "Reap's not fuckin' around anymore. We're hitting them back, ASAP."

"Okay. Anything from the meeting last night I should know?"

Gunner only smiled as he turned away. "I'm sure you'll find out everything you need to know today."

The conference room was already crowded by the time Gunner and I arrived. Normally, the press of so many bodies in a confined space would drive me to a panic attack. But as I squeezed my way in, I felt okay with only a few deep breaths. Not great by any means, but good enough to not look for an immediate escape route.

It wasn't just Steel Demons in the room—their women too. Tessa, Andrea, and Noelle stood huddled together, with Big G looking sour across the room from his ex-wife. General Bray's soldiers also lined the walls, standing at attention. The governor and Josh, bandages on the assistant's face and hands, talked with General Bray near a window.

I even spotted the Sons of Odin, the black raven and horned viking helmet on their cuts, to the right side of the room as they mingled.

"Shadow," T-Bone greeted with a lazy smile.

"Who invited you fuckers?" I returned.

They laughed as we all clasped fists and slapped each others' backs. Maybe I was starting to get the hang of this sense of humor thing.

"We're honorary Demons as far as I see it," Dyno grinned. "Saved your sorry asses enough times."

"Since you're Grudge's brother, you're a Son too," T-Bone said.

"Mari hasn't tested us to see if we're blood-related yet," I remarked. "Not that it matters."

"Mm-mm!" Grudge shook his head emphatically.

"Glad you agree, brother." I knocked my fist against his and went to stand next to him against the wall.

"Speaking of, where is your little lady?" T-Bone stroked his beard as he scanned the room.

I nearly corrected his assumption that she was mine, but decided against it. "Coming with Jandro soon."

Reaper's voice cut through the murmurings of conversations from the room only moments later. "Make a path, move! Give the VP some fucking room."

People jumped quickly out of the way, all talking fading to silence as they made their way inside. Over everyone's heads, I could see Mari holding on to Jandro's good arm, the other one still in a sling. Somehow, he still managed to get both arms through the holes of his cut.

His steps were slow and slightly unbalanced due to the walking boot encasing nearly the entire bottom half of his leg. Reaper walked on his other side, his eyes scanning the faces in the room as if daring anyone to say something out of line. But everyone only looked on with respect as the three of them made their way to the conference table.

Because of all the extra people here, this wasn't a church meeting in the traditional sense. But a gavel and a block still waited for Reaper at the end of the table, where he took his seat with Hades at his side. Mari helped Jandro settle into the seat next to him, then stepped back to stand with the others lining the wall.

Jandro nodded at me, indicating I should take the seat next to him. Mari smiled at me as I approached the chair, and Gunner took his place on the other side of Reaper. Our president hit the gavel once, the clack of wood echoing throughout the otherwise silent room.

"Thank you all for coming on such short notice," he began, his voice softer than any church meeting I'd attended before. "I invited you all here because this matter affects all of us." He paused for a deep breath. "Four Corners is in danger. And the people who want to topple this place are trying to do it from the inside."

Stony faces looked back at all of us sitting. Either everyone already knew, or at least suspected this, or was trying to look unafraid.

"We're facing a general who has also used MCs to do his dirty work for him," Reaper went on. "If we come at him with military force, he'll be ready. Expecting it, more likely. What we need to do is slip under his defenses, just like he did here. The only thing is," Reaper sighed, leaning back, "he'll recognize most of us. Fuck, any traveler approaching his territory from this direction will be regarded as suspicious. So we need to get creative. It's not just scouting we need anymore. We need to know what General Tash is thinking, planning, even feeling. We need someone to plant inside who can get us information. And we'll need them to stay there, for an extended amount of time."

My president took a moment to meet the gaze of everyone in the room. "This isn't going to be easy. I will order someone to do it, although I'd much rather not do so. I wanted to put it out to anyone, see if there's any volunteers or another solution that I'm missing. But no one is leaving this room until we have a mission set in stone."

Slick stepped forward. "How will this inside person get information to you, president?"

"We'll have rendezvous points where you can leave coded messages for either Horus or Munin to pick up."

"And how long will this assignment be?"

"As long as it takes," Reaper answered flatly. "Until we have enough information to invade Tash and wipe him out. Could be months, could be years."

"You're not going." Jandro cut Slick off from asking another question.

The youngest Demon's mouth flapped open. "Sir, I'm—"

"You've prospected for us long enough for one of Tash's inner circle to recognize you. Really, that goes for just about everyone rolling with the Demons, whether they have a patch or not." Jandro nodded his head toward Larkan. "Same for the Sons. Too recognizable."

"But not their women," Mari pointed out.

All four of us at the table whipped around at the same time. "You are *not* going," Reaper snarled. "It's completely out of the question."

"I know." Mari folded her hands demurely. "Tash's guards would recognize me from the Sandia outpost."

"What she says is true, though," Gunner piped up. "A woman might be our best chance of getting close to Tash and arouse the least suspicion."

Reaper made a noise of disagreement. "I don't like it. It's fucking dangerous."

"It'll be just as dangerous for a man," Gunner replied. "If not more so, because he'll be more likely to be interrogated the moment he steps foot in the territory."

"I'll do it."

Everyone's heads swiveled to the woman who spoke. Andrea, Dallas's widow, stepped forward, her face a calm, blank mask.

"Drea, no." Behind her, Tessa's face was white as a sheet, her arms holding her infant daughter starting to tremble.

"Andrea." Reaper's voice was heavy as he addressed her. "Not you. Tessa's right."

"You're both wrong," the woman retorted. "None of Tash's people have ever seen my face. I can charm his soldiers and make them tell me their secrets. It was what I did before Dallas and I got together. I'm the best person to do this, president."

"Your children need you," Reaper argued. "You're all they have left. It's not right for their mother to just leave them for months, if not longer. And that's *if* we get you back after this is over."

"They're big enough to get by without me, and to remember me if I don't return. The Steel Demons will look after them." Andrea remained tight-lipped, insistent. "Or did you forget that this club is a family, Reaper?"

A few beats of silence fell over the room, no one daring to interfere.

"No, I haven't forgotten," Reaper answered. "But they just lost their father, Drea. To lose their mother right after—"

"And *I* lost my husband," she cut him off. "One of your best, and the love of my life. He would *never* be hanging back, never have a second thought about hitting Tash where it hurt. If you called for battle, he'd be leading the charge."

"I know." Reaper closed his eyes, his shoulders sinking with the weight of Dallas's death. "I know, Drea."

"He wouldn't want me to hang back either," she added. "To sit here waiting for news, when I could be doing something for the good of all of us. When I'm the *only* one who can."

"There could still be someone else," Reaper protested.

"There isn't. All of your men will be recognized. The other women either don't have the skills I do, or their children are too young. I'm prepared, and I—" Her voice shook for a moment before she steeled herself with a breath. "I'm ready to avenge my husband."

Reaper didn't respond, the silence stretching on long and uncomfortably. Finally, he sighed and touched the handle on his gavel. "Are there any objections to Andrea carrying out the mission?"

Noelle and Tessa each held one of Andrea's hands, their faces twisted up in grimaces as they tried not to cry. The men in the room looked worried, some of them shaking their heads, but no one spoke up to object. Even Governor Vance and General Bray just observed the room silently.

As the seconds ticked by with no objections, Reaper lifted the gavel and brought it down with a firm crack on the table. "You honor us, Andrea," he said solemnly. "You honor your husband and your whole Steel Demons family."

The woman nodded sharply and stepped back into the crowd. "Just tell me when to go."

Reaper nodded, folding his fingers on the tabletop. "That brings us to the next step in our plan—getting you inside. At least one person should go with you, to ensure you get to the border with no issue and report back that you got safely inside. After that, you're on your own."

"Understood." Andrea said.

"Do I have any volunteers on taking Andrea to New Ireland?" Reaper asked the room. "Being unrecognized is not as essential. Ideally, you should be able to hang back while she gets inside, but the risk of death or torture is still high."

Much to everyone's surprise, Big G stepped forward. "I'll take her."

"G!" Poor Tessa looked like she was going to crumble to the floor. "What the fuck are you doing?"

"And why you?" Reaper peered at him shrewdly.

The large man released a breath, taking a moment to glance back at Tessa and Andrea huddled together.

"I know I've been on your shit list lately, president, and rightly so. Everyone here knows I'm not the best husband, and far from the best father. In your eyes, I haven't been the best Demon either. So let me correct that." He straightened, puffing his chest out. "Let me take this as a chance to start righting my wrongs. If I don't come back, I want my kids to remember me as a Demon who helped us win."

Reaper's eyes flicked to Andrea. "Do you have any objection to him taking you?"

She regarded Big G with a cool indifference at first, then looked at Tessa with a silent question I couldn't read. "No objection, president. I'm fine with it."

"Does anyone else object to Big G escorting Andrea on the mission?" When no response came, Reaper smacked the gavel once again. "Moving right along here," he sighed, scrubbing a hand down his face. "Now we need at least two scouts to oversee and hang farther back in case anything happens to either Big G or Andrea, and to step in and engage the enemy if necessary. Shadow?" He looked down the length of the table at me.

I knew this would be coming. In all likelihood, the mission would be carried out at night and he'd need me to see in the dark. I was also the most silent rider and least likely to get caught if it came to a fight.

"I accept, president." My answer came without hesitation, a heated thrill lighting up my senses. I hadn't been on a true mission since Blakeworth, and was eager to take out more enemies who threatened us.

My ears picked up a small sound, like a gasp behind me. Mari? My hands closed into fists on my lap, the reminder of her making me all the more determined to carry out my duty as a Steel Demon. She had been hurt, nearly killed by the enemy. I'd pick off any man who would follow through on an order to shoot her.

"You're leading the scouting team, then," Reaper said. "Who would you like to take with you?"

My gaze lifted to the Sons of Odin across the room, Grudge meeting my eyes.

"I'll take Grudge with me," I answered. The silent Son grinned as he stepped forward.

"Anyone else?"

It didn't take long for me to make a decision. "No, president. The two of us will get the job done."

"Excellent." Reaper smacked the gavel once again.

The rest of the meeting was less emotionally taxing. Maps were pulled out to decide on the best route to get Andrea into New Ireland. It would be a long, winding journey to make it look like she was coming from the northeast and not directly west. General Bray and his lieutenants also gave input on the best rendezvous point, somewhere outside the territory where Andrea could leave the coded messages for us to find.

The sun was setting by the time Reaper concluded the meeting. "Are we ready to do this tomorrow night?" he asked the room. When no one objected, he smacked the gavel down for the final time that day. "Church is adjourned. Those who need to, come back here at sunset tomorrow night."

I rose from the table, but stayed back while everyone filed out of the room. Reaper and Gunner helped Jandro out, while Mari came to stand next to me at the table.

"I won't ask you to stay." Her soft voice was nearly a whisper in the large, empty room. "But it doesn't make me worry any less."

Turning toward her slowly, I reached for her waist and pulled her closer without a single dissenting thought in my mind. Touching her had become normal, natural. Something I *needed*.

"You don't have to worry about me." I slid my hand up her back until my fingers touched the ends of her hair. "I didn't know what to expect in Blakeworth. But with Tash, I know exactly what to expect."

Her expression didn't change. If anything, the tension in her forehead grew even deeper. "Just make sure you come back. Even if Grudge has to drag you behind his bike through the desert."

"It won't come to that," I promised her. "We'll be back in four days at the most."

"You better." Her fingers slid between mine, slender and twig-like through my massive paws. "You can't miss the housewarming party."

"Oh, yeah." I heard others talking about how she and her men decided to move into the house the governor had offered them. "I wouldn't miss it. Congratulations, by the way," I added stiffly.

Her smile up at me was bright. "Congratulations to you too."

I frowned. "What do you mean?"

"Shadow." Mari propped her chin on my chest, sliding her arms around my ribs. "It's your house too."

"It is?"

She nodded.

"But." My chest was tight, my mind going off in all kinds of directions I didn't dare voice aloud. "I thought it was only for you and your men."

Mari grinned wider. "It is." She stretched on her tiptoes, leaning up until her lips came within kissing distance of mine. "You're mine, Shadow." Just as quickly, her feet planted on the floor again, the nervousness visible on her face. "That is, if you want to be."

My body felt it, but my brain seemed slow to catch up. I felt light, almost like I was floating. My pulse hammered and I wanted to laugh to release the sparks building in my chest. But my brain, my stupid brain, wouldn't let me believe the words she said.

"I'm...yours?"

She nodded. "Yes, I want you to be."

"Why?"

"Because," she laughed like it was obvious. "I love...how you make me feel. I admire your creativity, your loyalty, how sweet you are with me and my cat. When I'm not wrapped up in you, I wrap myself in your hoodie." Her touch slid down my arms, finding both of my hands. "I want to say good morning to you *every* morning."

I leaned my forehead down to hers. My stubborn brain was finally reconciling with my body's reactions. This brightness sparking under my skin, the smile I couldn't stop from spreading on my mouth. She wanted me.

Me.

"I...want to be yours." I placed her hand over my racing heart. "I still feel clueless about so many things, but I'll do my best to be a good partner to you. One you deserve." I brought her hand to my lips and kissed her small palm. "And you can have all my hoodies as long as you watch every sunset with me."

Her grin reflected mine. "Deal." She pulled away from me until her hands tugged mine toward the door leading out of the room. "Let's watch one now, before you leave me."

I tugged her back to me, catching her against my chest from the force of my pull. "I'll never leave you." I pressed a fast kiss to her mouth before releasing her. "Not without a promise that I'll come back."

"Hm." She practically skipped out the door, tossing a playful glance over her shoulder at me. "I'm gonna hold you to that."

MARIPOSA

"Get some antifreeze and put it in someone's drink if you need to kill them without being detected."

Andrea threw her head back and laughed, nearly falling out of her armchair. "How many times have you had to do that, Mari?"

"I plead the fifth," I snickered. "Oh wait, that doesn't exist anymore. Damn it!"

"You can always 'accidentally' smother a guy to death while you're sitting on his face," Noelle suggested. "Although, you'll need his limbs tied down, so make it like a kinky bondage session first."

"Better to use a pillow," I interjected. "You don't want things getting bitten off down there if he catches on."

Andrea howled with laughter, and even I couldn't smother my giggles entirely. The only one we couldn't seem to drag out from the dumps was Tessa, who barely cracked a smile as she rocked Vivian against her chest.

None of us could blame her. The father of her children and the woman she just rekindled a romance with were leaving on a dangerous mission in a few short hours. The probability was high that neither would come back soon, if ever.

The four of us were in one of the City Hall lounge rooms, usually reserved as sitting rooms for the male dignitaries to drink and smoke cigars. But us girls wanted to chat and get together before sending Andrea off.

And Big G. And Grudge and Shadow. My *Shadow,* I thought worriedly. We watched last night's sunset from a City Hall balcony until darkness and cold settled in. Our new house wasn't entirely furnished yet so we still had to spend another night in separate rooms in the B&B. By the time he returned from the mission, his new home would be moved in and ready.

Our new home.

"Don't look so sad, sweet cheeks." Andrea stood from her armchair, wobbling slightly from the drinks we'd all been consuming, before planting herself next to Tessa on the loveseat and pulling the young mother into a forced cuddle.

"I don't know how you all can be laughing right now." She leaned her head on Andrea's shoulder. "What if I never see you again?"

"Then we can remember the good times we had." Andrea planted a kiss on her forehead. "However brief they may have been."

"I've always laughed at the worst fuckin' times." Noelle helped herself to more whiskey from the coffee table. "Drove my moody-ass brothers nuts. Helps me deal with shit, I guess."

"That's really common, actually," I told her. "Cracking jokes at seemingly-inappropriate situations is a widely-studied coping mechanism."

"Alright, smart girl." Andrea wadded up a cocktail napkin and threw it at me. "What else should I know about potentially ending or saving lives?"

"Do you know how to give CPR?" I asked.

"Sure do. I taught myself from a book actually, when my son was born." Andrea's face turned thoughtful, her hands stroking lightly over Tessa's arms. "I should...I should see my kids one last time."

None of us were about to tell her no, as she slid out from behind Tessa and headed for the main doors of the building. She had said goodbye to her children right before coming here, but the finality of the situation seemed to sink in as the time grew near.

"Poor Drea." Noelle curled her feet underneath her. "It has to be so hard to do this."

"I told her that," Tessa said in a small voice. "She just said that was exactly *why* she had to. And that it's what Dallas would have done."

"She's being so brave," I said, swirling my *reposado* in my own glass. "I have to hand it to Big G too. He really stepped up."

"Yeah, *now* he does," Tessa scoffed. "Like I wasn't feeling shredded up about this enough."

"You still love him?" Noelle asked, never able to put a filter on that mouth.

"Not like I used to, but I still care about him." Tessa cradled Vivian's head against her shoulder. "He's my kids' father. There's always gonna be *something* there."

"It is nice to see him take initiative instead of just tagging along on the rides," Noelle relented. "Hopefully this is the start of him acting like a grown-up."

"If he comes back," Tessa mumbled.

"He will." I reached over and squeezed her knee. "He's stubborn as hell and built like a stone chimney. And he won't miss out on being here for his kids."

"What about your tall, dark, scary one?" Noelle turned to me, the alcohol making her extra chatty. "Scared for him?"

"He'll get it done," I answered, the tequila now jostling in my stomach.

"Not what I asked, sister." Noelle nudged me with her foot.

"Of course I'm scared," I sighed. "Why do you think I'm drinkin' with you two bitches?"

A sharp peal of laughter burst out of Tessa first, waking up a fussy, distressed Vivian, while Noelle just stared at me agape.

"Aw, shit!" Tessa fanned her face. "I needed that laugh."

"Someone's feisty on that tequila." Noelle chuckled. "I get it, sis. Sometimes cluckin' around like hens is the best therapy for when our men are out there doing stupid shit."

"Or women," Tessa corrected as she shushed Vivian.

"Or women, yes."

"It's different now." I rolled my glass between my palms, talking more to myself than either of them. "Back in Blakeworth...he wasn't mine, then. Not officially."

"Please tell me you've fucked him." Noelle, of course.

"Aside from the first time?" I shook my head. "No."

"What the shit!" Noelle flailed her arms and legs out dramatically, sliding from the armchair to the floor. "You had your whole romantic evening with him and didn't get some scarred, giant dick? Why the fuck not?"

His dick isn't scarred. I bit my tongue and chose against the snarky answer, despite what my tequila-driven urges wanted me to say. "I just wanted to have that moment with him, watching the sunset together."

"Bo-*ring,*" Noelle groaned. "Who says you can't watch a pretty sunset and get pounded at the same time?"

"No one," I laughed. "I dunno, it just didn't seem right at the time. I'd rather do it when we can relax and not have this dangerous mission hanging over our heads, you know?"

"Nah, I'm with Noelle on this one," Tessa chimed in. "There's no better sex than might-never-see-you-alive-again sex."

"Thank you!" My sister-in-law flipped her hair smugly.

"But," Tessa added, "the holy-shit-you're-alive-and-back-in-one-piece sex is pretty epic too. That's how this little lady was made." She patted Vivian's back.

That last statement seemed to do it. Tessa's face screwed up in a grimace, her lower lip wobbling as she willed herself not to cry. Noelle and I slid over to her at the same time, sandwiching her between us to wrap mother and baby in a cocoon of love and support.

"It's okay, mama." Noelle rested her cheek on the back of Tessa's head as she rocked her gently from side to side. "It sucks. It's not fair. Let it out."

"Why does it have to be *both* of them?" Tessa sniffed, accepting my tissue. "Goddamn it."

"We're still here," I said. "I know it's not the same, but we're here for you, honey. You're not alone."

"I know." She sniffed again, dabbing at her eyes. "Thanks, guys."

"And it's not forever," Noelle reminded her. "They'll be back. Both of them."

The three of us remained linked around each other until Andrea returned, her own eyes puffy and nose running. We opened our arms and brought her into our cuddle pile like she had never left. There we remained until one of Finn's lieutenants informed us that it was almost go-time, and that Andrea was needed in the conference room.

My heart beat a hard rhythm in my chest as the four of us stood up, hands linked as we followed him to the secured conference room. Noelle glanced at me, blinking back her own tears, but her mouth was hard and determined. I tried to funnel some of her strength to myself. We'd stay with our people until the last possible moment.

The room was already bustling with activity when we entered. Shadow, Jandro, Grudge, and Finn spoke quietly at one end of the table, leaning over a map in front of them. Big G, Reaper, Gunner, and another member of Finn's army spoke on another side of the room.

A few faces looked up as we stepped into the room. Some were friendly, others tense. It was no secret that most of Finn's people disagreed with how this mission would be carried out. But they'd never seen how an MC operated before.

"Ah, the woman of the hour," Finn greeted Andrea with a warm smile. "If you're ready, we'll just go over a few things one final time."

She nodded and broke away from us with a last squeeze of our hands. As Finn led her to look over the map, Shadow made his way over to me.

He was dressed from head to toe in black, for once not wearing his Steel Demons cut, but a plain one with no insignia. Under his cut and long-sleeved shirt, a stab-proof vest created a slightly bulky rectangle over his torso. It did nothing to diminish his intimidating stature, as evident by people getting out of his way as he crossed the room. Nor did it decrease the heat lighting me up as he got closer. I closed my fists until my nails bit into my palms. It was all I could do to not drag him off to another room and rip every piece of armor off of him.

My newest man didn't stop until his gloved hand reached my face, the other one drawing me against him by my hip. Our lips came together in the most fluid, natural way, like we were made to be linked together. My palms rested on his wide shoulders, toes barely touching the ground like his kiss would send me floating. With the vest between us, it felt like I couldn't get close enough, no matter how much I pressed my body to him.

"Wait," he said when we parted for a breath. With a turn of his head, he bit the fingertip of his glove to pull it off. The warmth of his bare hand against my cheek drew a shaky sigh from my chest. It hit me hard then, that this would be the last time in days that he'd touch me.

I leaned into his palm, reaching for another kiss, which he freely gave. The whole room was probably staring at us, but fuck if I cared. I wrapped around his neck tighter, tongue melding with his as I realized *he* didn't care if anyone watched us either.

"Keep kissing me like that," I whispered, forehead pressed to his. "And I really won't let you go."

He let out a soft hum as he kissed me again, slow and decadent, scar-tissued fingers caressing my cheek. "I'll be back before you know it."

"Not soon enough."

Our surroundings melted away, and I committed all of my senses to memorizing this man. Everything, from the slight flavor of coffee on his tongue to the scent of gunpowder and leather on him. The texture of his skin under my lips and hands and those mismatched eyes drinking me in like he wanted to memorize me in the same way.

"Tell me what you said last night." My hands trailed down and slid under the stab-proof vest. "I need to hear it again."

Shadow pulled his other glove off and cupped my face with both hands bare. "I'll never leave you." His breath hitched in his chest as he hesitated, then continued. "Because...I'm yours."

"Say it again," I pleaded shamelessly, desperately. My chest already ached with missing him. He didn't have the most dangerous job on the mission, but I knew my stomach wouldn't stop clenching until I saw his motorcycle riding into Four Corners again.

"I'll never leave you," he repeated. "I'll always come back."

Jandro walked up next to us at that point, hands behind his back and his face apologetic. "It's time, man."

Shadow nodded and slowly unwound from me, our fingertips the last to break away from each other. He pulled his gloves back on, then he and Grudge followed Andrea and Big G out the door.

A crowd of no less than thirty people watched their motorcycles take off just as dusk gave way to night. Shadow kept his headlight off, perfectly capable of seeing in the dark, with Grudge keeping his light dim as he followed Shadow's red brake light.

Jandro hugged me from behind as their lights and rumbling engines faded away into darkness.

"Did you tell him?" he asked with a warm kiss on my cheek.

"No," I sighed. "Maybe I should have, but I didn't want it to seem so...final."

"It won't be," he assured me. "You will when he comes back."

SHADOW

We rode exclusively at night, with Grudge and I avoiding the main roads. Andrea and Big G took the highways like normal, with us keeping watch from a distance. We even camped separately to not appear as though we were traveling together, which was fine with me. I didn't know Andrea well and didn't care for Big G's company. I appreciated Grudge's silence, although he was a chatty fucker with a pen and paper. And apparently, he loved terrible jokes.

What's orange and sounds like a parrot? He shoved his notepad at me, snickering.

"I dunno, Grudge. What?"

A carrot!

I choked on my drink, going into a coughing fit while he fell over with that silent laughter of his.

"Why haven't you picked up sign language?" I asked him one night. "Might be easier than writing all the time, right?"

I knew from our mission in Blakeworth, he and the Sons used hand signals to communicate quickly between each other. Beyond that, he made gestures for simple things and wrote down any thoughts that were more complex.

"Hmm." He shook his head and scribbled out a reply. *Nah. T & D would have to learn it too. Then translate 4 me. This is easier 4 everyone.*

"Still might not hurt to learn," I said. "I had a book on ASL back in Sheol. Taught myself the alphabet and a few phrases. Didn't really go deeper than that, though."

Grudge's mouth tightened and he shook his head. He clearly didn't want to be pressed on the subject, so I dropped it, sipping whiskey next to our campfire as he turned to a fresh page.

Miss her?

I swallowed, wondering if there was another word for the uncomfortable pangs in my chest from not having Mariposa around. I missed her while she worked at the hospital for an entire day. I missed her when I was alone at night in the B&B, knowing I wouldn't see her until morning while she was in the next room with her men.

But this feeling, like a tether stretching to its breaking point across the distance between me and her, felt different. It was deeper, sharper. A physical ache in my body that would only be soothed by having her near me again.

"Yes." I opted to give Grudge the simple answer. "A whole fucking lot."

Me too.

I looked at him across the campfire. Grudge often wrote his messages to be brief and to the point, which didn't always make his thoughts clear.

"You miss Mariposa, or someone else?"

He waved two fingers, indicating it was the second thing I said.

"T-Bone and Dyno?"

He shook his head, then waved his hands in a way that seemed to illustrate feminine curves.

"A woman?" I lifted my head from the saddlebag I was using as a pillow. "I didn't know you had one."

He shook his head again, quickly scrawling on his pad to elaborate. *I don't. Just miss one.*

"You should take the advice you gave me," I said, knocking back the rest of my drink. "Just put it out there and be yourself."

"Heh." Grudge made a noise of disagreement and shook his head again, but didn't write out another explanation.

We smothered the fire as daylight approached and took turns watching as the other man slept. When dusk began falling, we hit the road again.

Andrea and Big G doubled up on one motorcycle, taking the winding two-lane main road while Grudge and I kept them in our line of sight along the canyons above. Jandro had fitted our cafe racers with the thickest off-road tires and biggest damn mufflers he could find so we'd make minimal noise.

The two-day ride was a whole lot of nothing, with no direct contact with the other riders except for a quick flash of a mirror to let them know we were still there. It was late afternoon when we came within sight of New Ireland's northeastern border. Although it wasn't the border itself as much as we spotted the Irish flag flapping in the chilly wind.

Grudge and I rode to opposite embankments flanking the settlement. We were each a good hundred yards away from their perimeter, and would have no problem taking out anyone patrolling.

I parked next to some dense brush, took what I needed from my packs, and walked the bike *into* the bush. After grabbing some tumbleweeds and sticking them in at odd angles, I felt satisfied that my bike was adequately camouflaged. Ideally, no one would be walking around here anyway. I loaded the first of my rifles and made my way up to the top of the hill, crouched low and silent as a cat. Right before reaching the top, I lowered to my knees and crawled my way to the ledge until I had a clear view of the gate while lying on my stomach.

Big G and Andrea were, for the moment, out of sight. They were hidden at the base of Grudge's hillside, preparing to approach the gate with their disguises. Grudge flashed me an okay sign, indicating he had eyes on them. Nodding in return, I turned my attention to the final obstacle Andrea would be facing.

Twelve armed guards stood in front of the northeastern entrance alone, while a Jeep filled with more soldiers made its way slowly around the perimeter just outside the gate. This kind of security seemed excessive, almost like they were expecting an attack. I could only speculate that General Tash made many enemies due to how swiftly he trampled over cities and territories. Small uprisings of those he'd conquered had to be expected.

I tried to push away the thought of survivors marching up to this gate, probably wholly unprepared and armed with things like pitchforks. Just ordinary people who wanted justice for the atrocities committed against their loved ones. What kind of fate did they meet against these soldiers? The gravel road, surrounding sand, and perimeter walls were clean, even polished. There were no heads on spikes, no human remains littering the ground, no clues to indicate Tash's abject cruelty. Some unassuming refugee might stumble upon this place and even think they were safe.

Movement below me prompted my index finger to curl around my trigger—just resting, not yet squeezing. Andrea was making her way out, approaching the gate on foot and...

I looked up from my sights and blinked both eyes. "What the fuck?"

Big G was approaching the gate *with* her.

Looking across the valley to Grudge, he seemed just as confused as me. The plan was for Big G to cover Andrea as she went in *alone*. If there had been a change in plans, we sure as fuck weren't notified.

"God fucking damn it, Big G," I cursed under my breath as I pulled a small set of binoculars from my pocket.

Andrea was bound with her hands tied in front of her, Big G pulling roughly on her arm so much that she stumbled to keep up. She was scantily clad, the low-cut dress she wore her only possession. I figured she would make some kind of pitch as a service girl offering to entertain the soldiers, but to my knowledge, she didn't need Big G for that.

Unless he had plans of his own that he wanted to carry out once inside, which was the most likely answer. I muttered curses under my breath as the guards halted them at the gate and began asking questions. Big G acted without thinking or informing others who his actions might affect. The problem with him wasn't so much that he was insubordinate, but that he believed his ideas were much better than they actually were.

It felt like I held my breath through their long, ten-minute exchange standing outside the gate. Big G did most of the talking, while Andrea only answered questions when directly spoken to. My lungs released when the gates began to swing open but tightened up again when, just as I feared, Big G followed Andrea inside.

Grudge and I quickly lost our view of them as the gates slid closed. The two undercover Steel Demons were officially behind enemy lines. My mind raced, wondering what I should do. We weren't given orders for this situation and I didn't have a tactical mind like Gunner. We were supposed to come back with Big G alive or dead, unless circumstances prevented us from retrieving his body.

Anger coiled in my body. The fucker *knew* we were out here, they both did. They knew we couldn't leave.

I had to get back to my woman. I promised her.

Looking across the valley, I made sure I had Grudge's attention before making the ASL sign for *hours* with my left hand, then counted up to 24 with my right. To my relief, he nodded and made the *okay* sign that he understood. I sighed and shifted my legs underneath me, trying to prepare myself for the long day ahead as I marked where the shadows touched the ground next to me.

One full day. Big G would have twenty-four hours to do whatever the fuck and get out. If he wasn't outside that gate by this time tomorrow, we'd head home without him and he was on his own.

It must have been somewhere around hour twenty when I spotted movement down below. I rubbed my weary eyes and slapped myself awake, just as I'd done for the last several hours. A quick glance to the other embankment confirmed that Grudge was awake and watching too.

I waited with bated breath as the gates slid open, not knowing entirely who or what to expect coming through from the other side. My heart lifted slightly when I saw Big G being escorted out with a soldier on each side. He looked fine, not at all abused or in any distress. I didn't want to relax too soon, but whatever story he told to get in with Andrea must have worked. I couldn't wait until Reaper dragged that information out of him.

His escorts followed him roughly fifty feet outside of their perimeter before halting, their work done as they returned to stand at attention. Rather than continue on to where his bike was hidden, Big G stopped with them.

"Fucking get out of there," I muttered under my breath. "You big dumbshit, what the fuck are you doing?"

He dawdled, standing casually as he turned to face his two escorts. His mouth moved and his facial expressions looked as if he was cracking jokes, but I couldn't be sure. My finger curled around my rifle trigger, aiming at the empty space between him and the two soldiers. It was unnerving how familiar he was acting with Tash's men. Like they were friends.

My heart beat with ever-increasing punches to my ribcage. Big G was annoying and not very smart. But a traitor? Even if so, would he be dumb enough to act friendly with Tash's guards right in front of us?

The next movement came faster than my eyes could follow. All I saw was Big G swaying his upper body like he was leaning forward with laughter. Next, a gunshot rang out and one of the escorts clutched his chest as he fell to the ground.

All my senses heightened to focus on the scene below me, my whole body as tense as a tripwire. Big G shot the second escort before he had time to react, and then both men were on the ground. The first man who'd fallen had an empty holster.

Shocked stillness gave way to chaos. Shouts and running exploded from the front gate as Tash's guards realized two of their men were down, and the culprit was someone they just released.

Big G shouldered his stolen gun and fired into the soldiers running toward him. In the distance, a Jeep made a sharp U-turn and accelerated hard toward the lone gunman.

"For Dallas!" Big G shouted at the top of his lungs. "For the Sons of Odin! The Steel Demons wish you a long and prosperous fucking life!"

"Fucking idiot," I grumbled through my teeth. "Stupid goddamn fucking idiot."

The windshield of the oncoming Jeep shattered, but not from Big G, who was still focused on the men on foot ahead of him. Grudge had his long-barreled rifle pointed right at the vehicle and began picking off passengers and the driver.

Right, we still had to cover him, despite him outing himself like a fucking dumbass. I took careful aim at another swarm of soldiers heading for him, nailing their squadron leader right in his forehead.

"We're under attack!" someone yelled. "Snipers in the canyons! Get the Jeeps out there!"

Fuck, we couldn't afford to stick around. Why in God's fucking name would Big G endanger us like this?

It's a suicide mission, I realized.

He had to have known he wouldn't make it out of this alive, even with us covering him. But now Andrea was at risk, and we weren't expecting first contact from her for weeks.

Big G's body jerked as he received a bullet to his shoulder. He just switched hands on his gun and returned fire, his strength already leaving him. Grudge and I picked soldiers off as fast as we could, but there was no way we could get all of them. And now they knew our positions, and who we were affiliated with.

Everything about this mission had been fucked up. If Andrea wasn't subsequently captured because of this shit, I would consider it a miracle.

I pulled away from the ledge just as Big G fell to his knees. More soldiers were swarming in, and there was nothing we could do for him. Half-crawling, half-sliding down the hill on my side, I tried to ignore the feeling of abject failure in my gut. I had done my part, but it felt like I'd barely done shit. And now another one of our own was dead.

That pulled forth a lot of confusing feelings for me. I had never liked Big G, or even cared about him, really. But he was still a Steel Demon, a brother-in-arms. Foolish as his final actions were, he did it for the club. For the ones we lost.

I sprang to my feet at the bottom of the hill and took off running, hoping Grudge was already retreating too. Jerking my bike out of the bushes and weeds, I turned the ignition before even jumping on. I threw a leg over and hit the throttle hard, kicking up rocks and dust as I searched the fading daylight for Grudge.

I didn't dare turn my headlight on, and thankfully didn't need to. My silent brother raced down his hillside like a bat out of hell, hair and beard whipping back as he pushed his bike hard.

"Grudge!" I yelled, maneuvering closer to him.

He glanced at me, then made a panicked motion at something behind me. Before I could check my mirrors, a bright glare reflecting in them nearly blinded me. I looked over my shoulder to see the outlines of three Jeeps in my dust, with gigantic search lights mounted on top of their vehicles.

MARIPOSA

"They'll be okay, sugar." Reaper reached for my hand to stop me from pacing a hole into the floor, but I just moved further away from him to keep doing it.

"It's been five days," I said, not for the first time. "It wasn't supposed to take more than four. Something must have happened."

"Maybe, but it could be literally anything." Gunner moved into my direct path. "There's been thunderstorms out in that area, so they might've had to hunker down. They could've run out of gas and had to hitchhike. Don't worry until we've got something to worry about."

"No word for over twenty-four hours past their ETA *is* something to worry about!"

"*Bonita.*" Jandro tried next. "This is Shadow we're talking about, doing the best at what he does."

"Last time he did that, he nearly died, and guess who had to put him back together?" I shot back.

Without anything left to convince me, I resumed pacing the living room in my beautiful new house, too anxious to enjoy it. Moving and decorating had been my only distractions for the last few days. Reaper, in his persistent paranoia about Daren's dream, did not want me away from my men for even a moment. There was only so much I could do at the hospital without one of them hovering over me, so I took a few days off to get moved in.

Finn and Lis insisted on buying us furniture, introducing us to a lovely family of woodworkers who made everything by hand. In just three days, we had a brand new dining table, chairs, and bookshelves.

In their five years since arriving at Four Corners, my in-laws also accumulated dishes, blankets, rugs, wall-hangings, and other various knickknacks they were happy to pass along to us.

"It's the artist in me," Lis laughed. "I love collecting beautiful things and supporting my fellow craftsmen, but it's no good if they sit around collecting dust."

One of the most precious things she gave to me was a bronze sculpture made by her late husband, Carter. Like her, he'd been an accomplished metalsmith, but preferred creating large-scale sculptures over jewelry. Soon after settling in Four Corners, she and Finn recovered a small collection of Carter's pieces that he'd hidden away in storage.

"Lis, he made this for *you*!" I protested when she wheeled the heavy bronze piece into the house on a hand truck. "It's yours, you should keep it."

"Oh, I have a half dozen with a lot more sentimental value." She brought the hand truck upright carefully. "And anyway, I want all of my children to have something of his." She smiled at me, green eyes glittering. "It's like he's still here, watching over his family. Noelle has a favorite that I'll give to her when she has her own place."

"That's really lovely." I was touched, the will to fight her utterly squashed.

And it was a beautiful sculpture. It looked like a tree, each branch and leaf etched with exquisite details. The trunk however, was that of a woman's body. Not terribly unique subject matter for a male artist, but I loved how realistic the form was. Wide hips and thick thighs, softness to the belly, and even breasts that were not perfectly symmetrical. All the perceived imperfections made it even more beautiful. I considered asking my mother-in-law if she had been his muse for this particular piece, but decided against it.

Together we placed it in a corner between one of the first-story bedrooms and the stairs. I stared at the bronze tree woman now, for some reason fixating on the fact that the man who created her, who brought her to life from a shapeless hunk of metal, was dead.

Tonight was supposed to be our housewarming party, but the last thing I felt like doing was celebrating.

Is this how one of my men breaks my heart? I wondered. *By leaving and never coming back to me?*

I hadn't thought about Noelle's prophecy from Daren in weeks, brushing it off with every affectionate touch and word from my men since I first heard it. But Reaper's increasing fear about his own prophecy brought Noelle's harrowing words to the forefront of my mind. *You're going to get your heart broken. And not just by one man.*

"How long?"

"How long what, sugar?" Reaper once again reached for me from his spot on the couch. I relented this time, taking his hand.

"How long until you send a team to go find them? I want to go with, if it comes to that. They might need medical attention."

My husband sighed, tilting his head back, but at this point he knew better than to argue with me. "One more day. Another full twenty-four hours before we investigate." He pulled me over the couch's arm, sending me tumbling across his lap. "And if you're going, at least one of us will too. No excuses."

"Fine." I curled up against his chest, snuggling into the wall of hard muscle. "Fuck, I just want him to be okay."

"Have faith in Shadow, sugar." His hands braced around my hip and lower back. "He's tougher than all of us."

Gunner came to sit next to us. "I'll send Horus out that direction tomorrow morning, if that'll make you feel better."

I turned in Reaper's lap, leaning until I stretched between him and Gunner, and rested my head on Gunner's shoulder. "You're the best. Thank you."

"Jandro!" Reaper looked around behind him. "Where'd he go? It's not like him to miss a cuddle pile."

"Probably in the garage," I mused.

Like me, Jandro tried to smother his concern for Shadow by keeping busy. First, he assembled a brand-new luxurious chicken coop in our new backyard, then moved on to every tiny, minute motorcycle repair he could think of. It was getting late, and the birds were all tucked away in their insulated chicken-mansion, so I could only imagine Jandro would be off tinkering with something.

I was dozing off, cozy and warm from my men's bodies and the fire crackling in the stone fireplace, when a slamming door startled me awake.

"Riders coming into town," Jandro announced, heading to the sink to wash his hands. "Heard the engines and saw two headlights coming down over the hill."

"Two?" I jumped up from the couch, Reap and Gun quickly following. "Not three?"

"Pretty sure, yeah."

"You didn't see who they were?"

"We'll find out in a sec, *Mariposita*." He dried his hands on a towel and bent to plant a kiss on my forehead. "Too dark and too far away to see shit."

I went back to pacing, this time on the front porch. The air was chilly and I huddled my arms close as I listened for the approaching motorcycles. As the roars grew louder, I discerned that it was only one bike coming to this part of town. A single headlight hovering over the winding gravel road through the new development confirmed what I suspected. The rider could surely see me now, but it was too dark out and the headlight too blinding for me to see him.

Please be him, I silently begged. *Please let it be my Shadow.*

Freyja came out to join me on the porch, her eyes watching the road, but I didn't dare hope until I saw him with my own eyes.

And when I did, I burst into tears.

Shadow only had time to park the bike, but left it running as he jumped off. I took one step down the porch, but he closed the distance swiftly, pulling me into his chest with a squeezing, urgent hug.

"I told you I would." His lips moved over the crown of my head, planting kisses in my hair and wrapping my body in heat. "I'm here, see? I'm back."

"You are," I sniffled into his chest, my hands moving over him as if checking to make sure he was really there. "And you're..." I lifted my head, taking in the state of his leathers for the first time. "...filthy."

"Yeah," he laughed, releasing me to turn off the ignition on his bike. Under the porch light, I could see how he was caked in sand and dirt from the road. "It was a rough couple of days coming back."

"Who came with you?"

"Grudge," he answered. "He went back to the Sons and I came straight here. We uh," he sighed, clearly exhausted, "we lost Big G."

"And Andrea?"

"She made it inside, but…" He shook his head with another sigh. "I should give a full report to Reaper."

"Of course, but not yet." I grabbed his hands, pulling him up the porch to the front door. "You should clean up, eat, and rest. We gave you one of the downstairs bedrooms, I hope that's okay. I brought your stuff over from the B&B, everything's in there."

My fourth man smiled wearily at me as he followed my lead into our home. "Thank you, Mari. I'm…"

"Yes?" I closed the front door behind him and whirled around. "Take your boots off here. You're what, love?"

He just looked at me quietly, my hand still encased in his, rough fingers stroking over my palm.

"I'm so lucky to be yours."

The next day was spent spreading the word about Shadow and Grudge's return, and our housewarming party was rescheduled to that night. Jandro had gotten to know a butcher in town, and arranged to have a roasting pit dug in the backyard for a whole pig to serve that evening.

Reaper invited his father and the governor over early in the afternoon for Shadow's report, after he'd gotten a long shower and full night of sleep.

"Are you fuckin' shitting me?" I heard Reaper demand from the kitchen table.

"I wish I was, president," Shadow answered evenly.

"What the fuck, Big G?"

"I asked myself the same question many times."

"Has anyone told Tessa?" I popped my head into the doorway.

"I imagine Grudge has," Shadow said. "Considering they live in the same building."

"Sugar, make sure she comes over tonight." Reaper said, unofficially making me part of the meeting.

"I can ask her, but if she wants to be alone, I won't force her. She was afraid of this happening."

"Do what you can," he urged. "She should be around loved ones."

"I can ask Lis to hang out with her," Finn offered. "Losing husbands may be an unfortunate thing they have in common."

"I'm sorry for your lost man." The governor fiddled with his empty teacup and smiled at me appreciatively as I came to take it away. "It truly is tragic."

"I can't say it's completely unexpected," Reaper sighed. "I think he just couldn't pass up the chance to kill some of Tash's people and didn't think it through, as usual."

"Do you think Andrea's cover is compromised?" Finn asked.

"She is definitely a target, if she hasn't already been caught," Shadow said. "Big G referred to us and the Sons by name. They know she's at least affiliated with us."

"We won't know until the time to make first contact comes." Reaper drummed his fingers on the table. "If there isn't a message from her, that will be our answer."

"And what will you do if that happens?" Vance asked.

"Go back to square one." Reaper rubbed his hands over his face with a groan. "Again."

"Andrea's smart," I said over the running water in the kitchen sink. "She knows how to hide in plain sight and put on a persona. Even if G massively fucked up, she'll adapt and get her job done."

"Really?" Vance piped up. "How did she develop skills like that?"

Shadow and Reaper both hid smiles as I answered. "She was a high-end escort before meeting her husband."

"Ah." The governor's blush was precious. "I see."

The others chuckled at his discomfort while I made my way to

Shadow, standing behind him as I wrapped my arms around his neck. "What I want to know is why you took an extra day to get back to me."

"We were covering Big G when Tash's patrol spotted us," he said, hands sliding up to clasp mine resting on his chest. "We had to lead some Jeeps on a goose chase all over wild terrain, and lost at least half a day doing that." His head tilted back to look at me. "Fortunately we were faster, and Jeeps are gas guzzlers."

"Uh-huh." I made a show of sounding skeptical as I leaned down to kiss his forehead. "A very likely excuse."

"I missed you before I hit the road." He reached up to caress my cheek. "I was counting down the minutes until I'd be back with you."

"You're all, uh," the governor's voice cut in, "a very openly affectionate bunch."

Reaper laughed as he stood from the table. "Stay for the party, governor. You've seen how hard we fight." He came over to me, taking hold of my jaw as he pressed a hard kiss to my mouth. "Now you can see how hard we live."

The house started filling up with people a few hours later. Noelle and Lis came over to help prepare food, Gunner quickly sneaking in behind them. He darted into the downstairs bedroom we'd designated as the guest room, and quickly shoved something in the closet.

"Are you up to no good again?" I asked, leaning against the door jam.

"Always, baby girl." He grinned, kissing me in the doorway. "You'll see."

"Well, that isn't cryptic at all."

He just laughed, heading to the front door to let more people in. This time it was Tessa, another one of Andrea's friends, Elise, plus Tessa and Andrea's children. The young mother smiled as she walked in, but I saw the somberness in her eyes.

"Hey, honey." I pulled her into a hug. "Thanks for coming. I'm so sorry."

"You don't have to be." Her voice was raspy like she'd been crying. "I know you weren't the biggest fan of him. She'd never tell me, but I bet Noelle was celebrating."

"She wouldn't, Tess. And anyway, none of that matters." I held tightly on to her shoulders. "He was yours. You made your family with him. It's normal to mourn him, even if he wasn't perfect."

"Thanks, Mari. I am glad the other guys got back safe." She lifted Vivian out of her carseat, heading toward the backyard where the kids had gathered around the roasting pit. "Guess I'll go see what the excitement's about."

"Help yourself to anything." I squeezed her shoulder as she walked past me.

More Steel Demons trickled in over the next hour, the house growing loud and the mood celebratory. The Sons of Odin were among the last to arrive, T-Bone picking me up in a crushing hug as he planted a fat kiss on my cheek.

"Better put her down, T," Dyno laughed. "We're already getting the murder looks."

"Ah, these Demons don't scare me." T-Bone set me lightly on my feet. "They're all teddy bears under them cuts."

"Care to fuckin' repeat that?" Reaper came over, grinning, and already on his third glass of whiskey, which he took care not to spill as he hugged and greeted each of the Sons.

"I said you have a great house, Reap." T-Bone chuckled. "Congratulations."

"Thanks. You guys want a tour of the place?"

Grudge pointed at Reaper's whiskey and waggled his eyebrows.

"Drinks first? Yes, absolutely. Follow me, boys."

He led them through to the kitchen and soon after the party was well underway.

I looked out the kitchen window when I started making a plate of food, ignoring Hades begging for a bite at my side. We had enough room for a small pool in the backyard, and maybe a fire pit. I wanted more concrete out there too, with patio furniture and shady overhangs.

So it could be more like Sheol, I realized.

It would never be exactly the same, but I missed that part of our old home the most—having a place where everyone could gather and just celebrate being alive. The cold kept most people inside at this time of year, but a few kids ran around the backyard playing tag. Jandro talked with some guys over beers by the roasting pit. We had the essence of our old home, it just needed a few touches to make it a true Steel Demons party house.

"Can I have everyone's attention please!" Reaper called from the living room. "Where the fuck is Larkan?"

I followed the crush of people moving into the living room and promptly groaned. "Reaper, get off the coffee table!"

"It's fine, babe. She's sturdy." He bounced on the balls of his feet to demonstrate, sloshing his whiskey in the process.

I just covered my face with a hand while someone laughed and patted my shoulder sympathetically. If he broke our brand new table, it was on him to fix.

"Gun, get the thing. Where's Larkan at?"

"Right here, Pres." The prospect raised a beer from the middle landing of the stairs, his other arm around Noelle's shoulders.

"Get your grubby mitts off my sister and come down here, boy."

Larkan took his sweet time, knowing it would irritate Reaper. He polished off his beer and kissed Noelle, deep and full of tongue, to the sounds of cheers and wolf whistles. His smile as he came down the stairs was smug with a hint of curiosity. Surprisingly, Reaper didn't continue to rib him for it.

Gunner came out of the spare bedroom, carrying the wide, narrow box I saw him with earlier. He couldn't hold back his grin as he stood next to Reaper, facing Larkan and everyone else.

"I know we have traditions and customs and shit, but I'm drunk and I can't remember 'em now," Reaper began, earning laughs from everyone. "Gun, just open it and give it to 'im."

Gunner pulled open the top of the box, revealing a swath of black leather with the Steel Demons' grinning skull depicted. "Try it on, Lark."

Larkan's face had gone blank with shock when he saw the cut. He reached in slowly, with shaking hands, and held it up for everyone to see. It was indeed the cut of a fully patched-in SDMC member, with his name embroidered on the front. He slipped his arms through the holes and the whole house erupted in applause.

"I don't have a fuckin' road name for ya." Reaper waved his hand in front of him. "Nor an official job title for you yet, but everyone here knows you deserve this patch. You've saved our asses back at the Sandia outpost, and kept my old lady safe in Blakeworth. You're a Demon, Lark. You always have been, even before today. This is just sealin' the deal. Thanks for having our backs, brother."

"Thank you, Reaper," Larkan said so softly, it was almost a whisper.

My husband jumped down from the table and the two men clapped arms around each other in a rough hug. They clung to each other while everyone cheered, whistled, and applauded. When Larkan pulled away, he immediately turned to the stairs where Noelle beamed at him proudly.

"Baby, can you come here?" He extended a hand out to her.

A soft murmur of, *"Awww"* rose up from the onlookers as Noelle came down to join him.

"You better not embarrass me, you—"

Her words cut off abruptly when he dropped to one knee.

The *"Aww"*'s turned to gasps and hushed exclamations. Even I sucked in a breath and brought a hand to my chest.

"Marry me, Noelle." Larkan's eyes were only on her, his hands wrapped around her fingers. "Ever since you and Mari pulled me out of that wreck, I've only wanted two things in life. This cut, and for you to be my old lady."

"Are you...are you serious?" She stared at him, wide-eyed with disbelief.

"I've never been more serious in my life." He brought her fingers to his lips. "I don't have a ring yet, 'cause I wasn't exactly expecting this." He looked back at Reaper with a soft laugh. "But I told you, woman, I'd make you officially mine the moment I got a patch."

"I didn't think you'd do it so...literally," Noelle laughed nervously.

Everyone, Larkan included, seemed to hold their breath as they waited for an answer.

"I love you," he said, kissing her fingers again. "I want to spend the rest of my life taking care of you and whatever family we make."

"Too much information," Reaper muttered, earning a punch on the arm from Gunner.

"So what do you say, baby?" Larkan asked, his nerves starting to show.

Noelle grinned, wrapping her arms around his neck as she leaned over and kissed him, much like the way he did on the stairs.

"Of course I'll marry you, dummy."

The house erupted into cheers so loud, my ears started to ring. That still didn't stop me from joining in the noise as Larkan rose to his feet and picked up Noelle to kiss her again. Her palms against his cheeks, she broke the kiss and said loud enough for everyone to hear, "But pull this embarrassing shit again and I'll divorce your ass."

"We need a toast!" Reaper shouted over everyone's raucous laughter, trying not to bump into people as he headed into the kitchen.

The energy turned up several notches after the proposal. More drinks were flowing and everyone was excitedly congratulating the new couple. Even Tessa was smiling and hugging them both. I was glad and relieved she could feel at least some happiness tonight.

"Hey, Lark!" someone shouted across the room. Imagine my surprise to see that it was Shadow.

"What's up, dude?" the newest Demon grinned after releasing someone from a hug.

Shadow smiled back. "When do you want that tattoo?"

It only took a moment for Larkan to decide. "You good to do it right now?" He lifted up his T-shirt, revealing sculpted pecs and rows of abs. "Give it to me right here, man." He slapped his chest.

Shadow's grin grew wider. "Let me finish my drink and get set up."

"Wooo!" Larkan slid off his new cut and removed his shirt completely.

Much to Noelle's dismay, he whipped the shirt around his head a few times before tossing it in a random direction. He nearly fell over laughing when it landed on Governor Vance's head. Noelle placed a hand on her forehead and turned away, but I saw her shoulders shaking with laughter too.

"Have fun holding that wiggly one down," I said to Shadow as he headed toward his bedroom.

He paused to draw me in for a kiss, gently squeezing my waist. "I know a few tricks of the trade. He won't be nearly as solid as you, though."

His voice was low and warm, husky from just enough alcohol for a light buzz. I would have swooned if he hadn't been holding on to me. I stole a few more kisses before he released me, watching his wide shoulders swing through the door of his bedroom.

I was tipsy enough to consider following him, closing the door, and finally having our first moment alone since he got back. Preferably several moments. Even more preferably, all night long. I wanted him on top of me, inside me, all over my skin. Every taste of him leading up to now felt like meager scraps. Nothing was enough until we had consumed each other whole.

The tattoo would take a few hours, which felt like an eternity right then. I had already waited days, months really, to make this man truly mine. I was at the point where I didn't care who saw. If Shadow wanted to take me bent over the couch, I'd get into position before he finished the sentence.

Despite his growing comfort in social situations, I knew he wouldn't go that far. So I had to keep being a good hostess for the next few hours at least.

Considering people were still using our kitchen table to eat, Shadow decided to set Larkan up on the coffee table. People gathered around to watch, and the newest Demon turned out to be not as wiggly as I thought.

"Can you put Noelle's name on the skull's forehead?" he asked at one point.

"You better not!" Noelle cried from across the room.

"No," Shadow answered in his more serious tone. "The Demon can't be altered in any way. I can put her name somewhere else, though."

"My ass, then." Larkan nodded determinedly.

"We're divorced!" Noelle bellowed, unable to contain her laughter. "Shortest marriage ever!"

"Love you too, babe!" Larkan laced his hands behind his head as Shadow worked.

People started filtering out of the house as the darkest areas of the tattoo were getting filled in. Governor Vance, Finn, and Lis were among the first to leave, making cracks about being too old to party with us as they said their goodbyes.

The house had finally quieted down, with only a few guests remaining as Shadow made the finishing touches on Larkan. Most of them talked quietly with my other men across the house in the sunroom, which they were using as a smoking lounge.

My fourth man twisted and stretched, rolling his neck around on his shoulders once he finally put the tattoo gun down. Larkan thanked him and rolled off the coffee table, looking pretty exhausted himself.

"Had enough of socializing yet?" I asked Shadow, coming up behind him to rub his shoulders.

"Just about hit my limit, yeah." He turned to look at me. "That never includes you, though."

"Smart thing to say," I smirked, circling around him until I landed in his lap.

He snapped his gloves off and pulled me higher up his thigh, kissing me like a starving man. My pulse shot up, heat throbbing between my legs. He was just as responsive and giving as ever, but his kisses seemed far more eager than ever before.

Our lips parted slowly on a breath, his eyes meeting mine before flicking down slightly. I couldn't help myself from leaning in, tracing that scar tissue through his brow and eyelid with my lips.

"Come to my room with me?" he asked so softly, like he was afraid of what the answer might be.

I slid a hand up his chest, the organ inside pounding like a drum under my palm. That steady, firm beat contrasted with the buzzing in my body, the anticipation of finally being with him like a beehive in my chest.

"I'd love that, Shadow."

MARIPOSA

F ollowing Shadow into his room, I turned and locked the door behind me with a soft click. He stood in the center of the room when I turned back to face him, his face a mix of curiosity and apprehension.

"You okay?" I approached him, taking both of his hands.

His fingers squeezed around mine. "I'm just not sure what I'm supposed to do."

"That's okay." I offered him a smile. "We'll learn together. Do you want to sit down?"

He backed up slowly, lowering to sit at the edge of his bed. I placed a knee on either side of his thighs, lowering into his lap as my palms skimmed up his massive shoulders. In the familiar position, some tension drained out of him already, his gaze softening as his hands came around my back.

"You know how to kiss me," I told him, nudging my nose against his. "So why don't we start there?"

Shadow needed no further instruction, his lips finding mine with a soft press. I closed my eyes to return the pressure, seeking nothing but the taste of him. We had all the time in the world now. No dangerous mission to take him away tomorrow. None of our people with gunshots or stab wounds calling me away to the hospital. We were still on the brink of war with all the worries that came with that. But right now, it was just us.

He sighed when my fingers came up to stroke his neck and face, pushing his hair back and dragging my touch along his scalp. One day, he'd figure out how much I just loved touching him.

Kissing him left me breathless. He never rushed or tried to dominate my mouth, but savored each taste along with me. A strong hand left a trail of heat up my back, while the other encircled my waist and pulled me closer. Only after several minutes of kissing, when he'd utterly relaxed into a puddle in my arms, did I prompt him to escalate things further.

My lips trailed across his cheek to his ear. "Touch me anywhere you want to," I whispered, darting my tongue out against his earlobe. "I mean it. Anywhere."

He let out a shuddering groan as my tongue trailed down the side of his neck, sucking lightly at the rapid pulse. His fingers curled at my hip but didn't move for the longest time. I brought a kiss back to his mouth and then, his hand inched under my shirt to graze against my bare skin.

"Can I—"

I grabbed the hem of my top and flung it over my head before he could finish asking the question.

"Yes, Shadow." I palmed the sides of his neck, pulling another deep kiss from him. "Anything you ask me tonight, the answer is going to be yes."

He smiled, beautiful and unrestrained as his fingers now made tentative, exploratory trails of heat on my bare skin. Bolder now, he dragged kisses down the front of my throat. I tilted my head back to give him access, leaning into his hands still caressing me in relatively tame areas. One finger skimmed up my arm, over the tattoo he gave me, then hooked under the bra strap on my shoulder.

He dropped a kiss on my collarbone while slowly pulling the strap down over my arm. I knew he was giving me ample opportunity to stop him, to take back my enthusiastic *yes, anything*. But that was never going to happen.

I pulled my arm out when the strap reached my elbow and removed the other one myself. His gaze flicked back up to mine, our mouths finding each other in another sensual kiss as his hands slid around my ribcage to unhook my bra. He slid the garment out from between us and it fell discarded on the floor.

Hands and forearms covered my naked back as he crushed me to his chest, his kisses growing hungrier with each ragged breath. Just as he did with me, I grazed my fingertips along his waist and dipped them under the hem of his shirt.

"Can I?"

He froze for a moment, then leaned away from me to pull his shirt off his massive body.

For a few seconds, I could only stare and marvel. So, *so* many cuts that had healed and been reopened, overlapping on more that had healed and been reopened, with a few burns thrown in. So many of them were old and had stretched as his body grew. Scar tissue layered on itself again and again on top of muscle, like a type of armor. And probably to him, a kind of cage.

Shadow held his T-shirt in his fists like a barrier between us, his shoulders going rigid again. "I'll put this back on—"

"No." I grabbed the shirt from him and flung it away to the same dark corner where mine now resided. "Whatever you're thinking now, stop."

His brows lifted, eyes blinking as I tapped a finger to his forehead. "Stay out of there and just *be* with me." I placed that same hand on his chest, dragging it over the planes of muscles and scar tissue unabashedly. "I want you, Shadow." My other hand ran along the back of his shoulders, pulling him close to me again. "I want *all* of you."

My next kiss was forceful, shoving my tongue into his mouth while grinding on his erection to drive the point home. The next moan rumbling through him had my core clenching with need. He palmed my ass, squeezing and pulling me forward to increase the friction on him. Finally, *finally*, his touch slid up my ribs to fill his palms with my breasts.

I leaned into the scarred, calloused hands gently kneading and massaging, his breaths quieted as he watched for my response.

"What feels good here?" Shadow's teeth grazed along my shoulder, skimming back up to kiss my neck.

I had to bite back my whimper just at how sexy and low his voice was, never mind what his hands and mouth were already doing.

"That," I gasped when his thumb and forefinger closed around my nipple, the peak already aching. "Anything, really. You can kiss me there too."

He let out a soft hum as his lips trailed lower, kissing the swells of my breasts as his hands continued to explore different touches and my reactions. I was halfway convinced I was soaking through my pants *and* his by the time he pulled a nipple into his mouth.

"Yes!" My fingers curled into his hair at the light drag of teeth on the sensitive point, his tongue quick to soothe the light sting of pain away. "That feels so good..." I was downright drunk on him, this man treating me with such care when he'd gotten so little of it in his lifetime.

I ran my hands down his back when he moved on to my other nipple, resting my cheek on his forehead while I praised and touched him with abandon. At the first chance I got, I'd be kissing every one of those scars. He deserved to feel every bit as good as he was making me feel.

His lips returned to mine when both breasts were marked red from his mouth, nipples and clit thoroughly stimulated and buzzing with need.

"Do you want to lie down?" I asked between kisses.

"Okay," he grunted, already leaning us to the side.

Our kisses never stopped on the way down to the bed. Shadow landed on his side, arms still wrapped around me as I began my scar-kissing journey at the top of his chest.

"Mari?" His mouth rested against my hair, fingers gliding along my sides.

"Mm-hm?" I kissed a deep line cutting across his sternum, tongue flicking out to give it a little extra love.

A hand came under my chin, bringing my gaze up.

"Will you show me how to please you?" The question was asked shyly, his warm gaze resting on my lips with a flush in his cheeks.

I brought his hand to my lips, pressing kisses to the scars on his knuckles until his eyes met mine.

"You already please me *immensely*, just by being you." I kissed his mouth, letting my lips hover over his. "But I can show you how to make me come."

"Yes," he rasped, warm breath fanning over my lips as his eyes heated. "Show me how."

I laced my fingers through his, dragging our joined hands between my breasts and down my belly.

"What most men don't realize," I paused over my jeans, unlinking our hands to get my clothes off easier, "is how important foreplay is to getting us off."

"Is that so?" Shadow mused, flicking open the button and dragging my zipper down. Together we shimmied my pants and underwear down my hips and peeled them off my legs.

"Everything we just did." I touched his face, bringing his attention back upward. "The way you touch me, kiss me, all of that is at *least* half the battle. Making a woman come starts long before her pants come off."

"I'll remember that," he murmured, nuzzling his forehead to mine as he skimmed fingertips across my ribs. "I could do nothing but kiss you for days," he added with a sigh.

Like magnets, our lips connected again. Warm contentment passed through our kisses and it tasted nothing short of delicious on him. I guided his hand on my belly lower, inching toward the heat between my legs that ached for some attention from him. His breath hitched as I led him over my mound and bypassed my clit, despite craving the heaviness of that hand on it, preferably with my legs clamped around him. Instead I guided his fingers through my folds, letting him spread and caress the sensitive flesh.

"Fuck," he bit out, his breath choked. "You're so wet already."

Leaving his hand in place to explore, I returned my palm to his cheek. "Because you turn me on so fucking much."

His smile was shy, face turned down in the pillow next to mine, but those fingers between my legs stroked and caressed with confidence.

"What do you like here?" He gazed along the length of my body, taking in my reactions from my eyes to my toes.

"Exactly what you're doing," I breathed over his lips, an agonizing two inches away. "Don't stop."

He kissed me again, answering my silent plea. His tongue and fingers mirrored each other, stroking and licking, his touch becoming more refined as my body gave him more information. Shadow was incredible at reading me—I learned that from our first kiss. When a finger dipped inside me, I released a gasp, my hips bucking up against his hand.

"Are you okay?" A flash of worry crossed his face and I clamped my thighs around his hand before he could pull it away.

"Yes, yes." I wrapped an arm around the back of his head, pulling him back down to me. "More, Shadow. That feels so good."

With his mouth returned to mine, I directed his hand a bit more, sweeping his thumb over my clit in a motion that had me writhing. "Right there, that's the key to making me come." He hummed thoughtfully in response, his kisses moving to my neck as my instructions came out in breathy pants. "You can curl your fingers inside me—oh, fuck! Yes, Shadow. Just like that..."

Thank all the gods for Shadow being so keenly observant. He tried different angles, varying speeds, depths, and pressures—all of which drove me wild and left me trembling at the mercy of how he played my body.

"You're so beautiful to watch," he murmured, lips dragging a hot trail to my nipple.

I whimpered as he pulled the aching peak into his mouth, fingers gliding steadily in and out of me while his thumb teased my clit. My hips raised off the bed, pressing up into his hand to chase the feeling that crackled over me like electricity.

"Don't stop," I begged, clutching his arm like it would get me there faster. "Shadow, I'm so close."

"Holy fuck..." was the last thing I heard him utter before the blood pounding in my ears became a roar.

My release sent me shaking, pleasure exploding from my core outward like fireworks. Shadow thankfully didn't remove his hand from me until after my pleasure crested, the convulsions around his thick fingers so incredibly satisfying.

"Goddamn." Shadow caressed his hand up my thigh, watching in awe as the shivers wracked through me and my chest became heavy with ragged breaths. "How did that feel?"

"How does it feel when you come?" I grinned breathlessly.

"Pretty fuckin' good, but nothing that looks like that." He palmed my hip and my waist, my wetness on his fingers leaving glossy marks on my skin. "You can do that again, can't you?"

"You're just as bad as Reaper," I laughed, skimming both hands up his chest to wind around his neck. "Give me a minute to catch my breath."

"Fine." I felt his smile in his kiss and pulled him over me until his chest rested on mine with a comforting weight. "I'm not crushing you?" His hands slid under my back, holding me to him.

"No, I love how you feel." My lips found his forehead and eyelids, placing soft, lingering kisses there while I relished in his gentle sighs.

"I love how you feel." His forehead rested against my neck, placing small kisses on my collarbones. "I've never felt so...*good*."

I laughed lightly, scratching over his neck and upper back. "I haven't even done anything to you yet."

"You don't need to." He lifted up from me slightly, returning that mouth to my neck with just enough suction and bite to bring back my shivers. "Pleasing you is just...everything."

I spread my palms on Shadow's back, trying to pull him back down, but he resisted, grinning wickedly as his hand returned to the slick, sensitive flesh between my legs.

"Have you rested enough?"

I answered him with a groan and a deep, tongue-fucking kiss. I wanted his cock, not his hand, but he made no move to even adjust that bulge pressing against the front of his jeans. My leg hooked around his hip, seeing if he would go along with the friction of his pants sliding down, but he remained steadfast and focused on me.

"Can I kiss you here?" he whispered with a swipe of his thumb over my clit.

"Yes," I panted, hips lifting again as I grew dizzy with the realization that he really was going to make tonight all about me. It was both immensely touching and incredibly frustrating. *Shadow, you deserve to get your cock sucked, god damn it.*

He began his journey down my body slowly, rolling my breasts in his hands and savoring my nipples in his mouth like he never wanted to release them. The roughness of his beard awakened the sensitivity of my skin, large hands tracing over my ribs as his kisses moved lower. My eyes closed as I just sunk into the care and gentleness of his touch, fingers running over his scalp and neck.

"What's this from?"

My eyes flew open and I lifted my head. Shadow's black hair spilled like ink over my belly, his face level with the small scar next to my right hip.

"Oh, I got my appendix removed years ago. In high school, I think."

I had honestly forgotten about the scar. It had been a part of me for so long and had faded over the years. If the other guys had noticed it, they made no mention of it to me. They had all probably kissed it at some point and moved on to more interesting parts of me. But Shadow was fixated, inspecting it so closely that his nose pressed against my skin. He traced it with a fingertip and pressed a long kiss to the mark.

"It's beautiful," he murmured, eyes flicking up to mine. "Because it's part of you."

"Shadow, oh—!"

My words were stolen as his mouth fell to my pussy, devouring me with a long, pulling kiss. Hands gripped the outside of my thighs, spreading me open like he was seeking more of me to taste. His tongue dragged from my clit to my opening, lips sucking, kissing, tasting every part of me he could find.

"Shadow..." My thigh pulled against his grip, wanting to clamp around his head and already shaking from the building of another orgasm. It wasn't even from what he was *doing* specifically, just that he couldn't seem to get enough of me.

"Fuck, your taste," he groaned between kisses, nips, and sucks of my flesh. "I want you as a meal every day."

My laughter died on a moan as he slid those well-practiced fingers inside me, his tongue swirling a storm of pleasure around my clit before topping the aching point with a light kiss.

"More, please," I panted, my hips already rolling and fucking his hand as he stilled, amusement dancing in his eyes. "Fuck, I need to come. Shadow, please."

"Mm, I think I want to drag this one out." He kissed my appendectomy scar again, his hand inside me passive while my heels dug into the mattress, desperate for leverage.

"Don't be mean," I whined.

"If you're really not enjoying this, I'll stop." He turned his head and sucked a kiss along my inner thigh, smiling wickedly at my resulting trembles. "But I think you do like it."

"It's too good," I growled, my chest heavy. "You have no business being such a generous lover." I lifted my head to grin at him, to show I was kidding.

"You had no business being so good to me." He kissed my other thigh, lips making a trail to my hip crease. "To make me crave you, want you like I've never wanted anyone." His head rested on my leg for a brief moment, lips shining in my arousal as he looked up at me. "The least I can do is try to be worth the effort."

"Shadow." I sat up as far as I could, reaching for his face. He kissed my palms and that just amplified the yearning in my chest. "You were always worth the effort. I'm still stunned to be the first person to tell you that."

He hugged an arm around my leg, leaning his head against my knee as he stared at me with such pure adoration.

"Maybe it was supposed to be you," he whispered, lips gliding down toward my pussy again. "I can't imagine anyone else making me feel like you do."

My head dipped back as the warmth of his mouth hovered over my clit, his fingers stroking and pressing inside me again.

"Please..."

Finally, his lips sealed over my clit with a groan, the suction so hard and jolting that I cried out. His tongue slid over the hard spot with delicious pressure, aided by his fingers curling inside me and beckoning my orgasm.

"Yes, yes! Like that, don't stop."

He made wet, sucking sounds crashing his hand into me again and again. The moment my walls contracted around him, his moan against my flesh set me off like a stick of dynamite.

I thrashed and shivered, biting the pillow to keep from alerting the whole house as Shadow's mouth and hand rode out my orgasm. Even as I floated down from my finish, he licked my flesh and placed soft kisses on me before withdrawing his hand.

Looking down at him, his grin even looked a bit smug as he leaned against my thigh again. "Well, how was that?"

"Fucking shut up and come here," I laughed breathlessly, holding my arms out to him.

He only managed a few kisses on his way up my body before I tugged impatiently at his hair, laughing huskily as I drew his mouth up to mine and wrapped my arms around his back.

SHADOW

I wasn't a complete stranger to sex. But I'd never had this before—a woman flushed and panting underneath me. Breathless and smiling *because* of me.

From how she kept pulling me down, Mari seemed to like my weight on top of her. Her legs hugged around my waist, arms banded around my back, clinging to me with every kiss. As much as I was dying to sink into her, I was still worried about crushing her, with how fragile she felt underneath me.

"Again?" I mumbled through a kiss on her shoulder, my hand drifting down her body.

"No!" she laughed, nipping the side of my neck with that pain and pleasure mix that made my cock jolt. "You'll spoil me and make me selfish."

"I'm not sure that's possible." I rolled her breast in my hand, watching to see if she'd relent and let me make her come again.

And again.

And again, just for good measure.

Instead she glared at me playfully, tapping my arm. "Roll us over. I want to be on top."

I scooped my hands under her back, taking her with me as I rolled to my side and then my back. She straddled my legs, running her hands over me while sitting straight up. That touch and the view of her gave me a jarring sense of *deja vu*.

"What are you thinking?" Mari seemed to notice right away, fingers stroking over my abdomen before gliding back up to my chest.

"That we've been here before," I admitted.

"We have," she agreed. "Under very different circumstances."

I skimmed my hands up her thighs, taking my grip across her hips and behind to feel the curves of her ass before continuing on to her waist.

"I wanted to touch you like this so badly back then." Her small ribcage felt so fragile, like a bird's, against my palms. My touch reached her breasts, her nipples already tightening from the contact. "I was terrified of scaring you. I already felt guilty enough for—"

"I would've let you." She drew one of my hands up her chest, to her neck and face, turning to kiss my palm. "I thought about kissing you, wondered how you'd react to it."

"Probably not well. Just because I never let anyone get close to my face." I watched her bring my thumb to her lips, biting lightly over the tip. The pressure and light tinge of pain from her teeth made me swell underneath her.

"I like your face, Shadow. I have since I first saw it." She released my thumb, leaning over me with her hands braced on my chest. Her hair tickled my skin before her lips made contact on my sternum. "I like all of you, what's inside and outside." She sucked at the edge of my ribcage, no doubt leaving another dark hickey on me as the sweet tingles of pain expanded from the spot. "You're mine, and I'm happy to keep reminding you of the fact."

"Yours," I groaned, my breaths coming shorter as her kisses moved downward.

My cock was positively aching since she'd first planted herself in my lap, but I expected nothing from tonight except to learn from her. I was painfully aware of being behind the curve when it came to a woman's body, and would've been content to spend the night studying every square inch of Mari. But after only making her come twice, and now that her lips were trailing below my navel, it seemed she had other plans.

"What are you—mm!"

She rubbed the front of my jeans, my length jumping at the pressure of her touch, as if seeking her out.

"Making tonight a little less one-sided." I heard the smile in her voice as she pulled my zipper down.

"It's not one-si—mm, fuck. Mari, you don't have to."

"I know." Her finger dipped into the waistband of my boxer briefs, planting a kiss low on my hip. "But I'd like to, if you'd enjoy it."

My fists curled around the sheets as I sat up to get a better view. Her cheeks were still flushed, her long back stretched out between my legs and her cute ass in the air. She returned my gaze, smiling wider as I slid a pillow behind my back to stay propped up.

"I'll take that as a yes." She began shimmying my pants down, still watching me for a response.

"Oh. Yes, yes." I raised my hips to assist her. "I'd enjoy anything from you."

Her eyes fell to my length as she revealed me, those swollen, well-kissed lips pulling between her teeth. My apprehension returned while she finished stripping me bare. The size of my cock was just another reason on the long list of why women looked at me in fear.

But she stroked me from base to tip, the soft pressure from her palm so sweet I clutched the sheets with a groan.

"Has anyone ever touched you here?" Her fingers glided up and down my shaft, tongue wetting her lips as she stared at it.

"Once or twice," I admitted, my breath tight in my chest. It was only ever to get me hard, or to guide me inside.

For the first time in my life, I was at a woman's mercy and completely unafraid. I was eager for her touch, fighting the urge to jerk my hips through the grip of her hand.

"With their mouth?" she asked, bringing her smile closer to me.

"Uh, n-no," I stammered. "Never that."

Mari's eyes stayed locked on mine as her lips parted, tongue peeking out. Time seemed to move impossibly slow as she neared and I was certain I didn't breathe. Not until her tongue actually met the underside of my head, lips sliding over my crown.

"Ohh, Mar—fuck!"

The softest heat enveloped me, light suction pulling at my head and making me forget how to talk. Mari's tongue circled, licking the tip of me like an ice cream cone while my fists curled and twisted in the sheets.

"This good?" She asked the question tentatively, but her face was anything but. She liked watching me, I realized. She enjoyed putting her mouth on me just to see my reaction.

She *wanted* to please me too.

"So good," I said in a choked whisper, mesmerized at the sight of her. "Please don't stop."

That pink tongue traveled down my stiff length, swirling and licking with the heat of her mouth. She took her time, gliding those soft lips all over my cock like there was nothing else she'd rather do. Mari tasted me indulgently, like I was something *meant* to be enjoyed. She used both hands to stroke me, spreading the wetness from her mouth from base to tip.

I could only groan and curse under my breath, sometimes tipping my head back for a few seconds before I was desperate to watch her again. I had no instructions for her, none. While she so patiently led me through pleasing her, my words disappeared the moment she touched me. There were simply no words that existed for how this woman made me feel.

Mari's palms started twisting in opposite directions, working my length as her sweet mouth returned to my head. She hummed over me, sucking me in like a deep kiss, the vibration of her voice shivering up my back and down to my toes.

So, so good. Holy fuck, I didn't know it could be this good.

I ached to touch her, still a bit stunned that I could do so now without a stab of anxiety in my chest. Her hair spilled like a dark waterfall over my stomach and thigh, and I gathered up the silky strands to hold them out of her face.

Mari released me with a pop of her mouth, flushed and grinning with my dick resting on her lips as she panted for breath.

"Fuck, you're beautiful," I blurted out, my only coherent thought over the last five minutes.

She actually looked shy for a moment, eyes cast down while taking more sensual licks of me, hands still gliding up and down my shaft with sweet pressure.

"You're, um," her teeth came down over her lip, "a bit bigger than I'm used to."

"I'm sorry."

She laughed, leaning her head against my thigh. "Men everywhere would be jealous of you if they knew you had *this*."

"I don't care. I just don't want to hurt you."

"You won't, Shadow." Her mouth returned to me, hands resting on my thighs as she licked every stiff inch of me. "I know you won't. Because I know *you*."

Those lips sealed over my head again and I was fucking done for. She gripped my base, jerking upward as her mouth moved down, that tongue feeling like fucking heaven pressing on the underside.

"Oh fuck, Mari...fuck, yes..." Every word came out strangled, ripping out from my chest with a tight breath.

My hands sought out her shoulders, her back, her face, just desperate to feel more of her. I wanted her touch like a brand on me, as if it could erase my decades of scars. My greedy, frenzied touch found a breast and rolled her nipple between my fingers, palm kneading her soft flesh.

She moaned over me, taking me deeper in her mouth. I tapped the back of her throat and a growl dragged out of me. That couldn't have felt good for her, but her throat squeezed around my dick like—

"Oh God, Mari! Fuckkk..."

She sucked me down again, and—oh fuck—again. Her whole mouth slid over me, taking greedy gulps as she reached further down my shaft. My hips started bucking towards her face before I was aware of doing it, tapping the back of her throat eagerly for that tight feeling that made me see stars.

Stop, don't hurt her. Don't you dare fucking hurt her.

But every time I pulled back, she descended on me for more. Lips and hands now met each other on my shaft, her mouth so hot and wet and soft. Her cheeks hollowed out, sexy moans and whimpers floating up as she sucked me greedily.

"Mari, I'm so fucking close," I rasped. "Where do you want me to—ungh, God..."

She just stroked me faster, brows pinching with effort as she took me deeper, harder down her throat. Her breaths quickened too and she moaned even louder. No, she wouldn't really want me to finish in her mouth...would she?

"Mari," I tried again, keeping my grip on her shoulder as light as I could muster. "I'm about to come."

"Mm-hm," was the only reply I got before the sweet ache became overwhelming.

Sensation left my fingers and toes, the digits numb as pleasure concentrated in the base of my spine, licking out like flames of heat as Mari drew it out of me with her hands and mouth.

And then, sweet explosive release.

I was at her mercy, boneless as the sensitivity crashed over me, so intense it was almost painful. Her mouth never left me until I was utterly drained. Even as I began to soften, she licked me through the shivers and aftershocks.

My heart pounded like a drum, my whole body spent and rubbery like I'd just completed a workout. Mari crawled up the mattress, licking her lips and grinning as she slid down to nestle into my side, her cheek over my drumming heart.

"Again?" she joked, fingertips trailing over my chest.

I huffed out a breathless laugh, placing a kiss in her sweet-smelling hair. "I don't recover anywhere near as quickly as you do."

"In the morning, then." She lifted her head, brushing kisses over the scars that touched the edges of my tattoo.

"Not if I get you off first." My arm slid along her back, cupping her hip before I realized what she said. "Wait, morning?"

"Or in the middle of the night. Whenever someone wakes up first." She slid down a few inches, placing a kiss on one of my ribs before looking up, eyes brightening. "If you want to turn this into a race, it's on, Shadow."

"So, you're..." I hoped to every god listening that I wasn't misinterpreting this. "...spending the night with me?"

She looked bewildered before bringing a playful bite down on my nipple.

"Ow."

"Of course I am! You're not a booty call." Her hand slid across my abdomen, hugging around my waist. "That is, if you want me here."

"I do, yes." I wrapped both arms around her, drawing her mouth up toward mine with a hand under her jaw. "Stay with me."

"Happily," she murmured, fingertips grazing the scar on my cheek as our mouths connected.

Her kisses tasted softer now, if that was even possible. Our lips and tongues collided with a lazy satisfaction that I just wanted to sink into, to drown in. She sighed and hummed content little noises that I couldn't get enough of, hands stroking over me so gently. We kissed until the need for air forced us to separate, and even then I never wanted to stop tasting her skin.

"Mari?" I whispered against her forehead.

"Hm?"

"What's a booty call?"

She laughed into my neck, shoulders shaking before peppering more kisses on me.

"It's if I were to come see you to get laid and nothing else." Her fingertips danced over my chest. "I'd get what I want and then leave."

"Oh." I ran my fingers down her spine, feeling each of the bumps on her back. "You don't do that to anyone."

"No." She grinned up at me and tapped a finger to my nose. "You're stuck with me."

I pulled her closer until she was flush to me with a leg over mine. "I can think of far worse places to be stuck." *I was in one for over twenty years.*

No, I wouldn't let my mind go there tonight. At some point I would tell her, but not now. That long, miserable part of my life almost didn't seem real compared to this. In a single lifetime I'd somehow felt the deepest despair, and also the greatest joy I'd ever known—which was right now, and every moment with her.

It felt impossible for this woman, nestled in my arms and kissing me, to exist in the same universe as the ones who had carved into me like an animal. My brain still had to process that lips and hands were running tenderly over the same places I had bled for simply being born male. Mari was kissing my shoulder now, lips tracing years-old scars with the occasional soft lick from her tongue.

"I'm going to kiss all of these." Her smile was warm on my skin. "Just so you're aware."

"Huh," I mused. "You'll be here a long time."

She settled against my side, cheek resting over my heart. "That's the plan, Shadow."

I caressed a hand over her cheek, just taking in the face of this beautiful woman who saw something in me that she was determined to care for. "You really want me to be yours?"

"You *are* mine," she corrected. "If I have to suck your dick again to prove it, so be it."

"I thought you were going to do that anyway."

"I'll leave a hickey on your dick. There, double proving it."

I laughed, nudging my nose against hers. "I do like it when you mark me up with hickeys. It feels like you're claiming me."

"Then I'll keep doing it." Her eyelids blinked slowly, heavy with sleepiness as her palm settled over my chest. "I like seeing you happy, Shadow."

Stretching one arm over to the nightstand, I turned off the bedside lamp before returning my arm to wrap around her protectively.

"I'm happy because of you," I whispered, now that we were bathed in darkness. "I never thought it was possible but it feels like...you're healing me."

Mari curled into me, releasing a sigh as she settled against my body for sleep. "You deserve it."

As her breathing deepened and my own eyelids fell shut with fatigue, I wanted so badly to believe her.

MARIPOSA

A loud noise jolted me awake.

I had been so deeply asleep, I was only vaguely aware of the noises in the room until the bed lifted and I was suddenly rolling toward the opposite side. The whole world spun like I was in a hamster wheel until coming to a sudden, hard stop.

"What the—fuck, ow!"

Well, *now* I was awake. And, once I got my bearings, realized I was on the floor between the wall and the upturned bed.

Huh?

I knew *where* I was, but still couldn't make sense of anything. The room was completely dark. It had to be the middle of the night or very early morning. Was it an earthquake?

It wasn't until I heard the heavy footsteps pacing around the room, the pained groans, and the fists thumping at walls and whatever furniture was in the way, that started to clue me in.

Oh no.

"Shadow?" I called, my voice weak and timid.

No answer came except for more pacing, more thumps and bangs with the occasional whimper mixed in. I scooted along the floor, daring to peek around the upturned bedframe and mattress to look. What I saw broke my heart.

Shadow paced back and forth in the center of the room, no bigger than a six-by-six foot square, scratching at his arms as he whimpered and muttered to himself. He stopped abruptly to clutch at his head and release a pained cry into his hands. Then he swung his arms, catching the nearby chair and flinging it at the wall with a moan of pain I felt split my heart wide open.

My panicked gaze swept across the floor littered with his things. It was so dark, I could only make out rough shapes, but one bright object gave me all the answers— the bottle of his sleeping pills.

Oh no. Oh, Shadow!

The orange container had fallen off of the nightstand—which now lay in pieces on the other side of the room. His pills scattered along the floor, the bottle on its side against the baseboard. He must have forgotten to take one last night. It was the only explanation for this.

My sweet, brave man was in the grips of a nightmare.

"Fucking *stop*!" he bellowed, falling to his knees with his hands over his face. "I didn't *do* anything!" His chest wracked with a sob, a sound that made my heart shatter and want to run over and hold him, to love and soothe him. I went so far as to take three steps, my hand outstretched, before stopping myself and shrinking back against the wall.

Fifteen minutes. I remembered what Jandro told me when I first heard Shadow having a nightmare. These episodes only lasted for about fifteen minutes. Getting close to him during that time was dangerous, as Jandro had learned. I had to stay quiet and let the night terrors run their course. Then I'd have *my* Shadow back.

But it killed me to do nothing, to just watch him suffer instead of shaking him into awakeness. Every part of me yearned to touch him, to remind him that I was here and that he was safe. It went against every one of my instincts to do nothing, even if the suffering he endured was in his mind and no longer his body.

Shadow stayed on his knees, hands covering his face for a few long minutes before I started scooting out from my hiding place. He seemed calmer now that a bit of time passed since his last outburst. Maybe it was over.

My eyes drifted to his cut, now discarded on the floor. I reached for the soft leather, feeling around until I found one of the daggers he always kept hidden, just to protect myself if necessary. I hated that it was the same type of weapon that triggered him, but it was all I had.

I approached him slowly, the weapon low and slightly behind me so as not to alarm him with the sight of it.

"Shadow?" I called tentatively from several feet away.

His gaze snapped up to me, but there was no recognition in his eyes. He scowled cruelly, an expression I'd never once seen him wear. On his face, the same one I couldn't get enough of kissing, such a scowl looked downright terrifying.

"What do you want from me, bitch?" he ground out, the bitterness in his voice making him sound like a completely different person. "Haven't you taken enough already?"

"Shadow," I gasped, my heart now withering at how harshly he spoke to me. "It's me, Mari. I don't want to hurt you."

"I'm not falling for that again. Just leave me alone." He curled up into himself, arms wrapping around his knees like a child would.

I have to get out of this room, I realized.

He hadn't lashed out physically yet, but now I understood why Jandro locked him in his room back in Sheol. Shadow was wildly unpredictable in this state, his body curled up and muscles coiled so tight, like the smallest thing could set him off.

I pressed myself against the wall, following its path as I took slow steps heading for the door. He looked so sad but I couldn't help him, not while he was like this. When I reached the far corner of the room where my clothes had been discarded the night before, I hurriedly stepped into my underwear and jeans, keeping my eyes locked on him until I reached for my shirt. I had to set the blade down and did so without a sound, but the reflection of silver metal must have caught his eye.

Shadow's head snapped over to me, and he moved before I could blink. My mind could barely register his hand around my throat, the force with which he swung his arm and took me with him. The pain, the squeezing. The sudden lack of air making my lungs cry out. None of it could be real, not from him.

Shadow would never hurt me. The thought screamed in my head as I crashed to the floor, my forehead pounding as I tried to orient myself, tried to get away. *This isn't him.* Cruel fingers closed in my hair and yanked my head up as I screamed.

"Shadow, stop!" I cried, clawing desperately at his arm and fist. "Wake up!"

He pulled my head back by my hair, his grip callous and the angle of my neck so painful I thought it might break. Then he shoved me down as he released me, my forehead and nose slamming on the floor with pain that rattled my skull. Wetness coated my face, getting into my mouth and clogging my sinuses as I coughed and struggled to breath.

The weight of his grip came down on my head again and I fought desperately to scramble away across the floor, but he pulled me back, hair yanking painfully from my scalp.

"No, no, please! Help!"

Shadow pulled my head to the side, forcefully turning my whole body over onto my back. I let out a choked cry at the sight of him above me, pain stabbing through my head and whole body from his abuse. My heart felt just as abused, tearing, pulling, and screaming over this heartless man I didn't recognize.

The same eyes that watched me so carefully for any discomfort now radiated pure hatred. The same hands that pleased me so thoroughly were now instruments in hurting me as much as possible. Nothing hurt as much knowing the same person was capable of two such extremes.

"How does it feel?" he asked cruelly, lifting my head once again to let it thump back on the floor. "To be trapped and bleeding? To feel small and helpless?"

"Shadow, please..." I wheezed, coughing on the blood that trickled into my mouth from my nose, only to feel his other hand clasp around my throat.

"I've always wanted to do this," he continued, fingers pressing into my flesh. "To make you suffer as I have."

"HELLLP!" I screeched at the top of my lungs, knowing I wouldn't have a voice for much longer. "Somebody help me!"

"Mari!"

I heard thumping at the door, and saw the wood buckle as its hinges groaned to keep it in place.

"Reaper!" I called. "Help me! Hel—"

My cry choked off as Shadow's hand tightened, black dots swarming my vision as I struggled to breathe. Trapped in his nightmare, he didn't pay any attention to the door or how I pleaded and fought for my life. I kicked my legs out and clawed at his hand, but my strength was nothing compared to his.

Still I lashed out at him, fighting with everything I had left, even as my limbs grew heavier, his cruel scowl above me fading to blackness. Sensation started to leave my body, leaving me to sink into the worst heartbreak I'd ever felt. This loving, gentle man was literally killing me because of the abuse *he* had endured.

I'm so sorry, Shadow...

I knew the sleeping pills were only a band-aid solution to the nightmares. He pushed back when I broached the idea of getting more help, but I should have insisted. Maybe then we would have a normal night together, waking each other up with soft words, more kisses and exploring touches.

As the darkness began to swallow me up, I only wished that I hadn't been too late to save him.

REAPER

"Wake up."

"Huh?"

I blinked slowly to see Daren standing at the foot of the bed.

"Wake up, Rory. She needs you."

"Why, what's—"

Something cracked over the side of my face like a hand slapping me, and then I really did wake up.

"What the fuck?" I grumbled, rubbing my eyes.

Hades growled at my bedside, teeth glinting white in the dark room.

"What's gotten into you?" I peered at him.

A thumping sound came from somewhere in the house, making me pause and listen. It was only our third night in the new house, and Vance's builders insulated it like a fortress. I still couldn't tell exactly where noises were coming from.

I heard another thump, and then a scream. A woman's scream.

"Fuck, Mari!"

I shot out of bed, Hades already running down the hallway. Wearing nothing but my boxers, I somehow found the coordination in my panicked state to race down the stairs to Shadow's room. I jiggled the knob. Locked, of course. I jammed my shoulder hard into the door and it didn't budge. Fucking Vance just had to make every door in the house from solid oak.

"Shadow!" I yelled through the wood, slamming my fist against it. "Open the door!"

"No, no, please! Help!"

Mari's fear-stricken cry from inside spurred me into desperate, frantic action. My mind was blank except for the burning *need* to get her out. I tried my shoulder again, then a kick to the door, to no avail.

Fuck, fuck, fuck I had no time! What could I do?

"Helllp! Somebody help me!"

"Mari!" I slammed and clawed at the wood like I could tear through it. "Shadow, let her go! I'll fucking kill you if you don't!"

Her screams cut off with strangled coughs and wheezes. Crazed, desperate fear consumed me as I unleashed every ounce of my strength into that door. No, I could *not* lose her, but she was going to die if I didn't get in that room.

You'll have to break down the door, Reaper. She'll die if you don't.

I stopped assaulting the door and looked around behind me, eyes landing on the bronze sculpture next to the stairs just as Jandro, Gunner, and Hades came flying down from the second level.

"What's going on?" Jandro demanded.

"Bring that over," I said, pointing. "Fucking now!"

It took both of them to carry the heavy thing to me. Once in front of the door, the three of us held it like a battering ram, flat base toward the door, and started swinging.

"On three," I instructed, my chest already collapsing like a black hole at the silence in the room. "One, two, *three*!"

We used momentum and all of our strength to drive the bronze into the door. The wood splintered and buckled at the first hit, but didn't open. On the second try, it caved in and with a kick from Jandro, the damn door finally crashed open.

None of us stopped to assess, we just acted. We saw Shadow kneeling on the floor with his hand around Mari's throat, her face covered in blood and her body too fucking still. All three of us went straight for Shadow, but Jandro and Gunner were faster. While they pulled him off of her, tackling him to the ground, I feared the worst as I went to check on my wife.

"M-Mari..." I shook so fucking hard, my teeth chattered as I leaned over her to listen for breathing. But Jandro and Gunner were whaling on Shadow and I couldn't hear shit over the pounds of fists on flesh.

My trembling fingers felt along the side of her neck, and I wanted to scream at the feel of tacky blood on her skin. How the fuck could this have happened? How could we *let* this happen?

Her pulse was weak but steady under my fingers, and a shaky sigh of relief escaped me, my head dropping heavily.

"She's alive...she's alive." Coherency was flowing back to my brain now that I knew we still had her, at least for now. "We have to get her to the hospital."

"What do we do with him?" Gunner shook out his fist, his face full of disdain for Shadow, now lying passed out between him and Gunner. Jandro on the other hand, appeared torn, his face a grimace of pain as he looked between Mari and the friend we'd all wrongly trusted with her.

I didn't give a shit how he felt.

Once we got Mari stable, Shadow's life was mine to take.

"Throw him in the governor's jail at City Hall," I ordered, scooping Mari up carefully. "I'll deal with him later."

Dawn was peeking over the sky once Dr. Brooks came to update me, his sneakers squeaking over the tiled hospital floor. I rose up from the waiting room chair, Hades and I walking up to meet him.

"How is she?" I demanded before he could get a word out.

The doctor gave me an odd look, his brows knitting over the frames of his glasses, almost as if he was suspicious of me.

"She's doing okay, resting now. Some ligaments in her neck have torn, so she'll need to be in a neck brace for a few weeks and will be sore for a while. But she'll make a full recovery."

I will kill him. Then I'll bring him back to life so I can kill him again. He'll wish for the filthy cage he was born in when I'm done with him.

"Thank fuck." My head tipped backward, eyes closed in relief despite the rage roaring in my ears. "Can I see her?"

"Not tonight." The doctor was tight-lipped and firm. "She is sedated and the most important thing she needs right now is rest. And," he lifted his chin at me, "before you speak with her, we'll need to hear from her what happened."

I blinked at him. "I told you what happened."

"Yes, but," he sucked in a breath, "should your wife tell us a different version of events, we'll need to take her account into consideration. Everyone at this hospital has gotten to know Mariposa and cares deeply about her. We'll keep her safe."

The implication of his words sent my blood boiling. My fingers itched at my sides to swing into his judgmental face, but I knew that wouldn't help me.

"She is *my wife.*" My teeth felt like boulders grinding against each other.

"Yes, well, she wouldn't be the first woman on earth abused by a spouse."

"How dare you fucking—" I forced myself to stop, spinning away from the doctor before I crashed a fist through his jaw.

My breaths sawed in and out of my chest as I fought to keep myself from losing my shit. I had barely saved her in time, and now this overeducated prick was talking to me like I'd done this to her myself.

I fucking might as well have, I realized with despair. How could I not have seen this happening? Jandro had gotten dozens of black eyes and split lips from trying to subdue Shadow during his nightmares. We all should have known Mari wouldn't have been able to tame him completely. He was too much of a loose cannon, but Mari seemed to be doing so well with him that we got careless.

Now he hurt what was most precious to me. And I fucking let it happen.

"You're right about one thing, Dr. Brooks," I said, turning back to face him. He was still there, arms crossed and eyebrows raised at my concession. "I didn't lay a hand on her, but I also didn't protect her from the man that did this. And for that, I'm a shitty husband."

Dr. Brooks dipped his chin in a small nod of acknowledgment, the wrinkles smoothing out in his forehead.

"But I can promise you one thing, doctor." My hand drifted down to skim my fingertips along Hades' back. "I'm never allowing this to happen again."

MARIPOSA

O^{w.}

Oh fucking *ow*. Everything hurt. And I was so thirsty.

My eyelids weighed down like bricks as I tried to force them open. The first peek of light hurt too, sending a stabbing pain that ricocheted through my whole skull.

"Ah, Sleeping Beauty's waking up." Rhonda's voice was like a hug to my ears. "Take it easy, sweetheart. I know it hurts, I'm giving you a little something."

"Uh, wha..." I could barely get a whisper out, my throat was so dry.

"I got it for you, hon. Give me a sec."

I tried to look down at my hand, but the movement was stopped by something hard underneath my chin. Attempting to look to either side was also stopped. My sore fingertips flew up to my neck, touching the stiff piece of plastic holding me still. A dull ache ran from my fingertips down my arm, and I raised my hands to find bruised fingers and broken, jagged nails. A jolting reminder of what happened.

"How..." My whispery voice shook, as did my hands. "How did I...?"

"Survive? By a miracle. Drink up, sweetheart. I know you're parched."

Rhonda held the glass out in front of me, which thankfully had a straw. The sweet ache of cool water running down my throat awoke new pains, memories of being unable to breathe and feeling certain I would die.

Rhonda watched me shrewdly as I drank, her eyes like a hawk's. "I know you're in shock and in pain, but is there anything I need to know, Mariposa?"

"I..I..." *can't believe Shadow wouldn't recognize me, that he wouldn't stop.*

His face hovered with startling clarity in my mind, the mismatched eyes so full of hatred they were unrecognizable. Fresh pain sliced through my chest at the memories from earlier in the evening, when he made me feel so good, contrasted with when he hurt me so badly.

"Here's an easier question." Rhonda gripped the foot of my bed. "Do your injuries have anything to do with the biker president that won't leave the waiting room?"

Reaper! Reaper was here, which meant he had managed to get me out.

"No." I tried to clear my throat, wincing at how much it hurt to talk. "No, h-he didn't do this."

Rhonda nodded, accepting that answer. "He's been wanting to see you. Are you up for visitors?"

I tried to pull my head down in a nod, before remembering the neck brace holding me immobile. "Y-yes. You can let him in."

"Ten minutes, max," she told me sternly as she turned to leave. "You need to rest."

The moment I saw Reaper, all my frozen shock melted away. Fat tears rolled down my cheeks as he entered my room. By the time he reached my bedside and put his arms around me, I was full-on sobbing.

"Mari," he choked, his breaths ragged and green eyes filled with unspilled tears. "Fuck, baby, I—"

"You saved me," I rasped, cupping his face. "Thank all the gods you were there."

"I almost wasn't." He pressed his hand over mine, blinking and making a single tear track down his cheek. "If I had been even a minute late, he could've—"

"It's okay." I wiped his tear away and pulled him forward to kiss his forehead. "I'm okay, and I love you."

"You shouldn't be the one comforting me," he huffed, holding my hands and squeezing them like he'd never let go. "It's never happening again, sugar. I promise you. I never should have let it happen in the first place, but I'll spend every last breath I have protecting you. I swear."

His eyes hardened as he spoke, the ruthless scowl growing deeper on his face. I knew he was trying to make me feel safe, but the knot in my gut just twisted and contorted even tighter.

"What are you saying?" I asked.

Reaper's hands lowered to my lap. "Shadow is going to answer for what he did to you, of course."

"But he..." My brain spun, trying to reconcile all the conflicting feelings in my body, my heart, and my gut. Terror still gripped me, my brain flashing images of my last moments of consciousness in an attempt to process the trauma. My heart raced, the panic still running high. And right alongside those images and sensations, I saw the Shadow I knew. The one I loved and trusted just as much as any of my men. I may have felt all kinds of contradictory ways, but I knew one thing for certain— the truth.

"It was an accident, Reaper."

My husband's eyes were venomous as he straightened up, all tears gone in the wake of his hard set jaw. "Don't, Mari. Don't you dare defend him, not on this."

"He forgot to take a pill," I insisted. "I was so scared, more than I've been in my life, but he wasn't in his right mind—"

"Stop. Just stop." Reaper raised a hand, squeezing his eyes shut. "Are you listening to yourself?" he demanded, his pulse throbbing in his neck as he fought to keep his voice at a normal level. "He almost ki—fuck, I can't even say it, Mari."

"But he didn't," I argued. "Because you were there. This was what Daren was telling you about."

Rhonda pushed in before he could argue, which was excellent timing on her part. My husband's shoulders shook with rage and I knew this battle wasn't over.

"Alright, up and at 'em," the nurse held the door open. "Mari needs to rest."

Steeling himself with a deep breath, Reaper leaned in and planted a fast kiss on my lips. "I'll be back tomorrow. I love you."

"Love you..." My voice had already faded away, weariness sinking into my limbs.

I felt like a different person before even opening my eyes the next morning. Everything still hurt, but with more of a dull ache than the stabbing, blinding pain of the night before. Cracking my eyes open was easier, and it didn't even hurt to smile at the black cat lounging on my hospital bed.

"Hey, Freyja." My voice felt stronger too as I held my fingers out to her. She butted my hand with a loud purr, coming closer to rest in my lap. "I was about to thank the gods for strong drugs," I whispered, petting down her back. "But it's you healing me, isn't it? Healing us all."

I didn't get an answer besides an intense stare from those sharp green eyes. In the wake of what happened, I was hoping she'd have more to say. This cat had loved on Shadow since she first appeared to me. My connection to him had been guided by this goddess' presence, and now that connection was wounded, if not severed completely.

"Did you know this would happen?" I asked, stroking lightly over the cat's head. "Did you know he would..." My fingers began to shake, heart speeding up too fast in my chest. Accelerated physical healing apparently did nothing for my emotional state. At least *I* didn't have any nightmares yet. That, I could thank the drugs for.

His mind is still deeply wounded and has not healed. The warm, omniscient voice rolled over me moments later. *Regressions are to be expected with someone as fragile as him.* Freyja looked directly at me. *I would not have taken you, daughter. You still have much to do.*

"So, I wouldn't have died?"

The limits of the human body can be extended by the strength of the spirit, but even that is not infallible. The cat's ears flicked back and forth. *I would have held onto you for as long I could have managed. But there was no need.*

"Because Reaper was there, thanks to Daren." My fingers nervously curled and extended over the sheets. "He's not going to let Shadow get away with this. I'm worried, Freyja."

It felt wrong to feel worried. Shadow *did* attack me. I'd never felt so scared in my life and the roiling, sickening feeling in my gut was as strong as ever. If it were any other man who hurt me after spending the night together, there would be no questions. I'd let my men dole out whatever grueling punishment they saw fit. I'd happily never see the man again.

But this was Shadow. I felt guilty for feeling so afraid of him, and then gut-wrenching confusion about the guilt.

It was a simple mistake. One with terrible, painful consequences, but I'd bet my life he never would have raised a finger to harm me in his right mind. Wrapped up in each other that night, his sleeping pills were the furthest thing from my mind, and most likely his as well.

I turned over every moment of our evening in my mind. His touches had been so hesitant before they were confident, and even then, he made sure to be careful with me. None of that lined up with the cold, aggressive man who assaulted me.

"I still want to help him heal," I said to Freyja. "It'll have to be different, but we *can* make it happen. I know we can."

A soft knock rapped at my room door, and I looked up to see Reaper and Gunner shouldering their way in.

"There she is," Reaper said softly. "Looking a lot better already."

"Brought you these." Gunner produced the bouquet of flowers from behind his back with a lopsided smile. Red and golden sunflowers immediately brightened up the drab hospital room.

"Thank you, Gun." I beamed up at them. "I'll have Rhonda find a vase for them."

"You sound so much stronger too." Reaper leaned over the bed to kiss me, scratching Freyja as he pulled back. "Guess that's thanks to you, huh?"

The cat closed her eyes with a proud purr as Reaper moved aside so Gunner could kiss me.

"How are you, baby girl?" Gunner pulled a chair up next to my bed, blue eyes wide and searching my face, and I knew he didn't mean just physically.

"I'm...okay. Still kind of shaken, I guess."

He nodded, taking one of my hands to kiss. "We're never letting this happen to you again."

I swallowed, not wanting to argue with my men when they were only concerned and eager to take care of me.

"Where's Jandro?"

Gunner let out a disdainful scoff, dropping my hand. "With *him.*"

Reaper focused his gaze on me, not missing a single breath or twitch of my face. So much for not arguing. It seemed we'd be continuing our conversation where we left off.

"Where—" I swallowed, clearing my still-sore throat. "Where are you keeping him?"

"Contained," Reaper said flatly.

"And what will you do?"

Gunner took both of my hands, moving to sit next to me on my bed since I still couldn't turn my head to face him. "Mari...you have to understand, there's only one option, right?"

"What, kill him?" My eyes darted between his and Reaper's. I knew in my gut that was their answer to this, but I needed to hear it from them.

"It's not up for discussion." Reaper's voice was flat and emotionless. "I'll take no pleasure in doing it, but it has to be done."

"Reaper, you can't!" I pulled away from Gunner's hands to reach for his. "Love, please listen to me. He needs help."

"I don't give a fuck what *he* needs," he growled between his teeth. "Shadow had his chance to be with you and fucked it up beyond all repair. He already doesn't deserve the privilege of breathing right now."

"It was an *accident*!" I cried.

"Baby girl." Gunner stared at me, his voice low in an attempt to be calming. "It sucks what he's been through, yes. But there has to be consequences for what he did to you."

"Okay, I agree with that, but killing him is *not* the answer!" I grabbed for his arm. "Please listen to me, Gun. You know Shadow wouldn't hurt anyone, you both know that."

"He *did!*" Reaper yelled, so loud that he made the windows rattle in their panes. He turned away for a moment, scrubbing his hands down his face. Then he mumbled, "Gun, can we have a minute?"

Gunner frowned, but then nodded sharply. He bent down to kiss my forehead before turning and swiftly exiting the room. A long, uncomfortable silence stretched between me and Reaper, and I knew his temper was close to snapping. Not even Freyja could soothe the tension in the room.

"Do you still want to be with him?" The question came out of him so quietly, I nearly missed it.

"I'm not sure," I admitted. "I...I don't know about that, but I do want to keep helping him after...we have some time to move on from this."

"Move on from this?" Reaper repeated, incredulous.

"Sorry, I'm still tired and shaken up. I might not use the best words to fit the situation, okay?"

"Situation?" he went on. "For fuck's sake, Mari. Why do you keep downplaying this?"

"Because he didn't *mean* to do it!" I cried out, exasperated. "Yes, I was scared. Yes, it was awful, and my feelings are all confused but I'm sure of *that*, Reaper. And you know it, too. If he had only taken a pill—"

"Do I have to tell you what I saw?" Reaper's voice cracked. "Because I'll paint that picture. I broke the door to find him on top of you, his hands around your neck, your face covered in blood—"

"I know. I was there," I cut in, sounding more snippy than I intended. "I felt everything. I couldn't breathe and thought for sure I was going to die. I *know* how bad it was."

My husband's face crumpled with despair. "Then how can you excuse any of it?"

"I'm not," I sighed. "Something does need to happen. I'm not spending the night with him again until—"

"You are *never* seeing him again," Reaper snarled. "He is not worthy to be yours and never will be."

"That's *my* decision, Reaper."

"God damn, fuck everything." He lowered his head into his hands, fingers tearing through his hair. "I was really hoping you'd come to your senses after you got some rest."

"I have," I insisted. "I'm feeling a lot more certain about this now than yesterday."

"Mari, please..."

His voice softened to a whisper, a plea of desperation tugging at my heart. He dragged a chair next to my bed and sat down, tears filling his eyes as he took my hand. "Please try to understand where I'm coming from. I *love* you—"

"I love you too," I said.

"No, listen." He drew in a shaky breath, fingertip rubbing over the stone on my ring. "You are my *wife*. My whole world." One hand stretched out to caress my waist and lower abdomen. "I want to put my babies inside you and watch them grow." He huffed out a humorless laugh. "If I break a hip in forty years, I want it to be because I was chasing your fine ass. If he—" Reaper's breath stuttered as his grip tightened on my hand. "If he had taken all of that away from me...I don't know what I'd do, Mari. I'd have *nothing*. Do you understand?"

I turned toward him, sliding my hands up to his shoulders, caressing his neck and scalp. His arms came around my waist to hold me, his face in my chest.

"I love you so much," I whispered, brushing kisses across his forehead. "You're my husband in body and spirit, the father of my future children." My whole body felt heavy, like a pile of bricks, as I brought my lips to his ear. "But if you kill him—" My breath halted, stuck in my chest for a moment before I pushed through. "I'm sorry my love, but if you do this, I can't ever forgive you."

SHADOW

My head pounded like the worst fucking hangover. Which was odd, considering I made sure to keep my drinking under control at the party. I rubbed my temples with a groan, confused to find sticky, flaky blood stuck to my skin.

"What..." My eyes fluttered open with the quick realization that I was not in my bedroom. I was in a jail cell, the bars reminiscent of the cage I grew up in. And Mari was nowhere to be found.

"What the fuck?" I demanded of the barren, cold room as I scrambled to my feet. "What happened?"

No one was around to answer me. I inspected my hands and arms, cold dread seeping in at the state of myself. Dried blood and scratches covered my hands and forearms. Bruises and splinters were embedded in my skin. A throbbing in my head. I touched my face gingerly, feeling the swelling around my eye and jaw.

"Mari..."

I fell asleep next to her with no clothes on. Now I was alone, in a dark, dingy jail cell, dressed haphazardly in a pair of pants. A shirt had been crumpled and tossed onto the cot in my cell.

Panic gripped my chest, the sensation as unwelcome as it was familiar. I hadn't felt like this in weeks and now it was back with a vengeance.

Oh fuck, no. Fuck, what did I do?

I walked up to the iron bars, wrapping my hands around them as I took in my surroundings. The room had other jail cells, but mine was the only one occupied. There were no windows, so I had no idea what time of day it was or how long I'd been out. Nothing good came from me waking up in strange places and feeling like roadkill, I knew that much.

Did I take a sleeping pill?

The thought cut through me, anxiety slashing from my abdomen to my throat as I replayed the details of that night. My bottle of pills had been on the nightstand, like always. Then Mari came to my room with me and...I forgot about everything outside of being with her. She finished pleasing me and we talked, held each other. She started falling asleep and then I...

No...

No.

Oh please fucking God, no.

I slammed my forehead on a cross bar, wishing I could feel the pain rattling through my skull. I deserved it a hundred times over if I really...

Maybe I didn't. I could never, not to her.

But waking up alone in a cage never boded well for me.

Did I... Fuck, what if I...

I couldn't bring myself to complete the thought, a wave of nausea surging through me until bile coated my throat.

I'd never killed anyone by accident. Every life I took had been intentional and with purpose. But Mari...fucking sweet, beautiful Mari...

I was a dead man if I did. And also if I didn't, most likely. I didn't care. If I had a weapon nearby, I'd end my own life so Reaper wouldn't have to burden himself with the task. He could keep Mari safe—if she was still alive—while the vultures picked at me until I was forgotten. That would be better for everyone.

A door at the far end of the room opened, light pouring in from a hallway. I instantly recognized the silhouette of the man walking through and my heart dared to leap with a tiny spark of hope.

"Jandro!"

"Shadow," he greeted gruffly.

There was no humor in his voice—no easygoing, lighthearted demeanor as he came in and leaned against the bars of my neighboring cell to stare at me. His jaw was tense, muscles jumping in his arms like he was dying to take a swing at me.

No, the tension radiating off his body was more intense than that. He looked like he wanted to kill me.

"Jandro," I breathed, fists tightening around my bars. "What did I do?"

"You don't remember?"

"No." I rocked my forehead from side to side against the bars. "Mari and I...we fell asleep together and...then I woke up here."

He nodded without an ounce of sympathy. "One of your usual episodes then."

"Jandro..." I looked down at my bare feet, unable to meet his eye. "...did I hurt her?"

It felt like an eternity passed before he answered. "She's at the hospital, in stable condition. Reap and Gun are with her."

My stomach felt like it dropped out of my body. I'd never felt anything remotely like that sensation, like I was falling and also collapsing in on myself. Distantly, I was aware that I'd sunk to my knees against the cell bars, but my mind and thought process felt completely *out* of my body.

I hurt her.

Badly enough to put her in the hospital.

It felt like a boot was stomping down on my chest, impairing my breathing, and I wished for the feeling to kill me. To crush my ribcage and magically allow me to feel the pain of every bone breaking. I had hurt the person I cared about most.

"How...how bad is she?" Talking felt impossible but I forced the words out. I had to know.

"She's in a neck brace, pretty banged up. But she'll be okay."

A fucking neck brace. God, what kind of fucking monster am I?

"Fuck, Jandro..." I ground my teeth, banged my forehead on the metal bars, drew ragged anxiety-filled breaths, and none of it was enough. My stupid fucking body couldn't sense the pain I deserved for hurting her, couldn't keep the nightmares away for the one fucking night I forgot to take a pill.

"Reaper wants you executed." Jandro said, ignoring my outburst.

"Good. I'm ready any time."

"Yeah?"

"Yes." I pulled my face away from the bars, nothing but a throbbing sensation in my head. "Fuck, I'll do it myself so Reaper doesn't have to."

"So that's how it's gonna be, huh?" His voice betrayed some emotion for the first time since walking in. "You just gonna give up? Not make a case for yourself?"

"What case is there to make?" I cried. "She's his wife. *Your* wife! You all trusted me with her and I..." I couldn't bring myself to say or even imagine what I'd done to her.

"Did you take your meds?"

"No," I shook my head. "I forgot. I'm so fucking stupid. She'd be fine if I had just remembered to take a fucking pill."

Jandro let out an exhausted sigh, rubbing both hands down his face. "I don't know if it'll make a difference, but Reaper should know that."

"It doesn't make a difference to me," I said. "I don't deserve to walk out of here alive."

"Man, pissed as I am, fucking terrified as I was," Jandro spread his hands "you've whaled on me a number of times before Mari put you on those pills. And with me, it wasn't a big thing. I know you in your right mind wouldn't attack me for no reason." He paused, taking a long look at me. "And I know the real you wouldn't hurt Mari like that."

"But I *did*," I protested. "At least you could defend yourself against me. She's so...fuck, a fucking *neck brace*, Jandro!"

"I know. This whole situation is fucked." He rubbed the back of his neck. "But she is stronger than she looks. She'll be okay."

"Good, I hope so. But she shouldn't be forced to see me every day."

"Yeah, we'll have to do something about that." He leaned his head back against the bars. "And hear what she has to say when she wakes up."

"She can't..." I pressed my throat against a bar, wishing it was a sharp blade so it could decapitate me. "You can't let her have any sympathy toward me."

"Shadow—"

"I mean it, Jandro. If she doesn't want me executed, you can't take that into account."

"Don't you think *her* opinion is what counts most in this situation?"

"It does, but..." My head throbbed, but still with no pain. "I'm afraid she'll want to help me, not punish me. I don't deserve her help." *I don't deserve a single ounce of her kindness.*

"Maybe it doesn't have to be either or." Jandro's boot scuffled against the wall. "We can figure out a punishment that's also a form of rehabilitation."

"Ugh." I hated every minute of this, internally raging at my body for still being alive and drawing air. I needed to just stop existing so Mari could move on and live without fear. "Where's your gun? I just need to be fucking gone already."

"I purposely came unarmed because I know how much of a sneaky fucker you are." Jandro opened the sides of his cut to show me that his holsters were empty. "And there's one thing you're forgetting, my man."

"What?"

He paused to rub his jaw, seemingly struggling to get the words out. "If you do die, how's that gonna affect her?"

I unwrapped my hands from the bars to shrug. "She'll be relieved. She'll never have to see me and be afraid for her life again."

"Nah." My once-friend shook his head. "She would never celebrate your death. And for the record, neither would I."

"You and her," I scoffed. "Both of you. Too fucking good to me, and the ones I treated the worst."

"It's not that simple, man," he sighed. "Everyone fucks up. You know that."

"Right." I turned away, heading for the small cot now that I knew he wouldn't help end my life. "And her biggest fuck-up was me."

REAPER

I sat on the edge of my bed, turning my knife over in my hands. He hated blades. It would be especially cruel to kill him with one.

Did I *want* him to suffer? That was the question that kept turning over in my mind as I looked at my guns, knives, brass knuckles, and various other weapons spread out on the bed.

A quick death by a gunshot seemed almost too merciful after what he did to Mari. Some part of me felt gleeful at the expression he'd wear if I took my time cutting him up—to embroil him in the same horrors that gave him all those scars. I didn't know the full story, but I got the gist. Shadow couldn't feel pain, so using a knife to kill him would be more psychological torture than anything.

Mari deserved justice. She *would* forgive me for what I had to do. She had to. There were plenty of things about MC life she didn't care for, but accepted. She knew Python's death, and the manner in which he died, was necessary.

This one would be too, even if Shadow was nothing like Python.

"Fuck, man." I slid the knife into its sheath and tossed it away, picking up my handgun.

Shadow had been loyal, obedient, and efficient. His artistry created the symbol of the Steel Demons and he inked it onto every one of us.

He followed me everywhere, and I knew he would continue to do so. He took things so literally, living and breathing by our code, including to never harm another Steel Demon outside of Fight Night, unless it was in self-defense.

Until he took my wife to bed with him and put her in a neck brace.

I'd never wanted to kill anyone so badly, while at the same time wished there was another way.

Mari begged me not to, and fuck me, I *wanted* to give in. I yearned to tell her yes, I would spare him and we'd find another way to handle this. But then I'd see that thing around her neck, the cuts and bruising on her nose and forehead, her fingernails broken and splintered from how she scratched at him, and the white-hot rage would consume me.

Fuck that it was an accident. Fuck him being unmedicated. She nearly lost her life for no fucking reason.

And then there was the club I had to consider. What kind of leader would I be if I let my old lady's attacker get off with no consequence? While proving myself to them was the least of my worries, it still factored into my decision.

I slammed my clip into the gun, holstered my weapon and left the bedroom, Hades following dutifully at my side. He'd been silent since the day Eduardo stabbed me, and I wasn't sure what to make of it. Not that it mattered. I didn't need a god to tell me Shadow's life was mine to take.

Gunner supported me in this. Jandro probably didn't, but he would fall in line. Mari...

Forgive me, beautiful, I thought as I sat on my bike and turned the ignition. *I have to do this. For you.*

The ride to the jail felt both torturously long and far too short, my gun heavy and hot on my hip. Pulling up in front of the low brick building, I still couldn't decide if I wanted to drag this out or get it over with quickly.

Word might have spread at this point, but I wasn't about to make this a public display. I made the decision never to humiliate a man again like I did with Python. This would be taken care of quietly, a president avenging his old lady and handling business.

My boots felt like lead as I walked inside, the click of Hades' nails echoing over the concrete floor. Shadow didn't move at my approach. He sat like a statue on the edge of a cot in the far-right cell, forearms on his thighs and his head hanging low.

I paused in front of his cell door, waiting to see if he'd react to my presence at all. After a long silence, he spoke in a weak whisper, "I can do it myself, if you'd rather not carry that burden, Reaper."

"You'll address me as president," I said. "And it will be my pleasure to take your life with my own hands." A lie for him just as much as for me.

His head moved in the slightest nod. "Then I will accept your judgment, president."

My hand drifted to my holster, thumb flicking off the safety. "Any last words?"

"Just...I'm sorry." His white eye caught the sliver of light from the single bulb in the room as he looked up. "I wish I'd never hurt her. And...I hope she heals. And spends the rest of her life happy."

Shadow looked more broken down and beaten in that cell than when Jandro first brought him home. Like a caged animal waiting to die. I hesitated, fingers hovering over the pistol. Mari was the probably the best thing to walk into his life, aside from the club. Hell, she was the best thing in all of our lives. But Shadow never had family, friends, or the freedom of being a human until he came to live with us.

He had been dealt a shit hand in life and that was unfortunate. Ending his story here was sad from every angle, but a shitty upbringing didn't excuse him from abusing a defenseless woman. I brought the heartbreaking image of Mari in her hospital bed to mind, drawing on it for strength as my fingers wrapped around the pistol grip.

"I'll tell her you were remorseful," I said, pulling the gun from my holster. "And that you wish her well."

Shadow lowered his head. "Thank you, president." He said nothing else—no begging or pleading for his life. He truly believed this was what he deserved. That made this a little easier.

And yet, so much fucking harder.

I raised the gun, aiming it at his head. This close, one shot would be enough. But I'd take three just to be sure. With a deep breath, I squeezed around the trigger.

You will not reap.

My breath froze in my chest. I looked down at Hades, meeting those dark eyes looking straight through me.

His life is not yours to take. Do not reap.

"How can you tell me that?" I demanded. "How can I *not* take his life?"

He has not yet reached his end. Stay your hand.

I lowered the gun, turning to face the god at my side who was asking the impossible of me.

"You promised to protect her," I said. "And *he* almost took her life! Where were you then, huh?"

She was *protected. Her life was salvaged. The human Shadow's life must continue alongside hers.*

I crouched down, lowering my face to the dog's level. "I don't care. I will *not* obey. His life *is* mine to take." I returned to standing, spinning with my shooting arm outstretched toward Shadow's jail cell, to find a man blocking my shot.

He was a flash before my eyes, barely even an image, more of a hazy outline. I caught no details, just a murky silhouette before my gun was wrenched from my hand and tossed toward the door.

I pulled my hand back to my chest with a shout, the cramping painful and immediate. I was decently strong and always carried a good grip on my gun, but this thing broke my hold like I was a newborn.

This is my command, Hades bellowed, his voice like scraping metal in my head and clanging over every bar in the room. *You will* not *reap. His life. Is Not. Yours. To take.*

"Fuck you!" I yelled in the dog's face. He was completely impassive. Not even his ears went back. "I have fucking obeyed you, let me have this *one!*"

I went for the jail doors, deciding I'd strangle Shadow if I couldn't shoot him. Something hit me from the side with the force of a linebacker, and I went sprawling across the concrete floor.

Your human body will wear out if you continue this, Reaper. But I rule the dead and I am eternal. My word is law. Shadow's life will not be reaped until it is time.

"What about Mari's?" I hissed. "The next time he attacks her, will we get there in time? Huh? Or are you just gonna keep playing fast and loose with our lives?"

As long as Freyja, Horus, and I walk alongside you, those nearest to you will only die when their time comes.

"Swear to me," I said. "Promise me no one I love will have another brush with death. Especially not her. Swear it, fucking god!"

I owe you nothing beyond what I've said, human. You know the protection I offer. And you will carry out this command, and every one after, until our time together is finished.

The dog walked up to where I still sat on the floor, his presence almost unbearably heavy. More than a dog, more than a man, but an odd feeling like the whole pressure of the atmosphere sat on my chest.

Swear to me now, my reaper. His teeth bared, a low warning growl pulling from his throat. *You will obey. Shadow's life is not yours to take.*

"I...I will." The suffocating pressure on my chest eased just a little. "And...I will spare Shadow's life."

Hades backed away, his presence no longer closing in on me. *Return to Mariposa now. She is feeling much better.*

I climbed to my feet, shakily picking up my gun and returning it to my holster. Not bothering to look back at Shadow, I felt dazed as I left the building. Sweaty, feverish, and nauseous. *Did that just fucking happen? A god intervening on me taking a life?*

Hades was all dopey and smiling at my side again. He licked at my hand but I yanked it away, the thought of touching him just too fucking weird in that moment. I mounted my bike slowly, turning it on and guiding it back out to the road when I started to feel more normal.

Once I was a good distance away from the jail, the hospital looming into view, the wheels started turning in my head again.

I couldn't kill Shadow.

Which meant I had to do something else.

SHADOW

Disappointment didn't cover a fraction of what I felt.

Hades wouldn't allow me to die, and if I ventured a guess, that included by my own hand. So I'd be forced to live, and for what?

They could keep me here in this jail cell and that would work for me. Mariposa would never see me, and I'd reacquaint myself with a lifeless existence in a cage. That seemed like a fitting punishment.

I couldn't tell how much time had passed. I was brought six meals by people I didn't recognize, and barely touched the food. I was offered books to read, but refused them all. I passed the time by pacing my cage like I always used to. By staring at the walls—none of which had cracks that lead to glimpses of an outside sky. When I was feeling particularly masochistic, I thought back to all my moments with Mariposa.

I held on to every detail, sometimes wishing I had a pencil and sketchpad so I could draw my memories into something real. That one sketch I made of her was still in my room, and I yearned to fold and unfold the paper in my hands for one last look at her, stretched out and unafraid of me.

I often had to remind myself that I didn't deserve anything of hers, not even her likeness on a piece of paper. She had almost convinced me otherwise, but that truth would never change.

When the jailhouse door opened and booted footsteps approached my cell, I didn't react, thinking it was just my food for the day. But the footsteps stopped, my visitor motionless at my cell door, until I looked up.

Reaper stood there with something in his hand. He said nothing for several long moments and I wondered if he was going to make another attempt at killing me. If so, I couldn't blame him for trying.

"Have you decided what to do with me?" I asked after he continued to stand there and do nothing.

"Yes," he said, holding out the first item in his hand. "We have."

It was my cut, complete with my name and patches still affixed to it. So they had been in my room, and had probably searched through my things for all I knew. I just hoped my drawing of Mari hadn't been destroyed.

Reaper opened his hand and dropped the garment on the floor, the worn-out leather making a soft swishing sound as it hit the concrete. His eyes never left mine as he unscrewed the cap on the other item he held—a can of lighter fluid.

He bathed my cut in a generous amount of gasoline, the stench quickly filling the stale air of the jail. I watched as he emptied the can of flammable liquid all over the vest I designed and proudly wore for years. Even now, I'd pick that thing up from the floor and put it on if he asked me to.

Reaper tossed the empty can away, letting it clatter against the wall, before he took out a matchbox from his cut pocket. He removed a match, struck it against the side of the box, and dropped it onto my cut.

The leather caught fire in a deep *whoof* sound, fire consuming the cut in a sudden rush of heat. Flames licked the air almost to chest level between us, illuminating Reaper's face as we stared at each other across the blaze.

For a moment it reminded me of bonfires out on our rides, my brothers' faces lit up, glowing orange as they laughed, drank, and talked shit. But this wasn't any kind of unifying event. This fire was the opposite, a clear severing of me from him. Me from the club, and from everything that made me see how good life could be.

The one part of my life that had been worth living, burned away before my eyes.

Reaper stood there until my cut became nothing but ashes on the ground, the flames dying down slowly until there was nothing left to consume. Then he produced a set of keys from his pocket and proceeded to unlock my cell door.

"You have one hour to gather your belongings from your room," Reaper said. "And then you will ride. You'll ride as far as you can the fuck away from here. If I even hear whispers of you being near the Four Corners territory, I *will* end your life. And this time, no god will be able to stop me."

"Yes, president," I said numbly.

He opened my cage and headed for the door. "Two escorts are waiting for you outside."

I was every bit as numb on the way to the house—their *house, not yours anymore*—as when I watched my cut burn. My escorts were two soldiers from General Bray's army. Other than us, the place was empty. No one was around, not even for me to say good-bye to.

I stood in the doorway of my bedroom for a while, eyes just flicking around to the few things I owned. Aside from a few changes of clothes, weapons, and my tattooing equipment, I had nothing worth taking.

Where would I even go? What would I do?

The first thing I reached for though, was not any of my essentials. I went for the drawer in my nightstand, pulling it open to reveal the folded piece of paper in the bottom. I stuffed it in my pants pocket without looking at it. With my limited time, I just needed to know it was on me and safe.

My necessities were packed within minutes, all of it stuffed robotically into my saddlebags under the watchful eyes of my escorts. What to do with the rest of my time? I could just take off and not look back, be gone from the Steel Demons without a trace. That didn't feel right, but it wasn't like I could go around saying goodbyes either. Not face-to-face anyway.

A thought hit me as I eyed my guards. They were posted just inside of my door, still and solemn as statues. I couldn't do anything about them hovering over me, as much as I would have preferred privacy. I had limited time and a few things I wanted to say, so I had to make it count.

I pulled out my sketchbook and a pen, ripped out a blank page, sat down at the desk, and proceeded to write.

It was dusk as I went out to my motorcycle, everything I owned fitting on the vehicle that carried me, even saved me. My guards relieved themselves of their duty the moment my machine roared to life and I started on the road heading out of town. I switched my headlight on, deliberately turning down a side street in one of the smaller neighborhoods in search of someone, anyone who could do the one final thing I needed.

I almost gave up hope and started weighing the risks of doubling back to the house to leave the letter there. I'd be shot at, for sure. And even with Hades determined to make me live out my life until its natural end, I had my doubts about how far his protection would go.

My headlight caught a flash of reflective paint and my heart jumped. A horned skull grinned at me, shining in my light against the night falling. I accelerated to catch up and see who it was—Slick. Fuck, maybe the gods were looking out for me in some twisted way. I could not have run into anyone better.

"Slick!" I called out, slowing my bike alongside him. "I need a quick favor."

"Look Shadow, man." He shook his head, quickening his pace. "I'm sorry about everything, but I can't be seen talking to you. You're supposed to be gone and Reaper will—"

"I know. I'm on my way out now," I said, keeping pace with his hurried walking. "I just need you to give something to Jandro for me."

"Naw man, I can't—"

"Just this. Here." I pulled the letter out of my pocket and shoved it at him.

"Dude, I really—"

"Please, Slick!" Desperation bled into my voice. "Please just do this one thing for me. Jandro needs to get this and no one else."

The kid sighed heavily, finally stopping and whipping around to face me. "That's it?"

"Yes, I swear. Just give this to Jandro. He'll know what to do with it."

Looking both ways down the street first, Slick snatched the letter from my hand and stuffed it in his cut pocket. He barely looked at it, but I knew he caught the glimpse of Mari's name written on the front.

"I won't read it," he muttered. "Swear."

"I know you won't. You're..." I sighed, revving up my engine. This was the worst fucking time to get sentimental. "You're a good kid, Slick. I've always liked you."

"Thanks, Shadow." His head bobbed up and down in a nod, still looking from side to side. "Sorry to hear about...everything. Good luck out there."

"You too."

With nothing left to say, I picked my feet up from the ground, drove the bike forward, and never looked back.

MARIPOSA

I couldn't stop rolling my neck around on my shoulders. Having the brace off was both freeing and strange. Rhonda and Dr. Brooks couldn't believe that I requested to have it taken off after just three days, but they relented after much pestering. I had to act just as surprised as them, while my men and the animals stood by trying to hold back their grins.

With my arms wrapped around Reaper's waist, the chilly wind in my hair, and the rumble of the bike underneath us, it was such a relief to be heading home after my hospital stay.

Being laid up in that room, only allowed to go on short walks, gave me too much time to think, to circle back on what happened with Shadow again and again.

Ultimately, I knew I wanted to try things again with him, after some time. But I kept that between myself and Freyja. Reaper and Gunner would blow a gasket if they knew. Although I was pretty certain Jandro wouldn't.

My sweet VP had been the only one to visit Shadow, although he didn't share much about how he was or what the club's plans were. Jandro, usually full of smiles and warmth, was the most sullen and quiet I'd ever seen him. I knew he could see Reaper's point of view, but he was also Shadow's longest and closest friend. He had to feel some of the same conflicting feelings as I did.

Reaper avoided all talk of Shadow since I told him how I felt. He was not a man of inaction, so I hoped he would have some answers by the time I got home.

As far as I was concerned, Shadow was still mine. He'd be among the men at my side once he had time to work through his trauma. I knew in my heart he was remorseful and that was all that mattered to me. I didn't need to hear an apology right away. My chest ached at the thought of how much he surely blamed himself, how guilt-ridden he must have felt. He might never want to touch me again out of fear, and that thought hurt almost as much as the torn ligaments in my neck.

I wasn't ready to see him yet, but maybe soon. And eventually we'd be able to put this behind us.

Reaper pulled slowly up to our house, the lights in the windows warm and inviting. My fingers tightened for a moment around the edge of his cut.

"Is he...?"

"No, sugar." He brought my fingers to his lips and quickly kissed them before dismounting.

"Where is he?" I asked.

He looked at me, lips setting in a hard line before holding his arms out. "Let me help you off. I think Jandro's got dinner ready."

Avoiding the subject again. But I *was* tired and hungry, and let him lift me off the bike. After settling back in at home, I'd press him for information. But not right now.

Reaper led me inside, mumbling some excuse as he took off down the hall to his study.

"Baby girl!" Shirtless and barefoot, Gunner slid off the couch and came to greet me with an embrace and a smile. "Welcome home." He pulled me into his chest and I could have dozed off right then, perfectly content against his warm skin.

"It's good to be home," I sighed, squeezing around his waist.

He brought his hands to my face, tilting it up for kisses. I melted under the soft presses of his lips, always like gentle rain.

"What do you need? Food? A drink? Sleep?" He pecked kisses on my mouth between each question, making a smile pull across my lips.

"Hm, all of the above. In that order, please."

"Coming right up," he murmured, pulling away to holler toward the kitchen. "Jandrooo, make her a plate."

"What d'you think I'm doing, asshole?"

Gunner and I both flinched at the sound of his voice, full of malice and not a hint of Jandro's usual playfulness.

"He's in a shitty fuckin' mood," Gunner whispered.

"Let me go see him." I squeezed his hand before sliding past him into the kitchen. "Hey *guapito*," I said tentatively to the man hunched over the kitchen counter.

"Mariposita," Jandro muttered, rounding the counter toward me.

He wrapped me in a bear hug, pulling me tightly into his chest with his face buried in my neck. The hug was warm, affectionate with missing me, but I picked up on a deep sadness from him too.

"Jandro." I held tightly around his broad shoulders, one hand scratching over his scalp. "What's wrong, *mi amor?*"

He loosened his hold on me, pulling away to search my face intently, then looked to Gunner in the living room. "Did you fuckers *not* tell her?"

Cold dread filled me. "Tell me what? What's happened?"

"Reaper was going to," Gunner answered defensively.

"Fucking *when*?" Jandro roared.

"After she got settled back in and rested." Reaper re-emerged from his study, the harsh scowl he usually reserved for his club on his face.

"Tell me what?" I demanded, pulling away from Jandro. "What have you done?"

"Sugar—"

"Do not fucking *sugar* me. What did you *do*, Reaper?"

My husband's throat worked in a hard swallow but he didn't answer, which was telling enough. He did something that I wouldn't approve of, and my mind immediately jumped to the worst possible scenario.

No...

Oh no, no. How could he? I told him. I told him I wouldn't forgive him. Does he value our love so little?

"Check Shadow's room," Jandro said softly from behind me.

I headed that way immediately, snapping my arm away as Gunner tried to reach out and stop me.

"Mari, please—"

"Stop, Gunner," I growled. "Just fucking don't."

My feet carried me to the threshold of Shadow's room, the door wide open, which was unusual in itself. I felt along the inside wall for the light switch, my pulse accelerating with the realization that this was where everything went wrong.

The light flicked on, and I found myself staring at an empty room.

Completely barren, with none of Shadow's personal touches, as minimal as they were. No tattoo supplies scattered out on the desk. No sketchbook and pen on the nightstand. No black long-sleeved shirts hanging in the closet. Even the bed was stripped of all the sheets, with only a mattress remaining.

"What did you do?" I whispered to the empty room, then turning around slowly to face the two guilty men behind me. "What the *fuck* did you do?"

"I didn't kill him, if that's where your mind's going." Reaper's voice was laced with bitterness.

"Then where is he?" It took all of my resolve not to scream. "I'm getting sick of repeating myself. What did you do, Reaper?"

"I burned his cut," he snapped back. "The act of which eliminates him permanently from the Steel Demons. And told him to get the fuck out of here."

Blood rushed to my ears, filling my head with a dull, angry pulse. No, this could *not* be happening.

"What? Where?"

"Anywhere. Just told him to get as far away from you and us as possible." Reaper crossed his arms, looking defiant, if even proud. "Not that there's enough space in the world between us and him that would make me satisfied."

Gunner said nothing, but copied Reaper's stance, clearly aligned with his president. Only Jandro was sullen, fists at his sides as he looked blankly into the empty room.

"You...you sent him away?" My voice shook in a disbelieving whisper. "Just...cut him off and sent him out into the world?"

"Yes." Reaper lifted his chin. "I would have preferred something else but that didn't seem favorable to you."

My fear and disbelief shifted to an all-consuming anger. I stared at Reaper, standing there so proudly, wondering in that moment what I ever saw in this bloodthirsty, deceitful man.

"How could you?"

He narrowed his eyes. "Excuse me? I did this *for you.*"

"Right, even though you never told me this was your plan?"

Reaper sighed, scrubbing a hand down his face. "I knew you wouldn't want this, yes. But I did what you asked, and this was the best solution for everyone."

"The best solution?!" I screeched. "This club was everything to him, and you *burned* his cut?"

"He was no longer a Steel Demon the moment he put hands on you," Reaper growled. "That fact is not up for debate—only worthy men wear the patch. The only reason I didn't burn the tattoo off his body was because he wouldn't have felt it."

Something inside me snapped. Sending Shadow away was one thing, but knowing Reaper would have subjected him to torture, after everything he'd been through, changed everything. I didn't know this man standing in front of me. And I sure as hell did *not* love him.

"You fucking barbarian," I hissed. "I told you it was an accident and he needs help! And now you've cast him out into the world where he has no one and nothing?"

"I don't fucking care about him!" Reaper leaned toward me to yell, far enough that Jandro and Gunner had to pull back on his shoulders. "I care about *you*. You told me not to kill him and I respected that. Beyond that, it's *my* decision what happens to him, and I want him far away from *my* wife, my family."

"I wish he did kill me," I said, enjoying the look of shock on Reaper's face as I wrenched his ring off my finger. "Then I wouldn't have to live with a husband who's a heartless piece of shit!"

The ring clattered noisily to the floor, the sound echoing deafeningly throughout the whole house as my men stared at me in stunned silence. Desperate to get away, I slid past them and up the stairs to the master bedroom. I slammed the door behind me and sank to the floor, too weary to even collapse on the bed.

I sobbed noisily, releasing all my heartbreak through painful wracks of my chest and not caring who heard. Not even Freyja was here to comfort me. Maybe she could sense that I didn't want to be comforted. In that moment, I just wanted to wallow in the hurt.

It happened just like Noelle said—my heart had been broken by two men.

Shadow, at first for hurting me, then the fact that he was gone without a trace. And now Reaper, trying to act like a savior when he just hurt me worse.

Shadow...Oh, poor Shadow.

Where would he go? A fresh sob escaped me at the thought of him alone, trying to navigate a world filled with strangers. It would be lonely and isolating even for the most well-adjusted person. My chest ached so badly, like my very soul was splitting in half.

I cried until I had no strength left to sob with. My head ached and my whole body felt encased in cement. Tired of sitting against the door, I slid down to the floor on my side. If Shadow was out there all alone, with no friends or support, what right did I have to a comfortable bed?

My mind wouldn't shut off to sleep. The exhaustion would take me eventually, but all of their faces played on a reel through my mind, each one another prick of a needle through my heart.

Shadow kissing the scar on my belly, the warmth in his eyes when he asked me to stay. Then in contrast, his face full of hatred, eyes cold and unflinching as I begged for my life. Reaper with tears in his eyes. Reaper with no remorse. Gunner siding with him, which felt like another betrayal to me. And Jandro, my poor Jandro. The only one besides me with enough heart to care.

My head against the floor, I heard footsteps slowly ascend the stairs. A fresh bolt of anger struck through me. If any of them thought they could convince me this was the right thing to do, I wouldn't just discard their jewelry. I'd kick and punch my way out of here until I had some peace. I was sick of these men, even hated them in the moment.

The floorboards creaked under the weight of the footsteps. They approached the bedroom door slowly, as though unsure if they really wanted to see me or not. The footsteps paused just on the other side while I waited, listening while curled up on the ground.

"Mari? It's me."

Jandro.

Something in my chest lurched, and I pressed up from the floor. The sadness in his voice called to mine, and now I was desperate to not be alone.

I opened the door to let him in. He didn't say a word but pulled me into another embrace. And somehow, I found the strength to cry again.

Jandro let me sob on his shoulder, running his hands up and down my back. His body occasionally jerked with a rough breath and I knew he was fighting tears too.

"He's...he's gone..." It seemed to hit me hardest right then, that I would never see Shadow again.

"I know." Jandro's breath rattled shakily out of his chest. "I know. I'm so sorry."

"You couldn't have stopped him." I leaned my forehead into his neck, cradling my arms between his chest and mine. "Reaper would never let anyone get in his way."

Jandro stroked my back without saying any more, his breaths growing deeper and steadier. "He left something for you."

I lifted my head. "Shadow did?"

He nodded, reaching into his cut pocket and producing a folded piece of paper which read *Mariposa* in blocky handwriting. "I didn't read it. Promise."

I took the letter with both hands, unable to do anything but stare at my name on the front. So clearly, I could picture Shadow's hand moving across it as he wrote, the same way his hands moved over me as he tattooed me, pleased me.

"Do you want me to leave?" Jandro asked.

"No." I reached for his hand, walking us both toward the bed. "Stay with me?"

"*Siempre*," he whispered. *Always*.

We sank down on the mattress together, his touch drifting over my arms and waist. Always near, always supportive, even when I felt almost too afraid to open a letter. I took a few steadying breaths while he just held me, lips resting on the back of my head. Then with shaking hands, I unfolded the letter and began to read.

Mariposa,

I will never ask you to forgive me. I don't deserve it.

I'm sorry beyond what words can express for hurting you. You're one of the bravest, strongest people I've ever met, so I know you will recover, especially with the love of your men surrounding you. But I will carry this for the rest of my days. It's the least I can do after what I put you through.

You're always thinking of others before yourself, so please be assured that I will never allow this to happen again to another person. I'm not sure where I'll end up, but I'm making that promise to you now. No one will get hurt because of me.

Thank you for everything you've shown me. I'll always be grateful for your kindness and care, for taking a chance on me when no one else did. I hope what I did doesn't dampen your willingness to help others. There are people who need you, Mariposa. People more worthy of your kindness than me.

If I can make one request—heal from the pain I've caused you. Heal completely, like I was never in your life to begin with. Forget about me. Let me become nothing more than a faded scar from your past. I don't deserve the space in your mind. Live a long, happy life with your men who will always do right by you. I will never forget you, but please forget me.

Don't miss me. Don't be sad for me. It's better this way.

Shadow

My eyes started blurring with tears before I finished reading the first paragraph. By the time I reached the end, I was sobbing again.

Jandro wrapped tightly around me, pressing kisses into my hair and stroking me as he gently pulled me down on the bed. Finally, the exhaustion overtook me.

My face was hot. My head pounded. I'd been crying so hard, my eyes felt practically swollen shut as I started to rouse.

The heat on my face came from the late-morning sun streaming through the window. A bright, sunny day, as if the nightmarish last few days hadn't happened at all.

I stretched my sore, aching body, cracking my swollen eyes open to find toast and eggs on a plate on the nightstand, a mug of tea still steaming. Looking behind me, the sheets were rumpled on the bed but Jandro was missing. I allowed myself a smile, a small touch of warmth to soothe the deep ache in my chest as I scooted over to the food he left.

The eggs and toast were still warm, and I finished off the plate with the realization that I skipped dinner last night.

Fuck, last night.

A wave of regret hit me, clamping around the food in my stomach. I stretched out the fingers of my left hand, looking at the tan line left behind where my ring used to be.

I said awful things to Reaper, the man I promised to love forever. My hand closed into a fist, dropping down onto my thigh. I meant what I said in the moment, although my explosive anger had now given way to exhaustion and a deep, painful ache. He hurt me, so I wanted to hurt him back.

Guilt now consumed the regret, my sore eyes threatening to spill more tears if I wallowed in it. I'd never wanted to hurt someone I loved but he...

No. This is on you.

Reaper thought he was protecting me by sending Shadow away. He knew I'd be upset, but saw it as a fair trade-off for keeping me safe in the long term. I'd always known he was a man of absolution. He took no half-measures. His decisions were final, permanent. This was just another example of that.

I shook my head with a groan and rubbed my temples. He deserved an apology for what I said, for taking the ring off, but I wasn't ready to forgive him. I wasn't sure when or if that day would ever come.

A tapping sound brought my gaze up, and I spotted Horus peering at me through the window. As much as I didn't want to leave bed, I slipped out and went to slide the pane open. Chilly air rushed into the room, and I rubbed my arms against the cold.

Fresh air and sunlight will do you good, daughter.

Like Hades, Horus's voice sounded ancient. Powerful enough to rattle through my sore head, but right then he spoke with a gentleness, like a parent would to soothe a child. And he was right. I could already breathe easier, the cool air feeling like it revitalized my lungs and calmed the puffiness of my face.

"Do you know where he went?" I asked the falcon.

I see him, the bird answered. *I always do.*

"Is he okay?"

No. But he is alive.

I pulled in a deep breath, looking out over the landscape below my window.

"Will he come back?"

Not without a reason.

My gaze returned to the small, fearsome bird perched on my windowsill. He'd never come to me on his own, not without Gunner nearby, and had certainly never spoken to me before. But here he was now, like he'd been waiting for this moment to speak to me.

"I have to go find him." The words flew out of my mouth without a thought. "I have to give him a reason to come back."

Yes, Horus said, as though it were obvious. *But not yet, daughter.*

"When?"

I will tell you when the time is right. The bird fluffed up his feathers before smoothing them down again. *Shadow must learn to fly and he has only just opened his wings.*

Epilogue
Shadow

ONE WEEK LATER

I finally hit my breaking point where I needed to stop. Everything ached when I pulled up to the service center, another hotel from before the Collapse that had been converted into something between a hostel and brothel. I'd crashed in a few of them throughout my long, aimless journey, but never for more than a night. This time, I needed to stay in one place for a bit. A week or so to figure out what I would do next.

This particular service center also had a bar, from what the blinking neon lights in the windows claimed. Now that I could no longer be properly medicated, it was back to booze to chase away the nightmares.

Parking out front, I noticed a few motorcycles and muscle cars out in a side yard that had seen better days. They were cobwebbed and filthy, but some had to be in driving condition.

I pulled the front door open to a dark, smoke-filled bar. A middle-aged man with glasses wiped down the bar, while a much younger woman in ripped stockings, a miniskirt, and a cropped T-shirt stood on a stepladder to put away bottles. Lounging around in arm chairs and low couches scattered across the room, a few other women drank and talked. Service girls, naturally. A couple of whom looked pregnant.

"Welcome," the man called jovially to me. "What're you lookin' for? A drink? A room? A good time? All three?"

"Uh, just a drink and a room," I said, approaching the bar. "For a few nights, if that's available."

The woman next to him jumped down from her stepladder, whirling around to face me. She had dark makeup on and several piercings through her nose, lips, and eyebrows. "How're you payin'?"

"Well, I saw your junkyard out front. I know basic vehicle maintenance if you're looking to sell or get those running again."

The woman elbowed the older man, who shot her an annoyed look.

I cleared my throat. "I'm, uh, also a tattoo artist. I'll be happy to trade ink for room and board if that sounds fair."

"Ooh, tattoos?" The woman's eyebrows shot up, dark lips pulling into a smile. "Can you do any style?"

"Just about. I can show you flash art if you'd like."

"Oh, yes! Doc, let him stay." She put her elbows on the bar, cradling her face as she looked at the man. "You know I've been wanting to get some pretty sleeves."

"Uh huh." The guy pushed his glasses up his nose, taking another look at me. "You been in some fights, huh?" He gestured at my face.

Fuck. I'd forgotten to cover my scar with my hair. After Mariposa and I got closer, I fell out of the habit. She'd always push my hair aside to kiss me there anyway.

Don't think about that. It's over now. That chapter of your life is closed.

"None that I've started," was how I chose to answer. "I'm not a violent person. I won't bring any trouble to your establishment."

It felt like a lie, considering the reason I was at this center in the first place. But this place looked well-stocked with alcohol, so chances were high I could drink myself into oblivion, where I wasn't a danger to anyone.

The barman nodded at me, peering at me with more curiosity than the average person. "I believe you, son. Thing is, trouble tends to find us."

"Oh, yeah?" The woman had poured a drink and slid it across the bar to me. I raised it to my lips without bothering to ask what it was. "Thank you."

She winked at me. "Sure thing, handsome."

The gesture and affectionate name felt odd. No one talked to me like that except Mari.

"'Bout ten miles from here is one of those girls' camps," the man explained. "Where they train young females, children even, into being obedient and shit. Personally, I like my women with bite." He reached over to slap the barwoman's ass and she snarled, whirling around on him.

"Fuck off, dirty old man."

"Anyway," he continued. "We get a lot of runaways. Some of them stay and work. Most of them move on. And others," he paused with a sigh, "their captors come lookin' for 'em, dragging them back kicking and screaming. It's awful what they do to those girls and if they didn't come in here all guns blazing, I'd tell 'em to fuck off—"

"You're asking me for protection," I ventured.

"Well." He shrugged. "You look like a guy that can handle yourself."

I downed my drink, which turned out to be a cheap whiskey, mulling it over as I swallowed.

"I can handle traffickers trying to take women away," I conceded. "But my stay will be temporary. What I can do is teach some weapons skills, show the women how to defend themselves."

"So you're running from something." The barman's stare was probing, unabashedly trying to figure me out.

No thanks, guy. I almost killed the last person who tried to understand me.

"That's my offer." I chose to ignore his remark. "In exchange for one week's room and board."

"You got yourself a deal." Thankfully he didn't push the psychoanalysis and stuck his hand out. "Name's Bill Harman, but everyone around here calls me Doc."

I accepted his handshake, settling on giving him the name I decided on a couple hundred miles ago.

"Ivan."

"Ivan what?"

"Just Ivan," I repeated. "I'll grab my things and get settled in my room, if that'll be all."

"Ah, sure." Doc seemed a lot more hesitant about making a deal with me now, but he didn't argue. "Jen, get him a key, will ya?"

I turned and left the counter, heading back to my bike. Without my cut, my patches, and now not even my name, I felt like a stranger to myself. Like a new person had possessed my scarred-up husk and was trying to navigate the world without a past, and now with a completely uncertain future.

Because Shadow, the Steel Demons MC assassin, was dead.

It's not over yet! The ride continues in books 7-10.
Steel Demons MC Volume 3 is available now!

Start reading:
http://books2read.com/SDMCV3

Read on for exclusive bonus content!
In appreciation of all the amazing Steel Demons fans, Reaper allowed me to publish a few excerpts from his mother's journal. I hope you enjoy this peek into the past, and seeing how our surly president learned to share. ;)

Bonus content
Excerpts & letters from Alisa's journal

LETTER FROM FINN

MARCH 21, 2071

Hey Baby,

Holy shit!!! Oh my God, I can't even tell you how fucking happy I am. It was a shitty day out on the field, and coming back to base and finding your letter was exactly what I needed. I've been smiling for hours and I can't stop even now as I write this. I'm going to be a daddy!

God, I wish I could see you, touch you, kiss you, and especially on that belly. It's only been two weeks and I miss you so much already. This deployment is going to feel even longer, but I will put in the work for our family. I'll make you and our child proud, baby.

If it's a boy, do you think we could name him Rory? I'd love to have a son named after my grandfather. The last thing he told me before he passed was to take care of you. Did I ever tell you that? We'd only been dating for three months and you remember how reluctant I was to introduce you to my family? Well, it was because Granddad was the only one who really treated me like family. He wasn't feeling well

but he wanted to meet the special new girl in my life, no
matter what. I think he fell in love with you after just that
one dinner we had. I know I did! He passed a month later
and I was fighting everything not to cry in front of you. I
was still trying to impress you and be strong, hah. But you
held me that night and just let me mourn him. I'll never
forget that. I knew I'd make you wife then.

    I'm reminiscing a lot, baby, because the present honestly
sucks. I want to be anywhere but here, honestly. The military
is nothing like it used to be. We're nothing but glorified riot
police now. Today we threw tear gas at over 500 protesters.
They weren't being violent or anything, but we were ordered
to provoke them. I shit you not, our general's exact orders
were, "make these vermin too scared to ever gather in the
streets again". So many were just kids, teenagers who wanted
a chance to go college. It honestly doesn't feel like we're
protecting and serving the country anymore. We're just
armed guards for the politicians in that pristine, white
building.

    We'll talk about this more when I come home, but I'm
pretty sure I want out after this deployment. The next
contract is looking at yet another pay cut. They swore it
wouldn't happen again, and if it got proposed, it wouldn't be
voted on. Yet here we are. I might as well be a carpenter
again. Don't worry, though, babe. You and the little one are
my top priorities. If the military is the best option to provide
for my family, I'll stay. If there's another option, I'll do that.

    That's funny you ran into Carter! I haven't seen him in
so long, so I'm glad he's in town. We'll have to get together
when I'm back. He's all ripped and tattooed, huh? Trying to
make me jealous? Just kidding, we all know who knocked
you up.

In all seriousness, Alisa... I've been thinking for about an hour before writing this down. You and Carter are the two people I love and trust most. Please reach out to him. Talk to him. Let him know if you need anything, and I do mean anything.

If I'm being perfectly honest (and with you, I always am), I think he's always had a crush on you. He saw how happy we were together and wanted something like what we had. But of course, no other woman could compare to you. Smart, beautiful, kind, full of sunshine and love. Whenever we talked and you came up in conversation, he always smiled kind of sadly and told me how lucky I was. And it's true, baby. You're the best thing that's ever happened to me. This baby being the second best thing!

That's why it kills me to leave you and our child for these long six months. If I knew Carter was nearby, I would 100% ask him to watch over you. And if you two got closer, like inti-mately...it sounds weird but I don't think I would be upset. Like I said, I trust him and I trust you. If it were anyone else, absolutely not. But I'm serious, Alisa. I don't want you to feel alone. I don't want my best friend to keep settling for women who don't appreciate what a good guy he is.

I hope you're not mad by me saying this. I love you deeply and always will, no matter what happens! If there is still something between you and Carter when I get back, we'll figure it out. If you two remain strictly friends, that's great too. The three of us were always as thick as thieves, so we should be able to navigate this maturely, whatever the outcome may be.

I love you to the ends of the earth, my beautiful wife. I'm counting down the minutes until I can hold you and taste you again. I can't wait to see you and your adorable belly filled up with our baby! OUR baby! I still can't believe it. Believe me when I say you've made me the happiest man on earth. Your love is the most precious gift.

Always yours,
Finn

Alisa's Journal

March 30, 2071

I went to the doctor today. Everything went well and a lot of my fears were put to rest. I didn't tell them everything, but still, it was nice to vent to a living person.

I also wrote a letter to Finn, telling him pretty much everything I wrote in my last entry. That made me feel better too, and like I'm less alone. I didn't want to stress him out though, on top of everything else he has to worry about.

My metalsmithing class is going well! I'm getting better at saw piercings, and collecting pretty gemstones is such an addiction. It's pure luck that we moved to Tucson, home of the most amazing gem show in the world. I'm still hoarding stones from last year like some kind of dragon. I want to get better at smithing before I place them into jewelry settings.

I can't wait to go to the gem show again this year, but sad that Finn won't be there with me. He made fun of me for oohing and ahhing over pretty rocks last year, but it still won't be the same without him. Maybe I could go with some people from my class, if I get over being so damn shy.

Oh, I ran into Finn's friend Carter on my way out of the pharmacy the other day. And holy shit, he got so much hotter! I hadn't seen him in like two years, and he was kind of dorky and shy back then. But he's all buff and covered with tattoos now. I tried not to stare too much, but he was just as sweet as ever. He must have women hanging off of him all the time now. In fact, I hope he does! Last time I saw him, he was sad about the girl he dated leaving him for someone else. If she saw him now, I'm sure she's kicking herself for that! I really wish the best for him. In fact, it would be nice to see him around again. We talked outside the pharmacy for at least ten minutes catching up! I don't really have other friends in this town, and he's known Finn since they were kids.

I kind of wish I got his number, though that probably wouldn't be appropriate. It would be just as friends of course, but I don't want to give Finn anything to worry about.

Letter from Carter to Finn

May 19, 2071

Dear Finn,

Hey, man. Bet you're surprised to see a letter from me. It's been a while. I hope you're doing okay, given the state of the world, your job, and having to be separated from Alisa.

Fuck. This is so awkward. I wish I could talk to you in person about this, man to man. You were always there when I had to get something off my chest. But this feels fucking selfish.

It's the middle of the night, and your wife is asleep in my bed. Whatever you're imagining right now is exactly what happened.

Alisa showed me your letter, and expressed to me about how conflicted she felt. I told her the answer was simple. We'd hash this out when you got back from your deployment. That way, there would be no misinterpreting anything. Until then, she and I would just be friends. Only if we got in-person approval from you, would we pursue anything beyond the line of platonic friendship.

Obviously, that didn't happen. And I am so fucking sorry if that wasn't what your letter meant. We may have made a terrible mistake. What kills me is not knowing for sure. I wish I was strong enough to wait until you got back to talk to you about this.

Please don't blame Alisa for any of this. It was 100% me.

She's been sick with worry missing you. Her last few letters to you have gone unanswered. She hasn't received a phone call at the last scheduled time. She fears the worst, and honestly so do I.

I have been trying to be strong for her as best I can. As time passes though, it has gotten harder and harder to do so in a strictly platonic sense.

I'm sure you've always known I've had a small crush on your wife. Of course I love and respect you both, and would never cross the boundaries of your relationship. These past couple of weeks, I kept thinking back to your letter to justify the thoughts I've been having.

I made the first move with that flimsy justification as my reasoning. Alisa did not stop it from happening, but again, do not blame her, Finn. Please. She is vulnerable, lonely, and desperate for the father of her child to come home. I am merely a poor substitute that made myself available.

She wants to share equal blame, but I won't allow that. Your wife loves you. The world is going to shit, but you two have the most pure, strong connection I've ever seen between two people. Your growing family is going to be a much needed piece of brightness in the darkness to come. Don't let one mistake in a very stressful situation unravel your family.

If you want me gone when you return, I'll disappear. If you want me to stand against a wall so you can punch me in the face, I'll do that too.

You, Alisa, and your future son or daughter deserve the world. A much better one than what ours is shaping up to be.

Yours,
Carter

More journal excerpts and letters are available in Volume 3 of the Steel Demons MC omnibuses!

Start reading:
https://books2read.com/SDMCV3

ALSO BY CRYSTAL ASH

For a complete list of books by Crystal Ash, visit her Amazon page.

About the Author

Crystal Ash is a USA Today Bestselling Author from California. She loves writing steamy, heart-wrenching romance with tortured heroes, especially if they're in a reverse harem. Crystal's other loves include animals, mythology, and well-crafted alcohol, most of which can also be found in her stories.

When she's not writing, she's probably drinking craft beer with her husband or trying to coax her feral cat into accepting affection.

crystalashbooks.com

facebook.com/Crystal.Ash.Romance

instagram.com/crystalashbooks

amazon.com/author/crystalash

bookbub.com/profile/crystal-ash

Printed in the USA
CPSIA information can be obtained
at www.ICGtesting.com
LVHW050901131023
760813LV00004B/239